**Praise for #1 *New York Times*
bestselling author**

NORA ROBERTS

"Roberts is indeed a word artist, painting her story
and her characters with vitality and verve."
—*Los Angeles Daily News*

"There's no mystery about why Roberts is a
bestselling author of romances and mainstream
novels: she delivers the goods with panache and
wit."
—*Publishers Weekly*

"A consistently entertaining writer."
—*USA Today*

"Nora Roberts just keeps getting better and better."
—*Milwaukee Journal Sentinel*

"Roberts creates exceptional characters who...live on
in the reader's imagination and heart."
—*Publishers Weekly*

"It would be hard to pick any one book as
Ms. Roberts' best—such a feat defies human ability."
—*Romantic Times Magazine*

"John Grisham, watch your back!"
—*Entertainment Weekly*

"Roberts...is at the top of her game."
—*People Magazine*

Dear Readers,

I'm delighted with the publication of this collector's edition of *The Donovan Legacy*. It contains three very unusual stories I originally wrote for Silhouette Special Edition, all in one exciting volume.

All families share special bonds that bring them closer together and the Donovans—due to the extraordinary legacy they've inherited from their Celtic ancestors—have especially strong ties to one another. How would Morgana Donovan have faced the challenge of showing an unbelieving and irresistible Nash Kirkland the full strength of her powers, without her cousins Anastasia and Sebastian to cheer her on? As for Sebastian Donovan, even a worldly bachelor like him could use some advice from the women of his family to win the wary heart of beautiful Mary Ellen Sutherland. And even Anastasia Donovan, with her soothing strength and healing hands, knows that falling hard for a widowed single dad like Boone Sawyer won't be easy without an encouraging word now and then from one of her cousins.

All of the Donovans learn one vital truth: Love is the truest magic.

I hope you enjoy this collection of stories, as well as *Enchanted*, the newest book in *The Donovan Legacy*, also available this month from Silhouette Intimate Moments.

Sincerely,

NORA ROBERTS

THE DONOVAN LEGACY

Published by Silhouette Books

America's Publisher of Contemporary Romance

SILHOUETTE BOOKS

THE DONOVAN LEGACY

Copyright © 1999 by Harlequin Books S.A.

ISBN 0-373-48397-X

CAPTIVATED
Copyright © 1992 by Nora Roberts

ENTRANCED
Copyright © 1992 by Nora Roberts

CHARMED
Copyright © 1992 by Nora Roberts

Visit us at www.romance.net

Printed in U.S.A.

CONTENTS

THE DONOVAN LEGACY
by Nora Roberts

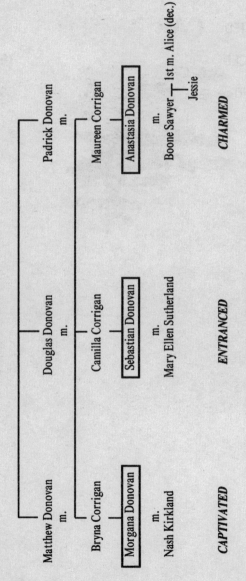

Matthew Donovan
m.
Bryna Corrigan

Douglas Donovan
m.
Camilla Corrigan

Padrick Donovan
m.
Maureen Corrigan

Morgana Donovan
m.
Nash Kirkland

Sebastian Donovan
m.
Mary Ellen Sutherland

Anastasia Donovan
m.
Boone Sawyer — 1st m. Alice (dec.)
Jessie

CAPTIVATED   *ENTRANCED*   *CHARMED*

*Look for ENCHANTED, a brand-new book in the Donovan Legacy
in November 1999, from Silhouette Intimate Moments!*

CAPTIVATED

Prologue

She was born the night the Witch Tree fell. With the first breath she drew, she tasted the power—the richness of it, and the bitterness. Her birth was one more link in a chain that had spanned centuries, a chain that was often gilded with the sheen of folklore and legend. But when the chain was rubbed clean, it held fast, tempered by the strength of truth.

There were other worlds, other places, where those first cries of birth were celebrated. Far beyond the sweeping vistas of the Monterey coast, where the child's lusty cry echoed through the old stone house, the new life was celebrated. In the secret places where magic still thrived—deep in the green hills of Ireland, on the windswept moors of Cornwall, deep in the caves of Wales, along the rocky coast of Brittany—that sweet song of life was welcomed.

And the old tree, hunched and gnarled by its age and its marriage to the wind, was a quiet sacrifice.

With its death, and a mother's willing pain, a new witch was born.

Though the choice would be hers—a gift, after all, can be refused, treasured or ignored—it would remain as much a part of the child, and the woman she became, as the color of her eyes. For now she was only an infant, her sight still dim, her thoughts still half-formed, shaking angry fists in the air even as her father laughed and pressed his first kiss on her downy head.

Her mother wept when the babe drank from her breast. Wept in joy and in sorrow. She knew already that she would have only this one girl child to celebrate the love and union she and her husband shared.

She had looked, and she had seen.

As she rocked the nursing child and sang an old song, she understood that there would be lessons to be taught, mistakes to be made. And she understood that one day—not so long from now, in the vast scope of lifetimes—her child would also look for love.

She hoped that of all the gifts she would pass along, all the truths she would tell, the child would understand one, the vital one.

That the purest magic is in the heart.

Chapter 1

There was a marker in the ground where the Witch Tree had stood. The people of Monterey and Carmel valued nature. Tourists often came to study the words on the marker, or simply to stand and look at the sculptured old trees, the rocky shoreline, the sunning harbor seals.

Locals who had seen the tree for themselves, who remembered the day it had fallen, often mentioned the fact that Morgana Donovan had been born that night.

Some said it was a sign, others shrugged and called it coincidence. Still more simply wondered. No one denied that it was excellent local color to have a self-proclaimed witch born hardly a stone's throw away from a tree with a reputation.

Nash Kirkland considered it an amusing fact and an interesting hook. He spent a great deal of his time studying the supernatural. Vampires and werewolves and things that went bump in the night were a hell of a way to make a living. And he wouldn't have had it any other way.

Not that he believed in goblins or ghoulies—or witches, if it came to that. Men didn't turn into bats or wolves at moonrise, the dead did not walk, and women didn't soar through the night on broomsticks. Except in the pages of a book, or in the flickering light and shadow of a movie screen.

There, he was pleased to say, anything was possible.

He was a sensible man who knew the value of illusions, and

the importance of simple entertainment. He was also enough of a dreamer to conjure images out of the shades of folklore and superstition for the masses to enjoy.

He'd fascinated the horror-film buff for seven years, starting with his first—and surprisingly successful—screenplay, *Shape Shifter*.

The fact was, Nash loved seeing his imagination come to life on-screen. He wasn't above popping into the neighborhood movie theater and happily devouring popcorn while the audience caught their breath, stifled screams or covered their eyes.

He delighted in knowing that the people who plunked down the price of a ticket to see one of his movies were going to get their money's worth of chills.

He always researched carefully. While writing the gruesome and amusing *Midnight Blood,* he'd spent a week in Rumania interviewing a man who swore he was a direct descendant of Vlad, the Impaler—Count Dracula. Unfortunately, the count's descendant hadn't grown fangs or turned into a bat, but he had proven to possess a wealth of vampire lore and legend.

It was such folktales that inspired Nash to spin a story—particularly when they were related by someone whose belief gave them punch.

And people considered him weird, he thought, grinning to himself as he passed the entrance to Seventeen Mile Drive. Nash knew he was an ordinary, grounded-to-earth type. At least by California standards. He just made his living from illusion, from playing on basic fears and superstitions—and the pleasure people took in being scared silly. He figured his value to society was his ability to take the monster out of the closet and flash it on the silver screen in Technicolor, usually adding a few dashes of unapologetic sex and sly humor.

Nash Kirkland could bring the bogeyman to life, turn the gentle Dr. Jekyll into the evil Mr. Hyde, or invoke the mummy's curse. All by putting words on paper. Maybe that was why he was a cynic. Oh, he enjoyed stories about the supernatural—but he, of all people, knew that was all they were. Stories. And he had a million of them.

He hoped Morgana Donovan, Monterey's favorite witch, would help him create the next one. For the past few weeks, between unpacking and taking pleasure in his new home, trying his skill at golf—and finally giving it up as a lost cause—and simply treasuring the view from his balcony, Nash had felt the urge to tell a tale of witchcraft. If there was such a thing as fate, he figured, it had done him a favor by plunking him down only a short, pleasant drive from an expert.

Whistling along with the car radio, he wondered what she'd be like. Turbaned or tasseled? Draped in black crepe? Or maybe she was some New Age fanatic who spoke only through Gargin, her channeler from Atlantis.

Either way, he wouldn't mind a bit. It was the loonies in the world that gave life its flavor.

He'd purposely avoided doing any extensive research on the witch. He wanted to form his own opinions and impressions, leaving his mind clear to start forming plot angles. All he knew was that she'd been born right here in Monterey, some twenty-eight years before, and she ran a successful shop that catered to people who were into crystals and herbs.

He had to give her two thumbs-up for staying in her home-town. After less than a month as a resident of Monterey, he wondered how he could ever have lived anywhere else. And God knew, he thought as his angular face creased in a grimace, he'd already lived just about everywhere.

Again, he had to thank his luck for making his scripts appealing to the masses. His imagination had made it possible for him to move away from the traffic and smog of L.A. to this priceless spot in northern California.

It was barely March, but he had the top down on his Jag, and the bright, brisk breeze whipped through his dark blond hair. There was the smell of water—it was never far away here—of grass, neatly clipped, of the flowers that thrived in the mild climate.

The sky was cloudless, a beautiful blue, his car was purring like a big, lean cat, he'd recently disentangled himself from a relationship that had been rushing downhill, and he was about to start a new project. As far as Nash was concerned, life was perfect.

He spotted the shop. As he'd been told, it stood neatly on the corner, flanked by a boutique and a restaurant. The businesses were obviously doing well, as he had to park more than a block away. He didn't mind the walk. His long, jeans-clad legs ate up the sidewalk. He passed a group of tourists who were arguing over where to have lunch, a pencil-slim woman in fuchsia silk leading two Afghan hounds, and a businessman who strolled along chatting on his cellular phone.

Nash loved California.

He stopped outside the shop. The sign painted on the window simply read WICCA. He nodded, smiling to himself. He liked it. The Old English word for witch. It brought to mind images of bent old women, trundling through the villages to cast spells and remove warts.

Exterior scene, day, he thought. The sky is murky with clouds, the wind rushes and howls. In a small, run-down village with broken fences and shuttered windows, a wrinkled old woman hurries down a dirt road, a heavy covered basket in her arms. A huge black raven screams as it glides by. With a flutter of wings, it stops to perch on a rusted gatepost. Bird and woman stare at each other. From somewhere in the distance comes a long, desperate scream.

Nash lost the image when someone came out of the shop, turned and bumped into him.

"Sorry," came the muffled apology.

He simply nodded. Just as well, Nash thought. It wouldn't do to take the story too far until he'd talked to the expert. For now, what he wanted was to take a good look at her wares.

The window display was impressive, he noted, and showed a flair for the dramatic. Deep blue velvet was draped over stands of various heights and widths so that it resembled a wide river with dark waterfalls. Floating over it were clusters of crystals, sparkling like magic in the morning sun. Some were as clear as glass, while others were of almost heartbreaking hues. Rose and aqua, royal purple, ink black. They were shaped like wands or castles or small, surrealistic cities.

Lips pursed, he rocked back on his heels. He could see how they would appeal to people—the colors, the shapes, the sparkle. That anybody could actually believe a hunk of rock held any kind of power was one more reason to marvel at the human brain. Still, they were certainly pretty enough. Above the clusters, faceted drops hung from thin wires and tossed rainbows everywhere.

Maybe she kept the cauldrons in the back.

The idea made him chuckle to himself. Still, he took a last look at the display before pushing open the door. It was tempting to pick up a few pieces for himself. A paperweight, or a sun-catcher. He might just settle for that—if she wasn't selling any dragon's scales or wolf's teeth.

The shop was crowded with people. His own fault, Nash reminded himself, for dropping in on a Saturday. Still, it would give him time to poke around and see just how a witch ran a business in the twentieth century.

The displays inside were just as dramatic as those glistening in the window. Huge chunks of rock, some sliced open to reveal hundreds of crystal teeth. Dainty little bottles filled with colored liquid. Nash was slightly disappointed when he read one label and discovered that it was a rosemary bath balm, for relaxing the senses. He'd hoped for at least one love potion.

There were more herbs, packaged for potpourri, for tea and for culinary uses, as well as candles in soft colors and crystals in all shapes and sizes. Some interesting jewelry—again leaning heavily on crystals—was sparkling behind glass. Artwork, paintings, statues, sculpture, all so cleverly placed that the shop might more accurately have been termed a gallery.

Nash, always interested in the unusual, took a fancy to a pewter lamp fashioned in the shape of a winged dragon with glowing red eyes.

Then he spotted her. One look had him certain that this was the very image of the modern witch. The sulky-looking blonde was holding a discussion with two customers over a table of tumbling stones. She had a luscious little body poured into a sleek black jumpsuit. Glittery earrings hung to her shoulders, and rings adorned every finger. The fingers ended in long, lethal-looking red nails.

"Attractive, isn't he?"

"Hmm?" The smoke-edged voice had Nash turning away from the dragon. This time one look had him forgetting the stacked young witch in the corner. He found himself lost for several heartbeats in a pair of cobalt blue eyes. "Excuse me?"

"The dragon." Smiling, she ran a hand over the pewter head. "I was just wondering if I should take him home with me." She smiled, and he saw that her lips were full and soft and unpainted. "Do you like dragons?"

"Crazy about them," he decided on the spot. "Do you shop in here often?"

"Yes." She lifted a hand to her hair. It was black as midnight and fell in careless waves to her waist. Nash made an effort and tried to put the pieces of her together. The ebony hair went with pale, creamy skin. The eyes were wide and heavily lashed, the nose was small and sharp. She was nearly as tall as he, and wand slender. The simple blue dress she wore showed taste and style, as well as subtle curves.

There was something, well, dazzling about her, he realized. Though he couldn't analyze what while he was so busy enjoying it.

As he watched, her lips curved again. There was something very aware as well as amused in the movement. "Have you been in Wicca before?"

"No. Great stuff."

"You're interested in crystals?"

"I could be." Idly he picked up a hunk of amethyst. "But I flunked my earth science course in high school."

"I don't think you'll be graded here." She nodded toward the stone he held. "If you want to get in touch with your inner self, you should hold it in your left hand."

"Oh, yeah?" To indulge her, he shifted it. He hated to tell her he didn't feel a thing—other than a shaft of pleasure at the way the dress skimmed around her knees. "If you're a regular here, maybe you could introduce me to the witch."

Brow lifted, she followed his look as he glanced at the blonde, who was finishing up her sale. "Do you need a witch?"

"I guess you could say that."

She turned those wonderful blue eyes on him again. "You don't look like the type who'd come looking for a love spell."

He grinned. "Thanks. I think. Actually, I'm doing some research. I write movies. I want to do a story on witchcraft in the nineties. You know...secret covens, sex and sacrifices."

"Ah." When she inclined her head, clear crystal drops swung

at her ears. "Nubile women doing ring dances sky-clad. Naked," she explained. "Mixing potions by the dark of the moon to seduce their hapless victims into orgies of prurient delights."

"More or less." He leaned closer and discovered that she smelled as cool and dark as a forest in moonlight. "Does this Morgana really believe she's a witch?"

"She knows what she is, Mr.—?"

"Kirkland. Nash Kirkland."

Her laugh was low and pleased. "Of course. I've enjoyed your work. I particularly liked *Midnight Blood*. You gave your vampire a great deal of wit and sensuality without trampling on tradition."

"There's more to being undead than graveyard dirt and coffins."

"I suppose. And there's more to being a witch than stirring a cauldron."

"Exactly. That's why I want to interview her. I figure she's got to be a pretty sharp lady to pull all this off."

"Pull off?" she repeated as she bent to pick up a huge white cat that had sauntered over to flow around her legs.

"The reputation," he explained. "I heard about her in L.A. People bring me weird stories."

"I'm sure they do." She stroked the cat's massive head. Now Nash had two pair of eyes trained on him. One pair of cobalt, and one of amber. "But you don't believe in the Craft, or the power."

"I believe I can make it into a hell of a good story." He smiled, putting considerable charm into it. "So, how about it? Put in a good word for me with the witch?"

She studied him. A cynic, she decided, and one entirely too sure of himself. Life, she thought, was obviously one big bed of roses for Nash Kirkland. Maybe it was time he felt a few thorns.

"I don't think that'll be necessary." She offered him a hand, long and slender and adorned with a single ring of hammered silver. He took it automatically, then hissed out a breath as a jolt of electricity zinged up to his shoulder. She just smiled. "I'm your witch," she said.

Static electricity, Nash told himself a moment later, after Morgana had turned away to answer a question from a customer about something called St. John's wort. She'd been holding that giant cat, rubbing the fur.... That was where the shock had come from.

But he flexed his fingers unconsciously.

Your witch, she'd said. He wasn't sure he liked her use of that particular pronoun. It made things a bit too uncomfortably intimate. Not that she wasn't a stunner. But the way she'd smiled at him when he jolted had been more than a little unnerving. It had also told him just why he'd found her dazzling.

Power. Oh, not *that* kind of power, Nash assured himself as he watched her handle a bundle of dried herbs. But the power some beautiful women seemed to be born with—innate sexuality and a terrifying self-confidence. He didn't like to think of himself as the kind of man who was intimidated by a woman's strength of will, yet there was no denying that the soft, yielding sort was easier to deal with.

In any case, his interest in her was professional. Not purely, he amended. A man would have to have been dead a decade to look at Morgana Donovan and keep his thoughts on a straight professional plane. But Nash figured he could keep his priorities in order.

Nash waited until she was finished with the customer, fixed a self-deprecating smile in place and approached the counter. "I wonder if you've got a handy spell for getting my foot out of my mouth."

"Oh, I think you can manage that on your own." Ordinarily she would have dismissed him, but there must be some reason she'd been drawn across the shop to him. Morgana didn't believe in accidents. Anyway, she decided, any man with such soft brown eyes couldn't be a complete jerk. "I'm afraid your timing's poor, Nash. We're very busy this morning."

"You close at six. How about if I come back then? I'll buy you a drink, dinner?"

Her impulse to refuse was automatic. She would have preferred to meditate on it or study her scrying ball. Before she could speak, the cat leapt onto the counter, clearing the four feet in that weightless soar felines accomplish so easily. Nash reached out absently to scratch the cat's head. Rather than walking off, insulted, or spitting bad-temperedly, as was her habit with strangers, the white cat arched sinuously under the stroking hand. Her amber eyes slitted and stared into Morgana's.

"You seem to have Luna's approval," Morgana muttered. "Six o'clock, then," she said as the cat began to purr lustily. "And I'll decide what to do about you."

"Fair enough." Nash gave Luna one last long stroke, then strolled out.

Frowning, Morgana leaned down until her eyes were level with the cat's. "You'd better know what you're about."

Luna merely shifted her not-inconsiderable weight and began to wash herself.

Morgana didn't have much time to think about Nash. Because she was a woman who was always at war with her impulsive nature, she would have preferred a quiet hour to mull over how best to deal with him. With her hands and mind busy with a flood of customers, Morgana reminded herself that she would have no trouble handling a cocksure storyteller with puppy dog eyes.

"Wow." Mindy, the lavishly built blonde Nash had admired, plopped down on a stool behind the counter. "We haven't seen a crowd like that since before Christmas."

"I think we're going to have full Saturdays throughout the month."

Grinning, Mindy pulled a stick of gum out of the hip pocket of her snug jumpsuit. "Did you cast a money spell?"

Morgana arranged a glass castle to her liking before responding. "The stars are in an excellent position for business." She smiled. "Plus the fact that our new window display is fabulous. You can go on home, Mindy. I'll total out and lock up."

"I'll take you up on it." She slid sinuously off the stool to stretch, then lifted both darkened brows. "My, oh, my...look at this. Tall, tanned and tasty."

Morgana glanced over and spotted Nash through the front window. He'd had more luck with parking this time, and was unfolding himself from the front seat of his convertible.

"Down, girl." Chuckling, Morgana shook her head. "Men like that break hearts without spilling a drop of blood."

"That's okay. I haven't had my heart broken in days. Let's see..." She took a swift and deadly accurate survey. "Six foot, a hundred and sixty gorgeous pounds. The casual type—maybe just a tad intellectual. Likes the outdoors, but doesn't overdo it. Just a few scattered sun streaks through the hair, and a reasonable tan. Good facial bones—he'll hold up with age. Then there's that yummy mouth."

"Fortunately I know you, and understand you actually do think more of men than you do puppies in a pet-store window."

With a chuckle, Mindy fluffed her hair. "Oh, I think more of them, all right. A whole lot more." As the door opened, Mindy shifted position so that her body seemed about to burst out of the jumpsuit. "Hello, handsome. Want to buy a little magic?"

Always ready to accommodate a willing woman, Nash flashed her a grin. "What do you recommend?"

"Well..." The word came out in a long purr to rival one of Luna's.

"Mindy, Mr. Kirkland isn't a customer." Morgana's voice was mild and amused. There were few things more entertaining than Mindy's showmanship with an attractive man. "We have a meeting."

"Maybe next time," Nash told her.

"Maybe anytime." Mindy slithered around the counter, shot Nash one last devastating look, then wiggled out the door.

"I bet she boosts your sales," Nash commented.

"Along with the blood pressure of every male within range. How's yours?"

He grinned. "Got any oxygen?"

"Sorry. Fresh out." She gave his arm a friendly pat. "Why don't you have a seat? I have a few more things to— Damn."

"Excuse me?"

"Didn't get the Closed sign up quick enough," she muttered. Then she beamed a smile as the door opened. "Hello, Mrs. Littleton."

"Morgana." The word came out in a long, relieved sigh as a woman Nash judged to be somewhere between sixty and seventy streamed across the room.

The verb seemed apt, he thought. She was built like a cruise ship, sturdy of bow and stern, with colorful scarves wafting around her like flags. Her hair was a bright, improbable red that frizzed cheerfully around a moon-shaped face. Her eyes were heavily outlined in emerald, and her mouth was slicked with deep crimson. She threw out both hands—they were crowded with rings—and gripped Morgana's.

"I simply couldn't get here a moment sooner. As it was, I had to scold the young policeman who tried to give me a ticket. Imagine, a boy hardly old enough to shave, lecturing me on the law." She let out huff of breath that smelled of peppermint. "Now then, I hope you have a few minutes for me."

"Of course." There was no help for it, Morgana thought. She was simply too fond of the batty old woman to make excuses.

"You're a dream. She's a dream, isn't she?" Mrs. Littleton demanded of Nash.

"You bet."

Mrs. Littleton beamed, turning toward him with a musical symphony of jaggling chains and bracelets. "Sagittarius, right?"

"Ah..." Nash heedlessly amended his birthday to suit her. "Right. Amazing."

She puffed out her ample bosom. "I do pride myself on being an excellent judge. I won't keep you but a moment from your date, dear."

"I don't have a date," Morgana told her. "What can I do for you?"

"Just the teensiest favor." Mrs. Littleton's eyes took on a gleam that had Morgana stifling a moan. "My grandniece. There's the matter of the prom, and this sweet boy in her geometry class."

This time she'd be firm, Morgana promised herself. Absolutely a rock. Taking Mrs. Littleton's arm, she edged her away from Nash. "I've explained to you that I don't work that way."

Mrs. Littleton fluttered her false eyelashes. "I know you *usually* don't. But this is such a worthy cause."

"They all are." Narrowing her eyes at Nash, who'd shifted closer, Morgana pulled Mrs. Littleton across the room. "I'm sure your niece is a wonderful girl, but arranging a prom date for her is frivolous—and such things have repercussions. No," she said when Mrs. Littleton began to protest. "If I did arrange it—

changing something that shouldn't be changed—it could affect her life."

"It's only one night."

"Altering fate one night potentially alters it for centuries." Mrs. Littleton's downcast look had Morgana feeling like a miser refusing a starving man a crust of bread. "I know you only want her to have a special night, but I just can't play games with destiny."

"She's so shy, you see," Mrs. Littleton said with a sigh. Her ears were sharp enough to have heard the faint weakening in Morgana's resolve. "And she doesn't think she's the least bit pretty. But she is." Before Morgana could protest, she whipped out a snapshot. "See?"

She didn't want to see, Morgana thought. But she looked, and the pretty young teenager with the somber eyes did the rest. Morgana cursed inwardly. Dragon's teeth and hellfire. She was as soppy as a wet valentine when it came to puppy love.

"I won't guarantee—only suggest."

"That will be wonderful." Seizing the moment, Mrs. Littleton pulled out another picture, one she'd cut from the high school yearbook at the school library. "This is Matthew. A nice name, isn't it? Matthew Brody, and Jessie Littleton. She was named for me. You will start soon, won't you? The prom's the first weekend in May."

"If it's meant, it's meant," Morgana said, slipping the photos into her pocket.

"Blessed be." Beaming, Mrs. Littleton kissed Morgana's cheek. "I won't keep you any longer. I'll be back Monday to shop."

"Have a good weekend." Annoyed with herself, Morgana watched Mrs. Littleton depart.

"Wasn't she supposed to cross your palm with silver?" Nash asked.

Morgana tilted her head. The anger that had been directed solely at herself shot out of her eyes. "I don't profit from power."

He shrugged, then walked toward her. "I hate to point it out, but she twisted you around her finger."

A faint flush crept into her cheeks. If there was anything she hated more than being weak, it was being weak in public. "I'm aware of that."

Lifting a hand, he rubbed his thumb over her cheek to wipe away the faint smear of crimson Mrs. Littleton had left there. "I figured witches would be tough."

"I have a weak spot for the eccentric and the good hearted. And you're not a Sagittarius."

He was sorry he had to remove his thumb from her cheek. Her skin was as cool and smooth as milk. "No? What, then?"

"Gemini."

His brow lifted, and he stuck his hand in his pocket. "Good guess."

His discomfort made her feel a little better. "I rarely guess. Since you were nice enough not to hurt her feelings, I won't take out my annoyance on you. Why don't you come in the back? I'll brew us some tea." She laughed when she saw his expression. "All right. I'll pour us some wine."

"Better."

He followed her through a door behind the counter into a room that served as storage, office and kitchenette. Though it was a small area, it didn't seem overly crowded. Shelves lined two walls and were stacked with boxes, uncrated stock and books. A curvy cherry desk held a brass lamp shaped like a mermaid, an efficient-looking two-line phone and a pile of paperwork held in place by a flat-bottomed glass that tossed out color and reflection.

Beyond that was a child-size refrigerator, a two-burner stove and a drop-leaf table with two chairs. In the single window, pots of herbs were crowded and thriving. He could smell...he wasn't sure what—sage, perhaps, and oregano, with a homey trace of lavender. Whatever it was, it was pleasant.

Morgana took two clear goblets from a shelf over the sink.

"Have a seat," she said. "I can't give you very much time, but you might as well be comfortable." She took a long, slim-necked bottle out of the refrigerator and poured a pale golden liquid into the goblets.

"No label?"

"It's my own recipe." With a smile, she sipped first. "Don't worry, there's not a single eye of newt in it."

He would have laughed, but the way she studied him over the rim of her glass was making him uneasy. Still, he hated to refuse a challenge. He took a sip. The wine was cool, faintly sweet, and smooth as silk. "Nice."

"Thank you." She took the chair beside him. "I haven't decided whether I'm going to help you or not. But I'm interested in your craft, particularly if you're going to incorporate mine into it."

"You like the movies," he said, figuring that gave him a head start. He hooked an arm around the back of the chair, scratching Luna absently with his foot as the cat wound around his legs.

"Among other things. I enjoy the variety of human imagination."

"Okay—"

"But," she went on, interrupting him, "I'm not sure I want my personal views going Hollywood."

"We can talk." He smiled again, and again she understood that he was a power to be reckoned with. As she considered that, Luna leapt onto the table. For the first time Nash noticed that the cat wore an etched round crystal around her neck. "Look, Morgana, I'm not trying to prove or disprove, I'm not trying to change the world. I just want to make a movie."

"Why horror and the occult?"

"Why?" He shrugged his shoulders. It always made him uncomfortable when people asked him to analyze. "I don't know. Maybe because when people go into a scary movie, they stop thinking about the lousy day they had at the office after the opening scream." His eyes lit with humor. "Or maybe because the first time I got past first base with a girl was when she wrapped herself all over me during a midnight showing of Carpenter's *Halloween.*"

Morgana sipped and considered. Maybe, just maybe, there was a sensitive soul under that smug exterior. There certainly was talent, and there was undeniably charm. It bothered her that she felt...pushed somehow, pushed to agree.

Well, she'd damn well say no if she chose to, but she'd test the waters first.

"Why don't you tell me about your story?"

Nash saw the opening and pounced. "I haven't got one to

speak of yet. That's where you come in. I like to have plenty of background. I can get a lot of information out of books." He spread his hands. "I already have some—my research tends to overlap and take me into all areas of the occult. What I want is the personal angle. You know, what made you get into witchcraft, do you attend ceremonies, what kind of trappings you prefer."

Morgana ran a fingertip thoughtfully around the rim of the goblet. "I'm afraid you're starting off with the wrong impression. You're making it sound as though I joined some sort of club."

"Coven, club.... A group with the same interests."

"I don't belong to a coven. I prefer working alone."

Interested, he leaned forward. "Why?"

"There are groups who are quite sincere, and those who are not. Still others dabble in things best left locked."

"Black magic."

"Whatever name you give it."

"And you're a white witch."

"You're fond of labels." With a restless move, she picked up her wine again. Unlike Nash, she didn't mind discussing the essence of her craft—but once she agreed to, she expected to have her thoughts received respectfully. "We're all born with certain powers, Nash. Yours is to tell entertaining stories. And to attract women." Her lips curved as she sipped. "I'm sure you respect, and employ, your powers. I do exactly the same."

"What are yours?"

She took her time, setting her goblet down, lifted her eyes to his. The look she leveled at him made him feel like a fool for having asked. The power was there—the kind that could make a man crawl. His mouth went so dry that the wine he was drinking could have been sand.

"What would you like, a performance?" The faintest hint of impatience had seeped into her tone.

He managed to draw a breath and shake himself out of what he would almost have thought was a trance—if he believed in trances. "I'd love one." Maybe it was twitching the devil's tail, but he couldn't resist. The color that temper brought to her cheeks made her skin glow like a freshly picked peach. "What did you have in mind?"

She felt the quick, unwelcome tug of desire. It was distinctly annoying. "Lightning bolts from the fingertips? Should I whistle up the wind or draw down the moon?"

"Dealer's choice."

The nerve of the man, she thought as she rose, the power humming hot in her blood. It would serve him right if she—

'Morgana."

She whirled, anger sizzling. With an effort, she tossed her hair back and relaxed. "Ana."

Nash couldn't have said why he felt as though he'd just avoided a calamity of major proportions. But he knew that, for an instant, his whole being had been so wrapped up in Morgana that he wouldn't have felt an earthquake. She'd pulled him right in, and now he was left, a little dazed, a little dull-witted, staring at the slim blond woman in the doorway.

She was lovely, and, though a head shorter than Morgana, she exuded an odd kind of soothing strength. Her eyes were a soft, calm gray, and they were focused on Morgana. In her arms she carried a box that was overflowing with flowering herbs.

"You didn't have the sign up," Anastasia said, "so I came in the front."

"Let me take that." Messages passed between the two women. Nash didn't have to hear them to know it. "Ana, this is Nash Kirkland. Nash, my cousin, Anastasia."

"I'm sorry to interrupt." Her voice, low and warm, was as soothing as her eyes.

"You're not," Morgana said as Nash got to his feet. "Nash and I were just finished."

"Just beginning," he told her. "But we can pick it up later. Nice to meet you," he said to Anastasia. Then he smiled at Morgana and tucked her hair behind her ear. "Till next time."

"Nash." Morgana set the box down and took out a small pot of blooms. "A gift." She offered it, and her sweetest smile. "Sweet peas," she explained. "To symbolize departure."

He couldn't resist. Leaning over the box, he touched his lips to hers. "For the hell of it." He sauntered out.

In spite of herself, Morgana chuckled.

Anastasia settled into a chair with a contented sigh. "Want to tell me about it?"

"Nothing to tell. He's a charming annoyance. A writer with very typical views on witches."

"Oh. *That* Nash Kirkland." To please herself, Anastasia picked up Morgana's half-full goblet and sipped. "The one who wrote that gory movie you and Sebastian dragged me to."

"It was really quite intelligent and sly."

"Hmm." Anastasia drank again. "And gory. Then again, you've always enjoyed that kind of thing."

"Watching evil is an entertaining way to reaffirm good." She frowned. "Unfortunately, Nash Kirkland does very superior work."

"That may be. I'd rather watch the Marx brothers." Automatically she walked over to check the herbs in Morgana's window. "I couldn't help but notice the tension. You looked as if you were about to turn him into a toad when I walked in."

The thought gave Morgana a moment of sterling pleasure. "I was tempted. Something about that smugness set me off."

"You're too easily set off. You did say you were going to work on control, didn't you, love?"

Scowling, Morgana snatched up Nash's glass. "He walked out of here on two legs, didn't he?" She sipped, and realized instantly it was a mistake. He'd left too much of himself in the wine.

A powerful man, she thought as she set the goblet down again. Despite the easy smile and the relaxed manner, a very powerful man.

She wished she'd thought to charm the flowers she'd given him, but she dismissed the idea immediately. Perhaps something was pushing them together, but she would deal with it. And she would deal with it, and with Nash Kirkland, without magic.

Chapter 2

Morgana enjoyed the peace of Sunday afternoons. It was her day to indulge herself—and from her first breath, Morgana had appreciated indulgences. Not that she avoided work. She had put a great deal of time and effort into seeing that her shop ran smoothly and turned a profit—without using her special skills to smooth her path. Still, she firmly believed that the proper reward for any effort was relaxation.

Unlike some business owners, Morgana didn't agonize over books and inventory and overhead. She simply did what she felt needed to be done, making sure she did it well. Then when she walked away from it—if only for an hour at a time—she forgot business completely.

It amazed Morgana that there were people who would spend a beautiful day inside, biting their nails over ledgers. She hired an accountant to do that.

She hadn't hired a housekeeper, but only because she didn't care for the idea of someone poking through her personal things. She, and only she, was their caretaker. Though her gardens were extensive—and she'd long ago accepted that she would never have the way with growing things that her cousin Anastasia had—she tended the blooms herself. She found the cycle—planting, watering, weeding, harvesting—rewarding.

She knelt now, in a strong stream of sunlight, at the extensive rockery where her herbs and spring bulbs thrived. There was the

scent of rosemary, of hyacinth, the delicacy of jasmine, the richness of anise. Music drifted through the windows, the penny
whistles and flutes of a traditional Irish folk tune, clashing cheerfully with the surge and thrust of water spewing up from the
rocks a few hundred yards behind her.

It was one of those precious and perfect days, with the sky
spread overhead like clear blue glass and the wind, light and
playful, carrying the scents of water and wildflowers. From beyond the low wall and sheltering trees at the front of her property, she could hear the occasional swish of a car as tourists or
natives took in the scenery.

Luna was sprawled nearby in a patch of sunlight, her eyes
slitted, nearly closed, her tail switching occasionally as she
watched birds. If Morgana weren't there, she might have tried
for a snack—for all her bulk, she could move like lightning. But
her mistress was very firm about such habits.

When the dog padded over to drop his head into Morgana's
lap, Luna gave a mutter of disgust and went to sleep. Dogs had
no pride.

Content, Morgana sat back on her heels, ruffling the dog's fur
with one hand as she surveyed her rockery. Perhaps she would
pluck a few sprigs—she was running low on angelica balm and
hyssop powder. Tonight, she decided. If there was a moon. Such
things were best done by moonlight.

For now, she would enjoy the sun, lifting her face to it, letting
its warmth and life pour over her skin. She could never sit here
without feeling the beauty of this spot, this place where she had
been born. Though she had traveled to many other lands, seen
many magic places, it was here she belonged.

For it was here, she had learned long ago, that she would find
love, share love, and bear her children. With a sigh, Morgana
closed her eyes. Those days could wait, she mused. She was
content with her life precisely as it was. When the time came
for it to change, she intended to remain fully in charge.

When the dog sprang to his feet, a warning growl humming
in his throat, Morgana didn't bother to look around. She'd
known he'd come. She hadn't needed the crystal or the black
mirror to tell her. Nor could she claim it was clairvoyance—that

was more her cousin Sebastian's territory. She'd needed only to be a woman to know.

She sat, smiling, while the dog sent out a series of rapid, unfriendly barks. She would see just how Nash Kirkland handled the situation.

How was a man supposed to react when the woman he'd come to see was being guarded by a…he was sure it couldn't really be a wolf, but it sure as hell looked like one. He was doubly sure that if she gave the word the sleek silver beast would take one long leap and go for his throat.

Nash cleared that throat, then jolted when something brushed his leg. Glancing down, he noted that Luna, at least, had decided to be friendly. "Nice dog you got there," he said cautiously. "Nice, big dog."

Morgana deigned to glance over her shoulder. "Out for a Sunday drive?"

"More or less."

The dog had subsided into those low, dangerous growls again. Nash felt a bead of sweat slide down his back as the mass of muscle and teeth stalked toward him to sniff at his shoes. "I, ah…" Then the dog looked up, and Nash was struck by the gleam of deep blue eyes against that silver fur. "God, you're a beauty, aren't you?" He held out a hand, sincerely hoping the dog would let him keep it. It was sniffed thoroughly, then rewarded with a lick.

Lips pursed, Morgana studied them. Pan had never so much as nipped anyone's ankle, but neither was he given to making friends so quickly. "You have a way with animals."

Nash was already crouched down to give the dog a brisk scratching. All throughout his childhood he'd yearned for a dog. It surprised him to realize that his boyhood desire had never quite faded. "They know I'm just a kid at heart. What breed is he?"

"Pan?" Her smile was slow and secret. "We'll just say he's a Donovan. What can I do for you, Nash?"

He looked over. She was in the sunlight, her hair bundled under a wide-brimmed straw hat. Her jeans were too tight, and her T-shirt was too baggy. Because she hadn't used gardening gloves, her hands were smeared with rich, dark earth. Her feet were bare. It hadn't occurred to him that bare feet could be sexy. Until now.

"Besides that," she said, with such an easy ripple of amusement in her voice that he had to grin.

"Sorry. My mind was wandering."

It didn't offend her to be found desirable. "Why don't you start with telling me how you found me?"

"Come on, honey, you know you've got a reputation." He rose to walk over and sit on the grass beside her. "I had dinner in the place beside your shop, struck up a conversation with my waitress."

"I'll bet you did."

He reached over to toy with the amulet she wore. An interesting piece, he thought, shaped like a half-moon and inscribed in—Greek? Arabic? He was no scholar. "Anyway, she was a fount of information. Fascinated and spooked. Do you affect a lot of people that way?"

"Legions." And she'd learned to enjoy it. "Did she tell you that I ride over the bay on my broomstick every full moon?"

"Close enough." He let the amulet drop. "It interests me how ordinarily intelligent people allow themselves to get caught up in the supernatural."

"Isn't that how you make your living?"

"Exactly. And, speaking of my living, I figure you and I started off wrong. How about a clean slate?"

It was hard to be annoyed with an attractive man on a beautiful day. "How about it?"

He thought it might be wise to take the conversation where he wanted by way of the back door. "You know a lot about flowers and stuff?"

"A few things." She shifted to finish planting a fresh pot of lemon balm.

"Maybe you can tell me what I've got in my yard, and what I should do about it?"

"Hire a gardening service," she said. Then she relented and smiled. "I suppose I might find time to take a look."

"I'd really appreciate it." He brushed at a smear of dirt on her chin. "You really could help me with the script, Morgana. It's no problem getting things out of books—anyone can do that.

What I'm looking for is a different slant, something more personal. And I—''

''What is it?''

''You have stars in your eyes,'' he murmured. ''Little gold stars…like sunlight on a midnight sea. But you can't have the sun at midnight.''

''You can have anything if you know how to get it.'' Those fabulous eyes held his. He couldn't have looked away to save his soul. ''Tell me what you want, Nash.''

''To give people a couple of enjoyable hours. To know they'll forget problems, reality, everything, when they step into my world. A good story's like a door, and you can go through it whenever you need to. After you've read it or seen it or heard it, you can still go back through it. Once it's yours, it's always yours.''

He broke off, startled and embarrassed. This kind of philosophizing didn't fit in with his carefree image. He'd had expert interviewers dig at him for hours without unearthing a statement as simple and genuine as that. And all she'd done was ask.

''And, of course, I want to make pots of money,'' he added, trying to grin. His head felt light, his skin too warm.

''I don't see that one desire has to be exclusive of the other. There have been storytellers in my family from the fairy days down to my mother. We understand the value of stories.''

Perhaps that was why she hadn't dismissed him from the outset. She respected what he did. That, too, was in her blood.

''Consider this.'' She leaned forward, and he felt the punch of something in his gut, something that went beyond her beauty. ''If I agree to help you, I refuse to let you fall back on the least common denominator. The old crone, cackling as she mixes henbane in the cauldron.''

He smiled. ''Convince me.''

''Be careful what you dare, Nash,'' she murmured, rising. ''Come inside. I'm thirsty.''

Since he was no longer worried about being chewed up by her guard dog, who was now strolling contentedly beside them, Nash took time to admire her house. He already knew that many of the homes along the Monterey Peninsula were extraordinary and unique. He'd bought one himself. Morgana's had the added allure of age and grace.

It was three stories of stone, turreted and towered—to suit a witch, he supposed. But it was neither Gothic nor grim. Tall, graceful windows flashed in the sunlight, and climbing flowers crept up the walls to twine and tangle in lacy ironwork. Carved into the stone were winged fairies and mermaids, adding charm. Lovely robed figures served as rainspouts.

Interior scene, night, he mused. Inside the topmost tower of the old stone house by the sea, the beautiful young witch sits in a ring of candles. The room is shadowy, with the light fluttering over the faces of statues, the stems of silver goblets, a clear orb of crystal. She wears a sheer white robe open to the waist. A heavy carved amulet hangs between the swell of her breasts. A deep hum seems to come from the stones themselves as she lifts two photographs high in the air.

The candles flicker. A wind rises within the closed room to lift her hair and ripple the robe. She chants. Ancient words, in a low, smoldering voice. She touches the photos to the candle flame.... No, scratch that. She...yeah, she sprinkles the photos with the glowing liquid from a cracked blue bowl. A hiss of steam. The humming takes on a slow, sinuous beat. Her body sways with it as she places the photos face-to-face, laying them on a silver tray. A secret smile crosses her face as the photos fuse together.

Fade out.

He liked it, though he figured she could add a bit more color to the casting of a love spell.

Content with his silence, Morgana took him around the side of the house, where the sound of water on rock rumbled and the cypress grove, trees bent and gnarled by time and wind, stood watch. They crossed a stone patio shaped like a pentagram, at whose top point stood a brass statue of a woman. Water gurgled in a tiny pool at her feet.

"Who's she?" Nash asked.

"She has many names." Moving to the statue, Morgana took up a small ladle, dipped it in the clear pool. She sipped, then poured the rest onto the ground for the goddess. Without a word, she crossed the patio again and entered a sunny, spotless kitchen. "Do you believe in a creator?"

The question surprised him. "Yeah, sure. I suppose." He shifted uncomfortably while she walked across a white tiled floor to the sink to rinse her hands. "This—your witchcraft—it's a religious thing?"

She smiled as she took out a pitcher of lemonade. "Life's a religious thing. But don't worry, Nash—I won't try to convert you." She filled two glasses with ice. "It shouldn't make you uncomfortable. Your stories are invariably about good and evil. People are always making choices, whether to be one or the other."

"What about you?"

She offered him his glass, then turned to walk through an archway and out of the kitchen. "You could say I'm always trying to check my less attractive impulses." She shot him a look. "It doesn't always work."

As she spoke, she led him down a wide hallway. The walls were decorated with faded tapestries depicting scenes from folklore and mythology, ornate sconces and etched plates of silver and copper.

She opted for what her grandmother had always called the drawing room. Its walls were painted a warm rose, and the tone was picked up in the pattern of the Bokhara rug tossed over the wide-planked chestnut floor. A lovely Adam mantel draped over the fireplace, which was stacked with wood ready to be put to flame should the night turn cool or should Morgana wish it.

But for now a light breeze played through the open windows, billowing the sheer curtains and bringing with it the scents of her gardens.

As in her shop, there were crystals, clusters and wands scattered around the room, along with a partial collection of her sculpture. Pewter wizards, bronze fairies, porcelain dragons.

"Great stuff." He ran his hand over the strings of a gold lap harp. The sound it made was soft and sweet. "Do you play?"

"When I'm in the mood." It amused her to watch him move around the room, toying with this, examining that. She appreciated honest curiosity. He picked up a scribed silver goblet and sniffed. "Smells like..."

"Hellfire?" she suggested. He set it down again, preferring a slender amethyst wand crusted with stones and twined with silver threads. "Magic wand?"

"Naturally. Be careful what you wish for," she told him, taking it delicately from his hand.

He shrugged and turned away, missing the way the wand glowed before Morgana put it aside. "I've collected a lot of this kind of thing myself. You might like to see." He bent over a clear glass ball and saw his own reflection. "I picked up a shaman's mask at an auction last month, and a—what do you call it?—a scrying mirror. Looks like we have something in common."

"A taste in art." She sat on the arm of the couch.

"And literature." He was poking through a bookshelf. "Lovecraft, Bradbury. I've got this edition of *The Golden Dawn*. Stephen King, Hunter Brown, McCaffrey. Hey, is this—?" He pulled out the volume and opened it reverently. "It's a first edition of Bram Stoker's *Dracula*." He looked over at her. "Will you take my right arm for it?"

"I'll have to get back to you on that."

"I always hoped he'd have approved of *Midnight Blood*." As he slipped the book back into place, another caught his eyes. "*Four Golden Balls. The Faerie King*." He skimmed a finger over the slim volumes. "*Whistle Up the Wind*. You've got her entire collection." Envy stirred in his blood. "And in first editions."

"You read Bryna?"

"Are you kidding?" It was too much like meeting an old friend. He had to touch, to look, even to sniff. "I've read everything she's written a dozen times. Anyone who thinks they're just for kids is nuts. It's like poetry and magic and morality all rolled into one. And, of course, the illustrations are fabulous. I'd kill for a piece of the original artwork, but she just won't sell."

Interested, Morgana tilted her head. "Have you asked?"

"I've filtered some pitiful pleas through her agent. No dice. She lives in some castle in Ireland, and probably papers the walls with her sketches. I wish..." He turned at Morgana's quiet laugh.

"Actually, she keeps them in thick albums, waiting for the grandchildren she hopes for."

"Donovan." He tucked his thumbs in his pockets. "Bryna Donovan. That's your mother."

"Yes, and she'd be delighted to know you approve of her work." She lifted her glass. "From one storyteller to another. My parents lived in this house off and on for several years. Actually, she wrote her first published work upstairs while she was pregnant with me. She always says I insisted she write the story down."

"Does your mother believe you're a witch?"

"It would be better to ask her that yourself, if you get the opportunity."

"You're being evasive again." He walked over to sprawl comfortably on the couch beside her. It was impossible not to be comfortable with a woman who surrounded herself with things he himself loved. "Let's put it this way. Does your family have any problem with your interests?"

She appreciated the way he relaxed, legs stretched, body at ease, as if he'd been making himself at home on her couch for years. "My family has always understood the need to focus energies in an individual direction. Do your parents have a problem with your interests?"

"I never knew them. My parents."

"I'm sorry." The mocking light in her eyes turned instantly to sympathy. Her family had always been her center. She could hardly imagine living without them.

"It wasn't a big deal." But he rose again, uneasy with the way she'd laid a comforting hand on his shoulder. He'd come too far from the bad old days to want any sympathy. "I'm interested in your family's reactions. I mean, how would most parents feel, what would they do if they found their kid casting spells. Did you decide to start dabbling as a child?"

Sympathy vanished like a puff of smoke. "Dabbling?" she repeated, eyes slitted.

"I may want to have a prologue, you know, showing how the main character got involved."

He was paying less attention to her than to the room itself, the atmosphere. As he worked out his thoughts, he paced. Not nervously, not even restlessly, but in a way that made it obvious that he was taking stock of everything he could see.

"Maybe she gets pushed around by the kid next door and turns him into a frog," he continued, oblivious to the fact that Morgana's jaw had tensed. "Or she runs into some mysterious woman who passes on the power. I kind of like that." As he roamed, he played with ideas, slender threads that could be woven into whole cloth for a story. "I'm just not sure of the angle I want to use, so I figured we'd start by playing it straight. You tell me what started you off—books you read, whatever. Then I can twist it to work as fiction."

She was going to have to watch her temper, and watch it carefully. When she spoke, her voice was soft, and carried a ring that made him stop in the center of the rug. "I was born with elvish blood. I am a hereditary witch, and my heritage traces back to Finn of the Celts. My power is a gift passed on from generation to generation. When I find a man of strength, we'll make children between us, and they will carry it beyond me."

He nodded, impressed. "That's great." So she didn't want to play it straight, he thought. He'd humor her. The stuff about elvish blood had terrific possibilities. "So, when did you first realize you were a witch?"

The tone of his voice had her temper slipping a notch. The room shook as she fought it back. Nash snatched her off the couch so quickly that she didn't have time to protest. He'd pulled her toward the doorway when the shaking stopped.

"Just a tremor," he said, but he kept his arms around her. "I was in San Francisco during the last big one." Because he felt like an idiot, he gave her a lopsided grin. "I haven't been able to be casual about a shake since."

So, he thought it was an earth tremor. Just as well, Morgana decided. There was absolutely no reason for her to lose her temper, or to expect him to accept her for what she was. In any case, it was sweet, the way he'd jumped to protect her.

"You could move to the Midwest."

"Tornados." Since he was here, and so was she, he saw no reason to resist running his hands up her back. He enjoyed the way she leaned into the stroke, like a cat.

Morgana tilted her head back. Staying angry seemed a waste

of time when her heart gave such an eager leap. It was perhaps unwise of them to test each other this way. But wisdom was often bland. "The East Coast," she said, letting her own hands skim up his chest.

"Blizzards." He nudged her closer, wondering for just an instant why she seemed to meld with him so perfectly, body to body.

"The South." She twined her arms around his neck, watching him steadily through a fringe of dark lashes.

"Hurricanes." He tipped the hat off her head so that her hair tumbled down to fill his hands like warm silk. "Disasters are everywhere," he murmured. "Might as well stay put and deal with the one that's yours."

"You won't deal with me, Nash." She brushed her lips teasingly over his. "But you're welcome to try."

He took her mouth confidently. He didn't consider women a disaster.

Perhaps he should have.

It was more turbulent than any earthquake, more devastating than any storm. He didn't feel the ground tremble or hear the wind roar, but he knew the moment her lips parted beneath his that he was being pulled in by some irresistible force that man had yet to put a name to.

She was molded against him, soft and warm as melted wax. If he'd believed in such things, he might have said her body had been fashioned for just this purpose—to mate perfectly with his. His hands streaked under her loose shirt to race over the smooth skin of her back, to press her even closer, to make sure she was real and not some daydream, some fantasy.

He could taste the reality, but even that had some kind of dreamy midnight flavor. Her mouth yielded silkily under his, even as her arms locked like velvet cords around his neck.

A sound floated on the air, something she murmured, something he couldn't understand. Yet he thought he sensed surprise in the whisper, and perhaps a little fear, before it ended with a sigh.

She was a woman who enjoyed the tastes and textures of a man. She had never been taught to be ashamed of taking pleasure, with the right man, at the right time. She hadn't ever learned to fear her own sexuality, but to celebrate it, cherish it, and respect it.

And yet now, for the first time, she felt the sly quickening of fear with a man.

The simplicity of a kiss filled a basic need. But there was nothing simple in this. How could it be simple, when excitement and unease were dancing together along her skin?

She wanted to believe that the power came from her, was in her. She was responsible for this whirlwind of sensation that surrounded them. Conjuring was often as quick as a wish, as strong as the will.

But the fear was there, and she knew it came from the knowledge that this was something beyond her reach, out of her control, past her reckoning. She knew that spells could be cast on the strong, as well as the weak. To break a charm took care. And action.

She slid out of his arms, moving slowly, deliberately. Not for an instant would she let him see that he had had power over her. She closed a hand over her amulet and felt steadier.

Nash felt like the last survivor of a train wreck. He jammed his hands in his pockets to keep himself from grabbing her again. He didn't mind playing with fire—he just liked to be sure he was the one holding the match. He knew damn well who'd been in charge of that little experiment, and it wasn't Nash Kirkland.

"You play around with hypnosis?" he asked her.

She was fine, Morgana told herself. She was just fine. But she sat on the couch again. It took an effort, but she managed a smile that was sultry around the edges. "Did I mesmerize you, Nash?"

Flustered, he paced to the window and back. "I just want to be sure when I kiss you that it's my idea."

Her head came up. The pride that swam in her blood was something else that was ageless. "You can have all the ideas you like. I don't have to resort to magic to make a man want me." She lifted a finger to touch the heat he'd left on her lips. "And if I decided to have you, you'd be more than willing." Under her finger, her lips curved. "Then you'd be grateful."

He didn't doubt it, and that scraped at his pride. "If I said something like that to you, you'd claim I was sexist and ego-centric.''

Lazily she picked up her glass. "The truth has nothing to do with sex or ego." The white cat jumped soundlessly on the back of the couch. Without taking her eyes off Nash, Morgana lifted a hand and stroked Luna's head. "If you're unwilling to take the risk, we can break off our...creative partnership."

"You think I'm afraid of you?" The absurdity of it put him in a slightly better mood. "Babe, I stopped letting my glands do the thinking a long time ago."

"I'm relieved to hear it. I'd hate to think of you as some calculating woman's love slave."

"The point is," he said between his teeth, "if we're going to work this out, we'd better have some rules."

He had to be out of his mind, Nash decided. Five minutes ago he had had a gorgeous, sexy, incredibly delicious woman in his arms, and now he was trying to think up ways to keep her from seducing him.

"No." Lips pursed, Morgana considered. "I'm not very good with rules. You'll just have to take your chances. But I'll make a deal with you. I won't lure you into any compromising situations if you'll stop taking smug little potshots at witchcraft." She combed her hair back with her fingers. "It irritates me. And I sometimes do things I regret when I'm irritated."

"I have to ask questions."

"Then learn to accept the answers." Calm but determined, she rose. "I don't lie—or at least I rarely do. I'm not sure why I've decided to share my business with you. Perhaps because there's something appealing about you, and certainly because I have a great deal of respect for a teller of tales. You have a strong aura—and a questing, if cynical, brain—along with a great deal of talent. And perhaps because those closest to me have approved of you."

"Such as?"

"Anastasia—and Luna and Pan. They're all excellent judges of character."

So he'd passed muster with a cousin, a cat and a dog. "Is Anastasia also a witch?"

Her eyes remained steady. "We'll discuss me, and the Craft in general. Ana's business is her own."

"All right. When do we start?"

They already had, she thought, and nearly sighed. "I don't work on Sundays. You can come by tomorrow night, at nine."

"Not midnight? Sorry," he said quickly. "Force of habit. I'd like to use a tape recorder, if that's all right."

"Of course."

"Should I bring anything else?"

"Tongue of bat and some wolfbane." She smiled. "Sorry. Force of habit."

He laughed and kissed her chastely on the cheek. "I like your style, Morgana."

"We'll see."

She waited until sundown, then dressed in a thin white robe. Forewarned was always best, she'd told herself when she'd finally broken down and slipped into the room at the top of the tower. She didn't like to admit that Nash was important enough to worry about, but since she was worrying, she might as well see.

She cast the protective circle, lit the candles. Drawing in the scent of sandalwood and herbs, she knelt in the center and lifted her arms.

"Fire, water, earth and wind, not to break and not to mend. Only now to let me see. As I will, so mote it be."

The power slid inside her like breath, clean and cool. She lifted the sphere of clear crystal, cupping it in both hands so that the light from the candles flickered over it.

Smoke. Light. Shadow.

The globe swam with them, and then, as if a wind had blown, cleared to a pure, dazzling white.

Within she saw the cypress grove, the ancient and mystical trees filtering moonlight onto the forest floor. She could smell the wind, could hear it, and the call of the sea some said was the goddess singing.

Candlelight. In the room. Inside the globe.

Herself. In the room. Inside the globe.

She wore the white ceremonial robe belted with a rope of

crystals. Her hair was unbound, her feet were bare. The fire had been lit by her hand, by her will, and it burned as cool as the moonlight. It was a night for celebration.

An owl hooted. She turned, saw its white wings flash and cut the dark like knives, she watched it glide off into the shadows. Then she saw him.

He stepped away from the trunk of a cypress, into the clearing. His eyes were full of her.

Desire. Demand. Destiny.

Trapped in the sphere, Morgana held out her arms, and took Nash into her embrace.

The walls of the tower room echoed with one brief curse. Betrayed—by herself—Morgana threw up a hand. The candles winked out. She stayed where she was, sulking in the dark.

She cursed herself, thinking she'd have been better off not knowing.

A few miles away, Nash woke from a catnap he'd taken in front of a blaring television. Groggy, he rubbed his hands over his face and struggled to sit up.

Hell of a dream, he thought as he worked out the kinks in his neck. Vivid enough to make him ache in several sensitive areas. And it was his own fault, he decided on a yawn as he reached absently for the bowl of popcorn he'd burned.

He hadn't made enough of an effort to get Morgana out of his mind. So if he was going to end up fantasizing about watching her do some kind of witch dance in the woods, about peeling her out of white silk and making love with her on the soft ground in the moonlight, he had no one to blame but himself.

He gave a quick shudder and groped for his lukewarm beer. It was the damnedest thing, he mused. He could have sworn he smelled candles burning.

Chapter 3

Morgana was already annoyed when she turned into her driveway Monday evening. An expected shipment had been delayed in Chicago, and she'd spent the last hour on the phone trying to track it down. She was tempted to deal with the matter her own way—nothing irked her more than ineptitude—but she was fully aware that such impulses often caused complications.

As it was, she'd lost valuable time, and it was nearly dusk before she parked her car. She'd hoped for a quiet walk among the trees to clear her mind—and, yes, damn it, to settle her nerves before she dealt with Nash. But that wasn't to be.

She sat for a moment, scowling at the gleaming black-and-chrome motorcycle in front of her car.

Sebastian. Perfect. Just what she *didn't* need.

Luna slid out of the car ahead of her to pad up the drive and rub herself against the Harley's back wheel.

"You would," Morgana said in disgust as she slammed the door. "As long as it's a man."

Luna muttered something that sounded uncomplimentary and stalked on ahead. Pan greeted them both at the front door with his wise eyes and his loving tongue. While Luna moved on, ignoring him, Morgana took a moment to stroke his fur before tossing her purse aside. She could hear the soft strains of Beethoven drifting from her stereo.

She found Sebastian exactly where she'd expected. He was

sprawled on her couch, booted feet comfortably crossed on her coffee table, his eyes half-closed and a glass of wine in his hand. His smile might have devastated an ordinary woman, with the way it shifted the planes and angles of his dusky face, curved those sculptured, sensuous lips, deepened the color of the heavy-lidded eyes that were as tawny and sharp as Luna's.

Lazily he lifted a long, lean-fingered hand in an ancient sign of greeting. "Morgana, my own true love."

He'd always been too handsome for his own good, she thought, even as a boy. "Make yourself at home, Cousin."

"Thank you, darling." He raised his glass to her. "The wine's excellent. Yours or Ana's?"

"Mine."

"My compliments." He rose, graceful as a dancer. It always irritated her that she had to tilt her head to keep her eyes level with his. At six-three, he had five full inches on her. "Here you go." He passed her the glass. "You look like you could use it."

"I've had an annoying day."

He grinned. "I know."

She would have sipped, but her teeth had clenched. "You know I hate it when you poke into my mind."

"I didn't have to." In a gesture of truce, he spread his hands. A ring with a square amethyst and intricately twisted gold winked on his little finger. "You were sending out signals. You know how loud you get when you're annoyed."

"Then I must be screaming now."

Since she wasn't drinking the wine, he took it back. "Darling, I haven't seen you since Candlemas." His eyes were laughing at her. "Haven't you missed me?"

The hell of it was, she had. No matter how often Sebastian teased her—and he'd been doing it since she was in the cradle—she enjoyed him. But that wasn't any reason to be too friendly too soon.

"I've been busy."

"So I hear." He chucked her under the chin because he knew it annoyed her. "Tell me about Nash Kirkland."

Fury snapped into her eyes. "Damn you, Sebastian, you keep your psychic fingers out of my brain."

"I didn't peek." He made a good show of looking offended. "I'm a seer, an artist, not a voyeur. Ana told me."

"Oh." She pouted a moment. "Sorry." She knew that, at least since he'd gained some maturity and control, Sebastian rarely invaded anyone's private thoughts. Unless he considered it necessary. "Well, there's nothing to tell. He's a writer."

"I know that. Haven't I enjoyed his movies? What's his business with you?"

"Research. He wants a witch tale."

"T-a-l-e, as in story, I hope."

She fought back a chuckle. "Don't be crude, Sebastian."

"Just looking out for my baby cousin."

"Well, don't." She tugged, hard, on a lock of his hair that lay over his collar. "I can look after myself. And he's going to be here in a couple of hours, so—"

"Good. That'll give you time to feed me." He swung a friendly arm over her shoulders. He'd decided she'd have to blast him out of the house to make him leave before meeting the writer. "I talked to my parents over the weekend."

"By phone?"

His eyes widened in shock. When he spoke, the faint wisps of Ireland that occasionally surfaced in his voice enlivened his tone. "Really, Morgana, you know how much they charge you for overseas calls? They positively soak you."

Laughing, she slipped an arm around his waist. "All right, I'll give you some dinner and you can catch me up."

She could never stay annoyed with him. After all, he was family. When one was different, family was sometimes all that could be relied on. They ate in the kitchen while he told her of the latest exploits of her parents, her aunts and uncles. By the end of an hour, she was completely relaxed again.

"It's been years since I've seen Ireland by moonlight," Morgana murmured.

"Take a trip. You know they'd all love to see you."

"Maybe I will, for the summer solstice."

"We could all go. You, Anastasia and me."

"Maybe." Sighing, she pushed her plate aside. "The problem is, summer's my business time."

"You're the one who tied yourself up with free enterprise."

There was the better part of a pork chop on her plate. Sebastian stabbed it and ate it himself.

"I like it, really. Meeting people. Even though some of them are weird."

He topped off their wineglasses. "Such as?"

She smiled and leaned forward on her elbows. "There was this little pest. He came around day after day for weeks. He claimed that he recognized me from another incarnation."

"A pathetic line."

"Yes. Fortunately, he was wrong—I'd never met him before, in any life. One night a couple of weeks ago, when I was closing up, he burst in and made a very strong, sloppy pass."

"Hmm." Sebastian finished off the last bite of pork. He was well aware that his cousin could take care of herself. That didn't stop him from being annoyed that some pseudo-New Ager had put the moves on her. "What'd you do?"

"Punched him in the stomach." She lifted her shoulders as Sebastian laughed.

"Style, Morgana. You have such style. You didn't turn him into a bullfrog?"

All dignity, she straightened. "You know I don't work that way."

"What about Jimmy Pakipsky?"

"That was different—I was only thirteen." She couldn't fight back the grin. "Besides, I turned him right back to a nasty little boy again."

"Only because Ana pleaded his case." Sebastian gestured with his fork. "And you left the warts on."

"It was the least I could do." She reached out to grab his hand. "Damn it, Sebastian, I have missed you."

His fingers curled tight around hers. "And I've missed you. And Anastasia."

She felt something—their bond was too old and too deep for her to miss it. "What is it, love?"

"Nothing we can change." He kissed her fingers lightly, then let them go. He hadn't intended to think about it, or to let his guard down enough to have his cousin tune in. "Got anything with whipped cream around here?"

But she shook her head. She had picked up grief. Though he

was skilled enough to block it from her now, she refused to let it pass. "The case you were working on—the little boy who'd been kidnapped."

The pain was sudden and sharp. He forced it away again. "They didn't get to him in time. The San Francisco police did everything they could, but the kidnappers had panicked. He was only eight years old."

"I'm sorry." There was a wave of sorrow. His, and her own. She rose to go over and curl into his lap. "Oh, Sebastian, I'm so sorry."

"You can't let it get to you." Seeking comfort, he rubbed his cheek against her hair. He could feel the sharper edges of his regret dulling because she shared it with him. "It'll eat you up if you do, but, damn it, I got so close to that kid. When something like this happens, you wonder why, why you've been given this gift if you can't make a difference."

"You have made a difference." She cupped his face in her hands. Her eyes were wet, and strong. "I can't count the times you've made a difference. It wasn't meant to be this time."

"It hurts."

"I know." Gently she stroked his hair. "I'm glad you came to me."

He hugged her tight, then drew her back. "Look, I came here to mooch a meal and have a few laughs, not to dump. I'm sorry."

"Don't be an ass."

Her voice was so brusque that he had to chuckle. "All right. If you want to make me feel better, how about that whipped cream?"

She gave him a smacking kiss between the eyes. "How about a hot fudge sundae?"

"My hero."

She rose and, knowing Sebastian's appetites, got out an enormous bowl. She also knew she would help him more by saying nothing else about the case. He would struggle past it and go on. Because there was no other way. Flicking her mind toward the living room, she switched channels on the stereo, moving from classical to rock.

"Better," Sebastian said, and propped his feet on an empty

chair. "So, are you going to tell me why you're helping this Kirkland with research?"

"It interests me." She heated a jar of fudge sauce in the conventional way. She used the microwave.

"Do you mean he interests you?"

"Somewhat." She scooped out a small mountain of French vanilla. "Of course, he doesn't believe in anything supernatural, he just exploits it for movies. I don't have a problem with that, really." Thoughtful, she licked ice cream from her thumb. "With the movies, I mean. They're very entertaining. His attitude, now… Well, I might have to adjust it before we're through."

"Dangerous ground, Cousin."

"Hell, Sebastian, life's dangerous ground." She poured a river of sauce over the mountain of ice cream. "We might as well have some fun with it." To prove her point, she covered the entire confectionary landscape with heaping clouds of whipped cream. With a flourish, she set the bowl in front of Sebastian.

"No nuts?"

She slapped a spoon into his hand. "I don't like nuts, and you're sharing." After sitting again, she dug deep into the sundae. "You'd probably like him," she said with her mouth full. "Nash. He has that relaxed sort of arrogance men think is so manly." Which, of course, it was, she thought resentfully. "And, obviously, he has a very fluid imagination. He's good with animals—Pan and Luna reacted very favorably. He's a big fan of Mother's, has a nice sense of humor, a good brain. And he drives a very sexy car."

"Sounds like you're smitten."

If she hadn't just swallowed, she would have choked. "Don't be insulting. Just because I find him interesting and attractive doesn't mean I'm—as you so pitifully put it—smitten."

She was sulking, Sebastian noted, pleased. It was always a good sign. The closer Morgana got to anger, the easier it was to slide information out of her. "So, have you looked?"

"Of course I looked," she shot back. "Merely as a precaution."

"You looked because you were nervous."

"Nervous? Don't be ridiculous." But she began to drum her fingers on the table. "He's just a man."

"And you, despite your gifts, are a woman. Shall I tell you what happens when men and women get together?"

She curled her fingers into fists to keep from doing something drastic. "I know the facts of life, thank you. If I do take him as a lover, it's my business. And perhaps my pleasure."

Happy that she'd lost interest in the ice cream, Sebastian nodded as he ate. "Trouble is, there's always a risk of falling in love with a lover. Tread carefully, Morgana."

"There's a difference between love and lust," she replied primly. From his spot under the table, Pan lifted his head and gave a soft woof.

"Speaking of which..."

Eyes full of warning, Morgana rose. "Behave yourself, Sebastian. I mean it."

"Don't worry about me. Go answer the door." The bell rang a heartbeat later. Chuckling to himself, Sebastian watched her stalk off.

Damn it, Morgana thought when she'd opened the front door. He looked so cute. His hair was tumbled by the wind. He carried a battered knapsack over one shoulder and had a hole in the knee of his jeans.

"Hi. I guess I'm a little early."

"It's all right. Come in and sit down. I just have a little...mess to clear up in the kitchen."

"What a way to speak about your cousin." Sebastian strolled down the hall, carrying the bowl of rapidly depleting ice cream. "Hello." He gave Nash a friendly nod. "You must be Kirkland."

Morgana narrowed her eyes but spoke pleasantly enough. "Nash, my cousin Sebastian. He was just leaving."

"Oh, I can stay for a minute. I've enjoyed your work."

"Thank you. Don't I know you?" His gaze changed from mild to shrewd as he studied Sebastian. "The psychic, right?"

Sebastian's lips quirked. "Guilty."

"I've followed some of your cases. Even some hard-boiled cops give you the credit for the arrest of the Yuppie Killer up in Seattle. Maybe you could—"

"Sebastian hates to talk shop," Morgana told him. There were dire threats in her eyes when she turned them on her cousin. "Don't you?"

"Actually—"

"I'm so glad you could stop by, darling." A quick jolt of power passed as she snatched the bowl out of his hands. "Don't be a stranger."

He gave in, thinking it was still early enough to stop by Anastasia's and discuss Morgana's current situation in depth. "Take care, love." He gave her a long kiss, lingering over it until he felt Nash's thoughts darken. "Blessed be."

"Blessed be," Morgana returned automatically, and all but shoved him out the door. "Now, if you'll just give me a minute, we can get started." She tossed her hair back, pleased when she heard him gun the engine of his motorcycle. "Would you like some tea?"

His brows were knitted, and his hands in his pockets. "I'd rather have coffee." He trailed after her as she walked toward the kitchen. "What kind of a cousin is he?"

"Sebastian? Often an annoying one."

"No, I mean..." In the kitchen he frowned at the remnants of their cozy dinner for two. "Is he a first cousin, or one of the three-times-removed sort?"

She set an old-fashioned iron kettle on the stove to heat, then started to load a very modern dishwasher. "Our fathers are brothers." Catching Nash's look of relief nearly had her chuckling. "In this life," she couldn't help but add.

"In this... Oh, sure." He set his knapsack aside. "So you're into reincarnation."

"Into it?" Morgana repeated. "Well, that's apt enough. In any case, my father, Sebastian's and Ana's were born in Ireland. They're triplets."

"No kidding?" He leaned a hip on the table as she opened a small tin. "That's almost as good as being the seventh son of a seventh son."

With a shake of her head, she measured out herbs for tea. "Such things aren't always necessary. They married three sisters," she went on. "Triplets also."

Nash rubbed Pan's head when the dog leaned against his leg. "That's great."

"An unusual arrangement, some might say, but they recognized each other, and their destiny." She glanced back with a smile before she set a small pot of tea aside to steep. "They were fated to have only one child apiece—a disappointment to them in some ways. Between the six of them, they had a great deal of love, and would have showered it over quantities of children. But it wasn't meant."

She added a pot of coffee to a silver tray where she'd arranged delicate china cups along with a creamer and sugar bowl, both in the shape of grinning skulls.

"I'll carry it in," Nash told her. As he hefted the tray, he glanced down. "Heirlooms?"

"Novelty shop. I thought they'd amuse you."

She led the way into the drawing room, where Luna was curled in the center of the sofa. Morgana chose the cushion beside her and gestured for Nash to set the tray on the table.

"Cream and sugar?" she asked.

"Both, thanks." Watching her use the grim containers, he was amused. "I bet you're a stitch around Halloween."

She offered him a cup. "Children come for miles to be treated by the witch, or try to trick her." And her fondness for children had her postponing her own All Hallows' Eve celebration every year until the last goody bag had been filled. "I think some of them are disappointed that I don't wear a pointed hat and ride out on my broomstick." The silver band on her finger winked in the lamplight as she poured a delicate amber tea brewed from jasmine flowers.

"Most people have one of two views on witches. It's either the hooked-nosed crone passing out poisoned apples, or the glittering spirit with a star-shaped wand telling you there's no place like home."

"I'm afraid I don't fit either category."

"Exactly why you're what I need." After setting his cup aside, he dug in his knapsack. "Okay?" he asked, setting his tape recorder on the table.

"Sure."

He punched the record button, then dug again. "I spent the

day slogging through books—the library, bookstores." He offered her a slim soft-cover volume. "What do you think about this?"

One brow arched, Morgana studied the title. "*Fame, Fortune and Romance: Candle Rituals for Every Need.*" She dropped the book into his lap smartly enough to make him wince. "I hope you didn't pay much for it."

"Six-ninety-five, and it comes off my taxes. You don't go in for this sort of thing, then?"

Patience, she told herself, slipping off her shoes and curling up her legs. The little red skirt she wore slid up to midthigh. "Lighting candles and reciting clever little chants. Do you really believe that any layman can perform magic by reading a book?"

"You gotta learn somewhere."

Snarling, she snatched it up again, flipped it open. "To arouse jealousy," she read, disgusted. "To win the love of a woman. To obtain money." She slapped it down again. "Think about this, Nash, and be grateful it doesn't work for everyone. You're a little strapped for cash, bills are piling up. You'd really like to have that new car, but the credit's exhausted. So, light a few candles, make a wish—maybe dance naked for effect. Abracadabra." She spread her hands. "You find yourself getting a check for ten thousand. Only problem is, your beloved grandmother had to die to leave it to you."

"Okay, so you've got to be careful how you phrase your charm."

"Follow me here," she said with a toss of her head. "Actions have consequences. You wish your husband were more romantic. Shazam, he's suddenly a regular Don Juan—with every woman in town. But you'll be noble, and cast a charm to stop a war. It works just fine, but as a result dozens of others spring up." She let out a huff of breath. "Magic is not for the unprepared or the irresponsible. And it certainly can't be learned out of some silly book."

"Okay." Impressed by her reasoning, he held up both hands. "I'm convinced. My point was that I could buy this in a bookstore for seven bucks. People are interested."

"People have always been interested." When she shifted, her hair slid down over her shoulder. "There have been times when their interest caused them to be hanged, burned or drowned.'' She sipped her tea. ''We're a bit more civilized today.''

''That's the thing,'' he agreed. ''That's why I want to write the story about now. Now, when we've got cellular phones and microwave ovens, fax machines and voice mail. And people are still fascinated with magic. I can go a couple of ways. Use lunatics who sacrifice goats—''

''Not with my help.''

''Okay, I figured that. Anyway, that's too easy...too, ah, ordinary. I've been thinking about leaning more toward the comic angle I used in *Rest In Peace,* maybe adding some romance. Not just sex.'' Luna had crawled into his lap, and he was stroking her, running long fingers down her spine. ''The idea is to focus on a woman, this gorgeous woman who happens to have a little extra. How does she deal with men, with a job, with...I don't know, grocery shopping? She has to know other witches. What do they talk about? What do they do for laughs? When did you decide you were a witch?''

''Probably when I levitated out of my crib,'' Morgana said mildly, and watched laughter form in his eyes.

''That's just the kind of thing I want.'' He settled back, and Luna draped herself over his legs like a lap rug. ''Must've sent your mother into shock.''

''She was prepared for it.'' When she shifted, her knees brushed his thigh. He didn't figure there was anything magical about the quick flare of heat he felt. It was straight chemistry. ''I told you I was a hereditary witch.''

''Right.'' His tone had her taking a deep breath. ''So, did it ever bother you? Thinking you were different?''

''*Knowing* I was different,'' she corrected. ''Of course. As a child, it was more difficult to control power. One often loses control through emotion—in the same way a woman might lose control of the intellect with certain men.''

He wanted to reach out and touch her hair, but he thought better of it. ''Does it happen often? Losing control?''

She remembered the way it had felt the day before, with his mouth on hers. ''Not as often as it did before I matured. I have a problem with temper, and I sometimes do things I regret, but there is something no responsible witch forgets. 'An it harm none,'" she quoted. "Power must never be used to hurt."

"So you're a serious and responsible witch. And you cast love spells for your customers."

Her chin shot out. "Certainly not."

"You took those pictures—that woman's niece, and the geometry heartthrob."

He didn't miss a trick, Morgana thought in disgust. "She didn't give me much choice." Because she was embarrassed, she set down her cup with a snap. "And just because I took the pictures doesn't mean I'm about to sprinkle them both with moondust."

"Is that how it works?"

"Yes, but—" She bit her tongue. "You're making fun of me. Why do you ask questions when you're not going to believe the answers?"

"I don't have to believe them to be interested." And he was— very. He found himself sliding a few inches closer. "So you didn't do anything about the prom?"

"I didn't say that." She sulked a little while he gave in and toyed with her hair. "I simply removed a small barrier. Anything else would have been interference."

"What barrier?" He didn't have a clue as to what moondust might smell like, but he thought it would carry the same perfume as her hair.

"The girl's desperately shy. I only gave her confidence a tiny boost. The rest is up to her."

She had a beautiful neck, slim and graceful. He imagined what it would be like to nibble on it. For an hour or two. Business, he reminded himself. Stick to business.

"Is that how you work? Giving boosts?"

She turned her head and looked directly into his eyes. "It depends on the situation."

"I've been reading a lot. Witches used to be considered the wise women of the villages. Making potions, charming, foretelling events, healing the sick."

"My speciality isn't healing, or seeing."

"What is your speciality?"

"Magic." Whether it was a matter of pride or annoyance, she wasn't sure, but she sent thunder walking across the sky.

Nash glanced toward the window. "Sounds like a storm coming."

"Could be. Why don't I answer some of your questions, so you can beat it home?"

Damn it, she wanted him gone. She knew what she'd seen in the scrying ball, and that with care, with skill, such things could sometimes be changed. But whatever was to be, she didn't want things moving so fast.

And the way he was touching her, just those long fingertips to her hair, had little flicks of fear lighting in her gut.

That made her angry.

"No hurry," he said easily, wondering whether, if he took a chance and kissed her again, he'd experience that same otherworldly sensation. "I don't mind a little rain."

"It's going to pour," she muttered to herself. She'd damn well see to it. "Some of your books might be helpful," she began. "Giving you history and recorded facts, a general outline of rituals." She poked a finger at the first one he'd given her. "Not this one. There are certain…trappings that are used in the Craft."

"Graveyard dirt?"

She rolled her eyes. "Oh, please."

"Come on, Morgana, it's a great visual." He shifted, slipping a hand over hers, wanting her to see as he saw. "Exterior scene, night. Our beautiful heroine wading through the fog, crossing over the shadows of headstones. An owl screams. In the distance echoes the long, ululant howl of a dog. Close-up of that pale, perfect face, framed by a dark hood. She stops by a fresh grave and, chanting, sifts a handful of newly turned earth into her magic pouch. Thunder claps. Fade out."

She tried, really tried, not to be offended. Imagine anyone thinking she skulked around graveyards. "Nash, I'm trying to remember that what you do is entertainment, and you're certainly entitled to a great deal of artistic license."

He had to kiss her fingers. Really had to. "So you don't spend much time in cemeteries."

She snagged her temper, and a bolt of desire. "I'll accept the fact that you don't believe what I am. But I will not, I absolutely will not, tolerate being laughed at.''

"Don't be so intense.'' He brushed the hair off her shoulder and gave the back of her neck a quick massage. "I admit, I usually do a better job at this. Hell, I did twelve hours of interviews with this whacked-out Rumanian who swore he was a vampire. Didn't have a mirror in the house. He made me wear a cross the whole time. Not to mention the garlic,'' Nash remembered with a grimace. "Anyway, I didn't have a problem humoring him, and he was a treasure chest of information. But you...''

"But me,'' she prompted, doing her best to ignore the fact that he was trailing a finger up her arm with the same skill and sensuousness he had used to stroke Luna.

"I just can't buy it, Morgana. You're a strong, intelligent woman. You've got style, taste—not to mention the fact that you smell terrific. I just can't pretend to believe that you believe all this.''

Her blood was starting to boil. She would not, simply could not, tolerate the fact that he could infuriate her and seduce her at the same time. "Is that what you do to get what you want? Pretend?''

"When some ninety-year-old woman tells me her lover was shot as a werewolf in 1922, I'm not going to call her a liar. I figure either she's a hell of a storyteller or she believes it. Either way it's fine with me.''

"As long as you get the angle for your movie.''

"That's my living. Illusion. And it doesn't hurt anyone.''

"Oh, I'm sure it doesn't, not when you walk away, then have a few drinks with the boys and laugh about the lunatic you interviewed.'' Her eyes were flaming. "Try it with me, Nash, and you'll get warts on your tongue.''

Because he could see that she was really angry, he swallowed his grin. "All I'm saying is, I know you've got a lot of data, a lot of facts and fantasy, which is exactly what I'm looking for. I figure building a reputation as a witch probably adds fifty percent to your sales annually. It's a great hook. You just don't have to play the game with me.''

"You think I pretend to be a witch to increase sales.'' She

was getting slowly to her feet, afraid that if she stayed too close she might do him bodily harm.

"I don't— Hey!" He jumped when Luna dug her claws into his thighs.

Morgana and her cat exchanged looks of approval. "You sit in my home and call me a charlatan, a liar and a thief."

"No." He unhooked himself from the cat and stood. "That's not what I meant at all. I just meant that you can be straight with me."

"Straight with you." She began to pace the room, trying and failing to regain control. On one hand he was seducing her without her willing it, and on the other he was sneering at her. He thought she was a fraud. Why, the insolent jackass was lucky she didn't have him braying and twitching twelve-inch ears. Smiling wickedly, she turned. "You want me to be straight with you?"

The smile relieved him, a little. He'd been afraid she'd start throwing things. "I just want you to know you can relax. You give me the facts, and I'll take care of the fiction."

"Relax," she said with a nod. "That's a good idea. We should both relax." Her eyes glowed as she stepped toward him. "Why don't we have a fire? Nothing like a cozy fire to help you relax."

"Good idea." And definitely a sexy one. "I'll light it."

"Oh, no." She laid a hand on his arm. "Allow me."

She whirled away, flung out both arms toward the hearth. She felt the cool, clear knowledge whip through her blood. It was an ancient skill, one of the first mastered, one of the last to be lost with age. Her eyes, then her mind, focused on the dry wood. In the next moment, flames erupted with a roar, logs snapped, smoke billowed.

Pleased, she banked it so that the hearth glowed with the cheerful blaze.

Lowering her arms, she turned back. It delighted her to see not only that Nash was white as a sheet, but also that his mouth had yet to close.

"Better?" she asked sweetly.

He sat on the cat. Luna howled her disapproval and stalked off, despite his muttered apology. "I think—"

"You look like you could use a drink." On a roll now, Morgana held out a hand. A decanter hopped off a table five feet away and landed on her palm. "Brandy?"

"No." He let out a deep breath. "Thanks."

"I believe I will." She snapped her fingers. A snifter drifted over and hung suspended in midair while she poured. It was showing off, she knew, but it was immensely satisfying. "Sure you don't want some?"

"Yeah."

With a shrug, she sent the decanter back. Glass clinked lightly against wood as it landed. "Now," she said, curling on the couch beside him. "Where were we?"

Hallucination, he thought. Hypnosis. He opened his mouth, but all he could manage was a stutter. Morgana was still smiling that sleek cat smile at him. Special effects. It was suddenly so clear, he laughed at his own stupidity.

"Gotta be a wire," he said, and rose to look for himself. "Hell of a trick, babe. Absolutely first-rate. You had me for a minute."

"Did I really?" she murmured.

"I hired some of the F/X guys to help me with this party last year. You should have seen some of the stuff we pulled off."

He picked up the decanter, looking for trips and levers. All he found was old Irish crystal and smooth wood. With a shrug, he walked over to crouch in front of the fire. He suspected she'd had a small charge set under the wood, something she could set off with a small device in the palm of her hand. Inspired, he sprang up.

"How about this? We bring this guy into town. He's a scientist, and he falls for her, then drives himself crazy trying to explain everything she does. Make it logical." His mind was leaping ahead. "Maybe he sneaks into one of her ceremonies. You ever been to one?"

She'd exorcised the temper, and she found only humor in its place. "Naturally."

"Great. You can give me inside stuff. We could have him see her do something off-the-wall. Levitate. Or this fire bit was good. We could have this bonfire, and she lights it without a match.

But he doesn't know for sure if it's a trick or real. Neither does the audience.''

She let the brandy slide warm into her system. Temper tantrums were so exhausting. ''What's the point of the story?''

''Besides some chills and thrills, I think it's a matter of, can this guy, this regular guy, deal with the fact that he's in love with a witch.''

Suddenly sad, she stared into her glass. ''You might ask yourself if a witch could deal with the fact that she's in love with an ordinary man.''

''That's just what I need you for.'' He sauntered over to drop down beside her. ''Not only the witch's angle, but the woman's, too.'' Comfortable again, he patted her knee. ''Now, let's talk about casting spells.''

With a shake of her head, she set the drink aside and laughed. ''All right, Nash. Let's talk magic.''

Chapter 4

He hadn't been lonely. How could he have been, when he'd spent hours that day poring over books, enlivening his mind and his world with facts and fantasies? Since childhood, Nash had been content with his own company. What had once been a necessity to survive had become a way of life.

The time he'd spent with his grandmother or his aunt, or his sporadic stays in foster homes, had taught him that he was much better off devising his own entertainment than looking to the adults in his life to devise some for him. More often than not, that entertainment had equaled chores, a lecture, solitary confinement or—in his grandmother's case—a swift backhand.

Since he'd never been permitted an abundance of playthings or playmates, he'd turned his mind into a particularly fine toy.

He'd often thought it had given him an advantage over better-endowed children. After all, the imagination was portable, unbreakable and amazingly malleable. It couldn't be taken away from you by an irritated adult when you had committed some infraction. It didn't have to be left behind when you were packed off to some other place.

Now that he could afford to buy himself whatever he liked—and Nash would have been among the first to admit that adult toys were a terrific source of entertainment—he was still content with the fluidity of imagination.

He could happily close himself off from the real world and

real people for hours at a stretch. It didn't mean he was alone,
not with all the characters and events racing around in his head.
His imagination had always been company enough. If he occasionally indulged in binges of parties and people, it was as much
to gather grist for the mill as it was to balance out those solitary
times.

But lonely? No, that was absurd.

He had friends now, he had control over his own destiny. It
was his choice, his alone, whether to stay or to go. It delighted
him that he had his big house to himself. He could eat when he
was hungry, sleep when he was tired, and toss his clothes wherever it suited him. Most of his friends and associates were un-
happily married or bitterly divorced and wasted a great deal of
time and effort complaining about their partners.

Not Nash Kirkland.

He was a single man. A carefree bachelor. A lone wolf who
was happy as a clam.

And what, he wondered, made a clam so damn happy, anyway?

Nash knew what made him happy. Being able to set his laptop
out on the patio table and work in the sunlight and fresh air,
with the drumming of water in the background. Being able to
toy with the treatment for a new screenplay without sweating
about time clocks or office politics or a woman who was waiting
for him to snap back and pay attention to her.

Did that sound like the lament of a lonely man?

Nash knew he'd never been meant for a conventional job, or
a conventional relationship. God knows his grandmother had
told him often enough he'd never amount to anything remotely
respectable. And she'd mentioned, more than once, that no decent woman with a grain of sense would have him.

Nash didn't figure that that stiff-necked woman would have
considered penning occult tales remotely respectable. If she were
still alive, she'd sniff and nod her head smugly at the fact that
he'd reached the age of thirty-three without taking a wife.

Still, he'd tried the other way. His brief and terrible stint as a
desk jockey with an insurance company in Kansas City had
proven that he would never be a nine-to-fiver. Certainly his last

attempt at a serious relationship had proven that he wasn't suited to the demands of permanence with a woman.

As that former lover, DeeDee Driscol, had sniped during their final battle, he was… How had she put it again? "You're nothing but a selfish little boy, emotionally retarded. You think since you're good in bed you can behave irresponsibly out of it. You'd rather play with your monsters than have a serious adult relationship with a woman."

She'd said a lot more, Nash remembered, but that had been the gist of it. He couldn't really blame her for throwing his irresponsibility at him. Or the marble ashtray, if it came to that. He'd let her down. He wasn't, as she'd hoped, husband material. And, no matter how much she'd altered and stitched during their six-month run, he just hadn't measured up.

So DeeDee was marrying her oral surgeon. Nash didn't think it was overly snide to chuckle at the idea that an impacted wisdom tooth had led to orange blossoms.

Better you than me, he told the nameless dentist. DeeDee was a bright, friendly woman with a cuddly body and a great smile. And she had the arm of a major-league outfielder when you ticked her off.

It certainly didn't make him lonely to think of DeeDee taking that long, slippery walk down the matrimonial aisle.

He was a free agent, a man-about-town, unattached, unencumbered, and pleased as punch. Whatever the hell that meant.

So why was he rattling around this big house like the last living cell in a dying body?

And, much more important, why had he started to pick up the phone a dozen times to call Morgana?

It wasn't their night to work. She'd been very firm about giving him only two evenings a week. And he had to admit, once they'd gotten past those initial rough spots, they'd cruised along together smoothly enough. As long as he watched the sarcasm.

She had a nice sense of humor, and a nice sense of drama—which was great, since he wanted both for the story. It wasn't exactly a sacrifice to spend a few hours a week in her company. True, she was adamant about insisting she was a witch, but that only made the whole business more interesting. He was almost disappointed that she hadn't set up any more special effects.

He'd exercised admirable control in keeping his hands off her. Mostly. Nash didn't figure touching her fingers or playing with her hair really counted. Not when he'd resisted that soft, sulky mouth, that long white throat, those high, lovely breasts....

Nash cut himself off, wishing he had something more satisfying to kick than the side of the sofa.

It was perfectly normal to want a woman. Hell, it was even enjoyable to imagine what it would be like to tangle up the sheets with her. But the way his mind kept veering toward Morgana at all hours of the day and night, making his work suffer in the process, was close to becoming an obsession.

It was time to get it under control.

Not that he'd lost control, he reminded himself. He'd been a saint. Even when she'd answered the door wearing those faded, raggedy cutoffs—a personal weakness of his—he'd slapped back his baser instincts. It was a bit lowering to admit that his reasoning had had less to do with altruism than with self-preservation. A personal entanglement with her would mess up the professional one. In any case, a woman who could knock him sideways with a single kiss was best treated with caution.

He had a feeling that that kind of punch would be a lot more lethal than DeeDee's deadly aim.

But he wanted to call her, to hear her voice, to ask if he could see her for just an hour or two.

Damn it, he was *not* lonely. Or at least he hadn't been until he'd shut off his machine and his tired brain to go for a walk on the beach. All those people he'd seen—the families, the couples, those tight little groups of belonging. And he'd been alone, watching the sun slide down into the water, longing for something he was sure he didn't really want. Something he certainly wouldn't know what to do with if he had it.

Some people weren't made to have families. That much Nash knew from firsthand experience. He'd decided long ago to avoid the mistake, and save some nameless, faceless child from being saddled with a lousy father.

But standing alone and watching those families had made him restless, had made the house he'd come home to seem too big and much too empty. It made him wish he'd had Morgana with him, so that they could have strolled along, hand in hand, by the water. Or sat on an old, bleached log, his arm tucked around her shoulders, as they watched the first stars come out.

On an oath, he yanked up the phone and punched out her number. His lips curved when he heard her voice, but the smile faded the moment he realized it was a recording, informing him that she was unavailable.

He thought about leaving a message, but hung up instead. What was he supposed to say? he asked himself. I just wanted to talk to you. I need to see you. I can't get you out of my mind.

Shaking his head, he paced the room again. Grim, beautiful masks from Oceania stared down at him from their place on the wall. In low cases, keen-edged knives with ornate handles glinted in the lamplight. To relieve some tension, Nash scooped up a voodoo doll and jammed a pin through its heart.

"See how you like it, bub."

He tossed it aside, jammed his hands in his pockets and decided it was time to get out of the house. What the hell, he'd go to the movies.

"It's your turn to buy the tickets," Morgana told Sebastian patiently. "Mine to spring for popcorn, and Ana's to choose the movie."

Sebastian scowled as they walked down Cannery Row. "I bought the tickets last time."

"No. You didn't."

Anastasia smiled when Sebastian appealed to her, but shook her head. "I bought them last time," she confirmed. "You're just trying to weasel out again."

"Weasel?" Insulted, he stopped in the middle of the sidewalk. "What a disgusting word. And I distinctly remember—"

"What you want to remember," Anastasia finished for him, tucking her arm through his. "Give it up, Cousin. I'm not passing on my turn."

He muttered something but started walking again, Morgana on one arm, Anastasia on the other. He really wanted to catch the new Schwarzenegger flick, and he was very much afraid that Ana was going to opt for the fluffy romantic comedy in theater two. Not that he minded romance, but he'd heard that Arnold had outdone himself this time, saving the entire planet from a group of evil, shape-shifting extraterrestrials.

"Don't sulk," Morgana said lightly. "You get to pick next time."

She liked the arrangement very much. Whenever the mood or their schedules allowed, the three cousins would take in a movie. Years of bickering, seething tempers and ruined evenings had resulted in the current system. It wasn't without its flaws, but it usually prevented a heated argument at the ticket booth.

"And no fair trying to influence," Anastasia added when she felt Sebastian pushing at her mind. "I've already decided."

"Just trying to keep you from wasting my money." Resigned, Sebastian glanced down at the smattering of people forming in line. His spirits lifted when he spotted the man who was strolling up from the opposite direction. "Well, well," he said. "Isn't this cozy?"

Morgana had already seen Nash, and wasn't sure whether she was annoyed or pleased. She'd managed to keep everything on an even keel during their meetings. No mean trick, she decided, considering the sexual sparks that crackled through the air whenever they got within two feet of each other.

She could handle it, she reminded herself, and offered Nash a smile. "Busman's holiday?"

His gloomy mood vanished. She looked like a dark angel, her hair flowing around her shoulders, the short red dress clinging to each curve. "More or less. I always like falling into someone else's movie when I'm struggling with one of my own." Though it took an effort to tear his eyes from Morgana's, he glanced at Sebastian and Anastasia. "Hi."

"It's nice to see you again." Anastasia stepped into line. "It's funny, the last time the three of us hit the movies, we saw your *Play Dead.*"

"Oh, yeah?"

"It was very good."

"She'd know," Sebastian put in. "Ana watched the last thirty minutes with her eyes closed."

"The highest of compliments." Nash shuffled his way down the line with them. "So, what're you going to see?"

Anastasia shot Sebastian a look as he pulled out his wallet. "The Schwarzenegger movie."

"Really?" Nash hadn't a clue why Sebastian was chuckling, but he smiled at Morgana. "Me, too."

Nash figured his luck was in when he settled down in the theater beside Morgana. It hardly mattered that he'd already seen the movie at its Hollywood premiere. He'd probably have ended up choosing it anyway. It was a hell of a show, as he recalled. Fast paced, with plenty of humor to leaven the violence, along with a nicely twisted coil of suspense. And there was a particular scene that had had the celebrity audience on the edge of their seats. If his luck held, Morgana would be cuddled up against him by the second reel.

As the lights dimmed, Morgana turned her head and smiled at him. Nash felt several of his brain cells melt and wished they still ran double features.

In the normal scheme of things, Nash took the long step out of reality the moment a movie caught his imagination. There was nothing he liked better than diving into the action. It rarely mattered whether it was his first shot at a film or he was visiting an old friend for the twentieth time—he was always at home in a movie. But tonight he kept losing track of the adventure on the screen.

He was much too aware of the woman beside him to click off reality.

Theaters had their own smell. The oily, not unpleasant aroma of what the concessions jokingly called butter over the warm fragrance of popcorn, the sweet tang of candies, the syrupy scent of spilled soft drinks. However appealing it was—and it had always been appealing to Nash—he couldn't get beyond the dreamy sexuality of Morgana's perfume.

The theater was cool, almost chilly. It had never made sense to him that the air-conditioning was so often turned toward frigid in a place where people would be sitting still for two hours. But the scent of Morgana's skin was hot, arousingly hot, as if she were sitting in a strong beam of sunlight.

She didn't gasp or jolt or huddle against him, no matter how much mayhem the invaders or the hero wrought. Instead, she kept her gaze fixed intently on the screen, nibbling occasionally from a dwindling container of popcorn.

At one point she did hiss a breath through her teeth and grip the armrest between them. Gallantly Nash covered her hand with his. She didn't look toward him, but she did turn her hand, palm up, and link her fingers with his.

She couldn't help it, Morgana thought. She wasn't made of stone. What she was was a flesh-and-blood woman who found the man beside her outrageously attractive. And sweet, damn it. There was something undeniably sweet about sitting in a darkened theater holding hands.

And what could it hurt?

She was being careful when they were alone, making sure things didn't move too quickly or in a direction not of her choosing. Not that she'd had to fight him off, Morgana reminded herself with a touch of resentment. He'd made no attempt to hold her, or kiss her again, or to seduce her in any way.

Unless she counted the fact that he always seemed to be touching her in that careless and friendly manner. The manner that had her tossing restlessly in bed for several hours after he'd left her last.

Her problem, she reminded herself, and tried to ignore the long, slow tug inside as Nash ran his thumb lazily up and down the side of her hand.

The up side was, she enjoyed working with him, helping him with his research. Not only because he was an amusing companion with a mind and talent she respected, but also because it was giving her the opportunity to explain what she was in her own way.

Of course, he didn't believe a word of it.

Not that it mattered, Morgana told herself, and lost track of the film as Nash's forearm rubbed warmly over hers. He didn't have to believe to incorporate her knowledge and write a good story. Yet it disappointed her, on some deep level. Having him believe, and accept, would have been so soothing.

When the world was saved and the lights came up, she slipped her hand from Nash's. Not that it hadn't felt nice keeping it there, but Morgana wasn't in the mood to risk any of Sebastian's teasing comments.

"Excellent choice, Ana," Sebastian told her.

"Say that again when my heart rate's normal."

Her cousin slipped an arm over her shoulders as they shuffled up the aisle. "Scare you?"

"Of course not." She refused to admit it this time. "Seeing that incredible body stripped to the waist for the best part of two hours is enough to give any woman a rush."

They moved into the brightly lit, noisy lobby. "Pizza," Sebastian decided. He glanced back at Nash. "You up for food?"

"I'm always up for food."

"Great." Sebastian pushed open the door and led them into the night. "You're buying."

They were quite a trio, Nash decided as the four of them devoured slices of pizza dripping with cheese. They argued about everything, from what kind of pizza to buy to which alien demise had been the most effective in the movie they'd just seen. He decided that Morgana and Sebastian enjoyed sniping at each other as much as they enjoyed the meal, with Anastasia slipping in and out of the role of referee.

It was obvious that the bond ran deep, for under the bickering and complaining was an inescapable stream of affection.

When Morgana said to Sebastian, "Don't be such a jerk, love," Nash sensed that she meant "jerk" and "love" in equal measure. Listening to it, Nash fought back the same little stab of envy he'd felt on the beach at sunset.

They were each only children, as he was. Yet they were not, as he was, alone.

Anastasia turned to him. Something flickered in her eyes for a moment that was so much like sympathy that he felt a wave of embarrassment. Then it was gone, and she was only a lovely woman with an easy smile.

"They don't mean to be rude," she said lightly. "They can't help themselves."

"Rude?" With her hair tucked around to spill over one shoulder, Morgana swirled her glass of heavy red wine. "It isn't rude to point out Sebastian's flaws. Not when they're so obvious." She slapped his hand away from the slice of pizza on her plate. "See that?" she asked Nash. "He's always been greedy."

"Generous to a fault," Sebastian said.

"Conceited," she said, grinning at her cousin while she took a healthy bite of pizza. "Bad-tempered."

"Lies." Contenting himself with his wine, Sebastian leaned back in his chair. "I'm enviably even-tempered. It's you who have always had the tantrums. Right, Ana?"

"Well, actually, you both—"

"She never grew out of it," Sebastian interjected. "As a child, when she didn't get her way, she'd wail like a banshee, or sulk in corners. Control was never her strong point."

"I hate to point this out," Anastasia told him, "but at least half the time Morgana was driven to wails it was because you'd provoked her."

"Naturally." Unrepentant, Sebastian shrugged. "It was so easy." He winked at Morgana. "Still is."

"I should never have let you down from the ceiling all those years ago."

Nash paused over his drink. "Excuse me?"

"A particularly nasty little prank," Sebastian explained. It still annoyed him that his cousin had gotten the better of him.

"Which you richly deserved." Morgana was pouting over her wine. "I'm not sure I've forgiven you yet."

Anastasia was forced to agree. "It was lousy of you, Sebastian."

Outnumbered, Sebastian relented. He could even, with an effort, dredge up some humor along with the memory. "I was only eleven years old. Little boys are entitled to be lousy. Anyway, it wasn't a real snake."

Morgana sniffed. "It looked real."

Chuckling, Sebastian leaned forward to tell Nash the tale. "We were all over at Aunt Bryna's and Uncle Matthew's for May Day. Admittedly, I was always looking for a way to get a rise out of the brat here, and I knew she was terrified of snakes."

"And it's just like you to exploit one small phobia," Morgana muttered.

"The thing was, the kid was fearless—except for this one thing." Sebastian's eyes, tawny as a cat's, glowed with humor. "So, seeing as boys will be boys, I plopped a rubber snake right in the center of her bed—while she was in it, of course."

Nash couldn't suppress the grin, but he did manage to turn

the laugh into a cough when he saw Morgana's arch look. "It doesn't seem so terrible."

"He made it hiss and wriggle," Ana put in, biting down on her lip to keep it from curving.

Sebastian sighed nostalgically. "I'd worked on that charm for weeks. Magic's never been my strong point, so it was a pretty weak attempt, all in all. Still—" he leered at Morgana "—it worked."

Nash discovered he had absolutely no comment to make. It appeared he wasn't sitting at a table with three sensible people after all.

"So, after I got finished screaming, and saw through what was really a very pitiful spell, I sent Sebastian to the ceiling, let him hang there, upside down." Her tone was smug and satisfied. "How long was it, darling?"

"Two hideous hours."

She smiled. "You'd still be there if my mother hadn't found you and made me bring you down."

"And for the rest of the summer," Anastasia put in, "the two of you tried to outdo each other, and you both stayed in trouble."

Sebastian and Morgana grinned at each other. Then Morgana tilted her head and sent Nash a sidelong glance. She could all but hear the wheels turning. "Sure you won't have a glass of wine?"

"No, thanks, I'm driving." They were putting him on, he realized. He flicked a smile at Morgana. Why should he mind? It made him part of the little group, and it gave him new angles for the story. "So, you, ah…played a lot of tricks on each other as kids?"

"It's difficult, when one has certain talents, to be content with ordinary games."

"Whatever we played," Sebastian said to Morgana, "you cheated."

"Of course I did." Unoffended, she passed him the rest of her pizza. "I like to win. It's getting late." She rose to kiss each of her cousins on the cheek. "Why don't you give me a ride home, Nash?"

"Sure." It was exactly what he'd had in mind.

"Be careful, Kirkland," Sebastian said lazily. "She likes to play with fire."

"So I've noticed." He took Morgana's hand and led her away.

Anastasia gave a little sigh and propped her chin on her hand. "With all the sparks popping back and forth between the two of them, I'm surprised we didn't have a blaze right here at the table."

"There'll be flames soon enough." Sebastian's eyes darkened, going fixed and nearly opaque. "Whether she likes it or not."

Instantly concerned, Ana put a hand on his. "She'll be all right?"

He wasn't seeing as clearly as he would have liked. It was always more difficult with family, and particularly with Morgana. "She'll have a few bumps and bruises." And he was sorry for it. Then his eyes cleared and the easy smile was back in place. "She'll get through it, Ana. As she said, Morgana likes to win."

Morgana wasn't thinking of battles or victories, but of how cool and silky the air felt blowing against her cheeks. With her head back, she stared up at a black sky haunted by a half-moon and dazzled by stars.

It was easy to enjoy. The fast, open car on the curving road, the shadowy moonlight and the sea-flavored air. And it was easy to enjoy him, this man who drove with a natural, confident flair, who played the radio too loud, who smelled of the night and all its secrets.

Turning her head, she studied his profile. Oh, she would have enjoyed running her fingers over that angular face, testing the shape of the bones, brushing a touch over that clever mouth, perhaps feeling the slight roughness of his chin. She would have enjoyed it very much.

So why did she hesitate? Though she'd never been promiscuous or seen every attractive man as a potential lover, she recognized the deeper desire to be his. And she had seen that it was to happen before much longer in any case.

That was her answer, Morgana realized. She would always rebel against being destiny's puppet.

But surely if she chose him for herself, if she kept the power in her own hands, it was not the same as being led by fate. She was, after all, her own mistress.

"Why did you go into town tonight?" she asked him.

"I was restless. Tired of myself."

She understood the feeling. It didn't spring up in her often, but when it did it was unbearable. "The script is going well?"

"Pretty well. I should have a treatment to send to my agent in a few days." He glanced toward her, then immediately wished he hadn't. She looked so beautiful, so alluring, with the wind in her hair and the moonlight sprinkling over her skin, that he didn't want to look away again. It wasn't a wise way to operate a moving vehicle. "You've been a lot of help."

"Does that mean you're through with me?"

"No. Morgana, I—" He stopped and swore, catching himself a moment after he passed her driveway. He backed up and turned in, but left the motor running. For a moment he sat brooding in silence, looking at the house, where only a single window glowed gold and the rest were black as pitch.

If she asked him in, he would go with her, would have to go. Something was happening tonight. Something had been happening since the moment he'd turned and looked into her eyes. It gave him the unsettling feeling that he was walking through someone else's script and the ending had yet to be written.

"You are restless," she murmured. "Out of character for you." On impulse, she reached over and switched off the ignition. The absence of the engine's purr had the silence roaring in his head. Their bodies brushed, and the promise of more sizzled hot in his gut. "Do you know what I like to do when I'm restless?"

Her voice had lowered, and it seemed liquid enough now to slide over his skin like mulled wine. He turned to see those vivid blue eyes glowing with moonlight. And his hands were already reaching for her.

"What?"

She eased away, slipping from his hands like a ghost. After opening her door, she walked slowly around to his side, leaned down until their lips nearly touched. "I take a walk." With her eyes still on his, she straightened and offered a hand. "Come with me. I'll show you a magic place."

He could have refused. But he knew if there was a man who wouldn't have stepped from the car and taken that offered hand he had yet to be born.

They crossed the lawn, walking away from the house where the single light glowed, and entered the mystic shadows and whispering silence of the cyprus grove. Moonlight flickered down, casting eerie silhouettes of the twisted branches on the soft forest floor. The faintest of breezes hummed through the leaves and made him think of the harp she kept in her drawing room.

Her hand was warm and firm in his as she moved forward, not with hurry, but with purpose.

"I like the night." She took a deep breath of it. "The scent and the flavor of night. Sometimes I'll wake in the dark, and come to walk here."

He could hear water on rock, a steady heartbeat of sound. For reasons he couldn't fathom, his own heart was thudding relentlessly in his chest.

Something was happening.

"The trees." The sound of his own voice seemed odd and secretive in the shadowy grove. "I fell in love with them."

She stopped walking to eye him curiously. "Did you?"

"I was up here on vacation last year. Wanted to get out of the heat. I couldn't get enough of the trees." He laid a hand on one, feeling the rough bark of a trunk that bent dramatically away. "I'd never been much of the nature type. I'd always lived in cities, or just outside them. But I knew I had to live somewhere where I could look out of my window and see these trees."

"Sometimes we come back where we belong." She began to walk again, her footsteps silent on the soft earth. "Some ancient cults worshiped trees like these." She smiled. "I think it's enough to love them, appreciate them for their age, their beauty, their tenacity. Here." She stopped again and turned to him. "This is the center, the heart. The purest magic is always in the heart."

He couldn't have said why he understood, or why he believed.

Perhaps it was the moon, or the moment. He knew only that he felt a stirring along the skin, a fluttering in his mind. And, from somewhere deep in memory, he knew he'd been here before. With her.

Lifting a hand, he touched her face, letting his fingertips trace from cheek to jaw. She didn't move, not forward or away. She only continued to watch him. And wait.

"I don't know if I like what's happening to me," he said quietly.

"What is happening to you?"

"You are." Unable to resist, he lifted his other hand so that her face was framed, a captive of his tensed fingers. "I dream about you. Even in the middle of the day I dream about you. I can't turn it off, or switch the scene around as I'd like. It just happens."

She lifted a hand to his wrist, wanting to feel the good, strong beat of his pulse. "Is that so bad?"

"I don't know. I'm real good at avoiding complications, Morgana. I don't want that to change."

"Then we'll keep it simple."

He wasn't certain if she had moved, or if he had, but somehow she was in his arms, and his mouth was drinking from hers. No dream had ever been so stirring.

Her tongue toyed with his, tempting him to plunge deeper. She welcomed him with a moan that sizzled in his blood. At last he pleasured himself by tasting the long line of her throat, sliding his tongue over the pulse that hammered there, nibbling the sensitive flesh under her jaw, until he felt the first quick, helpless shudder pass through her. And then he was diving, more deeply, more desperately, when his mouth again met hers.

How could she have thought she had any choice, any control? What they were bringing to each other here was as old as time, as fresh as spring.

If only it could be pleasure, nothing more, she thought weakly as sensations battered against her will. But even as her body throbbed with that pleasure, she knew it was much, much more.

Not once in her years as a woman had she given her heart. It had not been jealously guarded, because it had always been safe.

But now, with the moon overhead, with the silent old trees as witnesses, she gave it to him.

Her arms tightened at the swift, silvery ache. His name tumbled from her lips. In that moment, she knew why she had needed to bring him there, to her most private place. Where could it be more fitting for her to lose her heart than here?

For another moment, she held him close, letting her body absorb what he could give her, wishing she could have honored her word and kept it simple.

But it was not to be simple now. Not for either of them. All she could do was take the time that was still left and prepare them both.

When she would have drawn back, he pulled her in, taking her mouth again and again while images and sounds and needs whirled in his brain.

"Nash." She turned her head to rub her cheek soothingly against his. "It can't be now."

Her quiet voice slipped through the roaring in his brain. He had an urge to drag her to the ground, take her then and there, prove that she was wrong. It had to be now. It would be now. The wave of violence stunned him. Appalled, he loosened his grip, realizing his fingers were digging into her flesh.

"I'm sorry." He dropped his hands to his sides. "Did I hurt you?"

"No." Touched, she brought his hand to her lips. "Of course not. Don't worry."

He damn well would worry. He'd never, never been anything but gentle with a woman. There were some who might say he could be careless with feelings, and if it was true he was sorry for it. But no one would ever have accused him of being careless physically.

Yet he had nearly pulled her to the ground and taken what he so desperately needed, without a thought to her acceptance or agreement.

Shaken, he jammed his hands in his pockets. "I was right, I don't like what's happening here. That's the second time I've kissed you, and the second time I've felt like I had to. The same way I have to breathe or eat or sleep."

She would have to tread carefully here. "Affection is just as necessary for survival."

He doubted it, since he'd done without it for most of his life. Studying her, he shook his head. "You know, babe, if I believed you were really a witch, I'd say I was spellbound."

It surprised her that it hurt. Oh, not his words so much as the distance it put between them. Try as she might, she couldn't remember ever having been hurt by a man before. Perhaps that was what it meant to be in love. She hadn't guarded her heart before, but she could protect it now.

"Then it's fortunate you don't believe. It was just a kiss, Nash." She smiled, hoping the shadows would mask the sadness in her eyes. "There's nothing to fear in a kiss."

"I want you." His voice had roughened, and his hands were fisted in his pockets. There was a helplessness tangled with this need. Perhaps that was what had nearly touched off violence. "That might be dangerous."

She didn't doubt it. "When the time comes, we'll find out. Now I'm tired. I'm going in."

This time, when she walked through the grove, she didn't offer her hand.

Chapter 5

Morgana had opened the doors of Wicca for the first time five years and some months before Nash had walked through them looking for a witch. The success of the shop was due to Morgana's insistence on intriguing stock, her willingness to put in long hours, and her frank enjoyment of the game of buying and selling.

Since her family, for longer than anyone could clearly remember, had been financially successful, she could have spent her time in any number of idle pursuits while drawing from a number of trust funds. Her decision to become a businesswoman had been a simple one. She was ambitious enough, and more than proud enough, to want to earn her own living.

The choice of opening a shop had appealed to Morgana because it allowed her to surround herself with things she liked and enjoyed. She had also, from the first sale, found pleasure in passing those things along to others who would also enjoy them.

There were definite advantages to owning your own business. A sense of accomplishment, the basic pride of ownership, the constant variety of people who walked in and out of your life. But whenever there was an up side, there was also a down. If you were blessed with a sense of responsibility, it wasn't possible to simply shut the doors and pull down the shades when you were in the mood to be alone.

Among Morgana's many gifts was an undeniable sense of responsibility.

At the moment, she wished her parents had allowed her to become a flighty, self-absorbed, feckless woman. If they hadn't done such a good job raising her, she might have bolted the door, jumped in her car and driven away until this miserable mood passed.

She wasn't used to feeling unsettled. She certainly didn't like the idea that this uncomfortable mood had been brought on by a man. As long as she could remember, Morgana had been able to handle all members of the male species. It was—she smiled a little at the thought—a gift. Even as a child she'd been able to dance her way around her father and her uncles, getting her own way with a combination of charm, guilt and obstinacy. Sebastian had been tougher to manage, but she felt she'd at least broken even there.

Once she'd reached adolescence, she'd learned quickly how to deal with boys. What moves to make if she was interested, what moves to make if she was not. As the years had passed, it had been a simple matter of applying the same rules, with subtle variations, to men.

Her sexuality was a source of joy to her. And she was well aware that it equaled another kind of power. She would never abuse power. Her dealings with men, whether they led to friendship or to romance, had always been successful.

Until now. Until Nash.

When had she begun to slip? Morgana wondered as she wrapped and bagged a long, slim bottle of ginseng bath balm for a customer. When she'd followed that little tug on her sixth sense and crossed this very room to speak to him for the first time? When she'd bowed to that spark of curiosity and attraction and kissed him?

Perhaps she had made her first serious misstep only last night, by allowing herself to be led by pure emotion. Taking him into the grove, to that spot where the air hummed and the moon spilled.

She had taken no other man there before. She would take no other man there again.

At least, dreaming back, she could almost make herself believe it was the place and the night that had caused her to believe she had fallen in love.

She didn't want to accept that such a thing could happen to her so quickly, or leave her such little choice.

So she would refuse to accept and put an end to it.

Morgana could almost hear the spirits laughing. Ignoring the sensation, she walked around the counter to help a customer.

Throughout the morning, business was slow but steady. Morgana wasn't sure whether she preferred it when browsers drifted in or when she and Luna had the shop to themselves.

"I think I should blame you for the whole thing." Morgana braced her elbows on the table and leaned down until she was eye to eye with the cat. "If you hadn't been so friendly, I wouldn't have assumed he was harmless."

Luna merely switched her tail and looked wise.

"He's not the least bit harmless," Morgana continued. "Now it's too late to back out. Oh, sure," she said when Luna blinked, "I could tell him the deal's off. I could make up excuses why I couldn't meet with him anymore. If I wanted to admit I was a coward." She drew in a deep breath and rested her brow on the cat's. "I am not a coward." Luna gave Morgana's cheek a playful pat. "Don't try to make up. If this business gets any farther out of hand, it's on your head."

Morgana glanced up when the shop door opened. Her lips curved in relief when she spotted Mindy. "Hi. Is it two already?"

"Just about." Mindy tucked her purse behind the counter, then gave Luna a quick scratch between the ears. "So how's it going?"

"Well enough."

"I see you sold the big rose quartz cluster."

"About an hour ago. It's going to a good home, a young couple from Boston. I've got it in the back ready to pack for shipping."

"Want me to take care of it now?"

"No, actually, I could use a little break from retail. I'll do it while you mind the shop."

"Sure. You look a little down, Morgana."

She arched a brow. "Do I?"

"Yep. Let Madame Mindy see." Taking Morgana's hand, she peered, steely eyed, at the palm. "Aha. No doubt about it. Man trouble."

Despite the accuracy, the very annoying accuracy, of the statement, Morgana's lips twitched. "I hate to doubt your expertise in palmistry, Madame Mindy, but you always say it's man trouble."

"I play the odds," Mindy pointed out. "You'd be surprised how many people stick their hands in my face just because I work for a witch."

Intrigued, Morgana tilted her head. "I suppose I would."

"Well, lots of them are nervous about approaching you, and I'm safe. I guess they figure some of it might rub off, but not enough to worry about. Sort of like catching a touch of the flu or something, I guess."

For the first time in hours, a laugh bubbled up in Morgana's throat. "I see. I suppose it would disappoint them to learn I don't read palms."

"They won't hear it from me." Mindy lifted a jade-and-silver hand mirror to check her face. "But I'll tell you, honey, I don't need to be a fortune-teller to see a tall blond man with great buns and eyes to die for." She tugged a corkscrew curl toward the middle of her forehead before glancing at Morgana. "He giving you a rough time?"

"No. Nothing I can't handle."

"They're easy to handle." After setting the mirror aside, Mindy unwrapped a fresh stick of gum. "Until they matter." Then she flashed Morgana a smile. "Just say the word and I'll run interference for you."

Amused, Morgana patted Mindy's cheek. "Thanks, but I'll make this play on my own."

Her mood brighter, Morgana stepped into the back room. What was she worried about anyway? She *could* handle it. Would handle it. After all, she didn't know Nash well enough for him to matter.

He had plenty to keep him busy, Nash told himself. Plenty. He was sprawled on the sofa—six feet of faded, sagging cushions he'd bought at a garage sale because it was so obviously fashioned for afternoon naps. Books were spread over his lap and jumbled on the floor. Across the room, the agonies and pathos of an afternoon soap flickered on the television screen. A soft-drink bottle stood on the cluttered coffee table, should he want to quench his thirst.

In the next room, his computer sat sulking at the lack of attention. Nash thought he could almost hear it whine.

It wasn't like he wasn't working. Idly Nash ripped off a sheet of notepaper and began folding it. He might have been lying on the sofa, he might have spent a great deal of his morning staring into space. But he was thinking. Maybe he'd hit a bit of a snag in the treatment, but it wasn't like he was blocked or anything. He just needed to let it cook awhile.

Giving the paper a last crease, he narrowed his eyes, then sent the miniature bomber soaring. To please himself, he added sound effects as the paper airplane glided off, crash-landing on the floor in a heap of other models.

"Sabotage," he said grimly. "Must be a spy on the assembly line." Shifting for comfort, he began to build another plane while his mind drifted.

Interior scene, day. The big, echoing hangar is deserted. Murky light spills through the front opening and slants over the silver hull of a fighter jet. Slow footsteps approach. As they near, there is something familiar about them, something feminine. Stiletto heels on concrete. She slips in the entrance, from light into shadow. The glare and the tipped-down brim of a slouchy hat obscure her face, but not the body poured into a short red leather dress. Long, shapely legs cross the hangar floor. In one delicate hand, she holds a black leather case.

After one slow glance around, she goes to the plane. Her skirt hikes high on smooth white thighs as she climbs into the cockpit. There is purpose, efficiency, in her movements. The way she slips into the pilot's seat, spins the locks on the leather case.

Inside the case is a small, deadly bomb, which she secretes under the console. She laughs. The sound is sultry, seductive. The camera moves in on her face.

Morgana's face.

Swearing, Nash tossed the plane in the air. It did an immediate nosedive. What was he doing? he asked himself. Making up stories about her. Indulging in bad symbolism. So, sure, she'd climbed into his cockpit and set off an explosion. That was no reason to daydream about her.

He had work to do, didn't he?

Determined to do it, Nash shifted, sending books sliding to the floor. Using the remote, he switched off the television, then took up what was left of his notebook. He punched the play button on his recorder. It took less than five seconds for him to realize his mistake and turn it off again. He wasn't in any frame of mind to listen to Morgana's voice.

He rose, scattering books, then stepping over them. He was thinking, all right. He was thinking he had to get the hell out of the house. And he knew exactly where he wanted to go.

It was his choice, he assured himself as he snagged his keys. He was making a conscious decision. When a man had an itch, he was a lot better off scratching it.

Her mood had improved enough that Morgana could hum along with the radio she'd turned on low. This was just what she'd needed, she thought. A cup of soothing chamomile, an hour of solitude, and some pleasant and constructive work. After packing up the crystal cluster and labeling it for shipping, she pulled out her inventory ledger. She could have spent a happy afternoon sipping the soothing tea, listening to music and looking over her stock. Morgana was certain she would have done exactly that if she hadn't been interrupted.

Perhaps if she'd been tuned in, she would have been prepared to see Nash stride through the door. But it really didn't matter what she might have planned, as he stalked over to the desk, hauled her to her feet and planted a long, hard kiss on her surprised mouth.

"That," he said when he took a moment to breathe, "was my idea."

Nerve ends sizzling, Morgana managed a nod. "I see."

He let his hands slide down to her hips to hold her still. "I liked it."

"Good for you." She glanced over her shoulder and noted that Mindy was standing in the open doorway, smirking. "I can handle this, Mindy."

"Oh, I'm sure you can." With a quick wink, she shut the door.

"Well, now." Searching for composure, Morgana put her hands on his chest to ease him away. She preferred that he not detect the fact that her heart was pounding and her bones were doing a fast melt. That was no way to keep the upper hand. "Was there something else?"

"I think there's a whole lot else." His eyes on hers, he backed her up against the desk. "When do you want to get started?"

She had to smile. "I guess we could call this being direct and to the point."

"We'll call it whatever you like. I figure it this way." Because she was wearing heels and they were eye to eye, Nash had only to ease forward to nibble on her full lower lip. "I want you, and I don't see how I'm going to start thinking straight again until I spend a few nights making love with you. All kinds of love with you."

The stirring started deep and spread. She had to curl her fingers over the edge of the desk to keep her balance. But when she spoke her voice was low and confident. "I could say that once we did make love you'd never think straight again."

He cupped her face with one hand and brushed his lips over hers. "I'll take my chances."

"Maybe." Her breath hitched twice before she controlled it. "I have to decide whether I want to take mine."

His lips curved over hers. He'd felt her quick tremor of reaction. "Live dangerously."

"I am." She gave herself a moment to enjoy what he brought to her. "What would you say if I told you it wasn't the right time yet? And that we'd both know when it was the right time."

His hands slid up so that his thumbs teased the curves of her breasts. "I'd say you're avoiding the issue."

"You'd be wrong." Enchanted—his touch was incredibly gentle—she pressed her cheek to his. "Believe me, you'd be wrong."

"The hell with timing. Come home with me, Morgana."

She gave a little sigh as she drew away. "I will." She shook her head when his eyes darkened. "To help you, to work with you. Not to sleep with you. Not today."

Grinning, he leaned closer to give her earlobe a playful nip. "That gives me plenty of room to change your mind."

Her eyes were very calm, almost sad, when she stepped back. "You may change yours before it's done. Let me ask Mindy to take over for the rest of the day."

She insisted on driving herself, following behind him with Luna curled in her passenger seat. She would give him two hours, she promised herself, and two hours only. Before she left him, she would do her best to clear his mind so that he could work.

She liked his house, the overgrown yard that shouted for a gardener, the sprawling stucco building with arching windows and red tile for the roof. It was closer to the sea than hers, so the music of the water was at full pitch. In the side yard were a pair of cypresses bent close together, like lovers reaching for one another.

It suited him, she thought as she stepped out of her car, off the drive and into the grass that rose above her ankles. "How long have you lived here?" she asked Nash.

"Couple months." He glanced around the yard. "I need to buy a lawn mower."

He'd need a bush hog before much longer. "Yes, you do."

"But I kind of like the natural look."

"You're lazy." She felt some sympathy for the daffodils that were struggling to get their heads above the weeds. She walked to the front entrance with Luna streaming regally behind her.

"I have to get motivated," he told her as he pushed open the front door. "I've mostly lived in apartments and condos. This is the first regular house I've had to myself."

She looked around at the high, cool walls of the foyer, the rich, dark wood of the curving banister that trailed upstairs and along an open balcony. "At least you chose well. Where are you working?"

"Here and there."

"Hmm." She strolled down the hallway and peeked in the first archway. It was a large, jumbled living area with wide, uncurtained windows and a bare hardwood floor. Signs, Morgana thought, of a man who had yet to decide if he was going to settle in.

The furniture was mismatched and heaped with books, papers, clothes and dishes—possibly long forgotten. More books were shoved helter-skelter into built-in cases along one wall. And toys, she noted. She often thought of her own clutter as toys. Little things that gave her pleasure, soothed her moods, passed the time.

She noted the gorgeous, grim-faced masks that hung on the wall, an exquisite print of nymphs by Maxfield Parrish, a movie prop—one of the wolves' claws from *Shape Shifter,* she imagined. He was using it as a paperweight. A silver box in the shape of a coffin sat next to the Oscar he'd won. Both could have used a proper dusting. Lips pursed, she picked up the voodoo doll, the pin still sticking lethally out of its heart.

"Anyone I know?"

He grinned, pleased to have her there, and too used to his own disorder to be embarrassed by it. "Whatever works. Usually it's a producer, sometimes a politician. Once it was this bean-counting IRS agent. I've been meaning to tell you," he added as his gaze skimmed over her slim, short dress of purple silk, "you have great taste in clothes."

"Glad you approve." Amused, she set the unfortunate doll down, patted the mangled head, then picked up a tattered deck of tarot cards. "Do you read them?"

"No. Somebody gave them to me. They're supposed to have belonged to Houdini or someone."

"Hmm." She fanned them, felt the faint trickle of old power on her fingertips. "If you're curious where they came from, ask Sebastian sometime. He could tell. Come here." She held out the deck to him. "Shuffle and cut."

Willing to oblige, he did what she asked. "Are we going to play?"

She only smiled and took the cards back. "Since the seats are occupied, let's use the floor." She knelt, gesturing for him to join to her. After tossing her hair behind her back, she dealt out a Celtic Cross. "You're preoccupied," she said. "But your creative juices aren't dried up or blocked. There are changes coming." Her eyes lifted to his. They were that dazzling Irish blue that tempted even a sane man to believe anything. "Perhaps the biggest of your life, and they won't be easy to accept."

It was no longer the cards she read, but rather the pale light of the seer, which burned so much more brightly in Sebastian.

"You need to remember that some things are passed through the blood, and some are washed out. We aren't always the total of the people who made us." Her eyes changed, softened, as she laid a hand on his. "And you're not as alone as you think you are. You never have been."

He couldn't joke away what hit too close to home. Instead, he avoided the issue entirely by bringing her hand to his lips. "I didn't bring you here to tell my fortune."

"I know why you asked me here, and it isn't going to happen. Yet." With more than a little regret, she drew her hand free. "And it isn't really your fortune I'm telling, it's your present." Quietly she gathered up the cards again. "I'll help you, if I can, with what I can. Tell me about the problem in your story."

"Other than the fact that I keep thinking of you when I'm supposed to be thinking of it?"

"Yes." She curled up her legs. "Other than that."

"I guess it's a matter of motivation. Cassandra's. That's what I decided to call her. Is she a witch because she wanted power, because she wanted to change things? Was she looking for revenge, or love, or the easy way out?"

"Why would it be any of those things? Why wouldn't it be a matter of accepting the gifts she was given?"

"It's too easy."

Morgana shook her head. "No, it's not. It's easier, so much easier, to be like everyone else. Once, when I was a little girl, some of the mothers refused to let their children play with me. I was a bad influence. Odd. Different. It hurt, not being a part of the whole."

Understanding, he nodded. "I was always the new kid. Hardly in one place long enough to be accepted. Somebody always wants to give the new kid a bloody nose. Don't ask me why. Moving around, you end up being awkward, falling behind in school, wishing you'd just get old enough to get the hell out." Annoyed with himself, he stopped. "Anyway, about Cassandra—"

"How did you cope?" She had had Anastasia, Sebastian, her family, and a keen sense of belonging.

With a restless movement of his shoulders, he reached out to touch her amulet. "You run away a lot. And, since that just gets your butt kicked nine times out of ten, you learn to run away safe. In books, in movies, or just inside your own head. As soon as I was old enough, I got a job working the concession stand at a theater. That way, I'd get paid for watching movies." As troubled memories left his eyes, his face cleared. "I love the flicks. I just plain love them."

She smiled. "So now you get paid for writing them."

"A perfect way to feed the habit. If I can ever get this one whipped into shape." In one smooth movement, he took a handful of her hair and wrapped it around his wrist. "What I need is inspiration," he murmured, tugging her forward for a kiss.

"What you need," she told him, "is concentration."

"I'm concentrating." He nibbled and tugged at her lips. "Believe me, I'm concentrating. You don't want to be responsible for hampering creative genius, do you?"

"Indeed not." It was time, she decided, for him to understand exactly what he was getting into. And perhaps it would also help him open his mind to his story. "Inspiration," she said, and slid her hands around his neck. "Coming up."

And so were they. As she met his lips with hers, she brought them six inches off the floor. He was too busy enjoying the taste to notice. Sliding over him, Morgana forgot herself long enough to lose herself in the heat. When she broke the kiss, they were floating halfway to the ceiling.

"I think we'd better stop."

He nuzzled her neck. "Why?"

She glanced down deliberately. "I didn't think to ask if you were afraid of heights."

Morgana wished she could have captured the look on his face when he followed her gaze—the wide-eyed, slack-jawed comedy of it. The string of oaths was a different matter. As they ran their course, she took them gently down again.

His knees buckled before he got them under control. White faced, he gripped her shoulders. The muscles in his stomach were twanging like plucked strings. "How the hell did you do that?"

"A child's trick. A certain kind of child." She was sympathetic enough to stroke his cheek. "Remember the boy who cried wolf, Nash? One day the wolf was real. Well, you've been playing with—let's say the paranormal—for years. This time you've got yourself a real witch."

Very slowly, very sure, he shook his head from side to side. But the fingers on her shoulders trembled lightly. "That's bull."

She indulged in a windy sigh. "All right. Let me think. Something simple but elegant." She closed her eyes, lifted her hands.

For a moment she was simply a woman, a beautiful woman standing in the center of a disordered room with her arms lifted gracefully, her palms gently cupped. Then she changed. God, he could see her change. The beauty deepened. A trick of the light, he told himself. The way she was smiling, with those full, unpainted lips curved, her lashes shadowing her cheeks, her hair tumbling wildly to her waist.

But her hair was moving, fluttering gently at first as though teased by a playful breeze. Then it was flying, around her face, back from her face, in one long gorgeous stream. He had an impossible image of a stunning wooden maiden carved on the bow of an ancient ship.

But there was no wind to blow. Yet he felt it. It chilled along his skin, whisked along his cheeks. He could hear it whistle as it streaked into the room. When he swallowed, he heard a click in his throat, as well.

She stood straight and still. A faint gold light shivered around her as she began to chant. As the sun poured through the high windows, soft flakes of snow began to fall. From Nash's ceiling. They swirled around his head, danced over his skin as he gaped, frozen in shock.

"Cut it out," he ordered in a ragged voice before he sank to a chair.

Morgana let her arms drop, opened her eyes. The miniature blizzard stopped as if it had never been. The wind silenced and died. As she'd expected, Nash was staring at her as if she'd grown three heads.

"That might have been a bit overdone," she allowed.

"I— You—" He fought to gain control over his tongue. "What the hell did you do?"

"A very basic call to the elements." He wasn't as pale as he had been, she decided, but his eyes still looked too big for the rest of his face. "I didn't mean to frighten you."

"You're not frightening me. Baffling, yes," he admitted. He shook himself like a wet dog and ordered his brain to engage. If he had seen what he had seen, there was a reason. There was no way she could have gotten inside his house to set up the trick.

But there had to be.

He pushed out of the chair and began to search through the room. Maybe his movements were a bit jerky. Maybe his joints felt as though they'd rusted over. But he was moving. "Okay, babe, how'd you pull it off? It's great, and I'm up for a joke as much as the next guy, but I like to know the trick."

"Nash." Her voice was quiet, and utterly compelling. "Stop. Look at me."

He turned, and he looked, and he knew. Though it wasn't possible, wasn't reasonable, he knew. He let out a long, careful breath. "My God, it's true. Isn't it?"

"Yes. Do you want to sit down?"

"No." But he sat on the coffee table. "Everything you've been telling me. You weren't making any of it up."

"No, I wasn't making any of it up. I was born a witch, like my mother, my father, like my mother's mother, and hers, and back for generations." She smiled gently. "I don't ride on a broomstick—except perhaps as a joke. Or cast spells on young princesses or pass out poisoned apples."

It wasn't possible, really. Was it? "Do something else."

A flicker of impatience crossed her face. "Nor am I a trained seal."

"Do something else," he insisted, and cast his mind for options. "Can you disappear, or—"

"Oh, really, Nash."

He was up again. "Look, give me a break. I'm trying to help you out here. Maybe you could—" A book flew off the shelf and bopped him smartly in the head. Wincing, he rubbed the spot. "Okay, okay. Never mind."

"This isn't a sideshow," she said primly. "I only demonstrated so obviously in the first place because you're so thickheaded. You refused to believe, and since we seem to be developing some sort of relationship, I prefer that you do.'' She smoothed out the skirt of her dress. ''And now that you do, we can take some time to think it all through before we move on.''

''Move on,'' he repeated. ''Maybe the next step is to talk about this.''

''Not now.'' He'd already retreated a step, she thought, and he didn't even know it.

''Damn it, Morgana, you can't drop all this on me, then calmly walk out. Good God, you're a witch.''

''Yes.'' She flicked back her hair. ''I believe we've established that.''

His mind began to spin again. Reality had taken a long, slow curve. ''I have a million questions.''

She picked up her bag. ''You've already asked me several of those million. Play back your tapes. All of the answers I gave you were true ones.''

''I don't want to listen to tapes, I want to talk to you.''

''For now, it's what I want that matters.'' She opened her bag and took out a small, wand-shaped emerald on a silver chain. She should have known there was a reason she'd felt compelled to put it there that morning. ''Here.'' Moving forward, she slipped the chain over his head.

''Thanks, but I'm not much on jewelry.''

''Think of it as a charm, then.'' She kissed both of his cheeks. Warily he eyed it. ''What kind of a charm?''

''It's for clearing the mind, promoting creativity and— See the small purple stone above the emerald?''

''Yeah.''

''Amethyst.'' Her lips curved as they brushed his. ''For protection against witchcraft.'' With the cat already at her heels, Morgana moved to the archway. ''Go sleep for an hour, Nash. Your brain is tired. When you wake, you'll work. And when the time is right, you'll find me.'' She slipped out the door.

Frowning, Nash tilted the slender green stone up to examine it. Clear thinking. Okay, he could use some of that. At the moment, his thoughts were as clear as smoke.

He ran a thumb over the companion stone of amethyst. Protection against witchcraft. He glanced up, through the window, to see Morgana drive away.

He was pretty sure he could use that, as well.

Chapter 6

What he needed to do was think, not sleep. Though he wondered that any man could think after what had happened in the last fifteen minutes. Why, any of the parapsychologists he'd interviewed over the years would have been wild to have a taste of what Morgana had given him.

But wasn't the first rational step to attempt to disprove what he had seen?

He wandered back into the living room to squint at the ceiling for a while. He couldn't deny what he had seen, what he had felt. But perhaps, with time, he could come up with some logical alternatives.

Taking the first step, he assumed his favorite thinking position. He lay down on the sofa. Hypnotism. He didn't care to think that he could be put in a trance or caused to hallucinate, but it was a possibility. An easier one to believe now that he was alone again.

If he didn't believe that, or some other logical explanation, he would have to accept that Morgana was exactly what she had said she was all along.

A hereditary witch, possessing elvish blood.

Nash toed off his shoes and tried to think. His mind was full of her—the way she looked, the way she tasted, the dark, uncanny light that had been in her eyes before she'd closed them and lifted her arms to the ceiling.

The same light, he recalled now, that had come into her eyes when she'd done the trick with the brandy decanter.

Trick, he reminded himself as his heart gave a single unpleasant thud. It was wiser to assume they were tricks and try to logic out how she had produced them. Just how did a woman lift a hundred-and-sixty-five-pound man six feet off the floor?

Telekinesis? Nash had always thought there were real possibilities there. After his preliminary work on his script *The Dark Gift,* he'd come to believe there were certain people who were able to use their minds, or their emotions, to move objects. A more logical explanation than the existence of poltergeists, to Nash's way of thinking. And scientists had done exhaustive studies of pictures flying across the room, books leaping off shelves, and so forth. Young girls were often thought to possess this particular talent. Girls became women. Morgana was definitely a woman.

Nash figured a research scientist would need a lot more than his word that Morgana had lifted him, and herself, off the ground. Still, maybe he could...

He stopped, realizing he was thinking, reacting, the same way the fictional Jonathan McGillis thought and reacted in his story. Was that what Morgana wanted? he wondered.

Listen to the tapes, she'd told him. All right, then, that was what he'd do. Shifting, he punched buttons on his recorder until he'd reversed the tape inside and started it to play.

Morgana's smoky voice flowed from the tiny machine.

"It's not necessary to belong to a coven to be a witch, any more than it's necessary to belong to a men's club to be a man. Some find joining a group rewarding, comforting. Others simply enjoy the social aspects." There was a slight pause, then a rustling of silks as she shifted. "Are you a joiner, Nash?"

"Nope. Groups usually have rules somebody else made up. And they like to assign chores."

Her light laugh drifted into the room. "And there are those of us who prefer our own company, and our own way. The history of covens, however, is ancient. My great-great-grandmother was high priestess of her coven in Ireland, and her daughter after her. A sabbat cup, a keppen rod and a few other ceremonial items were passed down to me. You might have noticed the ritual dish on the wall in the hallway. It dates back to before the burning time.''

''Burning time?''

''The active persecution of witches. It began in the fourteenth century and continued for the next three hundred years. History shows that mankind usually feels the need to persecute someone. I suppose it was our turn.''

She continued to speak, he to question, but Nash was having a hard time listening to words. Her voice itself was so alluring. It was a voice meant for moonlight, for secrets, for hot midnight promises. If he closed his eyes, he could almost believe she was there with him, curled up on the couch beside him, those long, luscious legs tangled with his, her breath warm on his cheek.

He drifted off to sleep with a smile on his face.

When he awakened, nearly two hours had passed. Heavy-eyed and groggy, he scrubbed his hands over his face, then swore at the crick in his neck. He blinked at his watch as he pushed himself to a half-sitting, half-slouching position.

It shouldn't be a surprise he'd slept so heavily, he thought. He'd been burning energy on nothing but catnaps for the last few days. Automatically he reached out for the liter bottle and gulped down warm soda.

Maybe it had all been a dream. Nash sat back, surprised at how quickly those afternoon-nap fuzzies lifted from his brain. It could have all been a dream. Except... He fingered the stones resting against his chest. She'd left those behind, as well as a faint, lingering scent that was exclusively hers.

All right, then, he decided. He was going to stop backtracking and doubting his own sanity. She had done what she had done. He had seen what he had seen.

It wasn't so complicated, really, Nash thought. More a matter of adjusting your thinking and accepting something new. At one time people had believed that space travel was the stuff of fantasy. On the other hand, a few centuries back, witchcraft had been accepted without question.

Maybe reality had a lot to do with what century you happened to live in. It was a possibility that started his brain ticking.

He took another swallow, grimacing as he capped the bottle

again. He wasn't just thirsty, he realized. He was hungry. Famished.

And more, much more important than his stomach was his mind. The entire story seemed to roll out inside it, reel by reel. He could see it, really see it clearly, for the first time. With the quick thrum of excitement that always came when a story unfolded for him, he sprang up and headed for the kitchen.

He was going to fix himself one monster sandwich, brew the strongest pot of coffee on the planet, and then get to work.

Morgana sat on Anastasia's sunny terrace, envying and admiring her cousin's lush gardens and drinking an excellent glass of iced julep tea. From this spot on Pescadaro Point, she could look out over the rich blue water of Carmel Bay and watch the boats bob and glide in the light spring breeze.

Here she was tucked away from the tourist track, seemingly a world away from the bustle of Cannery Row, the crowds and scents of Fisherman's Wharf. Sheltered on the terrace by trees and flowers, she couldn't hear the rumble of a single car. Only birds, bees, water and wind.

She understood why Anastasia lived here. There was the serenity, and the seclusion, her younger cousin craved. Oh, there was drama in the meeting of land and sea, the twisted trees, the high call of the gulls. But there was also peace within the tumbling walls that surrounded the estate. Silent and steady ivy climbed the house. Splashy flowers and sweet-smelling herbs crowded the beds Ana tended so gently.

Morgana never failed to feel at ease here, and she was unfailingly drawn here whenever her heart was troubled. The spot, she thought, not for the first time, was so much like Anastasia. Lovely, welcoming, without guile.

"Fresh from the oven," Ana announced as she carried a tray through the open french doors.

"Oh, God, Ana—fudge cookies. My favorite."

With a chuckle, Anastasia set the tray on the glass table. "I had an urge to bake some this morning. Now I know why."

More than willing, Morgana took the first bite. Her eyes drifted closed as the smooth chocolate melted on her tongue. "Bless you."

"So." Ana took her seat so that she could look out over the gardens and grass to the bay. "I was surprised to see you out here in the middle of the day."

"I'm indulging in a long lunch break." She took another bite of cookie. "Mindy's got everything under control."

"Do you?"

"Don't I always?"

Ana laid a hand over Morgana's. Before Morgana could attempt to close them off, Ana felt the little wisps of sadness. "I can't help feeling how unsettled you are. We're too close."

"Of course you can't. Just as I couldn't help coming out here today, even though I knew I was bringing you problems."

"I'd like to help."

"Well, you're the herbalist," Morgana said lightly. "How about some essence of *Helleborus Niger?*"

Ana smiled. *Helleborus,* more commonly called Christmas rose, was reputed to have the power to cure madness. "Fearing for your sanity, love?"

"At least." With a shrug, she chose another cookie. "Or I could take the easy way out and mix up a blend of rose and angelica, a touch of ginseng, sprinkled liberally with moondust."

"A love potion?" Ana sampled a cookie herself. "For anyone I know?"

"Nash, of course."

"Of course. Things aren't going well?"

A faint line appeared between Morgana's brows. "I don't know how things are going. I do know I wish I wasn't so bloody conscientious. It's really a very basic procedure to bind a man."

"But not very satisfying."

"No," Morgana admitted, "I can't imagine it would be. So I'm stuck with the ordinary way." As she sipped the reviving tea, she watched the snowy sails billowing from the boats on the bay. She'd always considered herself that free, she realized. Just that free. Now, though she had done no binding, she, herself, was bound.

"To tell the truth, Ana, I've never given much thought to what it would be like to have a man fall in love with me. Really in love. The trouble is, this time my heart's too involved for comfort."

And there was little comfort she could offer, Anastasia thought, for this type of ailment. "Have you told him?"

Surprised by the quick aching in her heart, Morgana closed her eyes. "I can't tell him what I'm not entirely sure of myself. So I wait. Moonglow to dawn's light," she chanted. "Night to day, and day to night. Until his heart is twined with mine, no rest or peace can I find." She opened her eyes and managed a smile. "That always seemed overly dramatic before."

"Finding love's like finding air. We can't survive without it."

"But what's enough?" This was the question that had troubled her most in the days since she had left Nash. "How do we know what's enough?"

"When we're happy, I'd think."

Morgana thought the answer was probably true—but was it attainable? "Do you think we're spoiled, Ana?"

"Spoiled? In what way?"

"In our...our expectations, I suppose." Her hand fluttered up in a helpless gesture. "Our parents, mine, yours, Sebastian's. There's always been so much love there, support, understanding, respect. The fun of being in love, and the generosity. It's not that way for everyone."

"I don't think that knowing love can run deep and true, that it can last, means being spoiled."

"But wouldn't it be enough to settle for the temporary? For affection and passion?" She frowned, watching a bee court a stalk of columbine. "I think it might be."

"For some. You'd have to be sure it would be enough for you."

Morgana rose with a grumble of annoyance. "It's so exasperating. I hate not being in charge."

A smile tugged at Anastasia's mouth as she joined her cousin. "I'm sure you do, darling. As long as I can remember, you've pushed things along your own way, just by force of personality."

Morgana slanted her a look. "I suppose you mean I was a bully."

"Not at all. Sebastian was a bully." Ana tucked her tongue in her cheek. "We'll just say you were—are—strong willed."

Far from mollified, Morgana bent to sniff at a heavy-headed peony. "I suppose I could take that as a compliment. But being strong willed isn't helping at the moment." She moved along the narrow stone path that wound through tumbling blooms and tangled vines. "I haven't seen him in more than a week, Ana. Lord," she said. "That makes me sound like some whiny, weak-kneed wimp."

Ana had to laugh even as she gave Morgana a quick squeeze. "No, it doesn't. It sounds as though you're an impatient woman."

"Well, I am impatient," she admitted. "Though I was prepared to avoid him if necessary, it hasn't been necessary." She shot Ana a rueful look. "A little sting to the pride."

"Have you called him?"

"No." Morgana's lips formed into a pout. "At first I didn't because I thought it was best to give us both some time. Then..." She'd always been able to laugh at herself, and she did so now. "Well, then I didn't because I was so damn mad he hadn't tried to beat down my door. He has called me a few times, at the shop or at home. He fires off a couple of questions on the Craft, mutters and grumbles while I answer. Grunts, then hangs up." She jammed fisted hands in her skirt pockets. "I can almost hear the tiny little wheels in his tiny little brain turning."

"So he's working. I'd imagine a writer could become pretty self-absorbed during a story."

"Ana," Morgana said patiently, "try to keep with the program. You're supposed to feel sorry for me, not make excuses for him."

Ana dutifully smothered a grin. "I don't know what came over me."

"Your mushy heart, as usual." Morgana kissed her cheek. "But I forgive you."

As they walked on, a bright yellow butterfly flitted overhead. Absently Ana lifted a hand, and the swallowtail danced shyly into her palm. She stopped to stroke the fragile wings. "Why don't you tell me what you intend to do about this self-absorbed writer who makes you so damn mad?"

With a shrug, Morgana brushed a finger over a trail of wisteria. "I've been thinking about going to Ireland for a few weeks."

Ana released the butterfly with her best wishes, then turned to her cousin. "I'd wish you a good trip, but I'd also have to remind you that running away only postpones. It doesn't solve."

"Which is why I haven't packed." Morgana sighed. "Ana, before I left him, he believed I am what I am. I wanted to give him time to come to terms with it."

That was the crux of it, Ana thought. She slipped a comforting hand around Morgana's waist. "It may take him more than a few days," she said carefully. "He may not be able to come to terms with it at all."

"I know." She gazed out over the water to the horizon. One never knew exactly what lay beyond the horizon. "Ana, we'll be lovers before morning. This I know. What I don't know is if this one night will make me happy or miserable."

Nash was ecstatic. As far as he could remember, he'd never had a story flow out of his mind with the speed and clarity of this one. The treatment, which he'd finished in one dazzling all-nighter, was already on his agent's desk. With his track record, Nash wasn't worried about a sale—which, in a gleeful phone call, his agent had told him was imminent. The fact was, for the first time, Nash wasn't even thinking about the sale, the production, the ultimate filming.

He was too absorbed in the story.

He wrote at all hours. Bounding awake at 3:00 a.m. to attack the keyboard, slurping coffee in the middle of the afternoon with the story still humming like a hive of bees in his head. He ate whatever came to hand, slept when his eyes refused to stay open, and lived within the tilted reality of his own imagination.

If he dreamed, it was in surreal snatches, with erotic images of himself and Morgana sliding through the fictional world he was driven to create.

He would wake wanting her, at times almost unbearably. Then he would find himself compelled to complete the task that had brought them together in the first place.

Sometimes, just before he fell into an exhausted sleep, he thought he could hear her voice.

It's not yet time.

But he sensed the time was coming.

When the phone rang, he ignored it, then rarely bothered to

return any of the calls on his machine. If he felt the need for air, he took his laptop out to the patio. If he could have figured out a way, he'd have dragged it into the shower with him.

In the end, he snatched the hard copy from his printer as each page slid out. A few adjustments here, he thought, scrawling notes in the margins. A little fine-tuning there, and he'd have it. But as he read, he knew. He *knew* he'd never done better work.

Nor had he ever finished a project so quickly. From the time he'd sat down and begun the screenplay, only ten days had passed. Perhaps he'd slept only thirty or forty hours total in those ten days, but he didn't feel tired.

He felt elated.

After gathering the papers up, he searched for an envelope. Books, notes, dishes, all scattered as he dug through them.

He only had one thought now, and that was to take it to Morgana. One way or the other, she had inspired him to write it, and she would be the first person to read it.

He found a tattered manila envelope covered with notations and doodles. After dumping the papers inside, he headed out of his office. It was fortunate that he caught sight of himself in the mirror in the foyer.

His hair was standing on end, and he had the beginnings of a fairly decent beard. Which, as he rubbed a curious hand over his chin, made him wonder if he should give growing a real one a shot. All that might not have been too bad, but he was standing in the foyer, gripping a manila envelope—and wearing nothing but the silver neck chain Morgana had given him and a pair of red jockey shorts.

All in all, it would probably be best if he took the time to clean up and dress.

Thirty minutes later he rushed back downstairs, more conservatively attired in jeans and a navy sweatshirt with only one small hole under the left armpit. He had to admit, the sight of his bedroom, the bathroom and the rest of the house had come as quite a shock, even to him. It looked as though a particularly ragged army had billeted there for a few weeks.

He'd been lucky to find any clothes at all that weren't dirty or crumpled or hadn't been kicked under the bed. There certainly hadn't been a clean towel, so he'd had to make do with a trio of washcloths. Still, he'd located his razor, his comb and a matching pair of shoes, so it hadn't been all that bad.

It took him another frustrating fifteen minutes to unearth his keys. God alone knew why they were on the second shelf of the refrigerator beside a moldy peach, but there they were. He also noted that that very sad peach and an empty quart container of milk were all that was left after he took the keys.

There would be time to deal with that later.

Gripping the script, he headed out the door.

It wasn't until the engine sprang to life and the dash lit that Nash noticed it was nearly midnight. He hesitated, considered calling her first or just putting off the visit until morning.

The hell with it, he decided, and shot out of the drive. He wanted her now.

Only a few miles away, Morgana was closing the door behind her. She stepped out into the silvery light of the full moon. As she walked away from the house, the ceremonial robe drifted around her body, cinched at the waist with a belt of crystals. In her arms she carried a simple basket that contained everything she would need to observe the spring equinox.

It was a night of joy, of celebration, of thanksgiving for the renewal spring brought to the earth. But her eyes were troubled. In this night, where light and dark were balanced, her life would change.

She knew, though she had not looked again. There was no need to look, when her heart had already told her.

It was difficult to admit that she had nearly stayed inside. A challenge to fate, she supposed. But that would have been the coward's way. She would go on with the rite, as she and others like her had gone on for aeons.

He would come when he was to come. And she would accept it.

Twisted shadows stretched over the lawn as she moved toward the grove. There was the smell of spring in the night air. The nocturnal bloomers, the drift of the sea, the fragrance of earth she had turned herself for planting.

She heard the call of an owl, low and lonely. But she didn't look for the white wings. Not yet.

There were other sounds, the gentle breath of the wind easing through the trees, stroking leaves, caressing branches. And the murmur of music that only certain ears could hear. The song of the faeries, a song that was older than man.

She was not alone here, in the shadowy grove with the drift of stars swimming overhead. She had never been alone here.

As she approached the place of magic, her mood shifted, and the clouds drifted from her eyes. Setting the basket down, she took a moment for herself. Standing still, eyes closed, hands cupped loosely at her sides, she drew in the flavor and beauty of the night.

She could see, even with her eyes closed, the white moon sailing through the black sea of the sky. She could see the generous light it spilled onto the trees, and through them to her. And the power that bloomed inside her was as cool, as pure, as lovely, as the moonlight.

Serenely she opened the basket. From it she took a white cloth, edged in silver, that had been in her family for generations. Some said it had been a gift to Merlin from the young king he had loved. Once it was spread on the soft ground, she knelt.

A small round of cake, a clear flask containing wine, candles, the witch's knife with its scribed handle, the ceremonial dish and cup, a small halo woven from gardenia blossoms. Other blooms…larkspur, columbine, sprigs of rosemary and thyme. These she scattered, along with rose petals, over the cloth.

This done, she rose to cast the circle. She felt the power drumming in her fingertips, warmer now, more urgent. When the circle was complete, she set candles, pure as ice, along its edge. Fourteen in all, to symbolize the days between the moon's waxing and its waning. Slowly she walked beside them, holding out her hand.

One by one, the candles flickered to flame, then glowed steadily. Morgana stood in the center of the ring of light. She unhooked the belt of crystals. It slid onto the cloth like a rope of fire. She slipped her arms from the thin robe. It drifted to her feet like melting snow.

Candlelight gleamed gold on her skin as she began the ancient dance.

* * *

At five to midnight, Nash pulled up in Morgana's driveway. He swore, noting that not a single light glowed in a single window.

He'd have to wake her up, he thought philosophically. How much sleep did a witch need, anyway? He grinned to himself. He'd have to ask her.

Still, she was a woman. Women had a tendency to get ticked off if you dropped by in the middle of the night and got them out of bed. It might help to have something to pave the way.

Inspired, he tucked the envelope under his arm and began to raid her flower bed. He doubted she'd notice that he'd stolen a few blooms. After all, it seemed she had hundreds. Awash in the scent of them, he got carried away, gathering an overflowing armful of tulips and sweet peas, narcissi and wallflowers.

Pleased with himself, he adjusted the load and strolled to her front door. Pan barked twice before Nash could knock. But no light flicked on at the dog's greeting, or at the pounding Nash set up.

He glanced back to the driveway to assure himself her car was there and then pounded again. Probably sleeps like a stone, he thought, and felt the first pricklings of annoyance. There was something working in him, some urgency. He had to see her, and it had to be tonight.

Refusing to be put off, he laid the script on the stoop and tried the knob. Pan barked again, but to Nash the dog sounded more amused than aroused. Finding the door locked, Nash started around the side. He was damn well getting in, and getting to her, before the night was done.

A sudden rush of immediacy quickened his step, but somewhere between the front of the house and the side terrace he found himself looking toward the grove.

It was there he needed to go. Had to go. Though his brain told him it was utterly foolish to go traipsing into the woods at night, he followed his heart.

Perhaps it was the shadows, or the sighing of the wind, that had him moving so quietly. He felt somehow it would be blasphemous to make unnecessary noise. There was a quality in the air here tonight, and it was almost unbearably lovely.

Yet, with every step he took, the blood seemed to pound faster in his head.

Then he saw, in the distance, a ghostly shimmer of white. He started to call out, but a rustle of movement had him glancing up. There, on a twisted cypress branch, stood a huge white owl. As Nash watched, the bird glided soundlessly from its perch and flew toward the heart of the grove.

His pulse was drumming in his ears, and his heart was rapping hard against his ribs. He knew that, even if he turned and walked away, he would be drawn again to that same center.

So he moved forward.

She was there, kneeling on a white cloth. Moonlight poured over her like silver wine. Again he started to call her name, but the sight of her forming a circle of candles, jewels at her waist, flowers in her hair, struck him mute.

Trapped in the shadows, he stood as she made the small golden fires spark atop the snowy candles. As she disrobed to stand gloriously naked in the center of flames. As she moved into a dance so graceful it stopped his breath.

Moonlight slithered over her skin, tipped her breasts, caressed her thighs. Her hair rained, an ebony waterfall, down her back as she lifted her face to the stars.

And he remembered his dream, remembered it so vividly that the fantasy and the reality merged into one potent image, with Morgana dancing at its center. The scent of flowers grew so strong that he was nearly dizzy with it. For an instant, his vision dimmed. He shook his head to clear it and struggled to focus.

The image had changed. She was kneeling again, sipping from a silver cup while the flames from the candles rose impossibly high, surrounding her like golden bars. Through them he could see the shimmer of her skin, the glint of silver between her breasts, at her wrists. He could hear her voice, softly chanting, then rising so that it seemed to be joined by thousands of others.

For a moment, the grove was filled with a soft, ethereal glow. Different from light, different from shadow, it pulsed and shivered, glinting like the edge of a silver sword in the sun. He could feel the warmth of it bathing his face.

Then the candle flames ebbed once again to small points, and the sound of chanting echoed away into silence.

She was rising. She slipped the white robe on, belted it.

The owl, the great white bird he had forgotten in his fascination with the woman, called twice before gliding like a cloud through the night.

She turned, her breath rising high in her throat. He stepped from the shadows, his heart hammering in his breast.

For a moment she hesitated. A warning whispered to her. Tonight would bring her pleasure. More than she had known. And its price would be pain. More than she would wish.

Then she smiled and stepped from the circle.

Chapter 7

Thousands of thoughts avalanched into his brain. Thousands of feelings flooded into his heart. As she moved toward him, her robe flowing around her like moondust, all those thoughts, all those feelings, shivered down to one. Down to her.

He wanted to speak, to tell her something, anything, that would explain how he felt at that moment. But his heart stuttered in his throat, making words impossible. He knew this was more than the simple desire of a man for a woman, yet whatever was spiraling through him was so far out of his experience that he was sure he could never describe it, never explain it.

He knew only that in this place of magic, at this moment of enchantment, there was only one woman. Some quiet, patient voice was whispering inside his heart that there had always been only one woman and he had been waiting all his life for her.

Morgana stopped, only an arm span away. Soft, silent shadows waltzed between them. She had only to step into that lazy dance to be in his arms. He would not turn from her. And she was afraid she had gone beyond the point where it was possible for her to turn from him.

Her eyes remained on his, though the little fingers of nerves pinched her skin. He looked stunned, she realized, and she could hardly blame him. If he was feeling even a fraction of the needs and fears that were skidding through her, he had every right to be.

It would not be easy for them, she knew. After tonight, the bond would be sealed. Whatever decisions were made in the tomorrows, by both of them, that bond would not be broken.

She reached out to trail a hand over the flowers he still cradled in his arms. She wondered if he knew, by the blossoms he had chosen, that he was offering her love, passion, fidelity and hope.

"Blooms picked in moonlight carry the charms and secrets of the night."

He'd forgotten about them. Like a man waking from a dream, he glanced down. "I stole them from your garden."

Her lips curved beautifully. He wouldn't know the language of the flowers, she thought. Yet his hand had been guided. "That doesn't make their scent less sweet, or the gift less thoughtful." Lifting her hand from them, she touched his cheek. "You knew where to find me."

"I... Yes." He couldn't deny the urge that had brought him into the grove. "I did."

"Why did you come?"

"I wanted to..." He remembered his frantic rush to leave the house, his impatience to see her. But, no, it was more basic than that. And infinitely more simple. "I needed you."

For the first time, her gaze wavered. She could feel the need radiating from him like heat, to warm her and to tempt her. It could, if she did nothing to stop it, bind her to him so firmly that no charm, no spell, would ever free her.

Her power was not absolute. Her own wishes were not always granted. To take him tonight would be to risk everything, including her power to stand alone.

Until tonight, freedom had always been her most prized possession. Lifting her gaze to his again, she cast that possession away.

"What I give you tonight, I give with a free heart. What I take from you, I take without regrets." Her eyes glittered with visions he couldn't see. "Remember that. Come with me." She took his hand and drew him into the circle of light.

The moment he stepped through the flames, he felt the change. The air was purer here, its scent more vivid, as if they had climbed to the top of some high, untraveled cliff. Even the stars seemed closer, and he could see the trails of moonlight, silver-edged white streaks through the sheltering trees.

But she was the same, her hand firm in his.

"What is this place?" Instinctively he lowered his voice to a whisper, not in fear, but in reverence. It seemed to drift off, twining with the harp song that filled the air.

"It needs no name." She drew her hand from his. "There are many forms of magic," she said, and unfastened her belt of crystals. "We'll make our own here." She smiled again. "An it harm none."

Slowly she placed the crystal rope on the edge of the cloth, then turned to face him. With the moonlight silvering her eyes, she opened her arms.

She took him in, and the lips she offered were warm and soft. He could taste the lingering sweetness of the wine she had drunk, as well as her own richer, more potent flavor. He wondered that any man could survive without that heady, drugging taste. That any man would choose to. His head spun with it as she urged him to drink deeper.

On a moan that seemed to spring from his soul, he dragged her closer, crushing the flowers between them so that the night air swelled with their scent. His mouth branded hers before moving frantically over her face.

Behind her closed lids she could see the dance of candlelight, could see the single shadow her body and Nash's made sway. She could hear the deep, pure resonance of the breeze singing through the leaves, the night music that was its own kind of magic. And she heard the whisper of her name as it breathed through the lips that once again searched for hers.

But it was what she felt that was so much more real. This deep well of emotion that filled for him as it had never filled for anyone. As she gave him her heart for a second time, that well brimmed, then overflowed in a quiet, steady stream.

For a moment, she was afraid she might drown in it, and that fear brought on racking shudders. Murmuring to her, Nash drew her closer. Whether it was in need or comfort, Morgana didn't know, but she settled again. And accepted.

The captivator became the captivated.

He was struggling against some clawing beast prowling in his gut, demanding that he take her quickly, feed himself. He had never, never experienced such a violent surge of hunger for anything, or anyone, as he did for Morgana in that glowing circle of light.

He fisted his hands in her hair to keep them from tearing the robe from her. Some flicker shadowed by instinct told him she would accept the speed, respond to this gnawing appetite. But it wasn't the way. Not here. Not now.

Pressing his face to the curve of her neck, he held her close and fought it back.

Understanding didn't make her heartbeat less erratic. His desire to take warred with his desire to give, and both were ripe with power. His choice would make a difference. And, though she couldn't see, she knew that the texture of their loving tonight would matter to both of them in all the years to come.

"Nash, I—"

He shook his head, then leaned back and framed her face in his hands. They weren't steady. Nor was his breathing. His eyes were dark, intense. She wondered that they couldn't see into her and study her heart.

"You scare the hell out of me," he managed. "I scare the hell out of me. It's different now, Morgana. Do you understand?"

"Yes. It matters."

"It matters." He let out a long, unsteady breath. "I'm afraid I'll hurt you."

You will hurt me. The certainty of it shivered through her. The pain would come, no matter what defenses she used. But not tonight. "You won't." She kissed him gently.

No, he thought as his cheek rubbed against hers. He wouldn't. He couldn't. Though desire continued to beat in his blood, its tempo had slowed. His hands were steady again as he slipped the robe from her shoulders, followed it down her arms until they were both free of it.

The pleasure of looking at her was like a velvet fist pressed against his heart. He had seen her body before, when he had watched her dance naked in the circle. But that had been like a dream, as if she were some beautiful phantom just out of his reach.

Now she was only a woman, and his hand would not pass through if he tried to touch.

Her face first. He glided his fingertips over her cheeks, her lips, her jaw, and down the slender column of her throat. And she was real. Hadn't he felt her warm breath against his skin? Wasn't he now feeling the hammerbeat of her pulse when his fingers lingered?

Witch or mortal, she was his, to cherish, to enjoy, to pleasure. It was meant to be here, surrounded by the old, silent trees, by shadowed light. By magic.

Her eyes changed, as a woman's would when her system was crowded with desire and anticipation. He watched them as he trailed those curious fingers over the slope of her shoulders, down her arms and back again. Her breath began to shiver through her parted lips.

Just as lightly, just as slowly, his touch skimmed down to her breasts. Now her breath caught on a moan, and she swayed, but he made no move to possess her. Only skimming patiently over those soft slopes, brushing his thumbs over nipples that hardened and ached in response.

She couldn't move. If the hounds of hell had burst out of the trees, jaws snapping, she would have stood just as she was, body throbbing, eyes fixed helplessly on his. Did he know? Could he know what a spell he had cast over her with this exquisite tenderness?

There was nothing else for her but him. She could see only his face, feel only his hands. With each unsteady breath she took, she was filled with him.

He followed the line of her body, down her rib cage, detouring around to her back, where her hair drifted over his hands and her spine trembled under them. He wondered why he had thought it necessary to speak, when he could tell her so much more with a touch.

Her body was a banquet of slender curves, smooth skin, subtle muscles. But he no longer felt the urge to ravish. How much better it was, this time, to sample, to savor, to seduce. How much more power did a man need than to feel a woman's skin singing under his hands?

He skimmed over her hips, let his fingers glide over those

long, lovely thighs, changing the angle on the return journey so that he absorbed all the little bolts of pleasure at finding her already hot and damp for him.

When her knees buckled, he gathered her close, lowering her to the cloth so that he could begin the same glorious journey with his lips.

Steeped in sensation, she tugged his shirt away so that she could feel the wonder of his flesh sliding over hers. His muscles were taut, showing her that the gentleness he gave her took more strength than wild passion would have. She murmured something, and he brought his mouth back to hers so that she could slide the jeans over his hips, cast them away and make him as vulnerable as she.

Sweet, mindless pleasure. Long, lingering delights. The moon showered its fragile light as they offered each other the most precious of gifts. The scattered flowers they lay on sent up exotic perfumes to mix with the scent of the night. Though the breeze rustled the leaves, the encircling flames ran straight and true.

Even when passion gripped them, sending them rolling over crushed blooms and rumpled silk, there was no rush. Somewhere in the shadows, the owl called again, and the ring of flames shot up like lances. Closing them in, closing all else out.

Her body was shuddering, but there were no longer any nerves or fears. Her arms encircled him as he slipped inside her.

With his blood roaring in his head, he watched her eyes flutter open, saw those gold stars shining against the deep blue as magnificently as those overhead shone in the sky. He lowered his mouth to hers as they moved together in a dance older and more powerful than any other.

She felt the beauty of it, the magic that was more potent than anything she could conjure. He filled her utterly. Even when the ache drove them both, the tenderness remained. Two glistening tears slipped from her eyes as she arched for him, letting her body fly with that final staggering release. She heard him call out her name, like a prayer, as he poured himself into her.

When he buried his face in her hair, shuddering, she saw the flash of a shooting star, streaking like a flame through the velvet sky.

* * *

Time passed. Minutes, hours, it didn't concern him. All he knew was that she was as soft as a wish beneath him, her body relaxed but still curled into his. Nash thought it would be delightful for them to stay just like this until sunrise.

Then he thought, more practically, that he would probably end up smothering her.

When he started to shift, Morgana clamped herself around him like a vise. "Uh-uh," she said sleepily.

Since she insisted, he thought he might as well nibble on her neck. "I may be on the thin side, but I'd guess I have you by a good sixty pounds. Besides, I want to look at you."

He levered himself onto his elbows and pleased himself.

Her hair was spread out like tangled black silk on the white cloth. There were flowers caught in it, making him think of gypsies and faeries. And witches.

He let out a long, labored breath. "What happens when a mortal makes love to a witch?"

She had to smile, and did so slowly, sinuously. "Did you happen to notice the gargoyles on the tower of the house?" Nash's mouth opened, then closed again. Morgana let out a long, rich laugh as her fingers danced down his spine. "I love it when you're gullible."

He was feeling entirely too good to be annoyed. Instead, he played with her hair. "It seemed like a reasonable question. I mean, you are... I know you are. But it's still tough to swallow. Even after what I saw tonight." His eyes came back to hers. "I watched you."

She traced his lips with a fingertip. "I know."

"I've never seen anything more beautiful. You, the light. The music." His brows came together. "There was music."

"For those who know how to hear it. For those who are meant to hear it."

It wasn't so hard to accept, after everything else. "What are you doing here? It looked like some kind of ceremony."

"Tonight's the spring equinox. A magic night. What happened here, with us, was magic, too."

Because he couldn't resist, he kissed her shoulder. "It sounds like a tired line, but it's never been like this for me before. With anyone."

"No." She smiled again. "Not with anyone." Her pulse leapt as she felt him harden inside her. "Again," she murmured when his lips lowered to hers.

The night moved toward morning before they dressed. As Nash pulled on his sweatshirt, he watched Morgana gathering up the crushed and broken flowers.

"I guess we did them in. I'll have to steal you some more."

Smiling, she cradled them in her arms. "These will do nicely," she said. Nash's eyes widened when he saw that the flowers she held were now as full and fresh as when he had first picked them.

He passed a hand through his hair. "I don't think I'm going to get used to that anytime soon."

She merely placed them in his hands. "Hold them for me. I have to remove the circle." She gestured, and the candle flames died. As she took them from the ground, she chanted quietly.

"The circle cast in the moon's light is lifted now by my right. The work is done, with harm to none. With love and thanks I set thee free. As I will, so mote it be."

She set the last candle in the basket, then lifted the cloth. When it was folded, she put it away.

"That's, ah…all there is to it?"

She picked up the basket and turned to him. "Things are usually more simple than we believe." Morgana offered a hand, pleased when he curled his fingers around hers. "And, in the spirit of that simplicity, will you share my bed for what's left of the night?"

He brought their joined hands to his lips and gave her a simple answer. "Yes."

She couldn't get enough of him, Nash thought dreamily. During the night, they had turned to each other again and again. Drifting off to sleep, drifting into love while the moonlight faded. And now, when the sun was a pale red glow behind his closed lids, she was nuzzling his ear.

He smiled, murmuring to her as he let himself float toward wakefulness. Her head was a warm, welcome weight on his chest. The way she was tickling and teasing his ear told him she would not object to some lazy morning loving. More than willing to oblige her, he lifted a hand to stroke her hair. His hand stopped in midair.

How could her head be on his chest *and* her mouth be at his ear? Anatomically speaking, it just didn't figure. But then again, he'd seen her do several things that didn't figure in terms of the simple laws of the real world. But this was *too* weird. Even half-awake, his lively imagination bounced.

Would he open his eyes to look and see something so fantastic, so out of his realm, that it would send him screaming out into the night?

Day, he reminded himself. It was day. But that was hardly the point.

Cautiously he let his hand lower until it touched her hair. Soft, thick, but...God, the shape of her head was wrong. She'd changed. She'd...she'd shifted into... When her head moved under his hand, Nash let out a muffled cry and, with his heart skating into his throat, opened his eyes.

The cat lay on his chest, staring at him with unblinking—and somehow smug—amber eyes. Nash jolted when something cold slid over his cheek. He found that Pan was standing with his forelegs on the bed, his big silver head tilted curiously to one side. Before Nash could speak, the dog licked him again.

"Oh, boy." While Nash waited for his mind to clear and his pulse to settle, Luna stood, stretched, then padded up his chest to peer into his face. Her muttered purr seemed distinctly like a chuckle. "Okay, sure, you got me." He reached out with each hand to rub a furry head.

Pan took that for a welcome and leapt onto the bed. He landed—light-footed, fortunately—on Nash's most vulnerable area. With a strangled *oof,* Nash sat bolt upright, dislodging the cat and making her rap up against Pan.

Things looked dicey for a moment, with the animals glaring and growling at each other. But Nash was too concerned with getting his wind back to worry about the prospect of fur flying.

"Ah, playing with the animals?"

Sucking in air, Nash looked up to see Morgana standing in the doorway. The moment she was spotted, Luna flicked her tail in Pan's face, strolled over to a pillow, circled, sat and began to wash her hindquarters. Tail thumping, Pan plopped down. Nash figured he had about seventy pounds of muscle pinning his legs to the mattress.

"My pets seem very fond of you."

"Yeah. We're one happy family."

With a steaming mug in one hand, she crossed to the bed. She was already dressed, in a little red number with beads and embroidery on the wide shoulders, and tiny snaps running down the front until they ran out at the hem, which stopped several inches above her very sexy knees.

Nash wondered if he should undo the snaps one at a time, or in one quick yank. Then he caught a scent that was nearly as exotic and every bit as seductive as her perfume.

"Is that coffee?"

Morgana sat on the edge of the bed and sniffed the contents of the cup. "Yes, I believe it is."

Grinning, he reached out to toy with the end of the hair she'd woven into an intricate braid. "That was awfully sweet of you."

Her eyes mirrored surprise. "What was? Oh, you think I brought this in for you." Watching him, she tapped a fingertip against the mug. "That I brewed a pot of coffee, poured a cup and decided to serve it to you, in bed, because you're so damn cute."

Properly chastened, he sent one last, longing look at the mug. "Well, I—"

"In this case," she said, interrupting him, "you happen to be exactly right."

He took the cup she offered, watching her over the rim as he drank. He wasn't a coffee snob—couldn't afford to be, with the mud he usually made for himself—but he was sure this was the best cup to be found west of the Mississippi. "Thanks. Morgana..." He reached up to set one of the complex arrangements of beads and stones at her ears jangling. "Just how damn cute am I?"

She laughed, pushing the mug aside so that she could kiss him. "You'll do, Nash." More than do, she thought as she kissed him again. With that tousled, sun-streaked hair tumbled around a sleepy face, that surprisingly well-muscled chest tempting her above the tangle of sheets, and that very warm, very skilled mouth rubbing against hers, he did magnificently.

She pulled back, not without regret. "I have to go to work."

"Today?" Lazily he cupped his hand around the back of her neck to urge her closer. "Don't you know it's a national holiday?"

"Today?"

"Sure." She smelled like night, he thought. Like flowers that bloom only in starlight. "It's National Love-In Day. A tribute to the sixties. You're supposed to celebrate it by—"

"I get the picture. And that's very inventive," she said, closing her teeth over his bottom lip. "But I have a shop to run."

"That's very unpatriotic of you, Morgana. I'm shocked."

"Drink your coffee." She stood to keep from letting him change her mind. "There's food in the kitchen if you feel like breakfast."

"You could have gotten me up." He snagged her hand before she could retreat.

"I thought you could use the sleep, and I didn't want to give you any more time to distract me."

His eyes slanted up to hers as he nibbled on her knuckles. "I'd like to spend several hours distracting you."

Her knees went weak. "I'll give you a chance later."

"We could have dinner."

"We could." Her blood was beginning to hum, but she couldn't make herself pull her hand free.

"Why don't I pick something up, bring it by?"

"Why don't you?"

He opened her hand to press a kiss on the palm. "Seven-thirty?"

"Fine. You'll let Pan out, won't you?"

"Sure." His teeth grazed her wrist and sent her pulse soaring. "Morgana, one more thing."

Her body yearned toward his. "Nash, I really can't—"

"Don't worry." But he could see that she was worried, and it delighted him. "I'm not going to muss you up. It's going to be too much fun thinking about doing just that for the next few hours. I left something for you on the front stoop last night. I was hoping you'd find time to read it."

"Your script? You've finished?"

"All but some fine-tuning, I think. I'd like your opinion."

"Then I'll try to have one." She leaned over to kiss him again. "'Bye."

"See you tonight." He settled back with the cooling coffee, then swore.

Morgana turned at the doorway. "What?"

"My car's parked behind yours. Let me get some pants on."

She laughed. "Nash, really." With that, she strolled away. The cat jumped off the bed and followed.

"Yeah," Nash said to the now-snoozing Pan. "I guess she can take care of it."

Sitting back, he prepared to drink his coffee in solitary splendor. As he sipped, he studied the room. This was the first chance he'd taken to see what Morgana surrounded herself with in her most private place.

There was drama, of course. She walked with drama wherever she went. Here it was typified in the bold jewel colors she'd chosen. Turquoise for the walls. Emerald for the spread they had kicked aside during the night. Bleeding hues of both were in the curtains that fluttered at the windows. A daybed upholstered in sapphire stretched under one window. It was plumped with fat pillows of garnet, amethyst and amber. Arched over it was a slender brass lamp with a globe shaped like a lush purple morning glory. The bed itself was magnificent, a lake of tumbled sheets bordered by massive curved head and footboards.

Intrigued, Nash started to get up. Pan was still pinning his legs, but after a couple of friendly nudges, he rolled aside obligingly to snore in the center of the bed. Naked, mug in one hand, Nash began to wander the room.

A polished silver dragon stood on the nightstand, his head back, his tail flashing. The wick between his open jaws announced that he would breathe fire. She had one of those pretty mirrored vanities with a padded stool that Nash had always considered intensely feminine. He could imagine her sitting there, running the jewel-crusted silver-backed brush through her hair, or anointing her skin with the creams or lotions from one of the colorful glass pots that stood on it, winking in the sunlight.

Unable to resist, he picked one up, removing the long crystal top and sniffing. At that moment she was so much in the room with him, he could almost see her. That was the complexity and power of a woman's magic.

Reluctantly he recapped the bottle and set it aside. Damn it, he didn't want to wait through the day for her. He didn't want to wait an hour.

Easy, Kirkland, he lectured himself. She'd only been gone five minutes. He was acting like a man besotted. Or bewitched. That thought set off a niggling little doubt that he frowned over for a moment, then shoved aside. He wasn't under any kind of spell. He knew exactly what he was doing, and he was in complete control of his actions. It was just that the room held so much of her, and being in it made him want.

Frowning, he ran his fingers through a pile of smooth colored stones she kept in a bowl. If he was obsessing about her, that, too, could be explained. She wasn't an ordinary woman. After what he'd seen, with what he knew, it was natural for him to think about her more often than he might about someone else. After all, the supernatural was his forte. Morgana was living proof that the extraordinary existed in an ordinary world.

She was an incredible lover. Generous, free, outrageously responsive. She had humor and wit and brains, as well as an agile body. That combination alone could make a man sit up and beg. When you added the fairy dust, she became downright irresistible.

Plus, she'd helped him with his story. The more Nash thought about it, the more he was certain the script was his best work to date.

But what if she hated it? The idea jumped into his mind like a warty toad and had him staring into space. Just because they had shared a bed, and something else too intangible for him to name, didn't mean she would understand or appreciate his work.

What the hell had he been thinking of, giving it to her to read before he'd polished it?

Terrific, he thought in disgust and bent to snatch up his jeans. Now he had that to worry about for the next several hours. As he strode off to shower, Nash wondered how he had gotten in so deep that a woman could drive him crazy in so many ways.

Chapter 8

It was more than four hours later before Morgana had a chance for a cup of tea and a moment alone. Customers, phone calls, arriving shipments, had kept her busy enough that she'd had time enough only to glance at the first page or two of Nash's script.

What she saw intrigued her enough to have her resenting each interruption. Now she heated water and nibbled on tart green grapes. Mindy was in the shop, waiting on two college students. Since both students were male, Morgana knew Mindy wouldn't need any help.

With a sigh, she brewed the tea, set it to steep, then settled down with Nash's script.

An hour later, she'd forgotten the tea that grew cold in the pot. Fascinated, she flipped back to page one and began all over again. It was brilliant, she thought, and felt a surge of pride that the man she loved could create something so rich, so clever, so absorbing.

Talented, yes. She'd known he was talented. His movies had always entertained and impressed her. But she'd never read a screenplay before. Somehow she'd thought it would be no more than an outline, the bare bones that a director, actors, technicians, would flesh out for an audience. But this was so rich in texture, so full of life and spirit, that it didn't seem like words on paper at all. She could already see, and hear, and feel.

She imagined that, when those extra layers were added by the actors, the camera, the director, Nash might very well have the film of the decade on his hands.

It stunned her that the man she thought of as charming, a bit cocky and often full of himself had something like this inside him. Then again, it had rocked her the night before to discover that he had such deep wells of tenderness.

Setting the script aside, she leaned back in her chair. And she had always considered herself so astute, she thought with a little smile. Just how many more surprises did Nash Kirkland have up his sleeve?

He was working on the next one as hard as he could. Inspiration had struck, and Nash had never been one to let a good idea slip away.

He'd had a moment's twinge at the notion of leaving Morgana's back door unlocked. But he'd figured that with her reputation, and with the wolf-dog roaming the grounds, nobody would dare break in.

For all he knew, she'd cast some sort of protective spell over the house in any case.

It was going to be perfect, he told himself as he struggled to arrange an armload of flowers—purchased this time—in a vase. They seemed to take on a life of their own, stems jamming, heads drooping. After several tries, the arrangement still looked as though the flowers had been shoved into the container by a careless ten-year-old. By the time he'd finished, he'd filled three vases and was happy to admit he'd never be a set director.

But they smelled good.

A glance at his watch warned him that time was running short. Crouching in front of the hearth, he built a fire. It took him longer, and he imagined it took considerably more effort, than it would have taken Morgana, but at last the flames were licking cheerfully at the wood. A fire was hardly necessary, but he liked the effect.

Satisfied, he rose to check the scene he'd so carefully set. The table for two was laid with a white cloth he'd found in the drawer of the sideboard in Morgana's dining room. Though that room had had possibilities, with its soaring ceiling and its huge fireplace, he thought the drawing room more intimate.

The china was hers, too, and looked old and lovely, with little rosebuds hugging the edges of gleaming white plates. He'd arranged the heavy silverware and the crystal champagne glasses. All hers, as well. And folded the deep rose damask napkins into neat triangles.

Perfect, he decided. Then swore.

Music. How could he have forgotten the music? And the candlelight. He made a dash to the stereo and fumbled through a wide selection of CDs. Chopin, he decided, though he was more in tune with the Rolling Stones than with classical music. He switched it on and slipped the disc in, then nodded his approval after the first few bars. Then he went on a treasure hunt for candles.

Ten minutes later, he had over a dozen ranged throughout the room, glowing and wafting out the fragrances of vanilla, jasmine, sandalwood.

He'd barely had time to pat himself on the back when he heard her car. He beat Pan to the door by inches.

Outside, Morgana lifted a brow when she spotted Nash's car. But the fact that he was nearly a half hour early didn't annoy her. Not in the least. She was smiling as she crossed to the door, his script under one arm, a bottle of champagne in the other.

He opened the door and scooped her up into a long, luxurious kiss. Wanting his own greeting, Pan did his best to crowbar between them.

"Hi," Nash said when he freed her mouth.

"Hello." She handed Nash both bottle and envelope so that she could ruffle Pan's fur before closing the door. "You're early."

"I know." He glanced at the label on the bottle. "Well, well... Are we celebrating?"

"I thought we should." As she straightened, her braid slid over her shoulder. "Actually, it's a little congratulatory gift for you. But I'd hoped you'd share."

"Be glad to. What am I being congratulated for?"

She nodded toward the envelope in his hand. "For that. Your story."

He felt the little knot that had remained tight in his stomach all day loosen. "You liked it."

"No. I loved it. And once I sit down and take my shoes off I'll tell you why."

"Let's go in here." After shifting the bottle and envelope to one arm, he tucked the other around her. "How was business?"

"Oh, it's ticking right along. In fact, I may see if Mindy can squeak out another hour or two a day for me. We've been..." Her words trailed off as she stepped into the drawing room.

The candleglow was as mystic and romantic as moonbeams. It glinted on silver, tossed rainbows from crystal. Everywhere was the perfume of flowers and candle wax, and the haunting strains of violins. The fire smoldered gently.

It wasn't often she was thrown off balance so completely. Now she felt the sting of tears in the back of her throat, tears that sprang from an emotion so pure and bright she could hardly bear it.

She looked at him, and the flickering light tossed dozens of stars into her eyes. "Did you do this for me?"

A little off balance himself, he skimmed his knuckles over her cheek. "Must've been elves."

Her curving lips brushed his. "I'm very, very fond of elves."

He shifted until their bodies met. "How do you feel about screenwriters?"

Her arms slid comfortably around his waist. "I'm learning to like them."

"Good." As he settled into the kiss, Nash realized his arms were too encumbered to allow him to give it his best shot. "Why don't I get rid of this stuff, open the champagne?"

"That sounds like an excellent idea." With a long, contented sigh, she slipped out of her shoes while he walked over to pluck out a bottle already nestled in the ice bucket. He turned both hers and his around to show the identical labels.

"Telepathy?"

Moving toward him, she smiled. "Anything's possible."

He tossed the envelope aside, snuggled the second bottle in the ice, then opened the first with a cheerful pop and fizz. He poured, and then after handing her a glass, rang his against it. "To magic."

"Always," she murmured, and sipped. Taking his hand, she led him to the couch, where she could curl up close and watch the fire. "So, what did you do today besides call up some elves?"

"I wanted to show you my Cary Grant side."

With a chuckle, she brushed her lips over his cheek. "I like all of your sides."

Contented, he propped his feet on the coffee table. "Well, I spent a lot of time trying to get those flowers to look like they do in the movies."

She glanced over. "We'll concede that your talents don't run to floral arranging. I love them."

"I figured the effort was worth something." He entertained himself by toying with her earring. "I did a little fine-tuning on the script. Thought about you a lot. Took a call from my very excited agent. Thought about you some more."

She chuckled and laid her head on his shoulder. Home. She was home. Completely. "Sounds like a very productive day. What was your agent excited about?"

"Well, it seems he'd taken a call from a very interested producer."

Delight shimmered from her eyes as she sat up again. "Your screenplay."

"Right the first time." It felt a little odd.... No, Nash thought, it felt wonderfully odd to have someone so obviously excited for him. "Actually, it's the treatment, but since my luck's been running pretty well we've got a deal in the works. I'm going to let the script cook a couple of days and take another look. Then I'll ship it off to him."

"It's not luck." She tapped her glass to his again. "You've got magic. Up there." She laid a finger on his temple. "And in here." And on his heart. "Or wherever imagination comes from."

For the first time in his adult life, he thought he might blush. So he kissed her instead. "Thanks. I couldn't have done it without you."

With a light laugh, she settled back. "I'd hate to disagree with you. So I won't."

He ran an idle hand down the braid on her shoulder. It felt tremendously good, he realized, just to sit here like this at the end of the day with someone who was important to him. "Why don't you stroke my ego and tell me what you liked about it?"

She held out her glass so that he could top off her champagne. "I doubt your ego needs stroking, but I'll tell you anyway."

"Take your time. I wouldn't want you to leave anything out."

"All of your movies have texture. Even when there's blood splashing around or something awful scratching at the window, there's a quality that goes beyond being spooked or shocked. In this—though you're bound to set some hearts pumping with that graveyard scene, and that business in the attic—you go a step further." She shifted to face him. "It's not just a story of witchcraft and power or of conjuring forces, good and bad. It's about people, their basic humanity. Of believing in wonderful things and trusting your heart. It's a kind of funny celebration of being different, even when it's difficult. In the end, even though there's terror and pain and heartbreak, there is love. That's what we all want."

"You didn't mind that I had Cassandra casting spells with graveyard dirt or chanting over a cauldron?"

"Artistic license," Morgana said with a lifted brow. "I suppose I found it possible to overlook your creativity. Even when she was prepared to sell her soul to the devil to save Jonathan."

With a shrug, he drained his glass. "If Cassandra had the power of good, the story would hardly have enough punch if she didn't have at least one match with the power of evil. You see, there are some basic commandments of horror. Even though that's not exactly what this turned out to be, I think they still apply."

"Ultimate good against ultimate evil?" she suggested.

"That's one. The innocent must suffer," he added. "Then there's the rite of passage. That same innocent must spill blood."

"A manhood thing," Morgana said dryly.

"Or womanhood. I'm no sexist. And good must, through great sacrifice, triumph."

"Seems fair."

"There's one more. My personal favorite." He skimmed a fingertip up her neck. Chills chased it. "The audience should wonder, and keep wondering, if whatever evil that's been vanquished slinked free again after the final fade-out."

She pursed her lips. "We all know evil's always slinking free."

"Exactly." He grinned. "The same way we all wonder, from time to time, if there really is something drooling in the closet at night. After the lights go out. And we're alone." He nipped at her earlobe. "Or what's really rustling the bushes outside the cellar window or skulking in the shadows, ready, waiting, to ooze out and—"

When the doorbell rang, she jolted. Nash laughed. Morgana swore.

"Why don't I get it?" he suggested.

She made a stab at dignity and smoothed down her skirt. "Why don't you?"

When he walked out, she let go with a quick shudder. He was good, she admitted. So damn good that she, who knew better, had been sucked right in. She was still deciding whether to forgive him or not when Nash came back with a tall, gangly man hefting a huge tray. The man wore a white tux and a red bow tie. Stitched over his chest pocket was Chez Maurice.

"Set it right on the table, Maurice."

"It's George, sir," the man said in a sorrowful voice.

"Right." Nash winked at Morgana. "Just dish everything right on up."

"I'm afraid this will take me a moment or two."

"We've got time."

"The mocha mousse should remain chilled, sir," George pointed out. Nash realized that the poor man had a permanent apology stuck in his throat.

"I'll take it into the kitchen." Morgana rose to take the container. As she left them, she heard George murmuring sadly that the radicchio had been off today and they'd had to make do with endive.

"He lives for food," Nash explained when Morgana returned a few moments later. "It makes him weep to think how careless some of the new delivery boys are with the stuffed mushrooms. Bruising them heedlessly."

"Heathens."

"Exactly what I said. It seemed to put George in a better frame of mind. Or maybe it was the tip."

"So what has George brought us?" She wandered over to the table. "Endive salad."

"The radicchio—"

"Was off. I heard. Mmm. Lobster tails."

"À la Maurice."

"Naturally." She smiled over her shoulder as Nash pulled out her chair. "Is there a Maurice?"

"George was sorry to report that he's been dead for three years. But his spirit lives on."

She laughed and began to enjoy her food. "This is very inventive takeout."

"I'd considered a bucket of chicken, but I thought this would impress you more."

"It does." She dipped a bite of lobster in melted butter, watching him as she slipped it between her lips. "You set a very attractive stage." Her hand brushed lightly over his. "Thank you."

"Anytime." The fact was, he was hoping there'd be dozens of other times, dozens of other stages. With the two of them, just the two of them, as the only players.

He caught himself, annoyed that he was thinking such serious thoughts. Such permanent thoughts. To lighten the mood, he poured more champagne.

"Morgana?"

"Yes."

"There's something I've been wanting to ask you." He brought her hand to his lips, finding her skin much more alluring than the food. "Is Mrs. Littleton's niece going to the prom?"

She blinked first, then threw her head back with a rich laugh. "My God, Nash, you're a romantic."

"Just curious." Because he couldn't resist the way her eyes danced, he grinned. "Okay, okay. I like happily-ever-after as well as the next guy. Did she get her man?"

Morgana sampled another bite. "It seems Jessie worked up the courage to ask Matthew if he'd like to go to the prom with her."

"Good for her. And?"

"Well, I have this all secondhand from Mrs. Littleton, so it may not be precisely accurate."

Nash leaned forward to flick a finger down her nose. "Listen, babe, I'm the writer. You don't have to pause for dramatic effect. Spill it."

"My information is that he blushed, stuttered a bit, pushed up these cute horn-rim glasses he wears, and said he guessed so."

Solemnly Nash raised his glass. "To Jessie and Matthew."

Morgana lifted her own. "To first love. It's the sweetest."

He wasn't sure about that, since he'd been so successful in avoiding the experience. "What happened to your high school sweetheart?"

"What makes you think I had one?"

"Doesn't everyone?"

Morgana acknowledged that with a faint cock of her brow. "Actually, there was one boy. His name was Joe, and he played on the basketball team."

"A jock."

"I'm afraid Joe was second-string. But he was tall. Height was important to me in those days, as I loomed over half the boys in my class. We dated on and off through senior year." She sipped her wine. "And did a lot of necking in his '72 Pinto."

"Hatchback?" Nash asked between bites.

"I believe so."

"I like to get a clear visual." He grinned. "Don't stop now. I can see it. Exterior scene, night. The parked car on a dark, lonely road. The two sweethearts entwined, stealing desperate kisses as the radio sings out with the theme from *A Summer Place*."

"I believe it was *Hotel California*," she corrected.

"Okay. Then the last guitar riff fades...."

"I'm afraid that's about it. He went to Berkeley in the fall, and I went to Radcliffe. Height and a nice pair of lips just wasn't enough to keep my heart involved at a distance of three thousand miles."

Nash sighed for all men. "'Frailty, thy name is woman.'"

"I believe Joe recovered admirably. He married an economics major and moved to St. Louis. At last count, they'd produced three-fifths of their own basketball team."

"Good old Joe."

This time Morgana refilled the glasses. "How about you?"

"I never played much ball."

"I was talking about high school sweethearts."

"Oh." He leaned back, enjoying the moment—the fire crackling at his back, the woman smiling at him through the candlelight, the good-natured fizz of champagne in his head. "She was Vicki—with an *i*. A cheerleader."

"What else?" Morgana agreed.

"I mooned over her for nearly two months before I worked up the courage to ask her out. I was shy."

Morgana smiled over the rim of her glass. "Tell me something I can believe."

"No, really. I'd transferred in the middle of junior year. By that time all the groups and cliques are so firmly established it took a crowbar to break them up. You're odd man out, so you spend a lot of time watching and imagining."

She felt a stirring of sympathy, but she wasn't sure he'd welcome it. "And you spent time watching Vicki with an *i*."

"I spent a whole lot of time watching Vicki. Felt like decades. The first time I saw her do a *C* jump, I was in love." He paused to study Morgana. "Were you a cheerleader?"

"No. Sorry."

"Too bad. I still get palpitations watching *C* jumps. Anyway, I finally sweated up the nerve to ask her to the movies. It was *Friday the 13th*. The movie, not the date. While Jason was hacking away at the very unhappy campers, I made a fumbling pass. Vicki received. We were an item for the rest of the school year. Then she dumped me for this hood with a motorcycle and a tattoo."

"The hussy."

Shrugging philosophically, he polished off his lobster. "I heard she eloped with him and they went to live in a trailer park in El Paso. Which is no more than she deserved after breaking my heart."

Tilting her head, Morgana gave him a narrowed look. "I think you made it up."

"Only part of it." He didn't like to talk about his past, not with anyone. To distract her, he rose and changed the music.

Now it was slow, dreamy Gershwin. Coming back to the table, he took her hand to draw her to her feet. "I want to hold you," he said simply.

Morgana moved easily into his arms and let him lead. At first they merely swayed to the music, his arms around her waist, hers around his neck, their eyes on each other's. Then he guided her into a dance so that their bodies flowed together to the low throb of the music.

He wondered if he would always think of her in candlelight. It suited her so well. That creamy Irish skin glowed as fragilely as the rose-tipped china. Her hair, black as the night that deepened beyond the windows, was showered with little stars of light. There were more stars in her eyes, sprinkled like moondust over the deep midnight blue.

The first kiss was quiet, a soft meeting of lips that promised more. That promised anything that could be wished. He felt the champagne spin in his head as he lowered his mouth to hers again, as her lips parted beneath his like the petals of a rose.

Her fingers glided silkily along his neck, teasing nerves to the surface. A low moan sounded in her throat, a moan that had his blood humming in response. Her body moved against his as she deepened the kiss. Her eyes remained open, drawing him in.

He slid his hands up her back, aroused by her quick shudder of response. Watching her, wanting her, he tugged the band from the end of her braid, combing tensed fingers through to loosen the intricate coils. He could hear her breath catch, see her eyes darken, as he dragged her head back and plundered that wide, unpainted mouth.

She tasted danger and delight and desperation. The combination swirled inside her, a headier brew than any wine. His muscles were wire taut under her hands, and she shivered with a mixture of fear and pleasure at the thought of what would happen when they sprang free.

Desire took many forms. Tonight, she knew, it would not come as the patient, reverent exploration they had known before. Tonight, there were fires raging.

Something snapped. He could all but hear the chains on his control break. He pulled away, his hands still gripping her arms, his body a mass of aches and needs. She said nothing, only stood, her lips soft and swollen from his, her hair tumbled like restless night around her shoulders. Her eyes full of smoke and secret promises.

He dragged her back again. Even as his mouth was devouring hers, he lifted her off her feet.

She'd never believed she would allow herself to be swept away. She'd been wrong. As he strode from the room and up the stairs, both her mind and her body went willingly with him. Reckless and ready, she let her lips race over his face, down his throat and back up to meet his avid mouth.

He didn't pause at the bedroom door, not even when he saw that she'd brought the candles and music with them. The bed was centered in their glow, beckoning. He tumbled onto it with her.

Impatient hands, hungry mouths, desperate words. He couldn't get enough. There couldn't be enough to fill this gnawing need. He knew she was with him, flame for flame, demand for demand, but he wanted to push her further and faster, until there was nothing but blazing heat and wild wind.

She couldn't get her breath. The air was too heavy. And hot, so hot she wondered that her skin didn't burst into flames. She reached for him, thinking she would ask, beg, for a moment to stop and catch her sanity. Then his mouth crushed hers again and even the wish for reason was lost.

In a mindless haze of greed, he yanked his hand down the front of her dress. Snaps burst open like tiny explosions to reveal flushed skin and seductive black lace. With a breathless oath, he ripped the flimsy cloth aside so that her breasts spilled into his restless hands.

She cried out—not in fear or in pain, but in wonder—as his greedy mouth scorched her skin.

He was ruthless, relentless, reckless. Need sliced through him, hot knives of desire that cut all ties to the civilized. His hands moved over her, leaving aches and trembles in their wake.

Her response was not submission, not surrender, but rather a greed that swelled as ripely as his own. She took, she tormented, she tantalized.

They went tumbling over the bed, caught up in a war of passion, wild hands tugging and tearing at clothes, seeking the pleasure of flesh slicked from the heat. He did as he chose, releasing every dark fantasy that had spun in his mind. Touching, tasting, devouring.

She crested hard, clinging to him as the wave shot her up and left her wrecked. His name was a mindless chant through her trembling lips, a chant that ended on a sob when he sent her soaring again.

Dazed, she rose above him. He could see the candlelight shivering over her skin, and her eyes, dark and glazed with what he had given her. He knew he would die if he didn't have her tonight, tomorrow, a thousand tomorrows.

He pressed her back into the mattress, clamping his hands on hers. Breath heaving, he held on long enough for their eyes to meet. Was it challenge he saw in hers? Was it triumph?

Then he plunged deep. Her hands fisted beneath his, and her body rose up to meet him.

Speed. Power. Glory. They raced together, stroke for stroke, with a strength born of shattering needs. His mouth sought hers again in a bruising kiss. Her arms vised around him, those short, neat nails raking desperately down his back.

He felt her agile body convulse, heard her broken gasp of stunned pleasure. Then his mind went dim as he leapt off the razor's edge to follow her.

A long time later, he clawed his way back to reason. He'd rolled off her, wanting to let her breathe. Now she lay on her stomach, sprawled across the bed. Catching his own breath, he stared into the shadows, flipping back through his mind what had passed between them. He wasn't sure whether to be appalled or delighted.

He'd...well, he supposed *plundered* would be an apt word. He certainly hadn't been worried about the niceties. However much pleasure he'd found in making love with a woman before, he'd never slipped over the edge into madness. It had its points, he realized. But he wasn't sure how Morgana might feel about having had her clothes ripped off her.

Nash laid a tentative hand on her shoulder. She shuddered. Wincing, he took it away again. "Morgana...are you all right?"

She made some sound, something between a whimper and a

moan. He felt a quick stab of fear at the thought that she might be crying. Good going, Kirkland, he thought furiously, then tried again. He stroked a hand down her hair.

"Babe. Morgana. I'm sorry if I..."

He let his words trail off, not certain what to say. Slowly she turned her head, managed to lift up a limp hand far enough to rake the tangled hair out of her eyes. She blinked at him.

"Did you say something?"

"I was just... Are you okay?"

She sighed. It was a long, catlike sound that made his treacherous body twang. "Okay?" She seemed to roll the word around, testing it with her tongue. "I don't think so. Ask me again when I find the energy to move." She slid her hand over the tangled sheets to take his. "Are you?"

"Am I what?"

"Okay."

"I wasn't the one being plundered."

The word had a smile spreading lazily over her face. "No? I thought I did a pretty good job." She stretched and was pleased to see that her body was nearly in working order again. "Give me an hour and I'll try again."

Relief began to trickle through. "You're not upset?"

"Do I look upset?"

He thought it over. She looked like a cat who'd happily gorged on a gallon of cream. He didn't even realize he'd started to grin. "No, I guess not."

"Pleased with yourself, aren't you?"

"Maybe I am." He started to reach out to drag her closer and found his fingers tangled in what was left of her bra. "Are you?"

She wondered that the grin didn't split his face. He was watching her, all but whistling a tune as he spun the tattered lace on one finger. Morgana pushed up to her knees, noted his very satisfied eyes skimmed over her. "Do you know what, Nash?"

"No. What?"

"I'm going to have to wipe that grin off your face."

"Yeah? How?"

Tossing her hair back, she planted herself over him. Slowly, sinuously, she slid down. "Watch me."

Chapter 9

As far as Nash was concerned, life was a pretty good deal. He spent his days doing something he loved, and he was paid very well to do it. He had his health, a new home, and an interesting deal in the works. Best of all, he was enjoying an incredible affair with a fascinating woman. A woman who, he'd discovered in the past weeks, he was not only desperately attracted to, but considered a friend.

Nash had learned through trial and error that a lover you couldn't enjoy out of bed satisfied the body but left the spirit wanting. With Morgana, he'd found a woman he could laugh with, talk with, argue with and make love with, all with a sense of intimacy he'd never experienced before.

A sense of intimacy he hadn't realized he wanted before.

There were even times he forgot she was something more than a woman.

Now, as he finished the series of push-ups he forced himself to perform three times a week, he thought over their last few days together.

They'd taken a long, leisurely drive up to Big Sur to stand at an overlook, wind whipping their hair as they looked out over the staggering view of hills and water and cliffs. Like tourists, they'd taken snapshots with her camera, videos with his.

Though he'd felt a little foolish, he'd even scooped up a few pebbles—when she wasn't looking—to slip into his pocket as a souvenir of the day.

He'd tagged along while she'd poked around in the shops in Carmel—and had been good-naturedly resigned when she piled packages into his arms.

Lunch on the terrace of some pretty café, surrounded by flowers. Sunset picnics on the beach, sitting with his arm around her, her head on his shoulder, while the great red orb bled fire into the sky and then sank into the indigo sea.

Quiet kisses at dusk. Easy laughter. Intimate looks in crowded places.

It was almost as if he was courting her.

With a grunt, Nash let his arms relax. Courting? No, that wasn't what it was at all, he assured himself, rolling over on his back. They simply enjoyed each other's company, a great deal. But it wasn't courtship. Courtship had a sneaky habit of leading to marriage.

And marriage, Nash had decided long ago, was one experience he could do without.

A niggling doubt worked into his mind as he stood to flex the muscles he'd toned over the past half hour. Had he done anything to make her think that what they had together might lead to something...well, something legal and permanent? With DeeDee he had spelled out everything from the get-go, and still she'd been smugly certain she could change his mind.

But with Morgana he'd said nothing. He'd been too busy falling for her to be practical.

The last thing he wanted to do was hurt her. She was too important, she meant too much. She was...

Slow down, Kirkland, he warned himself uneasily. Sure, she was important. He cared about her. But that didn't mean he was going to start thinking about love. Love also had a nasty habit of leading to marriage.

Frowning, he stood in the middle of the room he'd set up with benches and weights. Sweat trickled unnoticed down his face as he cautiously took a peek at what was in his heart. Okay, yes, he cared about her. Maybe more than he'd ever cared about anyone. But that was a long way from orange blossoms, station wagons and a cozy cottage for two.

Rubbing a hand over his heart, he geared himself up for a closer look. Why did he think about her so often? He couldn't remember another woman intruding on his daily routine the way Morgana did. There were times when he stopped whatever he was doing just to wonder what she was doing. It had gotten so that he didn't sleep well unless she was with him. If he awakened in the morning and she wasn't there, he started the day with a nagging sense of disappointment.

It was a bad sign, he thought as he grabbed a towel to wipe his face. A sign he should have picked up on long before this. How come there'd been no warning bells? he wondered. No quiet little voice whispering in his ear that it was time to take a long, casual step in retreat.

Instead, he'd been moving forward in a headlong rush.

But he hadn't gone over the edge. Not Nash Kirkland. He took a deep breath and tossed the towel aside. It was just the novelty, he decided. Soon the immediacy of the feelings she brought out in him would fade.

As he walked off to shower, he assured himself, like any addict, that he was still in control. He could back off anytime.

But like fingers reaching for an itch, his mind kept worrying the problem. Maybe he was fine, maybe he was in control, but what about Morgana? Was she getting in too deep? If she was as tied up as he was, she could be imagining—what? A life in the burbs, monogrammed towels? A riding lawn mower.

The cool spray of water blasted his face. Nash found himself grinning.

And he'd said he wasn't sexist. Here he was worrying that Morgana was harboring delusions of marriage and family. Just because she was a woman. Ridiculous. She was no more interested in taking that deadly leap then he.

But as he let the water sluice over his head, he began to imagine.

Interior scene, day. The room is a jumbled heap of toys, clothes overflowing out of plastic hampers, dirty dishes. In a playpen dumped in the center of the room, a toddler squalls. Our hero walks in, a bulging briefcase in his hand. He wears a dark suit and a strangling tie. Wing tips. There is a weary cast to his face. A man who has faced problems all day and has come home to more.

"Honey," he says with an attempt at cheer, "I'm home."

The baby howls and rattles his cage. Resigned, our hero sets his briefcase aside and goes to pick up the screaming baby. The child's wet diaper sags.

"You're late again." The wife shuffles in. Her hair is a tangled mess around a face set in stern, angry lines. She wears a ratty bathrobe and a pair of fuzzy slippers. As our hero bounces the wet, screaming baby, the wife slaps her hands on her hips and begins to rattle off a list of all of his shortcomings, punctuated by announcements that the washing machine has overflowed, the sink is clogged, and she's pregnant—again.

Just as the scene he was creating began to ease both Nash's conscience and mind, it faded out, to be replaced by a new one.

Coming home with the scent of flowers and the sea in the air. Smiling because you were almost where you wanted to be. Needed to be. Starting up the walk, carrying a bouquet of tulips. The door opens, and she stands there, her hair pulled back in a sleek ponytail, her lips curved in welcome. She cradles a pretty, dark-haired child on her hip, a child who giggles and holds out its pudgy arms. He cuddles the child, smelling talc and baby and his wife's subtle perfume.

"We missed you," she says, and lifts her face for a kiss.

Nash blinked. With a wrench of his wrist, he shut off the water, then shook his head.

He had it bad, he admitted. But, since he knew that second scene was more of a fantasy than anything he'd ever written, he was still in control.

When he stepped out of the shower, he wondered how soon she would be there.

Morgana punched down on the accelerator and leaned the car into a curve. If felt good...no, it felt fabulous, to be buzzing along the tree-lined road with the windows down and the sea breeze blowing through her hair. What made it fabulous was that she was going somewhere to be with someone who had made a difference in her life.

She'd been content without him. Perhaps she would have gone

on being content if she had never met him. But she had, and nothing was ever going to be the same again.

She wondered if he knew how much it meant that he accepted her for what she was. She doubted it. She hadn't known how much it could mean until it had happened. And, as for Nash, he had a habit of looking at things at a skewed angle and seeing the humor in them. She imagined he saw her...talents as some kind of great joke on science. And perhaps they were, in a way.

But the important thing, to her, was that he knew, and accepted. He didn't look at her as if he expected her to grow a second head at any moment. He looked at her as a woman.

It was easy to be in love with him. Though she had never considered herself a romantic, she had come to appreciate all the books, the songs, the poetry, written to celebrate the caprices of the heart. It was true that when you were in love, the air smelled clearer, the flowers sweeter.

On a whim, she wished a rose into her hand, smiling as she sniffed the delicate closed bloom. Her world felt like that, she realized. Like a rose that was just about to open.

It made her feel foolish to think like that. Giddy, light-headed. But her thoughts were her own, she reminded herself. Until she made them someone else's. It occurred to her that, sooner or later, she would have to share them with Nash.

She couldn't be sure how long it would be before complications set in, but for now it was glorious simply to enjoy the soft spread of emotion glowing inside her.

As she pulled into his driveway, she was smiling. She had a few surprises for Nash, starting with her plan for this balmy Saturday night. She reached for the bag on the seat beside her, and Pan stuck his head over her shoulder.

"Just give me a minute," she told him, "and you can get out and see what's what. Luna will show you around."

From her perch on the floor of the passenger seat, Luna glanced up, eyes slitted.

"If you don't behave, I'll dump you both back home. You'll have only yourselves for company until Monday."

As she stepped from the car, she felt a flicker, like a curtain fluttering over her mind. She stood, one hand resting on the door, absorbing a wash of wind, a whisper of sound. The air thickened, grayed. There was no dizziness. It was as if she had stepped from sunshine into shadows, shadows where mysteries waited to be solved. She strained to see beyond that mist, but it lay heavy, teasing her with hints and glimpses only.

Then the sun was back, and there was only the sound of water rushing against rock.

Though she hadn't Sebastian's gift for precognition, or Anastasia's empathetic tendencies, she understood.

Things were about to change. And soon. Morgana also understood that those changes might not be something she would have wished for.

Shaking off the mood, she started up the walk. Tomorrow could always be changed, she reminded herself. Especially if one concentrated on now. Since now equaled Nash, she was willing to fight to keep it.

He opened the door before she reached it and stood, hands tucked in his pockets, smiling at her. "Hi, babe."

"Hi." Dangling the bag from one hand, she linked an arm around his neck and curved her body to his for a kiss. "Do you know how I feel?"

"Yeah." He skimmed his hands down her sides to her hips. "I know exactly how you feel. Fantastic."

She chuckled and pushed the last lingering doubts aside. "As it happens, you're right." Riding on pure emotion, she handed him the rose.

"For me?" He wasn't exactly sure what a man's response should be when a woman gave him a rosebud.

"Absolutely for you." She kissed him again while Luna strolled territorially into the house. "How would you like to spend an evening—" she moved her mouth seductively to his ear "—an entire evening...doing something—" voice breathy, she walked her fingers up his chest "—decadent?"

His blood leapt in his veins and roared in the ear she was tormenting. "When do we get started?"

"Well." She rubbed against him, tilting her head back just enough to look into his eyes. "Why waste time?"

"God, I love an aggressive woman."

"Good. Because I've got big plans for you..." She caught

his lower lip in her teeth, sucked gently. "Babe. And it's going to take hours."

He wondered if he'd ever breathe normally again. He hoped not. "Want to start here and work our way inside?"

"Uh-uh." She eased away, sliding her hand down and gripping his waistband to pull him inside with her. Pan padded in behind them, decided he wouldn't get much attention from either of them and moved along to check out the house. "We can't do what I have in mind outside. Follow me." Tossing him a sultry look over her shoulder, she started upstairs.

"You bet."

He made a grab for her at the top of the stairs. After a moment's debate, she let him catch her. Sliding into the kiss was like sliding into a hot tub. Full of heat and bubbles. But when he tugged on her zipper, she eased herself away.

"Morgana..."

She only shook her head and strolled into the bedroom.

"I've got a treat for you, Nash." Reaching into the bag, she pulled out a thin shimmer of black silk and tossed it carelessly on his bed. He glanced at it, back at her. He could imagine her wearing it.

He could imagine taking it off of her.

His fingertips began to tingle.

"I made a stop on the way over. Picked up a few...things."

Without taking his eyes off her, he laid the rose on the dresser. "So far, I like it."

"Oh, it gets better." She pulled something else out of the bag and handed it to him. Nash frowned at the plastic video case. A grin flickered on his mouth.

"Adult movies?"

"Read the title."

Amused, he turned the case over. And let out a whoop. "*The Crawling Eye?*" His grin flashed as he looked over at her.

"Approve?"

"Approve, hell—this is great! A classic. I haven't seen it in years."

"There's more where that came from." She upended the bag on the bed. Scattered among a handful of toiletries were three more tapes. Nash snatched them up like a kid grabbing for packages under the Christmas tree.

"*An American Werewolf in London, Nightmare on Elm Street, Dracula.* This is great." Laughing, he scooped her against him. "What a woman. You want to spend the evening watching horror flicks?"

"With a few lengthy intermissions."

This time he unzipped her dress with one quick motion. "Tell you what—let's start the whole thing off with an overture."

She laughed as they tumbled onto the bed. "I love a good overture."

Nash couldn't imagine a more perfect weekend. They watched movies—among other things—until dawn. Slept late, then had a lazy, and sloppy, breakfast in bed.

He couldn't imagine a more perfect woman. Not only was she beautiful, smart and sexy, but she also appreciated the subtleties of a movie like *The Crawling Eye.*

He didn't even mind the fact that she'd put him to work Sunday afternoon. Puttering around the yard, mowing, weeding, planting, took on a whole new meaning when he could look over and see her kneeling in the grass wearing one of his T-shirts and a pair of his jeans hitched up at the waist with twine.

It made him wonder what it would be like, what it could be like, if she were always there. Within reach.

Nash lost track of the weeding he'd been assigned, and, nuzzling the dog, who had trotted over to butt his head against his chest, he just watched Morgana.

She was humming. He didn't recognize the tune, but it sounded exotic. Some witch's song, he supposed. Handed down through time. She was magic. Even without the talents she'd inherited, she would be magic.

She'd tucked her hair up under his battered Dodgers cap. There wasn't a touch of makeup on her face. His jeans bagged around her hips. Still, she looked erotic. Black lace or faded denim, her sensuality radiated like sunlight.

More, there was a purity to her face, a confidence, an awareness of self, that he found utterly irresistible.

He could imagine her kneeling there, in that very spot, a year from now. Ten years. And still setting off that stirring in his blood.

My God. His hand slid bonelessly from the dog's head. He was in love with her. Really in love. Totally caught in the big, scary *L* word.

And what the hell was he going to do about it?

In control? he thought, dazed. Able to back off anytime? What a crock.

He rose on unsteady legs. The clutching in his stomach was plain fear. And it was for both of them. She glanced over, tipping the cap down so that the brim shaded her eyes.

"Something wrong?"

"No. No, I...I was going to go in and get us something cold."

He all but ran into the house, leaving Morgana staring after him.

Coward. Wimp. Idiot. All the way into the kitchen, he cursed himself. After filling a glass with water, he gulped it down. Maybe it was a touch of sun. A lack of sleep. An overactive libido.

Slowly he set the glass aside. Like hell. It was love.

Step right up, ladies and gentlemen. Step right up and see an average man transformed into a puddle of nerves and terror by the love of a good woman.

He bent over the sink and splashed water on his face. He didn't know how it had happened, but he was going to have to deal with it. As far as he could see, there was no place to run. He was a grown man, Nash reminded himself. So he would do the adult thing and face it.

Maybe he should just tell her. Straight out.

Morgana, I'm crazy about you.

Blowing out a breath, he dashed more water onto his face. Too weak. Too ambivalent.

Morgana, I've come to realize that what I feel for you is more than attraction. Even more than affection.

This time his breath hissed out. Too wordy. Too damn stupid.

Morgana, I love you.

Simple. To the point. And scary as hell.

He majored in scary, he reminded himself. He ought to be

able to pull this off. Straightening his shoulders, bracing his system, he started out of the kitchen.

The wall phone shrilled and nearly had him jumping out of his shoes.

"Easy, boy," he muttered.

"Nash?" Morgana stood in the kitchen doorway, eyes full of curiosity and concern. "Are you all right?"

"Me? Yeah, yeah, I'm great." He dragged a nervous hand through his hair. "How about you?"

"Fine," she said slowly. "Are you going to answer the phone?"

"The phone?" While his mind scattered in a thousand directions, he glanced at the ringing phone. "Sure."

"Good. I'll fix us that cold drink while you do." Still frowning at him, she walked to the refrigerator.

Nash didn't notice that his palms were wet until he picked up the receiver. Forcing a grin, he wiped his free hand on his jeans.

"Hello." The excuse for a smile faded instantly. Stunned, Morgana paused with one hand on a soft-drink bottle and the other on the refrigerator door.

She'd never seen him look like this. Cold. His eyes had frosted over. Ice over velvet. Even as he leaned back against the counter, there was tension in every line of his body.

Morgana felt a shudder rush down her spine. She'd known he could be dangerous, and the man she was staring at now had stripped off all the easygoing charm and good-natured humor. Like one of the characters Nash might have conjured out of his imagination, this man was capable of quick and bloodless violence.

Whoever was on the other end of the telephone should have been grateful for the distance between them.

"Leeanne." He said the name in a flat, gelid tone. The voice rattling brightly in his ear set his teeth on edge. Old memories, old wounds, swam to the surface. He let her ramble for a moment, until he was sure he had himself under control. "Just cut to the chase, Leeanne. How much?"

He listened to the wheedling, the whining, the recriminations. His responsibilities, he was reminded. His obligations. His family.

"No, I don't give a damn. It's not my fault you got hung up with another loser." His lips curved in a humorless smile. "Yeah, right. Bad luck. How much?" he repeated, barely lifting a brow at the requested amount. Resigned, he pulled open a drawer and rummaged until he found a tattered scrap of paper and the stub of an old pencil. "Where do I send it?" He scribbled. "Yes, I've got it. Tomorrow." He tossed the paper onto the counter. "I said I would, didn't I? Just drop it. I've got things to do. Sure. You bet."

He hung up and started to let loose with a stream of oaths. Then he focused on Morgana. He'd forgotten she was there. When she started to speak, he shook his head.

"I'm going for a walk," he said abruptly, and slammed out of the screen door.

Carefully Morgana set the bottle she still held on the counter. Whoever had called had done more than anger him, she realized. She had seen more than anger in his eyes. She had seen grief, too. One had been as vicious as the other.

Because of it, she blocked her first inclination, to go after him. She would give him a few minutes alone first.

His long strides ate up the ground quickly. He stalked over the grass that had given him so much pleasure when he had mowed it only an hour before, passed without noticing the flowers that were already lapping up the sun now that they were free of choking weeds. Automatically he headed for the tumble of rocks at the edge of his property that separated his land from the bay.

This was another reason he'd been drawn to this place. The combination of wildness and serenity.

It suited him, he supposed as he dug his hands deep in his pockets. On the surface he was a relaxed, contented man. Those qualities usually extended deeper. But often, maybe too often, there was a recklessness swarming inside him.

Now he dropped down on a rock and stared out over the water. He would watch the gulls, the waves, the boats. And he would wait until he felt that contentment again.

He drew a deep breath, cleansing. *Thank God* was all he could think. Thank God he hadn't spoken of his feelings to Morgana.

All it had taken was one phone call from the past to remind him that there was no place for love in his life.

He would have told her, he realized. He would have gone with the impulse of the moment, and told her he loved her. Maybe—probably—he would have started to make plans.

Then he would have messed it up. No doubt he would have messed it up. Sabotaging relationships was in his blood.

His hands curled and uncurled as he struggled to level again. Leeanne, he thought with a short, bitter bark of laughter. Well, he would send her the money, and she would fade out of his life. Again. Until the money ran out.

And that pattern would repeat itself over and over again. For the rest of his life.

"It's beautiful here," Morgana said quietly from behind him.

He didn't jolt. He just sighed. Nash supposed he should have expected her to follow him. And he supposed she would expect some sort of explanation.

He wondered how creative he might be. Should he tell her Leeanne was an old lover, someone he'd pushed aside who wouldn't stay aside? Or maybe he'd weave some amusing tale about being blackmailed by the wife of a Mafia don, with whom he'd had a brief, torrid affair. That had a nice ring.

Or he could work on her sympathies and tell her Leeanne was a destitute widow—his best friend's widow—who tapped him for cash now and again.

Hell, he could tell her it had been a call for the policemen's fund. Anything. Anything but the bitter truth.

Her hand brushed his shoulder as she settled on the rock beside him. And demanded nothing. Said nothing. She only looked out over the bay, as he did. Waiting. Smelling of night. Of smoke and roses.

He had a terrible urge to simply turn and bury his face at her breast. Just to hold her and be held until all this helpless anger faded away.

And he knew that, no matter how clever he was, how glib, she would believe nothing but the truth.

"I like it here," he said, as if several long, silent minutes hadn't passed between her observation and his response. "In

L.A. I looked out of my condo and saw another condo. I guess I didn't realize I was feeling hemmed in until I moved here."

"Everyone feels hemmed in from time to time, no matter where they live." She laid a hand on his thigh. "When I'm feeling that way, I go to Ireland. Walk along an empty beach. When I do, I think of all the people who have walked there before, and will walk there again. Then it occurs to me that nothing is forever. No matter how bad, or how good, everything passes and moves on to another level."

"'All things change; nothing perishes,'" he mumbled.

She smiled. "Yes, I'd say that sums it up perfectly." Reaching over, she cupped his face in her hands. Her eyes were soft and clear, and her voice was full of comfort ready to be offered. "Talk to me, Nash. I may not be able to help, but I can listen."

"There's nothing to say."

Something else flicked into her eyes. Nash cursed himself when he recognized it as hurt. "So, I'm welcome in your bed, but not into your mind."

"Damn it, one has nothing to do with the other." He wouldn't be pushed, wouldn't be prodded or maneuvered into revealing parts of himself he chose to keep hidden.

"I see." Her hands dropped away from his face. For a moment she was tempted to help him, to spin a simple charm that would give him peace of mind. But it wasn't right; it wouldn't be real. And she knew using magic to change his feelings would only hurt them both. "All right, then. I'm going to go finish the marigolds."

She rose. No recriminations, no heated words. He would have preferred them to this cool acceptance. As she took a step away, he grabbed her hand. She saw the war on his face, but offered nothing but silence.

"Leeanne's my mother."

Chapter 10

His mother.

It was the anguish in his eyes that had Morgana masking her shock. She remembered how cold his voice had been when he spoke to Leeanne, how his face had fallen into hard, rigid lines. Yet the woman on the other end of the telephone line had been his mother.

What could make a man feel such distaste and dislike for the woman he owed his life to?

But the man was Nash. Because of that, she worked past her own deeply ingrained loyalty to family as she studied him.

Hurt, she realized. There had been as much hurt as anger in his voice, in his face, then. And now. She could see it plainly now that all the layers of arrogance, confidence and ease had been stripped away. Her heart ached for him, but she knew that wouldn't lessen his hurt. She wished she had Anastasia's talent and could take on some of his pain.

Instead, she kept his hand in hers and sat beside him again. No, she was not an empath, but she could offer support, and love.

"Tell me."

Where did he begin? Nash wondered. How could he explain to her what he had never been able to explain to himself?

He looked down at their joined hands, at the way her strong

fingers entwined with his. She was offering support, understanding, when he hadn't thought he needed any.

The feelings he'd always been reluctant to voice, refused to share, flowed out.

"I guess you'd have to know my grandmother. She was—" he searched for a polite way of putting it "—a straight arrow. And she expected everyone to fly that same narrow course. If I had to choose one adjective, I'd go with intolerant. She'd been widowed when Leeanne was about ten. My grandfather'd had this insurance business, so she'd been left pretty well off. But she liked to scrape pennies. She was one of those people who didn't have it in her to enjoy life."

He fell silent, watching the gulls sweep over the water. When his hand moved restlessly in hers, Morgana said nothing, and waited.

"Anyway, it might sound kind of sad and poignant. The widow with two young girls to raise alone. Until you understand that she liked being in charge. Being the widow Kirkland and having no one to answer to but herself. I have to figure she was pretty rough on her daughters, holding holiness and sex over their heads like lightning bolts. It didn't work very well with Leeanne. At seventeen she was pregnant and didn't have a clue who the father might have been."

He said it with a shrug in his voice, but Morgana saw beneath it. "You blame her for that?"

"For that?" He looked at her, his eyes dark. "No. Not for that. The old lady must have made her life hell for the best part of nine months. Depending on who you get it from, Leeanne was a poor, lonely girl punished ruthlessly for one little slip. Or my grandmother was this long-suffering saint who took her sinful daughter in. My own personal opinion is that we had two selfish women who didn't give a damn about anyone but themselves."

"She was only seventeen, Nash," Morgana said quietly.

Anger carved his face into hard, unyielding lines. "That's supposed to make it okay? She was only seventeen, so it's okay that she bounced around so many guys she didn't know who got her pregnant. She was only seventeen, so it's okay that two days after she had me she took off, left me with that bitter old woman without a word, without a call or even a thought, for twenty-six years."

The raw emotion in his voice squeezed her heart. She wanted to gather him close, hold him until the worst of it passed. But when she reached out, he jerked away, then stood.

"I need to walk."

She made her decision quickly. She could either leave him to work off his pain alone, or she could share it with him. Before he could take three strides, she was beside him, taking his hand again.

"I'm sorry, Nash."

He shook his head violently. The air he gulped in was as sweet as spring, and yet it burned like bile in his throat. "I'm sorry. No reason to take it out on you."

She touched his cheek. "I can handle it."

But he wasn't sure he could. He'd never talked the whole business through before, not with anyone. Saying it all out loud left an ugly taste in his mouth, one he was afraid he'd never be rid of. He took another careful breath and started again.

"I stayed with my grandmother until I was five. My aunt, Carolyn, had married. He was in the army, a lifer. For the next few years I moved around with them, from base to base. He was a hard-nosed bastard—only tolerated me because Carolyn would cry and carry on when he got drunk and threatened to send me back."

Morgana could imagine it all too clearly. The little boy in the empty middle, controlled by everyone, belonging to no one. "You hated it."

"Yeah, I guess that hits the center. I didn't know why, exactly, but I hated it. Looking back, I realize that Carolyn was as unstable as Leeanne, in her own way. One minute she'd fawn all over me, the next she'd ignore me. She wasn't having any luck getting pregnant herself. Then, when I was about eight or nine, she found out she was going to have a kid of her own. So I got shipped back to my grandmother. Carolyn didn't need a substitute anymore."

Morgana felt her eyes fill with angry tears at the image of the child, helpless, innocent, being shuffled back and forth between people who knew nothing of love.

"She never looked at me like a person, you know? I was a mistake. That was the worst of it," he said, as if to himself. "The way she drummed that point home. That every breath I took, every beat of my heart was only possible because some careless, rebellious girl had made a mistake."

"No," Morgana said, appalled. "She was wrong."

"Yeah, maybe. But things like that stick with you. I heard a lot about the sins of the father, the evils of the flesh. I was lazy, intractable and wicked—one of her favorite words." He sent Morgana a grim little smile. "But that was no more than she expected, seeing as how I'd been conceived."

"She was a horrible woman," Morgana bit out. "She didn't deserve you."

"Well, she'd have agreed with you on the second part. And she made me understand just how grateful I should be that she put food in my belly and a roof over my head. But I wasn't feeling very grateful, and I ran away a lot. By the time I was twelve, I got slipped into the system. Foster homes."

His shoulders moved restlessly, in a small outward showing of the turmoil within. He was pacing back and forth over the grounds, his stride lengthening as the memories worked on him.

"Some of them were okay. The ones that really wanted you. Others just wanted the check you brought in every month, but sometimes you got lucky and ended up in a real home. I spent one Christmas with this family, the Hendersons." His voice changed, took on a hint of wonder. "They were great—treated me just like they treated their own kids. You could always smell cookies baking. They had the tree, the presents under it. All that colored paper and ribbon. Stockings hanging from the mantel. It really blew me away to see one with my name on it.

"They gave me a bike," he said quietly. "Mr. Henderson bought it secondhand and took it down to the basement to fix it up. He painted it red. Bug-eyed, fire-engine red, and he'd polished all the chrome. He put a lot of time into making that bike something special. He showed me how to hook baseball cards on the spokes."

He sent her a sheepish look that had Morgana tilting her head. "What?"

"Well, it was a really great bike, but I didn't know how to

ride. I'd never had a bike. Here I was, nearly twelve years old, and that bike might as well have been a Harley hog for all I knew."

Morgana came staunchly to his defense. "That's nothing to be ashamed of."

Nash sent her an arch look. "Obviously you've never been an eleven-year-old boy. It's pretty tough to handle the passage into manhood when you can't handle a two-wheeler. So, I mooned over it, made excuses not to ride it. I had homework, I'd twisted my ankle, it looked like rain. Thought I was pretty clever, but she—Mrs. Henderson—saw right through me. One day she got me up early, before anyone else was awake, and took me out. She taught me. Held the back of the seat, ran along beside me. Made me laugh when I took a spill. And when I managed to wobble down the sidewalk on my own, she cried. Nobody'd ever..." He let his words trail off, embarrassed by the scope of emotion that memory evoked.

Tears burned the back of her throat. "They must have been wonderful people."

"Yeah, they were. I had six months with them. Probably the best six months of my life." He shook off the memory and went on. "Anyway, whenever I'd get too comfortable, my grandmother would yank the chain and pull me back. So I started counting the days until I was eighteen, when nobody could tell me where to live, or how. When I got free, I was damn well going to stay that way."

"What did you do?"

"I wanted to eat, so I tried a couple of regular jobs." He glanced at her, this time with a hint of humor in his eyes. "I sold insurance for a while."

For the first time since he'd begun, she smiled. "I can't picture it."

"Neither could I. It didn't last. I guess when it comes right down to it, I've got the old lady to thank for trying writing as a career. She used to whack me good whenever she caught me scribbling."

"Excuse me." Morgana was certain she must have misunderstood. "She hit you for writing?"

"She didn't exactly understand the moral scope of vampire

hunters," he said dryly. "So, figuring it was the last thing she'd want me to do, I kept right on doing it. I moved to L.A., managed to finesse a low-level job with the special-effects guys. Then I worked as a script doctor, met the right people. Finally managed to sell *Shape Shifter*. My grandmother died while that was in production. I didn't go to the funeral."

"If you expect me to criticize you for that, I'll have to disappoint you."

"I don't know what I expect," he muttered. Stopping beneath a cypress, he turned to her. "I was twenty-six when the movie hit. It was…well, we'll risk a bad pun and call it a howling success. Suddenly I was riding the wave. My next script was picked up. I got myself nominated for a Golden Globe. Then I started getting calls. My aunt. She just needed a few bills to tide her over. Her husband had never risen above sergeant, and she had three kids she wanted to send to college. Then Leeanne."

He scrubbed his hands over his face, wishing he could scrub away the layers of resentment, of hurt, of memory.

"She called you," Morgana prompted.

"Nope. She popped up on my doorstep one day. It would have been ludicrous if it hadn't been so pathetic. This stranger, painted up like a Kewpie doll, standing at my front door telling me she was my mother. The worst part was that I could see me in her. The whole time she was standing there, pouring out the sad story of her life, I wanted to shut that door in her face. Bolt it. I could hear her telling me that I owed her, how having me had screwed up her life. How she was divorced for the second time and running on empty. So I wrote her out a check."

Tired, he slid down the tree and sat on the soft ground beneath. The sun was hanging low, the shadows stretching long. Morgana knelt beside him.

"Why did you give her money, Nash?"

"It was what she wanted. I didn't have anything else for her, anyway. The first payment lasted her almost a year. In between, I'd get calls from my aunt, or one of my cousins." He tapped a fisted hand on his thigh. "Months will go by, and you'll think you've got your life pretty well set. But they don't let you forget what you've come from. If the price for that's a few thousand now and again, it's not a bad bargain."

Morgana's eyes heated. "They have no right, no right to take pieces of you."

"I've got plenty of money."

"I'm not talking about dollars. I'm talking about you."

His gaze locked on hers. "They remind me who—what—I am."

"They don't even know you," she said furiously.

"No, and I don't know them. But that doesn't mean a hell of a lot. You know about legacies, Morgana. About what comes down in the blood. Your inheritance is magic. Mine's self-interest."

She shook her head. "Whatever we inherit, we have the choice of using it, or discarding it. You're nothing like the people you came from."

He took her by the shoulders then, his fingers tense. "More than you think. I've made my choices. Maybe I stopped running away because it never got me anywhere. But I know who I am. That's someone who does best alone. There's no Henderson family in my future, Morgana. Because I don't want it. Now and again, I write out a check. Then I can close that all off so it's just me again. That's the way I want it. No ties, no obligations, no commitments."

She wouldn't argue with him, not when the pain was so close to the surface. Another time she could show him how wrong he was. The man holding her now was capable of tenderness, of generosity, of sweetness—none of which had been given to him. All of which he'd found for himself.

But she could give him something. If only for a short time.

"You don't have to tell me who you are, Nash." Gently she brushed his hair from his face. "I know. There's nothing you can't give that I'll ask for. Nothing you don't want to give that I'll take." She lifted her amulet, closed his hand over it, and hers over his. Her eyes deepened as they stared into his. "That's an oath."

He felt the metal grow warm in his hand. Baffled, he looked down to see it pulsing with light. "I don't—"

"An oath," she repeated. "One I can't break. There's something I want you to take, that I can give. Will you trust me?"

Something was stealing over him. Like a shadow cast by a

cloud, it was cool and soft and weightless. His tensed muscles relaxed; his eyes grew pleasantly heavy. As from a great distance, he heard himself speak her name. Then he glided into sleep.

When he awakened, the sun was warm and bright. He could hear birdsong, and the babbling music of water running over rock. Disoriented, he sat up.

He was in a wide, rolling meadow of wildflowers and dancing butterflies. A few feet away, a gentle-eyed deer stopped her peaceful walk to study him. There was the lazy drone of bees and the whisper of wind through the high, green grass.

With a half laugh, he rubbed a hand over his chin, half expecting to find a beard like Rip Van Winkle's. But there was no beard, and he didn't feel like an old man. He felt incredible. Standing, he looked out over the acres of flowers and waving grass. Above, the sky was a rich blue bowl, the deep blue of high spring.

Something stirred in him, as gently as the wind stirred the grass. After a moment, he recognized it. Serenity. He was utterly at peace with himself.

He heard the music. The heartbreaking beauty of harp song. The smile was already curving his lips as he followed it, wading through the meadow grass and flowers, startling butterflies.

He found her on the banks of the brook. Sun flashed off the water as it tumbled over smooth, jewel-colored rocks. The full white skirts of her dress pooled over the grass. Her face was shaded by a wide-brimmed hat, tipped flirtatiously over one eye. In her lap was a small golden harp. Her fingers caressed the strings, coaxing out music that floated over the air.

She turned her head, smiled at him, continued to play.

"What are you doing?" he asked her.

"Waiting for you. Did you rest well?"

He crouched beside her, then lifted a hesitant hand to her shoulder. She was real. He could feel the warmth of her skin through the silk. "Morgana?"

Her eyes laughed up at his. "Nash?"

"Where are we?"

She stroked the harp again. Music soared, spreading like the wings of a bird. "In dreams," she told him. "Yours and mine."

After setting the harp aside, she took his hands. "If you want to be here, we can stay awhile. If you want to be somewhere else, we can go there."

She made it sound so easy, so natural. "Why?"

"Because you need it." She brought his hand to her lips. "Because I love you."

He didn't feel the scrabble of panic. Her words slid easily into his heart, making him smile. "Is it real?"

She rubbed her cheek over his hand, then kissed it again. "It can be. If you want it." Her teeth grazed lightly over his skin, sparking desire. "If you want me."

He drew the hat from her head, tossing it aside as her hair rained down over her shoulders and back. "Am I spellbound, Morgana?"

"No more than I." She cupped his face in her hands to bring his lips to hers. "I want you," she murmured against his mouth. "Love me here, Nash, as though it were the first time, the last time, the only time."

How could he resist? If it was a dream, so be it. All that mattered was that her arms welcomed him, her mouth tempted him.

She was everything a man could want, all silk and honey, melting against him. Her body seemed boneless as he laid her back on the soft green grass.

There was no time here, and he found himself pleased to linger over little things. The velvet flow of her hair under his hands, the teasing flavors at the corners of her mouth, the scent of her skin along her jaw. She yielded to him, a malleable fantasy of silks and scents and seduction. Her quiet sigh sweetened the air.

He couldn't know how easy it had been, Morgana thought as his mouth drank from hers. As different as they were, their dreams were the same. For this hour, or two, they could share each other, and the peace she had wrapped them in.

When he lifted his head, she smiled at him. His eyes darkened as he traced the shape of her face with a fingertip. "I want it to be real," he said.

"It can be. Whatever you take from here, whatever you want for us, can be."

Testing, he brought his lips to hers again. It was real, as was the feeling that flooded him when those lips parted for his. He sank deep into that long, luxurious melding of lips and tongues. Beneath his, her heart beat fast and true. When his hand covered it, he felt its rhythm leap.

Slowly, wanting to spin out the moment, he unfastened the tiny pearls that ranged down her bodice. Beneath, she was all warm, soft skin. In fascination, he explored the textures as her breath quickened.

Satin and silk. The color of rich cream.

His eyes flicked back to hers as his fingertips skimmed. Through the fringe of dark lashes, her irises had deepened, hazed. Lightly he brushed his lips over the soft slopes of her breasts.

Honey and rose petals.

With a murmur of approval, he teased her flesh with lazy, openmouthed kisses, circling in until he could roll his tongue over the aching peaks. He nipped, knowing by her gasp that he was holding her at that dazzling point between pleasure and pain.

He drew her in, driving them both quietly mad with teeth and tongue. Her hands were in his hair, gripping hard. And he felt her body arch, go taut, then shudder into pliancy. When he lifted his head to look at her, her eyes were glazed with shock and delight.

"How—?" She shivered again, throbbing with the aftermath of that fast, unexpected crest.

"Magic," he said, pressing his lips to her heated flesh again. "Let me show you."

He took her places she'd never seen. As she gloried in each dizzying journey, her hands and lips moved freely over him. When she trembled, so did he.

A mixing of sighs, a melding of bodies. A murmured request, a breathless answer. Fired by need, she pulled his shirt away to taste the hot, damp flesh of his heaving chest.

Where there was fire, there was joy—in feeling his blood leap for her, his pulse quicken.

Within the small slice of paradise she had conjured, they made their own. Each time his mouth came to hers, the spell grew stronger. Possessive, persuasive, her hands streaked over him, and she rejoiced in the way his muscles bunched and quivered at her touch.

He wanted—needed—her to be as desperate as he. With his heart pounding in his ears, he began a torturous journey down her torso, streaking toward the center of her heat. His teeth scraped the sensitive skin of her thigh, dragging a broken moan from her.

Her hands fisted in the grass as his tongue pleasured and plundered. Blind with need, she cried out as he drove her from peak to shattering peak. As her body writhed and arched, he steeped himself in her.

Damp flesh slid over damp flesh as he began the return journey. When his mouth crushed down on hers, he sheathed himself in her. And his vision dimmed as he felt her open for him, surround him, welcome him.

Fighting back the grinding need, he moved slowly, savoring, watching the flickers of pleasure on her face, feeling her pulse throb as she rose to meet him.

The breath sighed out between her lips. Her eyes fluttered open. They stayed on his while her hands slid down his arms. With their fingers locked, they tumbled past reason together.

When she felt his body shatter, when his muscles went to water, he rested his head between her breasts. Lulled by the beat of her heart, he let his eyes close. He began to sense the world beyond Morgana. The warm sun on his back, the call of birds, the scent of flowers growing wild on the banks of the rushing brook.

Beneath him, she sighed and lifted a hand to stroke his hair. She had given him peace, and she had found pleasure. And she had broken one of her firmest rules by manipulating his emotions.

Perhaps it had been a mistake, but she wouldn't regret it.

"Morgana."

She smiled at the husky murmur. "Sleep now," she told him.

In the dark, he reached for her. And found the bed empty. Groggy, he forced his heavy eyes open. He was in bed, his own bed, and the house held the heavy hush of predawn.

"Morgana?" He didn't know why he said her name when he knew she wasn't there.

Dreaming? Fumbling with the sheets, he pushed himself out of bed. Had he been dreaming? If it had been only a dream, nothing in the waking world had ever seemed more real, more vivid, more important.

To clear his head, he walked to the window and breathed deeply of the cool air.

They'd made love—incredible love—in a meadow beside a stream.

No, that was impossible. Leaning on the sill, he gulped in air like water. The last thing he remembered clearly, they had been sitting under the tree in the side yard, talking about—

He jolted back. He'd told her everything. The whole ugly business about his family had come pouring out of him. Why the hell had he done that? Dragging a hand through his hair, he paced the room.

That damned phone call, he thought. But then he recalled abruptly that the phone call had stopped him from making an even bigger mistake.

It would have been worse if he'd told Morgana he loved her— a lot worse than telling her about his parentage and upbringing. At least now she wouldn't get any ideas about where their relationship was headed.

In any case, it was done, and it couldn't be taken back. He'd just have to live with the fact that it embarrassed the hell out of him.

But after that, after they had been sitting in the yard. Had he fallen asleep?

The dream. Or had it been a dream? It was so clear in his mind. He could almost smell the flowers. And he could certainly remember the way her body had flowed like water under his hands. More, much more, he could remember feeling as though everything he had done up to that point in his life had been leading to that moment. To the moment when he could lie on the grass with the woman he loved, and feel the peace of belonging.

Illusions. Just illusions, he assured himself as panic began to set in. He'd just fallen asleep under the tree. That was all.

But what the hell was he doing back in his room, in the middle of the night—alone?

She'd done it. Giving in to unsteady legs, he lowered to the bed. All of it. Then she'd left him.

She wasn't getting away with it. He started to rise, then dropped down again.

He could remember the peace, the utter serenity, of waking with the sun on his face. Of walking through the grass and seeing her playing the harp and smiling at him.

And when he'd asked her why, she'd said...

She'd said she loved him.

Because his head was reeling, Nash clamped it between his hands. Maybe he'd imagined it. All of it. Morgana included. Maybe he was back in his condo in L.A., and he'd just awakened from the granddaddy of all dreams.

After all, he didn't really believe in witches and spells. Gingerly he lowered one hand and closed it around the stone that hung from a chain around his neck.

The hell he didn't.

Morgana was real, and she loved him. The worst part was, he loved her right back.

He didn't want to. It was crazy. But he was in love with her, so wildly in love that he couldn't get through an hour without thinking about her. Without wishing for her. Without imagining that maybe, just maybe, it could work.

And that was the most irrational thought in the whole irrational business.

He needed to think it all through, step by step. Giving in to fatigue, he lay back to stare at the dark.

Infatuated. That was what he was. Infatuation was a long way from love. A long, safe way. She was, after all, a captivating woman. A man could live a long, happy life being infatuated by a captivating woman. He'd wake up every morning with a smile on his face, knowing she belonged to him.

Nash began to weave a pretty fantasy. And brought himself up short.

What the hell was he thinking of?

Her, he thought grimly. He was always thinking of her.

Maybe the best thing to do would be to take a little vacation, a quick trip to anywhere to shake her out of his system.

If he could.

The niggling doubt lay in his gut like a stone.

How did he know, even before he began, that he wouldn't be able to shake her out?

Because it wasn't infatuation, he admitted slowly. It wasn't even close to infatuation. It was the big four-letter word. He wasn't in lust. He'd taken the big leap. He was in love.

She'd made him fall in love with her.

That thought had him sitting straight up. She'd made him. She was a witch. Why hadn't it ever occurred to him that she could cast her spells, snap her fingers and have him groveling at her feet?

Part of him rejected the notion as absurd. But another part, the part that had grown out of fear and self-doubt, plucked at the idea. The longer he considered it, the darker his thoughts became.

In the morning, he told himself, he was going to face off with a witch. When he was done, he'd clear the decks, and Nash Kirkland would be exactly where he wanted to be.

In control.

Chapter 11

It felt odd not going in to open the shop Monday morning. It also felt necessary, not just for her weary body, but also for her mind. A call to Mindy eased Morgana's conscience. Mindy would pick up the slack and open the shop at noon.

It didn't bother her too much to take a day off. But she would have preferred to steal a day when she felt better. Now she walked downstairs wrapped in her robe, feeling light-headed and queasy, with the restless night weighing heavily on her.

The die had been cast. Matters had been taken out of her hands. With a weary sigh, Morgana wandered into the kitchen to brew some tea. It had never really been in her hands. The awkward thing about power, she mused, was that you could never let yourself become so used to wielding it that you forgot there were bigger, more vital powers than your own.

Pressing a gentle hand to her stomach, she walked to the window while the kettle heated. She wondered if she sensed a storm in the air, or if it was merely her own unsettled thoughts. Luna curled in and out of her legs for a moment, then sensed her mistress's mood and padded off.

She hadn't chosen to be in love. She certainly hadn't chosen to have this avalanche of emotion barrel down on her and sweep her away. To have her life changed. It was nothing less than that now.

There was always a choice, of course. And she had made hers.

It wouldn't be easy. The most important things rarely were.

Heavy-limbed, she turned to the stove to make the tea. It had barely had time to cool in her cup before she heard the front door open.

"Morgana!"

Resigned, Morgana poured two more cups just as her cousins came into the kitchen. "There." Anastasia shot Sebastian a look as she hurried to Morgana. "I told you she wasn't feeling well."

Morgana kissed her cheek. "I'm fine."

"I said you were fine," Sebastian put in, digging a cookie out of the jar on the counter. "Just grumpy. You were sending out signals loud enough and cranky enough to drag me out of bed."

"Sorry." She offered him a cup. "I guess I didn't want to be alone."

"You're not well," Ana insisted. Before she could probe deeper, Morgana stepped away.

"I had a restless night, and I'm paying for it this morning."

Sebastian sipped his tea. He'd already taken in the pale cheeks and shadowed eyes. And he was getting a flicker of something else, something Morgana was working hard to block. Patient, and always willing to match his will against hers, he settled back.

"Trouble in paradise," he said, just dryly enough to make her eyes flash.

"I can handle my own problems, thanks."

"Don't tease her, Sebastian." Anastasia set a warning hand on his shoulder. "Have you argued with Nash, Morgana?"

"No." She sat. She was too tired not to. "No," she said again. "But it is Nash who worries me. I learned a few things about him yesterday. About his family."

Because she trusted them as much as she loved them, Morgana told them everything, from the call from Leeanne to the moment beneath the cypress. What had happened after that, because it belonged only to her and to Nash, she kept to herself.

"Poor little boy," Anastasia murmured. "How awful to feel unwanted and unloved."

"And unable to love," Morgana added. "Who could blame him for being afraid to trust his feelings?"

"You do."

Her gaze shot up to meet Sebastian's. It was no use cursing

him for being so perceptive. Or so right. "Not really blame. It hurts, and it saddens, but I don't blame him for it. I'm just not sure how to love someone who can't, or won't, love me back."

"He needs time," Ana told her.

"I know. I'm trying to figure out how much time I can give him. I made a vow. Not to take more than he wanted to give." Her voice thickened, and she swallowed to clear it. "I won't break it."

Her defenses slipped. Quick as a whip, Sebastian snatched her hand. He looked deep, and then his fingers went lax on hers. "My God, Morgana. You're pregnant."

Furious at the intrusion, and at her own wavering emotions for permitting it, she sprang to her feet. But even as she started to spew at him, she saw the concern and the worry in his eyes.

"Damn it, Sebastian. That's an announcement a woman particularly likes to make for herself."

"Sit down," he ordered, and he would have carried her to a chair himself if Anastasia hadn't waved him off.

"How long?" Ana demanded.

Morgana only sighed. "Since the spring equinox. I've only been sure for a few days."

"Are you well?" Before Morgana could answer, Ana spread a hand over Morgana's belly. "Let me." With her eyes on Morgana's, Anastasia searched. She felt the warm flesh beneath the robe, the throb of pulse, the flow of blood. And the life, not yet formed, sleeping. Her lips curved. "You're fine," she said. "Both of you."

"Just a little sluggish this morning." Morgana laid a hand over hers. "I don't want you to worry."

"I still say she should sit down, or lie down, until her color's back." Sebastian scowled at both of them. The idea of his cousin, his favorite sparring partner, being fragile and with child made him uneasy. With a light laugh, Morgana bent over to kiss him.

"Are you going to fuss over me, cousin?" Pleased, she kissed him again, then sat. "I hope so."

"With the rest of the family in Ireland, it's up to Ana and me to take care of you."

Morgana murmured an absent thank-you as Ana refilled her cup. "And what makes you think I need to be taken care of?"

Sebastian shrugged the question away. "I'm the eldest here," he reminded her. "And, as such, I want to know what Kirkland's intentions are."

Ana grinned over her cup. "Lord, Sebastian, how medieval. Do you intend to run him through for trifling with your cousin?"

"I don't find this whole situation quite the hoot you do." His eyes darkened when his cousins rolled theirs. "Let's clear it up, shall we? Morgana, do you want to be pregnant?"

"I am pregnant."

He pressed a hand on hers until she looked at him again. "You know very well what I mean."

Of course she did. She let out another sigh. "I've only had a day or two to think of it, but I have thought of it, carefully. I realize that I can undo what's been done. Without shame. I know the idea upsets you, Ana."

Ana shook her head. "The choice has to be yours."

"Yes, it does. I took precautions against conception. And fate chose to ignore them. I've searched my heart, and I believe I was meant to have the child. This child," she said with a faint curve of the lips. "At this time, and with this man. However unsettled I feel, however afraid I am, I can't shake that belief. So, yes, I want to be pregnant."

Satisfied, Sebastian nodded. "And Nash? How does he feel about it?" He didn't wait for her to speak. It only took a heartbeat for him to know. His voice thundered to the roof. "What in the name of Finn do you mean, you haven't told him?"

Her glare was sharp enough to cut ten men off at the knees. "Keep out of my head, or I swear I'll turn you into a slug."

He merely lifted a brow. "Just answer the question."

"I've only just come to be certain myself." Tossing back her hair, she rose. "And, after yesterday, I couldn't simply drop the news on him."

"He has a right to know," Ana said quietly.

"All right." Her temper bubbled until she clenched her hands into fists. "I'm going to tell him. When I'm ready to tell him. Do you think I want to bind him this way?" It shocked her to feel a tear slip down her cheek. She brushed it away impatiently.

"That's a choice he has to make for himself." Sebastian had already decided that, if Nash chose incorrectly, he would take great pleasure in breaking several vital bones—the conventional way.

"Sebastian's right, Morgana." Concerned but firm, Ana rose again to wrap her arms around her cousin. "It's his choice to make, as it was yours. He can't make it if he doesn't know the choice exists."

"I know." To comfort herself, Morgana laid her head on Ana's shoulder. "I'll go this morning and tell him."

Sebastian rose to stroke a hand down Morgana's hair. "We'll be close."

She was able to smile with a trace of her usual verve. "Not too close."

Nash rolled over in bed and muttered into his pillow. Dreams. He was having so many dreams. They were flitting in and out of his head like movie scenes.

Morgana. Always Morgana, smiling at him, beckoning to him, promising him the incredible, and the wonderful. Making him feel whole and strong and hopeful.

His grandmother, her eyes bright with anger, whacking him with her ubiquitous wooden spoon, telling him over and over again that he was worthless.

Riding a bright red bike down a suburban sidewalk, the wind in his hair and the sound of flipping, flapping baseball cards thrumming in the spokes.

Leeanne, standing close, too close, with her hand out, reminding him that they were blood. That he owed her, owed her, owed her.

Morgana, laughing that wild, wicked laugh, her hair billowing back like a cloud while she streaked over the dark waters of the bay on her broomstick.

Himself, plunged into a steaming cauldron with his grandmother stirring the stew with that damned spoon. And Morgana's voice—his mother's voice?—cackling like one of the Weird Sisters from Shakespeare.

"Double, double, toil and trouble."

He sat up with a jolt, breathing fast and blinking against the streaming sunlight. He lifted shaking hands to his face and rubbed hard.

Great. Just dandy. In addition to everything else, he was losing his mind.

Had she done that to him, as well? he wondered. Had she insinuated herself into his mind to make him think what she wanted him to think? Well, she wasn't going to get away with it.

Nash stumbled out of bed and tripped over his own shoes. Swearing, he kicked them aside and headed blindly for the shower. As soon as he'd pulled himself together, he and the Gorgeous Witch of the West were going to have a little chat.

While Nash was holding his head under the shower, Morgana pulled up in his driveway. She'd come alone. When she'd refused to let Luna accompany her, the cat had stalked off, tail twitching in indignation. Sighing, Morgana promised herself she'd make it up to her. Maybe she'd run by Fisherman's Wharf and pick up a seafood feast to soften the cat's heart.

In the meantime, she had her own heart to worry about.

Tilting down the rearview mirror, she took a careful study of her face. With a sound of disgust, she leaned back. What had made her think she could cover the signs of strain and worry with simple cosmetics?

She pressed her lips together and looked toward his house. She wasn't going to let him see her like this. She wasn't going to go to him with this kind of news when she appeared vulnerable and needy.

He had enough people pulling his strings.

She remembered that she'd once thought he was a completely carefree man. Perhaps, for long periods of time, he was. He'd certainly made himself believe so. If Nash was entitled to his front, then so was she.

After taking a long, soothing breath, Morgana crooned a quiet chant. The shadows vanished from under her eyes, the color crept back into her cheeks. As she stepped out of the car, all signs of a restless night had been erased. If her heart was beating too quickly, she would deal with it. But she would not let him see that she was miserably in love and terrified.

There was an easy smile on her face as she rapped on his door. A slick, sweaty fist was lodged in her gut.

Cursing, Nash jammed one leg then the other into jeans. "Just a damn minute," he mumbled as he yanked them up. He stalked down the steps barefoot and bare chested, all but growling at the thought of a visitor before coffee. "What?" he demanded as he flung open the door. Then he stopped dead, staring.

She looked as fresh and beautiful as the morning. As sultry and sexy as midnight. Nash wondered how it was that the damp still clinging to his skin didn't turn to steam.

"Hi." She leaned in to brush his lips with hers. "Did I get you out of the shower?"

"Just about." Off balance, he slicked his fingers through his dripping hair. "Why aren't you at the shop?"

"I'm taking the day off." She sauntered in, willing herself to keep her voice natural and her muscles relaxed. "Did you sleep well?"

"You should know." At the mild surprise in her eyes, his temper strained. "What did you do to me, Morgana?"

"Do to you? I did nothing *to* you." She made the effort to smile again. "If I'm not mistaken, you're in dire need of coffee. Why don't I fix some?"

He grabbed her arm before she could turn toward the kitchen. "I'll fix it myself."

She measured the anger in his eyes and nodded slowly. "All right. Would you rather I came back later?"

"No. We'll settle this now." When he strode down the hallway, Morgana squeezed her eyes tight.

Settle it, she thought with a vivid premonition of disaster. Why did that phrase sound so much like "end it"? Bracing, she started to follow him into the kitchen, but found her courage fading. Instead, she turned into the living room and sat on the edge of a chair.

He needed his coffee, she told herself. And she needed a moment to regroup.

She hadn't expected to find him so angry, so cold. The way he'd looked when he'd spoken to Leeanne the day before. Nor had she had any idea how much it would hurt to have him look at her with that ice-edged and somehow aloof fury.

She rose to wander the room, one hand placed protectively over the life beginning in her womb. She *would* protect that life, she promised herself. At all costs.

When he came back, a steaming cup in his hand, she was standing by the window. Her eyes looked wistful. If he hadn't known better, he would have said she looked hurt, even vulnerable.

But he did know better. Surely being a witch was the next thing to being invulnerable.

"Your flowers need water," she said to him. "It isn't enough just to plant them." Again her hand lay quietly over her stomach. "They need care."

He gulped down coffee and scalded his tongue. The pain helped block the sudden need to go to her and take her into his arms, to whisk away the sadness he heard in her voice. "I'm not much in the mood to talk about flowers."

"No." She turned, and the traces of vulnerability were gone. "I can see that. What are you in the mood to talk about, Nash?"

"I want the truth. All of it."

She gave him a small, amused smile, turning her palms up questioningly. "Where would you like me to begin?"

"Don't play games with me, Morgana. I'm tired of it." He began to pace the room, his muscles taut enough to snap. His head came up. If she had been fainter of heart, the look in his eyes would have had her stumbling back in defense. "This whole business has been one long lark for you, hasn't it? Right from the beginning, from the minute I walked into your shop, you decided I was a likely candidate." God, it hurt, he realized. It hurt to think of everything he'd felt, everything he'd begun to wish for. "My attitude toward your…talents irritated you, so you just had to strut your stuff."

Her heart quivered in her breast, but her voice was strong. "Why don't you tell me what you mean? If you're saying I showed you what I am, I can't deny it. I can't be ashamed of it."

He slapped the mug down so that coffee sloshed over the sides and onto the table. The sense of betrayal was so huge, it overwhelmed everything. Damn it, he loved her. She'd made him love her. Now that he was calling her on it, she just stood there, looking calm and lovely.

"I want to know what you did to me," he said again. "Then I want you to undo it."

"I told you, I didn't—"

"I want you to look me in the eye." On a wave of panic and fury, he grabbed her arms. "Look me in the eye, Morgana, and tell me you didn't wave your wand or chant your charm and make me feel this way."

"What way?"

"Damn you, I'm in love with you. I can't get through an hour without wanting you. I can't think about a year from now, ten years from now, without seeing you with me."

Her heart melted. "Nash—"

He jerked back from the hand she lifted to his cheek. Stunned, Morgana let it fall back to her side. "How did you do it?" he demanded. "How did you get inside me like this, to make me start thinking of marriage and family? What was the point? To play around with the mortal until you got tired of him?"

"I'm as mortal as you," she said steadily. "I eat and sleep, I bleed when I'm cut. I grow old. I feel."

"You're not like me." He bit off the words. Morgana felt her charm slipping, the color washing out of her cheeks.

"No. You're right. I'm different, and there's nothing I can do to change it. Nothing I would do. If you're finding that too difficult to accept, then let me go."

"You're not going to walk out of here and leave me like this. Fix it." He gave her a brisk shake. "Undo the spell."

The illusion fell away so that she stared at him with shadowed eyes. "What spell?"

"Whatever one you used. You got me to tell you things I've never told anyone. You stripped me bare, Morgana. Didn't you think I'd figure out that I'd never have told you about my family, my background, if I'd been in my right mind? That was mine." He released her, and turned away to keep from doing something drastic. "You tricked it out of me, just like you tricked all the rest. You used my feelings."

"I never used your feelings," she began furiously, then stopped, paling even more.

When he noted the look, his lips thinned. "Really?"

"All right, I used them yesterday. After your mother called, after you'd told me all those things, I wanted to give you some peace of mind."

"So it was a spell."

Though her chin came up, he wavered. She looked so damn fragile just then. Like glass that would shatter at his touch. "I let my emotions rule my judgment. If I was wrong, as it's obvious now I was, I apologize."

"Oh, fine. Sorry I took you for a ride, Nash." He jammed his hands into his pockets. "What about the rest?"

She lifted a shaky hand to her hair. "The rest of what?"

"Are you going to stand there and tell me you didn't cause all of this, manipulate my feelings? Make me think I was in love with you, that I wanted to start a life with you? God, have children with you?" Because he still wanted it, still, his anger grew. "I know damn well it wasn't my idea. No way in hell."

The hurt sliced deep. But, as it cut, it freed something. His anger, his sense of betrayal and confusion, was nothing compared to what bubbled inside her. She reined it in with a light hand as she studied him.

"Are you saying that I bound you to me with magic? That I used my gifts for my own gain, charmed you into loving me?"

"That's just what I'm saying."

Morgana released the reins. Color flooded back into her face, had her eyes gleaming like suns. Power, and the strength it brought, filled her. "You brainless ass."

Indignant, he started to snap back. His words came out like the bray of a donkey. Eyes wide, he tried again while she swooped around the room.

"So you think you're under a spell," she muttered, her fury making books fly through the room like literary missiles. Nash ducked and scrambled, but he didn't managed to avoid all of them. As one rapped the bridge of his nose, he swore. He felt a moment's dizzy relief when he realized he had his own voice back.

"Look, babe—"

"No, you look. *Babe.*" On a roll now, she had a gust of wind tossing his furniture into a heap. "Do you think I'd waste my gifts captivating someone like you? You conceited, arrogant jerk. Give me one reason I shouldn't turn you into the snake you are.''

Eyes narrowed, he started toward her. ''I'm not going to play along with this.''

''Then watch.'' With a flick of her hand she had him shooting back across the room, two feet above the floor, to land hard in a chair. He thought about getting up, but decided it was wiser to get his breath back first.

To satisfy herself, she sent the dishes soaring in the kitchen. Nash listened to the crashing with a resigned sigh.

''You should know better than to anger a witch,'' she told him. The logs in his fireplace began to spit and crackle with flame. ''Don't you know what someone like me, someone without integrity, without scruples, might do?''

''All right, Morgana.'' He started to rise. She slapped him back in the chair so hard his teeth rattled.

''Don't come near me, not now, not ever again.'' Her breath was heaving, though she was struggling to even it. ''I swear, if you do, I'll turn you into something that runs on four legs and howls at the moon.''

He let out an uneasy breath. He didn't think she'd do it. Not really. And it was better to take a stand than to whimper. His living room was a shambles. Hell, his life was a shambles. They were going to have to deal with it.

''Cut it out, Morgana.'' His voice was admirably calm and firm. ''This isn't proving anything.''

The fury drained out of her, leaving her empty and aching and miserable. ''You're quite right. It isn't. My temper, like my feelings, sometimes clouds my judgment. No.'' She waved a hand before he could rise. ''Stay where you are. I can't trust myself yet.''

As she turned away, the fire guttered out. The wind died. Quietly Nash breathed a sigh of relief. The storm, it appeared, was over.

He was very wrong.

''So you don't want to be in love with me.''

Something in her voice had his brows drawing together. He

wanted her to turn around so that he could see her face, but she stood with her back to him, looking out the window.

"I don't want to be in love with anyone," he said carefully, willing himself to believe it. "Nothing personal."

"Nothing personal," she repeated.

"Look, Morgana, I'm a bad bet. I like my life the way it was."

"The way it was before you met me."

When she said it like that, he felt like something slimy that slithered through the grass. He checked his hands to make certain he wasn't. "It's not you, it's me. And I... Damn it, I'm not going to sit here and apologize because I don't like being spellbound." He got to his feet gingerly. "You're a beautiful woman, and—"

"Oh, please. Don't strain yourself with a clever brush-off." The words choked out of her as she turned.

Nash felt as though she'd stuck a lance in his heart. She was crying. Tears were streaming out of her brimming eyes and flowing down her pale cheeks. There was nothing, nothing, he wanted more at that moment than to take her in his arms and kiss them away.

"Morgana, don't. I never meant to—" His words were cut off as he rapped into a wall. He couldn't see it, but she'd thrown it up between them, and it was as solid as bricks and mortar. "Stop it." His voice rose on a combination of panic and self-disgust as he rammed a hand against the shield that separated them. "This isn't the answer."

Her heart was bleeding. She could feel it. "It'll do until I find the right one." She wanted to hate him, desperately wanted to hate him for making her humiliate herself. As the tears continued to fall, she laid both hands on her stomach. She had more than herself to protect.

He spread his own impotent hands against the wall. Odd, he thought, he felt as though it was he who had been closed off, not her. "I can't stand to see you cry."

"You'll have to for a moment. Don't worry, a witch's tears are like any woman's. Weak and useless." She steadied herself, blinking them away until she could see clearly. "You want your freedom, Nash?"

If he could have, he'd have clawed and kicked his way through to her. "Damn it, can't you see I don't know what I want?"

"Whatever it is, it isn't me. Or what we've made together. I promised I wouldn't take more than you wanted to give me. And I never go back on my word."

He felt a new kind of fear, a rippling panic at the thought that what he did want was about to slip through his fingers. "Let me touch you."

"If you thought of me as a woman first, I would." For herself, she laid a hand on the wall opposite his. "Do you think, because of what I am, that I don't need to be loved as any man loves any woman?"

He shoved and strained against the wall. "Take this damn thing down."

It was all she had—a poor defense. "We crossed purposes somewhere along the line, Nash. No one's fault, I suppose, that I came to love you so much."

"Morgana, please."

She shook her head, studying him, drawing his image inside her head, her heart, where she could keep it. "Maybe, because I did, I somehow drew you in. I've never been in love before, so I can't be sure. But I swear to you, it wasn't intentional, it wasn't done to harm."

Furious that the tears were threatening again, she backed away. For a moment she stood—straight, proud, powerful.

"I'll give you this, and you can trust what I say. Whatever hold I have on you is broken, as of this instant. Whatever feelings I've caused in you through my art, I cast away. You're free of me, and of all we made."

She closed her eyes, lifted her hands. "Love conjured is love false. I will not take, nor will I make. Such cast away is nothing lost. Your heart and mind be free of me. As I will, so mote it be."

Her eyes opened, glittered with fresh tears. "You are more than you think," she said quietly. "Less than you could be."

His heart was thudding in his throat. "Morgana, don't go like this."

She smiled. "Oh, I think I'm entitled to at least a dramatic exit, don't you?" Though she was several feet away, he would have sworn he felt her lips touch him. "Blessed be, Nash," she said. And then she was gone.

Chapter 12

He had no doubt he was going out of his mind. Day after day he prowled the house and the grounds. Night after night he tossed restlessly in bed.

She'd said he was free of her, hadn't she? Then why wasn't he?

Why hadn't he stopped thinking about her, wishing for her? Why could he still see the way she had looked at him that last time, with hurt in her eyes and tears on her cheeks?

He tried to tell himself she'd left him charmed. But he knew it was a lie.

After a week, he gave up and drove by her house. It was empty. He went to the shop and was told by a very cool and unfriendly Mindy that Morgana was away. But she wouldn't tell him where, or when she would be back.

He should have felt relief. That was what he told himself. Doggedly he pushed thoughts of her aside and picked up the life he'd led before her.

But when he walked the beach, he imagined what it would be like to stroll there with her, a toddler scampering between them.

That image sent him driving down to L.A. for a few days.

He wanted to think he felt better there, with the rush and the crowds and the noise. He took a lunch with his agent at the Polo Lounge and discussed the casting for his screenplay. He went alone to clubs and fed himself on music and laughter. And he wondered if he'd made a mistake in moving north. Maybe he belonged in the heart of the city, surrounded by strangers and distractions.

But, after three days, his heart yearned for home, for the rustle of wind and the whoosh of water. And for her.

He went back to the shop, interrogating Mindy ruthlessly enough to have customers backing off and murmuring. She wouldn't budge.

At his wits' end, he took to parking in her driveway and brooding at her house. It had been nearly a month, and he comforted himself with the thought that she had to come back sometime. Her home was here, her business.

Damn it, he was here, waiting for her.

As the sun set, he braced his elbows on the steering wheel and rested his head in his hands. That was just what he was doing, he admitted. Waiting for her. And he wasn't waiting to have a rational conversation, as he'd tried to convince himself he was over the past weeks.

He was waiting to beg, to promise, to fight, to do whatever it took to put things right again. To put Morgana back in his life again.

He closed his hand over the stones he still wore around his neck and wondered if he could will her back. It was worth a shot. A better idea than putting an ad in the personals, he thought grimly. Shutting his eyes, he focused all his concentration on her.

"Damn it, I know you can hear me if you want to. You're not going to shut me out this way. You're not. Just because I was an idiot is no reason to..."

He felt a presence, actually felt it. He opened his eyes cautiously, turned his head and looked up into Sebastian's amused face.

"What is this?" Sebastian mused. "Amateur night?"

Before he could think, Nash was shoving the car door open. "Where is she?" he demanded, taking Sebastian's shirt in his fists. "You know, and one way or the other you're going to tell me."

Sebastian's eyes darkened dangerously. "Careful, friend. I've been wanting to go one-on-one with you for weeks."

The notion of a good, nasty fight appealed to Nash enormously. "Then we'll just—"

"Behave," Anastasia commanded. "Both of you." With delicate hands, she pushed the men apart. "I'm sure you'd enjoy giving each other bloody noses and black eyes, but I'm not going to tolerate it."

Nash fisted his frustrated hands at his sides. "I want to know where she is."

With a shrug, Sebastian leaned on the hood of the car. "Your wants don't carry much weight around here." He crossed his feet at the ankles when Anastasia stepped between them again. "You're looking a little ragged around the edges, Nash, old boy." And it pleased him no end. "Conscience stabbing at you?"

"Sebastian." Ana's quiet voice held both censure and compassion. "Don't snipe. Can't you see he's unhappy?"

"My heart bleeds."

Ana laid a hand on Nash's arm. "And that he's in love with her?"

Sebastian's response was a short laugh. "Don't let the hangdog look twist your feelings, Ana."

She shot Sebastian an impatient glare. "For heaven's sake, you only have to look."

Reluctantly, he did. As his eyes darkened, he clamped a hand on Nash's shoulder. Before Nash could shrug it angrily away, Sebastian laughed again. "By all that's holy, he is." He shook his head at Nash. "Why the devil did you make such a mess of it?"

"I don't have to explain myself to you," Nash muttered. Absently he rubbed a hand over his shoulder. It felt as though it had been sunburned. "What I have to say, I'll say to Morgana."

Sebastian was softening, but he didn't see any reason to make it easy. "I believe she's under the impression that you've already had your say. I don't know that she's in any condition to listen to your outrageous accusations again."

"Condition?" Nash's heart froze. "Is she sick?" He grabbed Sebastian by the shirtfront again, but the strength had left his hands. "What's wrong with her?"

A look passed between the cousins, so brief, so subtle, that it went unnoticed. "She's not ill," Ana said, and tried not to be furious with Morgana for not telling Nash about the child. "In fact, she's quite well. Sebastian meant that she was upset by what happened between you the last time."

Nash's fingers loosened. When he had his breath back, he nodded. "All right, you want me to beg. I'll beg. I have to see her. If after I've finished crawling she boots me out of her life, I'll live with it."

"She's in Ireland," Ana told him. "With our family." Her smile curved beautifully. "Do you have a passport?"

Morgana was glad she'd come. The air in Ireland was soothing, whether it was the balmy breeze that rolled down from the hills or the wild wind that whipped across the channel.

Though she knew it would soon be time to go back and pick up her life again, she was grateful for the weeks she'd had to heal.

And for her family.

Stretched out on the window seat in her mother's sitting room, she was as much at home, and at peace, as she could be anywhere in the world. She felt the sun on her face, that luminous sun that seemed to belong only to Ireland. If she looked through the diamond panes of glass, she could see the cliffs that hacked their way down to the rugged beach. And the beach, narrow and rough, stretching out to the waves. By changing the angle, she could see the terraced lawn, the green, green grass scattered with a profusion of flowers that stirred in the wind.

Across the room, her mother sat sketching. It was a cozy moment, one that reminded Morgana sweetly of childhood. And her mother had changed so little in the years between.

Her hair was as dark and thick as her daughter's, though she wore it short and sleek around her face. Her skin was smooth, with the beautiful luster of her Irish heritage. The cobalt eyes were often dreamier than Morgana's, but they saw as clearly.

When Morgana looked at her, she was washed by an intense flood of love. "You're so beautiful, Mother."

Bryna glanced up, smiled. "I won't argue, since it feels so good to hear that from a grown daughter." Her voice carried the charming lilt of her homeland. "Do you know how wonderful it is to have you here, darling, for all of us?"

Morgana raised a knee and linked her hands around it. "I know how good it's been for me. And how grateful I am you haven't asked me all the questions I know you want to."

"And so you should be. I've all but had to strike your father mute to keep him from badgering you." Her eyes softened. "He adores you so."

"I know." Morgana felt weak tears fill her eyes again, and she tried to blink them away. "I'm sorry. My moods." With a shake of her head, she rose. "I don't seem to be able to control them."

"Darling." Bryna held out both hands, waiting until Morgana had crossed the room to link hers with them. "You know you can tell me anything, anything at all. When you're ready."

"Mother." Seeking comfort, Morgana knelt down to rest her head in Bryna's lap. She gave a watery smile as her hair was stroked. "I've come to realize recently how very lucky I am to have had you, all of you. To love me, to want me, to care about what happens to me. I haven't told you before how grateful I am for you."

Puzzled, Bryna cradled her daughter. "Families are meant to love and want and care."

"But all families don't." Morgana lifted her head, her eyes dry now and intense. "Do they?"

"The loss is theirs. What's hurting you, Morgana?"

She gripped her mother's hands again. "I've thought about how it must feel not to be wanted or loved. To be taught from childhood that you were a mistake, a burden, something only to be tolerated through duty. Can anything be colder than that?"

"No. Nothing's colder than living without love." Her tone gentled. "Are you in love?"

She didn't have to answer. "He's been hurt so, you see. He never had what you, what all of you, gave me, what I took for granted. And, despite it all, he's made himself into a wonderful man. Oh, you'd like him." She rested her cheek on her mother's palm. "He's funny and sweet. His mind is so, well, fluid. So ready to test new ideas. But there's a part of him that's closed off. He didn't do it, it was done to him. And, no matter what my powers, I can't break that lock." She sat back on her heels. "He doesn't want to love me, and I can't—won't—take what he doesn't want to give."

"No." Bryna's heart broke a little as she looked at her daughter. "You're too strong, too proud, and too wise for that. But people change, Morgana. In time…"

"There isn't time. I'll have his child by Christmas."

All the soothing words Bryna had prepared slipped away down her throat. All she could think was that her baby was carrying a baby. "Are you well?" she managed.

Morgana smiled, pleased that this should be the first question. "Yes."

"And certain?"

"Very certain."

"Oh, love." Bryna rose to her feet to rock Morgana against her. "My little girl."

"I won't be little much longer."

They laughed together as they broke apart. "I'm happy for you. And sad."

"I know. I want the child. Believe me, no child has ever been wanted so much. Not only because it's all I might ever have of the father, but for itself."

"And you feel?"

"Odd," Morgana said. "Strong one moment, terrifyingly fragile the next. Not ill, but sometimes light-headed."

Understanding, Bryna nodded. "And you say the father is a good man."

"Yes, he's a good man."

"Then, when you told him, he was just surprised, unprepared…" She noted the way Morgana glanced away. "Morgana, even when you were a child you would stare past my shoulder when you were preparing to evade."

Wincing at the tone, Morgana met her mother's eyes again. "I didn't tell him. Don't," she pleaded before Bryna could launch into a lecture. "I had intended to, but it all fell apart. I know it was wrong not to tell him, but it was just as wrong to hold him to me by the telling. I made a choice."

"The wrong choice."

Morgana's chin angled as her mother's had. "My choice, right or wrong. I won't ask you to approve, but I will ask you to respect. And I'll also ask you not to tell anyone else just yet. Including Father.''

"Including Father what?" Matthew demanded as he strode into the room, the wolf that was Pan's sire close at his heels.

"Girl talk," Morgana said smoothly and moved over to kiss his cheeks. "Hello, handsome."

He tweaked her nose. "I know when my women are keeping secrets."

"No peeking," Morgana said, knowing Matthew was nearly as skilled at reading thoughts as Sebastian. "Now, where's everyone else?"

He wasn't satisfied, but he was patient. If she didn't tell him soon, he would look for himself. He was, after all, her father.

"Douglas and Maureen are in the kitchen, arguing over who's fixing what for lunch. Camilla's rousting Padrick at gin." Matthew grinned, wickedly. "And he's not taking it well. Accused her of charming the cards."

Bryna managed a smile of her own. "And did she?"

"Of course." Matthew stroked the wolf's silver fur. "Your sister's a born cheat."

Bryna sent him a mild look. "Your brother's a poor loser."

Morgana laughed and linked arms with them both. "And how the six of you managed to live in this place together and not be struck by lightning is a mystery to me. Let's go down and make some more trouble."

There was nothing like a group meal with the Donovans to lift her mood. And a mood lift was precisely what Morgana needed. Watching with affection the squabbling, the interplay between siblings and spouses, was better than front-row seats at a three-ring circus.

She was well aware that they didn't always get along. Just as she was aware that, whatever the friction, they would merge together like sun and light in the face of a family crisis.

She didn't intend to be a crisis. She only wanted to spend some time being with them.

They might have been two sets of triplets, but there was little physical resemblance between the siblings. Her father was tall and lean, with a shock of steel-gray hair and a dignified bearing. Padrick, Anastasia's father, stood no higher than Morgana, with the husky build of a boxer and the heart of a prankster. Douglas was nearly six-four, with a receding hairline that swept back dramatically into a widow's peak. Eccentricity was his hobby. At the moment, he was sporting a magnifying glass around his neck that he peered through when the whim took him.

He'd only removed his deerstalker hat and cape because his wife, Camilla, had refused to eat with him otherwise.

Camilla, often thought of as the baby of the brood, was pretty and plump as a pigeon, and she had a will of iron. She matched her husband's eccentricities with her own. This morning, she was trying out a new hairstyle of blazing orange curls that corkscrewed around her head. A long eagle feather dangled from one ear.

Maureen, as skilled a medium as Morgana had ever known, was tall and stately and had an infectious, bawdy laugh that could rattle the rafters.

Together with Morgana's serene mother and dignified father, they made a motley crew. Witches all. As she listened to them bicker around her, Morgana was nearly swamped with love.

"Your cat's been climbing the curtains in my room again," Camilla told Maureen with a wave of her fork.

"Pooh." Maureen shrugged her sturdy shoulders. "Just hunting mice, that's all."

Camilla's massive curls jiggled. "You know very well there's not a mouse in this house. Douglas cast them out."

"And did a half-baked job," Matthew muttered.

"Half-baked." Camilla huffed in her husband's defense. "The only thing half-baked is this pie."

"Aye, and Doug made that, as well," Padrick interjected and grinned. "But I like my apples crunchy."

"It's a new recipe." Douglas peered owlishly through his magnifying glass. "Healthy."

"The cat," Camilla insisted, knowing very well she'd lose control of the conversation.

"Cat's healthy as a horse," Padrick said cheerfully. "Isn't that right, lamb chop?" He sent his wife a lusty wink. Maureen responded with an equally lusty giggle.

"I don't give a tinker's damn about the cat's health," Camilla began.

"Oh, now, now..." Douglas patted her chubby hand. "We don't want a sick cat around, do we? Reenie will brew him up a nice remedy."

"The cat's not sick," Camilla said in a strangled voice. "Douglas, for heaven's sake, keep up."

"Keep up with what?" he demanded, indignant. "If the cat's not sick, what in Finn's name is the problem? Morgana, lass, you're not eating your pie."

She was too busy grinning. "It's wonderful, Douglas. I'm saving it." She sprang up, dancing around the table to smack kisses on every cheek. "I love you, all of you."

"Morgana," Bryna called as her daughter spun out of the room. "Where are you going?"

"For a walk on the beach. For a long, long walk on the beach."

Douglas scowled through his glass. "Girl's acting odd," he pronounced. Since the meal was nearly over, he plucked up his hat and dropped it on his head. "Don't you think?"

Nash was feeling odd. Perhaps it had something to do with the fact that he hadn't slept in two days. Traveling steadily for approximately twenty hours in planes, trains, cabs and shuttle buses might have contributed to the dazed, dreamlike state he was currently enjoying. Still, he'd managed to get from the West Coast to the East, to catch another plane in New York and snatch a little twilight sleep crossing the Atlantic. Then there'd been the train south from Dublin and a frantic search for a car he could buy, rent or steal to carry him the last jarring miles from Waterford to Castle Donovan.

He knew it was important to stay on the right side of the road. Or rather the wrong side. He wondered why the devil it should matter, when the rutted, ditch-lined dirt track he was currently bouncing along couldn't remotely be considered a road of any kind.

And the car, which he'd managed to procure for the equivalent of twelve hundred American dollars—nobody could say the Irish weren't shrewd bargainers—was threatening to break apart on

him at every bump. He'd already lost the poor excuse for a
muffler, and was making enough noise to wake the sleeping
dead.

It wasn't that the land didn't have style and grace, with its
towering cliffs and its lush green fields. It was that he was afraid
he'd end up staggering up the final hill with nothing but a steering wheel in his hands.

Those were the Knockmealdown Mountains to the west. He
knew because the same slippery horse trader who'd sold him the
car had been expansive enough to offer directions. The mountains to the west, St. George's Channel to the east, and you'll
trip right over the Donovans before teatime.

Nash was beginning to believe he'd find himself buried in a
peat bog before teatime.

"If I live," Nash mumbled. "If I find her and I live, I'm
going to kill her. Slowly," he said with relish, "so she knows
I mean it."

Then he was going to carry her off to some dark, quiet place
and make love with her for a week. Then he was going to sleep
for a week, wake up and start all over again.

If, he reminded himself, he lived.

The car sputtered and bucked and jolted his bones. He wondered how many of his internal organs had been shifted. Gritting
his teeth, Nash cursed and cajoled and threatened the stuttering
car up a rise. When his mouth fell open, he slammed on the
brakes. The act managed to slow his descent. As he slid down
the hill, he didn't notice the smell of rubber burning, or see the
smoke beginning to pour out of the hood.

His eyes were all for the castle.

He hadn't really expected a castle, despite the name. But this
was the real McCoy, perched high on the cliffs, facing the arrogant sea. Gray stone glittered in the sun, with flashing chips
of quartz and mica. Towers lanced into the pearly sky. From the
topmost, a white flag flew. Nash saw with awe and amazement
that it was a pentagram.

He blinked his eyes, but the structure remained, as fanciful as
something from one of his movies. If a mounted knight had burst
across the drawbridge—by God, there *was* a drawbridge—Nash
wouldn't have turned a hair.

He started to laugh, as delighted as he had been stunned. Recklessly, he punched the gas, and when the steering locked, drove straight into a ditch.

Calling up every oath he knew, Nash climbed out of what was left of the car. Then he kicked it and watched the rusted fender clatter off.

He squinted against the sun and judged that he was about to add a good three-mile hike to his travel arrangements. Resigned, he snagged his duffel bag out of the rear seat and started to walk.

When he saw the white horse gallop across the bridge, he set himself to the task of deciding whether he was hallucinating or whether it was real. Though the horseman wasn't wearing armor, he was striking—lean and masculine with a waving silver mane. And Nash was not surprised to note the hawk clamped to the leather glove of his left arm.

Matthew took one look at the man staggering up the road and shook his head. "Pitiful. Aye, Ulysses, pitiful. Wouldn't even make you a decent meal." The hawk merely blinked in agreement.

At first glimpse, Matthew saw a disheveled, unshaven, bleary-eyed man with a knot forming on his forehead and a line of blood trickling down his temple.

Since he'd seen the fool drive into the ditch, he felt honor-bound to set him right again. He pulled up his mount and stared haughtily down at Nash.

"Lost, are you, lad?"

"No. I know just where I'm going. There." He lifted a hand and gestured.

Matthew lifted a brow. "Castle Donovan? Don't you know the place is lousy with witches?"

"Yeah. That's just why I'm going."

Matthew shifted in the saddle to reassess the man. He might be disheveled, but he wasn't a vagrant. His eyes might be bleary with fatigue, but there was a steely glint of determination behind them.

"If you'll pardon my saying so," Matthew continued, "you don't look to be in any shape to battle witches at the moment."

"Just one," Nash said between his teeth. "Just one particular witch."

"Hmm. Did you know you're bleeding?"

"Where?" Nash lifted a hand gingerly, looked at his smeared fingers in disgust. "Figures. She probably cursed the car."

"And who might you be speaking of?"

"Morgana. Morgana Donovan." Nash wiped his fingers on his grimy jeans. "I've come a long way to get my hands on her."

"Mind your step," Matthew said mildly. "It's my daughter you're speaking of."

Tired, aching, and at the end of his tether, Nash stared back into the slate-gray eyes. Maybe he'd find himself turned into a squashed beetle, but he was taking his stand.

"My name's Kirkland, Mr. Donovan. I've come for your daughter. And that's that."

"Is it?" Amused, Matthew tilted his head. "Well, then, climb up and we'll go see about that." He sent the hawk soaring, then offered his gloved hand. "It's pleased I am to meet you, Kirkland."

"Yeah." Nash winced as he hauled himself onto the horse. "Likewise."

The journey took less time on horseback than it would have on foot—particularly since Matthew shot off at a gallop. The moment they were across the drawbridge and into the courtyard, a tall, dark-haired woman rushed out of a doorway.

Grinding his teeth, Nash jumped down and started toward her. "You've got a lot to answer for, babe. You cut your hair. What the hell do you—" He skidded to a halt as the woman stood her ground, watching him with bemused eyes. "I thought you were...I'm sorry."

"I'm flattered," Bryna countered. With a laugh, she looked toward her husband. "Matthew, what have you brought me?"

"A young man who drove into a ditch and seems to want Morgana."

Bryna's eyes sharpened as she took another step toward Nash. "And do you? Want my daughter?"

"I... Yes, ma'am."

A smile flirted around her lips. "And did she make you unhappy?"

"Yes— No." He let out a heavy sigh. "I did that all by myself. Please, is she here?"

"Come inside." Bryna gently took his arm. "I'll fix your head, then send you to her."

"If you could just—" He broke off when he saw a huge eye peering at him from the doorway. Douglas dropped his magnifying glass and stepped out of the shadows.

"Who the devil is this?"

"A friend of Morgana's," Bryna told him, nudging Nash inside.

"Ah. The girl's acting odd," Douglas said, giving Nash a hearty clap on the back. "Let me tell you."

Morgana let the brisk, chill wind slap her face and sneak through the heavy knit of her sweater. It was so cleansing, so healing. In a few more days, she would be ready to go back and face reality again.

With a small, helpless sound, she sat on a rock. Here, alone, she could admit it. Had to admit it. She would never be healed. She would never be whole. She would go on and make a good life for herself and the child, because she was strong, because she was proud. But something would always be missing.

But she was through with tears, through with self-pity. Ireland had done that for her. She'd needed to come here, to walk this beach and remember that nothing, no matter how painful, lasts forever.

Except love.

Rising, she started back, watching the water spray on rocks. She would brew some tea, perhaps read Camilla's tarot cards or listen to one of Padrick's long, involved stories. Then she would tell them, as she should have told them all along, about the baby.

And, being her family, they would stand behind her.

How sorry she was that Nash would never experience that kind of union.

She sensed him before she saw him. But she thought her mind was playing tricks on her, teasing her because she was pretending to be so fearless. Very slowly, her pulse hammering in a hundred places, she turned.

He was coming down the beach, in long, hurried strides. The spray had showered his hair, and droplets of water were gleaming on it. His face was shadowed with a two-day beard, and there was a neat white bandage at his temple. And a look in his eyes that had her heart screaming into her throat.

In defense, she took a step back. The action stopped him cold. She looked... The way she looked at him. Oh, her eyes were dry. There were no tears to tear up his gut. But there was a glint in them. As if—as if she was afraid of him. How much easier it would have been if she'd leapt at him, clawing and scratching and cursing.

"Morgana."

Giddy, she pressed a hand over the secret she held inside. "What happened to you? You're hurt?"

"It's..." He touched his fingers to the bandage. "Nothing. Really. I had a car fall apart on me. Your mother put something on it. On my head, I mean."

"My mother?" Her gaze flickered over his shoulder, toward the towers of the castle. "You've seen my mother?"

"And the rest of them." He managed a quick smile. "They're...something. Actually, I ditched the car a couple of miles from the castle. Literally. That's how I met your father." He knew he was babbling, but he couldn't stop. "Then they were taking me in the kitchen and pouring tea into me and... Hell, Morgana, I didn't know where you were. I should have. You told me you came to Ireland to walk the beach. I should have known. I should have known a lot of things."

She braced a hand on the rock for balance. She was deathly afraid she was about to have a new experience and faint at his feet. "You've come a long way," she said dully.

"I would have been here sooner, but— Hey." He jumped forward as she swayed. The shock came first, that she felt so frighteningly fragile in his arms.

But her arms were strong enough as she pushed at him. "Don't."

Ignoring her, Nash pulled her close and buried his face in her hair. He drew in her scent like breath. "God, Morgana, just give me a minute. Let me hold you."

She shook her head, but her arms, her treacherous arms, were already wrapping hard around him. Her moan was not of protest, but of need, when his mouth rushed to hers and took. He sank into her like a parched man into a clear, cool lake.

"Don't say anything," he murmured as he rained kisses over her face. "Don't say anything until I've told you what I have to tell you."

Remembering what he had told her before, she struggled against him. "I can't go through this again, Nash. I won't."

"No." He caught her hands by the wrists, his eyes burning into hers. "No walls this time, Morgana. On either side. Your word."

She opened her mouth to refuse, but there was something in his eyes she was powerless against. "You have it," she said briefly. "I want to sit down."

"Okay." He let her go, thinking it might be best if he wasn't touching her while he was struggling to fight his way clear of the morass he'd made of things. When she sat on the rock, folded her hands in her lap and lifted her chin, he remembered he'd given serious thought to murdering her.

"No matter how bad things were, you shouldn't have run away."

Her eyes widened and gleamed. "I?"

"Yes, you," he shot back. "Maybe I was an idiot, but that's no reason for making me suffer the way you did when you weren't there when I came to my senses."

"So, it's my fault."

"That I've been going out of my mind for the last month? Yeah, it is." He blew out a breath between his teeth. "Everything else, all the rest of it's on my head." He took a chance and touched a hand to her cheek. "I'm sorry."

She had to look away or weep. "I can't accept your apology until I know what it's for."

"I knew you'd make me crawl," he said in disgust. "Fine, then, I'm sorry for all the stupid things I said."

Her lips curved a little. "All of them?"

Out of patience now, he hauled her back to her feet. "Look

at me, damn it, I want you to look at me when I tell you I love you. That I know it has nothing to do with charms or spells, that it never did. That all it has to do with is you, and me."

When she closed her eyes, he felt panic skitter up his spine. "Don't shut me out, Morgana. I know that's what I did to you. I know it was stupid. I was scared. Hell, I was terrified. Please." He cupped her face in his hands. "Open your eyes and look at me." When she did, he let out a shudder of relief. He could see it wasn't too late. "This is a first for me," he said carefully. "First I have to ask you to forgive me for the things I said. I can tell you that I didn't mean them, that I was just using them to push you way, but that's not the point. I did say them."

"I understand being afraid." She touched her hand to his wrist. "If it's forgiveness you want, you have it. There's no need to hold it back from you."

"Just like that?" He pressed his lips to her brow, her cheeks. "You don't want to maybe turn me into a flounder for three or four years?"

"Not for a first offense." She drew back, praying they could find some light and friendly plane to walk on for a little while. "You've had a long trip, and you're tired. Why don't we go back in? The wind's picking up, and it's nearly teatime."

"Morgana." He held her still. "I said I loved you. I've never said that to anyone before. Not to anyone in my life before you. It was hard the first time, but I think it might get easier as we go."

She looked away again. Her mother would have recognized it as evasion. Nash saw it as dismissal. "You said you loved me." His voice tightened, and so did his grip.

"Yes, I did." She met his eyes again. "And I do."

He gathered her close again to rest his brow on hers. "It feels good," he said in a wondering voice. "I didn't know how damn good it would feel to love someone, to have her love me back. We can go from here, Morgana. I know I'm not a prize, and I'll probably mess up. I'm not used to having someone there for me. Or for being there for someone else. But I'll give it all I've got. That's a promise."

She went very still. "What are you saying?"

He stepped back, nervous all over again, and stuck his hands in his pockets. "I'm asking you to marry me. Sort of."

"Sort of?"

He swore. "Look, I want you to marry me. I'm not doing a good job of asking. If you want to wait until I've set the stage, gotten down on one knee with a ring in my pocket, okay. It's just...I love you so much, and I didn't know I could feel this way, be this way. I want a chance to show you."

"I don't need a stage, Nash. And I wish it could be simple."

His fingers clenched. "You don't want to marry me."

"I want a life with you. Oh, yes, I want that very much. But it isn't only myself you'd be taking."

For a moment, he was baffled. Then his face cleared with a smile. "You mean your family, and the, ah, Donovan legacy. Babe, you're everything I want, and more. The fact that the woman I love is a witch just adds some interest to the situation."

Touched, she lifted a hand to his cheek. "Nash, you're perfect. Absolutely perfect for me. But it's not only that you'd be taking on." Her eyes stayed level on his. "I'm carrying your child."

His face went utterly blank. "What?"

She didn't need to repeat it. She watched as he staggered back and dropped onto the rock where she had sat earlier.

He gulped in air before he managed to speak again. "A baby? You're pregnant? You're having a child?"

Outwardly calm, she nodded. "That about sums it up." She gave him a moment to speak. When he didn't, she forced herself to go on. "You were very clear about not wanting a family, so I realize this changes things, and..."

"You knew." He had to swallow to make his voice rise above the sound of wind and sea. "That day, the last day, you knew. You'd come to tell me."

"Yes, I knew. I'd come to tell you."

On unsteady legs, he got up to walk to the verge of the water. He remembered the way she'd looked, the things he'd said. He'd remember for a long time. Was it any wonder she'd left him that way, keeping the secret inside her?

"You think I don't want the baby?"

Morgana moistened her lips. "I understand you'd have

doubts. This wasn't planned by either of us." She stopped, appalled. "I didn't plan it."

Eyes fierce, he whipped back to her. "I don't often make the same mistake twice, and certainly not with you. When?"

She folded her hands over her belly. "Before Christmas. The child was conceived that first night, on the spring equinox."

"Christmas," he repeated. And thought of a red bike, of cookies baking, of laughter and a family that had nearly been his. A family that could be his. She was offering something he'd never had, something he'd wished for only in secret.

"You said I was free," he said carefully. "Free of you, and everything we'd made together. You meant the baby."

Her eyes darkened, and her voice was strong and beautiful. "This child is loved, is wanted. This child is not a mistake, but a gift. I would rather it be mine alone than to risk that for one instant of its life it would not feel cherished."

He wasn't sure he could speak at all, but when he did, the words came straight from the heart. "I want the baby, and you, and everything we made together."

Through a mist of tears she studied him. "Then you have only to ask."

He walked back to her, laid his hand over where hers rested. "Give me a chance" was all he said.

Her lips curved when his moved to meet them. "We've been waiting for you a long time."

"I'm going to be a father." He said it slowly, testingly, then let out a whoop and scooped her off her feet. "We made a baby."

She threw her arms around his neck and laughed. "Yes."

"We're a family."

"Yes."

He kissed her long and hard before he began to walk. "If we do a good job with the first, we can have more, right?"

"Absolutely. Where are we going?"

"I'm taking you back and putting you to bed. With me."

"Sounds like a delightful idea, but you don't have to carry me."

"Every bloody step. You're having a baby. My baby. I can see it. Interior scene, day. A sunny room with pale blue walls."

"Yellow."

"Okay. With bright yellow walls. Under the window stands a gleaming antique crib, with one of those funny mobiles hanging over it. There's a sound of gurgling, and a tiny, pudgy hand lifts up to grab at one of the circling..." He stopped, his face whipping around to Morgana's. "Oh, boy."

"What? What is it?"

"It just hit me. What are the chances? I mean how likely is it that the baby will, you know, inherit your talent?"

Smiling, she curled a lock of his hair around her finger. "You mean, what are the chances of the baby being a witch? Very high. The Donovan genes are very strong." Chuckling, she nuzzled his neck. "But I bet she has your eyes."

"Yeah." He took another step and found himself grinning. "I bet she does."

*   *   *   *   *

ENTRANCED

Prologue

He understood his power early. What coursed through his blood and made him what he was did not have to be explained to him. Nor did he have to be told that this gift was one not possessed by everyone.

He could see.

The visions were not always pleasant, but they were always fascinating. When they came—even when they came to a small child whose legs were still unsteady—he accepted them as easily as he accepted the sun's rising each morning.

Often his mother would crouch on the floor with him, her face close to his, her eyes searching his eyes. Mixed with her great love was a hope that he would always accept the gift, and that he would never be hurt by it.

Though she knew better, on both counts.

Who are you? He could hear her thoughts as clearly as if she had spoken aloud. *Who will you be?*

They were questions he couldn't answer. Even then he understood that it was more difficult to see into yourself than to see into others.

As time passed, the gift did not prevent him from racing and running and teasing his young cousins. Though often, quite often, he strained against its limitations and tried for more, it did not keep him from enjoying an ice-cream cone on a summer afternoon, or from laughing at cartoons on a Saturday morning.

He was a normal, active, mischievous boy with a sharp, sometimes devious mind, a strikingly handsome face set off by hypnotic gray-blue eyes, and a full mouth that was quick to smile.

He went through all the stages that lead a boy toward manhood. The scraped knees and the broken bones, the rebellions large and small, the first jumpy heartbeat at the smile of a pretty girl. Like all children, he grew into an adult, moved away from his parents' domain and chose his own.

And the power grew, as he did.

He considered his life a well-adjusted and comfortable one.

And he accepted, as he always had, the simple fact that he was a witch.

Chapter 1

She dreamed of a man who was dreaming of her. But he wasn't sleeping. She could see, with a perfect clarity that was extremely undreamlike, that he was standing by a wide, dark window, with his arms relaxed by his sides. But his face was very tense, very purposeful. And his eyes... They were so deep, so unrelenting. Gray, she thought as she twisted in sleep. But not quite gray. There were hints of blue, as well. The color of them reminded her of rocks hacked out of a high cliff one moment, and of the soft, calm waters of a lake the next.

Strange—how strange—she knew that his face was taut and tensed, but she couldn't see it. Just those eyes, those fascinating, disturbing eyes.

And she knew he was thinking of her. Not just thinking of her, but somehow seeing her. As if she had walked up to the other side of that glass, stood there looking back at him through the wide windowpane. Somehow she was certain that if she lifted a hand to that glass her fingers would pass right through it until they found his.

If she chose to.

Instead, she thrashed, tangling the sheets and muttering in her sleep. Even in dreams Mel Sutherland didn't care for the illogical. Life had rules, very basic rules. She firmly believed you were better off following them.

So she didn't reach for the glass, or for him. She rolled, almost violently, knocking a pillow to the floor and willing the dream away.

It faded, and, both relieved and disappointed, she dropped deeper into a dreamless sleep.

A few hours later, with the night vision tucked away in her subconscious, she snapped awake at the clattering bell of the Mickey Mouse alarm clock at her bedside. One expert slap silenced it. There was no danger that she would snuggle down in the bed and slide back into sleep. Mel's mind was as regulated as her body.

She sat up, indulging in one huge yawn as she dragged her fingers through her tousled cap of dark blond hair. Her eyes, a rich, mossy green she'd inherited from a father she couldn't remember, were blurry for only a moment. Then they focused on the twisted sheets.

Rough night, she thought, kicking her legs free of them. And why not? It could hardly have been expected that she'd sleep like a baby, not with what she had to do today. After blowing out one long breath, she plucked a pair of gym shorts from the floor and yanked them on under the T-shirt she'd slept in. Five minutes later, she was stepping out into the soft-aired morning for her daily three-mile jog.

As she went out, she kissed the tips of her fingers and tapped them against the front door. Because it was her place. Hers. And even after four years she didn't take it for granted.

It wasn't much, she thought as she limbered up with a few stretches. Just a little stucco building tucked between a Laundromat and a struggling accounting firm. But then, she didn't need much.

Mel ignored the whistle from the car that passed, its driver grinning appreciatively at her long, leanly muscled legs. She didn't jog for her looks. She jogged because routine exercise disciplined the mind and the body. A private investigator who allowed either to become sluggish would find herself in trouble. Or unemployed. Mel didn't intend to be either.

She started out at an easy pace, enjoying the way her shoes slapped the sidewalk, delighted by the pearly glow in the eastern sky that signaled the start of a beautiful day. It was August, and she thought of how miserably hot it would be down in L.A. But here, in Monterey, there was perpetual spring. No matter what the calendar said, the air was as fresh as a rosebud.

It was too early for there to be much traffic. Here in the downtown area it would be a rare thing for her to pass another jogger. If she'd chosen any of the beaches, it would have been a different matter. But Mel preferred to run alone.

Her muscles began to warm. A thin layer of sweat gleamed healthily on her skin. She increased her pace slightly, falling into a familiar rhythm that had become as automatic as breathing.

For the first mile, she kept her mind empty, letting herself observe. A car with a faulty muffler rattled by, with no more than a token hesitation at a stop sign.

An '82 Plymouth sedan, dark blue. The mental list was just to keep in practice. Dented driver's door. California license Able Charlie Robert 2289.

Someone was lying facedown on the grass of the park. Even as Mel broke her stride, he sat up, stretched and switched on a portable radio.

College student hitchhiking cross-country, she decided, picking up her pace again even as she made a note of his backpack...blue, with an American flag on the flap...and his hair color...brown...and... *Name That Tune,* she thought as the music began to fade behind her.

Bruce Springsteen. "Cover Me."

Not too shabby, Mel thought with a grin as she rounded a corner.

She could smell bread from the bakery. A fine, yeasty good-morning scent. And roses. She drew them in—though she would have suffered torture before admitting she had a weakness for flowers. Trees moved gently in the early breeze, and if she concentrated, really concentrated, she could just scent the sea.

And it was good, so very good, to feel strong and aware and alone. It was good to know these streets and to know she belonged here. That she could stay here. That there would be no midnight rambles in a battered station wagon at her mother's whim.

Time to go, Mary Ellen. Time to head out. I've just got a feeling we should head north for a while.

And so they would go, she and the mother she adored, the mother who would always be more of a child than the daughter who huddled on the ripped and taped front seat beside her. The headlights would cut down the road, leading the way to a new place a new school, new people.

But they would never settle, never have time to become a part of anything but the road. Soon her mother would get what she always called "Those itchy feet." And off they would go again.

Why had it always felt as if they were running *away,* not running *to?*

That, of course, was all over. Alice Sutherland had herself a cozy travel trailer—which would take Mel another twenty-six months to pay off—and she was happy as a clam, bopping from state to state and adventure to adventure.

As for Mel, she was sticking. True, L.A. hadn't worked out, but she'd gotten a taste of what it was like to put down roots. And she'd had two very frustrating and very educational years on the LAPD. Two years that had taught her that law enforcement was just her cup of tea, even if writing parking tickets and filling out forms was not.

So she had moved north and opened Sutherland Investigations. She still filled out forms—often by the truckload—but they were *her* forms.

She'd reached the halfway point of her run and was circling back. As always, she felt that quick rush of satisfaction at the knowledge that her body responded so automatically. It hadn't always been so—not when she was a child, too tall, too gangly, with elbows and knees that just begged to be banged and scraped. It had taken time and discipline, but she was twenty-eight now, and she'd gotten her body under control. Yes, sir. It had never been a disappointment to Mel that she hadn't bloomed and rounded. Slim and sleek was more efficient. And the long, coltish legs that had once invited names like Stretch and Beanpole were now strong, athletic and—she could admit privately—worth a second look.

It was then that she heard the baby crying. It was a fussy, impatient sound that bounded through an open window of the apartment building beside her. Her mood, buoyed by the run, plummeted.

The baby. Rose's baby. Sweet, pudgy-cheeked David.

Mel continued to run. The habit was too ingrained to be broken. But her mind filled with images.

Rose, harmless, slightly dippy Rose, with her fuzzy red hair and her easy smile. Even with Mel's natural reserve, it had been impossible to refuse her friendship.

Rose worked as a waitress in the little Italian restaurant two blocks from Mel's office. It had been easy to fall into a casual conversation—particularly since Rose did most of the talking—over a plate of spaghetti or a cup of cappuccino.

Mel remembered admiring the way Rose hustled trays, even though her pregnant belly strained against her apron. And she remembered Rose telling her how happy she and her Stan were to be expecting their first child.

Mel had even been invited to the baby shower, and though she'd been certain she would feel awkward and out of place at such a gathering, she'd enjoyed listening to the oohs and aahs over the tiny clothes and the stuffed animals. She'd taken a liking to Stan, too, with his shy eyes and slow smiles.

When David had been born, eight months ago, she'd gone to the hospital to visit. As she'd stared at the babies sleeping, bawling or wriggling in their clear-sided cribs, she'd understood why people prayed and struggled and sacrificed to have children.

They were so perfect. So perfectly lovely.

When she'd left, she was happy for Rose and Stan. And lonelier than she'd ever been in her life.

It had become a habit for her to drop by their apartment from time to time with a little toy for David. As an excuse, of course, an excuse to play with him for an hour. She'd fallen more than a little in love with him, so she hadn't felt foolish exclaiming over his first tooth, or being astounded when he learned to crawl.

Then that frantic phone call two months before. Rose's voice, shrill and nearly incoherent.

"He's gone. He's gone. He's gone."

Mel had made the mile from her office to the Merrick home in record time. The police had already been there. Stan and Rose had been clutched together on the sofa like two lost souls in a choppy sea. Both of them crying.

David was gone. Snatched off his playpen mat as he napped

in the shade on the little patch of grass just outside the rear door of their first-floor apartment.

Now two months had passed, and the playpen was still empty.

Everything Mel had learned, everything she'd been trained to do and her instincts had taught her, hadn't helped get David back.

Now Rose wanted to try something else, something so absurd that Mel would have laughed—if not for the hard glint of determination in Rose's usually soft eyes. Rose didn't care what Stan said, what the police said, what Mel said. She would try anything, anything, to get her child back.

Even if that meant going to a psychic.

As they swept down the coast to Big Sur in Mel's cranky, primer-coated MG, she took one last shot at talking sense to Rose.

"Rose..."

"There's no use trying to talk me out of this." Though Rose's voice was low, there was steel in it that had only surfaced over the last two months. "Stan's already tried."

"That's because we both care about you. Neither one of us want to see you hurt by another dead end."

She was only twenty-three, but Rose felt as old as the sea that spread out beneath them. As old as the sea, and as hard as the rocks jutting out from cliffs beside them. "Hurt? Nothing can come close to hurting me now. I know you care, Mel, and I know it's asking a lot for you to go with me today..."

"It's not—"

"It is." Rose's eyes, always so bright and cheery before, were shadowed with a grief and a fear that never ended. "I know you think it's nonsense, and maybe it's even insulting, since you're doing all you can do to find David. But I have to try. I have to try just anything."

Mel kept her silence for a moment, because it shamed her to realize that she *was* insulted. She was trained, she was a professional, and here they were cruising down the coast to see some witch doctor.

But she wasn't the one who had lost a child. She wasn't the one who had to face that empty crib day after day.

"We're going to find David, Rose." Mel took her hand off the rattling gearshift long enough to squeeze Rose's chilled fingers. "I swear it."

Instead of answering, Rose merely nodded and turned her head to stare out over the dizzying cliffs. If they didn't find her baby, and find him soon, it would be all too easy just to step out over one of those cliffs and let go of the world.

He knew they were coming. It had nothing to do with power. He'd taken the phone call from the shaky-voiced, pleading woman himself. And he was still cursing himself for it. Wasn't that why he had an unlisted number? Wasn't that why he had one of those handy machines to answer his calls whenever anyone dug deep enough to unearth that unlisted number?

But he'd answered that call. Because he'd felt he had to. Known he had to. So he knew they were coming, and he'd braced himself to refuse whatever they would ask of him.

Damn it, he was tired. He'd barely gotten back to his home, to his life, after three grueling weeks in Chicago helping the police track down what the press had so cleverly dubbed the South Side Slicer.

And he'd seen things, things he hoped he'd never see again.

Sebastian moved to the window, the wide window that looked out over a rolling expanse of lawn, a colorful rockery, and then a dizzying spill of cliffs dropping down to the deep sea.

He liked the drama of the view, that dangerous drop, the churning water, even the ribbon of road that sliced through the stone to prove man's wiliness, his determination to move on.

Most of all, he liked the distance, the distance that provided him relief from those who would intrude, not only on his space, but also on his thoughts.

But someone had bridged that distance, had already intruded, and he was still wondering what it meant.

He'd had a dream the night before, a dream that he'd been standing here, just here. But there had been a woman on the other side of the glass—a woman he wanted very badly.

But he'd been so tired, so used up, that he hadn't gathered up the force to focus his concentration. And she'd faded away.

Which, at the moment, was just fine with him.

All he really wanted was sleep, a few lazy days to tend his horses, toy with his business, interfere in the lives of his cousins.

He missed his family. It had been too long this time since he'd been to Ireland to see his parents, his aunts and uncles. His cousins were closer, only a few miles down that winding cliff road, but it felt like years rather than weeks, since he'd seen them.

Morgana was getting so round with the child she carried. No, children. He grinned to himself, wondering if she knew there were twins.

Anastasia would know. His gentler cousin knew all there was to know about healing and folk medicines. But Ana would say nothing unless Morgana asked her directly.

He wanted to see them. Now. He even had a hankering to spend some time with his brother-in-law, though he knew Nash was hip-deep in his new screenplay. Sebastian wanted to hop on his bike, rev it up and whoosh up to Monterey and surround himself with family and the familiar. He wanted, at all costs, to avoid the two women who were even now heading up the hill toward him. Coming to him with needs and pleas and hopelessness.

But he wouldn't.

He wasn't an unselfish man, and he never claimed he was. He did, however, understand the responsibilities that went hand in hand with his gift.

You couldn't say yes to everyone. If you did, you'd go quietly mad. There were times when you said yes, then found your way blocked. That was destiny. There were times when you wanted to say no, wanted desperately to say no, for reasons you might not understand. And there were times when what you wanted meant nothing compared to what you were meant to do.

That, too, was destiny.

He was afraid, uncomfortably afraid, that this was one of those times when his desires meant nothing.

He heard the car straining its way up his hill before he saw it. And nearly smiled. Sebastian had built high and built solitary, and the narrow, rutted lane leading up to his home was not welcoming. Even a seer was entitled to some privacy. He spotted the car, a smudge of dull gray, and sighed.

They were here. The quicker he turned them back, the better.

He started out of the bedroom and down the steps, a tall man, nearly six-five in his booted feet, lean of hip and wide of shoulder. His black hair swept dramatically back from his forehead and fell over the collar of his denim shirt, curling a bit there. His face was set in what he hoped were polite but inaccessible lines. The strong, prominent bones gifted to him by his Celtic ancestors jutted against skin made dusky by his love of the sun.

As he walked down, he trailed a hand along the silky wood of the banister. He had a love for texture, as well, the smooth and the rough. The amethyst he wore on one hand winked richly.

By the time the car had chugged its way to the top of the drive and Mel had gotten over her first astonishment at the sight of the eccentric and somehow fluid structure of wood and glass he called home, Sebastian was standing on the porch.

It was as if a child had tossed down a handful of blocks and they had landed, by chance, in a fascinating pattern of ledges that had then fused together. That was what she thought as she stepped out of the car and was assaulted by the scents of flowers, horses and the trailing wind from the sea.

Sebastian's gaze flicked over Mel, and lingered a moment as his eyes narrowed. With the faintest of frowns, he looked away and focused on Rose.

"Mrs. Merrick?"

"Yes. Mr. Donovan." Rose felt a bubble rise to her throat that threatened to boil into a sob. "It's so kind of you to see me."

"I don't know if it's kind or not." He hooked his thumbs in the front pockets of his jeans as he studied them. Rose Merrick wore a plain, painfully neat blue dress that hung a bit on her hips. As if she'd recently lost weight. She'd taken some care with her makeup, but, judging by the way her eyes were shining, it wouldn't last long.

He struggled against sympathy.

The other woman hadn't bothered overmuch with appearances, which made her all the more intriguing. Like Sebastian, she was wearing jeans and boots, both well used. The T-shirt she'd tucked into the waistband of her jeans had probably been a bright red at one time, but was now faded with many washings.

She wore no jewelry, no cosmetics. What she did wear—and Sebastian saw it as clearly as he did the color of her hair and eyes—was attitude. *Bad* attitude.

You're a tough one, aren't you... He scanned for her name and was thudded by a whirl of feeling—a kind of mental static— that told him this one was in as much emotional turmoil as Rose Merrick.

Terrific.

Rose was already moving forward. Sebastian was trying to stand aside, to remain dispassionate, but he knew he was losing. She was fighting those tears, the ones he could feel burning out of her heart.

There was nothing on earth that weakened a man like a courageous woman.

"Mr. Donovan. I won't take up much of your time. I just need..."

Even as her words trailed off, Mel was by her side. The look she shot at Sebastian was anything but friendly. "Are you going to let us come in and sit down, or are we just going to..."

Now she was the one whose words trailed off. It wasn't threatening tears that robbed her of her voice. It was utter shock.

His eyes. It was all she could think for an instant, and indeed she thought it so clearly, so violently, that Sebastian heard the words echo in his own mind.

Ridiculous, she told herself, regaining control. It was a dream. That was all. Some silly dream she was mixing up with reality. It was just that he had the most beautiful eyes. The most uncomfortably beautiful eyes.

He studied her for a moment more, and, though curious, he didn't look beyond her face. She was, even in the harsh sunlight, quite attractive. Perhaps it was the defiance he saw so clearly in her steady green eyes, or the lift of her chin, with its faint and oddly sexy cleft. Attractive, yes, he decided, even if she did wear her hair inches shorter than his own. Even if it did look as though she hacked at it herself with a pair of kitchen shears.

He turned away from her and offered Rose a smile.

"Please, come in," he said, and gave her his hand. He left Mel to follow.

She did, and he might have been amused to see the way she

swaggered up those steps and into the high-ceilinged great room, with its skylights and open balcony. She frowned a bit, wishing she didn't find it so appealing, those warm, honey-toned walls that made the light so soft and sexy. There was a low, wide couch, long as a river, done in a lustrous royal blue. He led Rose to it, over a lake-sized rug of bleeding pastels, while Mel checked out his living quarters.

It was neat as a pin without appearing viciously organized. Modern sculptures of marble, wood and bronze were interspersed with what were surely valuable antiques. Everything was large scale, with the result that, despite its size, the room was cozy.

Here and there, set with apparent casualness on those polished antiques, were clusters of crystals—some large enough to strain a man's back lifting them, others tiny enough to fit in a child's palm. Mel found herself charmed by them, the way they winked and gleamed, shaped like ancient cities, slender wands, smooth globes or rough mountains.

She found Sebastian watching her with a kind of patient amusement, and she shrugged. "Some digs."

His lips curved, joining the humor in his eyes. "Thanks. Have a seat."

The couch might be as long as a river, but she chose a chair across the island of an ornately carved coffee table.

His eyes stayed on Mel another moment, and then he turned to Rose. "Can I get you some coffee, Mrs. Merrick? Something cold?"

"No. No, please don't bother." The kindness was worse, somehow, undermining her desperate control. "I know this is an imposition, Mr. Donovan. I've read about you. And my neighbor, Mrs. Ott, she said how you were so helpful to the police last year when that boy went missing. The runaway."

"Joe Cougar." Sebastian sat beside her. "Yes, he thought he'd give San Francisco a try, and drive his parents crazy. I suppose youth enjoys risks."

"But he was fifteen." Rose's voice broke and pressing her lips together, she shored it up again. "I—I don't mean his parents wouldn't have been frightened, but he was fifteen. My David's only a baby. He was in his playpen." She sent Sebastian a look of desperate pleading. "I only left him for a minute when the phone rang. And he was right by the door, sleeping. It wasn't as if he was out on the street, or left in a car. He was right by the open door, and I was only gone a minute."

"Rose." Though her personal preference was to keep her distance from Sebastian, Mel got up to sit beside her friend. "It's not your fault. Everyone understands that."

"I left him," Rose said flatly. "I left my baby, and now he's gone."

"Mrs. Merrick. Rose. Were you a bad mother?" Sebastian asked the question casually, and saw the horror bloom in Rose's eyes. And the fury light in Mel's.

"No. No. I love David. I only wanted to do my best for him. I only—"

"Then don't do this." He took her hand, and his touch was so gentle, so comforting, that the threatening tears retreated a little. "You're not to blame for this. Trying to make it so you are won't help find David."

Mel's fury fizzled out like a wet firecracker. He'd said exactly the right thing, in exactly the right way.

"Will you help me?" Rose murmured. "The police are trying. And Mel...Mel's doing everything she can, but David's still gone."

Mel, he mused. An interesting name for a long, slim blonde with a chip on her shoulder.

"We're going to get David back." Agitated, Mel sprang up again. "We have leads. They may be slim, but—"

"We?" Sebastian interrupted. He got a quick image—here, then gone—of her with a gun gripped in both hands, her eyes as cold as frozen emeralds. "Are you with the police Miss—?"

"Sutherland. Private." She snapped the words at him. "Aren't you supposed to know things like that?"

"Mel..." Rose said with quiet warning.

"That's all right." He patted Rose's hand. "I can look, or I can ask. With relative strangers, it's more polite to ask than to intrude, don't you think?"

"Right." With what was certainly a snort, Mel dropped into a chair again.

"Your friend's a cynic," Sebastian commented. "Cynicism

can be very valuable, as well as very rude." He started to steel himself to tell Rose he couldn't help. He simply couldn't open himself to the trauma and risk of looking for another lost little boy.

Mel changed everything. Just, he supposed, as she was meant to.

"I don't consider it cynicism to recognize a charlatan masquerading as a samaritan." Her eyes were hot when she leaned forward. "This psychic business is as phony as a ten-dollar magician in a shiny suit pulling rabbits out of his hat."

His brow quirked. It was the only sign of interest or irritation. "Is that so?"

"A scam's a scam, Mr. Donovan. A young child's future is at stake, and I won't have you playing your mumbo-jumbo games to get your name in the papers. I'm sorry, Rose." She stood, almost vibrating with anger. "I care about you, and I care about David. I just can't stand by and watch this guy hose you."

"He's my baby." The tears Rose had been battling spilled over. "I have to know where he is. I have to know if he's all right. If he's scared or happy. He doesn't even have his teddy bear." Rose buried her face in her hands. "He doesn't even have his teddy bear."

Mel cursed herself, cursed her temper, cursed Sebastian Donovan, cursed the world in general. But when she knelt beside Rose, both her hands and voice were gentle.

"I'm sorry. Honey, I'm sorry. I know how scared you are. I'm scared, too. If you want Mr. Donovan to—" she almost choked on the word "to help, then he'll help." She raised her furious, defiant face to Sebastian's. "Won't you?"

"Yes." He nodded slowly, feeling fate take his hands. "I will."

He managed to persuade Rose to drink some water and dry her eyes. While Mel stared grimly out the window, Rose took a small yellow teddy bear out of her bag.

"This is David's. His favorite. And this…" She fumbled with a wallet sized snapshot. "This is his picture. I thought— Mrs. Ott said you might need something."

"It helps." He took the toy and felt a vicious pull in his gut that he recognized as Rose's grief. He would have to go through, and beyond, that. But he didn't look at the photograph. Not yet. "Leave it with me. I'll be in touch." He helped her to her feet. "You have my word. I'll do what I can."

"I don't know how to thank you. For trying. Just knowing you are... Well, it gives me something else to hope for. We, Stan and me, we've got some money saved."

"We'll talk about it later."

"Rose, wait in the car for me," Mel said it quietly, but Sebastian could see that she was feeling anything but quiet. "I'll pass on what information I have to Mr. Donovan. It may help him."

"All right." A smile ghosted around Rose's mouth. "Thank you."

Mel waited until Rose was out of earshot, then turned and fired. "How much do you think you can squeeze out of her for this kind of a con? She's a waitress. Her husband's a mechanic."

He leaned lazily against the doorjamb. "Ms. Sutherland, does it appear I need money?"

She made another derisive sound. "No, you've got just buckets, don't you? It's all just a game for you."

He curled his fingers around her arm with a steely strength that caught her off guard. "It's not a game." His voice was so low, so filled with suppressed violence, that she blinked. "What I have, what I am, is no game. And stealing children from their playpens is no game, either."

"I won't see her hurt again."

"We can agree on that. If you're so against this, why did you bring her?"

"Because she's my friend. Because she asked me to."

He accepted that with a slight nod. Loyalty was something else he could feel pumping out of her. "And my private number? You dug that up, as well?"

Her lip curled in something close to a sneer. "That's my job."

"And are you good at it?"

"Damn right."

"Fine. I'm also good at mine, and we're going to be working together."

"What makes you think—?"

"Because you care. And if there's a chance—oh, even the slimmest chance—that I'm what I claim to be, you won't want to risk ignoring it."

She could feel the heat from his fingers. It seemed to sizzle right through the skin to her bones. It occurred to her that she was afraid. Not physically. It was deeper than that. She was afraid because she'd never felt this kind of power before.

"I work alone."

"So do I," he said calmly. "As a rule. We're going to break the rules." He reached in, quick as a snake. He wanted one thing, one small thing, to rub her nose in. Finding it, he smiled. "I'll be in touch very soon. Mary Ellen."

He had the pleasure of seeing her mouth fall open, of seeing her eyes narrow as she thought back, struggling to remember if Rose had used her full name. But she couldn't remember, couldn't be sure. Shaken, she jerked away.

"Don't waste my time, Donovan. And don't call me that." With a toss of her head, she strode to the car. She might not be psychic, but she knew he was grinning.

Chapter 2

Sebastian didn't go back inside, not even after he had watched the little gray car trail down the ribbon of Highway 1. He stood on the porch, both amused and faintly irritated by the sizzles of anger and frustration Mel had left behind to spark in the air.

Strong-willed, he mused. And just brimming with energy. A woman like that would exhaust a peaceful man. Sebastian considered himself a peaceful man. Not that he wouldn't mind poking at her a bit, the way a young boy pokes at glowing embers to see how often he can get a flame to shoot up.

It was often worth the risk of a few minor burns to make fire.

At the moment, however, he was just too tired to enjoy it. He was already angry with himself for having agreed to become involved. It was the combination of the two women that had done it to him, he thought now. The one with her face so full of fears and desperate hope, the other so vivid with fury and sneering disbelief. He could have handled one or the other, he thought as he descended the steps. But being caught in the middle of all that conflicting emotion, the sheer depth of it, had defeated him.

So he would look. Though he had promised himself a long, quiet break before taking on another case, he would look. And he would pray to whatever god was listening that he could live with what he might see.

But for now, he would take some time—one long, lazy morning—to heal his fatigued mind and ragged soul.

There was a paddock behind the house, attached to a low, gleaming white stable. Even as he approached, he heard the whicker of greeting. The sound was so ordinary, so simple and welcoming that he smiled.

There they were, the sleek black stallion and the proud white mare, standing so still that he thought of two elegantly carved chess pieces, one ebony, one alabaster. Then the mare flicked her tail in a flirtatious gesture and pranced to the fence.

They could leap it, he knew. Both had done so more than once, with him in the saddle. But there was a trust between them, an understanding that the fence was not a cage but a home.

"There's a beauty." Sebastian lifted a hand to stroke her cheek, her long, graceful neck. "Have you been keeping your man in line, Psyche?"

She blew into his hand. In her dark eyes he saw pleasure, and what he liked to think was humor. She whinnied softly when he swung over the fence. Then she stood patiently while he passed his hands over her flanks, down over her swollen belly.

"Only a few more weeks," he murmured. He could almost feel the life inside her, sleeping. Again he thought of Morgana, though he doubted his cousin would care to be compared to a pregnant horse, even as fine an Arabian as Psyche.

"Has Ana been taking good care of you?" He nuzzled against the mare's neck, comforted by her quiet good nature. "Of course she has."

He murmured and stroked for a while, giving her the attention they had both missed while he'd been away. Then he turned and looked at the stallion, who stood alert, his handsome head high.

"And you, Eros, have you been tending to your lady?"

At the sound of his name, the horse reared to paw the air, trumpeting a cry that was rich in power and almost human. The display of pride had Sebastian laughing as he crossed to the stallion.

"You've missed me, you gorgeous beast, admit it or not." Still laughing, Sebastian slapped the gleaming flank and sent Eros dancing around the paddock. On the second trip around,

Sebastian grabbed a handful of mane and swung onto the restless mount, giving them what they both wanted. A fast, reckless ride.

As they soared over the fence, Psyche watched them, her eyes as indulgent—and as superior—as a mother watching little boys wrestling.

Sebastian felt better by the afternoon. The hollowness he'd brought back from Chicago was gradually being filled. But he continued to avoid the little yellow teddy bear sitting lonely on the long, empty sofa. And he had yet to look at the photograph.

In the library, with its coffered ceiling and its walls of books, he sat at a massive mahogany desk and toyed with some paperwork. At any given time, Sebastian might have between five and ten businesses of which he was either sole owner or majority partner. They were hobbies to him—real estate, import-export firms, magazines, a catfish farm in Mississippi that amused him, and his current pet, a minor-league baseball team in Nebraska.

He was shrewd enough to make a healthy profit, wise enough to leave day-to-day management in the hands of experts, and capricious enough to buy and sell on a whim.

He enjoyed what money could give him, and he often used those profits lavishly. But he had grown up with wealth, and amounts of money that would have startled many were hardly more than numbers on paper to him. The simple game of mathematics, the increasing or decreasing, was a never-ending source of entertainment.

He was generous with pet charities, because he believed in them. His donations were a matter not of tax breaks or philanthropy, but of morals.

It would probably have embarrassed him, and it would certainly have irritated him, to be thought of as an unshakably moral man.

He pleased himself until sunset, working, reading, toying with a new spell he hoped to perfect. Magic was his cousin Morgana's speciality. Sebastian could never hope to equal her power there, but his innate competitive streak kept him struggling to try.

Oh, he could make fire—but that was a witch's first and last skill. He could levitate, but that, too, was an elementary talent. Beyond that and a few hat tricks—that was Mel sneaking back into his mind again—he was no magician. His gift was one of sight.

In much the same way that a brilliant actor might yearn to sing and dance, Sebastian yearned to cast spells.

After two hours with little success, he gave up in disgust. He fixed himself an elaborate meal for one, put some Irish ballads on the stereo and uncorked a three-hundred-dollar bottle of wine with the same casualness another man might show in popping open a can of beer.

He indulged in a lengthy whirlpool, his eyes closed, his mind a blessed blank as the water jetted around him. After slipping into a silk pajama bottoms, he pleased himself by watching the sun set in bleeding reds. And then he waited for night to steal across the sky.

It couldn't be put off any longer. With some reluctance, Sebastian went downstairs again. Rather than flick on lights, he lit candles. He didn't need the trappings of the art, but there was comfort in tradition.

There was the scent of sandalwood and vanilla. Because they reminded him of his mother's room at Castle Donovan, they never failed to soothe him. The light was shadowy, inviting power.

For several long moments, he stood by the sofa. With a sigh— very like a laborer might make on hefting a pick—he looked at the photograph of David Merrick.

It was a charming, happy face, one that would have made Sebastian smile if his concentration hadn't been focused. Words gathered in his head, ancient words, secret words. When he was sure, he set the picture aside and lifted the sad-eyed yellow bear.

"All right, David," he murmured, and his voice echoed hollowly through the empty rooms. "Let me see."

It didn't happen with a blaze of light or a flash of understanding. Though it could. It could. He simply drifted. His eyes changed, from smoke to slate to the color of storm clouds. They were fixed, unblinking, beyond the room, beyond the walls, beyond the night.

Images. Images. Forming and melting like wax through his mind. His fingers were gentle on the child's toy, but his body had stiffened like stone. His breathing remained steady, slowing, evening out as it would in sleep.

To begin, he had to fight past the grief and fear that shimmered through the toy. Without losing concentration, he had to slip past the visions of the weeping mother clutching the bear, of a dazed-eyed father holding them both.

Oh, but these were strong, these emotions of sorrow and terror and fury. But strongest of all, as always, was the love.

Even that faded as he skimmed past, going deeper, going back.

He saw, with a child's eyes, and a child's wonder.

A pretty face, Rose's face, leaning over the crib. A smile, soft words, soft hands. Great love. Then another, a man's face, young, simple. Hesitant fingers, rough and callused. Here, too, was love. Slightly different from the mother love, but just as deep. This was tinted with a kind of dazed awe. And... Sebastian's lips curved. And a wish to play catch in a nice backyard.

The images slid, one into the other. Fussy crying at night. Formless fears, soon soothed by strong, caring hands. Nagging hungers sated by warm mother's milk from a willing breast. And pleasures, such delight in colors, in sounds, in the warmth of sunlight.

Health, robust health, in a body straining to grow as a babe's did in that first dazzling year of life.

Then heat, and a surprising, baffling pain. Aching, throbbing in the gums. The comfort of being walked, rocked, sung to.

And another face, soft with a different kind of love. Mary Ellen, making the yellow bear dance in front of his eyes. Laughing, her hands tender and hesitant as she gathered him up, holding him high in the air and pressing tickling kisses to his belly.

From her, a longing, too unformed in her own mind to be seen clearly. All emotion and confusion.

What is it you want? Sebastian wanted to ask her. What is it you're afraid you can't have?

Then she faded away from him like a chalk portrait washed away in a shower of rain.

Sleeping. Dreaming easy dreams, with a slash of sunlight just beyond your fisted hand and the shade cool and soft as a kiss. Peace, utter peace.

When it was broken, there was sleepy irritation. Small, healthy lungs filled to cry, but the sound was cut off by a hand. Unfamiliar hands, unfamiliar smell, and then irritation turned to fear. The face— There was only a glimpse, and Sebastian struggled to freeze that image in his mind for later.

Being carried, held too tightly, and bundled in a car. The car smells of old food and spilled coffee and the sweat of the man.

Sebastian saw it, felt it, as one image stuttered into the next. He lost whole patches as the child's terror and tears exhausted him into sleep.

But he saw. And he knew where to begin.

Morgana opened the shop promptly at ten. Luna, her big white cat, slinked in between her feet, then settled down in the center of the room to groom her tail. Knowing the summer trade, Morgana went directly behind the counter to check the cash register. Her belly bumped gently against the glass, and she chuckled.

She was getting as big as a house. And she loved it. Loved the full, weighted sensation of carrying life. The life she and Nash had created between them.

She remembered how just that morning her husband had pressed kisses to that growing mound, then jerked back, eyes wide, as whoever was sleeping inside kicked.

"Jeez, Morgana, a foot." He'd cupped a hand over the lump, grinning. "I can practically count the toes."

As long as there's five to each foot, she thought now, and she was smiling when her door jingled open.

"Sebastian." Fresh pleasure filled her face as she held out both arms to him. "You're back."

"A couple of days ago." He took her hands, kissed them soundly, then drew back, wiggling his brows as he studied her. "My, my, aren't we huge!"

"Aren't we just?" She patted her belly as she skirted around the counter toward him.

Pregnancy hadn't dimmed her sexuality. If anything, it had enhanced it. She—as they say about brides and expectant mothers—glowed. Her fall of black, curling hair rained down the back of an unapologetically red dress that showed off excellent legs.

"I don't have to ask if you're well," he commented. "I can see that for myself."

"Then I'll ask you. I've already heard you helped clean up Chicago." She said it with a smile, but there was quiet concern in her eyes. "Was it difficult?"

"Yes. But it's done." Before he could say more, before he was certain he wanted to, a trio of customers strolled in to explore the crystals and herbs and statuary. "You're not working here alone?"

"No, Mindy will be here any minute."

"Mindy is here," her assistant announced, bounding into the shop wearing a white catsuit and a flirtatious smile for Sebastian. "Hello, handsome."

"Hi, gorgeous."

Instead of heading out of the shop, or ducking into the back room as was his habit when customers filed in, Sebastian prowled around, fiddling restlessly with crystals, sniffing at candles. Morgana took advantage of the first lull to join him again.

"Looking for some magic?"

He frowned, a smooth, obsidian ball in his hand. "I don't need visual aids."

Morgana tucked her tongue in her cheek. "Having trouble with another spell, darling?"

Though he was very taken with it, Sebastian set the ball down. He'd be damned if he'd give her the satisfaction. "I leave the casting to you."

"Oh, if only you would." She picked up the ball and handed it to him. Morgan knew her cousin too well. "Here, a gift. There's nothing like obsidian for blocking out those bad vibrations."

He let the globe run from palm to fingertips and back. "I suppose, being a shop owner, you'd be up on who's who in town at the moment."

"More or less. Why?"

"What do you know about Sutherland Investigations?"

"Sutherland?" Her brow creased in thought. "It's familiar. What is it, a detective agency?"

"Apparently."

"I think I... Mindy, didn't your boyfriend have some business with Sutherland Investigations?"

Mindy barely glanced up from ringing a sale. "Which boyfriend?"

"The intellectual-looking one, with the hair. Insurance."

"Oh, you mean Gary." Mindy beamed at her customer. "I hope you enjoy it. Please come back. Gary's an *ex*-boyfriend," she added. "Much too possessive. Sutherland does a lot of stuff for the insurance company he works for. Gary says she's as good as they get."

"She?" Morgana glanced back at Sebastian with a cool smile. "Ah."

"There's no 'ah.'" He tweaked her nose. "I've agreed to help someone, and Sutherland is involved."

"Hmm. Is she pretty?"

"No," he said with perfect sincerity.

"Ugly, then."

"No. She's...unusual."

"The very best kind. What are you helping her with?"

"A kidnapping." The teasing light went out of his eyes. "A baby."

"Oh." Automatically she covered her own with her hands. "I'm sorry. The baby... Is the baby... Do you know?"

"He's alive. And well."

"Thank God." Even as she closed her eyes in relief, she remembered. "The baby? Is it the one who was taken from his playpen, from his own backyard, just a couple of months ago?"

"That's right."

She took his hands. "You'll find him, Sebastian. You'll find him soon."

He nodded. "I'm counting on it."

It just so happened that Mel was at that very moment in the process of typing up a bill for Underwriter's Insurance. They had her on a monthly retainer—which kept the wolf from the door—but in the previous few months she had had some additional billable expenses. She also had a fading bruise on her left shoulder where a man supposedly suffering from whiplash and slipped discs had popped her a good one when he'd discovered her taking pictures of him changing a flat tire.

A tire she had herself discreetly deflated.

Bruises aside, it had been a good week's work.

If only everything were so simple.

David. She simply couldn't get David out of her head. She knew better—had been trained better. Personal involvements meant you messed up. Thus far, she'd only proven that rule.

She'd canvassed Rose's neighborhood, questioning people who had already been interviewed by the police. And, like the police, she'd come up with three different descriptions of a car that had been parked half a block from Rose's apartment. She also had four markedly different descriptions of a "suspicious character."

The term made her smile a little. It was so detective-novel. She'd certainly learned that life was much blander than fiction. In reality, investigative work consisted of mountains of paperwork, hours of sitting in a parked car fighting boredom while you waited for something to happen, making phone call after phone call, talking to people who didn't want to talk. Or—often worse—people who talked too much and had nothing to say.

And, occasionally, there was the extra added excitement of being pushed around by a two-hundred-pound gorilla in a neck brace.

Mel wouldn't have traded it for a mountain of gold dust.

But what good was it, she wondered, what good was making a living doing what you loved, and having the talent to do a good job of it, if you couldn't help a friend? There hadn't been so many friends in her life that she could take Rose and Stan for granted. They had given her something just by being there, by sharing David with her. The connection to family that she'd always done without.

She would have walked through fire to bring David back to them.

After tossing the billing aside, she picked up a file that hadn't been off her desk in two months. It was neatly labeled David Merrick, and its contents were miserably thin.

All his vital statistics were there—his height and weight and coloring. She had his footprints and his fingerprints. She knew his blood type and was aware of the tiny dimple on the left side of his mouth.

But the reports didn't say that the dimple deepened so sweetly when he laughed. It couldn't describe the engaging sound of that laughter, or how it felt when he pressed that soft, damp mouth to yours in a kiss. It didn't say how his pretty brown eyes sparkled when you lifted him high over your head to play airplane.

She knew how empty she felt, how sad and frightened. Just as she knew that if she multiplied those emotions by a thousand it wouldn't come close to what Rose was living with every hour of every day.

Mel opened the folder and drew out the formal studio shot of David at six months. It had been taken only a week before the kidnapping. He was grinning at the camera, his pudgy chin creased in a smile as he clutched the yellow bear she had bought for him on the day he'd come home from the hospital. His hair had begun to thicken, and it was the shade of ripening strawberries.

"We're going to find you, baby. We're going to find you and bring you home real soon. I swear it."

She put the picture away again, quickly. She had to, if she was to have any hope of proceeding in a calm and professional manner. Mooning over his picture wouldn't help David, any more than hiring a psychic with a pirate's mouth and spooky eyes would.

Oh, the man irritated her. Irritated her from the top of her head down to the soles of her feet and every possible inch between. That look on his face, that not-quite-a-smirk, not-quite-a-grin set to his mouth made her want to plant her fist there.

And his voice, smooth, with just a whisper of an Irish brogue, set her teeth on edge. There was such cool superiority in it. Except when he'd spoken to Rose, she remembered. Then it had been gentle and kind and unflaggingly patient.

Just setting her up, Mel told herself, and stepped over a pile of phone books to get to the doorway, where a refrigerator held a monstrous supply of soft drinks—all loaded with caffeine. He had just been setting Rose up, offering her hope when he had no right to.

David would be found, but he would be found by logical,

meticulous police work. Not by some crackpot visionary in six-hundred-dollar boots.

She was just taking an angry swig when those boots walked through her door.

She said nothing, just continued to lean in the doorway, the bottle to her lips and her eyes shooting tiny green darts. Sebastian closed the door marked Sutherland Investigations behind him and took a lazy look around.

As offices went, he'd seen worse. And he'd certainly seen better. Her desk was army-surplus gray steel, functional and tough, but far from aesthetically pleasing. Two metal file cabinets were shoved against a wall that would have benefited from a coat of paint. There were two chairs, one in a lurid purple, the other a faded print, on either side of a skinny table that held ancient magazines and was scarred with sundry cigarette burns.

On the wall behind them, as out of place as an elegant woman in a waterfront dive, was a lovely watercolor of Monterey Bay. The room smelled inexplicably like a spring meadow.

He caught a glimpse of the room behind her and saw that it was a tiny and unbelievably disordered kitchen.

He couldn't resist.

Tucking his hands in his pockets, he smiled at her. "Some digs."

She took another drink, then dangled the bottle between two fingers. "Have you got business with me, Donovan?"

"Have you got another bottle of that?"

After a moment, she shrugged, then stepped over the phone books again to snatch one out of the refrigerator. "I don't think you came down off your mountain for a drink."

"But I rarely turn one down." He twisted off the top after she handed him the bottle. He skimmed his gaze over her, taking in the snug jeans and the scarred boots, then moving back up, to the tipped-up chin, with its fascinating little center dip, all the way to the distrustful dark green eyes. "You certainly look fetching this morning, Mary Ellen."

"Don't call me that." Though she'd meant merely to sound firm, the words gritted out between her teeth.

"Such a lovely, old-fashioned name." He tilted his head, baiting her. "Then again, I suppose Mel suits you better."

"What do you want, Donovan?"

The teasing light faded. "To find David Merrick."

She was almost fooled. Almost. The simple statement sounded so sincere, so keenly honest, that she nearly reached out. Snapping herself back, she sat on the corner of her desk and studied him.

"It's just you and me now, pal. So let's cut to the chase. You don't have any stake in this. I humored Rose because I couldn't find a way to talk her out of going to you, and because it gave her some temporary comfort. But I know your kind. Maybe you're too slick for the obvious con. You know the sort—send me twenty bucks and I'll change your life. Let me help you obtain money, power and great sex for only a small monetary contribution."

She gestured with the bottle, then drank again. "You're not the small-change sort. More the beluga and Dom Perignon type. I suppose you get your jollies by going into trances around crime scenes and spouting out clues. Maybe you even hit a few from time to time, so good for you. But you're not going to get your jollies out of Rose and Stan's unhappiness. You're not going to use their little boy as an ego boost."

He was only mildly annoyed. Sebastian assured himself that he didn't give a tinker's dam what this smart-mouthed green-eyed bimbo thought of him. The bottom line was David Merrick.

But his fingers had tightened on the bottle, and his voice, when he spoke, was entirely too soft.

"Have me all figured out, do you, Sutherland?"

"You bet your buns I do." Arrogance came off her in waves as she sat on the corner of the desk. "So let's not waste each other's time. If you feel you're owed something for hearing Rose out yesterday, bill me. I'll see you get what's coming to you."

He said nothing for a moment. It occurred to him that he'd never had the urge to throttle a woman before. Excepting his cousin Morgana. But now he imagined closing his hands around Mel's long, tanned throat. And he imagined very well.

"It's a wonder you don't stagger with that chip on your shoulder." He set the half-empty bottle down. Then, pushing impatiently through the chaos on her desk, he unearthed a pencil and a sheet of paper.

"What're you doing?" she asked when he cleared a small space and began to sketch.

"Drawing you a picture. You seem like the kind who needs visuals."

She frowned. Watching the careless way his hand streaked over the paper, she frowned deeper. She'd always envied and resented people who could draw so effortlessly. She continued to drink, telling herself she wasn't interested. But her gaze continued to be pulled back to the face emerging from the lines and curves he made.

Despite herself, she leaned closer. Somewhere in the back of her mind it registered that he smelled like horses and leather. Sleek, groomed horses, and oiled leather. The deep purple of his amethyst caught her eye. She stared at it, half-hypnotized by the way it glinted in that twist of gold on his little finger.

Artist's hands, she thought dimly. Strong and capable and elegant. She reminded herself they would probably be soft, as well—accustomed to opening champagne or undoing a lady's fancy buttons.

"I often do both at the same time."

"What?" More than a little dazed, she looked up and saw that he had stopped drawing. He was simply standing, closer than she'd realized. And watching.

"Nothing." His lips curved, but he was annoyed with himself for probing. He'd simply been curious as to why she'd been staring at his hands. "Sometimes it's best not to think too loudly." While she was chewing that over, he handed her the sketch. "This is the man who took David."

She wanted to dismiss the drawing, and the artist. But there was something eerily right about it. Saying nothing, she walked behind her desk and opened David's folder. Inside were four police sketches. She chose one, comparing it to Sebastian's work.

His was more detailed, certainly. The witness hadn't noticed that little C-shaped scar under the left eye or the chipped front tooth. The police artist hadn't captured that expression of glittery panic. But, essentially, they were the same man—the shape of the face, the set of the eyes, the springy hair beginning to recede.

So he has a connection on the force, she told herself, trying to settle her jumping nerves. He got hold of a copy of the sketch, then embellished it a bit.

She tossed the sketch down, then settled in her chair. It squeaked rustily when she leaned back. "Why this one?"

"Because that's the one I saw. He was driving a brown Mercury. An '83 or '84. Beige interior. The back seat's ripped on the left side. He likes country music. At least that's what he had playing on the car radio when he drove off with the child. East," he murmured, and his eyes sharpened to a knife edge for just a heartbeat. "Southeast."

One of the witnesses had reported a brown car. Nondescript but unfamiliar, parked near Rose's apartment. Several days running, he'd said.

And Sebastian could have gotten that information from the police, as well, Mel reminded herself. She'd called his bluff, and he was just pushing buttons.

But if he wasn't…if there was the slightest chance…

"A face and a car." She tried to sound disinterested, but the faintest of tremors in her voice betrayed her. "No name, address and serial number?"

"You're a tough sell, Sutherland." It would be easy to dislike her, he thought, if he couldn't see—feel—how desperately she cared.

What the hell. He'd dislike her on principle.

"A child's life is at stake."

"He's safe," Sebastian said. "Safe and well cared for. A little confused, and he cries more than he did. But no one's hurt him."

She felt the breath clog up in her lungs. She wanted to believe that—that much, if nothing more.

"You're not going to talk to Rose about this," she said steadily. "It'll drive her crazy."

Ignoring her, Sebastian went on. "The man who took him was afraid. You could smell it. He took him to a woman somewhere… East." It would come. "And she dressed him in Oshkosh overalls and a red striped shirt. He was in a car seat and had a ring of plastic keys to play with. They drove most of the day, then stopped at a motel. It had a dinosaur out front. She fed him, bathed him, and when he cried she walked him until he fell asleep."

"Where?" she asked.

"Utah." He frowned a little. "Arizona, maybe, but probably Utah. The next day they drove, still southeast. She's not afraid. It's just business. They go to a mall—someplace in Texas. East Texas. It's crowded. She sits on a bench. A man sits beside her. He leaves an envelope on the bench and pushes David away in his stroller.

"The same routine the following day. David's tired of traveling and bewildered by all the strange faces. He wants home. He's taken to a house. A big stone house with old, leafy trees in the yard. South. It feels like Georgia. He's given to a woman who holds him and cries a little, and a man who holds them both. He has a room there, with blue sailboats on the wall and a mobile over the crib of circus animals. They call him Eric now."

Mel was very pale when she managed to speak. "I don't believe you."

"No, but there's a part of you that wonders if you should. Forget what you think of me, Mel. Think of David."

"I am thinking of David." She sprang to her feet, the sketch clutched in her hand. "Give me a name, then. Give me a damn name."

"Do you think it works like that?" he tossed back. "Demand and answer? It's an art, not a pop quiz."

She let the sketch float back to the desk. "Right."

"Listen to me." He slapped his hands down on the desk, hard enough to make her jolt in reaction. "I've been in Chicago for three weeks, watching some monster slice people to ribbons in my head. Feeling his glee while he did it. Using up everything I am, everything I have, to find him before he could do it again. If I'm not working fast enough to suit you on this, Sutherland, that's too damn bad."

She backed off. Not because she was afraid of this sudden burst of temper. Because she saw something in his face, some trace of his weary horror at what he'd been through.

"Okay." She took a deep breath. "Here are the facts. I don't believe in psychics or witches or things that go bump in the night."

He had to smile. "You'll have to meet my family sometime."

"But," she continued, as if he hadn't spoken, "I'll use anything, any resource. Hell, we can use a Ouija board if it'll help get David back." She picked up the sketch again. "I've got a face. I'll start with that."

"*We'll* start with that."

Before she could come up with a suitable response, the phone rang. "Sutherland Investigations. Yeah, it's Mel. What's going down, Rico?"

Sebastian watched her attention sharpen, saw a slight smile tug at her lips. Why, she is pretty, he realized with a kind of annoyed surprise.

"Hey, babe, you can trust me." She began to write on a pad in messy, hurried scribbles. "Yeah, I know where it is. Isn't that dandy?" She listened again, nodding to herself and muttering now and then. "Come on, come on, I know the drill. I never heard of you, never saw that pretty face of yours. I'll leave your fee at O'Riley's." She paused and laughed. "In your dreams, baby."

When she hung up, Sebastian could feel the excitement shooting off her in sparks. "Take a walk, Donovan. I've got to go to work."

"I'll go with you." It was said on impulse, and almost immediately regretted. He would have taken it back if her reaction had been less scathing. She laughed again.

"Listen, pal, this isn't amateur hour. I don't need the extra baggage."

"We're going to be working together—for a hopefully brief duration. I know what I can handle, Sutherland. I haven't got a clue about you. I'd like to see you in action."

"You want action?" She nodded slowly. "All right, hotshot. Wait here. I've got to change first."

Chapter 3

She'd changed, all right, Sebastian thought less than ten minutes later. The woman who walked in from the back room in a pumpkin-colored leather skirt the length of a place mat was a sharp left turn away from the one who'd walked out.

Those legs were, well, just short of miraculous.

She'd done something to her face, as well. Her eyes seemed huge and heavy. Slumberous, he supposed was the word. Her mouth was dark and slick. She'd fluffed and fiddled with her hair. Now, rather than looking careless, it was tousled in a way that suggested she'd just gotten out of bed—and would be more than willing to tumble back in.

Two glittery gold balls hung from her ears, nearly touching the shoulders of a snug black tank top. Snug enough, Sebastian thought, to make any man not currently in a coma realize there was nothing beneath it but woman.

SEX! The word steamed into his mind in big, bold letters. This was wild, uninhibited and casually available sex.

He was certain he was about to make some snide comment, or perhaps say something rudely suggestive. But that wasn't what came out of his mouth.

"Where in the name of Finn do you think you're going dressed like that?"

Mel cocked one penciled eyebrow. "In the name of who?"

He made a dismissive gesture and tried to keep his eyes off

her legs. Whatever fragrance she'd dumped all over herself made his tongue want to hang out. "You look like a—"

"Yeah." Pleased, she grinned and turned in a saucy circle. "It's my floozy look. Works like a charm. Most guys don't care if you're pretty or not if you show enough skin and cover the rest with something tight."

He shook his head. He didn't want to try to decipher that. "Why are you dressed like that?"

"Tools of the trade, Donovan." She shifted the oversize purse on her shoulder. Inside it, she carried another tool of the trade. "If you're going with me, let's hit it. I'll fill you in on the way."

It wasn't excitement he felt from her now. That she had banked. As she climbed into her car—and Lord, her skirt slithered up another inch—he caught bolts of anticipation, quicksilver streaks of fun. The kind Sebastian imagined another kind of woman might feel embarking on a shopping spree.

But Mel wasn't like any kind of woman he'd ever before encountered.

"Okay," she said as he settled into the passenger seat. "Here's the deal."

She shot away from the curb, and her driving was as quick and competent as her explanation.

There had been a rash of local robberies over the past six weeks. All electronics—televisions, VCRs, stereo equipment. A good many of the victims had been insured by Underwriter's. The police had a few leads, but nothing solid. And since no single home had been hit for more than a few hundred at a shot, it wasn't exactly number one on their hit list.

"Underwriter's is your average happy insurance company," she commented as she winked through an amber light. "Which means they really hate to pay claims. So I've been working on it for the last few weeks."

"Your car needs a tune-up," Sebastian told her when the engine made a gagging sound.

"Yeah. Anyway, I did some poking around, and what do you know? Turns out there's a couple of guys selling TVs and such out of the back of a van. Oh, not around here. They bop over to Salinas or down to Soledad."

"How did you find out?"

She shot him a mild smile. "Legwork, Donovan. Miles and miles of legwork."

Despite his better judgment, his gaze dropped down to those long, tanned thighs. "I'll bet."

"So I've got this snitch. He's had a few unfortunate run-ins with the cops, and he's a little leery. But he kind of took to me. Because I'm private, I guess."

Sebastian coughed, cleared his throat. "Oh, yeah. I'm sure that's it."

"He's got connections," she went on. "Seeing as he did some time for B and E—breaking and entering," she explained. "And some petty larceny."

"You have fascinating friends."

"It's a good life," she said, with a laugh in her voice. "He passes me some information, I pass him a few bills. Mostly it keeps him from picking locks. He hangs down at the docks. Strictly nontourist areas. There's a bar down there where he happened to be tossing back a few last night. Got chummy with this guy who was already soused. My friend likes a drink better if somebody else is paying for it. They got intimate in that happy way drunks do, and he finds out this guy's flush because he just hauled a load of electronic entertainment down to King City. Now, because they're the best of friends, he takes my snitch around the back of the bar to this dump of a warehouse. And what do you suppose is inside?"

"Previously owned electronics at a discount price."

Amused, she chuckled. "You catch on, Donovan."

"So why don't you just call the cops?"

"Hey, these guys might not be the James Gang, but it's a pretty good bust." Her lips were curved as she downshifted. "My bust."

"I suppose it's occurred to you that they might be... uncooperative."

When she smiled again, something hot and beautiful leapt into her eyes. "Don't worry, Donovan. I'll protect you. Now, here's what I want you to do."

When they pulled up in front of the bar a few minutes later, Sebastian had the game plan. He didn't like it, but he had it. A fastidious man, he looked dubiously at the low-slung, windowless establishment.

Seedy, he thought, but supposed that a good many bars looked seedy in the light of day. He had a feeling this one would look equally seedy in the dead of night.

It was built of cinder blocks that some enterprising soul had painted green. The paint, a particularly hideous shade, was peeling badly and showed the gray beneath, the way an old, peeling scab shows the pasty skin underneath.

It was barely noon, but there were nearly a dozen cars in the gravel lot.

Mel dropped her keys in her purse while she frowned at Sebastian. "Try to look less..."

"Human?" he suggested.

Elegant was the word she'd had in mind, but she'd be damned if she'd use it. "Less *Gentleman's Quarterly*. And for God's sake don't order any white wine."

"I'll restrain myself."

"Just follow the bouncing ball, Donovan, and you'll do fine."

What he followed were her swaying hips, and he wasn't sure he'd do fine at all.

The smell of the place assaulted him the moment Mel pulled open the door. Stale smoke, stale beer, stale sweat. There was a rumbling sound from the jukebox, and, though Sebastian had very eclectic tastes in music, he hoped he wouldn't be subjected to that surly sound for long.

Men were lined up at the bar—the kind of men with burly forearms littered with tattoos. This particular artwork ran heavily in favor of snakes and skulls. There was a clatter as four oily-looking characters shot nine ball. Some glanced up, their gazes sliding over Sebastian with a kind of smirking derision and lingering on Mel, longer and with more affection.

He picked up on scattered thoughts—easy enough, since the average IQ of the patrons hovered below three digits. His lips twitched once. He hadn't realized there were so many ways to describe a...lady.

The lady in question, one of three currently enjoying the atmosphere, sauntered up to the bar and wiggled her leather-clad bottom onto a stool. That wide, slicked mouth was pursed in a sexy pout. "Least you can do is buy me a beer," she said to Sebastian in a breathy little voice that caught him off guard. Her eyes narrowed briefly in warning, and he remembered his cue.

"Listen, sweetcakes, I told you it wasn't my fault."

Sweetcakes? Mel stopped herself from rolling her eyes. "Sure, nothing is. You get canned, it's not your fault. You lose a hundred bucks playing poker with your slimy friends, it's not your fault. Give me a beer, will you?" she called to the bartender, and crossed those long, lovely legs.

Trying to hulk a bit, Sebastian held up two fingers, then slid onto the stool beside her. "I told you... Didn't I tell you that creep had it in for me at work? And why don't you get off my back?"

"Oh, sure." She sniffed as the beers were slapped down in front of them. When Sebastian reached for his back pocket, it occurred to her that his wallet was probably worth more than the combined liquid assets of the bar's patrons. And that it was likely filled with plenty of the green stuff, along with a few flashy gold credit cards.

She hissed at him.

He understood instantly, and that would give her some food for thought later. His hand hesitated, then dropped away.

"Tapped out again?" she said, a sneer in her voice. "Isn't that just swell?" With obvious reluctance, she dug into her bag and unearthed two ragged dollar bills. "You're such a loser, Harry."

Harry? Sebastian's frown was entirely authentic. "I'll have some coming in. I got ten on the game."

"Oh, sure, sure. You'll be rolling in it." She gave him her back and, sipping at the mug of beer, scanned the room.

She had Rico's description. It took her less than two minutes to zero in on the man Rico's pal had called Eddie. Eddie was a real fun guy, according to Rico's drinking partner. He was the day man, the one who doled the merchandise out for transport and sale. And, according to Rico, he had a real soft spot for the ladies.

Mel swung her leg in time with the music and made sure she caught Eddie's eye. She smiled, fluttered, and sent out conflicting signals.

To Eddie her smile said: Hey there, big guy. I've been looking for someone just like you all my life.

To Sebastian, who had tuned in to her just enough to keep her from surprising him, it was: Fat, hairless jerk.

He turned and took a look for himself. Hairless, true, Sebastian thought. But it wasn't all fat stuffed into that sleeveless T-shirt. There was plenty of muscle mixed in.

"Listen, honey." Sebastian put a hand on Mel's shoulder and had it shrugged off.

"I'm tired of excuses, Harry. Sick and damn tired. They're all just a crock. You got no money. You lose all of mine. You can't even put fifty together to get the TV fixed. And you know how much I like my shows."

"You watch the tube too much, anyway."

"Oh, fine." She was fired up now, and she swung around to face him. "I work my butt off waiting tables half the night, and you give me grief because I like to sit down, put my feet up and watch a little TV. It don't cost nothing to watch."

"It's going to cost fifty bucks."

She shoved him, sliding off the stool as she did. "You just lost twice that in a damn card game, and some of it was mine."

"I said get off my back." He was getting into it now, almost enjoying it. Maybe it was because he remembered he'd been instructed to push her around a little. "Whine and bitch, that's all you do." He grabbed her, trying to make a good show of it. Her head fell back and her eyes were bright with defiance. That...sexy? Oh, yes, very sexy—mouth moved into a pout, and he had to struggle to stay in character.

She saw something in his eyes, very briefly, very powerfully. Mel's heart tripped right up to her throat and beat there like a big brass drum.

"I don't have to take this crap from you." He gave her a good shake, as much to settle himself as for effect. "If you don't like the way things are, you can try the door."

"You better take your hands off me." She made her voice tremble. It was embarrassing, but necessary. "I told you what would happen if you ever hit me again."

Hit her? Good Lord! "Just get your butt outside, Crystal." He started to push her toward the door and found his face pressed against a beefy chest covered in a sweaty T-shirt that announced that its owner was A Hard Driving Man.

"The little lady wants hands off, jerkface."

Sebastian looked up into Eddie's wide smile. Mel was sniffling beside him, really laying it on. Hoping for more even ground, Sebastian rose from the stool so that he and the knight errant were eye-to-eye.

"Mind your own business."

Eddie knocked him back on the stool with one blow. Sebastian was certain he was going to feel the imprint of the heel of that sledgehammer hand on his chest for years to come.

"You want I should take him out and mess him up, sweetheart?"

Mel dried her lashes and seemed to consider it. She hesitated just long enough to make Sebastian sweat. "No." She laid a trembling hand on Eddie's arm. "He ain't worth it." Fluttering, she turned her admiring face up to his. "You're awfully nice. There's hardly any gentlemen left in this world a girl can count on."

"Why don't you come on and sit down at my table?" He put a tree-trunk arm around her waist. "I'll buy you a drink and you can take a load off."

"That's real sweet."

She sauntered off with him. Wanting to put on a good show, Sebastian made as if to follow them. One of the contestants at the pool table grinned and slapped a cue on his palm. Suitably warned, Sebastian skulked down to the end of the bar and nursed his beer.

She made him wait an hour and a half. He couldn't even order a second beer without breaking his cover and was enduring nasty looks from the bartender as he nibbled on peanuts and made the last half inch of his drink last forever.

He'd just about had it. His idea of a good time was not sitting in a smelly bar watching some sumo wrestler paw the woman he'd come with. Even if he didn't have any emotional investment. And even, he thought darkly, if that woman giggled with every appearance of enjoyment every time one of those ham-sized hands rubbed her leg.

It would serve her right if he just strolled out, caught himself a cab and left her to it.

In Mel's opinion, everything was going just fine. Fine and dandy. Sir Eddie, as she called him—much to his delight—was getting slowly and steadily drunk. Not pie-eyed, just nice and vulnerable. And he was doing plenty of talking. Men just loved to brag to an eager woman—especially when they were juiced.

He'd just come into a nice chunk of change, so Eddie said. And maybe she'd like to help him spend a little of it.

She'd love to. Of course, she had to get to work in a couple of hours, and she didn't finish her shift until one, but after that...

When she had him softened up, she gave him a sob story. How she and Harry had been together for almost six whole months. How he ran through money like water and kept her from having a good time. She didn't ask for much. Just some pretty clothes and a few laughs. And now it was really bad, just plain awful, because her TV had broken down. Here she'd been saving up for a VCR so she could tape shows while she worked, and now the TV was on the fritz. Worse, Harry had blown his money and hers on cards, so now she didn't even have the fifty to fix the set.

"I really like to watch, you know?" She toyed with her second beer. Eddie was working on number seven. "In the afternoon they got these shows, and all the women have these pretty clothes. Then they switch me to the day shift and I miss out. I can never catch up with what's happening. And you know..." She leaned forward, confidentially, so that her breasts rubbed against his forearm. "Tney got these love scenes on them. Watching them just gets me so...hot."

Eddie watched her tongue peek out and run around her lips. He plainly thought he'd died and gone to heaven. "I guess it's not much fun watching something like that all alone."

"Be more fun with somebody." She gave him a look that told him he was the only possible somebody. "If I had a set that worked, it might be nice. I like daytime, you know. When everybody else is working or shopping, and you can be...in bed." Sighing, she ran her fingertip around her mug.

"It's daytime now."

"Yeah. But I haven't got a TV." She giggled, as if it were a great joke.

"I might be able to help you with that, baby."

She let her eyes widen, then brought her lashes coyly down. "Aw, gee, that's really sweet of you, Eddie. I couldn't let you give me the fifty. It wouldn't be right."

"What do you want to toss money at an old set for, anyway? You can have a new one."

"Oh, yeah." She snorted into her beer. "And I could have me a diamond tiara, too."

"Can't help you on that, but I can get you a set."

"Come on." She shot him a disbelieving look and let her hand rest on his knee. "How?"

He puffed out his massive chest. "Just so happens, I'm in the business."

"You sell TVs?" She cocked her head and had her eyes blinking in fascination. "You're pulling my leg."

"Not now." He winked. "Maybe later."

Mel laughed heartily. "Oh, you're a card, Sir Eddie." She drank again, sighed again. "I wish you weren't fooling. If you could get me one, I'd be awfully grateful."

He leaned closer. She could smell the beer and smoke on his breath. "How grateful?"

Mel wiggled toward him, put her mouth to his ear and whispered a suggestion that would have made the worldly Sebastian stutter.

Short of breath, Eddie finished off his beer in one gulp and grabbed her hand. "Come on, sweet thing. I got something to show you."

Mel went along, not bothering to glance in Sebastian's direction. She sincerely hoped that what Eddie was about to show her was a television.

"Where're we going?" she asked as he led her to the back of the building.

"My office, babe." A sly wink. "Me and my partners got a little business back here."

He took her over a rubble of broken bottles, trash and piles of gravel to another concrete building, perhaps half the size of the bar. After three raps on the door, it was opened by a skinny man of about twenty wearing horn-rims and carrying a clipboard.

"What's the deal, Eddie?"

"The lady needs a TV." He swung his arm over Mel's shoulder and squeezed. "Crystal, honey, this is Bobby."

"'Meetcha," Bobby said with a bounce of his head. "Look, Eddie, I don't think this is a good idea. Frank's going to be mad as hell."

"Hey, I got as much right as Frank." Eddie bulled his way in.

Ah, Mel thought, and sighed. For real.

The fluorescent bulbs overhead shone down on the blank single eyes of more than a dozen televisions. They sat cheek by jowl with CD players, VCRs, stereo systems. Tossed in for good measure were several boom boxes, personal computers, telephone answering machines, and one lonely microwave oven.

"Wow!" She clapped her hands together. "Oh, wow, Eddie! Look at all this! It's like a regular department store."

Full of confidence, and swaying only a little, Eddie winked at the nervous Bobby. "We're what you call suppliers. We don't do any retail out of here. This is just like our warehouse. Go ahead, look around."

Still playing her role, Mel walked over to the televisions, running her hands over their screens as if her fingers were walking in mink.

"Frank's not going to like this," Bobby hissed.

"So what he don't know he don't have to not like. Right, Bobby?"

Bobby, who was outweighed by a hundred pounds, nodded. "Sure, Eddie. But bringing a broad in here—"

"She's okay. Great legs, but not much brains. I'm going to give her a set—and then I'm going to get lucky." He moved past Eddie to join Mel. "See one you like, baby?"

"Oh, they're great. Really great. Do you mean I can really have one? Just pick one out and have it?"

"Why, sure." He gave her a quick, intimate squeeze. "We got this breakage insurance. So I'll just have old Bobby there put down like one got busted. That's all there is to it."

"Really?" She tossed her head, moving just far enough out

of reach that she could easily slip a hand into her bag. "That's great, Eddie. But it looks to me like you're the one who's busted."

She pulled out a nickel-plated .38.

"A cop!" Bobby nearly screeched the words, while Eddie's face settled into a thoughtful frown. "Jeez, Eddie, she's a cop!"

"There you go. Don't," she warned as Bobby edged to the door. "Just have a seat, Bobby. On the floor there. And sit on your hands, will you?"

"You bitch," Eddie said, in a considering voice that put Mel on guard. "I should've smelled cop."

"I'm private," she told him. "That might be the reason." She gestured with the gun. "Let's take it outside, Eddie."

"No woman's going to double-cross me—gun or no gun."

He lunged.

She didn't want to shoot him. She really didn't. He wasn't anything more than a fat, second-rate thief, and he didn't deserve a bullet. Instead, she twisted, veering left and counting on her speed and agility and his beer-induced sluggishness.

He missed and rammed headlong into a twenty-five inch screen. Mel wasn't sure who was the victor, but the screen cracked like an egg, and Eddie went down hard.

There was a sound behind her. When she whirled she had time to see Sebastian wrap an arm around Bobby's throat. One quick squeeze had him dropping the hammer he'd been lifting over Mel's head.

"It probably wouldn't have made a dent," Sebastian said between his teeth as Bobby crumpled bonelessly to the concrete floor. "You didn't tell me you had a gun."

"I didn't think I had to. You're supposed to be psychic."

Sebastian picked up the hammer, tapping it gently against his palm. "Keep it up, Sutherland."

She merely shrugged and took another look at the loot. "Nice haul. Why don't you go call the cops? I'll keep an eye on these two."

"Fine." He was sure it was too much to expect her to thank him for saving her from a concussion, or worse. The best he could do was slam the door behind him.

* * *

It was nearly an hour later when Sebastian stood by and watched Mel sitting on the hood of her car. She was going over the fine details with what appeared to be a very disgruntled detective.

Haverman, Sebastian remembered. He'd run into him once or twice.

Then he dismissed the cop and concentrated on Mel.

She'd pulled off the earrings and was still rubbing her lobes from time to time. Most of the goo on her face had been wiped off with tissue. Her unpainted mouth and naturally flushed cheeks made a devastating contrast with the big, heavy-lidded eyes.

Pretty? Had he granted her pretty? Sebastian wondered. Hell, she was gorgeous. In the right light, at the right angle, she was drop-dead gorgeous. Then she might turn and be merely mildly attractive again.

That held an odd and disturbing sort of magic.

But he didn't care how she looked, he reminded himself. He didn't care, because he was plenty peeved. She'd dragged him into this. It didn't matter that he'd volunteered to come along. Once he had, she'd set the rules, and he'd had plenty of time to decide he didn't like them.

She'd gone alone into that storage building with a man built like two fullbacks. And she'd had a gun. No little peashooter, either, but a regular cannon.

What the hell would she have done if she'd had to use it? Or—Lord—if that mountain of betrayed lust had gotten it away from her?

"Look," Mel was saying to Haverman. "You've got your sources, I've got mine. I got a tip. I followed it up." She was moving her shoulders carelessly, but, oh, she was enjoying this. "You've got no beef with me, Lieutenant."

"I want to know who put you on to this, Sutherland." It was a matter of principle for him. He was a cop, after all, a *real* cop. Not only was she a PI, she was a female PI. It just plain grated on him.

"And I don't have to tell you." Then her lips quirked, because the idea was so beautiful, so inspired. "But, since we're pals, I'll clue you in." She jerked her thumb toward Sebastian. "He did."

"Sutherland..." Sebastian began.

"Come on, Donovan, what does it hurt?" This time she smiled and brought him in on the joke. "This is Lieutenant Haverman."

"We've met."

"Sure." Now Haverman was not only piqued but deflated. Women PIs and psychics. What was law enforcement coming to? "I didn't think missing TVs was your gig."

"A vision's a vision," Sebastian said complacently, and had Mel hooting.

"So how come you passed it to her?" It didn't sit right with him. "You always come to the cops."

"Yeah." Sebastian shot a glittering look at Mel over his shoulder. "But she's got better legs."

Mel laughed so hard she nearly fell off the car. Haverman grumbled a little more and then stalked off. After all, he thought, he had two suspects in hand—and if he tried to shake Donovan, he'd have the chief on his case.

"Good going, slick." Still chuckling, Mel gave Sebastian a friendly bop on the shoulder. "I didn't think you had it in you."

He merely lifted a brow. "There are a great many things you might be surprised I have in me."

"Yeah, right." She twisted her head to watch Haverman climb in his car. "The lieutenant's not such a bad guy. He just figures PIs belong in the pages of a book, and women belong one step away from the oven." Because the sun was warm and the deed had been done well, she was content to sit on the car for few minutes and enjoy the small triumph. "You did good... Harry."

"Thanks, Crystal," he said, and tried not to let his lips twitch into a smile. "Now, I'd appreciate it if next time you filled me in on the entire plan before we start."

"Oh, I don't think there's a next time coming soon. But this was fun."

"Fun." He said the word slowly, understanding that that was precisely what she meant. "You really enjoyed it. Dressing up like a tart, making a scene, having that muscle-bound throwback drool on you.''

She offered a bland smile. "I'm entitled to some on-the-job benefits, aren't I?"

"And it was fun, I suppose, to nearly have your head cracked open?"

"Nearly's the key." Feeling more kindly toward him, she patted his arm. "Come on, Donovan, loosen up. I said you did good."

"That, I take it, is your way of thanking me for saving your thick skull."

"Hey, I could've handled Bobby fine, but I appreciate the backup. Okay?"

"No." He slapped his hands down on the hood on either side of her hips. "It is not okay. If this is a taste of how you do business, you and I are going to set some rules."

"I've got rules. My rules." His eyes were the color of smoke now, she thought. Not the kind that had hung listlessly at the ceiling of the bar, but the sort that plumes up into the night from a crackling good bonfire. "Now back off, Donovan."

Make me. He hated—no, detested—the fact that the childish, taunting phrase was the first thing to pop into his head. He wasn't a child. And neither was she—sitting there, daring him with that insolent lift to her chin and that half smirk on her beautiful mouth.

His right hand fisted. It was tempting to give her one good pop on that damnably arrogant chin. But her mouth seemed a better notion. And he had a much more satisfying idea about what could be done with it.

He snatched her off the hood of the car so quickly that she didn't think to use any of the defensive countermoves that were second nature to her. She was still blinking when his arms came around her, when one hand cupped firmly on the back of her head, fingers spread.

"What the hell do you think—?"

That was it. The words clicked off as completely as her brain the moment his mouth clamped over hers. She didn't break away or shift her body to one side to toss him over her shoulder. She didn't bring her knee up in a way that would have had him dropping to his and gasping. She simply stood there and let his lips grind her mind to mush.

He was sorry she'd pushed him beyond his own rules. Grabbing unwilling women was not on Sebastian's list of things to do. And he was sorry—desperately sorry, because she didn't taste the way he'd been certain she would. A woman with a personality like Mel's should have had a vinegary flavor. She should have tasted prickly and tart.

Oh, but she was sweet.

It wasn't sugar he thought of, or the kind of gooey candy that came wrapped in gold foil. It was honey, rich, thick, wild honey that you were compelled to lick off your finger. The kind that, even as a child, he'd never been able to resist.

When her lips opened for his, he dived in. Wanting more.

His hands weren't soft. That was the first wayward thought that stumbled into her brain. They were hard and strong and just a little rough. She could feel those fingers pressed against the back of her neck. The skin there seemed to be on fire.

He pulled her closer, so that their bodies made one long shadow on the littered gravel. As sensations swarmed through her system, she threw her arms around him and gave him back desire for desire.

It was different now. She thought she heard him curse before he changed the angle of the kiss, his teeth scraping over her lips and nearly making her cry out from the bolt of pleasure. Her heart was beating in her head, echoing in her ears like a train picking up speed in a tunnel.

It would break through any moment, break out of the dark and into the light, and then she would—

"Hey!"

The shout didn't even register. The movement of Sebastian's lips on hers did, a movement that was at first her name, and then another oath.

"Hey!"

Sebastian heard the shout, and the crunch of footsteps on gravel. He could cheerfully have committed murder. He kept one arm around Mel's waist and his hand firm on her neck as he turned his head and stared into a grizzled face under a Dodgers baseball cap.

"Go away." The order was close to a snarl. "Go very far away."

"Listen, bud, I just wanna know how come the bar's closed."

"They ran out of vodka." He could already feel Mel retreating from him, and would have sworn again if it would have done any good.

"Well, hell, all I want's a lousy beer." Having successfully destroyed the mood, the Dodgers fan clumped back to his pickup and drove off.

Mel had crossed her arms over her breasts and was cupping her elbows as if she were warding off a brisk wind.

"Mary Ellen…" Sebastian began.

"Don't call me that." Staggered, she jerked back and came up hard against her car.

Her lips were vibrating. She wanted to press her hand against them to make it stop, but she didn't dare. Her pulse was beating in her throat in a quick, jumpy rhythm. She wanted that to stop, too, to slow and even out until it was normal and as it should be.

God. Good God. She'd been all over him, practically climbing on him. Letting him touch her.

He wasn't touching her now, but he looked like he might. Pride prevented her from shifting away, but she braced, ready to block another assault on her senses.

"Why did you do that?"

He resisted the urge to dip in and see what she was really feeling, to compare it to what was going on inside him. But he'd already taken unfair advantage. "I haven't the vaguest idea."

"Well, don't get any more ideas." She was surprised that his answer hurt. What had she expected? she asked herself. Did she think he might have said he'd been unable to resist her? That he'd been overwhelmed with passion? She lifted her chin.

"I can handle being pawed on the job, but not on my own time. Clear?"

His eyes flashed—once. Then, with more restraint than she could have imagined, he lifted his hands, palms out. "Clear," he repeated. "Hands off."

"All right, then." She wasn't going to make a big deal out of it, she decided as she dug in her bag for her keys. It was over. And it hadn't meant a thing to either of them. "I've got to get back, make some calls." When he took a step forward, her head snapped up, as if she were a deer scenting a wolf.

"I'm just opening your door," Sebastian said, though he discovered he wasn't the least bit displeased by her reaction.

"Thanks." She climbed in and slammed it herself. She had to clear her throat to be certain her voice would be careless. "Climb aboard, Donovan. I've got places to go."

"Question," he said after he slipped in beside her. "Do you eat?"

"Mostly when I'm hungry. Why?"

There was a wariness in her eyes that he was enjoying a great deal. "Seeing as all I've had since this morning was bar nuts, I was thinking late lunch, early dinner. Why don't you stop off somewhere? I'll buy you a burger."

She frowned over that for a moment, poking the suggestion for pitfalls. "I could use a burger," she decided. "But we'll go dutch."

He smiled and settled back his seat. "Whatever you say, Sutherland."

Chapter 4

Mel spent most of the morning doing door-to-doors in Rose's neighborhood with Sebastian's sketch in her hand. By that afternoon, the score was three positive IDs, four offers of coffee and one lewd proposition.

One of the positive IDs also corroborated Sebastian's description of the car, right down to the dented door. And that gave Mel a very uncomfortable feeling.

It didn't stop her from backtracking. There was a name on her list that continued to nag at her. Mel had a hunch Mrs. O'Dell in apartment 317 knew more than she was saying.

For the second time that day Mel knocked on the dull brown door, wiped her feet on the grass-green welcome mat with the white daisy in the corner. From inside she could hear the whining of children and the bright applause of a television game show.

As it had before, the door opened a few inches, and Mel looked down into the chocolate-smeared face of a young boy. "Hi. Is your mom home?"

"She don't let me say to strangers."

"Right. Maybe you could go get her."

Bumping a sneakered foot against the doorjamb, the boy seemed to consider. "If I had a gun, I could shoot you."

"Then it looks like this is my lucky day." She crouched down until they were eye-to-eye. "Chocolate pudding, right?" she said, studying the smears around his mouth. "Did you get that from licking the spoon after your mom made it?"

"Yeah." He shifted his feet and began to eye her with more interest. "How'd you know that?"

"Elementary, my dear puddingface. The smears are pretty fresh, and it's too close to lunch for your mom to let you have a whole bowl."

The boy tilted his head. "Maybe I snuck it."

"Maybe," Mel agreed. "But then you'd be pretty dumb not to wash off the evidence."

He started to grin when his mother swooped down from behind. "Billy! Didn't I tell you not to answer the door?" She hauled him back one-handed. The other arm was full of a wiggling girl with teary eyes. Mrs. O'Dell sent Mel one impatient look. "What are you doing back around here? I told you everything I could already."

"You were a big help, Mrs. O'Dell. It's my fault, really. I'm just trying to put everything in order," Mel continued, slipping into the cluttered living room as she spoke. "I hate to bother you again, especially since you were so helpful before."

Mel almost choked on that. Mrs. O'Dell had been suspicious, unfriendly and curt. Just, Mel thought as she warmed up her apologetic smile, as the lady was going to be now.

"I looked at your picture." Mrs. O'Dell jiggled her daughter on her hip. "I told you everything I know. Just like I told the police."

"I know. And I'm sure it's inconvenient to have your busy day constantly interrupted." Mel stepped over a platoon of G.I. Joes that had been overrun by a miniature fire truck. "But you see, your living room windows look right down on where the perpetrator was allegedly parked."

Mrs. O'Dell set her daughter down, and the little girl toddled toward the TV and sat down hard on her diapered bottom. "So?"

"Well, I couldn't help but notice how clean your windows are. The cleanest ones in the entire building. You know, if you look up here from down on the street, they shine like diamonds."

The flattery smoothed away Mrs. O'Dell's frown. "I take

pride in my home. I don't mind clutter—with two kids you're going to have plenty of that. But I don't tolerate dirt."

"Yes, ma'am. It seems to me that to have windows looking like that you'd have to keep after them."

"You're telling me. Living this close to the water, you get that salt scum." With a mother's radar, she shot a look over her shoulder. "Billy, don't let the baby put those dirty soldiers in her mouth. Give her your truck."

"But, Mom..."

"Just for a little while." Satisfied that she would be obeyed, Mrs. O'Dell glanced back. "Where was I?"

"Salt scum," Mel prompted.

"Sure. And the dust and dirt that comes from having cars going up and down the road. Fingerprints." She nearly smiled. "Seems I'm always chasing somebody's fingerprints."

Yeah, Mel thought. Me too.

"I know it must take a lot of work to keep your place up like this, raising two kids."

"Not everyone thinks so. Some people figure if you don't carry a briefcase and commute to some office every day you're not working."

"I've always thought holding together a home and family is the most important career there is."

Mrs. O'Dell took the dust rag that was hanging out of the back pocket of her shorts and rubbed at the surface of a table. "Well."

"And the windows," Mel said, gently leading her back. "I was wondering how often you have to wash them."

"Every month, like clockwork."

"You'd have a real good view of the neighborhood."

"I don't have time to spy on my neighbors."

"No, ma'am. But you might notice things, casually."

"Well, I'm not blind. I saw that man hanging around. I told you that."

"Yes, you did. I was thinking, if you happened to be washing the windows, you might have noticed him down there. I imagine it would take you about an hour to do the job..."

"Forty-five minutes."

"Uh-huh. Well, if he was down there that long, sitting in his car, it would have struck you as unusual, wouldn't it?"

"He got out and walked around."

"Oh?" Mel wondered if she dared take out her notepad. Better to talk now and write it all down later, she decided.

"Both days," Mrs. O'Dell added.

"Both days?"

"The day I did the windows, and the day I washed the curtains. I really didn't think anything of it. I don't poke around into other people's business."

"No, I'm sure you don't." But I do, Mel thought, her heart hammering. I do. And I just need a little more. "Do you remember which days you noticed him?"

"Did the windows the first of the month, like always. A couple days later, I noticed the curtains were looking a little dingy, so I took them down and washed them. Saw him across the street then, walking down the sidewalk."

"David Merrick was taken on the fourth of May."

Mrs. O'Dell frowned again, then glanced at her children. When she was satisfied they were squabbling and not paying any attention, she nodded. "I know. And, like I told you before, it just breaks my heart. A little baby like that, stolen practically out of his mother's arms. I haven't let Billy go out alone all summer."

Mel laid a hand on her arm to make a connection, woman to woman. "You don't have to know Rose Merrick to understand what she's going through. You're a mother."

It got through to her. Mel could see it in the way moisture sprang to Mrs. O'Dell's eyes. "I wish I could help. I just didn't see anything more than that. All I remember is thinking that this neighborhood should be safe. That you shouldn't have to be afraid to let your children walk across the street to play with a friend. You shouldn't have to worry every day that someone's going to come back and pick out your child and drive away with him."

"No, you shouldn't. Rose and Stan Merrick shouldn't be wondering if they'll ever see their son again. Someone drove away with David, Mrs. O'Dell. Someone who was parked right under your window. Maybe you weren't paying attention at the time, but if you'd clear your mind for a minute and think back... You might have noticed his car, some little thing about his car.''

"That beat-up old thing? I didn't pay any mind to it.''

"It was black? Red?''

Mrs. O'Dell shrugged. "Dirty is what it was. Might have been brown. Might have been green, under all that grime.''

Mel took a leap of faith. "Out-of-state plates, I imagine.''

After a moment's consideration, Mrs. O'Dell shook her head. "Nope. I guess I might have wondered why he was just sitting down there. Sometimes your mind wanders when you're working, and I was thinking he might have been visiting someone, waiting for them to get home. Then I was figuring he hadn't come all that far 'cause he had state plates.''

Mel banked down her excitement and mentally crossed her fingers. "I always used to play this game when I was a kid. My mom and I traveled a lot, and she tried to give me things to do. I guess you know how car trips are with kids.''

Mrs. O'Dell rolled her eyes. For the first time, there was a trace of humor in them. "Oh, do I.''

"I always tried to make words out of the letters on plates. Or come up with funny names for what the initials stood for.''

"We do the same thing with Billy. He's old enough. But the baby...''

"Maybe you noticed the license number, casually, while you were working. Without even thinking about it, if you know what I mean.''

And Mel could see that she did try for a minute. Her lips pursed, her eyes narrowed. Then she made an impatient movement with her dust rag and closed down. "I've got a lot of more important things on my mind. I saw it was a California plate, like I said, but I didn't stand there and play games with it.''

"No, of course not, but sometimes you pick up things without even knowing it. Then, when you think back—''

"Miss—''

"Sutherland,'' Mel told her.

"I'd like to help you. Really. My heart goes out to that poor woman and her husband. But I make a habit of minding my own business and keeping to my own. Now there's nothing else I can tell you, and I'm falling behind schedule.''

Recognizing the wall she'd just hit, Mel took out a business card. "If you remember anything about the plate, anything at all, would you call me?"

Billy piped up. "Said cat."

"Billy, don't interrupt when people are talking."

He shrugged and drove his fire truck up his sister's leg to make her giggle.

"What said cat?" Mel asked.

"The car did." Billy made engine noises. "*K-a-t*, that spells *cat*," he chanted, and had his mother sighing.

"You don't spell *cat* with a k. It's *c-a-t*. I can't believe you'll be going into the second grade and—"

Mel put a hand on Mrs. O'Dell's arm. "Please," she murmured, then squatted down in front of Billy. "Did you see the car down there Billy, the dirty brown car?"

"Sure. When I came home from school it was there. Freddy's mom had the pool."

"Car pool," Mrs. O'Dell said quietly.

"She let me off right behind it. I don't like riding with Freddy, 'cause he pinches."

"Did you play the license plate game with the brown car?" Mel asked.

"I like it when they make words. Like *cat*."

"You're sure it was that brown car? Not some other car you saw on the drive home from school?"

"No, 'cause it was parked just out front the whole week Freddy's mom drove me. Sometimes it was on the other side of the street. Then it wasn't there anymore when Mom had the pool."

"Do you remember the numbers, Billy?"

"I don't like numbers. Letters are better. *K-a-t*," he repeated. Then he looked up at his mother. "If it doesn't spell *cat*, what does it spell?"

With a grin, Mel kissed him right on the chocolate-smeared mouth. "This time it spells *thanks*. Thanks a lot."

Mel was practically singing when she walked back into Sutherland Investigations. She had something. Maybe it was only half of a license plate, and maybe the information had come from a six-year-old, but she had something.

She switched her answering machine to playback, then nipped into the kitchen for a soft drink. Her self-satisfied smile remained as she jotted down the messages.

Good solid investigative work, she told herself. That was the way you got things done. Persistence didn't hurt. She didn't imagine the police had managed to get anywhere near Billy O'Dell, or that they would have considered him a viable witness.

Solid investigative work, persistence—and hunches. Mel believed in hunches, just as she believed they were part of an investigator's makeup. But that was a far cry from psychic visions.

Her smile tilted toward a smirk as she thought of Sebastian. Maybe he had gotten lucky with the sketch and the car. But maybe it was just as she'd thought before. A connection on the force could have given him that data.

She wouldn't mind rubbing his nose in this new information.

Not that he was all bad, she thought, feeling charitable. He'd been okay when they'd shared a burger the evening before. No more come-ons—which she'd been positive she would have nipped in the bud. And he hadn't gotten spooky on her, either.

Actually, she remembered, they'd talked. Mostly books and movies, those old conversational standbys. But he had been interesting. When he wasn't irritating her, his voice was rather pleasant, with that whisper of a brogue.

A brogue that had deepened when he'd murmured to her, his lips sliding over hers.

Annoyed, she shook herself. She wasn't going to think about that. She'd been kissed before, and she wasn't against the practice. She simply preferred to choose her own time and place.

And if she hadn't had a reaction quite like that before, it was because he'd taken her so completely by surprise.

That wouldn't happen again, either.

In fact, the way things were going, she wasn't going to need Sebastian Donovan and his hocus-pocus any longer. She had a few contacts at the Department of Motor Vehicles, and once she called in with the partial plate she would...

Her thoughts trailed off as Sebastian's voice flowed out of her answering machine.

"Ah, Sutherland, sorry I missed you. Out sleuthing, I suppose."

She made a face at the machine. An immature reaction, she readily admitted. But the laughter in his voice demanded it.

"I thought you might be interested in some new information. I've been working on the car. The left rear tire's nearly bald—which could give our man a great deal of trouble, since his spare is flat."

"Give me a break, Donovan," she muttered. She rose, deciding to turn off the machine, and the voice.

"Oh, by the way, the car has California plates. KAT 2544." Mel's mouth fell open as her finger hesitated on the button.

"I thought you might be able to work your detective magic with that tidbit. Let me know what you come up with, won't you, love? I'll be home this evening. Good hunting, Mary Ellen."

"Son of a—" She gritted her teeth and switched the machine off.

She didn't like it. She didn't like it one damn bit, but she downshifted and started up the narrow, bumpy lane to Sebastian's house. Not for a minute did she believe he'd dreamed the plate number—or whatever term he would use—but, since he'd given her the tip, she felt obliged to do a follow-up.

When she reached the top of his lane, she was torn between elation at the progress she'd made and irritation at having to deal with him again. She'd be professional, she promised herself as she pulled between a muscular-looking Harley and a late-model minivan.

After climbing the steps, she gave a brisk knock on the door. The knocker she used was a brass figure of a snarling wolf. Intrigued, Mel played with it for a moment while she waited. When there was no response, Mel did what came naturally. She peeked in the windows.

She saw no one, only the lofty living room on one side and a very impressive library on the other. If her conscience had allowed, she would have turned away and gone home. But to do so would be both cowardly and petty. Instead, she went back down the steps and started around the house.

Mel spotted him standing inside a paddock, his arm intimately around a slim blonde in snug jeans. They were laughing, and the sound they made together was as intimate as their stance.

The quick bolt of heat baffled her. She didn't give a hang if he had a lady. She didn't care if he had a bloody harem. This was business.

But the fact that he would kiss a woman senseless one day and be snuggled up to another the next told Mel just what kind of a man Sebastian Donovan was.

A creep.

Despite it, she would be professional. Digging her hands into her pockets, she strode across the lawn toward the weathered fence.

"Hey, Donovan."

They both turned, man and woman. Mel could see that the female was not only slim and blond, but lovely, too. Absolutely lovely, with calm gray eyes and a soft, full mouth that was already curved in a half smile.

Mel felt like a big mongrel dog faced with a glossy purebred.

As she scowled, Mel saw him murmur something to the woman, kiss her smooth temple, then come over to lean against the fence.

"How you doing, Sutherland?"

"I got your message."

"I assumed you did. Ana, this is Mel Sutherland, a private investigator. Mel, Anastasia Donovan. My cousin."

"It's nice to meet you." Ana held out a hand as Mel approached the fence. "Sebastian's told me about the case you're working on. I hope you find the child quickly."

"Thanks." Mel accepted the hand. There was something so soothing about the voice, about the touch, that she felt half of her tension dissolve. "I'm making some progress."

"The boy's parents must be frantic."

"They're scared, but they're holding up."

"I'm sure it helps them, having someone who cares so much trying to help."

Anastasia stepped back, wishing she could do something to

help. But, like Sebastian, she had learned she couldn't be all things to all people.

"I'm sure you have business," she continued.

"I don't want to interrupt." Mel flicked a glance at Sebastian, then looked over his shoulder to where the horses stood. The quick pleasure showed in her face before she looked away again. "I only need a minute."

"No, take your time." Graceful as a doe, Ana vaulted over the fence. "I was just leaving. Will you make the movies tomorrow night, Sebastian?"

"Whose turn is it?"

"It's Morgana's. She said she felt like murder, so we're going to see a thriller."

"I'll meet you." He leaned over the fence to give her another kiss. "Thanks for the tansy."

"My pleasure. Welcome home. Nice to meet you, Mel."

"Yeah. Nice to meet you." Mel pushed her hair out of her eyes and watched Anastasia cross the lawn.

"Yes, she is lovely, isn't she?" Sebastian said lightly. "And as lovely inside as out."

"You seemed pretty close, for cousins."

His lips curved. "Yes, we are. Ana, Morgana and I spent a great deal of our childhood together, here and in Ireland. And, of course, when you have something in common, something that separates you from what's termed the norm, you tend to stick together."

Lifting a brow, Mel turned back to him. "You want me to believe she's psychic, too?"

"Not precisely. Ana has a different talent." He reached out to brush at Mel's bangs himself. "But you didn't come here to talk about my family."

"No." She shifted slightly, just out of reach, and tried to decide on the least humiliating way to thank him. "I checked out the plate. I already had half of it myself when I got the message."

"Oh?"

"I turned up a witness." No way was she going to admit how hard she'd worked to come up with those three little letters. "So anyway, I called my contact at the DMV, had it checked out."

"And?"

"And the car's registered to a James T. Parkland. The address is in Jamesburg." Propping one booted foot on a low rail, she leaned on the fence while the breeze ruffled her hair. She liked the smell of horses. Just watching them relaxed her. "I took a ride down there. He'd skipped. Landlady was pretty talkative, since he'd ducked two months' rent."

The mare walked over to the fence and bumped Mel's shoulder. Automatically she lifted a hand to stroke down the smooth white cheek. "I got an earful on Jimmy. He was the kind of guy who just invited trouble. Not a bad-looking boy—and I quote—but always had his pockets turned out. Always seemed to scrape up enough for a six-pack, though. The landlady claims to have taken a...motherly interest in him...but I have a hunch it wasn't quite so platonic. Otherwise she wouldn't be so steamed."

"Two months' rent," Sebastian reminded her, watching the way Mel's hand rubbed over the horse.

"Uh-uh. This was personal. She had that bitter tone a woman gets when she's been dumped."

Sebastian tilted his head, trusting Mel's intuition. "Which made her more talkative—to a sympathetic ear."

"You bet. She said he liked to gamble. Mostly on sports, but any game would do. He'd gotten in pretty deep over the last few months, started having visitors." She flicked Sebastian a glance. "The kind who have broken noses and lumps under their suit coats where their guns ruin the line. He tried to hit her for some quick cash, but she claimed she was tapped out. Then he said how he had a line on how to get himself out of it, once and for all. Last few days he was there, he was real nervous, jumpy, hyped up. Then he split. The last time she saw him was a week before David's kidnapping."

"An interesting story."

"It gives me something to work with. I figured you'd want to know."

"What's the next step?"

"Well, it hurts, but I turned over what I had to the local cops. The more people we have looking for old Jimmy, the better."

Sebastian ran a hand over Psyche's flank. "He's about as far away from Monterey as you can get and still stay in the country.''

"Yeah, I figure he's—''

"I don't figure.'' Sebastian turned those compelling eyes of his on her. "I know. He's traveling in New England, too nervous to settle yet.''

"Look, Donovan...''

"When you searched his room, did you notice that the second drawer down on his dresser had a loose pull?''

She had, but she said nothing.

"I'm not playing parlor games with you, Mel,'' Sebastian said impatiently. "I want to get that boy back, and quickly. Rose is losing hope. Once she loses it completely, she may very well do something drastic.''

Instant fear. It gripped Mel by the throat with vicious fingers. "What do you mean?''

"You know what I mean. Use what influence you have. See that the Vermont and New Hampshire police look for him. He's driving a Toyota now. Red. The plates are the same.''

She wanted to dismiss it, but she couldn't. "I'm going to go see Rose.''

Before she could back away from the fence, Sebastian laid a hand over hers. "I called Rose a couple of hours ago. She'll be all right for a while longer.''

"I told you I didn't want you to feed her any of this business.''

"You work your way, I'll work mine.'' His hand tightened on Mel's. "She needed something, a little something to hold on to, to get her through another night when she goes in and looks at an empty crib. I gave it to her.''

She felt something from him, something so akin to her own fear and frustration that she relented. "All right, maybe it was the thing to do. I can't second-guess you there. But if you're right about Parkland being in New England...''

"You won't get first shot at him.'' Sebastian smiled, relaxed now. "And that just burns the hell right out of you.''

"You hit that one dead on.'' She hesitated, then let out a long breath and decided to tell it all. "I got hold of an associate in Georgia.''

"You have far-reaching connections, Sutherland."

"I spent about twenty years knocking around the country. Anyway, there's a lawyer there, and he put me on to an investigator he trusts. As a professional courtesy, he's going to do some checking."

"Does that mean you're accepting the fact that David's in Georgia?"

"It means I'm not taking any chances. If I was sure, I'd go myself."

"When you are, and when you do, I'll go with you."

"Right." And there would be reports of frost in hell. There was nothing else she could do tonight, Mel thought. But she had a good beginning. Which was more, she was forced to admit, than she'd had before Sebastian had come along. "Is this head business of yours, this ESP, like what they study at Columbia, places like that?"

He had to smile. It was simply her nature to try to logic out the intangible. "No. Not quite. What you're referring to is that added sense most people have—to some extent—and usually chose to ignore. Those little flashes of insight, premonition, déjà vu. What I am is both less and more."

She wanted something more tangible, more logical, but she doubted she'd get it. "Seems pretty weird to me."

"People are often frightened by what they consider weird. There have been times throughout history when people have been frightened enough to hang or burn or drown those who seemed different." He studied her carefully, his hand still over hers on the rail. "But you aren't frightened, are you?"

"Of you?" Her laugh was quick. "No, I'm not scared of you, Donovan."

"You may be before it's done," he said, half to himself. "But I often feel it's best to live in the present, no matter what you know about tomorrow."

Mel flexed her fingers, nearly gasping at a sudden flash of heat that seemed to jump from his palm into her hand. His face remained calm.

"You like horses."

"What?" Uneasy, she pulled her hand free. "Yeah, sure. What's not to like?"

"Do you ride?"

She moved her shoulders. The heat was gone, but her hand felt as though she'd held it too close to a candle flame. "I've been on one before. Not in the last few years, though."

Sebastian said nothing, but the stallion's head came up, as if he'd heard a signal. He trotted over to the fence, pawing the ground.

"This one looks like he's got a temper." But, even as she said it, Mel was laughing and reaching out to touch. "You know you're beautiful, don't you?"

"He can be a handful," Sebastian commented. "But he can also be gentle if he chooses. Psyche'll be foaling in a few weeks, so she can't be ridden. But if you'd like, you can take a turn on Eros."

"Sometime, maybe." She dropped her hand before the temptation to take him up on it here and now proved too much to resist. "I'd better get going."

He nodded before the temptation to ask her to stay, to stay with him, proved too much to resist. "Tracking down Parkland that quickly was good work."

She was surprised enough to flush a little at the compliment. "It was routine. If I can trace the route to David, that'll be good work."

"We'll start in the desert." And soon, he thought. Very soon. "Sutherland, how about the movies?"

She blinked. "Excuse me?"

"I said how about the movies." He shifted his body toward hers, only the slightest bit. Mel couldn't have said why the movement seemed so much like a threat. Or why the threat seemed so exciting. "Tomorrow night," he continued. "My cousins and I are going. I think you might find my family interesting."

"I'm not much on socializing."

"This would be worth your while." He vaulted the fence as gracefully as Ana had, but this time Mel didn't think of a deer. She thought of a wolf. Now, without the fence between them, the threat, and the excitement, ripened. "A couple of hours of entertainment—to clear your mind. Afterward, I think you and I might have somewhere to go."

"If you're going to talk in riddles, we won't get anywhere."

"Trust me on this." He cupped a hand on her cheek. His fingers lay there as lightly as butterfly wings, but she found it impossible to brush them away. "An evening with the Donovans will be good for both of us."

She knew her voice would be breathless before she spoke, and she damned him for it. He only had his hand on her face. "I've pretty well decided nothing about you could be good for me."

He smiled then, thinking how flattering the evening light was to her skin, how caution added an odd attraction to her eyes. "It's a invitation to the movies, Mel, not a proposition. At least not precisely like the one you dodged this morning from the lonely man on the third floor of Rose's building."

Wary, she stepped back. It could have been a good guess. A remarkably good one. "How did you know about that?"

"I'll pick you up in time for the nine-o'clock show. Maybe I'll explain it to you." He held up a hand before she could refuse. "You said you weren't afraid of me, Sutherland. Prove it."

It was a perfect ploy. She understood that they both knew it. "I pay my own way. This isn't a date."

"No, indeed."

"Okay, then. Tomorrow night." She took a backward step, then turned. It was easier to think, she realized, when she wasn't facing him, or staring into those patient, amused eyes. "See you."

"Yes," he murmured. "You certainly will."

As he watched her walk away, his smile slowly faded. No, it wasn't a date. He doubted there would be anything as simple as a date in their relationship. And, though he was far from comfortable with the idea, he already knew they would have a relationship.

When he'd had his hand over Mel's, just before she yanked it away from that sudden flare of heat, he'd seen. He hadn't looked, not voluntarily, but he'd seen.

The two of them in the last rosy light of dusk. Her skin like ripe peaches under his hands. Fear in her eyes, fear and something stronger than fear. Through the open windows the first stirrings of the night creatures, those secret songs of the dark.

And he'd seen where they had been. Where they would be, however each of them tried to refuse it.

Frowning, Sebastian turned his head and looked up to the wide window glinting now in the lowering sunlight. Beyond the window was the bed where he slept, where he dreamed. The bed he would share with Mel before the summer was over.

Chapter 5

Mel had plenty to keep her occupied throughout the day. There was the mopping up of a missing-persons case, the groundwork for a possible insurance fraud for Underwriter's, and the little boy who had stopped by to hire her to find his lost dog.

She'd agreed to take the case of the missing pooch, for a retainer of two dollars and seven cents—mostly pennies. It did her heart good to see the boy go off, assured the matter was in professional hands.

She ate what passed for dinner at her desk. Munching on potato chips and a fat dill pickle, she made follow-up calls to the local police, and to the authorities in Vermont and New Hampshire. She touched base with her counterpart in Georgia, and hung up dissatisfied.

Everybody was looking for James T. Parkland. Everybody was looking for David Merrick. And nobody was finding them.

After a check of her watch, she called the local pound with a description of the missing mutt and her young client's name and phone number. Too restless to stay inside, she took the Polaroid snapshot the boy had given her of his canine best friend and made the rounds.

Three hours later, she located Kong, an aptly named mixed breed of astonishing proportions, snoozing in the storeroom of a shop on Fisherman's Wharf.

Using a length of twine donated by the shopkeeper, Mel managed to lead Kong to her car and stuff him into the passenger seat. Worried that the dog might leap out during the drive back to her office, Mel strapped him in with the seat belt and had her face bathed with a big wet tongue.

"Lot of nerve you've got," she muttered as she climbed in beside him. "Don't you think I figured out you went AWOL to cruise chicks? That kid of yours is worried sick about you, and where do I find you? Cozied up in a shell shop with pastrami on your breath."

Rather than appearing chastised, the dog seemed to grin, his tongue lolling out of the corner of his mouth, his head lifted to the wind, as Mel maneuvered through the parking lot.

"Don't you know the meaning of loyalty?" she asked him. Kong shifted his bulky body, laid his massive head on her shoulder and moaned. "Sure, sure. I know your kind, buster. Love the one you're with. Well, you can forget about me. I'm on to you."

But she lifted a hand from the gearshift to scratch his ears.

Sebastian was just parking his motorcycle when Mel pulled up in front of her office. He took one look at her and at the hundred and fifty pounds of muscle and fur riding beside her in the tiny car and grinned.

"Just like a woman. Here I think we're going out and you've picked yourself up another date."

"He's more my type." She finger-combed her hair away from her face, used her arm to wipe the dog kisses off her cheek, then located the end of the twine. "What are you doing here, anyway? Oh," she said before he could answer. "Movies. Right. I forgot."

"You sure know how to flatter a man, Sutherland." He moved out of her way when she unbuckled the dog's seat belt. "Nice dog."

"I guess. Come on, Kong, ride's over." She tugged and pulled, but the dog merely sat there, panting and grinning—and, she noted, shedding dusty yellow hairs on her seat.

Enjoying the performance, Sebastian leaned on the hood of her car. "Ever consider obedience school?"

"Reform school," she muttered. "But he's not mine." Mel

gritted her teeth and put her back into it. "Belongs to a client. Damn it, Kong, get your butt out."

As if he'd merely been waiting for her to ask, the dog responded by jumping out, ramming Mel back into Sebastian. He caught her neatly around the waist as she lost her footing. While she worked on getting her breath back, Mel scowled at the dog, who now sat placidly on the sidewalk.

"You're a real jerk, you know that?" she said to Kong. As if he agreed wholeheartedly, the dog went through his repertoire of tricks. Lying down, rolling over, then sitting up again with one paw lifted to shake.

She laughed before she realized her back was still nestled against Sebastian's chest. His very hard chest. Automatically she brought her hands down to his and pried them off.

"Let go."

Sebastian ran his hands up her arms once before she managed to break away. "You sure are touchy, Sutherland."

She tossed her head. "Depends on who's doing the touching." Wanting to wait until her heartbeat leveled, she swiped halfheartedly at the dog hairs clinging to her jeans. "Look, do me a favor and stay out here with fur-face while I make a call. There's a kid who, for reasons that escape me, actually wants this mutt back."

"Go ahead." Sebastian crouched down and ran his elegant hands over the dusty fur.

Only minutes after Mel came back out, a young boy rushed down the sidewalk, a red leash trailing behind him.

"Oh, wow. Kong. Oh, wow."

In response, the dog leapt to his feet, barking happily. He rushed the boy—like a fullback blocking a tight end. They went down on the sidewalk in a delighted, rolling heap.

With one arm hooked over Kong's massive neck, the boy grinned up at Mel. "Gee, lady, you sure are a real detective and all. Just like on TV. Thanks. Thanks a lot. You did real good."

"Thanks." Mel held out a hand to accept the boy's formal handshake.

"Do I owe you anymore?"

"No, we're square. You ought to get him one of those tags

with his name and your phone number on it. In case he decides to hit the road again.''

''Okay. Yeah, okay.'' He hooked the red leash onto King's collar. ''Wait till Mom sees. Come on, Kong, let's go home.'' They went off at a dash, the dog pulling the boy behind him. ''Thanks,'' he called out again, and his laughter echoed on the evening air.

''He's right,'' Sebastian murmured, not bothering to resist the urge to run his fingers through her hair. ''You did good.''

She shrugged, wishing she weren't so moved by the tone of his voice, by the touch of his hand. ''I earn my keep.''

''I bet you made a bundle on that one.''

Laughing a little, she turned her head. ''Hey, I made two dollars and seven cents. That ought to buy me some popcorn at the flicks.''

He cut off her laughter by touching his lips to hers. It wasn't a kiss...really...she thought. It was...friendlier.

''What did you do that for?''

''Just one of those things.'' Sebastian straddled his bike, then tossed her a helmet. ''Climb on, Sutherland. I hate to be late for the movies.''

All in all, it wasn't a bad way to unwind. Mel had always enjoyed the movies. They had been one of her favorite recreations as a child. It didn't matter if you were the new kid in school once the lights went out and the screen flickered into life.

Movie theaters were comfortingly familiar anywhere in the country. The smell of popcorn and candy, the sticky floors, the shufflings people made as they settled down to watch. Whatever movie was playing in El Paso was probably entertaining patrons in Tallahassee, too.

Mel had been drawn back to them time and time again during her mother's wanderings, stealing a couple of hours a week where it didn't matter where she was. Or who she was.

She felt the same sense of anonymity here, with the moody music and shadowy suspense on the screen. A killer was stalking the streets, and Mel—along with the other viewers—was content to sit back and watch the ancient duel of good against evil.

She sat between Sebastian and his cousin, Morgana. His gorgeous cousin Morgana, Mel had noted.

She'd heard the rumors about Morgana Donovan Kirkland. The rumors that whispered she was a witch. Mel had found them laughable—and only found them more so now. Morgana was anything but a cackling crone ready to jump on board a broomstick.

Still, she imagined the rumors added to the business Morgana pulled in at her shop.

On the other side of Morgana was her husband, Nash. Mel knew he was a successful and highly respected screenwriter, one who specialized in horror scripts. His work had certainly scared a few muffled screams from Mel—and made her laugh at herself.

Nash Kirkland didn't seem the Hollywood type to her. He struck her as open and easygoing—and very much in love with his wife.

They held hands during the movies. But not with the sloppy sort of mush that would have made Mel uncomfortable. Instead, there was a quiet, steady bond of affection in the gesture that she envied.

On the other side of Sebastian was Anastasia. Mel wondered why a woman as hauntingly lovely as Ana didn't have a date. Then she reminded herself that such a thought was sexist and stupid. Not every woman—herself included—found it necessary to go everywhere hanging on to the arm of a man.

Mel dug into her popcorn and settled into the movie.

"You going to eat all that?"

"Hmm?" Distracted, she turned her head. Then jerked it back quickly. She'd practically been lip-to-lip with Sebastian. "What?"

"You going to share, or what?"

She stared a moment. Wasn't it odd how his eyes seemed to glow in the dark? When he tapped a finger on the box of popcorn in her lap, she blinked.

"Oh, yeah. Help yourself."

He did, enjoying her reaction to him every bit as much as the buttery popcorn.

She smelled...fresh. Sebastian kept part of his mind on the twists and turns of the plot and let the rest wander at will. He found it pleasant to be able to scent her soap-and-water skin over the aromas of the theater. If he let himself, he could hear her pulse beating. Steady, very steady, and strong—and then a quick jerk and flutter when the action heated up on-screen.

What would her pulse do if he touched her now? If he were to shift his body and take that wide, unpainted mouth with his own?

He thought he knew. He thought he could wait and see.

But he couldn't quite resist a gentle poke into her own thoughts.

Idiot! If she knows somebody's after her, why is she bopping down the street in the dark? How come they always have to make women either dumb or helpless? There she goes—running into the park. Oh, sure, it makes perfect sense to haul her butt into the bushes where he can slit her throat. Ten to one she trips... Yep.

Oh, well, that one deserves to get iced.

She crunched on more popcorn, and Sebastian heard her wish absently that she'd added more salt.

Her thoughts stuttered to a halt, then tangled into confusion. What he was reading in her head he could see on her face.

She sensed him. She didn't understand what it was, but she sensed an intrusion and was instinctively blocking it.

The fact that she did, the fact that she could, intrigued him. It was very rare for anyone outside his family to feel his scannings.

There was some power here, he mused. Untapped, and certainly denied. He toyed with the idea of pushing a little deeper. Beside him, Ana stirred.

"Don't be rude, Sebastian," she said gently.

Relenting, reluctantly, he gave himself over to the movie.

He reached for some popcorn, and his fingers brushed Mel's. She flinched. He grinned.

"Pizza," Morgana said when they stepped outside. "With the works."

Nash ran a hand down her hair. "I thought you said you wanted Mexican."

She smiled, patting her belly. "We changed our minds."

"Pizza," Ana agreed. "No anchovies." She smiled at Mel. "How about it?"

Mel felt herself linked in this ring of good fellowship. "Sure. That sounds—"

"We can't," Sebastian interrupted, laying a hand on her shoulder.

Curious, Morgana pursed her lips. "I've never known you to turn down food, darling." She shot a quick, humorous look at Mel. "Cousin Sebastian has outrageous appetites. You'd be amazed."

"Mel's much too practical-minded to be amazed," Sebastian said coolly. "What astonishes, she merely dismisses."

"He's only baiting you." Ana gave Sebastian a quick dig in the ribs. "We've seen so little of you lately. Can't you spare another hour, Sebastian?"

"Not tonight."

"Well, I can..." Mel began.

"I'll see the lady home." Nash winked at Mel. "I don't have any problem taking on three beautiful women alone."

"You're such a generous man, darling." Morgana patted her husband's cheek. "But I think Sebastian has other plans for his lady."

"I'm not his—"

"Exactly." He tightened his grip on Mel's shoulder. "We'll do it next time." He kissed both of his cousins. "Blessed be." And he propelled Mel down the sidewalk toward his bike.

"Listen, Donovan, we said this wasn't a date, and maybe I'd have liked to go along with them. I'm hungry."

He unsnapped a helmet, then dropped it on her head. "I'll feed you eventually."

"I'm not a horse," Mel muttered, fastening the helmet. "I can feed myself." Pouting only a little, she glanced over her shoulder at the retreating trio as she climbed behind Sebastian onto the bike. It wasn't all that often that she went out with a group—and particularly a group she felt so comfortable with. But if she was annoyed with Sebastian for breaking it up early, she had to be grateful to him for including her in the first place.

"Don't sulk."

"I never sulk." She rested her hands lightly on his hips for balance as he drove away from the curb.

She enjoyed the feeling of the bike—the freedom of it, and the risk. Perhaps, when her cash flow was a little more fluid, she'd look into getting one for herself. Of course, it would be more practical to have her car painted and tuned first. Also, there was that leak in the bathroom that needed to be dealt with. And she really wanted some new surveillance equipment. The high-tech stuff cost the earth.

But she might be able to swing it in another year or so. The way things were going, her books ended nearly every month in the black. Breaking up that burglary ring and saving Under-writer's a hefty chunk in claims might just shake a bonus loose.

She let her mind drift in that direction, her body automatically leaning with Sebastian's in the curves. Mel wasn't aware that her hands had slid more truly around his waist, but Sebastian was.

She liked the sensation of the wind in her face, on her skin. And, though she wasn't proud of it, she enjoyed the way her body fit snug to his with the bike vibrating seductively beneath them.

He had a very....interesting body. It was difficult not to notice, Mel thought, since they were sharing such a small space. His back was muscled beneath the butter-smooth leather jacket. His shoulders were quite wide—or maybe they only seemed so because his hips were lean and narrow.

There were muscles in his arms, as well. Not that she was overly impressed with that sort of thing, she reminded herself. It was just that it surprised her that someone in his line of work—so to speak—was so well built.

More like a tennis player than an oracle.

Then again, she supposed he had plenty of time for working out, or riding his horses, or whatever form of exercise he preferred, between visions.

She began to wonder what it might be like to own her own horse.

It wasn't until she realized he was swinging onto the east-bound ramp of 156 that she came to attention.

"Hey!" She rapped her fingers on his helmet. "Hey, Daniel Boone, the trail's back that way."

He heard her clearly enough, but shook his head. "What? Did you say something?"

"Yeah, I said something." But she did precisely as he'd hoped she would. She wiggled closer on the seat and leaned against him. He felt every curve. "I said you're going the wrong way. My place is back there, about ten miles back there."

"I know where you live."

She huffed and kept her voice lifted over the purr of the engine. "Then what are we doing out here?"

"Nice night for a drive."

Yeah, maybe it was, but nobody had asked her. "I don't want to go for a drive."

"You'll want to go on this one."

"Oh, yeah? Well, where are we going?"

Sebastian zipped around a sedan and punched it up to sixty. "Utah."

It was a good ten miles before Mel managed to close her mouth.

Three o'clock in the morning, in the ghastly light of the parking lot of a combination convenience store and gas station. Mel's bottom felt as though it had been shot full of novocaine.

But her mind wasn't numb. She might have been tired, cranky and sore after riding on the back of a bike for four hours, but her mind was functioning just fine.

Right now she was using it to develop ways of murdering Sebastian Donovan and making it the perfect crime.

It was a damn shame she hadn't brought her gun. Then she could just shoot him. Clean and quick. On some of the roads they'd been traveling, she could dump the body into a gully where it might not be found for weeks. Possibly years.

Still, it would be more satisfying to beat him to death. He had her by a few inches, and maybe fifty pounds, but she thought she could take him.

Then she could ditch the bike, hop a bus and be back in her office bright and early the next morning.

Mel stretched her legs by pacing the parking lot. Occasionally a semi rattled by, using the back roads to avoid weighing stations. Apart from that, it was dark and quiet. Once she heard something that sounded suspiciously like a coyote, but she dismissed it.

Even out here in the boonies, she assured herself, people had dogs.

Oh, he'd been clever, she thought now, kicking an empty soda can out of her way. He hadn't stopped the bike until they'd been past Fresno. Not exactly walking distance back to Monterey.

And when she'd hopped off, punched him and let loose with a string of curses that should have turned his ears blue, he'd simply waited her out. Waited her out, and then gone on to explain that he'd wanted to follow James T. Parkland's trail.

He'd needed to see the motel where David had stayed with the first woman he'd been passed to.

As if there were a motel. Mel kicked the hapless can again. Did he really expect her to believe they would drive up to some dumb motel with a dinosaur out front?

Right.

So, here she was, tired, hungry and numb from the waist down, stuck on some back road with a crazy psychic. She was two hundred and fifty miles from home, and she had eleven dollars and eighty-six cents on her person.

"Sutherland."

Mel whirled and caught the candy bar he tossed her. She would have cursed him then, but she had to snag the soft drink can that came looping after it.

"Look, Donovan…" Since he was busy with the gas pump, she stalked over, ripping the wrapper off the candy bar as she went. "I've got a business to run. I have clients. I can't be running around half the night with you chasing wild geese."

"You ever done any camping?"

"What? No."

"I've done some up in the Sierra Nevadas. Not far from here. Very peaceful."

"If you don't turn this bike around and take me back, you're going to have an eternity of peace. Starting now."

When he looked at her, really looked, she saw that he didn't appear tired at all. Oh, no. Rather than suffering from four hours of traveling, he looked as if he'd just spent a week at some exclusive spa.

Under the relaxation, the calm, was a drumming excitement that took hold of her pulse and set it hopping. Resenting every minute of it, Mel took a healthy bite of chocolate.

"You're crazy. Certifiable. We can't go to Utah. Do you know how far it is to Utah?"

He realized the temperature had dropped considerably. Sebastian peeled off his jacket and handed it to her. "To the place we want, from Monterey? About five hundred miles." He clicked off the pump, replaced the nozzle. "Cheer up, Sutherland, we're more than halfway there."

She gave up. "There must be a bus depot around here," she muttered, tugging on his jacket as she headed toward the harshly lit store.

"This is where he stopped off with David." Sebastian spoke quietly, and she stopped in her tracks. "Where they made the first switch. He didn't make the kind of time we did, what with traffic, nerves, and watching the rearview mirror for cops. The meet was set for eight."

"This is bull," Mel said, but her throat was tight.

"The night man recognized him from the sketch. He noticed him because Jimmy parked all the way across the lot, even though there were spaces just out front. And he was nervous, so the night man kept an eye on him, thinking he might try to shoplift. But Jimmy paid."

Mel watched Sebastian carefully as he spoke. When he was finished, she held out a hand. "Give me the sketch."

With his eyes on hers, Sebastian reached in the top pocket of the jacket. Through the lining, his hand brushed lightly over her breast, lingering for a heartbeat before he lifted the folded sketch out.

She knew she was breathing too fast. She knew she was feeling more than that brief, meaningless contact warranted. To compensate, she snatched the paper out of his hand and strode toward the store.

As she went inside to verify what he had just told her, Sebastian secured his gas cap and rolled the bike away from the pumps.

It took her less than five minutes. She was pale when she returned, her eyes burning dark in her face. But her hand was steady when she tucked the sketch away again. She didn't want to think, not yet. Sometimes it was better to act.

"All right," she told him. "Let's go."

She didn't doze. That could be suicide on a bike. But she did find her mind wandering, with old images passing over new. It was all so familiar, this middle-of-the-night traveling. Never being quite sure where you were going or what you would do when you got there.

Her mother had always been so happy driving down nameless roads with the radio blaring. Mel could remember the comfort of stretching out on the front seat, her head in her mother's lap, and the simplicity of trusting that somehow they would find a home again.

Heavy with fatigue, her head dropped to Sebastian's back. She jerked up, forcing her eyes wide.

"Want to stop for a while?" he called to her. "Take a break?"

"No. Keep going."

Toward dawn he did stop, refueling himself with coffee. Mel opted for a caffeine-laden soft drink and wolfed down a sugar-spiked pastry.

"I feel I owe you a decent meal," Sebastian commented while they took a five-minute breather somewhere near Devil's Playground.

"This *is* my idea of a decent meal." Content, she licked sugar and frosting off her fingers. "You can keep the pheasant under glass."

Her eyes were shadowed. He was sorry for that, but he'd acted on instinct—an instinct he'd known was right. When he slipped an arm around her, she stiffened, but only for a moment. Perhaps she recognized that the gesture was one of friendly support and nothing more.

"We'll be there soon," he told her. "Another hour."

She nodded. She had no choice but to trust him now. To trust him, and the feeling inside her. What Mel would have called a gut hunch. "I just want to know it's worth it. That it's going to make a difference."

"We'll have that answer, too."

"I hope so. I hope the answer's yes." She turned her face into him, her lips brushing over his throat. There was a flare of warmth, of flavor, before her gritty eyes widened. "I'm sorry. I'm punchy." She would have moved away, far away, but his arm merely tightened around her.

"Relax, Mel. Look. Sun's coming up."

They watched the dawn bloom together, his arm around her and her head resting lightly against his shoulder. Over the desert, the colors rose up from the horizon, bleeding into the sky and tinting the low-hanging clouds. Dull sand blushed pink, then deepened to rose before it slowly became gilded. In another hour, the baking sun would leech the color out of the landscape. But for now, for just this single hushed moment, it was as lovely as any painting.

She felt something here, watching this ageless transition with his arm around her. A communion. The first gentle fingers of a bond that needed no words for understanding.

This time, when he kissed her, his mouth soft and seeking, she didn't resist and she didn't question. The moment itself justified it. She was too tired to fight whatever was growing inside her. She was too dazed by the magic of dawn over the desert to refuse what he asked of her.

He wanted to ask for more—knew that at this moment, in this place, he could ask. But he could sense her fatigue, her confusion, and her nagging fears for a friend's child. So he kept the kiss easy, a comfort to both of them. When he released her, he understood that what they had begun would not be broken.

Without a word, they mounted the bike again and headed east, toward the sun.

In southern Utah, not far from the Arizona border—and near enough to Vegas for an easy trip to lose a paycheck—was a hot little huddle of storefronts. The town, such as it was, had a gas station, a tiny café that offered corn tortillas, and a twenty-five unit motel with a plaster brontosaurus in the center of the gravel lot.

"Oh," Mel whispered as she stared at the sadly chipped dinosaur. "Oh, sweet Lord." As she eased off the bike, her legs were trembling from more than travel fatigue.

"Let's go see if anyone's awake." Sebastian took her arm to pull her toward the check-in desk.

"You did see it, didn't you?"

"It seems that way, doesn't it?" When she swayed, he wrapped a supporting arm around her waist. Odd that she would suddenly seem so fragile. "We'll get you a bed while we're at it."

"I'm all right." She'd go into shock later, Mel promised herself. Right now she needed to keep moving. Together they walked through the door and into the fan-cooled lobby.

Sebastian rang the bell on the desk. Moments later, they heard the shuffle of slippered feet behind a faded flowered curtain.

A man in a white athletic shirt and baggy jeans wandered out, his eyes puffy with sleep, his face unshaven.

"Help you?"

"Yes." Sebastian reached for his wallet. "We need a room. Unit 15." He laid down crisp green cash.

"Happens it's empty." The clerk reached for a key from the pegboard behind him. "Twenty-eight a night. Café down the road there serves breakfast twenty-four hours. You want to sign here?"

After he had, Sebastian laid another twenty on the counter, with David's picture on top of it. "Have you see this boy? It would have been three months ago."

The clerk looked longingly at the twenty. David's picture might have been a sheet of glass. "Can't remember everybody comes through."

"He was with a woman. Attractive, early thirties. A redhead, driving a midsize Chevy."

"Maybe they was through. I mind my business and nobody else's."

Mel nudged Sebastian aside. "You look like a pretty sharp guy to me. I'd think if a good-looking lady like that came through here, with a cute little baby, you'd notice. Maybe you'd tell her where she could buy spare diapers, or get fresh milk."

He shrugged his shoulders and scratched. "I don't look into anybody else's trouble."

"You'll look to your own, though." Mel's voice had toughened, enough for the clerk to look up warily. "Now, when Agent Donovan— I mean Mr. Donovan." The clerk's eyes widened. "When he asked you if you'd seen that little boy, I think you were going to think it over. Weren't you?"

The clerk licked his lips. "You cops? FBI or something?"

Mel only smiled. "We'll say 'or something' and keep everything mellow."

"I run a quiet place here."

"I can see that. That's why I know if that woman stopped off here with the kid, you'd remember. I don't guess you get all that much traffic."

"Look, she only spent one night. She paid cash in advance, kept the kid pretty quiet through the night and went on her way first thing in the morning."

Mel fought back the ragged edge of hope and kept her voice cool. "Give me a name, pal."

"Hell's bells, how'm I supposed to remember names?"

"You keep records." Mel put a fingertip on the twenty and inched it across the counter. "Records of registered guests, and any phone calls they might make from their rooms. Why don't you dig it up for us? My partner might even give you a bonus."

Muttering oaths, the clerk pulled a cardboard box from behind the desk. "Got phone records here. You can look through the register yourself."

Mel reached for the registration book, then put her hands behind her back and let Sebastian do it. She was ready to admit he'd find what they were looking for quicker than she would.

Sebastian homed in on the name. "Susan White? I don't suppose she showed you any ID?"

"Paid cash," the clerk mumbled. "Jeezie peezie, you expect me to frisk her or something? One long-distance call," he announced. "Went through the operator."

Mel dug in her purse for her notepad. "Date and time." She scribbled them down. "Now listen, friend, and this is the bonus question—no jive. Would you state under oath that this child...and look carefully—'' she held up David's picture ''—this child was brought into this motel last May?''

The clerk shifted uncomfortably. "If I had to, I would. I don't want to go to court or nothing, but she brought him. I remember he had that dimple there and that funny reddish hair."

"Good job." She wasn't going to cry—oh, no, she wasn't. But she walked outside while Sebastian replaced the photo and passed the clerk another twenty.

"Okay?" he asked when he joined her.

"Sure. Fine."

"I need to see the room, Mel."

"Right."

"You can wait out here if you want."

"No. Let's go."

She didn't speak again, not when they walked down the broken sidewalk, not when he unlocked the door and stepped inside its stuffy walls. She sat on the bed, clearing her mind while Sebastian used his for what he did best.

He could see the baby, sleeping on a pallet on the floor, whimpering a bit in his confusing dreams.

She'd left the light on in the bathroom so that she could see easily if the child woke and began to cry. She'd watched a little television, made her call.

But her name wasn't Susan White. She'd used so many over the years that it was difficult for Sebastian to pick up on the true one. He thought it was Linda, but it wasn't Linda now, and it wasn't Susan, either.

And it hadn't been more than a few weeks before that when she had transported still another baby.

He would have to tell Mel about that once she'd rested.

When he sat on the bed beside her, put a hand on her shoulder, she continued to stare straight ahead.

"I don't want to know right now how you did it. I might sometime, but not now. Okay?"

"Okay."

"She had him here in this room."

"Yes."

"And he isn't hurt?"

"No."

Mel wet her lips. "Where did she take him?"

"Texas, but she doesn't know where he was taken from there. She's only one leg of the trip."

Mel took two deep, careful breaths. "Georgia. Are you sure it's Georgia?"

"Yes."

Her hands fisted on her lap. "Where? Do you know where?"

He was tired, more tired than he wanted to admit. And it would drain him even more to look now. But she needed him to. Not in here, he thought. There was too much interference in here, too many sad stories in this sad little room.

"I have to go outside. Leave me alone for a minute."

She just nodded, and he left her. Time passed, and she was relieved to find that the need to cry went with it.

Mel didn't see tears as weak, particularly. She saw them as useless.

So her eyes were dry when Sebastian came back into the room.

She thought he looked pale, and suddenly tired. Odd that she hadn't noticed the fatigue around his eyes a few moments ago. Then again, she reminded herself, she hadn't been looking at him very carefully.

She did so now, and because she did she felt compelled to rise and go to him. Perhaps the lack of roots and family had made her a person wary of outward displays of affection. She'd never been a toucher, but she reached out now, taking both his hands in hers.

"You look like you need the bed more than I do. Why don't you sack out for an hour? Then we'll figure out what to do next."

He didn't answer, only turned her hands over and stared at her palms. Would she believe how many things he could see there?

"Tough shells aren't necessarily thick ones," he said quietly, lifting his gaze to hers. "You've got a soft center, Mel. It's very attractive."

Then he did something that left her both shaken and speechless. He lifted her hands to his lips. No one had ever done that before, and she discovered that what she'd assumed was a silly affectation was both moving and seductive.

"He's in a place called Forest Park, a suburb a little south of Atlanta."

Her fingers tightened on his, then relaxed. If she had never taken anything in her life on faith before, she would take this.

"Stretch out on the bed." Her voice was brisk, her hands firm, as she nudged him over to it. "I'm going to call the FBI and the nearest airport."

Chapter 6

She slept like a stone. Sebastian sipped a little more wine, kicked back in his chair and watched Mel. She was stretched out on the sofa across from him in the main cabin of his private plane. She hadn't argued when he'd suggested having his pilot fly to Utah to pick them up for the trip east. She'd simply nodded distractedly and continued to scribble notes on her ever-present pad.

The moment they'd hit cruising height, she'd ranged her long body out on the couch, closed her eyes and gone under, as quickly and easily as an exhausted infant. He understood that energy, like any power, had to be recharged, and he'd left her alone.

Sebastian had indulged in a long shower and changed into some of the spare clothes he kept aboard the Lear. While he enjoyed a light lunch, he made a few phone calls. And waited.

It was an odd journey, to say the least. Himself and the sleeping woman, hurtling away from the sun after a night of racing toward it. When it was over, there would be broken hearts and mended ones. Fate always charged a fee.

And he would have crossed a continent with a woman he found annoying, desirable, and incomprehensible.

She stirred, murmured something, then opened her eyes. He watched the cloudy green sharpen and focus as she pushed past the disorientation. She stretched once—it was a brisk, business-like movement, and it was incredibly sexy—then rolled herself to a sitting position.

"How much longer?" Her voice was still husky with sleep, but he could see the energy pouring back.

"Less than an hour."

"Good." After running a hand through her hair, she lifted her head, scenting the air. "Do I smell food?"

He had to smile. "In the galley. There's a shower to starboard if you want to wash up."

"Thanks."

She chose the shower first. It wasn't easy, but she didn't want to act unduly impressed that the man could snap his fingers and call up his own plane—a plane fitted out with deep pile carpeting, its own cozy bedroom and a galley that made her kitchen at home look like someone's closet. Obviously the psychic business paid well.

She should have checked his background, Mel thought now as she wrapped herself in a robe and tiptoed into the bedroom. But she'd been so sure that she would be able to talk Rose out of using him that she hadn't bothered. Now here she was, some thirty thousand feet up, with a man she knew much too little about.

She'd remedy that the moment they touched down in Monterey again. Though, of course, if things went as she hoped, there would be no need to. Once David was back where he belonged, her association with Sebastian Donovan would be over.

Still, she might run a background check on him, just out of curiosity.

Lips pursed, Mel poked into his closet. He liked silk and cashmere and linen, she discovered. Spotting a denim shirt, she yanked it out. At least he had something practical, and she sure could use some fresh clothes.

She tugged it on, then whipped around to the doorway. For a moment, she had thought he was there, had been sure of it. Then she realized it was his scent, clinging still to the shirt that was now brushing softly against her skin.

What was that fragrance, exactly? Experimentally she lifted her arm to sniff the sleeve. Nothing she could quite pinpoint.

Something wild, erotic. Something you'd expect to catch just a whiff of in the forest in the dark of the moon.

Annoyed with herself, she pulled on her jeans. If this kept up, she'd actually start believing in witches.

After rolling the sleeves of the borrowed shirt up to her elbows, she went to investigate the galley. She helped herself to a banana, ignored a jar of caviar and tossed some ham and cheese on a piece of bread.

"Got any mustard?" she called out, then swallowed a gasp when she felt his body bump against hers. He'd made no more sound than a ghost.

He reached over her head for a jar and handed it to her. "Want some wine?"

"I guess." She slathered mustard on the bread, wishing there was a little more room to maneuver away from him in the small space. "I borrowed a shirt. Okay?"

"Sure." He poured her wine and topped off his own glass. "You rested well."

"Yeah, well, it helps the time pass." The plane danced in some turbulence. His hand came down to steady her and stayed on her arm. "The pilot said there'd be a few bumps." Testing both of them, he rubbed his thumb over the inside of her elbow. The pulse there was fast and steady. "We'll be starting our descent soon."

She lifted her face to his. Studying him, she felt what she had felt in the desert. The beginning of something. Mel wondered if she'd be less restless if she were able to see the end as well.

"Then we'd better sit down. And strap in."

"I'll take your wine."

With a long breath of relief, she picked up her plate and followed him. As she dug happily into the sandwich, she noticed him smiling at her. "Problem?"

"I was just thinking that I really do owe you an actual meal."

"You don't owe me." She took a sip of wine, and then, because it was so different, so delightfully different, from what she was used to, she sipped again. "I like paying my own way."

"I've noticed."

Mel tilted her head. "Some guys are intimidated by that."

"Really?" A smile played around his lips. "I'm not. Still,

after we're finished, maybe you'd agree to dinner. A celebration of a job well done.''

"Maybe," she said over a mouthful of sandwich. "We can flip to see who buys.''

"Lord, you are charming." He chuckled and stretched out his legs, pleased she'd chosen the seat facing him rather than the one beside him. Now he could look his fill when she was awake. "Why private investigations?''

"Hmmm?''

His lips curved again. "It's time I asked, don't you think? What made you choose your profession?''

"I like to figure things out." She moved her shoulders and started to rise to take her empty plate away. But he stood up and took it into the galley himself.

"It's that simple?''

"I believe in the rules." The seats were roomy, so she tucked her legs up and crossed them. She was comfortable, she realized. Refreshed from the nap, and from a surge of hope that had yet to fade. Easy in his company. Well, she supposed, anything was possible.

"And I think when you break the rules somebody should make you pay for it." She felt the subtle shift and change in the cabin as the plane began its descent into Atlanta. "I also like to figure things out—by myself. That's why I only made a pretty good cop but I make a really good PI.''

"So, you're not a team player.''

"Nope." She cocked her head. "Are you?''

"No." He smiled into his wine. "I suppose not." Then, abruptly, his eyes were intense again, focused on her. Into her, she thought. "But rules often change, Mel. The lines between right and wrong sometimes blur. When that happens, how do you choose?''

"By knowing what things shouldn't change, what lines can't be blurred—or crossed. You just feel it.''

"Yeah." With that sudden flash of power banked again, he nodded. "You just feel it.''

"It has nothing to do with being psychic." She thought she understood just where he was leading her. She wasn't ready to give him quite that much rope. "I don't go in for visions or second sight or whatever you call it."

He lifted his glass in toast. "But you're here, aren't you?"

Her eyes remained level. If he expected her to squirm, he'd be disappointed. "Yeah, I'm here, Donovan. I'm here because I won't risk not following up any lead—no matter how slim, or how weird."

He continued smiling. "And?"

"And because maybe I'm willing to consider that you might have seen or felt something. Or maybe you just had a good gut hunch. I believe in hunches."

"So do I, Mel." The plane bumped down on the runaway. "So do I."

It was always difficult to turn over the reins to another. Mel didn't mind cooperating with local authorities or the FBI, but she preferred doing it on her own terms. For David's sake, she had to bite her tongue a dozen times during the interview with Federal Agent Thomas A. Devereaux.

"I have reports on you, Mr. Donovan. Several, in fact, from associates of mine who consider you not only trustworthy but something of a wonder."

Mel thought Sebastian sat in the small, beige-toned office like a king at his court. He responded to Devereaux's statement with a slight nod.

"I've been involved in a few federal investigations."

"Most recently in Chicago," Devereaux said, flipping through a file. "A bad mess up there. A pity we couldn't stop it sooner."

"Yes." It was all Sebastian would say. Not all of those images had faded.

"And you, Ms. Sutherland." Devereaux rubbed his round, bald head, then poked a finger at the nosepiece of his glasses. "The local authorities in California seem to find you competent enough."

"I can sleep easy now." She ignored Sebastian's warning glance and leaned forward. "Can we bypass the introductions, Agent Devereaux? I have friends back in California who are desperate. David Merrick's only a few miles away—"

"That's yet to be determined." Devereaux set one file aside

and picked up another. "We had all pertinent information faxed in after your call. A federal investigator has already interviewed your witness at the...Dunes Motel in Utah." He pushed his glasses up again. "He positively identified David Merrick's picture. We're working on IDing the woman."

"Then why are we sitting here?"

Devereaux peered over the rims of his glasses, which had already slid down his nose again. "Do you expect us to knock on every door in Forest Park and ask if they've recently stolen a baby?" Anticipating her, he held up a pudgy finger. "We have data coming in right now on male children between the ages of six and nine months. Adoption records, birth certificates. We're looking into who has moved into the area, with a child, within the last three months. I have no doubt that by morning we'll have narrowed it down to a manageable few."

"Morning? Listen, Devereaux, we've just spent the best part of twenty-four hours getting here. Now you're going to tell us to wait until morning?"

Devereaux leveled a look at Mel. "Yes. If you give us the name of your hotel, we'll contact you with any further developments."

Mel popped out of her chair. "I know David. I can identify him. If I did a sweep of the area, set up some surveillance—"

Devereaux cut her off. "This is a federal case. We may very well want you to identify the boy. However, we have copies of his prints to substantiate." While Mel bit her tongue, Devereaux shifted his gaze from her to Sebastian. "I'm moving on this under the advice of Special Agent Tucker in Chicago—who I've known for more than twenty years. Because he puts some stock in this psychic business, and because I have a grandson about David's age, I'm not going to advise the two of you to go back to California and leave this alone."

"We appreciate your help, Agent Devereaux." Sebastian rose and took Mel by the elbow, squeezing hard before she could hurl whatever insult was in her mind. "I've made reservations at the Doubletree. We'll wait for your call."

Satisfied, Devereaux stood and offered a hand.

"I should have spit in it," Mel grumbled a few moments later when they walked out into the torrid Atlanta evening. "The Fee-bies always treat PIs like mongrel dogs."

"He'll do his job."

"Right." She was distracted enough to let him open the door of the car they'd rented at the airport. "Because some pal of his took a shine to you in Chicago. What did you do up there, anyway?"

"Not enough." Sebastian shut her door and rounded the hood. "I don't suppose you feel like a quiet drink in the hotel bar and a leisurely dinner."

"Not on your life." She snapped her seat belt into place. "I need a pair of binoculars. Must be a sporting goods store around here someplace."

"I imagine I could find one."

"A long-range camera," she said to herself, pushing up the sleeves of her borrowed shirt. "A federal case," she muttered. "Well there's no law that says I can't take a nice drive through the 'burbs, is there?"

"I don't believe there is," Sebastian said as he pulled into traffic. "Perhaps a walk, as well. Nothing quite like a walk in a nice neighborhood on a summer evening."

She turned her head to beam a smile at him. "You're all right, Donovan."

"That kind of flattery will last me a lifetime."

"Can you—?" Mel bit her lip and swallowed the question as they drove slowly down the tree-lined streets of Forest Park.

"Can I tell which house?" Sebastian finished for her. "Oh, eventually."

"How—?" She cut that thought off, as well, and lifted the binoculars.

"How does it work?" He smiled and turned left, in what appeared to Mel to be an unstudied decision. "That's a bit complicated to explain. Perhaps sometime, if you're still interested, I'll try."

When he pulled over to the curb and stopped, she frowned. "What are you doing?"

"They often walk him here after dinner."

"What?"

"They like to take him out in the stroller after dinner, before his bath."

Before she realized what she meant to do, Mel reached out, put a hand on his cheek to turn his face to hers. She blinked once, stunned by the flash of power in his eyes. How dark they were, she thought. Nearly black. When she managed to speak, her voice was barely a whisper.

"Where is he?"

"In the house across the street. The one with the blue shutters and the big tree in the front yard." He grabbed her wrist before she could reach for the doorhandle. "No."

"If he's in there, I'm going in and getting him. Damn it, let go of me."

"Think." Because he understood that she would feel long before she would think, he pressed her back against the seat with both hands on her shoulders. No easy task, he thought grimly. She might be as slim as a wand, but she was strong. "Hellfire, Mel, listen to me. He's safe. David's safe. You'll only complicate and confuse things by bursting in there and trying to take him from them."

Her eyes blazed as she strained against him. He thought she looked like a goddess, ready to fling lightning from her fingertips. "They stole him."

"No. No, they didn't. They don't know he was stolen. They think he was given away, or they've convinced themselves he was because they were desperate for a child. Haven't you ever been desperate enough to take a shortcut, to overlook that blurred line and grab what you wanted?"

Furious, she could only shake her head. "He's not their child."

"No." His voice gentled, as did his hold. "But for three months he has been. He's Eric to them, and they love him very much. Enough to pretend he was meant to be theirs."

She struggled to control her breathing. "How can you ask me to leave him with them?"

"Only for a little while longer." He stroked a hand over her cheek. "I swear Rose will have him back before tomorrow night."

She swallowed, nodded. "Let go of me." When he did, she

picked up the binoculars with unsteady hands. "You were right to stop me. It's important to be sure."

She focused on the wide bay window, seeing pastel walls through gauzy curtains. She saw a baby swing, and a maroon couch with a clutter of toys scattered over it. With her lips pressed together, Mel watched a woman walk into view. A trim brunette in walking shorts and a cotton blouse. The woman's hair swung prettily as she turned her head to laugh at someone out of sight.

Then she held out her arms.

"Oh, God. David."

Mel's knuckles whitened on the field glasses as she saw a man pass David to the woman's waiting arms. Behind the filmy curtains, she saw David's smile.

"Let's take a walk," Sebastian said quietly, but she shook her head.

"I need some pictures." Hands steady again, Mel set the glasses aside and took up the camera, with its telescopic lens. "If we can't convince Devereaux to move, maybe these will."

Patiently she took half a roll, waiting when they moved out of view, snapping when they walked in front of the window again. Her chest hurt. There was such terrible pressure there that she rubbed the heel of her hand against it.

"Let's walk." She set the camera down on the floor of the car. "They may bring him out soon."

"If you try to snatch him—"

"I'm not stupid," she told him sharply. "I wasn't thinking before. I know how it needs to be done."

They got out on opposite sides, then rejoined on the sidewalk.

"It might look less conspicuous if you held my hand." Sebastian held his out to hers. She studied it dubiously, then shrugged.

"Wouldn't hurt, I guess."

"You have such a romantic heart, Sutherland." He swung their joined hands up to his lips and kissed her fingers. The rude name she called him only made him smile. "I've always enjoyed neighborhoods like this without ever wanting to live in one. Tidy lawns. A neighbor pruning roses over the fence." He inclined his head toward a young boy speeding down the street on a bike.

"Kids out playing. Barbecue smoke, and children's laughter in the air."

She'd always longed for a niche in such a place. Not wanting to admit it to him, or to herself, she shrugged. "Crabgrass. Nosy neighbors spying through the front blinds. Bad-tempered dogs."

As if she'd called it up, one came barreling across a lawn, barking deep in its throat. Sebastian merely turned his head and stared. The dog stumbled to a halt, whimpered a little, then skulked away with his tail between his legs.

Impressed, Mel pursed her lips. "Nice trick."

"It's a gift." Sebastian released her hand and put an arm around her shoulders. "Relax," he murmured. "You don't have to worry about him."

"I'm fine."

"You're tight as a drum. Here." He shifted his hand, moving it to the base of her neck. When Mel felt his fingertips prod gently, she tried to shake him off.

"Look, Donovan—"

"Shhh. It's another gift." He did something, even with her wiggling away. She felt the tensed muscles of her shoulders go fluid.

"Oh," she managed.

"Better?" He tucked her under his arm again. "If I had more time—God knows, if I had you naked—I'd work all the kinks out." He grinned down into her astonished face. "It seems only fair to let you in on some of my thoughts from time to time. And I have been thinking about getting you naked quite a bit."

Flustered, mortally afraid she might blush, she looked straight ahead. "Well, think about something else."

"It's hard. Particularly when you look so fetching in my shirt."

"I don't like flirtations," she said under her breath.

"My dear Mary Ellen, there's a world of difference between a flirtation and a direct statement of desire. Now, if I were to tell you what lovely eyes you have, how they remind me of the hills in my homeland—that would be flirting. Or if I mentioned that your hair is like the gold in a Botticelli painting, or that your skin is as soft as the clouds that drift over my mountain some evenings—that could be construed as flirting."

There was an odd, distinctly uncomfortable fluttering in her stomach. She wanted it to stop.

"If you said any of those things I'd think you'd lost your mind."

"Which is exactly why I opted for the direct approach. I want you in bed. My bed." Under one of the spreading oaks, he stopped, turning her into his arms before she could so much as sputter. "I want to undress you. Touch you. I want to watch you come alive when I'm inside you." He leaned down to catch her lower lip between his teeth. "And then I want to do it all over again." He felt her shudder and turned the nip into a long, searching kiss. "Direct enough?"

Her hands were against his chest, fingers spread. She had no idea how they'd gotten there. Her mouth felt swollen and stung and hungry. "I think…" But, of course, she couldn't think at all, and that was the problem. Her blood was pounding so hard that she wondered people didn't come out of their houses to see what the racket was about. "You're crazy."

"For wanting you, or for saying it?"

"For…for thinking I'd be interested in a quick tumble with you. I hardly know you."

He caught her chin with his fingers. "You know me." He kissed her again. "And I didn't say anything about quick."

Before she could speak again, he tensed. "They're coming out," he said, without turning around. Over his shoulder she could see the door open and the brunette pushing out a stroller. "Let's cross the street. You can get a good look as they walk by."

She'd tensed up again. Sebastian kept an arm around her shoulders, as much in warning as in support. She could hear the man and woman talking to each other. It was the light, happy conversation of two young parents with a healthy baby. Their words were nothing but a blur. Without thinking, she slipped an arm around Sebastian's waist and held on.

Oh, he'd grown! She felt tears rush stinging to her eyes and willed them back. He was moving quickly beyond baby to toddler. There were little red hightops on his feet, scuffed, as if he might have been walking already. His hair was longer, curling around his round, rosy face.

And his eyes... She stopped, had to bite back his name. He was looking at her as he rolled along in the bright blue stroller. Looking right at her, and there was a smile, a smile of recognition, in his eyes. He squealed, held out his arms.

"My boy likes pretty women," the man said with a proud grin as they rolled David past.

Rooted to the spot, Mel watched David crane his neck around the stroller, saw his lips move into a pout. He let out a wail of protest that had the woman crooning to him.

"He knew me," Mel whispered. "He remembered me."

"Yes, he did. It's difficult to forget love." He caught her as she took a stumbling step forward. "Not now, Mel. We'll go call Devereaux."

"He knew me." She found her voice muffled against a cool linen shirt. "I'm all right," she insisted, but she didn't try to break away.

"I know you are." He pressed his lips to her temple, stroked a hand over her hair and waited for her tremors to pass.

It was one of the most difficult things she'd ever done, standing on the sidewalk in front of the house with the blue shutters and the big tree in the yard. Devereaux and a female agent were inside. She'd watched them go in, through the door opened by the young brunette. She'd still been in her robe, Mel remembered, and there had been a flicker of fear, or perhaps knowledge, in her eyes as she bent to retrieve the morning paper.

She could hear weeping now, deep, grieving tears. Her heart wanted to hold rock hard against it, but it couldn't.

When would they come out? Stuffing her hands in her pockets, she paced the sidewalk. It had already been too long. Devereaux had still insisted that they wait until morning, and she'd had hardly a wink of sleep at the hotel. It was well over an hour since they'd gone inside.

"Why don't you sit in the car?" Sebastian suggested.

"I couldn't sit."

"They won't let us take him yet. Devereaux explained the procedure. It'll take hours to do the blood test and the print checks."

"They'll let me stay with him. They'll damn well let me stay with him. He's not going to be with strangers." She pressed her lips together. "Tell me about them," she blurted out. "Please."

He'd expected her to ask, and he turned away from the house to look into Mel's eyes as he told her. "She was a teacher. She resigned when David came to them. It was important to her to spend as much time with him as possible. Her husband is an engineer. They've been married eight years, and have been trying to have a child almost since the start. They're good people, very loving to each other, and with room in their hearts for a family. They were easy prey, Mel."

He could see in her face the war between compassion and fury, between right and wrong. "I'm sorry for them," she whispered. "I'm sorry to know that anyone would exploit that kind of love, that kind of need. I hate what's been done to everyone involved."

"Life isn't always fair."

"Life isn't usually fair," she corrected.

She paced some more, casting dark, desperate looks at the bay window. When the door opened, she shifted to her toes, ready to dash. Devereaux strode toward her.

"The boy knows you?"

"Yes. I told you he recognized me when he saw me yesterday."

He nodded. "He's upset, wailing pretty good, making himself half-sick, what with Mr. and Mrs. Frost carrying on. We've got the woman calming down. Like I told you, we'll have to take the boy in until we can check the matches and clear up the paperwork. Might be easier for him if you went in for him, drove along with Agent Barker."

"Sure." Her heart began to pound in her throat. "Donovan?"

"I'll follow you."

She went inside, fighting to shield her heart and mind from the hopeless weeping beyond a bedroom door. She walked down a hallway, stepping over a plastic rocking horse and into the nursery.

Where the walls were pale blue and painted with sailboats. Where the crib by the window held a circus mobile.

Just as he'd said, she thought as her mouth went dry. Exactly as he'd said.

Then she tossed all that aside and reached down for the crying David.

"Oh, baby." She pressed her face to his, drying his cheeks with her own. "David, sweet little David." She soothed him, brushing his damp hair back from his face, grateful the agent's back was to her so that he couldn't see her own eyes fill.

"Hey, big guy." She kissed his trembling lips. He hiccuped, rubbed his eyes with his fists, then let out a tired sigh as his head dropped to her shoulder. "That's my boy. Let's go home, huh? Let's go home and see Mom and Dad."

Chapter 7

"I'll never be able to thank you. Never." Rose stood looking out her kitchen window. In the courtyard beyond, her husband and son sat in a patch of sunlight, rolling a bright orange ball around. "Just looking at them makes me..."

"I know." Mel slipped an arm around her shoulders. As they watched in silence, listening to David laugh, Rose brought her hand up to Mel's and squeezed tight. "They look real good out there, don't they?"

"Perfect." Rose dabbed her eyes with a tissue and sighed. "Just perfect. When I think how afraid I was that I'd never see David again—"

"Then don't think. David's back where he belongs."

"Thanks to you and Mr. Donovan." Rose moved away from the window, but her gaze kept going back to it again and again. Mel wondered how long it would be before Rose would feel comfortable with David out of her sight. "Can you tell me anything about the people who had him, Mel? The FBI were very sympathetic and kind, but..."

"Tight-lipped," Mel finished. "They were good people, Rose. Good people who wanted a family. They made a mistake, trusted someone they shouldn't have trusted. But they took good care of David."

"He's grown so. And he's been trying to take a few steps." There was a bitterness, a sharp tang of bitterness in the back of her throat, at having missed those three precious months of her son's life. But with it was a sorrow for another mother in another city with an empty crib to face. "I know they loved him. And I know how hurt and afraid she must be now. But it's worse for her than it was for me. She knows she'll never have him back." She laid her fisted hands on the counter. "Who did this to us, Mel? Who did this to all of us?"

"I don't know. But I'm working on it."

"Will you work with Mr. Donovan? I know how concerned he is."

"Sebastian?"

"We talked about it a little when he stopped by."

"Oh?" Mel thought she did nonchalance very well. "He came by?"

Rose's face softened. She looked almost as she had in those carefree days before David's abduction. "He brought David his teddy bear, and this cute little blue sailboat."

A sailboat, Mel mused. Yes, he would have thought of that. "That was nice of him."

"He just seemed to understand both sides of it, you know? What Stan and I went through, what those people in Atlanta are going through right now. All because there's someone out there who doesn't care about people at all. Not about babies or mothers or families. He only wants to make money on them." Her lips trembled then firmed. "I guess that's why Mr. Donovan wouldn't let me and Stan pay him anything."

"He didn't take a fee?" Mel asked, struggling to sound disinterested.

"No, he wouldn't take a dime." Recalling other duties, Rose opened the oven to check on her meat loaf. "He said Stan and I should send what we thought we could afford to one of the homeless shelters."

"I see."

"And he said he was going to think about following up on the case."

"The case?"

"He said...something like it wasn't right for babies to be stolen out of cribs and sold off like puppies. That there were some lines you couldn't cross."

"Yes, there are." Mel snatched up her bag. "I have to go, Rose."

Surprised, Rose shut the oven door. "Can't you stay for dinner?"

"I really can't." She hesitated, then did something she rarely did, something she wished she could do with more ease. She kissed Rose's cheek. "There's something I have to take care of."

She supposed she should have done it before. But they'd been back in Monterey for only a couple of days. Mel skimmed through a low-lying cloud on her way up the mountain. It wasn't as if he'd gone out of his way to come and see her, she thought. He'd gone by Rose's apartment, but he hadn't driven a few more blocks to hers.

Obviously he hadn't meant any of that nonsense he'd been spouting about finding her attractive, about wanting her. All that stuff about her eyes and her hair and her skin. Mel drummed her fingers on the gearshift. If he'd meant any of it, he'd have made a move by now. She wished he had. How could she decide if she would block it or not if he didn't bother to make a move?

So she'd beard the wolf in his den. There were obligations to fulfill, statements to be made, and questions to be answered.

Certain she was ready for all of that, Mel turned into Sebastian's bumpy lane. Halfway up she hit the brakes as a horse and rider leapt in front of her. The black stallion and the dark man on his back bounded across the gravel track in a flash of muscle and speed. At the sight of the gleaming horse and the golden-skinned man with his ebony hair flying in the wind, she was tossed back centuries to when there were dragons to be slain and magic sung in the air.

Mel sat openmouthed as they thundered up the rocky slope, through a pocket of mist and back into the stream of sun. No centaur had ever looked more magnificent.

As the echoes of hoofbeats died away, she nudged her car up the lane. This was reality, she reminded herself. The engine groaned and complained at the incline, coughed, sputtered, then finally crept its way up to the house.

As she expected, Sebastian was in the paddock, rubbing Eros

down. Dismounted, he looked no less magnificent, no less mystical. Energy and life vibrated from him. The excitement of the ride was still on his face, in his eyes. The strength of it was in the rippling muscles of his back and forearms as he cooled down his mount.

Mel thought that if she touched him now her fingers would burn.

"Nice day for a ride, I guess."

Sebastian looked over Eros's withers and smiled. "Most are. I'm sorry I didn't greet you, but I hate to stop Eros when he has his head."

"It's all right," She was glad he hadn't. Mel was dead certain she wouldn't have managed more than a stutter if he'd spoken to her astride that horse. "I just stopped by to see if you had a few minutes to clear things up."

"I think I could find some time for you." He patted the stallion's left flank, and then, resting the horse's knee on his thigh, began to clean the hoof. "You've seen Rose?"

"Yes, I've just come from there. She said you'd been by. You brought David a sailboat."

Sebastian glanced up, then moved to the next hoof. "I thought it might help ease some of his confusion to have something familiar from those weeks he was away."

"It was very…kind."

He straightened, then moved on to the front leg. "I have my moments."

On more solid ground now, Mel braced a boot on the lowest rung of the fence. "Rose said you wouldn't take a fee."

"I believe I pointed out before that I don't need the money."

"I'm aware of that." Mel leaned on the fence, running her fingers down Eros's neck. Nothing magical there, she assured herself. Just a magnificent beast in his prime. Much like his master. "I did some checking. You have your fingers in a lot of pies, Donovan."

"That's one way of putting it."

"I guess it's easier to make money when you've got a bundle behind you to start with."

He examined the last hoof. "I suppose. And it would follow it would be easier to lose money under the same conditions."

"You got me there." She tilted her head as he straightened again. "That business in Chicago. It was rough."

She saw the change in his face and was sorry for it. This wasn't something he took lightly or brushed off in a matter of days. "It was difficult, yes. Failure is."

"But you helped them find him. Stop him."

"Five lives lost isn't what I term a success." He gave Eros a slap on the rump to send him trotting off. "Why don't you come inside while I clean up?"

"Sebastian."

He knew it was the first time she'd used his given name. It surprised him enough to have him pausing, one hand on the fence, his body poised to vault.

"Five lives lost," she said quietly. Her eyes were dark with understanding. "Do you know how many saved?"

"No." He came over the fence, landing lightly in front of her. "No, I don't. But it helps that you'd ask." He took her arm, his fingers sliding from shoulder to elbow to wrist. "Come inside."

She liked it out here, where there was plenty of room to maneuver. Should maneuvering be necessary. But it seemed foolish and undeniably weak not to go in the house with him.

"There is something I want to talk with you about."

"I assumed there was. Have you had dinner?"

"No."

"Good. We'll talk while we eat."

They went in through the side of the house, climbing onto a redwood deck flanked with pots spilling over with impatiens and going through a wide glass door directly into the kitchen. It was all royal blue and white, and as sleek and glossy as a page out of a high-fashion magazine. Sebastian went directly to a small glass-fronted refrigerator and chose a chilled bottle of wine from a rack inside.

"Have a seat." He gestured to a stool at the tiled work island. After uncorking the wine, he poured her a glass. "I need to clean up," he said, setting the wine on the counter in front of her. "Be at home."

"Sure."

The moment he was out of the room, she was off the stool. Mel didn't consider it rude. It was innate curiosity. There was no better way to find out what made people tick than by poking around their personal space. And she desperately wanted to know what made Sebastian Donovan tick.

The kitchen was meticulously neat, spotless counters and appliances, the dishes in their glass-fronted cupboards arranged according to size. The room didn't smell of detergent or disinfectant, but of...air, she decided, fresh, faintly herb-scented.

There were several clusters of herbs hanging upside down in front of the window over the sink. Mel sniffed at them, finding their aroma pleasant and vaguely mysterious.

She opened a drawer at random and found baking utensils. She tried another and found more kitchen gadgets neatly stacked.

Where was the clutter? she wondered as she frowned around the room. And the secrets one always found jumbled with it?

Not so much discouraged as intrigued, she slipped back onto the stool and picked up her wine a moment before he came into the room again.

He wore black now—snug coal-colored jeans and a black shirt rolled up to his elbows. His feet were bare. When he picked up the wine to pour his own glass, Mel realized he looked like what he claimed to be.

A wizard.

Smiling, he tapped his glass to hers, leaning close to stare into her eyes. "Will you trust me?"

"Huh?"

His smile widened. "To choose the menu."

She blinked, took a hasty sip of wine. "Sure. I'll eat most anything."

As he began gathering ingredients and pots and pans, she let out a slow, relieved breath. "You're going to cook?"

"Yes. Why?"

"I figured you'd just call out for something." Her brows drew together as he poured oil in a skillet. "It's an awful lot of trouble."

"I enjoy it." Sebastian snipped some herbs into a bowl. "It relaxes me."

Mel scratched her knee and gave the mixture he was making a doubtful look. "You want me to help you?"

"You don't cook."

She lifted a brow. "How do you know?"

"I got a glimpse of your kitchen. Garlic?"

"Sure."

Sebastian crushed the clove with the flat of his knife. "What did you want to talk to me about, Mel?"

"A couple of things." She shifted in her chair, then rested her chin on her hand. Odd, she hadn't realized she would enjoy watching him cook. "Things turned out the way they were supposed to for Rose and Stan and David. What's that you're putting in there?"

"Rosemary."

"It smells good." So did he, she thought. Gone was the sexy leather-and-sweat scent he'd carried with him after the ride. It had been replaced by that equally sexy forest fragrance that was both wild and utterly male. She sipped her wine again, relaxing enough to toe off her boots. "For Mr. and Mrs. Frost back in Georgia, things are pretty awful right now."

Sebastian scooped tomato and garlic and herbs into a skillet. "When someone wins, someone usually loses."

"I know how it works. We did what we had to do, but we didn't finish."

He coated boneless chicken breasts before laying them in a pan. He liked the way she sat there, swinging one leg lazily and watching his culinary preparations with a careful eye. "Go on."

"We didn't get the one who matters, Donovan. The one who arranged the whole thing. We got David back, and that was the most important thing, but we didn't finish. He's not the only baby who's been stolen."

"How do you know?"

"It's logical. An operation that slick, that pat. It wasn't just a one-shot deal."

"No." He topped off their glasses, then poured some of the wine onto the chicken. "It's not."

"So, here's the way I see it." She pushed off the stool. Mel felt she thought better on her feet. "The Frosts had a contact. Now, they might have been able to turn the feds onto him, or he could be long gone. I'd go with long gone." She stopped pacing to tilt her head.

Sebastian nodded. "Continue."

"Okay. It's a national thing. A real company. Got to have a lawyer, someone to handle the adoption papers. Maybe a doctor, too. Or at least someone with connections in the fertility business. The Frosts had all kinds of fertility tests. I checked."

Sebastian stirred and sniffed and checked, but he was listening. "I imagine the FBI checked, as well."

"Sure they did. Our pal Devereaux's right on top of things. But I like to finish what I start. You've got all these couples trying to start a family. They'll try anything. Regulate their sex lives, their diets, dance naked under the full moon. And pay. Pay all kinds of money for tests, for operations, for drugs. And if none of it works, they'll pay for a baby."

She came back to the island to sniff at one of the pots herself. "Good," she murmured. "I know it's usually on the up-and-up. A reputable adoption agency, a reputable lawyer. And, in most cases, it's the right thing. The baby gets a loving home, the biological mother gets a second chance, and the adoptive parents get their miracle. But then you have the slime factor. The sleaze-ball who always finds a way to make a buck off someone else's tragedy."

"Why don't you put a couple of plates on the table by the window? I'm listening."

"Okay." She puttered around the kitchen, following his instructions for china, for flatware, for napkins, as she continued to theorize. "But this isn't just any pennyante sleaze. This is a smart one, slick enough to pull together an organization that can snatch a kid from one coast, pass him along like a football cross-country and bounce him into a nice, affluent home thousands of miles away."

"I haven't found anything to argue about yet."

"Well, he's the one we have to get to. They haven't picked up Parkland yet, but I figure they will. He's not a pro. He's just some jerk who tried to find a quick way to pay off a debt and keep his kneecaps intact. He won't be much of a lead when they find him, but he'll be something. I have to figure the feds will keep him under wraps."

"So far your figuring seems flawless. Take the bottle and sit."

She did, curling her legs under her on the corner bench by

the window. "It's not likely the feds would cut a PI much of a break."

"No." Sebastian set platters down on the table, pasta curls tanged with tomatoes and herbs, the wine-braised chicken, thick slabs of crusty bread.

"They'd cut you one. They owe you."

Sebastian served Mel himself. "Perhaps."

"They'd give you a copy of Parkland's statement when they nab him. Maybe even let you talk to him. If you said you were still interested in the case, they'd feed you information."

"Yes, they might." Sebastian sampled the meal and found it excellent. "But am I still interested?"

She clamped a hand over his wrist before he could slice off another bite of tender chicken. "Don't you like to finish what you start?"

He lifted his eyes to hers and looked deep, so deep that her fingers trembled once before they slid away. "Yes, I do."

Uneasy, she broke a piece of bread. "Well, then?"

"I'll help you. I'll use whatever connections I may have."

"I appreciate it." Though she was careful not to touch him again, her lips curved, her eyes warmed. "Really. I'll owe you for this."

"No, I don't think so. Nor will you when you hear my conditions. We'll work together."

She dropped the bread. "Look, Donovan, I appreciate the offer, but I work alone. Anyway, your style—the visions and stuff—it makes me nervous."

"Fair enough. Your style—guns and stuff—makes me nervous. So, we compromise. Work together, deal with each other's…eccentricities. After all, it's the goal that's important, isn't it?"

She mulled it over, poking at the food on her plate. "Maybe I did have an idea that would work better as a couple—a childless couple." Still wary, she glanced up at him. "But if we did agree to compromise, for this one time, we'd have to have rules."

"Oh, absolutely."

"Don't smirk when you say that." With her mind clicking away, she dug into the meal. "This is good." She scooped up another bite. "Really good. It didn't look like all that much trouble."

"You flatter me."

"No, I mean…" She laughed and shrugged and ate some more. "I guess I thought fancy food meant fancy work. My mother worked as a waitress a lot, and she'd bring home all this food from the kitchen. But it was mostly in diners and fast-food joints. Nothing like this."

"Your mother's well?"

"Oh, sure. I got a postcard last week from Nebraska. She travels around a lot. Itchy feet."

"Your father?"

The faintest of hesitations, the briefest shadow of sadness. "I don't remember him."

"How does your mother feel about your profession?"

"She thinks it's exciting—but then, she watches a lot of TV. What about yours?" Mel lifted her glass and gestured. "How do your parents feel about you being the wizard of Monterey?"

"I don't think I'd term it quite that way," Sebastian said after a moment. "But, if they think of it, I imagine they're pleased that I'm carrying on the family tradition."

Mel huffed into her wine. "What are you, like a coven?"

"No," he said gently, unoffended. "We're like a family."

"You know, I wouldn't have believed any of it if I hadn't… Well, I was there. But that doesn't mean I swallow the whole deal." Her eyes flashed up to his, careful and calculating. "I did some reading up, about tests and research and that kind of thing. A lot of reputable scientists believe there's something to psychic phenomena."

"That's comforting."

"Don't be snide," she said, shifting in her seat. "What I mean is, they know they don't completely understand the human mind. That's logical. They look at EEG patterns and EMGs and stuff. You know, they study people who can guess what's on the face of a card without lifting it up, things like that. But that doesn't mean they go in for witchcraft or prophesies or fairy dust."

"A little fairy dust wouldn't hurt you," Sebastian murmured. "I'll have to speak to Morgana about it."

"Seriously," Mel began.

"Seriously." He took her hand. "I was born with elvin blood. I am a hereditary witch who can trace his roots back to Finn of the Celts. My gift is of sight. It was not asked for or demanded, but given. This has nothing to do with logic or science or dancing naked in the moonlight. It is my legacy. It is my destiny."

"Well," Mel said after a long moment. And again: "Well." She moistened her lips and cleared her throat. "In these studies they tested things like telekinesis, telepathy."

"You want proof, Mel?"

"No— Yes. I mean, if we are going to work together on this thing, I'd like to know the extent of your...talent."

"Fair. Think of a number from one to ten. Six," he said before she could open her mouth.

"I wasn't ready."

"But that was the first number that popped into your mind."

It was, but she shook her head. "I wasn't ready." She closed her eyes. "Now."

She was good, he thought. Very good. Right now she was using all her will to block him out. To distract her, he nibbled on the knuckle of the hand he still held. "Three."

She opened her eyes. "All right. How?"

"From your mind to mine." He rubbed his lips over her fingers. "Sometimes in words, sometimes in pictures, sometimes only in feelings that are impossible to describe. Now you're wondering if you had too much wine, because your heart's beating too fast, your skin is warm. Your head's light."

"My head's fine." She jerked her hand from his. "Or it would be if you'd stay out of it. I can feel..."

"Yes." Content, he sat back and lifted his glass. "I know you can. It's very rare, without a blood connection, for anyone to feel me, particularly on such a light scan. You have potential, Sutherland. If you care to explore it, I'd be happy to assist you."

She couldn't quite mask the quick shudder that passed through her. "No, thanks. I like my head just the way it is." Experimentally she put a hand to it while watching Sebastian. "I don't like the idea of anybody being able to read my mind. If we're going to go through with this temporary partnership, that's the number one rule."

"Agreed. I won't look inside your mind unless you ask me to." Noting the doubt in her eyes, he smiled. "I don't lie, Mel."

"Witch's creed?"

"If you like."

She didn't, but she would take him at his word. "Okay, next—we share all information. No holding back."

His smile was both charming and dangerous. "I'm more than willing to agree we've held back long enough."

"We're professional. We keep it professional."

"When appropriate." He touched the rim of his glass to hers. "Is sharing a meal considered professional?"

"We don't have to be ridiculous. What I mean is, if we're going to go under posing as a married couple wanting a child, we don't let the act—"

"Blur those lines of yours," he finished for her. "I understand. Do you have a plan?"

"Well, it would help if we had the cooperation of the FBI."

"Leave that to me."

She grinned. It was exactly what she'd hoped for. "With them backing us up, we can establish a solid identity. Papers, backgrounds, IRS files, the works. We need to come to the attention of the organization, so we'll have to be affluent, but not so high-profile as to scare them off. We should be new in the community we choose. No ties, no family. We'll have to be put on the waiting list of several reputable adoption agencies. Have records from fertility clinics and doctors. Once they've gotten to Parkland or one of the others, we'll have a better idea where to set up, and how."

"There might be an easier way."

"What?"

He waved her aside. "I'll get to it. This could take quite a lot of time."

"It could. It would be worth it."

"We compromise. I work out where we begin, when and how, you handle the procedure from there."

She hesitated, aware she'd never be any good at compromise. "If you pick the when, where and how, it has to be for solid reasons, and I have to accept them."

"All right."

"All right." It seemed simple enough. If there was a frisson of excitement working through her, it was the anticipation of an interesting and rewarding job. "I guess I could help you deal with all these dishes."

She rose, started to stack the delicate china with the competence her waitress mother had taught her. Sebastian put a hand on her arm. The frisson erupted into a flare.

"Leave them."

"You cooked," she said, and strode quickly to the sink. A little room, she thought. A little room and some busywork was all she needed to stay on an even keel. "And from the looks of this kitchen, you're not the type who leaves dirty dishes hanging around."

He was behind her when she turned, and his hands came to her shoulders to prevent her from dodging away. "So, I'll be unpredictable."

"Or you could hire some elves to scrub up," she muttered.

"I don't employ any elves—in California." When her look sharpened, he began to knead her shoulders. "You're tensing up on me, Mel. During dinner you were quite relaxed. You even smiled at me several times, which I found a very pleasant change."

"I don't like people touching me." But she didn't move away. After all, there was nowhere to go.

"Why not? It's merely another form of communication. There are many. Voices, eyes, hands." His slid over her shoulders, turning the muscles there to water. "Minds. A touch doesn't have to be dangerous."

"It can be."

His lips curved as his fingers skimmed down her back. "But you're no coward. A woman like you meets a dangerous situation head-on."

Her chin came up, as he'd known it would. "I came here to talk to you."

"And we've talked." He nudged her closer so that he had only to bend his head to press his lips to the faint cleft in the center of that strong chin. "I enjoyed it."

She would not be seduced. She was a grown woman with a mind of her own, and seduction was, always had been, out of the question. She lifted a hand to his chest, where it lay, fingers spread, neither resisting or inviting.

"I didn't come to play games."

"Pity." His lips hovered a breath from hers before he tilted his head and brushed them under her jaw. "I also enjoy games. But we can save them for another time."

It was becoming very difficult to breathe. "Look, maybe I'm attracted to you, but that doesn't mean…anything."

"Of course not. Your skin's unbelievably delicate just here, Mary Ellen. It's as if your pulse would bruise the flesh if it continued to beat so hard."

"That's ridiculous."

But when he tugged her shirt free of her waistband to let his hands roam up her back, she felt as delicate as a dandelion puff. With a sound that was somewhere between a moan and a sigh, she arched back against him.

"I'd nearly lost my patience," he murmured against her throat. "Waiting for you to come to me."

"I didn't. I haven't." But her arms had wound around him, and her fingers were tangled in his hair. "This isn't why I'm here."

But hadn't she known? Somewhere inside, hadn't she known?

"I have to think. This could be a mistake." But even as she said it, her mouth was moving hungrily over his. "I hate to make mistakes."

"Mmm… Who doesn't?" He cupped his hands under her hips. With a murmur of acceptance, she scooted up, wrapping her legs around his waist. "This isn't one."

"I'll figure it out later," she said as he carried her out of the kitchen. "I really don't want this to mess up the other business. It's too important. I want that to work, I really want that to work, and I'd hate myself if I messed it up just because…"

On a groan, she pressed her mouth to his throat. "I want you. I want you so much."

Her words started a drumbeat in his head, slow, rhythmic, seductive. He dragged her head back with one hand so that he could plunder her mouth. "One has nothing to do with the other."

"It could." She rocked against him as he started up the steps.

Her breath was already coming in pants as her eyes met his. "It should."

"Then so be it." He kicked open the door to the bedroom. "Let's break some rules."

Chapter 8

She had never been one to throw caution to the winds. To take risks, certainly, but always knowing the consequences. There was no way to figure the odds now, not with him. Again, it was up to instinct. Although her head told her to cut her losses and run, something else, something closer to the bone, urged her to stay.

To trust.

She was still wrapped around him, throbbing at every point a pulse could beat. It wasn't shyness that had her hesitating. She had never considered herself overly sexual or more than average in looks, so she felt she had nothing to be shy about. It was a sudden certainty that this was vital that had her taking one last long look at him.

And what she saw was exactly what she wanted.

Her lips curved slowly. When she started to slide down him, he braced her back against the bedpost so that when her feet touched the floor she was trapped between the smooth, carved wood and his body.

His eyes stayed on hers as his hands moved slowly upward, fingertips sliding over thighs, hips, the sides of her breasts, her throat, temples. She shuddered once before his fists closed, vise-like, in her hair and his mouth crushed down on hers.

His body was pressed against her so truly that she felt every line and curve. She sensed that the power inside it was that of a wolf on a leash, ready to tear free. But it was his mouth that drove her mind to the edge of reason. Insatiable and possessive, it drew from hers every nuance of emotion. Desires and doubts, fears and longings. She felt her will being passed to him like a gift.

He felt that instant of surrender, when her body was both limp and firm against his, when her lips trembled, then sought more of what he wanted to give. The hunger sliced through him like a silver blade, cleaving the civilized from the desperate and leaving him quivering like a stallion that scents his mate.

He reared his head back, and she saw that his eyes were dark as midnight, full of reckless needs and heedless wants. And power. She trembled, first in fear, then again, in glorious delight.

It was that answer he saw. And it was that answer he took.

With one violent swipe, he tore her shirt to tatters. Her gasp was muffled against his mouth. Even as they tumbled onto the bed, his hands were everywhere, bruising and stroking, taking and tormenting.

In answer she dragged at his shirt, popping buttons, rending seams, as they rolled over the sheets. When she felt his flesh against hers, she let out a long, breathless sigh of approval.

He gave her little time to think, and none to question. He was riding her into a storm filled with thunderclaps and flashing lights and howling winds. She knew it was physical. There was nothing magical about the skill of his hands, the drugging taste of his mouth. But oh, it seemed like magic to be whisked away, beyond the ordinary, beyond even the simple beauty of a rosy dusk and the stirrings of night birds just waking.

Where he took her was all dazzling speed and unspeakable pleasure. A whisper of some language she couldn't understand. An incantation? Some lover's promise? The sound alone was enough to seduce her. A touch, rough or gentle, was accepted with delight. The taste of him, hot and salty on her lips, cool and soothing on her tongue, was enough to make her ravenous for more.

So generous, his hazy mind thought. So strong, so giving. In the lowering light her skin was gilded like a warrior goddess's prepared for battle. She was slim and straight, agile as a fantasy, responsive as a wish. He felt her strangled gasp against his ear, the sudden convulsive dig of her nails into his back as her body shuddered from the climax he gave her.

Even as her limp hand slid from his damp shoulder he was racing over her again. Wild to taste, crazed to make her blood pump hot again until he could hear her breath rasping out his name.

He braced over her, shaking his head until his vision cleared, until he could see her face, her eyes half-closed and drugged with pleasure, her lips swollen from his and trembling on each breath.

"Come with me," he told her.

As her arms encircled, he drove himself inside her. And he knew, as they raced together, that some spells require nothing more than a willing heart.

She thought she heard music. Lovely, soothing. Heart music. Mel didn't know where the phrase had come from, but she smiled at the thought of it and turned.

There was no one to turn to.

Instantly awake, she sat up in the dark. Though the night was ink black, she knew she was alone in the room. Sebastian's room. Being with him had been no dream. Nor was being alone now a dream.

She groped for the light beside the bed and shielded her eyes until they had adjusted.

She didn't call out his name. It would have made her feel foolish to speak it in an empty bed in a shadowy room. Instead she scrambled up, found his shirt crumpled on the floor. Tugging her arms through the sleeves, she followed the music.

It came from no real direction. Though soft as a whisper, it seemed to surround her. Odd, no matter how she strained to hear, she couldn't be sure if she was hearing voices raised in song, or strings, flutes, horns. It was simply sound, a lovely vibration on the air that was both eerie and beautiful.

She flowed with it, following instinct. The sound grew no louder, no softer, but it did seem to become more fluid, washing over her skin, sliding into her mind as she followed a corridor that snaked left, then climbed a short flight of stairs.

She saw the glow of candlelight, an ethereal flicker that built to a golden flood as she approached a room at the end of the hallway. There was a scent of warm wax, of sandalwood, of pungent smoke.

She wasn't aware she was holding her breath when she stopped in the doorway and looked.

The room wasn't large. She thought the word *chamber* would be more appropriate, but she wasn't sure why such a quaint term came to mind. The walls were a pale, warm-toned wood, burnished now with the mystical lights of dozens of slim white candles.

There were windows, three in the shape of crescent moons. She remembered seeing them from the outside and realized that the room was at the topmost part of the house, facing the cliffs and the sea.

Above, a twinkling of stars could be seen through the skylights he'd opened to the night and the air. There were chairs and tables and stands, all of them looking as if they belonged in some medieval castle, rather than a modern home in Big Sur. On them she saw orbs of crystal, colorful bowls, scribed silver mirrors, slender wands of clear glass, and goblets encrusted with glittering stones.

She didn't believe in magic. Mel knew there was always a false drawer in the magician's chest and an ace of hearts up his sleeve. But standing there, in the doorway of that room, she felt the air pulse and throb as if it were alive with a thousand hearts.

And she knew that there was more, here in this world she thought she knew, than she had ever dreamed of.

Sebastian sat in the center of the room, in the center of a silver pentagram inlaid in the wooden floor. His back was to her, and he was very still. Her curiosity had always been strong, but she discovered something stronger—her need to give him his privacy.

But, even as she stepped back from the doorway, he spoke to her.

"I didn't mean to wake you."

"You didn't." She toyed with one of the few buttons left on his shirt. "The music did. Or I woke up and heard it, and wondered..." She looked around, baffled. She could see no recording device, no stereo. "I wondered where it was coming from."

"The night." He rose. Though she'd never considered herself a prude, she found herself flushing when he stood naked in the candlelight, holding a hand out for her.

"I'm naturally nosy, but I didn't mean to intrude."

"You didn't." Her hesitation had him lifting a brow, then stepping forward to take her hand. "I needed to clear my mind. I couldn't do it beside you." He brought her palm to his lips, pressing them at the center. "Too many thoughts clouding the issue."

"I guess I should've gone home."

"No." He leaned down to kiss her, lightly, sweetly. "No, indeed."

"Well, the thing is..." She backed away a little, wishing she had something to do with her hands. "I don't usually do this sort of thing."

She looked so young, he thought, and so frail, standing there in his shirt, with her hair mussed from love and sleep, and her eyes too wide.

"Should I say that, since you decided to make an exception with me, you do this sort of thing very well?"

"You don't have to." Then her lips turned up. She had done well. They had done incredibly well. "But I don't guess it hurts. Do you usually sit naked on the floor in candlelight?"

"When the spirit moves me."

More comfortable now, she began moving around the room, picking up objects. Lips pursed, she examined a centuries-old scrying mirror. "Is this supposed to be magic stuff?"

In that moment, watching her peer suspiciously at the priceless, he adored her. "That was said to belong to Ninian."

"Who?"

"Ah, Sutherland, your education is sadly lacking. Ninian was a sorceress, reputed to have imprisoned Merlin in his cave of crystal."

"Yeah?" She took a closer look, found it a pretty piece, then set it down to study a globe of smoky quartz. "So what do you use this stuff for?"

"Enjoyment." He had no need for scrying mirrors or crystal balls in order to see. He kept them around him out of an appreciation of tradition and a sense of aesthetics. It amused him to see her frown and squint at the tools of power.

There was something he wanted to give her, a small gift. He hadn't forgotten the fleeting sadness he'd seen in her eyes when she'd told him she didn't remember her father.

"Would you like to see?"

"See what?"

"To see," he said gently, and walked to her. "Come." He took the globe in one hand, her fingers in the other, and drew her back to the center of the room.

"I don't really think—"

"Kneel." He nudged her down with him. "Past or future, Mel? Which would you like?"

With a nervous laugh, she settled back on her heels. "Aren't you supposed to be wearing a turban?"

"Use your imagination." He touched a hand to her cheek. "The past, I think. You prefer taking care of your own future."

"You got that right, but—"

"Put your hands on the globe, Mel. There's nothing to be afraid of."

"I'm not afraid." She squirmed a little, let out a long breath. "It's just a piece of glass. It's weird, that's all," she muttered as she took the crystal. Sebastian put his hands under hers and smiled.

"My aunt Bryna, Morgana's mother, gave me this ball as a christening gift. It was, for me, somewhat like training wheels on a bicycle."

It was cool in her hands, smooth and as cool as lake water. "I had this ball when I was a kid. A black plastic one. You were supposed to ask it questions, then you could shake it and this writing would float up toward this opening. It usually said something like, answer unclear, try again."

Again he smiled, finding her nerves endearing. The power was flowing into him, sweet as wine, easy as a spring breeze. This was a simple thing he would show her. "Look inside," he said, and his voice echoed oddly in the small room. "And see."

She was compelled to do so. At first she saw only a pretty ball with internal fractures glinting rainbows back at her. Then there were shadows, shadows within shadows, forms shifting, colors bleeding.

"Oh," she murmured, for the glass was no longer cool, but as warm as a sunbeam.

"Look," he said again, and it seemed his voice was inside her head. "With your heart."

She saw her mother first, but young, so young, and brightly pretty, despite the heavy use of eyeliner and a lipstick several shades too pale. It was the laughter in her face that brought the prettiness through the cosmetics. Her hair was blond, shoulder-length and straight as a pin. She was laughing at a young man in a white uniform, a sailor's cap perched jauntily on his head.

The man was holding a child of about two who was dressed in a frilly pink dress with black strapped shoes and lacy white socks.

Not just any child, Mel thought as her heart thudded in her throat. Me. The child is me.

In the background was a ship, a big gray naval vessel. There was a band playing something rousingly military, and there were people milling about, talking all at once. She couldn't hear the words, only the sounds.

She saw the man toss her in the air, toss her high. In the candlelit room her stomach leaped and dropped giddily. And here was love and trust and innocence. His eyes beaming up at her with pride and humor and excitement. Strong hands around her. A whiff of after-shave. A giggly laugh tickling her throat as she was caught close.

She watched the images shift. Saw her parents kiss. Oh, the sweetness of it. Then the boy who had been her father gave them a jaunty salute, tossed his duffel bag over his shoulder and walked toward the ship.

The ball in her hand was only pretty glass with inner fractures glinting rainbows back at her.

"My father." Mel might have dropped the globe if Sebastian's hands hadn't held firm. "It was my father. He...he was in the Navy. He wanted to see the world. He left that day from Norfolk. I was only two, I don't remember. My mother said we went down to see him off, and that he'd been excited."

Her voice broke, and she gave herself a minute. "A few

months later there was a storm in the Mediterranean, and he was lost at sea. He was only twenty-two. Just a boy, really. She has pictures, but you can't tell from pictures.'' Mel stared into the globe again, then slowly looked up at Sebastian. ''I have his eyes. I never realized I have his eyes.''

She closed them a moment, waiting until her system leveled a bit. ''I did see it, didn't I?''

''Yes.'' He lifted a hand to her hair. ''I didn't show you to make you sad, Mary Ellen.''

''It didn't. It made me sorry.'' On a sigh, she opened her eyes again. ''Sorry I can't remember him. Sorry that my mother remembers too much and that I never understood that before. And it made me happy to have seen him, and them together—all of us together—even once.'' She slipped her hands away, leaving the ball in his. ''Thank you.''

''It was a small thing, after what you brought me tonight.''

''What I brought?'' she asked as he rose to replace the ball.

''Yourself.''

''Oh, well...'' Clearing her throat, she got to her feet. ''I don't know if I'd put it like that.''

''How would you put it?''

She looked back at him and felt that new helpless fluttering in her stomach. ''I don't know, exactly. We're both adults.''

''Yes.'' He started toward her, and she surprised herself by edging back.

''Unattached.''

''So it seems.''

''Responsible.''

''Admirably.'' He danced his fingers over her hair. ''I've wanted to see you in candlelight, Mary Ellen.''

''Don't start that.'' She brushed his hand away.

''What?''

''Don't call me Mary Ellen, and don't start that violin-and-candlelight business.''

His eyes stayed on hers as he trailed a finger down her throat. ''You object to romance?''

''Not object, exactly.'' Her emotions were too close to the surface, much too close, after what she had seen in the globe. She needed to make certain they had their ground rules. ''I just don't need it. I don't know what to do with it. And I think we'll deal better if we know where we stand.''

"Where do we stand?'' he asked, slipping his hands around her waist.

"Like I said, we're responsible, unattached adults. And we're attracted to each other.''

He touched his lips to her temple. "So far I find nothing to argue about.''

"And as long as we handle this relationship sensibly—''

"Oh, we may run into trouble there.''

"I don't see why.''

He skimmed his hands up her rib cage until his thumbs circled her nipples. "I don't feel particularly sensible.''

Her knees buckled. Her head fell back. "It's just a matter of…establishing priorities.''

"I have my priorities.'' He teased her lips apart with his tongue. "Top of the list is making love with you until we're both a puddle of useless flesh.''

"Good.'' She went willingly when he pulled her to the floor. "Good start.''

She really worked better with lists. By the following evening, Mel was huddled at her desk, doing her best to put one together. It was the first free hour she'd had since speeding away from Sebastian's house at 10:00 a.m., already frazzled and behind schedule.

She was never behind schedule. Of course, she'd never had an affair with a witch before. It was obviously a month for firsts.

If she hadn't had an appointment, paperwork and a court appearance waiting, she might not have left his house at all. He'd certainly done everything in his power to discourage her, she remembered, tapping her pencil against her smiling lips.

The man definitely had a lot of power.

But work was work, she reminded herself. She had a business to run.

The best news of the day was that the New Hampshire State Police had picked up James T. Parkland. And there was a certain sergeant, grateful for her tip and annoyed with the federal take-over, who was being very cooperative.

He'd faxed Mel a copy of Parkland's statement on the sly.

It was a start.

She had the name of the high roller who'd held Parkland's IOU, and she intended to put it to good use. With any luck, she'd be spending a few days in Lake Tahoe.

She needed to bring Devereaux around. He'd want to use his own agents on any kind of a sting, and she had to come up with several solid reasons why she and Sebastian would make better bait.

Her assistance and cooperation in the Merrick case would work in her favor, but Mel didn't think it would swing the deal. Her record was good, she didn't do flashy work—and she sensed that Devereaux would disapprove of a hotdogging PI. Her partnership with Sebastian was in her favor, as well. And the fact that she was perfectly willing to let the feds take the lion's share of credit for the collar would add a little weight to her side of the scales.

"Open for business?" Sebastian asked as he pushed open the door.

She struggled to ignore the quick, giddy fluttering in her stomach, and she smiled. "Actually, I'm closing for the day in five minutes."

"Then my timing's good. What's this?" Taking her hand, he pulled her to her feet to examine the trim peach-colored suit she wore.

"Court appearance late this afternoon." She moved her shoulders restlessly as he toyed with the pearls at her throat. "Divorce case. Kind of nasty. So you want to go in looking as much like a lady as possible."

"You succeeded."

"Easy for you to say. It takes twice as much time and trouble to dress like a lady as it does to dress like a normal person." She rested a hip on the desk and handed him a sheet of paper. "I got a copy of Parkland's statement."

"Quick work."

"As you can see, he's a pretty pathetic type. He was desperate. He didn't mean to hurt anybody. He was over his head. Gambling problem. Afraid for his life." She gave a quick, unladylike opinion of his excuses. "I'm surprised he didn't toss out how his father had traumatized him by not giving him a little red wagon for Christmas.''

"He'll pay," Sebastian said. "Pathetic or not."

"Right, because he was also stupid. Taking David across the state line really upped the ante." She kicked off her shoes and rubbed her calf with her foot. "Now he claims he got the offer of the job over the phone."

"Sounds reasonable."

"Sure. Want a drink?"

"Mmm." Sebastian read over the statement again while she moved into the kitchen.

"Five thousand dollars for snatching a kid. Pretty paltry, compared with the sentence he's facing. So." She turned, found Sebastian in the doorway and offered him a soft drink. "He owes thirty-five hundred to this casino up in Tahoe, and he knows if he doesn't make a payment soon, he's going to have his face rearranged in a way that might not be pleasing. So he scouts out a kid."

He was following her, but Sebastian was also interested in her personal habitat. "Why David?" he asked as he walked past her into the adjoining room.

"I looked into that. Stan worked on his car about five months ago. Stan'll show off pictures of David to anyone who doesn't run for cover. So when Parkland figured snatching a kid was better than plastic surgery the hard way, he figured a mechanic's kid might be the ticket. David's cute. Even a sleaze like Parkland would have realized a pretty baby makes an impression on a buyer."

"Um-hmm." Sebastian rubbed a hand over his chin as he studied her bedroom. He assumed it was a bedroom, as there was a narrow, unmade bed in the center of it. It also appeared to be a living room, as there was an overstuffed chair piled with books and magazines, a portable TV on a wobbly plant stand, and a lamp in the shape of a trout. "Is this where you live?"

"Yeah." She kicked a pair of boots out of the way. "Maid's year off. And so," she continued, dropping down on a chest decorated with stickers of most, if not all, of the fifty states, "he took the job, got all his instructions from Mr. X over the phone.

Met the redhead at the prearranged drop and exchanged David for an envelope of cash.''

"What's this?"

Mel glanced over. "It's a Bullwinkle bank. Didn't you ever watch Bullwinkle?"

"I believe I did," Sebastian mused, shaking the moose before setting it aside again. "Hokey smokes."

"That's the one. Anyway—"

"And this?" He gestured to a poster tacked to the wall.

"Underdog. Wally Cox used to do the voice. Are you paying attention to me?"

He turned and smiled. "I'm riveted. Do you know it takes a bold soul to mix purple and orange in one room?"

"I like bright colors."

"And red striped sheets."

"They were on sale," she said impatiently. "You turn the light off when you sleep, anyway. Look, Donovan, how long are we going to discuss my decor?"

"Only a moment or two." He picked up a bowl shaped like the Cheshire cat. She'd tossed odds and ends into it. A straight pin, a safety pin, a couple of loose buttons, a .22 bullet, a coupon for the soft drinks she seemed to live on, and what looked to Sebastian to be a lock pick.

"You're not the tidy sort, are you?"

"I use up my organizational talents in business."

"Um-hmm." He set the bowl down and picked up a book. *"The Psychic Handbook?"*

"Research," she said, and scowled. "I got it out of the library a couple of weeks ago."

"What did you think?"

"I think it has very little to do with you."

"I'm sure you're right." He set it aside again. "This room has very much to do with you. Just as that streamlined office out there does. Your mind is very disciplined, like your file cabinet."

She wasn't sure if it was a compliment or not, but she recognized the look in his eye. "Look, Donovan..."

"But your emotions," he continued, moving toward her, "are very chaotic, very colorful."

She batted his hand away when he toyed with her pearls. "I'm trying to have a professional conversation."

"You closed up shop for the day. Remember?"

"I don't have regular hours."

"Neither do I." He flipped open a button of her suit jacket. "I've been thinking about making love with you ever since I finished making love with you this morning."

Her skin was going hot, and she knew her attempts to stop him from undoing her jacket were halfhearted at best. "You must not have enough on your mind."

"Oh, you're quite enough. I have started on some arrangements that should please you. Professionally."

She turned her head just in time to avoid his mouth. "What arrangements?"

"A long conversation with Agent Devereaux and his superior."

Her eyes flew open again as she struggled away from his hands. "When? What did they say?"

"You could say the stew's simmering. It'll take a couple of days. You'll have to be patient."

"I want to talk to him myself. I think he should—"

"You'll have your shot at him tomorrow. The next day, at the latest." He drew her hands behind her back, handcuffing her wrists with his fingers. "What's going to happen will happen soon enough. I know the when, I know the where."

"Then—"

"Tonight, it's just you and me."

"Tell me—"

"I'm going to show you," he murmured. "Show you just how easy it is to think of nothing else, to feel nothing else. To want nothing else." With his eyes on hers, he teased her mouth. "I wasn't gentle with you before."

"It doesn't matter."

"I don't regret it." He nipped lightly at her lower lip, then soothed the small pain with his tongue. "It's just that seeing you tonight, in your quiet little suit, makes me want to treat you like a lady. Until it drives you crazy."

Her laugh was breathless as his tongue danced up her throat. "I think you already are."

"I haven't even started."

With his free hand, he nudged the jacket from her shoulder. She wore a sheer pastel blouse underneath that made him think of summer teas and formal garden parties. While his mouth roamed over her face and throat, he traced his fingers over the sheer cloth and the lace beneath.

Her body was already quivering. She thought it ridiculous that he held her arms captive, that she allowed it. But there was a dreamy excitement at having him touch her this way, slowly, experimentally, thoroughly.

She felt his breath against her flesh as he opened her blouse, and the moist warmth of his tongue cruising over the tops of her breast just above, then just beneath, the chemise. She knew she was still standing, her feet on the floor, her legs pressed back against the bed, but it felt like floating. Floating, while he lazily savored her as if she were a banquet to be sampled at his whim.

Her skirt slithered down her legs. His hand trailed up. Her murmur of approval was low and long as his fingers toyed seductively with the hook of her garter.

"So unexpected, Mary Ellen." With one expert flick, he unsnapped the front.

"Practical," she said on a gasp as his fingers skimmed up toward the heat. "Cheaper this way, because I'm always... running them."

"Delightfully practical."

Struggling against the need to rush, he laid her back on the bed. In the name of Finn, how could he have known that the sight of that strong, angular body in bits of lace would rip his self-control to shreds?

He wanted to devour, to conquer, to possess.

But he had promised her some tenderness.

He knelt over her, lowered his mouth to hers, and kept his word.

And he was right. In mere moments she understood he was so very right. It was easy to think of nothing but him. To feel nothing but him. To want nothing but him.

She was rocked in the cradle of his gentleness, her body as alive as it had been the night before, certainly as desired as it had been but with the added aspect of being treasured for a femininity she so often forgot.

He savored her, and sent her gliding. He explored and showed her new secrets of herself. All the rush and fury they had indulged in the night before had shifted focus. Now the world was slow, the air was soft, and passion was languid.

And when she felt his heart thudding wildly against hers, when his murmurs became urgent, breathless, she understood that he was as seduced as she by what they made together.

She opened for him, drawing him in, heat to heat, pulse to pulse. When his body shuddered, it was she who cradled him.

Chapter 9

"We're wasting time."

"On the contrary," Sebastian said, pausing at a shop window to examine an outfit on a stylized, faceless mannequin. "What we're doing is basic, even intricate, groundwork for the operation."

"Shopping?" She made a disgusted sound and hooked her thumbs in her front pockets. "Shopping for an entire day?"

"My dear Sutherland, I'm quite fond of the way you look in jeans, but as the wife of an affluent businessman you need a more extensive wardrobe."

"I've already tried on enough stuff to clothe three women for a year. It'll take a tractor-trailer to deliver it all to your house."

He gave her a bland look. "It was easier to convince the FBI to cooperate than it is you."

Because that made her feel ungrateful and petty, she squirmed. "I'm cooperating. I've been cooperating for hours. I just think we have enough."

"Not quite." He gestured toward the dress in the display. "Now this would make a statement."

Mel chewed on her lower lip as she studied it. "It has sequins."

"You have religious or political objections to sequins?"

"No. It's just that I'm not the glittery type. I'd feel like a jerk. And there's hardly anything to it." She flicked her gaze over the tiny strapless black dress, which left the mannequin's white legs bare to midthigh. "I don't see how you could sit down in it."

"I seem to recall a little number you wore to go to a bar a few weeks ago."

"That was different. I was working." At his patient, amused look, she grimaced. "Okay, okay, Donovan, you made your point."

"Be a good soldier," he said, and patted her cheek. "Go in and try it on."

She grumbled and muttered and swore under her breath, but she was a good soldier. Sebastian roamed the boutique, selecting accessories and thinking of her.

She didn't give a hang for fashion, he mused, and was more embarrassed than pleased that she could now lay claim to a wardrobe most woman would envy. She would play her part, and play it well. She would wear the clothes he'd selected and be totally oblivious to the fact that she looked spectacular in them.

As soon as it was possible, she would slip back into her jeans and boots and faded shirts. And be equally oblivious to the fact that she looked equally spectacular in them.

By Merlin's beard, you have it bad, Donovan, he thought as he chose a silver evening bag with an emerald clasp. His mother had once told him that love was more painful, more delightful and more unstoppable when it came unexpectedly.

How right she had been.

The last thing he'd expected was to feel anything more than an amused attraction for a woman like Mel. She was tough, argumentative, prickly and radically independent. Hardly seductive qualities in a woman.

She was also warm and generous, loyal and brave, and honest.

What man could resist an acid-tongued woman with a caring heart and a questing mind? Certainly not Sebastian Donovan.

It would take time and patience to win her over completely. He didn't have to look to know. She was much too cautious—and, despite her cocky exterior, too insecure—to hand over her heart with both hands until she was sure of its reception.

He had time, and he had patience. If he didn't look to be sure, it was because he felt it would be unfair to both of them. And because, in a deep, secret chamber of his own heart, he was afraid he would look and see her walking away.

"Well, I got it on," Mel griped behind him. "But I don't see how it's going to stay up for long."

He turned. And stared.

"What is it?" Alarmed, she slapped a hand to the slight swell of her breasts above the glittery sequins and looked down. "Do I have it on backwards or something?"

The laugh did the trick of starting his heart again. "No. You wear it very well. There's nothing that raises a man's blood pressure as quickly as a long, slim woman in a black dress."

She snorted. "Give me a break."

"Perfect, perfect." The saleswoman came over to pluck and peck. Mel rolled her eyes at Sebastian. "It fits like a dream."

"Yes," he agreed. "Like a dream."

"I have some red silk evening pants that would be just darling on her."

"Donovan," Mel began, a plea in her voice, but he was already following the eager clerk.

Thirty minutes later, Mel strode out of the store. "That's it. Case closed."

"One more stop."

"Donovan, I'm not trying on any more clothes. I'd rather be staked to an anthill."

"No more clothes," he promised.

"Good. I could be undercover on this case for a decade and not wear everything."

"Two weeks," he told her. "It won't take longer than two weeks. And by the time we've made the rounds at the casinos, the clubs, attended a few parties, you'll have made good use of the wardrobe."

"Two weeks?" She felt excitement begin to percolate through the boredom. "Are you sure?"

"Call it a hunch." He patted her hand. "I have a feeling that what we do in Tahoe will be enough to set the dominoes tumbling on this black-market operation."

"You never told me exactly how you convinced the feds to let us go with this."

"I have a history with them. You could say I called in a few favors, made some promises."

She stopped to look in another store window, not to peruse the wares, but because she needed a moment to chose her words. "I know I couldn't have gotten them to back me without you. And I know that you don't really have a stake in any of this."

"I have the same stake as you." He turned her to face him. "You don't have a client, Sutherland. No retainer, no fee."

"That doesn't matter."

"No." He smiled and kissed her brow. "It doesn't. Sometimes you're involved simply because there's a chance you can make a difference."

"I thought it was because of Rose," Mel said slowly. "And it is, but it's also because of Mrs. Frost. I can still hear the way she was crying when we took David away."

"I know."

"It's not that I'm a do-gooder," she said, suddenly embarrassed. He kissed her once more.

"I know. There are rules." He took her hand, and they began to walk again.

She took her time, keeping her voice light, as she touched on something that had been nagging at her brain for days.

"If we can really get set up by the end of the week, we'll be sort of living together for a while."

"Does that bother you?"

"Well, no. If it doesn't bother you." She was beginning to feel like a fool, but it was important she make him understand she wasn't the kind of woman who mixed fantasy with reality. "We'll be pretending that we're married. That we're in love and everything."

"It's convenient to be in love when you're married."

"Right." She let out a huff of breath. "I just want you to know that I can play the game. I can be good at it. So you shouldn't think that..."

He toyed with her fingers as they walked. "Shouldn't think what?"

"Well, I know that some people can get carried away, or mix up the way things are with the way they're pretending they are. I just don't want you to get nervous that I'd do that."

"Oh, I think my nerves can stand the pretense of you being in love with me."

He said it so lightly that she scowled down at the sidewalk. "Well, good. Fine. Just so we know where we stand."

"I think we should practice." He whipped her around so that she collided with him.

"What?"

"Practice," he repeated. "So we can be sure you can pull off the role of the loving wife." He held her a little closer. "Kiss me, Mary Ellen."

"We're out on the street. We're in public."

"All the more reason. It hardly matters how we behave privately. You're blushing."

"I am not."

"You certainly are, and you'll have to watch that. I don't think it would embarrass you to kiss a man you've been married to for—what is it? Five years. And, according to our established cover, we lived together a full year before that. You were twenty-two when you fell in love with me."

"I can add," she muttered.

"You wash my socks."

Her lips quirked. "The hell I do. We have a modern marriage. You do the laundry."

"Ah, but you've given up your career as an ad executive to make a home."

"I hate that part." She slipped her arms around his neck. "What am I supposed to do all day?"

"Putter." He grinned. "Initially, we'll be on vacation, establishing our new home. We'll spend a lot of time in bed."

"Well, all right." She grinned back. "Since it's for a good cause."

She did kiss him then, long and deep, dancing her tongue over his, feeling his heart pick up its beat and race with hers. Then, slowly, she inched away.

"Maybe I wouldn't kiss you like that after five years," she mused.

"Oh, yes, you will." He took her arm and steered her into his cousin's shop.

"Well, well..." Morgana set down a malachite egg she'd

been polishing. She'd had an excellent view of the show through her display window. "Another few minutes of that and you'd have stopped traffic."

"An experiment," Sebastian told her. "Morgana knows about the case." Even as Mel's brows drew together, he was continuing. "I don't keep secrets from my family."

"There's no need to worry." Morgana touched Sebastian's arm, but her eyes were on Mel. "We don't keep secrets from each other, but we've had plenty of experience in being... discrete with outsiders."

"I'm sorry. I'm not used to taking people into my confidence."

"It's a risky business," Morgana agreed. "Sebastian, Nash is in the back, grumbling about unloading a shipment. Run along and keep him company for a minute, will you?"

"If you like."

As Sebastian went into the back room, Morgana moved to the door and turned the Closed sign over. She wanted a moment of privacy. "Nash has gotten very protective," she said, turning back. "He worries about me handling boxes and lifting inventory."

"I guess that's natural. In your condition."

"I'm strong as an ox." She smiled and shrugged. "Besides, there are other ways of maneuvering heavy merchandise."

"Hmm" was all Mel could think of to say.

"We don't make a habit of flaunting what we are. Sebastian uses his gift publicly, but people think of it as something one might read about in a supermarket tabloid. They don't really understand what he is or what he has. As for me, the whispers and rumors are good business. And Ana...Ana has her own way of dealing with her talents."

"I really don't know what I'm supposed to say." Mel lifted her hands, then dropped them again. "I don't know if I'll ever take all this in. I never even bought into the tooth fairy."

"That's a pity. Then again, it seems to me that a very practical mind would be unable to deny what it sees. What it knows."

"I can't deny that he's different. That he has abilities...gifts. And that..." Frustrated, she let her words trail off again. "I've never met anyone like him before."

Morgana gave a low laugh. "Even among the different, Sebastian is unique. One day, perhaps, we'll have time for me to tell you stories. He was always competitive. It continues to infuriate him that he can't cast a decent spell with any real finesse."

Fascinated, Mel stepped closer. "Really?"

"Oh, yes. Of course, I don't tell him just how frustrating it is for me to have to go through all manner of stages to get even a glimpse of the things he can see simply by looking." She waved it away. "But those are old family rivalries. I wanted a moment with you because I realize that Sebastian trusts you enough, obviously cares for you enough, to have opened that part of his life to you."

"I..." Mel blew out a breath. What next? "We're working together," she said carefully. "And you could say that we have a kind of relationship. A personal relationship."

"I'm not going to intrude—overmuch—in that personal relationship. But he is family, and I love him very much. So I have to tell you—don't use this power you have to hurt him."

Mel was flabbergasted. "But you're the witch," she blurted out. Then she blinked. "What I mean is—"

"You said what you meant, aptly. Yes, I am a witch. But I'm also a woman. Who understands power better?"

Mel shook her head. "I don't know what you mean. And I certainly don't know how you think I could possibly hurt Sebastian. If you think I've put him in any danger by involving him in this case—"

"No." Eyes thoughtful, Morgana lifted a hand. "You really don't understand." Morgana's lips curved as her eyes cleared. It was obvious, beautifully obvious, that Mel hadn't a clue that Sebastian was in love with her. "How fascinating," she murmured. "And how delightful."

"Morgana, if you'd just make yourself clear..."

"Oh no, I'd hate to do that." She took both of Mel's hands. "Forgive me for confusing you. We Donovans tend to be protective of each other. I like you," she said with a charming smile. "Very much. I hope we'll be good friends." She gave Mel's hands a squeeze. "I'd like to give you something."

"It isn't necessary."

"Of course not," Morgana agreed, moving toward a display case. "But when I chose this stone, I knew that I would want it to belong to just the right person. Here." She took a slender blue wand attached to a thin silver chain out of the case.

"I can't take that. It must be valuable."

"Value's relative. You don't wear jewelry." Morgana slipped the chain over Mel's head. "But think of this as a talisman. Or a tool, if you like."

Though she'd never been particularly attracted to the things people hung from their ears or crowded on their fingers, she lifted the blue stone to eye level. It wasn't clear, but she could see hints of light through it. In length it was no longer than her thumbnail, but the hues in the stone ranged from pale blue to indigo. "What is it?"

"It's a blue tourmaline. It's an excellent aid for stress." And it was also an excellent channel for joining love with wisdom. But Morgana said nothing of that. "I imagine you have plenty of that in your work."

"My share, I guess. Thanks. It's nice."

"Morgana." Nash poked his head out of the storeroom door. "Oh, hi, Mel."

"Hello."

"Babe, there's this nut on the phone who wants to know something about green dioptaste on the fourth chakra."

"Customer," Morgana corrected wearily. "It's a customer, Nash."

"Yeah, right. Well this customer wants to expand his heart center." Nash winked at Mel. "Sounds pretty desperate to me."

"I'll take it." She gestured for Mel to follow.

"Know anything about chakras?" Nash murmured to Mel as she walked through the doorway.

"Do you eat it or dance to it?"

He grinned and patted her on the back. "I like you."

"There seems to be a lot of that going around."

Morgana walked into a room beyond. Mel studied the kitchenette, where Sebastian had made himself at home at a wooden table with a beer.

"Want one?"

"You bet." There was the smell of herbs again, from little

pots growing on the windowsill. Morgana's voice rose and fell from the next room. "It's an interesting shop."

Sebastian handed her a bottle. "I see you picked up a trinket already."

"Oh." She fingered the stone. "Morgana gave it to me. It's pretty, isn't it?"

"Very."

"So." She turned to Nash. "I really didn't get a chance to tell you before. I love your movies. Especially *Shape Shifter*. It blew me away."

"Yeah?" He was rooting around in the cupboards for cookies. "It has a special place in my heart. Nothing like a sexy lycanthrope with a conscience."

"I like the way you make the illogical logical." She took a sip of beer. "I mean, you make the rules—they might be really weird rules—but then you follow them."

"Mel's big on rules," Sebastian put in.

"Sorry." Morgana stepped back in. "A slight emergency. Nash, you ate all the cookies already."

"All?" Disappointed, he closed the cupboard door.

"Every crumb." She turned to Sebastian. "I imagine you're wondering if the package came in."

"Yes."

She reached into her pocket and took out a small box of hammered silver. "I think you'll find it quite suitable."

He rose to take it from her. Their eyes met, held. "I trust your judgment."

"And I yours." She took his face in her hands and kissed him. "Blessed be, cousin." In a brisk change of mood, she reached for Nash. "Darling, come out in the shop with me. I want to move some things."

"But Mel was just feeding my ego."

"Heavy things," she said, and gave his hand a tug. "We'll see you soon I hope, Mel."

"Yes. Thanks again." The moment the door closed behind them, she looked at Sebastian. "What was that all about?"

"Morgana understood that I preferred to do this alone." He rubbed his thumb over the box as he watched her.

Mel's smile went a little nervous around the edges. "It's not going to hurt, is it?"

"Painless," he promised. At least for her. He opened the box, and offered it.

She peeked in, and would have taken a quick step away if she hadn't been standing with her back to the counter. Inside the ornate little box was a ring. Like the necklace Morgana had given her, it was silver, thin glistening wires woven into an intricate pattern around a center stone of delicate pink with a green rind rim.

"What is it?"

"It's also tourmaline," he told her. "What's called watermelon tourmaline, because of its colors." He took it out. Held it to the light. "Some say it can transfer energy between two people who are important to each other. On a practical level, which I'm sure will interest you, they're used in industry for electrical tuning circuits. They don't shatter at high frequencies like other crystals."

"That's interesting." Her throat was very dry. "But what's it for?"

Though it was not quite the way he might have liked it, it would have to do for now. "A wedding ring," he said, and put it into her hand.

"Excuse me?"

"We would hardly have been married five years without you having a ring."

"Oh." Surely she was just imagining that the ring was vibrating in her palm. "That makes sense. Sure. But why not a plain gold band?"

"Because I prefer this." With his first show of impatience, he plucked the ring out of her hand and shoved it on her finger.

"Okay, okay, don't get testy. It just seems like a lot of trouble when we could have gone by any department store and picked up—"

"Shut up."

She'd been busy playing with the ring as she spoke, but now she looked up, narrow-eyed. "Look, Donovan—"

"For once." He lifted her to her toes. "For once, do something my way without arguing, without questioning, without making me want to strangle you.''

Her eyes heated. "I was stating my opinion. And if this is going to work, we'd better get one thing clear right now. There's no your way, there's no my way. There can only be our way.''

Since no amount of searching helped him come up with an argument, he released her. "I have a remarkably even temper,'' he said, half to himself. "It very rarely flares, because power and temper are a dangerous mix.''

Pouting a bit, she rubbed her arms where his fingers had dug in. "Yeah. Right.''

"There's one rule, one unbreakable rule, that we live by in my world, Sutherland. 'An it harm none.' I take that very seriously. And for the first time in my life I've come across someone who tempts me to whip up a spell that would have her suffering from all manner of unpleasant discomforts.''

She sniffed and picked up her beer again. "You're all wind, Donovan. Your cousin told me you're lousy at spells.''

"Oh, there are one or two I've had some luck with.'' He waited until she'd taken a good swallow of beer, then concentrated. Hard.

Mel choked, gasped and grabbed for her throat. It felt as though she'd just swallowed a slug of pure Kentucky moonshine.

"Particularly spells that involve the mind,'' Sebastian said smugly while she fought for breath.

"Cute. Real cute.'' Though the burning had faded, she set the beer aside. There was no point in taking chances. "I don't know what you're all bent out of shape about, Donovan. And I'd really appreciate it if you'd hold the tricks for Halloween, or April Fool's Day, or whenever you all break out for a few laughs.''

"Laughs?'' He said it much too quietly, taking a step forward. Mel took one to meet him, but whatever they might have done was postponed as the side door swung open.

"Oh.'' Anastasia, with her hair blowing into her eyes, held the door open with a hip as she balanced a tray of dried flowers. "Excuse me.'' She didn't need to go any closer to feel the tempers rattling like sabers in the air. "I'll come back later.''

"Don't be silly.'' Sebastian nudged Mel aside—none too

gently—and took the tray from his cousin. "Morgana's in the shop."

Hastily, Ana brushed her wayward hair away from her face. "I'll just go tell her I'm here. Nice to see you again, Mel." Ingrained manners had her offering a smile. Then her gaze fixed on the ring. "Oh. How beautiful. It looks like…" She hesitated, flicking a glance at Sebastian. "It looks like it was made for you."

"I'm just kind of borrowing it for a few weeks."

Ana looked at Mel again, and her eyes were kind. "I see. I doubt if I could bear to give something that wonderful back. May I?" Gently Ana took Mel's fingertips and lifted her hand. She recognized the stone as one Sebastian had owned and treasured most of his life. "Yes," she said. "It looks perfect on you."

"Thanks."

"Well, I only have a few minutes, so I'd better let you finish your argument." She tossed Sebastian a quick smile and went out into the shop.

Mel sat on the edge of the table and tilted her head. "Wanna fight?"

He picked up her half-finished beer. "There doesn't seem to be much point in it."

"No, there's not. Because I'm not mad at you. I'm nervous. I've never done anything this big before. Not that I'm afraid I can't handle it."

He sat on the table beside her. "Then what?"

"I guess it's the most important thing I've ever done, and I really…I really care about making it work. Then there's this other thing."

"What other thing?"

"This you-and-me thing. It's important, too."

He took her hand in his. "Yes, it is."

"And I don't want the lines between these two important things to be blurred or mixed up, because I really care about… I really care," she finished.

He brought her fingers to his lips. "So do I."

Sensing that the mood was friendly again, she smiled. "You know what I like about you, Donovan?"

"What?"

"You can do stuff like that—kissing-my-hand stuff. And not look goofy doing it."

"You humble me, Sutherland," he said in a strained voice. "You positively humble me."

Hours later, when the night was quiet and the moonlight dim, she turned to him in sleep. And in sleep her arms slid around him, her body curved to his. He brushed the hair back from her temples as she nestled her head on his shoulder. He rubbed his thumb over the stone on her finger. If he left it there, let his mind drift, he could join her in whatever dream her heart was weaving. It was tempting, almost as tempting as waking her.

Before he could decide which to choose, he had a flash of the stables, the smell of hay and sweat and the distressed whicker of the mare.

Mel blinked awake as she felt him pull away. "What? What?"

"Go back to sleep," he ordered, reaching for a shirt.

"Where are you going?"

"Psyche's ready to foal. I'm going to the stables."

"Oh." Without thinking, she climbed out to search for her clothes. "I'll go with you. Should we call the vet?"

"Ana will come."

"Oh." She fumbled with her buttons in the dark. "Should I call her?"

"Ana will come," he said again, and left her to finish dressing.

Mel hurried after him, pulling on boots on the run. "Should I, like, boil water or something?"

Halfway down the stairs, he stopped and kissed her. "For coffee. Thanks."

"They always boil water," she mumbled, trudging into the kitchen. By the time the coffee was scenting the room, she heard the sound of a car. "Three cups," Mel decided, figuring it was useless to question how Anastasia had known to come.

She found both cousins in the stables. Ana was kneeling beside the mare, murmuring. Beside her were two leather pouches and a rolled cloth.

"She's all right, isn't she?" Mel asked. "I mean, she's healthy?"

"Yes." Ana stroked Psyche's neck. "She's fine. Just fine." Her voice was as soothing as a cool breeze in the desert. The mare responded to it with a quiet whinny. "It won't take long. Relax, Sebastian. It's not the first foal to be born in the world."

"It's her first," he shot back, feeling foolish. He knew it would be all right. He could have told them what sex the foal would be. But that didn't make it any easier to wait while his beloved Psyche suffered through the pangs.

Mel offered him a mug. "Have some coffee, Papa. You could always go pace in the next stall with Eros."

"You might keep him calm, Sebastian," Ana tossed over her shoulder. "It'll help."

"All right."

"Coffee?" Mel eased into the stall to offer Ana a mug.

"Yes, a little." She sat back on her heels to sip.

"Sorry," Mel said when she saw Ana's eyes go wide. "I tend to make it strong."

"It's all right. It'll last me for the next couple of weeks." She opened a pouch and shook some dried leaves and petals into her hand.

"What's that?"

"Just some herbs," Ana said as she fed them to the mare. "To help her with the contractions." She chose three crystals from the other pouch and placed them on the mare's quivering side. She was murmuring now in Gaelic.

The crystals should slide off, Mel thought, staring at them. It was gravity, basic physics. But they remained steady, even as the laboring horse shuddered.

"You have good hands," Ana said. "Stroke her head."

Mel complied. "I really don't know anything about birthing. Well, I had to learn the basics when I was a cop, but I never... Maybe I should..."

"Just stroke her head," Ana repeated gently. "The rest is the most natural thing in the world."

Perhaps it was natural, Mel thought later as she, Sebastian, Ana and the mare labored to bring the foal into the world. But it was also miraculous. She was slick with sweat, her own and the horse's, wired from coffee, and giddy with the idea of helping life into the light.

A dozen times throughout the hours they worked she saw the changes in Ana's eyes. From cool calm gray to smoky concern. From warm amusement to such deep, depthless compassion that Mel's own eyes stung in response.

Once she'd been sure she saw pain in them, a wild, terrified pain that faded only after Sebastian spoke sharply to his cousin.

"Only to give her a moment's relief," she'd said, and Sebastian had shaken his head.

After that it had happened quickly, and Mel had scrambled to help.

"Oh, wow" was the best she could do as she stared at the mare going about the business of cleaning her new son. "I can't believe it. There he is. Just like that."

"It's always a fresh amazement." Ana picked up her pouches and her medical instruments. "Psyche's fine," she continued as she rolled the instruments in the apron she'd put on before the birthing. "The colt, too. I'll come back around this evening for another look, but I'd say mother and son are perfect."

"Thank you, Ana." Sebastian pulled her against him for a hug.

"My pleasure. You did very well for your first foaling, Mel."

"It was incredible."

"Well, I'm going to get cleaned up and head home. I think I'll sleep till noon." Ana kissed Sebastian's cheek, and then, just as casually, kissed Mel's. "Congratulations."

"What a way to spend the night," Mel murmured, and leaned her head against Sebastian's shoulder.

"I'm glad you were here."

"So am I. I never saw anything born before. It makes you realize just how fantastic the whole business is." She yawned hugely. "And exhausting. I wish I could sleep till noon."

"Why don't you?" He tilted his head to kiss her. "Why don't we?"

"I have a business to run. And, since I'm going to be away from it for a couple of weeks, I have a lot of loose ends to tie up."

"You have one to tie up here."

"I do?"

"Absolutely." He swung her up, stained shirt, grubby hands and all. "A few hours ago I was lying in bed thinking about sneaking into one of your dreams with you, or just waking you up."

"Sneaking into one of my dreams?" She gave him a hand by pushing open the door. "Can you do that?"

"Oh, Sutherland, have some faith. In any case," he continued, carrying her straight through the kitchen and into the hall. "Before I did either, we were distracted. So, before you go in to work to tie up loose ends, we'll tie some of our own right here."

"Interesting thought. You may not have noticed, however, that we're both a mess."

"I've noticed." He marched through the master bedroom into the bath. "We're going to have a shower."

"Good idea. I think— Sebastian!"

She shrieked with laughter as he stepped into the shower stall, fully dressed, and turned on the water.

"Idiot. I still have my boots on."

He grinned. "Not for long."

Chapter 10

Mel wasn't sure how she felt about being Mrs. Donovan Ryan. It certainly seemed to her that Mary Ellen Ryan—her cover persona—was a singularly boring individual, more interested in fashion and manicures than in anything of real importance.

She had to agree it was a good setup. Damn good, she mused as she stepped out onto the deck of the house and studied the glimmer of Lake Tahoe under the moonlight.

The house itself was nothing to sneeze at. Two sprawling levels of contemporary comfort, it was tastefully furnished, decorated with bold colors to reflect the style of its owners.

Mary Ellen and Donovan Ryan, formerly of Seattle, were a modern couple who knew what they wanted.

What they wanted most, of course, was a child.

She'd been impressed with the house when they'd arrived the day before. Impressed enough to comment on the fact that she hadn't expected the FBI to be able to provide such cozy digs so quickly. It was then that Sebastian had casually mentioned that it was one of his properties—something he'd had a whim to pick up about six months before.

Coincidence or witchcraft? Mel thought with a grimace. You be the judge.

"Ready for a night on the town, sweetheart?"

Her grimace turned into a scowl as she turned to Sebastian.

"You're not going to start calling me all those dopey names just because we're supposed to be married."

"Heaven forbid." He stepped out on the deck, looking—Mel was forced to admit—about as gorgeous as a man could get in his black dinner suit. "Let's have a look at you."

"I put it all on," she said, struggling not to grumble. "Right down to the underwear you set out."

"You're such a good sport." The sarcasm was light and friendly, and made her lips twitch into a reluctant smile. Taking her hand, he turned her in a circle. Yes, he thought, the red evening pants had been an excellent choice. The fitted silver jacket went quite well with them, as did the ruby drops at her ears. "You look wonderful. Try to act like you believe it."

"I hate wearing heels. And do you know what they did to my hair?"

His lips curved as he flicked a finger over it. It was sleeked back in a sassy, side-parted bob. "Very chic."

"Easy for you to say. You didn't have some maniacal woman with a French accent glopping up your head with God knows what, spraying stuff on it, snipping and crimping and whatnot until you wanted to scream."

"Hard day, huh?"

"That's not the half of it. I had to get my nails done. You have no idea what that's like. They come at you with these little scissors and probes and files and smelly bottles, and they talk to you about their boyfriends and ask personal questions about your sex life. And you have to act like you're just enjoying the hell out of it. I almost had to have a facial." She shuddered with complete sincerity. "I don't know what they'd have done to me, but I said I had to get home and fix dinner."

"A narrow escape."

"If I really had to go to a beauty parlor once a week for the rest of my life I think I'd slit my throat."

"Buck up, Sutherland."

"Right." She sighed, feeling better. "Well, it wasn't hard to start spreading it around how I had this wonderful husband and this great new house and how we'd been trying for years to have a baby. They just lap that kind of stuff up. I went on about how we'd had all these tests and had been trying these fertility drugs, and how long the lists were at adoption agencies. They were very sympathetic.''

"Good job."

"Better, I got the name of two lawyers and a doctor. The doctor's supposed to be some miracle gynecologist. One of the lawyers was the manicurist's cousin, and the other was supposed to have helped the sister-in-law of this lady getting a permanent, to adopt two Romanian babies last year."

"I believe I follow that," Sebastian said after a moment.

"I figured we should check it out. Tomorrow I'm going to the health club. While they're pummeling me, I can go through the routine."

"There's no law that says you can't enjoy a sauna and massage while you're at it."

She hesitated, and was grateful that the roomy pockets of the evening pants made a home for her hands. "It makes me feel... I know you're putting a lot of your money into this."

"I have plenty." He tipped a finger under her chin. "If I didn't want to use it this way, I wouldn't. I remember how Rose looked when you brought her to me, Mel. And I remember Mrs. Frost. We're in this together."

"I know." She curled her fingers around his wrist. "I should be thanking you instead of complaining."

"But you complain so well." When she grinned, he kissed her. "Come on, Sutherland. Let's gamble. I'm feeling lucky."

The Silver Palace was one of Tahoe's newest and most opulent hotel casinos. White swans glided in the silvery waters of the lobby pool, and man-sized urns exploded with exotic flowers. The staff was dressed in spiffy tuxedos with trademark silver ties and cummerbunds.

They passed a number of elegant shops displaying everything from diamonds and furs to T-shirts. Mel figured they'd aligned them close enough to the casino to tempt any winners to put their money back into the hotel.

The casino itself was crowded with sound, the chink-chink of coins pouring out of slots echoing from the high ceilings. There was the hubbub of voices, the clatter of the roulette wheels, the smell of smoke and liquor and perfumes. And, of course, of money.

"Some joint," Mel commented, taking a gander at the knights and fair ladies painted on the windowless walls.

"What's your game?"

She shrugged. "They're all sucker's games. Trying to win against the house is like trying to row upstream with one oar. You might make some progress, but the current's going to carry you down sooner or later."

He nipped lightly at her ear. "You're not here to be practical. We're on our second honeymoon, remember? Sweetie pie?"

"Yuck," she said distinctly through a bright, loving smile. "Okay, let's buy some chips."

She opted to start off with the slots, deciding they were mindless enough to allow her to play while still absorbing her surroundings. They were there to make contact with Jasper Gumm, the man who'd held Parkland's IOU. Mel was well aware it could take several nights to reach that next step.

She lost steadily, then won back a few dollars, automatically feeding the coins back into the machine. She found there was something oddly appealing about the whoosh and jingle, the occasional squeal from another player, the bells and lights that rang and flashed when someone hit the jackpot.

It was relaxing, she realized, and tossed a smile over her shoulder to Sebastian. "I don't guess the house has to worry about me breaking the bank."

"Perhaps if you went at it less...aggressively." He put a hand over hers as she pulled the lever. Lights whirled. Bells clanged.

"Oh!" Her eyes went huge as coins began to shoot into the basket. "Oh, wow! That's five hundred!" She did a little dance, then threw her arms around him. "I won five hundred dollars." She gave him a big, smacking kiss, then froze with her mouth an inch from his. "Oh, God, Donovan, you cheated."

"What a thing to say. Outwitting a machine isn't cheating." He could see her sense of fair play warring with her elation. "Come on, you can lose it back at blackjack."

"I guess it's okay. It's for a higher cause."

"Absolutely."

Laughing, she began to scoop the coins into the bucket beside the machine. "I like to win."

"So do I."

They scoped out the tables, sipping champagne and playing the part of an affectionate couple on a night out. She tried not to take it too seriously, the attention he paid her, the fact that his hand was always there when she reached for it.

They were lovers, yes, but they weren't in love. They cared for and respected each other—but that was a long way from happily-ever-after. The ring on her finger was only a prop, the house they shared only a cover.

One day she would have to give the ring back and move out of the house. They might continue to see each other, at least for a time. Until his work and hers took them in different directions.

People didn't last in her life. She'd come to accept that. Or always had before. Now, when she thought of heading off in that different direction alone, without him, there was an emptiness inside her that was almost unbearable.

"What is it?" Instinctively he put a hand at the base of her neck to rub. "You're tensing up."

"Nothing. Nothing." Even with the rule about him not looking into her mind, he was much too perceptive. "I guess I'm impatient to move. Let's try this table. See what happens."

He didn't press, though he was quite certain that something more than the case was troubling her. When they took their seats at a five-dollar table, he slipped an arm around her shoulders so that they played the cards together.

She played well, he noted, her practical nature and quick wits keeping her even with the house for the first hour. He could see by the casual way she scanned the room that she was taking everything in. The security guards, the cameras, the two-way glass on the second level.

Sebastian ordered more champagne and began to do his own probing.

The man next to him was sweating over a seventeen and worrying that his wife suspected he was having an affair. His wife sat next to him, chain-smoking and trying to imagine how the dealer would look naked.

Sebastian fastidiously left her to it.

Next to Mel was a cowboy type tossing back bourbon and branch water while he won at a slow but steady pace. His mind was a jumble of thoughts about treasury bonds, livestock and the spread of cards. He was also wishing that the little filly beside him had come to the table alone.

Sebastian smiled to himself, wondering how Mel would feel about being called a little filly.

As he mentally roamed the table, Sebastian got impressions of boredom, excitement, desperation and greed. He found what he wanted in the young couple directly across from him.

They were from Columbus, on the third night of their honeymoon. They were barely old enough to be at the tables, they were deliriously in love, and they had decided, after much calculation, that the excitement of gambling was worth the hundred-dollar stake.

They were down to fifty now, and they were having the time of their lives.

Sebastian saw the husband—Jerry was his name—hesitating over hitting fifteen. He gave him a little push. Jerry signaled for another card and went pop-eyed when he pulled a six.

With a subtle and enjoyable magic, Sebastian had young Jerry doubling his stake, then tripling it, while the young couple gasped and giggled over their astonishing luck.

"They're sure raking it in," Mel commented.

"Mmm." Sebastian sipped his wine.

Oblivious to the gentle persuasion, Jerry began to up his bets. Word spread, as it does in such places, that there was a winner at table three. People began to mill around, applauding and slapping the baffled Jerry on the shoulder as his winnings piled up to three thousand.

"Oh, Jerry!" His new wife, Karen, clung to him. "Maybe we should stop. It's almost enough for a down payment on a house. Maybe we should just stop."

Sorry, Sebastian thought, and gave her a little mental nudge.

Karen bit her lip. "No. Keep going." She buried her face against his shoulder and laughed. "It's like magic."

The comment had Mel looking up from her own cards and sending Sebastian a narrow-eyed look. "Donovan."

"Shh." He patted her hand. "I have my reasons."

Mel began to understand them as the nearly delirious Jerry hovered at the ten-thousand dollar mark. A husky man in a tuxedo approached the table. He had a dignified bearing to go with smoothly tanned skin, a sun-tipped mustache and expertly styled hair. Mel was certain he was the kind of man most women would look at more than twice.

But she took an instant dislike to his eyes. They were pale blue, and, though they were smiling, she felt a quick chill race up her spine.

"Bad business," she muttered, and felt Sebastian's hand close over hers.

The crowd that had gathered cheered again as the dealer lost to Jerry on nineteen.

"This seems to be your lucky night."

"Boy, I'll say." Jerry looked up at the newcomer with dazed eyes. "I've never won anything before in my life."

"Are you staying at the hotel?"

"Yeah. Me and my wife." He gave Karen a squeeze. "This is the first night we tried the tables."

"Then allow me to congratulate you personally. I'm Jasper Gumm. This is my hotel."

Mel slanted Sebastian a look. "Pretty sneaky way to get a look at him."

"A roundabout route," he agreed. "But an enjoyable one."

"Hmm... Have your young hero and heroine finished for the evening?"

"Oh, yes, they're quite finished."

"Excuse me a minute." Taking her glass, Mel got up to stroll around the table. Sebastian had been right. The young couple were already making noises about cashing in and were busily thanking Gumm.

"Be sure to come back," Gumm told them. "We like to think that everyone at the Silver Palace walks away a winner."

When Gumm turned, Mel made certain she was directly in his path. A quick movement, and her champagne splattered.

"Oh, I beg your pardon." She brushed at his damp sleeve. "How clumsy of me."

"Not at all. It was my fault." Easing away from the dispersing crowd, he took out a handkerchief to dry her hand. "I'm afraid

I was distracted.'' He glanced at her empty glass. ''And I owe you a drink.''

''No, that's kind of you, but it was nearly empty.'' She flashed him a smile. ''Fortunately for your suit. I suppose I was a little curious about all those chips. My husband and I were across the table from that young couple. And not having nearly their luck.''

''Then I definitely owe you a drink.'' Gumm took her arm just as Sebastian walked up.

''Darling, you're supposed to drink the champagne, not pour it on people.''

As if she were flustered, she laughed and ran a hand down his arm. ''I've already apologized.''

''No harm done,'' Gumm assured them as he offered Sebastian a hand. ''Jasper Gumm.''

''Donovan Ryan. My wife, Mary Ellen.''

''A pleasure. Are you guests of the hotel?''

''No, actually, we've just moved to Tahoe.'' Sebastian sent an affectionate glance to Mel. ''We're taking a few days as a kind of second honeymoon before we get back to business.''

''Welcome to the community. Now I definitely must replace that champagne.'' He signalled to a roving waitress.

''It's very kind of you.'' Mel glanced around approvingly. ''You have a wonderful place here.''

''Now that we're neighbors, I hope you'll enjoy the facilities. We have an excellent dining room.'' As he spoke, Gumm took stock. The woman's jewelry was discreet and expensive. The man's dinner suit was expertly tailored. Both of them showed the panache of quiet affluence. Just the type of clientele he preferred.

When the waitress returned with a fresh bottle and glasses, Gumm poured the wine himself. ''What business are you in, Mr. Donovan?''

''Real estate. Mary Ellen and I spent the last few years in Seattle, and we decided it was time for a change. My business allows me to be flexible.''

''And yours?'' Gumm asked Mel.

''I've recently retired, at least for a while. I thought I'd like keeping a home.''

''Ah, and children.''

"No." Her smile wobbled as she looked down at her glass. "No, not yet. But I think the weather here, the sun, the lake... would be a wonderful place to raise a family." There was a trace, just a hint, of desperation in her voice.

"I'm sure. Please enjoy the Silver Palace. Don't be strangers."

"Oh, I'm sure we'll be back," Sebastian assured him. "Nicely done," he murmured to Mel when they were alone.

"I thought so. Do you think we should go back to the tables for a while or just wander about looking moon-eyed at each other?"

He chuckled, started to pull her close for a kiss, then stopped, his hand on her shoulder. "Well, well...sometimes things just fall neatly into place."

"What?"

"Drink your champagne, my love, and smile." He turned her gently, keeping his arm around her as they wandered toward the roulette table. "Now look over there, to the woman Gumm is speaking with. The redhead by the staircase."

"I see her." Mel leaned her head against Sebastian's shoulder. "Five-five, a hundred and ten, light complexion. Twenty-eight, maybe thirty years old."

"Her name's Linda—or it is now. It was Susan when she checked into the motel with David."

"She's—" Mel nearly took a step forward before she stopped herself. "What's she doing here?"

"Sleeping with Gumm, I imagine. Waiting for the next job."

"We have to find out how much they know. How close they are to the top." Grimly she finished off the champagne. "You work your way, I'll work mine."

"Agreed."

When Mel saw that Linda was heading for the ladies' lounge, she shoved her empty glass into Sebastian's hand. "Hold this."

"Of course, darling," he murmured to her retreating back.

Mel bided her time, sitting at one of the curvy dressing tables, freshening her lipstick, powdering her nose. When Linda sat at the table next to hers, she began the process all over again.

"Shoot," Mel said in disgust, examining her fingers. "I chipped a nail."

Linda sent her a sympathetic glance. "Don't you hate that?"

"I'll say, especially since I just had them done this morning. I have the worst luck with them." She searched through her bag for the nail file she knew wasn't there. "Your nails are gorgeous."

"Thank you." The redhead held up a hand to examine. "I have a marvelous manicurist."

"Do you?" Mel shifted and crossed her legs. "I wonder... My husband and I just moved here from Seattle. I really need to find the right beautician, health club, that sort of thing."

"You can't do better than right here at the hotel for either. Nonguest membership fees for the health club are a bit pricey, but believe me, it's well worth it." She fluffed at her luxuriant mane. "And the beauty shop is top-notch."

"I appreciate that. I'll look into it."

"Just tell them Linda sent you, Linda Glass."

"I will," Mel said as she rose. "Thanks a lot."

"No problem." Linda slicked on lip gloss. If the woman joined the club, she thought, she'd get a nice commission. Business was business.

A few hours later, Mel was flopped on her stomach in the center of the bed, making a list. She wore a baggy pajama top, her favored lounging choice, and had already disarranged her sleek coiffure into tousled spikes with restless fingers.

She'd be using the Silver Palace's facilities, all right, she thought. Starting tomorrow, she would join their health club, check out their beauty parlor. And, Lord help her, make an appointment for a facial, or whatever other torture they had in mind.

With any luck, she could be cozied up to Linda Glass and exchanging girl talk within twenty-four hours.

"What are you up to, Sutherland?"

"Plan B," she said absently. "I like to have a plan B in reserve in case plan A bombs. Do you think leg waxing hurts?"

"I wouldn't hazard a guess." He ran a fingertip down her calf. "However, yours feel smooth enough to me."

"Well, I have to be prepared to spend half my day in this place, so I have to have something for them to do to me." She cocked her head to look up at him. He was standing beside the bed, wearing the bottoms of the baggy pajamas and swirling a brandy.

I guess we look like a unit, she thought. Like an actual couple having a little chat before bedtime.

The idea had her doodling on the pad. "Do you really like that stuff?"

"Which stuff?"

"That brandy. It always tastes like medicine to me."

"Perhaps you've never had the right kind." He handed her the snifter. Mel braced up on her elbows to sample it while he straddled her and sat back on his heels. "You're still tense," he commented, and began to rub her shoulders.

"A little wired, maybe. I guess I'm starting to think this really may work—the job, I mean."

"It's going to work. While you're having your incredibly long and lovely legs waxed, I'm going to be playing golf—at the same club Gumm belongs to."

Far from convinced the brandy had anything going for it, she looked back over her shoulder. "Then we'll see who finds out more, won't we?"

"We will indeed."

"There's this spot on my shoulder blade." She arched like a cat. "Yeah, that's it. I wanted to ask you about that couple tonight. The big winners."

"What about them?" He pushed the shirt up out of his way and pleased himself by exploring the long, narrow span of her back.

"I know it was your way of getting Gumm to the table, but it doesn't seem exactly straight, you know? Making him win ten thousand."

"I merely influenced his decisions. And I imagine Gumm's taken in much more than that by selling children."

"Yeah, yeah, and I can sort of see the justice in that. But that couple—what if they try to do it again and lose their shirts? Maybe they won't be able to stop, and—"

He chuckled, pressing his lips to the center of her back. "I'm more subtle than that. Young Jerry and Karen will put a down payment on a nice house in the suburbs, astonish their friends with their good fortune. They'll both agree that they've used up all of their luck on this one shot, and rarely gamble again. They'll have three children. And they'll have a spot of fairly serious marital trouble in their sixth year, but they'll work it out.''

"Well." Mel wondered if she'd ever get used to it. "In that case.''

"In that case," he murmured, running his lips down her spine. "Why don't you put it out of your mind and concentrate on me?''

Smiling to herself, she set the brandy on the chest at the foot of the bed. "Maybe I could." She flipped, then twisted, getting a solid grip before shoving him back on the bed. With her hands clamped on his, she leaned down until they were nose-to-nose. "Gotcha.''

He grinned, then nipped her lower lip. "Yes, you do.''

"And I might just keep you a while." She kissed the tip of his nose, then his cheek, his chin, his lips. "The brandy tastes better on you than it does in the glass.''

"Try again, just to be sure.''

With humor bright in her eyes, she lowered her mouth to his and sampled long and deep. "Mmm-hmm. A definite improvement. I do like your taste, Donovan." She linked her fingers with his, pleased that he made no move to break the contact when she slid down to nibble at his throat.

She teased him, toying with his desire and her own as she savored his flesh. Warm here, cooler there, the rich beat of a pulse beneath her lips. She enjoyed the shape of his body, the width of his shoulders, the hard, smooth chest, the quick quiver of his flat belly under her touch.

She liked the way her hand looked gliding over him, her skin shades lighter than his, the ring glowing with its meld of colors against the silver. Rubbing her cheek over him, she felt not just passion, but a deep, drugging emotion that welled up like wine and clouded her senses.

Her throat stung with it, her eyes burned, and her heart all but melted out of her chest.

With a sigh, she brought her lips back to his.

It was she who was the witch tonight, he thought, wallowing

in her. She who had the power and the gift. She had taken his heart, his soul, his needs, his future, and had them cupped delicately in her hands.

He murmured his love for her, again and again, but the language of his blood was Gaelic, and she didn't understand.

They moved together, flowing over the bed as if it were an enchanted lake. As the moon began to set, shifting night closer to day, they were lost in each other, surrounded by the magic each brought to the other.

When she rose over him, her body glimmering in the lamplight, her eyes dark with desires, heavy with pleasures, he thought she had never looked more beautiful. Or more his.

He reached for her. And she answered. Their bodies blended. The moment was sweet and fine and fierce.

She arched back, taking more of him, shuddering with the glory of it.

Their hands met, and held, gripping firm as they rose toward the next pinnacle.

When they could go no higher, when he had emptied himself into her and their flesh was weak and wet from love, she slid down to him, hardly aware that her eyes were damp. She buried her face at his throat, shivering as his arms came around her.

"Don't let go," she murmured. "All night. Don't let go all night."

"I won't."

He held her while her heart struggled with the knowledge that it loved, and until her body gave way to weariness and slept.

Chapter 11

It wasn't so difficult to get a look at the appointment books for the beauty shop and health club in the Silver Palace. If you smiled enough and tipped enough, Mel knew, you could get a look at most anything. And by tipping a little more, it was easy to match her schedule with Linda Glass's.

That was the simple part. The hard part for Mel was the prospect of spending an entire day wearing a leotard.

When she took her place in the aerobics class with a dozen other women, she sent a friendly smile in Linda's direction.

"So, you're giving it a try." The redhead checked to see that her mane was still bundled attractively in its band.

"I really appreciate the tip," Mel responded. "With the move, I've missed over a week. It doesn't take long to get out of shape."

"Don't I know it. Whenever I travel—" She broke off when the instructor switched on a recorder. Out poured a catchy rock ballad.

"Time to stretch, ladies." All smiles and firm muscles, the instructor turned to face the mirror at the head of the class. "Now, reach!" she said in her perky voice as she demonstrated.

Mel followed along through the stretches and the warm-up and into the more demanding routines. Though she considered herself in excellent shape, she had to give all her attention to the moves. Obviously she'd plopped herself down in a very advanced class, and there was a matter of grace and style, as well as endurance.

Before the class was half-over, she developed a deep loathing for the bouncy instructor, with her pert ponytail and cheerful voice.

"One more leg lift, and I'm jumping her," Mel muttered. Although she hadn't meant to speak aloud, it was apparently the perfect move. Linda flashed her a grim smile.

"I'm right behind you." She panted as she executed what the instructor gleefully called hitch kicks. "She can't be over twenty. She deserves to die."

Mel chuckled and puffed. When the music stopped, the women sagged together in a sweaty heap.

After pulse checks and cool-downs, Mel dropped down next to Linda and buried her face in a towel. "That's what I get for taking ten days off." With a weary sigh, Mel lowered the towel. "I can't believe I scheduled myself for an entire day."

"I know what you mean. I've got weight training next."

"Really?" Mel offered her a surprised smile. "So do I."

"No kidding?" Linda blotted her neck, then rose. "I guess we might as well go suffer through it together."

They moved from weights to stationary bikes, from bikes to treadmills. The more they sweated, the friendlier they became. Conversation roamed from exercise to men, from men to backgrounds.

They shared a sauna and a whirlpool, and ended the session with a massage.

"I can't believe you gave up your career to keep a house." Stretched on the padded table, Linda folded her arms under her chin. "I can't imagine it."

"I'm not used to it myself." Mel sighed as the masseuse worked her way down her spine. "To tell you the truth, I haven't quite figured out what to do with myself yet. But it's a kind of experiment."

"Oh?"

She hesitated, just enough to let Linda know it was a sensitive subject. "You see, my husband and I have been trying to start a family. No luck. Since we've gone through the whole route of tests and procedures without results, I had this idea that if I quit for a while, maybe shucked off some of the career tension...well, something might happen.''

"It must be difficult.''

"It is. We both—I suppose since we're only children ourselves and don't have anyone but each other, we really want a large family. It seems so unjust, really. Here we have this wonderful house, we're solid financially, and our marriage is good. But we just can't seem to have children.''

If the wheels were clicking in Linda's head, she masked it with sympathy. "I guess you've been trying for a while now.''

"Years. It's really my fault. The doctors have told us there's a very slim chance that I'd be able to conceive.''

"I don't mean to offend you, but have you ever thought of adoption?''

"Thought about it?'' Mel managed a sad smile. "I can't tell you how many lists we're on. Both of us agree that we could love a child that wasn't biologically ours. We feel we have so much to give, but...'' She sighed again. "I suppose it's selfish, but we really want a baby. It might be a little easier to adopt an older child, but we're holding out. We've been told it could take years. I don't know how we'll handle all those empty rooms.'' She made her eyes fill, then blinked away the tears. "I'm sorry. I shouldn't go on about it. I get maudlin.''

"That's all right.'' Linda stretched her arm between the tables to squeeze Mel's hand. "I guess no one can really understand like another woman.''

They shared an iced juice and a spinach salad for lunch. Mel allowed Linda to guide the conversation gently back to her personal life. As the naive and deeply emotional Mary Ellen Ryan, she poured out information about her marriage, her hopes, her fears. She sprinkled in a few tears for good measure, and bravely wiped them away.

"You aren't thinking marriage yourself?'' Mel asked.

"Me? Oh, no.'' Linda laughed. "I tried it once, a long time ago. It's too confining for me. Jasper and I have a very nice arrangement. We're fond of each other, but we don't let it interfere with business. I like being able to come and go as I please.''

"I admire you.'' *You coldhearted floozy.* "Before I met Donovan, I had the idea that I'd go it alone through life, carving out my niche. Not that I regret falling in love and getting married, but I guess we all envy the woman who makes her own.''

"It suits me. But you're doing all right. You've got a guy who's crazy about you, and he's done well enough that you've got a nice home. Just about perfect.''

Mel looked down at her empty glass. "Just about.''

"Once you have that baby, it'll be perfect.'' Linda patted her hand. "Take my word for it.''

Mel dragged herself home, tossing her gym bag one way and kicking her shoes the other.

"There you are.'' Sebastian was looking down from the upstairs balcony. "I was about to send out a search party.''

"You'd do better with a stretcher.''

His smile faded. "Are you hurt?'' He was already starting down the steps. "I knew I should've kept an eye on you.''

"Hurt?'' She all but growled at him. "You don't know the half of it. I had the aerobics instructor from hell. Her name was Penny, if that gives you a clue. And she was cute as a damn button. Then I got handed over to some Amazon queen named Madge who put me on weights and all these hideous shiny machines. I pumped and lifted and squatted and crunched.'' Wincing, she pressed a hand to her stomach. "And all I've had to eat all day is a few stingy leaves.''

"Aw.'' He kissed her brow. "Poor baby.''

Her eyes narrowed. "I'm in the mood to punch someone, Donovan. It could be you.''

"How about if I fix you a nice snack?''

Her lips moved into a pout. "Have we got any frozen pizza?''

"I sincerely doubt it. Come on.'' He put a friendly arm around her shoulders as he led her into the kitchen. "You can tell me all about it while you eat.''

She dropped down agreeably at the smoked glass kitchen table. "It was quite a day. You know she—Linda—does this whole routine twice a week?'' Inspired, Mel popped up again to root through the cupboards for a bag of chips. "I don't know why anybody'd want to be that healthy,'' she said with her mouth full. "She seems okay, really. I mean, when you talk to her, she comes across as a normal, bright lady.'' Eyes grim, she sat again. "Then you keep talking, and you get to see that she's plenty bright. She's also cold as a fish.''

"I take it you talked quite a bit." Sebastian glanced up from his construction of a king-size sandwich.

"Hell, yes. I spilled my guts to her. She knows how I lost my parents when I was twenty. How I met you a couple years later. The whole love-at-first-sight routine. And you were pretty romantic." She crunched into a chip.

"Was I?" He set the sandwich and a glass of her favorite soft drink in front of her.

"You bet. Showered me with roses, took me dancing and for long moonlit walks. You were nuts about me.''

He smiled as she bit hungrily into the sandwich. "I'm sure I was.''

"You begged me to marry you. Lord, this is good." She closed her eyes and swallowed. "Where was I?''

"I was begging you to marry me.''

"Right." She gestured with her glass before drinking. "But I was cautious. I did move in with you eventually, and then I let you wear me down. You've done everything to make my life a fairy tale since.''

"I sound like a terrific guy.''

"Oh, yeah. I really played that up. We are the world's happiest couple. Except for our one heartbreak." She frowned but kept on eating. "You know, in the beginning I was starting to feel pretty bad about stringing her along. I knew it was a job, an important job, but it just seemed so calculating. She was nice, friendly, and I felt uncomfortable the way I was setting her up.''

She reached for the chips again, nibbling as she worked through her own thoughts. "Then, once I brought up the baby business, I could practically see her go sharp, you know? All those soft edges just cleaved away. She was still smiling and sympathetic and friendly as hell, but she was clicking it all into that brain of hers and figuring the angles. So I didn't feel bad about letting her pry more information out of me. I want her, Donovan.''

"You'll be seeing her again soon?''

"Day after tomorrow. At the beauty parlor, for the works.''

With a little moan, Mel pushed her plate away. "She thinks I'm a woman trying to fill the time on her hands." She grimaced. "Shopping was mentioned."

"How we suffer for our work."

"Very funny. Since you spent the morning hitting a little white ball around."

"I don't suppose I mentioned that I detest golf."

"No." She grinned. "Good. Tell me how it went."

"We ran into each other on the fourth tee. Quite by accident, of course."

"Of course."

"So we ended up playing the rest of the course together." Sebastian picked up her half-finished drink and sipped. "He finds my wife quite charming."

"Naturally."

"We discussed business, his and mine. He's interested in making some investments, so I made a few real estate suggestions."

"Clever."

"I do have some property in Oregon I've been thinking about selling. Anyway, we had a drink afterward and discussed sports and other manly things. I managed to drop into the conversation the fact that I hoped to have a son."

"Not just a kid?"

"As I said, it was a manly sort of event. A son to carry on the name, to play ball with, slipped more seamlessly into the conversation."

"Girls play ball," she muttered. "Never mind. Did he pick up on it?"

"Only quite delicately. I fumbled a bit, looked distressed, and changed the subject."

"Why?" She straightened in her chair. "If you had him on the line, why'd you cut him loose?"

"Because it felt right. You'll have to trust me on this, Mel. Gumm would have been suspicious if I'd taken him into my confidence so quickly. With you and the woman it's different. More natural."

She mulled it over, and, though she was still frowning, nodded. "All right. I'm inclined to agree. And we've certainly laid the groundwork."

"I spoke with Devereaux just before you got in. They should have a full work-up on Linda Glass by tomorrow, and he'll let us know as soon as Gumm makes a move to check out our story."

"Good enough."

"Also, we're invited to dine with Gumm and his lady on Friday evening."

Mel cocked a brow. "Even better." She leaned forward to kiss him. "You did good work, Donovan."

"I suppose we make a fair team. Have you finished eating?"

"For now."

"Then I think we should prepare for Friday night."

"Prepare what?" She shot him a suspicious look as he pulled her to her feet. "If you're going to start fiddling around with what I'm supposed to wear..."

"Not at all. It's this way," he told her as they walked out of the kitchen. "We're going to be a devoted and deliriously happy married couple."

"Yeah, so?"

"Madly in love," he continued, drawing her toward the stairs.

"I know the drill, Donovan."

"Well, I firmly believe in the Method school of acting. So I'm quite sure it will help our performance if we spend as much time as possible making love."

"Oh, I see." She turned, twining her arms around his neck and backing into the bedroom. "Well, like you said, we have to suffer for our work."

Mel was certain that one day she would look back and laugh. Or at least she would look back with the grim satisfaction of having survived.

Since going into law enforcement she had been kicked, cursed, slugged and insulted, had doors slammed in her face and on her foot. She'd been threatened, propositioned and, on one memorable occasion, she'd been shot at.

All of that was nothing compared to what was being done to her in the Silver Woman.

The hotel's exclusive and expansive beauty salon offered everything from a wash and set to something exotically—and terrifyingly—termed body wrapping.

Mel hadn't had the courage for that one, but she was getting the treatment from head to toe—and every inch between.

She arrived moments before Linda and, falling back on her established persona, greeted the woman like an old friend.

During leg waxing—which, Mel discovered quickly enough, did hurt—they discussed clothes and hairstyles. Smiling through gritted teeth, Mel was glad she'd boned up for hours the night before with fashion magazines.

Later, while whatever pungent glop the beautician smeared on her face hardened, Mel chatted about how much she was enjoying living in Tahoe.

"Our view of the lake is incredible. I really can't wait until we get to know more people. I love to entertain."

"Jasper and I can introduce you around," Linda offered as the pedicurist buffed her toenails. "Being in the hotel business, we know just about everyone you'd want to know."

"That would be marvellous." Mel chanced a look down and tried to look pleased, rather than horrified, that her toenails were being painted fuchsia. "Donovan mentioned to me that he met Jasper on the golf course at the club. Donovan just loves playing golf," she said, hoping it trapped him into spending hours on the green. "It's more a passion than a hobby."

"Jasper's the same way. I can't work up an interest in it myself." She began to chat about different people she wanted Mel to meet, and about how they might get together for tennis or sailing.

Mel agreed animatedly, wondering if a person could actually die of boredom.

Her face was scrubbed clean, and cream was slathered on. Some sort of oil was squirted all over her hair, and then plastic was wrapped around it.

"I just love being pampered this way," Linda murmured. They were both lying back in soft chairs, having their hands massaged and their nails done.

"Me too," Mel said, and prayed they were nearly finished.

"I suppose that's why this job suits me. Most of the time I

work nights, so my days are free. And I can make use of all the hotel's benefits.''

"Have you worked here long?"

"Almost two years now." She sighed. "It's never dull."

"I imagine you meet all sorts of fascinating people."

"The high-powered sort. That's what I like. From what you were saying the other day, your husband doesn't sound like small change.''

Mel would have grinned, but she settled for an indulgent smile. "Oh, he does very well. You could say that Donovan has the magic touch.''

They were rinsed, their scalps were massaged—Mel actually found it quite enjoyable—and it was nearly time for the finishing touches. She realized that if Linda didn't probe soon she would have to find an opening to bring up the subject herself.

"You know, Mary Ellen, I was thinking about what you told me the other day.''

"Oh." Mel feigned discomfort. "I'm so sorry about that, Linda, dumping on you that way, and so soon after we'd met. I guess I was feeling a little lost and homesick.''

"Nonsense." Linda waved her glorious nails. "I think we just hit it off, that's all. You were comfortable with me.''

"Yes, I was. But I'm more than a little embarrassed to think that I bored you with all that business about my personal life.''

"I wasn't bored at all. I was touched." Her voice was smooth as silk, with just the right touch of sympathy. Mel felt her hackles rising. "And it made me think. Please tell me if I'm getting too personal. But have you ever considered private adoption?''

"You mean going through a lawyer who works with unwed mothers?" Mel gave a long, wistful sigh. "Actually, we did try that route once, about a year ago. We weren't quite sure it was right. It wasn't that the money was a problem, but we were concerned about the legality, and the morality. But it all seemed perfect. We even went so far as to have an interview with the mother. Our hopes were very high. Too high. We picked our names, and window-shopped for baby things. It really looked as if it was going to happen. At the last minute, she backed out.''

Mel bit her lower lip, as if to steady herself.

"That must have been dreadful for you.''

"We both took it very hard. To get that close and then... nothing. We haven't discussed trying that way again since."

"I can understand that. But, as it happens, I do know of someone who's had a great deal of luck placing babies with adoptive parents."

Mel closed her eyes. She was afraid they would fill with derision, not hope. "A lawyer?"

"Yes. I don't know him personally, but, as I said, you meet a lot of people in this business, and I've heard. I don't want to promise, or get your hopes up, but if you'd like I could check."

"I'd be very grateful." Mel opened her eyes and met Linda's in the mirror. "I can't tell you how grateful."

An hour later, Mel swung out of the hotel and into Sebastian's arms. She laughed as he dipped her back for an exaggerated kiss.

"What are you doing here?"

"Playing the dutiful, lovesick husband come to fetch his wife." He held her at arm's length and smiled. Her hair was fluffed into a sexy, windblown look, her eyes were deepened and enlarged with blending shadows, and her lips were the same slick fuchsia as her nails. "In the name of Finn, Sutherland, what have they done to you?"

"Don't smirk."

"I'm not. You look extraordinary. Stunning. Just not quite like my Mel." He tipped her chin up for another kiss. "Who is this elegant, polished woman I'm holding?"

Not as annoyed as she wanted to be, she pulled a face. "You'd better not make fun after what I've been through. I actually had a bikini wax. It was barbaric." Chuckling, she linked her hands around his neck. "And my toenails are pink."

"I can't wait to see." He kissed her again, lightly. "I have news."

"Me too."

"Why don't I take a walk with my gorgeous wife and tell her how Gumm's been putting out feelers on the estimable Ryans of Seattle?"

"All right." She linked her fingers with his. "And I'll tell you how, out of the goodness of her heart, Linda Glass is going to help us make contact with a lawyer. About a private adoption."

"We do work well together."

"Yes, we do, Donovan." Pleased with herself, she strolled beside him. "We certainly do."

From the presidential suite on the top floor of the Silver Palace, Gumm watched through the window. "A charming couple," he commented to Linda.

"They're certainly loopy for each other." She sipped champagne as Sebastian and Mel walked off hand in hand. "The way she looks when she says his name almost makes me wonder if they're really married."

"I've had copies of the marriage certificate and other papers faxed in. It all seems in order." He tapped his fingers to his lips. "If they were a plant, I can't imagine they'd be so easily intimate."

"Plant?" Linda gave him a worried look. "Come on, Jasper, why would you even consider it? There's no way back to us."

"The business with the Frosts concerns me."

"Well, it's too bad they lost the kid. But we got our fee, and we didn't leave a trail."

"We left Parkland. I haven't been able to locate him."

"So he dropped off the edge of the world." Linda shrugged and moved over to press her body to Gumm's. "You've got nothing to worry about there. You held his note, and it was legit."

"He saw you."

"He wasn't seeing much of anything, as panicked as he was. Plus, it was dark, and I was wearing a scarf. Parkland doesn't worry me." She touched her lips to his. "We've got the touch, babe. Being in an organization like this, we've got so many covers and trapdoors, they'll never come close to us. And the money..." She loosened his tie. "Just think how that money keeps pouring in."

"You do like the money, don't you?" He tugged down the zipper of her dress. "We've got that in common."

"We've got lots in common. This could be a big one for us.

We pass the Ryans along, there will be a nice fat commission in it. I guarantee they'll pay the maximum for a kid. The woman's desperate to be a mommy.''

"I'll do a little more checking." Still calculating, he sank with her onto the couch.

"No harm in that, but I'm telling you, Jasper, these two are primed. No way we can lose. No way."

Mel and Sebastian became a convivial foursome with Gumm and Linda. They dined out, enjoyed the casino, lunched at the club and indulged in rousing doubles matches at tennis.

Ten days of the high life was making Mel edgy. Several times she ventured to ask Linda about the lawyer she had spoken of and was told, kindly, to be patient.

They were introduced to dozens of people. Some of them Mel found interesting and attractive, others slick and suspicious. She spent her days following the routine of a well-to-do woman with time and money on her hands.

And her nights with Sebastian.

She tried not to concern herself with her heart. She had a job to do, and if she'd fallen in love doing it, that was her problem to solve.

She knew he cared for her, just as she knew he desired her. It was a worry that he seemed so fond of the woman she pretended to be—a woman she would cease to be as soon as the job was over.

Not quite like my Mel. My Mel, he had said. There was hope in that, and she wasn't above clinging to it.

And as much as she wished the case were closed and justice served, she began to dread the day when they would go home, no longer married by design.

Whatever her personal needs and private hopes, she couldn't allow herself to put them ahead of what they were trying to do.

Following a suggestion of Linda's, Mel agreed to give a party. After all, she was supposed to be an enthusiastic entertainer, a whiz of a homemaker and a society gem.

As she struggled into her little black dress, she prayed she wouldn't make some telltale faux pas that showed her up as a phony.

"Damnation," she swore as Sebastian strolled into the bedroom.

"Problem, darling?"

"Zipper's stuck." She was half in and half out of the dress, flushed, harried and mad as a cat. He was sorely tempted to help her the rest of the way out of it, rather than in.

He gave the zipper a flick that sent it up to its home, halfway up her back. "All done. You're wearing the tourmaline," he said, reaching over her shoulder to touch the stone between her breasts.

"Morgana said it was good for stress. I need all the help I can get." Turning, she slipped regretfully into the heels, which brought them eye-to-eye. "It's stupid, but I'm really nervous. The only kind of parties I've ever given involved pizza and beer. Did you see all that stuff downstairs?"

"Yes, and I also saw the caterers who will take care of it."

"But I'm, like, the hostess. I'm supposed to know what to do."

"No, you're supposed to tell other people what to do, then take all the credit."

She smiled a little. "That's not so bad. It's just that something's got to happen soon. I'll go out of my mind if it doesn't. Linda keeps making cryptic remarks about being able to help, but I feel like I've been spinning wheels for the last week."

"Patience. We take the next step tonight."

"What do you mean?" She caught at his sleeve. "We said no holding back. If you know something, have seen something, tell me."

"It doesn't always work like a perfect mirror of events. I know the person we're looking for will be here tonight, and I'll recognize who it is. We've played the game well so far, Mel. And we'll play it out."

"All right." She took a deep breath. "What do you say, honey bun? Shall we go down and get ready to greet our guests?"

He winced. "Don't call me honey bun."

"Shoot, and I thought I was getting the hang of it." She started down, then stopped with a hand pressed to her stomach. "Oh, Lord, there's the bell. Here we go."

* * *

It wasn't really so bad, Mel discovered as the party flowed through the house and onto the deck. Everyone seemed to be having a dandy old time. There was some nice classical music—of Sebastian's choosing—playing in the background. The night was balmy enough that they could leave the doors wide and allow the guests to roam in and out. The food, if she did say so herself, was excellent. And, if she didn't recognize half of the canapés, it hardly mattered. She accepted the compliments graciously.

There was wine and laughter and interesting conversation. Which she supposed made for a pretty good party. And it was nice to watch Sebastian move through the room, to look over and see him smile at her, or to have him stop beside her for a touch or a private word.

Anyone looking at us would buy it, she thought. *We're the world's happiest couple, madly in love with each other.*

She could almost buy it herself, when his gaze moved in her direction and his eyes warmed, sending those secret signals up her spine.

Linda glided up, looking drop-dead gorgeous in a white off-the-shoulder gown. "I swear, the man can't keep his eyes off you. If I could find his twin, I might give marriage another shot after all."

"There's no one else like him," Mel said, sincerely enough. "Believe me, Donovan's one of a kind."

"And he's all yours."

"Yes. All mine."

"Well, besides being lucky in love, you throw a wonderful party. Your house is beautiful." And, Linda calculated, worth a good half a million on the market.

"Thank you, but I really owe you for recommending the caterer. He's a jewel."

"Anything I can do." She squeezed Mel's hand and gave her a long look. "I mean that."

Mel was quick. "Do you...have you... Oh, I don't mean to nag, but I haven't been able to think about anything else for days."

"No promises," she said, but then she winked. "There is

someone I'd like you to meet. You did say I could invite some people."

"Of course." She slipped on her hostess mask. "You know, I feel this is your party as much as mine. You and Jasper have become such good friends."

"And we're fond of you, too. Come over this way, so I can introduce you." Keeping Mel's hand in hers, Linda began weaving through the guests. "I'll bring her back," she said, laughing. "I just need to steal her a moment. Ah, here you are, Harriet. Harriet dear, I want you to meet your hostess and my friend, Mary Ellen Ryan. Mary Ellen, Harriet Breezeport."

"How do you do?" Mel took the slim, pale hand gently. The woman was well into her sixties and had a fragile air that was accented by her snow-white hair and half glasses.

"Delighted to meet you. So kind of you to invite us." Her voice was hardly more than a whisper. "Linda told me how charming you are. This is my son, Ethan."

He was nearly as pale as his mother, and wire-thin. His handshake was brisk, and his eyes were as black as a bird's. "Lovely party."

"Thank you. Why don't I find you a chair, Mrs. Breezeport? And something to drink?"

"Oh, I would dearly love a little wine." The woman smiled wispily. "I don't want to be any bother."

"Not at all." Mel took her arm and led her to a chair. "What can I get you?"

"Oh, Ethan will take care of it. Won't you, Ethan?"

"Of course. Excuse me."

"A good boy," Harriet said as her son walked off to the buffet table. "Takes such good care of me." She smiled up at Mel. "Linda tells me you've recently moved to Tahoe."

"Yes, my husband and I moved from Seattle. It's quite a change."

"Indeed, indeed. Ethan and I sometimes vacation here. We keep a nice little condo."

They chatted while Ethan brought back a plate with a few choice canapés and a small glass of wine. Linda had already slipped off when Mel glanced over and saw Sebastian approaching.

"This is my husband." Mel slipped a hand through his arm. "Donovan, this is Harriet and Ethan Breezeport."

"Linda said you were a dashing figure." Harriet offered a hand. "I'm afraid I've been hoarding your charming wife."

"I'm often guilty of that myself. In fact, I have to steal her for a moment. A small problem in the kitchen. Enjoy yourselves."

He nudged Mel along and then, finding no private spot, ducked with her into a closet.

"Donovan, for God's sake..."

"Shh." In the dim light, his eyes were very bright. "It's her," he said quietly.

"Who's her, and why are we standing in the closet?"

"The old woman. She's the one."

"The one?" Mel's mouth fell open. "Excuse me, do you expect me to believe that that fragile old lady is the head of a babynapping ring?"

"Exactly." He kissed her astonished mouth. "We're closing in, Sutherland."

Chapter 12

Mel met Harriet Breezeport twice more over the next two days, once for tea and again at a party. If it hadn't been for her faith in Sebastian, Mel would have laughed at the idea of the whispery-voiced matron as the head of a criminal organization.

But she did have faith in him, so she watched, and played her part.

It was Devereaux who fed them the information that neither Harriet nor Ethan Breezeport owned a condo in Tahoe. Nor, in fact, was there any record that either party existed.

Still, when the contact came, it came from neither of them, but from a tanned young man with a tennis racket. Mel had just finished a match with Linda and was waiting over a glass of iced tea for Sebastian to complete a round of golf with Gumm. The man approached, wearing tennis whites and a dazzling smile.

"Mrs. Ryan?"

"Yes?"

"I'm John Silbey. A mutual acquaintance pointed you out. I wonder if I could have a word with you?"

Mel hesitated, as she imagined a happily married woman might when approached by a strange man. "All right."

He sat, laying the tennis racket across his tanned knees. "I realize this is a bit unorthodox, Mrs. Ryan, but, as I said, we have mutual acquaintances. I've been told you and your husband might be interested in my services.''

"Really?" She arched a brow coolly, but her heart was picking up rhythm. "You don't look like a gardener, Mr. Silbey, though my husband and I are quite desperate for one.''

"No, indeed." He laughed heartily. "I'm afraid I can't help you there. I'm a lawyer, Mrs. Ryan.''

"Oh?" She tried for hopeful confusion, and apparently pulled it off. Silbey leaned a little closer and spoke gently.

"This isn't the usual way I solicit clients, but when you were pointed out to me just now, I thought it might be a good opportunity for us to become acquainted. I'm told you and your husband are interested in a private adoption.''

She moistened her lips and rattled the ice in her glass for good measure. "I... We've hoped," she said slowly. "We've tried. It's been very difficult. All the agencies we've tried have such long waiting lists.''

"I understand.''

And she could see that he did, and that he was very pleased to find her emotional, desperate and primed. He touched her hand in sympathy.

"We tried going through a lawyer before, but the whole thing fell through at the last minute." She pressed her lips together, as if to steady them. "I'm not sure I could handle that kind of disappointment again.''

"It's wrenching, I'm sure. I would hate to get your hopes up before we discuss this in more detail, but I can tell you that I've represented several women who have, for one reason or another, required the placement of their child. What they want for them is a good home, a loving home. It's my job to find that, Mrs. Ryan. And when I do, I have to say, it's one of the most rewarding experiences a man can have.''

And one of the most lucrative, Mel thought, but she smiled tremulously. "We want very much to provide a good and loving home for a child, Mr. Silbey. If you could help us...I can't begin to tell you how grateful we'd be.''

He touched her hand again. "Then, if you're agreeable, we'll talk further.''

"We could come to your office, anytime you say.''

"Actually, I'd like to meet you and your husband under less restrictive circumstances. At your home, so that I can assure my client on how you live, how you are together as a couple, in your own habitat."

"Of course, of course," she said, brimming with excitement. *Don't have an office, do you, bucko?* "Whenever it's convenient for you."

"Well, I'm afraid I'm booked for the next couple of weeks."

"Oh." She didn't have to feign disappointment. "Oh, well, I suppose we've waited this long…"

He waited a moment, then smiled kindly. "I could spare an hour this evening, unless you—"

"Oh, no." She grabbed his hand in both of hers. "That would be wonderful. I'm so grateful. Donovan and I… Thank you, Mr. Silbey."

"I hope I'll be able to help. Is seven o'clock all right with you?"

"It's fine." She blinked out tears of gratitude.

When he left her, she stayed in character, certain there would be someone watching. She dabbed at her eyes with a tissue, pressed a hand to her lips. Sebastian found her sniffing into her watery iced tea.

"Mary Ellen." The sight of her red-rimmed eyes and trembling lips brought instant concern. "Darling, what's wrong?" The moment he took her hands, the jolt of excitement nearly rocked him back on his heels. Only sheer willpower kept the astonishment from showing.

"Oh, Donovan." She scrambled to her feet, spotting Gumm over his shoulder. "I'm making a scene." Laughing, she wiped at the tears. "I'm sorry, Jasper."

"Not at all." Gallantly he offered a silk handkerchief. "Has someone upset you, Mary Ellen?"

"No, no." She gave a little shuddering sob. "It's good news. Marvelous news. I'm just overreacting. Would you excuse us, Jasper? Give my regrets to Linda. I really need to speak with Donovan alone."

"Of course." He walked off to give them their privacy, and Mel buried her face in Sebastian's shoulder.

"What the hell is going on?" he demanded in a soothing murmur as he stroked her hand.

"Contact." All damp eyes and shaky smiles, she drew her head back. "This sleazy lawyer—hell, I doubt he is a lawyer—just plopped himself down and offered to help us with a private adoption. Look delighted."

"I am." He kissed her for his own enjoyment, and for the benefit of their audience. "What's the deal?"

"Out of the goodness of his heart, and in consideration of a desperate woman, he's agreed to come by tonight and discuss our needs in more detail."

"Very obliging of him."

"Oh, yes. I may not have your gifts, but I could read his mind well enough. One look at me and he thought patsy. I could almost hear him calculating his take. Let's go home." She slipped an arm around him. "The air around here is really bad."

"Well?" Linda asked Gumm as they watched Sebastian and Mel walk away.

"Like shooting fish in a barrel." Pleased with himself, he signaled to a waiter. "They're so giddy with the idea, they'll ask the minimum amount of questions and pay the maximum fee. He might be a little more cautious, but he's so besotted with her he'd do anything to make her happy."

"Ah, love." Linda sneered. "It's the best scam in town. You got the merchandise picked out?"

Gumm ordered drinks then sat back to light a cigarette. "He wants a boy, so I think we'll oblige him, since he's paying top dollar. We've got a nurse in New Jersey ready to select a healthy male right out of the hospital."

"Good. You know, I'm fond of Mary Ellen. Maybe I'll throw her a shower."

"An excellent idea. I wouldn't be surprised if in a year or two they'd be in the market again." He checked his watch. "I'd better call Harriet and tell her she can start pushing buttons."

"Better you than me," Linda said with a grimace. "The old bag gives me the creeps."

"The old bag runs a smooth setup," he reminded her.

"Yeah, and business is business." Linda picked up the glass

the waiter set in front of her and raised it in a toast. "To the happy mommy-and-daddy-to-be."

"To an easy twenty-five grand."

"Better." Linda touched her glass to his. "Much better."

Mel knew her part and was ready when Silbey arrived promptly at seven. Her hand trembled a bit as she accepted his. "I'm so glad you could come."

"It's my pleasure."

She led him into the sprawling living room, chattering brightly. "We've only been in the house a couple of weeks. There are still a lot of changes I want to make. There's a room upstairs that would make a wonderful nursery. I hope... Donovan." Sebastian stood across the room, pouring a drink. "Mr. Silbey is here."

Sebastian knew his part, as well. He appeared to be reserved and nervous as he offered Silbey a drink. After a few social inanities, they sat, Sebastian and Mel close together on the sofa, hands linked in mutual support.

All solicitude, Silbey opened his briefcase. "If I could just ask you a few questions? Get to know you a bit?"

They filled in their established backgrounds while Silbey took notes. But it was their body language that told the tale. The quick, hopeful glances exchanged, the touches. Silbey continued the interview, completely unaware that every word he spoke was being transmitted to two federal agents in an upstairs room.

Clearly pleased with the progress he was making, Silbey sent them an encouraging look. "I have to say, in my personal and professional opinion, you would make excellent parents. The selecting of a home for a child is a very delicate matter."

He pontificated for a while on stability, responsibility, and the special requirements of raising an adopted child. Mel's stomach turned even as she beamed at him.

"I can see that you've both thought this through very seriously, very thoroughly. There is, however, a point you may want to discuss at more length. The expenses. I know it sounds crass, putting a price on something we should consider a miracle. But there is a reality to be accepted. There's a matter of medical expenses and compensation to the mother, my fee, court costs and filing—all of which I will handle.''

"We understand,'' Sebastian said, wishing he was free to wring Silbey's neck.

"I'll require a twenty-five-thousand-dollar retainer, and another hundred and twenty-five thousand at the end of the legalities. This will include all the expenses of the mother.''

Sebastian started to speak. He was, after all, a businessman. But Mel gripped his hand tighter and hit him with a pleading glance.

"The money won't be a problem,'' he said, and touched her cheek.

"All right then.'' Silbey smiled. "I have a client. She's very young, unmarried. She wants very much to finish college, and has come to the difficult decision that raising a child on her own would make this impossible. I'll be able to provide you with her medical background, and that of the father. She's quite firm that there be no other information divulged. With your permission, I will tell her about you, and give her my recommendation.''

"Oh.'' Mel pressed her fingers to her lips. "Oh, yes.''

"To be frank, you're exactly the kind of parents she was hoping for. I believe we'll be able to complete this with everyone's best interest served.''

"Mr. Silbey.'' Mel leaned her head against Sebastian's shoulder. "When...I mean, how soon would we know? And the child— What can you tell us?''

"I'd say you'd know within forty-eight hours. As far as the child...'' He smiled benignly. "My client is due to deliver any day. I have a feeling my call is going to ease her mind tremendously.''

By the time they had walked Silbey to the door, Mel had shed a few more tears. The moment she was alone with Sebastian, fury burned her eyes dry.

"That sonofa—''

"I know.'' He put his hands on her shoulders. She was vibrating like a plucked string. "We'll get them, Mel. We'll get them all.''

"You're damn right we will.'' She paced to the stairs and back. "You know what this means, don't you? They're going to steal a baby, an infant, probably right out of a hospital or clinic.''

"Logical as always," he murmured, watching her carefully.

"I can't stand it." She pressed a hand to her churning stomach. "I can't bear the idea of some poor woman lying in a hospital bed being told her baby's been stolen."

"It won't take long." He wanted to slip into her thoughts, to see for himself just what was in her head. But he'd given his word. "We have to play this through."

"Yeah." That was just what she was going to do. He wouldn't approve, she decided. And neither would the feds. But there were times you had to follow your heart. "We'd better make sure the boys upstairs got all of that." She took a deep breath. "Then I think we should do what any happy, expectant couple would do."

"Which is?"

"Go out and tell our dearest friends. And celebrate."

Mel sat in the lounge at the Silver Palace with a glass of champagne in her hand and a smile on her lips. "To new and valued friends."

Linda laughed and clinked glasses. "Oh, no, to the happy parents-to-be."

"We'll never be able to thank you." She looked from Linda to Gumm. "Both of you."

"Nonsense." Gumm patted her hand. "Linda merely made an inquiry to a friend. We're both delighted such a small gesture reaped such benefits."

"We still have to sign papers," Sebastian pointed out. "And wait for the mother's approval."

"We're not going to worry about any of that." Linda waved details away. "What we have to do now is plan a baby shower. I'd love to give you one, Mary Ellen, up in the penthouse."

Though she was getting damned tired of weeping, Mel let her eyes fill. "That's so..." Tears spilled over as she got to her feet. "Excuse me." An emotional wreck, she rushed off to the ladies' room. As she'd hoped, Linda followed her a moment later.

"What an idiot I am."

"Don't be silly." Linda sat beside her, slipped an arm around her. "They say expectant mothers are apt to cry at the drop of a hat."

With a shaky laugh, Mel dried her eyes. "I suppose. Would you mind terribly getting me a drink of water before I try to repair the damage?"

"Sit right there."

Mel figured she had twenty seconds at best, so she moved fast. She flipped open Linda's beaded evening bag, pushed through past lipstick and perfume and gripped the penthouse key. She was slipping it into the pocket of her evening pants when Linda came back with a cup.

"Thanks." Mel smiled up at her. "Thanks a lot."

The next step was to get away from the group for at least twenty minutes without being detected. She suggested a celebratory dinner, with a little gambling as an appetizer. Always the gracious host, Gumm insisted on making the arrangements in the dining room himself. Marking time, Mel managed to slip away from Sebastian and Linda in the crowd at the crap table.

She took the express elevator, keeping well to the back of the glass walls. The top floor was silent as she stepped out. Mel checked her watch, then fit the key into the lock of the penthouse.

She didn't need much. With the evidence they already had, she needed only enough to link Gumm and Linda with Silbey or the Breezeports. She judged Gumm as a man who kept records on everything—and kept them cleverly.

Maybe it was rash, she thought as she headed straight for a huge ebony desk. But the idea of them even now plotting to steal a baby fired her blood. She wasn't going to stand by while someone else went through what Rose and Stan had experienced. Not while there was a chance she could make a difference.

She found nothing in the desk of interest and used up five of her allotted twenty minutes in the search. Undaunted, she moved on, checking tables for false bottoms, locating a wall safe behind a section of books. She would have loved to have the time and the talent to lift that lock, but she had to admit defeat. With less than three minutes to go, she found what she was looking for in plain sight.

The second bedroom of the suite served as a fussily decorated office that Linda used as a convenience. There, on top of her French provincial desk, was a leather-bound account book.

At first glance, it seemed like nothing more than it purported to be, a daily record of deliveries for the hotel shops. Mel had nearly put it down again in disgust when she noted the dates.

Merchandise acquired 1/21. Tampa. Picked up 1/22. Little Rock. Delivered 1/23. Louisville. Accepted COD 1/25. Detroit. Commission $10,000.

Breathing shallowly, Mel flipped pages.

Merchandise acquired 5/5. Monterey. Picked up 5/6. Scuttlefield. 5/7. Delivered 5/8. Lubbock. Accepted COD 5/11. Atlanta. Commission $12,000.

David, she thought, and didn't bother to hold back a string of oaths. It was right there, all the dates and cities. And more. Babies listed like packages to be shipped and paid for on delivery.

Tight-lipped, she skimmed the pages and let out a hiss between her teeth.

H.B. ordered new blue package, West Bloomfield, New Jersey. Pick up between 8/22 and 8/25. Standard route, acceptance and final payment expected by 8/31. Estimated commission $25,000.

"You bitch," Mel muttered as she closed the book. She struggled against the urge to break something, and scanned the room instead. When she was certain nothing was out of place, she started for the door.

"Oh, she's probably off having another crying jag," Linda said as she walked through the main door of the penthouse into the parlor. "He'll find her."

Mel took a quick look around and opted for the closet.

"I can't say I'm looking forward to spending the evening with her," Gumm said. "I doubt she'll talk about anything but booties and baby formula."

"We can take it, lover. Especially for twice our usual fee." Her voice faded a bit as she walked toward the opposite bedroom. "I think it was a good idea to arrange for dinner up here. The more grateful and emotional they are, the less they'll think. Once they have the kid, they won't question anything."

"Harriet's thoughts exactly. She already has Ethan putting the wheels in motion. I was surprised when she came down to take a look at them for herself, but she's a little more cautious since the Frost affair."

Mel kept her breath slow and even. She pressed her fingers against the stone of her ring. Communication between people who are important to each other, she remembered, and shut her eyes. Well, here's hoping. Come on, Donovan, get your butt up here and bring the marines.

It was risky, she knew, but she thought the odds were in her favor. Reaching into her bag, she felt the comforting bulk of her weapon. Not that way. She took a deep, bracing breath and put the account book in instead of taking the revolver out. She set her bag on the floor, then opened the closet.

"They'll pass the merchandise to our contact in Chicago," Gumm was saying.

"I'd like to pick him up in Albuquerque," Linda put in. "I could always use an extra couple of thousand for the run." Her head snapped up as Mel deliberately bumped a chair. "What the hell?"

Gumm was in the room like a shot, twisting the struggling Mel's arms behind her. "Let me go! Jasper, you're hurting me."

"People who break into other people's homes often get hurt."

"I—I was just lying down for a while." She made her eyes dart crazily to make the lie all the more ridiculous. "I didn't think you'd mind."

"What have we got here?" Linda asked.

"A plant. I should have known. I should have smelled it."

"Cop?" Linda considered.

"Cop?" Eyes wide with alarm, Mel twisted. "I don't know what you're talking about. I was just resting."

"How'd she get in?" Jasper demanded, and Mel let the key she was holding slip out of her hands.

"Mine." Swearing in disgust, Linda bent to pick it up. "She must have palmed it."

"I don't know what—" Jasper cut off Mel's protest with a backhand that left her head ringing. She decided it was time to drop one act for another.

"Okay, okay, you don't have to play rough." She shuddered and swallowed audibly. "I'm just doing my job."

Jasper shoved her into the parlor and onto the sofa. "Which is?"

"Look, I'm just an actress. I took a gig with Donovan. He's a PI." Stall, Mel thought. Stall, stall, stall, because he was coming. She knew he was. "I only did what he told me to do. I don't care what you're into. And I got an appreciation for a good scam."

Gumm moved to the desk and took a pistol from the top drawer. "What are you doing in here?"

"Man, you don't need that," she said, swallowing. "He said I should get the key and come up to look around. He thought there might be some papers in the desk there." She gestured toward the ebony desk. "It seemed like a real kick, you know. And he's paying me five grand for the job."

"A two-bit actress and a PI," Linda said furiously. "What the hell do we do now?"

"What we have to do."

"Look, look, you say the word and I'm out of here. I mean out of the state." Mel tried for a tawdry kind of charm. "I mean, it was great while it lasted, the clothes and all, but I don't want any trouble. I didn't hear anything, I didn't see anything."

"You heard plenty," Gumm countered.

"I got a bad memory."

"Shut up," Linda snapped, and Mel shrugged.

"We'll have to contact Harriet. She's back in Baltimore seeing to the details of the last job." Gumm ran his hands through his hair. "She's going to be very unhappy. She'll have to call off the nurse. We can't take a kid without a buyer."

"Twenty-five thousand down the tubes." Linda sent Mel a look of avid dislike. "I was actually pretty fond of you, Mary Ellen." She walked over to lean into Mel's face, squeezing a hand around her throat. "As it is now, I'm going to get a lot of satisfaction out of letting Jasper take care of you."

"Hey, listen…"

"Shut up." She shoved Mel back. "You'd better arrange for someone to do it tonight. And to pick up the PI, too. I think a little spat in their house, maybe. A nice murder-suicide."

"I'll take care of it."

At the knock on the door, Mel made to scramble up and as expected had Linda clamp a hand over her mouth.

"Room service, Mr. Gumm."

"The damn dinner," he muttered. "Take her in the other room and keep her quiet. I'll handle this."

"A pleasure." Linda took the gun Gumm handed her and gestured Mel into the next room.

Smoothing back his hair, Gumm went to the door, then gestured for the waiter to roll in the room-service tray. "Don't bother to set up. Our guests haven't arrived yet."

"Yes, they have." Sebastian strolled in. "Jasper, I'd like you to meet Special Agent Devereaux. FBI."

In the next room, Linda swore and Mel grinned. "Excuse me," she said politely, tramped hard on Linda's foot and knocked the gun aside.

"Sutherland," Sebastian said with restrained fury from the doorway. "You've got some explaining to do."

"In a minute." To please herself, she turned and rammed her fist into Linda's astonished face. "That one was for Rose," she said.

He wasn't happy with her. Sebastian made that abundantly clear through the rest of that evening, through all the explanations. Devereaux wasn't exactly thrilled himself, though she thought it was small-minded of him, since she'd all but wrapped the evidence in a bow and handed it to him.

Sebastian had a right to be annoyed, she supposed. She'd acted on her own. But she was the professional. Besides, it had worked out exactly as she'd planned, so what was his problem?

She asked him just that several times, as they packed up for the trip home, as they flew back to Monterey, as he dropped her off at her office.

His only answer was one of his long, enigmatic looks. The last thing he said to her left her miserable and silent.

"I kept my word, Mary Ellen. You didn't. As a matter of trust, it comes down to that."

That had been two days before, she thought as she brooded at her desk. And there hadn't been a peep from him since.

She'd even swallowed her pride and called him, only to get his answering machine. It wasn't that she felt she owed him an apology, exactly. But she did think he deserved another chance to be reasonable.

She toyed with the idea of going to Morgana or Anastasia and asking them to intercede. But that was too weak. All she wanted to do was to put things back on an even keel between them.

No, no, she wanted much more than that, Mel admitted. And that was what was killing her.

Only one way to do it, she told herself, and kicked back from her desk. She would hunt him down, pin him to the wall if necessary, but she would make him listen to her.

All the way along the winding mountain road she practiced what she would say and how she would say it. She tried being tough, experimented with being quiet and solemn, and even took a shot at being penitent. When that didn't sit well, she opted for aggressive tactics. She'd just march right up to his door and tell him to cut out the silent routine. She was tired of it.

If he wasn't there, she'd wait.

He was there, all right, she discovered as she reached the top of his lane. But he certainly wasn't alone. There were three other cars in the drive, including what appeared to be the longest stretch limo in the known world.

She stepped out of her car and stood beside it, wondering what to do next.

"I told you, didn't I tell you?" Mel looked around and spotted a pretty woman in a flowing tea-length dress. "A green-eyed blonde," she said, a definite smack of satisfaction in her Irish voice. "I told you something was bothering him."

"Yes, dear." The man beside her was tall and gangly, his graying hair receding into a dramatic widow's peak. He looked rather dashing in jodhpurs and top boots. A Victorian quizzing glass dangled from a string around his neck. "But it was I who told you it was a female."

"Nevertheless." The woman glided across the grounds with both plump hands held out to Mel. "Hello, hello, and welcome."

"Ah, thanks. I'm, ah, looking for..."

"Of course you are," the woman said with a breezy laugh. "Anyone could see that, couldn't they, Douglas?"

"Pretty," he said in response. "Not a pushover." He peered at her with eyes that were so much like Sebastian's that Mel began to put two and two together. "He didn't tell us about you, which speaks for itself."

"I suppose," she said after a moment. His parents, she thought, sinking. A family reunion was no place for a confrontation. "I don't want to disturb him when he has company. Maybe you could tell him I stopped by."

"Nonsense. I'm Camilla, by the way. Sebastian's mother." She took Mel's arm and began to lead her toward the house. "I quite understand your being in love with him, my dear child. I've loved him myself for years."

Panicked, Mel looked for a route of escape. "No, I— That is...I really think I should come back later."

"No time like the present," Douglas said, and gave her a friendly nudge through the door. "Sebastian, look what we've brought you." He brought the glass to his eye and peered around owlishly. "Where is that boy?"

"Upstairs." Morgana breezed in from the direction of the kitchen. "He'll be... Oh, hello."

"Hi." The frost on the greeting told Mel it had been a bad idea to come. "I was just...leaving. I didn't realize your family was visiting."

"Oh, they drop in now and again." After she took one long look into Mel's eyes, Morgana's smile warmed. "Stepped in it, did you?" she murmured. "That's all right. He'll come around."

"I really think I should—"

"Meet the rest of the family," Camilla said gaily and kept Mel's arm in an iron grip as she marched her toward the kitchen.

There were glorious scents in the air, and roomsful of people. A tall, queenly woman was laughing raucously as she stirred something on the stove. Nash was on a stool beside a lean middle-aged man with steel-gray hair. When the man glanced up at her, she felt like a moth on a pin.

"Hey, Mel." Nash sent her a wave, and she was thrust into the fray. Introductions followed, Camilla taking charge territorially.

"My brother-in-law, Matthew," she began, gesturing to the man beside Nash. "My sister Maureen at the stove." Maureen waved an absent hand and sniffed at her brew. "And my sister, Bryna."

"Hello." A woman every bit as stunning as Morgana stepped forward to take Mel's hand. "I hope you're not too befuddled by all this. We all dropped in quite unexpectedly just this morning."

"No, no, really. I don't want to intrude. I should really just—"

Then it was too late. Sebastian walked in, flanked by Ana and a short, husky man with twinkling eyes.

"Ah, Sebastian." Bryna kept Mel's hand. "More company. Mel, this is Padrick, Ana's father."

"Hello." It was easier to look at him than Sebastian. "Nice to meet you."

He strolled right up and pinched her cheek. "Stay for dinner. We'll put some meat on your bones. Maureen, my moonflower, what is that tantalizing scent?"

"Hungarian goulash."

Padrick winked at Mel. "And not a single eye of newt in the batch. Guaranteed."

"Yes, well, I appreciate the invitation, but I really can't stay." She took a chance and glanced at Sebastian. "I'm sorry," she fumbled when he just continued to gaze at her with those quiet, inscrutable eyes. "I shouldn't have... I mean, I really should have called first. I'll catch you later."

"Excuse us," he said to the group at large, gripping Mel's arm as she tried to dash by. "Mel hasn't seen the foal since the birthing."

Though she knew it was cowardly, she shot one desperate glance behind her as he pulled her out of the door. "You have company."

And that company moved as a unit to the kitchen window to watch the goings-on.

"Family isn't company," he said. "And, since you've come all this way, I have to believe you have something to say."

"Well, I do, and I'll say it when you stop dragging me."

"Fine." He stopped near the paddock where the foal was busily nursing. "Say it."

"I wanted to... I talked to Devereaux. He said Linda copped

a plea and spilled everything. They've got enough on Gumm and the Breezeports to put them away for a long time. They've got a line on a handful of others, like Silbey, too.''

''I'm aware of all that.''

''Oh, well, I wasn't sure.'' She stuck her hands in her pockets. ''It's going to take some time to locate all the children, and get them back where they belong, but... It worked, damn it,'' she blurted out. ''I don't know what the hell you're so bent out of shape about.''

His voice was deceptively mild. ''Don't you?''

''I did what I thought was best.'' She kicked at the ground, then strode over to the fence. ''They'd already made plans to snatch another kid. It was right in the book.''

''The book you went in and found. On your own.''

''If I'd told you what I was going to do, you'd have tried to stop me.''

''Wrong. I would have stopped you.''

She frowned back at him. ''See? By doing it my way, we saved a lot of heartache.''

''And risked more.'' The anger he'd been struggling to hold back flared. ''There was a bruise on your cheek.''

''A qualified job risk,'' she shot back. ''And it's my cheek.''

''Good God, Sutherland. She had a gun on you.''

''Only for a minute. Hell, Donovan, the day I can't handle a sap like Linda Glass is the day I retire. I'm telling you I just couldn't take the idea of them snatching another baby, so I went with the gut.'' Her eyes were so eloquent, some of his anger died. ''I know what I'm doing, and I also know it seems like I was cutting you out. But I wasn't. I called you.''

He took a calming breath, but it failed to work. ''And if I'd been too late?''

''Well, you weren't, so what's the point?''

''The point is, you didn't trust me.''

''The hell I didn't. Who else was I trusting when I stood in that closet and tried to use the ring or whatever connection we had to get you and the feds up there? If I hadn't trusted you, I would've slipped right out the door with the book.'' She grabbed at his shirt and shook him. ''It was because I trusted you that I played it out that way. Staying there, letting them catch me—

because I knew I could trust you to back me up. I tried to explain it all to you before. I knew they'd tell me things Devereaux could use, and with the book as a backup, we'd have them cold."

Steadying himself, he turned away. As angry as he was, he saw the truth in that. Perhaps it wasn't the kind of trust he'd wanted, but it was trust. "You could have been hurt."

"Sure. I could be hurt every time I take a case. That's what I do. That's what I am." She swallowed, struggling to clear an obstruction in her throat. "I had to accept you, and what you are. And believe me, it was no snap. If we're going to be... friends, the same goes."

"You may have a point. But I still don't like your style."

"Fine," she snapped back, blinking her vision clear. "Same goes."

At the kitchen window, Camilla shook her head. "He always was stubborn."

"Ten pounds she wears him down." Padrick pinched his wife's bottom affectionately. "Ten pounds and no tricks."

Ana shushed him. "We won't be able to hear."

Mel let out a shaky breath. "Well, we know where we stand anyway. And I'm sorry."

"Excuse me?" He turned and was astonished by the tears he saw on her face. "Mary Ellen—"

"Don't. I'm going to get this out." She wiped furiously at the tears. "I have to do what I think is right. And I still think what I did was right, but I'm sorry you're so angry with me, because I... Oh, I hate this." She scrubbed her hands over her face, evading him when he reached for her. "Don't. I don't want you to. I don't need to be patted or soothed, even if I am acting like a baby. You were mad, and I guess I can't blame you for it, or for dropping me cold."

"Dropping you cold?" He nearly laughed. "I left you alone, and well out of harm's way, until I could be certain I could restrain myself from throttling you or present you with an ultimatum you might have tossed back in my face."

"Whatever." She sniffed and regained some control. "I guess what I did hurt you, and I didn't mean it to."

He smiled a little. "Same goes."

"Okay." There had to be some way to finish this with a little dignity intact. "Anyway, I wanted to clear the air, and to tell you I think we did a good job. Now that it's done, I figured I'd better return this." It was hard, one of the hardest things she'd ever done, to pull his ring from her finger. "Looks like the Ryans are getting a divorce."

"Yes." He took the ring back and held it warm in the palm of his hand as he considered her. It wasn't necessary to dip into her thoughts to see that she was suffering. It wasn't particularly noble, but the fact that she was pleased him very much. "It seems a pity." He brushed his knuckles over her cheek. "Then again, I much prefer you to her."

She blinked. "You do?"

"Very much. I was beginning to find her a little dull. She'd never argue with me, and she was forever having her nails done." Gently he cupped a hand behind her head and drew her closer. "She certainly wouldn't have been caught dead in those jeans."

"Guess not," she murmured, leaning into him, into the kiss.

She felt herself tremble, felt the tears welling up again as she threw her arms around him. "Sebastian. I need..." She tightened her hold as her lips clung to his.

"Tell me."

"I want— Oh, Lord, you scare me." She drew back, her eyes wet and terrified. "Just read my mind, will you? For God's sake, just look at what I'm feeling and give me a break."

His eyes darkened, his hands moved up to cup her face. He looked, and found everything he'd been waiting for. "Again," he murmured, taking her mouth. But this time the kiss was gentle, coaxing. "Can't you tell me? Can't you say the words? They're the truest magic."

"I don't want you to feel like I'm boxing you in. It's just that I..."

"I love you," he finished for her.

"Yeah." She managed a weak smile. "You could say I blurred the lines. I wasn't going to bring it up, but it seemed like I should. Only fair that I should be up-front. Pretty awkward when you've got a houseful of people."

"All of whom have their noses pressed up to the kitchen window and are enjoying this nearly as much as I."

"Who—?" She spun around, flushed and stumbled backward. "Oh, Lord. Look, I'm going. I really can't believe I did this." Unnerved, she lifted a hand to tug at her hair. And saw the ring back on her finger. As she stared at it, he stepped forward.

"I gave the stone to Morgana. A stone I've treasured most of my life. I asked her to have a ring made out of it. For you. For you," he repeated, waiting until she lifted her eyes to his. "Because you were the only woman I wanted to wear it. You were the only woman I wanted to share my life with. Twice now I've put it on your finger, and both times it was a pledge to you." He held out his hand, offering. "No one, in any time, in any place, will love you more."

Her eyes were dry now, and her nerves were suddenly calm as the day. "Do you mean it?"

His lips curved. "No, Sutherland. I'm lying."

With a laugh, she launched herself into his arms. "Tough break. I've got witnesses." The spontaneous applause from the kitchen made her laugh again. "Oh, I do love you, Donovan. I'm going to do my best to make your life eventful."

He swung her in one giddy circle. "I know." After one last long kiss, he took her by the hand. "Come, meet your family again. We've all been waiting for you."

*   *   *   *   *

CHARMED

Prologue

Magic exists. Who can doubt it, when there are rainbows and wildflowers, the music of the wind and the silence of the stars? Anyone who has loved has been touched by magic. It is such a simple and such an extraordinary part of the lives we live.

There are those who have been given more, who have been chosen to carry on a legacy handed down through endless ages. Their forebears were Merlin the enchanter, Ninian the sorceress, the faerie princess Rhiannon, the Wegewarte of Germany and the jinns of Arabia. Through their blood ran the power of Finn of the Celts, the ambitious Morgan le Fay, and others whose names were whispered only in shadows and in secret.

When the world was young and magic as common as a raindrop, faeries danced in the deep forests, and—sometimes for mischief, sometimes for love—mixed with mortals.

And they do still.

Her bloodline was old. Her power was ancient. Even as a child she had understood, had been taught, that such gifts were not without price. The loving parents who treasured her could not lower the cost, or pay it themselves, but could only love, instruct and watch the young girl grow to womanhood. They could only stand and hope as she experienced the pains and the joys of that most fascinating of journeys.

And, because she felt more than others, because her gift demanded that she feel more, she learned to court peace.

As a woman, she preferred a quiet life, and was often alone without the pain of loneliness.

As a witch, she accepted her gift, and never forgot the responsibility it entailed.

Perhaps she yearned, as mortals and others have yearned since the beginning, for a true and abiding love. For she knew better than most that there was no power, no enchantment, no sorcery, greater than the gift of an open and accepting heart.

Chapter 1

When she saw the little girl peek through the fairy roses, Anastasia had no idea the child would change her life. She'd been humming to herself, as she often did when she gardened, enjoying the scent and the feel of earth. The warm September sun was golden, and the gentle whoosh of the sea on the rocks below her sloping yard was a lovely background to the buzzing of bees and the piping of birdsong. Her long gray cat was stretched out beside her, his tail twitching in time with some feline dream.

A butterfly landed soundlessly on her hand, and she stroked the edge of its pale blue wings with a fingertip. As it fluttered off, she heard the rustling. Glancing over, she saw a small face peeping through the hedge of fairy roses.

Ana's smile came quickly, naturally. The face was charming, with its little pointed chin and its pert nose, its big blue eyes mirroring the color of the sky. A pixie cap of glossy brown hair completed the picture.

The girl smiled back, those summer-sky eyes full of curiosity and mischief.

"Hello," Ana said, as if she always found little girls in her rosebushes.

"Hi." The girl's voice was bright, and a little breathless. "Can you catch butterflies? I never got to pet one like that before."

"I suppose. But it seems rude to try unless one invites you."

She brushed the hair from her brow with her forearm and sat back on her heels. Ana had noticed a moving van unloading the day before, and she concluded she was meeting one of her new neighbors. "Have you moved into the house next door?"

"Uh-huh. We're going to live here now. I like it, 'cause I get to look right out my bedroom window and see the water. I saw a seal, too. In Indiana you only see them in the zoo. Can I come over?"

"Of course you can." Ana set her garden spade aside as the girl stepped through the rosebushes. In her arms was a wriggling puppy. "And who do we have here?"

"This is Daisy." The child pressed a loving kiss to the top of the puppy's head. "She's a golden retriever. I got to pick her out myself right before we left Indiana. She got to fly in the plane with us, and we were hardly scared at all. I have to take good care of her and give her food and water and brush her and everything, 'cause she's my responsibility."

"She's very beautiful," Ana said soberly. And very heavy, she imagined, for a little girl of five or six. She held out her arms. "May I?"

"Do you like dogs?" The little girl kept chattering as she passed Daisy over. "I do. I like dogs and cats and everything. Even the hamsters Billy Walker has. Someday I'm going to have a horse, too. We'll have to see about that. That's what my daddy says. We'll have to see about that."

Utterly charmed, Ana stroked the puppy as she sniffed and licked at her. The child was as sweet as sunshine. "I'm very fond of dogs and cats and everything," Ana told her. "My cousin has horses. Two big ones and a brand-new baby."

"Really?" The child squatted down and began to pet the sleeping cat. "Can I see them?"

"He doesn't live far, so perhaps one day. We'll have to ask your parents."

"My mommy went to heaven. She's an angel now."

Ana's heart broke a little. Reaching out, she touched the shiny hair and opened herself. There was no pain here, and that was a relief. The memories were good ones. At the touch, the child looked up and smiled.

"I'm Jessica," she said. "But you can call me Jessie."

"I'm Anastasia." Because it was too much to resist, Ana bent down and kissed the pert nose. "But you can call me Ana."

Introductions over, Jessie settled down to bombard Ana with questions, filtering information about herself through the bright chatter. She'd just had a birthday and was six. She would be starting first grade in her brand-new school on Tuesday. Her favorite color was purple, and she hated lima beans more than anything.

Could Ana show her how to plant flowers? Did her cat have a name? Did she have any little girls? Why not?

So they sat in the sunshine, a bright pixie of a girl in pink rompers and a woman with garden dirt smearing her shorts and her lightly tanned legs, while Quigley the cat ignored the playful attentions of Daisy the dog.

Ana's long, wheat-colored hair was tied carelessly back, and the occasional wisp worked free of the band to dance in the wind around her face. She wore no cosmetics. Her fragile, heart-breaking beauty was as natural as her power, a combination of Celtic bones, smoky eyes, the wide, poetically sculptured Donovan mouth—and something more nebulous. Her face was the mirror of a giving heart.

The pup marched over to sniff at the herbs in her rockery. Ana laughed at something Jessica said.

"Jessie!" The voice swept over the hedge of roses, deeply male, and touched with exasperation and concern. "Jessica Alice Sawyer!"

"Uh-oh. He used my whole name." But Jessie's eyes were twinkling as she jumped to her feet. There was obviously little fear of reprisals.

"Over here! Daddy, I'm right over here with Ana! Come and see!"

A moment later, there was a man towering over the fairy roses. No gift was needed to detect waves of frustration, relief and annoyance. Ana blinked once, surprised that this rough-and-ready male was the father of the little sprite currently bouncing beside her.

Maybe it was the day or two's growth of beard that made him look so dangerous, she thought. But she doubted it. Beneath that dusky shadow was a sharp-featured face of planes and angles, a full mouth set in grim lines. Only the eyes were like his daughter's, a clear, brilliant blue, marred now by an expression of impatience. The sun brought out glints of red in his dark, tousled hair as he dragged a hand through it.

From her perch on the ground, he looked enormous. Athletically fit and disconcertingly strong, in a ripped T-shirt and faded jeans sprung at the seams.

He cast one long, annoyed and unmistakably distrustful glance at Ana before giving his attention to his daughter.

"Jessica. Didn't I tell you to stay in the yard?"

"I guess." She smiled winningly. "Daisy and I heard Ana singing, and when we looked, she had this butterfly right on her hand. And she said we could come over. She has a cat, see? And her cousin has horses, and her other cousin has a cat *and* a dog."

Obviously used to Jessie's rambling, her father waited it out. "When I tell you to stay in the yard, and then you're not there, I'm going to worry."

It was a simple statement, made in even tones. Ana had to respect the fact that the man didn't have to raise his voice or spout ultimatums to get his point across. She felt every bit as chastened as Jessie.

"I'm sorry, Daddy," Jessie murmured over a pouting lower lip.

"I should apologize, Mr. Sawyer." Ana rose to lay a hand on Jessie's shoulder. After all, it looked as if they were in this together. "I did invite her over, and I was enjoying her company so much that it didn't occur to me that you wouldn't be able to see where she was."

He said nothing for a moment, just stared at her with those water-clear eyes until she had to fight the urge to squirm. When he flicked his gaze down to his daughter again, Ana realized she'd been holding her breath.

"You should take Daisy over and feed her."

"Okay." Jessie hauled the reluctant pup into her arms, then stopped when her father inclined his head.

"And thank Mrs...?"

"Miss," Ana supplied. "Donovan. Anastasia Donovan."

"Thank Miss Donovan for putting up with you."

"Thank you for putting up with me, Ana," Jessie said with singsong politeness, sending Ana a conspirator's grin. "Can I come back?"

"I hope you will."

As she stepped through the bushes, Jessie offered her father a sunny smile. "I didn't mean to make you worry, Daddy. Honest."

He bent down and tweaked her nose. "Brat." Ana heard the wealth of love behind the exasperation.

With a giggle, Jessie ran across the yard, the puppy wriggling in her arms. Ana's smile faded the moment those cool blue eyes turned back to her.

"She's an absolutely delightful child," Ana began, amazed that she had to wipe damp palms on her shorts. "I do apologize for not making certain you knew where she was, but I hope you'll let her come back to visit me again."

"It wasn't your responsibility." His voice was cool, neither friendly nor unfriendly. Ana had the uncomfortable certainty that she was being weighed, from the top of her head to the bottom of her grass-stained sneakers. "Jessie is naturally curious and friendly. Sometimes too much of both. It doesn't occur to her that there are people in the world who might take advantage of that."

Equally cool now, Ana inclined her head. "Point taken, Mr. Sawyer. Though I can assure you I rarely gobble up young girls for breakfast."

He smiled, a slow curving of the lips that erased the harshness from his face and replaced it with a devastating appeal. "You certainly don't fit my perception of an ogre, Miss Donovan. Now I'll have to apologize for being so abrupt. She gave me a scare. I hadn't even unpacked yet, and I'd lost her."

"Misplaced." Ana tried another cautious smile. She looked beyond him to the two-story redwood house next door, with its wide band of windows and its curvy deck. Though she was content in her privacy, she was glad it hadn't remained empty long. "It's nice to have a child nearby, especially one as entertaining as Jessie. I hope you'll let her come back."

"I often wonder if I *let* her do anything." He flicked a finger over a tiny pink rose. "Unless you replace these with a ten-foot wall, she'll be back." And at least he'd know where to look if she disappeared again. "Don't be afraid to send her home when she overstays her welcome." He tucked his hands in his pockets. "I'd better go make sure she doesn't feed Daisy our dinner."

"Mr. Sawyer?" Ana said as he turned away. "Enjoy Monterey."

"Thanks." His long strides carried him over the lawn, onto the deck and into the house.

Ana stood where she was for another moment. She couldn't remember the last time the air here had sizzled with so much energy. Letting out a long breath, she bent to pick up her gardening tools, while Quigley wound himself around her legs.

She certainly couldn't remember the last time her palms had gone damp just because a man had looked at her.

Then again, she couldn't recall ever being looked at in quite that way before. Looked at, looked into, looked through, all at once. A very neat trick, she mused as she carried the tools into her greenhouse.

An intriguing pair, father and daughter. Gazing through the sparkling glass wall of the greenhouse, she studied the house centered in the next yard. As their closest neighbor, she thought, it was only natural that she should wonder about them. Ana was also wise enough—and had learned through painful experience—to be careful not to let her wondering lead to any involvement beyond a natural friendliness.

There were precious few who could accept what was not of the common world. The price of her gift was a vulnerable heart that had already suffered miserably at the cold hand of rejection.

But she didn't dwell on that. In fact, as she thought of the man, and of the child, she smiled. What would he have done, she wondered with a little laugh, if she had told him that, while she wasn't an ogre—no, indeed—she was most definitely a witch.

In the sunny and painfully disorganized kitchen, Boone Sawyer dug through a packing box until he unearthed a skillet. He knew the move to California had been a good one—he'd convinced himself of that—but he'd certainly underestimated the time, the trouble and the general inconvenience of packing up a home and plopping it down somewhere else.

What to take, what to leave behind. Hiring movers, having his car shipped, transporting the puppy that Jessie had fallen in love with. Justifying his decision to her worried grandparents, school registration—school shopping. Lord, was he going to have to repeat that nightmare every fall for the next eleven years?

At least the worst was behind him. He hoped. All he had to do now was unpack, find a place for everything and make a home out of a strange house.

Jessie was happy. That was, and always had been, the most important thing. Then again, he mused as he browned some beef for chili, Jessie was happy anywhere. Her sunny disposition and her remarkable capacity to make friends were both a blessing and a bafflement. It was astonishing to Boone that a child who had lost her mother at the tender age of two could be unaffected, so resilient, so completely normal.

And he knew that if not for Jessie he would surely have gone quietly mad after Alice's death.

He didn't often think of Alice now, and that fact sometimes brought him a rush of guilt. He had loved her—God, he had loved her—and the child they'd made together was a living, breathing testament to that love. But he'd been without her now longer than he'd been with her. Though he had tried to hang on to the grief, as a kind of proof of that love, it had faded under the demands and pressures of day-to-day living.

Alice was gone, Jessie was not. It was because of both of them that he'd made the difficult decision to move to Monterey. In Indiana, in the home he and Alice had bought while she was carrying Jessie, there had been too many ties to the past. Both his parents and Alice's had been a ten-minute drive away. As the only grandchild on both sides, Jessie had been the center of attention, and the object of subtle competition.

For himself, Boone had wearied of the constant advice, the gentle—and not so gentle—criticism of his parenting. And, of course, the matchmaking. The child needs a mother. A man needs a wife. His mother had decided to make it her life's work to find the perfect woman to fit both bills.

Because that had begun to infuriate him, and because he'd realized how easy it would be to stay in the house and wallow in the memories it held, he'd chosen to move.

He could work anywhere. Monterey had been the final choice because of the climate, the life-style, the schools. And, he could admit privately, because some internal voice had told him this was the place. For both of them.

He liked being able to look out of the window and see the water, or those fascinatingly sculptured cypress trees. He certainly liked the fact that he wasn't crowded in by neighbors. It was Alice who had enjoyed being surrounded by people. He also appreciated the fact that the distance from the road was enough to muffle the sound of traffic.

It just felt right. Jessie was already making her mark. True, it had given him a moment of gut-clutching fear when he'd looked outside and hadn't seen her anywhere. But he should have known she would find someone to talk to, someone to charm.

And the woman.

Frowning, Boone settled the top on the skillet to let the chili simmer. That had been odd, he thought as he poured a cup of coffee to take out on the deck. He'd looked down at her and known instantly that Jessie was safe. There had been nothing but kindness in those smoky eyes. It was his reaction, his very personal, very basic reaction, that had tightened his muscles and roughened his voice.

Desire. Very swift, very painful, and totally inappropriate. He hadn't felt that kind of response to a woman since... He grinned to himself. Since never. With Alice it had been a quiet kind of rightness, a sweet and inevitable coming together that he would always treasure.

This had been like being dragged by an undertow when you were fighting to get to shore.

Well, it had been a long time, he reminded himself as he watched a gull glide toward the water. A healthy reaction to a beautiful woman was easily justified and explained. And beautiful she'd been, in a calm, classic manner that was the direct opposite of his violent response to her. He couldn't help but resent it. He didn't have the time or inclination for any kind of reaction to any kind of woman.

There was Jessie to think of.

Reaching in his pocket, he took out a cigarette, lit it, hardly aware he was staring across the lawn at the hedge of delicate roses.

Anastasia, he thought. The name certainly suited her. It was old-fashioned, elegant, unusual.

"Daddy!"

Boone jolted, as guilty as a teenager caught smoking in the boys' room by the high school principal. He cleared his throat and gave his pouting daughter a sheepish grin.

"Give your old man a break, Jess. I'm down to half a pack a day."

She folded her arms. "They're bad for you. They make your lungs dirty."

"I know." He tamped the cigarette out, unable to take even a last drag when those wise little eyes were judging him. "I'm giving them up. Really."

She smiled—it was a disconcertingly adult sure-you-are smile—and he jammed his hands in his pockets. "Give me a break, Warden," he said in a passable James Cagney imitation. "You ain't putting me in solitary for snitching one drag."

Giggling, already forgiving him for the lapse, she came over to hug him. "You're silly."

"Yeah." He cupped his hands under her elbows and lifted her up for a hearty kiss. "And you're short."

"One day I'm going to be big as you." She wrapped her legs around his waist and leaned back until she was upside down. It was one of her favorite pastimes.

"Fat chance." He held her steady as her hair brushed the deck. "I'm always going to be bigger." He pulled her up again, lifting her high and making her squeal with laughter. "And smarter, and stronger." He rubbed the stubble of his beard against her while she wriggled and shrieked. "And better-looking."

"And ticklish!" she shouted in triumph, digging her fingers into his ribs.

She had him there. He collapsed on the bench with her. "Okay, okay! Uncle!" He caught his breath, and caught her close. "You'll always be trickier."

Pink-cheeked, bright-eyed, she bounced on his lap. "I like our new house."

"Yeah?" He smoothed her hair, as always enjoying the texture of it under his palm. "Me too."

"After dinner, can we go down to the beach and look for seals?"

"Sure."

"Daisy, too?"

"Daisy, too." Already experienced with puddles on the rug and chewed-up socks, he glanced around. "Where is she?"

"She's taking a nap." Jessie rested her head against her father's chest. "She was very tired."

"I bet. It's been a big day." Smiling, he kissed the top of Jessie's head, felt her yawn and settle.

"My favorite day. I got to meet Ana." Because her eyes were heavy, she closed them, lulled by the beating of her father's heart. "She's nice. She's going to show me how to plant flowers."

"Hmm."

"She knows all their names." Jessie yawned again, and when she spoke again her voice was thick with sleep. "Daisy licked her face and she didn't even mind. She just laughed. It sounded pretty when she did. Like a fairy," Jessie murmured as she drifted off.

Boone smiled again. His daughter's imagination. His gift to her, he liked to think. He held her gently while she slept.

Restless, Ana thought as she strolled along the rocky beach at twilight. She simply wasn't able to stay inside, working with her plants and herbs, when she was dogged by this feeling of restlessness.

The breeze would blow it out of her, she decided, lifting her face to the moist wind. A nice long walk and she'd find that contentment again, that peace that was as much a part of her as breathing.

Under different circumstances she would have called one of her cousins and suggested a night out. But she imagined Morgana was cozily settled in with Nash for the evening. And at this stage of her pregnancy, she needed rest. Sebastian wasn't back from his honeymoon yet.

Still, it had never bothered her to be alone. She enjoyed the solitude of the long, curved beach, the sound of water against rock, the laughing of the gulls.

Just as she had enjoyed the sound of the child's laughter, and the man's, drifting to her that afternoon. It had been a good sound, one she didn't have to be a part of to appreciate.

Now, as the sun melted, spilling color over the western sky, she felt the restlessness fading. How could she be anything but content to be here, alone, watching the magic of a day at rest?

She climbed up to stand on a driftwood log, close enough to the water that the spray cooled her face and dampened her shirt. Absently she took a stone out of her pocket, rubbing it between her fingers as she watched the sun drop into the flaming sea.

The stone warmed in her hand. Ana looked down at the small, waterlike gem, its pearly sheen glinting dully in the lowering light. Moonstone, she thought, amused at herself. Moon magic. A protection for the night traveler, an aid to self-analysis. And, of course, a talisman, often used to promote love.

Which was she looking for tonight?

Even as she laughed at herself and slipped the stone back into her pocket, she heard her name called.

There was Jessie, racing down the beach with the fat puppy nipping at her heels. And her father, walking several yards behind, as if reluctant to close the distance. Ana took a moment to wonder if the child's natural exuberance made the man appear all the more aloof.

She stepped down from the log and, because it was natural, even automatic, caught Jessie up in a swing and a hug. "Hello again, sunshine. Are you and Daisy out hunting for faerie shells?"

Jessie's eyes widened. "Faerie shells? What do they look like?"

"Just as you'd suppose. Sunset or sunrise—that's the only time to find them."

"My daddy says faeries live in the forest, and usually hide because people don't always know how to treat them."

"Quite right." She laughed and set the girl on her feet. "But they like the water, too, and the hills."

"I'd like to meet one, but Daddy says they hardly ever talk to people like they used to 'cause nobody really believes in them but kids."

"That's because children are very close to magic." She looked up as she spoke. Boone had reached them, and the sun setting at his back cast shadows over his face that were both dangerous and appealing. "We were discussing faeries," she told him.

"I heard." He laid a hand on Jessie's shoulder. Though the gesture was subtle, the meaning was crystal-clear. *Mine.*

"Ana says there are faerie shells on the beach, and you can only find them at sunrise or sunset. Can you write a story about them?"

"Who knows?" His smile was soft and loving for his daughter. When his gaze snapped back to hers, Ana felt a shudder down her spine. "We've interrupted your walk."

"No." Exasperated, Ana shrugged. She understood that he meant she had interrupted theirs. "I was just taking a moment to watch the water before I went in. It's getting chilly."

"We had chili for dinner," Jessie said, grinning at her own joke. "And it was *hot!* Will you help me look for faerie shells?"

"Sometime, maybe." When her father wasn't around to stare holes through her. "But it's getting too dark now, and I have to go in." She flicked a finger down Jessie's nose. "Good night." She gave a cool nod to her father.

Boone watched Ana walk away. She might not have gotten chilled so quickly, he thought, if she'd worn something to cover her legs. Her smooth, shapely legs. He let out a long, impatient breath.

"Come on, Jess. Race you back."

Chapter 2

"I'd like to meet him."

Ana glanced up from the dried petals she was arranging for potpourri and frowned at Morgana. "Who?"

"The father of this little girl you're so enchanted with." More fatigued than she cared to admit, Morgana stroked her hand in a circular motion over her very round belly. "You're just chock-full of information on the girl, and very suspiciously lacking when it comes to Papa."

"Because he doesn't interest me as much," Ana said lightly. To a bowl filled with fragrant leaves and petals she added lemon for zest and balsam for health. She knew very well how weary Morgana was. "He's every bit as standoffish as Jessie is friendly. If it wasn't obvious that he's devoted to her, I'd probably dislike him instead of being merely ambivalent."

"Is he attractive?"

Ana lifted a brow. "As compared to?"

"A toad." Morgana laughed and leaned forward. "Come on, Ana. Give."

"Well, he isn't ugly." Setting the bowl aside, she began to look through the cupboard for the right oil to mix through the potpourri. "I guess you'd say he has that hollow-cheeked, dangerous look. Athletic build. Not like a weight lifter." She frowned, trying to decide between two oils. "More like a...a long-distance runner, I suppose. Rangy, and intimidatingly fit."

Grinning, Morgana cupped her chin in her hands. "More."

"This from a married woman about to give birth to twins?"

"You bet."

Ana laughed, chose an oil of rose to add elegance. "Well, if I have to say something nice, he does have wonderful eyes. Very clear, very blue. When they look at Jessie, they're gorgeous. When they look at me, suspicious."

"What in the world for?"

"I haven't a clue."

Morgana shook her head and rolled her eyes. "Anastasia, surely you've wondered enough to find out. All you'd have to do is peek."

With a deft and expert hand, Ana added drops of fragrant oil to the mixture in the bowl. "You know I don't like to intrude."

"Oh, really."

"And if I was curious," she added, fighting a smile at Morgana's frustration, "I don't believe I'd care to see what was rolling around inside Mr. Sawyer's heart. I have a feeling it would be very uncomfortable to be linked with him, even for a few minutes."

"You're the empath," Morgana said with a shrug. "If Sebastian was back, he'd find out what's in this guy's mind anyway." She sipped more of the soothing elixir Ana had mixed for her. "I could do it for you if you like. I haven't had cause to use the scrying mirror or crystal for weeks. I may be getting stale."

"No." Ana leaned forward and kissed her cousin's cheek. "Thank you. Now, I want you to keep a bag of this with you," she said as she spooned the potpourri into a net bag. "And put the rest in bowls around the house and the shop. You're only working two days a week now, right?"

"Two or three." She smiled at Ana's concern, even as she waved it off. "I'm not overdoing, darling, I promise. Nash won't let me."

With an absent nod, Ana tied the bag securely. "Are you drinking the tea I made up for you?"

"Every day. And, yes, I'm using the oils religiously. I'm carrying rhyolite to alleviate emotional stress, topaz against external stresses, zircon for a positive attitude and amber to lift my spirits.'' She gave Ana's hand a quick squeeze. "I've got all the bases covered.''

"I'm entitled to fuss.'' She set the bag of potpourri down by Morgana's purse, then changed her mind and opened the purse herself to slip it inside. "It's our first baby.''

"Babies,'' Morgana corrected.

"All the more reason to fuss. Twins come early.''

Indulging in a single sigh, Morgana closed her eyes. "I certainly hope these do. It's getting to the point where I can hardly get up and down without a crane.''

"More rest,'' Ana prescribed, "and very gentle exercise. Which does not include hauling around shipping boxes or being on your feet all day waiting on customers.''

"Yes, ma'am.''

"Now let's have a look.'' Gently she laid her hands on her cousin's belly, spreading her fingers slowly, opening herself to the miracle of what lay within.

Instantly Morgana felt her fatigue drain away and a physical and emotional well-being take its place. Through her half-closed eyes she saw Ana's darken to the color of pewter and fix on a vision only Ana could see.

As she moved her hands over her cousin's heavy belly and linked with her, Ana felt the weight within her and, for one incredibly vivid moment, the lives that pulsed inside the womb. The draining fatigue, yes, and the nagging discomfort, but she also felt the quiet satisfaction, the burgeoning excitement, and the simple wonder of carrying those lives. Her body ached, her heart swelled. Her lips curved.

Then she *was* those lives—first one, then the other. Swimming dreamlessly in that warm, dark womb, nourished by the mother, held safe and fast until the moment when the outside would be faced. Two healthy hearts beating steady and close, beneath a mother's heart. Tiny fingers flexing, a lazy kick. The rippling of life.

Ana came back to herself, came back alone. "You're well. All of you.''

"I know.'' Morgana twined her fingers with Ana's. "But I feel better when you tell me. Just as I feel safe knowing you'll be there when it's time.''

"You know I wouldn't be anywhere else." She brought their joined hands to her cheek. "But is Nash content with me as midwife?"

"He trusts you—as much as I do."

Ana's gaze softened. "You're lucky, Morgana, to have found a man who accepts, understands, even appreciates, what you are."

"I know. To have found love was precious enough. But to have found love with him." Then her smile faded. "Ana, darling, Robert was a long time ago."

"I don't think of him. At least not really of him, but of a wrong turn on a particularly slippery road."

Indignation sharpened Morgana's eyes. "He was a fool, and not in the least worthy of you."

Rather than sadness Ana felt a chuckle bubble out of her. "You never liked him. Not from the first."

"No, I didn't." Frowning, Morgana gestured with her glass. "And neither did Sebastian, if you recall."

"I do. As I recall Sebastian was quite suspicious of Nash, too."

"That was entirely different. It *was,*" she insisted as Ana grinned. "With Nash, he was just being protective of me. As for Robert, Sebastian tolerated him with the most insulting sort of politeness."

"I remember." Ana shrugged. "Which, of course, put my back up. Well, I was young," she said with a careless gesture. "And naive enough to believe that if I was in love I must be loved back equally. Foolish enough to be honest. And foolish enough to be devastated when that honesty was rewarded with disbelief, then outright rejection."

"I know you were hurt, but there's little doubt you could do better."

"None at all," Ana agreed, for she wasn't without pride. "But there are some of us that aren't meant to mix with outsiders."

Now there was frustration, as well as indignation. "There have been plenty of men, with elfin blood and without, who've been interested in you, cousin."

"A pity I haven't been interested in them." Ana laughed.

"I'm miserably choosy, Morgana. And I like my life just as it is."

"If I didn't know that to be true, I'd be tempted to work up a nice little love spell. Nothing binding, mind," she said with a glint in her eye. "Just something to give you some entertainment."

"I can find my own entertainment, thanks."

"I know that, too. Just as I know you'd be furious if I dared to interfere." She pushed away from the table and rose, regretting for a moment her loss of grace. "Let's take a walk outside before I head home."

"If you promise to put your feet up for an hour when you get there."

"Done."

The sun was warm, the breeze balmy. Both of which, Ana thought, would do her cousin as much good as the long nap she imagined Nash would insist his wife take when she returned home.

They admired the late-blooming larkspur, the starry asters and the big, bold zinnias. Both had a deep love of nature that had come through the blood and through upbringing.

"Do you have any plans for All Hallows' Eve?" Morgana asked.

"Nothing specific."

"We were hoping you'd come by, at least for part of the evening. Nash is going all out for the trick-or-treaters."

With an appreciative laugh, Ana clipped some mums to take inside. "When a man writes horror films for a living, he's duty bound to pull out the stops for Halloween. I wouldn't miss it."

"Good. Perhaps Sebastian will join you and me for a quiet celebration afterward." Morgana was bending awkwardly over the thyme and verbena when she spotted the child and dog skipping through the hedge of roses.

She straightened. "We have company."

"Jessie." Pleased but wary, Ana glanced over to the house beyond. "Does your father know where you are?"

"He said I could come over if I saw you outside and you weren't busy. You aren't busy, are you?"

"No." Unable to resist, Ana bent down to kiss Jessie's cheek.

"This is my cousin, Morgana. I've told her you're my brand-new neighbor."

"You have a dog and a cat. Ana told me." Jessie's interest was immediately piqued. Then her gaze focused, fascinated, on the bulge of Morgana's belly. "Do you have a baby in there?"

"I certainly do. In fact, I have two babies in there."

"Two?" Jessie's eyes popped wide. "How do you know?"

"Because Ana told me." With a laugh, she laid a hand on her heavy stomach. "And because they kick and squirm too much to be only one."

"My friend Missy's mommy, Mrs. Lopez, had one baby in her tummy, and she got so fat she could hardly walk." Out of brilliant blue eyes, Jessie shot Morgana a hopeful glance. "She let me feel it kick."

Charmed, Morgana took Jessie's hand and brought it to her while Ana discouraged Daisy from digging in the impatiens. "Feel that?"

Giggling at the movement beneath her hand, Jessie nodded. "Uh-huh! It went pow! Does it hurt?"

"No."

"Do you think they'll come out soon?"

"I'm hoping."

"Daddy says babies know when to come out because an angel whispers in their ear."

Sawyer might be aloof, Morgana thought, but he was also very clever, and very sweet. "That sounds exactly right to me."

"And that's their special angel, forever and ever," she went on, pressing her cheek to Morgana's belly in the hope that she could hear something from inside. "If you turn around really quick, you maybe could get just a tiny glimpse of your angel. I try sometimes, but I'm not fast enough." She peered up at Morgana. "Angels are shy, you know."

"So I've heard."

"I'm not." She pressed a kiss to Morgana's belly before she danced away. "There's not a shy bone in my body. That's what Grandma Sawyer always says."

"An observant woman, Grandma Sawyer," Ana commented while wrestling Daisy into her arms to prevent her from disturbing Quigley's afternoon nap.

Both women enjoyed the energetic company as they walked among the flowers—or rather as they walked and Jessie skipped, hopped, ran and tumbled.

Jessie reached for Ana's hand as they started toward the front of the house and Morgana's car. "I don't have any cousins. Is it nice?"

"Yes, it's very nice. Morgana and Sebastian and I practically grew up together, kind of like brothers and sisters do."

"I know how to get brothers and sisters, 'cause my daddy told me. How do you get cousins?"

"Well, if your mother or father have brothers or sisters, and they have children, those children are your cousins."

Jessie digested this information with a frown of concentration. "Which are you?"

"It's complicated," Morgana said with a laugh, opting to rest against her car for a moment before getting in. "Ana's and Sebastian's and my father are all brothers. And our mothers are sisters. So we're kind of double cousins."

"That's neat. If I can't have cousins, maybe I can have a brother or sister. But my daddy says I'm a handful all by myself."

"I'm sure he's right," Morgana agreed as Ana chuckled. Brushing her hair back, Morgana glanced up. There, framed in one of the wide windows on the second floor of the house next door, was a man. Undoubtedly Jessie's father.

Ana had described him well enough, Morgana mused. Though he was more attractive, and certainly sexier, than her cousin had let on. That very simple omission made her smile. Morgana lifted a hand in a friendly wave. After a moment's hesitation, Boone returned the salute.

"That's my daddy." Jessie pinwheeled her arms in greeting. "He works up there, but we haven't unpacked all the boxes yet."

"What does he do?" Morgana asked, since it was clear Ana wasn't going to.

"Oh, he tells stories. Really good stories, about witches and fairy princesses and dragons and magic fountains. I get to help sometimes. I have to go because tomorrow's my first day of school and he said I wasn't supposed to stay too long. Did I?"

"No." Ana bent down to kiss her cheek. "You can come back anytime."

"Bye!" And she was off, gamboling across the lawn, with the dog racing behind her.

"I've never been more charmed, or more worn out," Morgana said as she climbed into her car. "The girl's a delightful whirlwind." Smiling out at Ana, she jiggled her keys. "And the father is certainly no slouch."

"I imagine it's difficult, a man raising a little girl alone."

"From the one glimpse I had, he looked up to it." She gunned the engine. "Interesting that he writes stories. About witches and dragons and such. Sawyer, you said?"

"Yes." Ana blew tousled hair out of her eyes. "I guess he must be Boone Sawyer."

"It might intrigue him to know you're Bryna Donovan's niece—seeing as they're in the same line of work. That is, if you wanted to intrigue him."

"I don't," Ana said firmly.

"Ah, well, perhaps you already have." Morgana put the car in reverse. "Blessed be, cousin."

Ana struggled with a frown as Morgana backed out of the drive.

After driving to Sebastian's to give his horses their morning feeding and grooming, Ana spent most of the next morning delivering her potpourris, her scented oils, her medicinal herbs and potions. Others were boxed and packaged for shipping. Though she had several local customers for her wares, including Morgana's shop, Wicca, a great portion of her clientele was outside the area.

Anastasia's was successful enough to suit her. The business she'd started six years before satisfied her needs and ambitions and allowed her the luxury of working at home. It wasn't for money. The Donovan fortune, and the Donovan legacy, kept both her and her family comfortably off. But, like Morgana with her shop and Sebastian with his many businesses, Ana needed to be productive.

She was a healer. But it was impossible to heal everyone. Long ago she had learned it was destructive to attempt to take on the ills and pains of the world. Part of the price of her power was knowing there was pain she could not alleviate. She did not reject her gift. She used it as she thought best.

Herbalism had always fascinated her, and she accepted the fact that she had the touch. Centuries before, she might have been the village wise woman—and that never failed to amuse her. In today's world, she was a businesswoman who could mix a bath oil or an elixir with equal skill.

If she added a touch of magic, it was hers to add.

And she was happy, happy with the destiny that had been thrust on her and with the life she had made from it.

Even if she'd been miserable, she thought, this day would have lifted her spirits. The beckoning sun, the caressing breeze, the faintest taste of rain in the air, rain that would not fall for hours—and then would fall gently.

Wanting to take advantage of the day, she decided to work outside, starting some herbs from seed.

He was watching her again. Bad habit, Boone thought with a grimace as he glanced down at the cigarette between his fingers. He wasn't having much luck with breaking bad habits. Nor was he getting a hell of a lot of work done since he'd looked out of the window and had seen her outside.

She always looked so…elegant, he decided. A kind of inner elegance that wasn't the least diminished by the grass-stained cutoffs and short-sleeved T-shirt she wore.

It was in the way she moved, as if the air were wine that she drank lightly from as she passed through it.

Getting lyrical, he mused, and reminded himself to save it for his books.

Maybe it was because she was the fairy-princess type he so often wrote about. There was that ethereal, otherworldly air about her. And the quiet strength in her eyes. Boone had never believed that fairy princesses were pushovers.

But there was still this delicacy about her body—a body he sincerely wished he hadn't begun to dwell upon. Not a frailty, but a serene kind of femininity that he imagined would baffle and allure any male who was still breathing.

Boone Sawyer was definitely breathing.

Now what was she doing? he wondered, crushing out his cigarette impatiently and moving closer to the window. She'd gone into the garden shed and had come out again with her arms piled high with pots.

Wasn't it just like a woman to try to carry more than she should?

Even as he was thinking it, and indulging in a spot of male superiority, he saw Daisy streak across her lawn, chasing the sleek gray cat.

He had a hand on the window, prepared to shoot it up and call off the dog. Before he could make the move, he saw it was already too late.

In slow motion, it might have been an interesting and well-choreographed dance. The cat streaked like gray smoke between Ana's legs. She swayed. The clay pots in her arms teetered. Boone swore, then let out a sigh of relief when she righted them, and herself, again. Before the breath was out, Daisy plowed through, destroying the temporary balance. This time Ana's feet were knocked completely out from under her. She went down, and the pots went up.

Though he was already swearing, Boone heard the crash as he leapt through the terrace doors and down the steps to the lower deck.

She was muttering what sounded to him like exotic curses when he reached her. And he could hardly blame her. Her cat was up a tree, spitting down on the yipping dog. The pots she'd been carrying were little more than shards scattered over the grass and the edge of the patio where the impact had taken place.

Boone winced, cleared his throat. "Ah, are you all right?"

She was on her hands and knees, and her hair was over her eyes. But she tossed it back and shot him a long look through the blond wisps. "Dandy."

"I was at the window." This certainly wasn't the time to admit he'd been watching her. "Passing by the window," he corrected. "I saw the chase and collision." Crouching down, he began to help her pick up the pieces. "I'm really sorry about Daisy. We've only had her a few days, and we haven't had any luck with training."

"She's a baby yet. No point in blaming a dog for doing what comes naturally."

"I'll replace the pots," he said, feeling miserably awkward.

"I have more." Because the barking and spitting were getting desperate, Ana sat back on her heels. "Daisy!" The command was quiet but firm, and it was answered instantly. Tail wagging furiously, the pup scrambled over to lick at her face and arms. Refusing to be charmed, Ana cupped the dog's face in her hands. "Sit," she ordered, and the puppy plopped her rump down obligingly. "Now behave yourself." With a little whine of repentance, Daisy settled down with her head on her paws.

Almost as impressed as he was baffled, Boone shook his head. "How'd you do that?"

"Magic," she said shortly, then relented with a faint smile. "You could say I've always had a way with animals. She's just happy and excited and roaring to play. You have to make her understand that some activities are inappropriate." Ana patted Daisy's head and earned an adoring canine glance.

"I've been trying bribery."

"That's good, too." She stretched out under a trellis of scarlet clematis, looking for more broken crockery. It was then that Boone noticed the long scratch on her arm.

"You're bleeding."

She glanced down. There were nicks on her thighs, too. "Hard to avoid, with pots raining down on me."

He was on his feet in a blink and hauling Ana to hers. "Damn it, I asked you if you were all right."

"Well, really, I—"

"We'll have to clean it up." He saw there was more blood trickling down her legs, and he reacted exactly as he would if it were Jessie. He panicked. "Oh, Lord." He scooped an amazed Ana into his arms and hurried toward the closest door.

"Honestly, there's absolutely no need—"

"It's going to be fine, baby. We'll take care of it."

Half amused, half annoyed, Ana huffed out a breath as he pushed his way into the kitchen. "In that case, I'll cancel the ambulance. If you'd just put me—" He dropped her into one of the padded ice-cream chairs at her kitchen table. "Down."

Nerves jittering, Boone raced to the sink for a cloth. Efficiency, speed and cheer were the watchwords in such cases, he knew. As he dampened the cloth and squirted it with soap, he took several long breaths to calm himself.

"It won't look so bad when we get it cleaned up. You'll see." After pasting a smile on his face, he walked back to kneel in front of her. "I'm not going to hurt you." Gently he began to dab at the thin line of blood that had dripped down her calf. "We're going to fix it right up. Just close your eyes and relax." He took another long breath. "I knew this man once," he began, improvising a story as he always did for his daughter. "He lived in a place called Briarwood, where there was an enchanted castle behind a high stone wall."

Ana, who had been on the point of firmly telling him she could tend to herself, stopped and did indeed relax.

"Growing over the wall were thick vines with big, razor-sharp thorns. No one had been to the castle in more than a hundred years, because no one was brave enough to climb that wall and risk being scraped and pricked. But the man, who was very poor and lived alone, was curious, and day after day he would walk from his house to the wall and stand on the tips of his toes to see the sun gleam on the topmost towers and turrets of the castle."

Boone turned the cloth over and dabbed at the cuts. "He couldn't explain to anyone what he felt inside his heart whenever he stood there. He wanted desperately to climb over. Sometimes at night in his bed he would imagine it. Fear of those thick, sharp thorns stopped him, until one day in high summer, when the scent of flowers was so strong you couldn't take a breath without drinking it in, that glimpse of the topmost towers wasn't enough. Something in his heart told him that what he wanted most in the world lay just beyond that thorn-covered wall. So he began to climb it. Again and again he fell to the ground, with his hands and arms pricked and bleeding. And again and again he pushed himself up."

His voice was soothing, and his touch—his touch was anything but. As gentle as he was with the cool cloth, an ache began to spread, slow and warm, from the center of her body outward. He was stroking her thighs now, where the sharp edge of a shard had nicked the flesh. Ana closed her hand into a fist, the twin of which clenched in her stomach.

She needed him to stop. She wanted him to go on. And on.

"It took all of that day," Boone continued in that rich, mesmerizing storyteller's voice. "And the heat mixed sweat with the blood, but he didn't give up. Couldn't give up, because he knew, as he'd never known anything before, that his heart's desire, his future and his destiny, lay on the other side. So, with his hands raw and bleeding, he used those thorny vines and dragged himself to the top. Exhausted, filled with pain, he stumbled and fell down and down, to the thick, soft grass that flowed from the wall to the enchanted castle.

"The moon was up when he awoke, dazed and disoriented. With the last of his strength, he limped across the lawn, over the drawbridge and into the great hall of the castle that had haunted his dreams since childhood. When he crossed the threshold, the lights of a thousand torches flared. In that same instant, all his cuts and scrapes and bruises vanished. In that circle of flame that cast shadow and light up the white marble walls stood the most beautiful woman he had ever seen. Her hair was like sunlight, and her eyes like smoke. Even before she spoke, even before her lovely mouth curved in a welcoming smile, he knew that it was she he had risked his life to find. She stepped forward, offered her hand to him, and said only, 'I have been waiting for you.'"

As he spoke the last words, Boone lifted his gaze to Ana's. He was as dazed and disoriented as the man in the story he had conjured up. When had his heart begun to pound like this? he wondered. How could he think when the blood was swimming in his head and throbbing in his loins? While he struggled for balance, he stared at her.

Hair like sunlight. Eyes like smoke.

And he realized he was kneeling between her legs, one hand resting intimately high on her thigh, and the other on the verge of reaching out to touch that sunlight hair.

Boone rose so quickly that he nearly overbalanced the table. "I beg your pardon," he said, for lack of anything better. When she only continued to stare at him, the pulse in her throat beating visibly, he tried again. "I got carried away when I saw you were bleeding. I've never been able to take Jessie's cuts and scrapes in stride.'' Struggling not to babble, he thrust the cloth at her. "I imagine you'd rather handle it yourself."

She accepted the cloth. She needed a moment before she dared speak. How was it possible that a man could stir her so desperately with doctoring and a fairy tale, then leave her fighting to find a slippery hold on her composure when he apologized?

Her own fault, Ana thought as she scrubbed—with more force than was really necessary—at the scrape on her arm. It was her gift and her curse that she would feel too much.

"You look like you should be the one sitting down," she told him briskly, then rose to go to the cupboard for one of her own medications. "Would you like something cold to drink?"

"No... Yes, actually." Though he doubted that a gallon of ice water would dampen the fire in his gut. "Blood always makes me panic."

"Panicked or not, you were certainly efficient." She poured him a glass of lemonade from the fat pitcher she fetched from the refrigerator. "And it was a very nice story." She was smiling now, more at ease.

"A story usually serves to calm both Jessie and me during a session with iodine and bandages."

"Iodine stings." She expertly dabbed a tobacco-brown liquid from a small apothecary jar onto her cleaned cuts. "I can give you something that won't, if you like. For your next emergency."

"What is it?" Suspicious, he sniffed at the jar. "Smells like flowers." And so did she.

"For the most part it is. Herbs, flowers, a dash of this and that." She set the bottle aside, capped it. "It's what you might call a natural antiseptic. I'm an herbalist."

"Oh."

She laughed at the skeptical look on his face. "That's all right. The majority of people only trust healing aids they can buy at the drugstore. They forget that people healed themselves quite well through nature for hundreds of years."

"They also died of lockjaw from a nick from a rusty nail."

"True enough," she agreed. "If they didn't have access to a reputable healer." Since she had no intention of trying to convert him, Ana changed the subject. "Did Jessie get off for her first day of school?"

"Yeah, she was raring to go. I was the one with the nervous stomach." His smile came and went. "I want to thank you for being so tolerant of her. I know she has a tendency to latch on to people. It doesn't cross her mind that they might not want to entertain her."

"Oh, but she entertains me." In an automatic gesture of courtesy, she took out a plate and lined it with cookies. "She's very welcome here. She's very sweet, unaffected and bright, and she doesn't forget her manners. You're doing a marvelous job raising her."

He accepted a cookie, watching her warily. "Jessie makes it easy."

"As delightful as she is, it can't be easy raising a child on your own. I doubt it's a snap even with two parents when the child is as energetic as Jessie. And as bright." Ana selected a cookie for herself and missed the narrowing of his eyes. "She must get her imagination from you. It must be delightful for her to have a father who writes such lovely stories."

His eyes sharpened. "How do you know what I do?"

The suspicion surprised her, but she smiled again. "I'm a fan—actually, an avid fan—of Boone Sawyer's."

"I don't recall telling you my first name."

"No, I don't believe you did," Ana said agreeably. "Are you always so suspicious of a compliment, Mr. Sawyer?"

"I had my reasons for settling quietly here." He set the half-empty glass down on the counter with a little clink. "I don't care for the idea of my neighbor interrogating my daughter, or digging into my business."

"Interrogating?" She nearly choked on the word. "Interrogating Jessie? Why would I?"

"To get to know a little more about the rich widower in the next house."

For one throbbing moment, she could only gape. "How unbelievably arrogant! Believe me, I enjoy Jessie's company, and I don't find it necessary to bring you into the conversation."

What he considered her painfully transparent astonishment made him sneer. He'd handled her type before, but it was a disappointment, a damned disappointment, for Jessie. "Then it's odd that you'd know my name, that I'm a single parent, and my line of work, isn't it?"

She wasn't often angry. It simply wasn't her nature. But now she fought a short, vicious war with temper. "You know, I doubt very much you're worth an explanation, but I'm going to give you one, just to see how difficult it is for you to talk when you have to shove your other foot in your mouth." She turned. "Come with me."

"I don't want—"

"I said come with me." She strode out of the kitchen, fully certain he would follow.

Though annoyed and reluctant, he did. They moved through an archway and into a sun-drenched great room dotted with the charm of white wicker furniture and chintz. There were clusters of glinting crystals, charming statues of elves and sorcerers and faeries. Through another archway and into a cozy library with a small Adam fireplace and more mystical statuary.

There was a deep cushioned sofa in raspberry that would welcome an afternoon napper, daintily feminine lace curtains dancing in the breeze that teased through an arching window, and the good smell of books mixed with the airy fragrance of flowers.

Ana walked directly to a shelf, rising automatically to her toes to reach the desired volumes. *"The Milkmaid's Wish,"* she recited as she pulled out one book after another. *"The Frog, the Owl and the Fox. A Third Wish for Miranda."* She tossed a look over her shoulder, though tossing one of the books would have been more satisfactory. "It's a shame I have to tell you how much I enjoy your work."

Uncomfortable, he tucked his hands in his pockets. He was already certain he'd taken a wrong turn, and he was wondering if he could find a suitable way to backtrack. "It isn't often grown women read fairy tales for pleasure."

"What a pity. Though you hardly deserve the praise, I'll tell you that your work is lyrical and valuable, on both a child's and an adult's level." Far from mollified, she shoved two of the books back into place. "Then again, perhaps such things are in my blood. I was very often lulled to sleep by one of my aunt's stories. Bryna Donovan," she said, and had the pleasure of seeing his eyes widen. "I imagine you've heard of her."

Thoroughly chastised, Boone let out a long breath. "Your aunt." He flicked his gaze over the shelf and saw several of Bryna's stories of magic and enchanted lands alongside his. "We've actually corresponded a few times. I've admired her work for years."

"So have I. And when Jessie mentioned that her father wrote stories about fairy princesses and dragons, I concluded the Sawyer next door was Boone Sawyer. Grilling a six-year-old wasn't necessary."

"I'm sorry." No, actually, he was much more embarrassed than sorry, but that would have to do. "I had an...uncomfortable experience not long before we moved, and it's made me overly sensitive." He picked up a small, fluidly sculpted statue of an enchantress, turning it in his fingers as he spoke. "Jessie's kindergarten teacher...she pumped all sorts of information out of the kid. Which isn't too hard, really, since Jessie's pump's always primed."

He set the statue down again, all the more embarrassed that he felt this obligation to explain. "But she manipulated Jessie's feelings, her natural need for a mother figure, gave her all sorts of extra attention, requested several conferences to discuss Jessie's unusual potential, even going so far as to arrange a one-on-one with me over dinner where she... Suffice it to say she was more interested in an unattached male with a nice portfolio than she was in Jessie's feelings or her welfare. Jessie was very hurt by it."

Ana tapped a finger on the edge of one of his books before replacing it. "I imagine it was a difficult experience for both of you. But let me assure you, I'm not in the market for a husband. And, if I were, I wouldn't resort to manipulations and maneuvers. I'm afraid happy-ever-after has been too well indoctrinated in me for that."

"I'm sorry. After I get those feet out of my mouth, I'll try to come up with a better apology."

The way she lifted her brow told him he wasn't out of the woods yet. "I think the fact that we understand each other will do. Now I'm sure you want to get back to work, and so do I."

She walked past him into a tiled foyer and opened the front door. "Tell Jessie to be sure to drop by and let me know how she likes school."

Here's your hat, what's your hurry, Boone thought as he stepped out. "I will. Take care of those scratches," he added, but she was already closing the door in his face.

Chapter 3

Good going, Sawyer. Shaking his head, Boone sat down in front of his word processor. First his dog knocks her down in her own yard, then our blundering hero barges into her house uninvited to play with her legs. To cap it, he insults her integrity and insinuates that she's using his daughter to try to trap him.

All in one fun-filled afternoon, he thought in disgust. It was a wonder she hadn't pitched him bodily out of her house rather than simply slamming the door in his face.

And why had he acted so stupidly? Past experience, true. But that wasn't the root of it, and he knew it.

Hormones, he decided with a half laugh. The kind of raging hormones better suited to a teenager than a grown man.

He'd looked up at her face in that sun-washed kitchen, feeling her skin warm under his hand, smelling that serenely seductive scent she exuded, and he'd wanted. He'd craved. For one blinding moment, he'd imagined with perfect clarity what it would be like to drag her off that curvy little chair, to feel that quick jerk-shudder of reaction as he devoured that incredibly soft-looking mouth.

That instant edge of desire had been so sharp, he'd needed to believe there was some outside force, some ploy or plot or plan to jumble his system so thoroughly.

Safest course, he realized with a sigh. Blame her.

Of course, he might have been able to dismiss the whole thing if it hadn't been for the fact that at that moment he'd looked up into her eyes and seen the same dreamy hunger he was feeling. And he'd felt the power, the mystery, the titanic sexuality, of a woman on the point of yielding.

His imagination had a great deal of punch, he knew. But what he'd seen, what he'd felt, had been utterly real.

For a moment, for just a moment, the tensions and needs had had that room humming like a harp string. Then he'd pulled back—as he should. A man had no business seducing his neighbor in her kitchen.

Now he'd very likely destroyed any chance of getting to know her better—just when he'd realized he very much wanted to get to know Miss Anastasia Donovan.

Pulling out a cigarette, Boone ran his fingers over it while he thought through various methods of redemption. When the light dawned, it was so simple he laughed out loud. If he'd been looking for a way into the fair maiden's heart—which he wasn't, exactly—it couldn't have been more perfect.

Pleased with himself, he settled down to work until it was time to pick up Jessie at school.

Conceited jerk. Ana worked off her temper with mortar and pestle. It was very satisfying to grind something—even if it was only some innocent herbs—into a powder. Imagine. *Imagine* him having the idea that she was...on the make, she decided, sneering. As if she'd found him irresistible. As if she'd been pining away behind some glass wall waiting for her prince to come. So that she could snare him.

The gall of the man.

At least she'd had the satisfaction of thumbing her nose at him. And if closing a door in anyone's face was out of character for her, well, it had felt wonderful at the time.

So wonderful, in fact, that she wouldn't mind doing it again.

It was a damn shame he was so talented. And it couldn't be denied that he was a wonderful father. They were traits she couldn't help but admire. There was no denying he was attractive, magnetically sexual, with just a dash of shyness tossed in for sweetness, along with the wild tang of untamed male.

And those eyes, those incredible eyes that just about stopped your breath when they focused on you.

Ana scowled and tightened her grip on the pestle. Not that she was interested in any of that.

There might have been a moment in the kitchen, when he was stroking her flesh so gently and his voice blocked out all other sound, that she found herself drawn to him.

All right, aroused by him, she admitted. It wasn't a crime.

But he'd certainly shut that switch off quickly enough, and that was fine by her.

Beginning this instant, and from now on, she would think of him only as Jessica's father. She would be aloof if it killed her, friendly only to the point where it eased her relationship with the child.

She enjoyed having Jessie in her life, and she wasn't about to sacrifice that pleasure because of a basic and very well justified dislike of Jessie's father.

"Hi!"

There was that pixie face peeping through Ana's screen door. Even the dregs of temper were difficult to hold on to when she was faced with those big smiling eyes.

Ana set the mortar and pestle aside and smiled back. She supposed she had to be grateful that Boone hadn't let the altercation that afternoon influence him to keep Jessie away.

"Well, it looks like you survived your first day of school. Did school survive you?"

"Uh-huh. My teacher's name is Mrs. Farrell. She has gray hair and big feet, but she's nice, too. And I met Marcie and Tod and Lydia and Frankie, and lots of others. In the morning we—"

"Whoa." With a laugh, Ana held up both hands. "Maybe you should come in and sit down before you give me the day's events."

"I can't open the door, 'cause my hands are full."

"Oh." Ana obligingly pushed open the screen. "What have you got there?"

"Presents." On a huff of breath, Jessie dropped a package on the table. Then she held up a large crayon drawing. "We got to draw pictures today, and I made two. One for Daddy and one for you."

"For me?" Touched, Ana accepted the colorful drawing on the thick beige paper that brought back some of her own school memories. "It's beautiful, sunshine."

"See, this is you." Jessie pointed out a figure with yellow hair. "And Quigley." Here a childish, but undeniably clever, depiction of a cat. "And all the flowers. The roses and the daisies and the lark things."

"Larkspur," Ana murmured, misty-eyed.

"Uh-huh. And all the others," Jessie continued. "I couldn't remember all the names. But you said you'd teach me."

"Yes, I will. It's just lovely, Jessie."

"I drew Daddy one of our new house with him standing out on the deck, because he likes to stand there best. He put it on the refrigerator."

"An excellent idea." Ana walked over to center the picture on the refrigerator door, anchoring it with magnets.

"I like to draw. My daddy draws real good, and he said my mommy drew even better. So I come by it naturally." Jessie slipped her hand into Ana's. "Are you mad at me?"

"No, sweetheart. Why would I be?"

"Daddy said Daisy knocked you down and broke your pots, and you got hurt." She studied the scratch on Ana's arm, then kissed it solemnly. "I'm sorry."

"It's all right. Daisy didn't mean it."

"She didn't mean to chew up Daddy's shoes, either, and make him say swear words."

Ana bit her lip. "I'm sure she didn't."

"Daddy yelled, and Daisy got so nervous she peed right on the rug. Then he chased her around and around the house, and it looked so funny that I couldn't stop laughing. And Daddy laughed, too. He said he was going to build a doghouse outside and put Daisy and me in it."

Ana lost any hope of taking it all seriously, and she laughed as she scooped Jessie up. "I think you and Daisy would have a great time in the doghouse. But if you'd like to save your father's shoes, why don't you let me help you work with her?"

"Do you know how? Can you teach her tricks and everything?"

"Oh, I imagine. Watch." She shifted Jessie to her hip and

called Quigley out from his nap beneath the kitchen table. The cat rose reluctantly, stretched his front legs, then his back, then padded out. "Okay, sit." Heaving a feline sigh, he did. "Up." Resigned, Quigley rose on his haunches and pawed the air like a circus tiger. "Now, if you do your flip, I might just open a can of tuna fish later, for your dinner."

The cat seemed to be debating with himself. Then—perhaps because the trick was small potatoes compared to tuna—he leapt up, arching his back and flipping over to land lightly on his feet. While Jessie crowed with laughter and applauded, Quigley modestly cleaned his paws.

"I didn't know cats could do tricks."

"Quigley's a very special cat." Ana set Jessie down to give Quigley a stroking. He purred like a freight train, nuzzling his face against her knee. "His family's in Ireland, like most of mine."

"Does he get lonely?"

Smiling, Ana scratched under Quigley's jaw. "We have each other. Now, would you like a snack while you tell me about the rest of your day?"

Jessie hesitated, tempted. "I don't think I can, 'cause it's close to dinner, and Daddy— Oh, I almost forgot." She rushed back to the table to pick up a package wrapped in candy-striped paper. "This is for you, from Daddy."

"From..." Unconsciously Ana linked her hands behind her back. "What is it?"

"I know." Jessie grinned, her eyes snapping with excitement. "But I can't tell. Telling spoils the surprise. You have to open it." Jessie picked it up and thrust it at Ana. "Don't you like presents?" Jessie asked when Ana kept her hands clasped tight behind her back. "I like them best of anything, and Daddy always gives really good ones."

"I'm sure he does, but I—"

"Don't you like Daddy?" Jessie's lower lip poked out. "Are you mad at him because Daisy broke your pots?"

"No, no, I'm not mad at him." Not for the broken pots, anyway. "It wasn't his fault. And, yes, of course I like him— That is, I don't know him very well, and I..." Caught, Ana decided, and she worked up a smile. "I'm just surprised to get a present when it's not my birthday." To please the child, Ana took the gift and shook it. "Doesn't rattle," she said, and Jessie clapped and giggled.

"Guess! Guess what it is!"

"Ah...a trombone?"

"No, no, trombones are too big." Excitement had her bouncing. "Open it. Open it and see."

It was the child's reaction that had her own heart beating a shade too fast, Ana assured herself. To please Jessie, she ripped the paper with a flourish. "Oh."

It was a book, a child's oversize book with a snowy white cover. On the front was a beautiful illustration of a golden-haired woman wearing a sparkling crown and flowing blue robes.

"The Faerie Queen," Ana read. "By Boone Sawyer."

"It's brand-new," Jessie told her. "You can't even buy it yet, but Daddy gets his copies early." She ran a hand gently over the picture. "I told him she looks like you."

"It's a lovely gift," Ana said with a sigh. And a sneaky one. How was she supposed to stay irritated with him now?

"He wrote something inside for you." Too impatient to wait, Jessie opened the cover herself. "See, right there."

To Anastasia, with hopes that a magic tale works as well as a white flag. Boone.

Her lips curved. It was impossible to prevent it. How could anyone refuse a truce so charmingly requested?

Which was, of course, what Boone was counting on. As he shoved a packing box out of his way with his foot, he glanced through the window toward the house next door. Not a peep.

He imagined it might take a few days for Ana to calm down, but he thought he'd made a giant stride in the right direction. After all, he didn't want any antagonism between himself and Jessie's new friend.

Turning back to the stove, he lowered the heat on the boneless chicken breasts he had simmering, then deftly began to mash potatoes.

Jessie's number one favorite he thought, as he sent the beaters whirling. They could have mashed potatoes every night for a year and the kid wouldn't complain. Of course, it was up to him to vary the menu, to make sure she got a healthy meal every night.

Boone poured in more milk and grimaced. He had to admit, if there was one part of parenting he would cheerfully give up, it was the pressure of deciding what they were to eat night after night.

He didn't mind cooking it so much, it was that daily decision between pot roast, baked chicken, pork chops and all the others. Plus what to serve with it. Out of desperation, he'd begun to clip recipes—secretly—in hopes of adding some variety.

At one time he'd seriously considered hiring a housekeeper. Both his mother and his mother-in-law had urged him to, and then they'd gone into one of their competitive huddles on how to choose the proper woman to fit the bill. But the idea of having someone in the house, someone who might gradually take over the rearing of his daughter, had deterred him.

Jessie was his. One hundred percent his. Despite dinner decisions and grocery shopping, that was the way he liked it.

As he added a generous slice of butter to the creamy potatoes, he heard her footsteps racing across the deck.

"Good timing, frog face. I was just about to give you a whistle." He turned, licking potatoes from his finger and saw Ana standing in the doorway, one hand on Jessie's shoulder. The muscles in his stomach tightened so quickly that he nearly winced. "Well, hello."

"I didn't mean to interrupt your cooking," Ana began. "I just wanted to thank you for the book. It was very nice of you to send it over."

"I'm glad you like it." He realized he had a dishcloth tucked in his jeans and hastily tugged it out. "It was the best peace offering I could think of."

"It worked." She smiled, charmed by the sight of him hovering busily over a hot stove. "Thanks for thinking of me. Now, I'd better get out of your way so you can finish cooking your dinner."

"She can come in, can't she?" Jessie was already tugging on Ana's hand. "Can't she, Daddy?"

"Sure. Please." He shoved a box out of her way. "We

haven't finished unpacking yet. It's taking longer than I thought it would."

Out of politeness, and curiosity, Ana stepped inside. There were no curtains on the window as yet, and a few packing boxes littered the stone colored floor tiles. But ranged along the royal blue countertop there was a glossy ceramic cookie jar in the shape of Alice's white rabbit, a teapot of the mad hatter, and a dormouse sugar bowl. Potholders, obviously hooked by a child's hand, hung on little brass hooks. The refrigerator's art gallery was crowded with Jessie's drawings, and the puppy was snoozing in the corner.

Unpacked and tidy, no, she thought. But this was already a home.

"It's a great house," she commented. "I wasn't surprised when it sold quickly."

"You want to see my room?" Jessie tugged on Ana's hand again. "I have a bed with a roof on it, and lots of stuffed animals."

"You can take Ana up later," Boone put in. "Now you should go wash your hands."

"Okay." She looked imploringly at Ana. "Don't go."

"How about a glass of wine?" Boone offered when his daughter raced off. "A good way to seal a truce."

"All right." Drawings rustled as he opened the fridge. "Jessie's quite an artist. It was awfully sweet of her to draw a picture for me."

"Careful, or you'll have to start papering the walls with them." He hesitated, the bottle in his hand, wondering where he'd put the wineglasses, or if he'd unpacked them at all. A quick search through cupboards made it clear that he hadn't. "Can you handle chardonnay in a Bugs Bunny glass?"

She laughed. "Absolutely." She waited for him to pour hers, and his—Elmer Fudd. "Welcome to Monterey," she said, raising Bugs in a toast.

"Thanks." When she lifted the glass to her lips and smiled at him over the rim, he lost his train of thought. "I... Have you lived here long?"

"All my life, on and off." The scent of simmering chicken and the cheerful disarray of the kitchen were so homey that she relaxed. "My parents had a home here, and one in Ireland. They're based in Ireland for the most part now, but my cousins and I settled here. Morgana was born in the house she lives in, on Seventeen Mile Drive. Sebastian and I were born in Ireland, in Castle Donovan."

"Castle Donovan."

She laughed a little. "It sounds pretentious. But it actually is a castle, quite old, quite lovely, and quite remote. It's been in the Donovan family for centuries."

"Born in an Irish castle," he mused. "Maybe that explains why the first time I saw you I thought, well, there's the faerie queen, right next door in the rosebushes." His smiled faded, and he spoke without thinking. "You took my breath away."

The glass stopped halfway to her lips. Those lips parted in surprised confusion. "I..." She drank to give herself a moment to think. "I suppose part of your gift would be imagining faeries under bushes, elves in the garden, wizards in the treetops."

"I suppose." She smelled as lovely as the breeze that brought traces of her garden and hints of the sea through his windows. He stepped closer, surprised and not entirely displeased to see the alarm in her eyes. "How's that scratch? Neighbor." Gently he cupped his hand around her arm, skimmed his thumb up until he felt the pulse inside her elbow skitter. Whatever was affecting him was damn well doing the same to her. His lips curved. "Hurt?"

"No." Her voice thickened, baffling her, arousing him. "No, of course it doesn't."

"You still smell of flowers."

"The salve—"

"No." The knuckles of his free hand skimmed just under her chin. "You always smell of flowers. Wildflowers and sea foam."

How had she come to be backed against the counter, his body brushing hers, his mouth so close, so temptingly close, that she could all but taste it?

And she wanted that taste, wanted it with a sudden staggering force that wiped every other thought out of her head. Slowly, her eyes on his, she brought her hand to his chest, spread it over his heart where the beat was strong. Strong and wild.

And so would the kiss be, she thought. Strong and wild, from the first instant.

As if to assure her of that, he grabbed a fistful of her hair, tangling his fingers in it. It was warm, as he'd known it would be, warm as the sunlight it took its shade from. For a moment, his entire being was focused on the kiss to come, the reckless pleasure of it. His mouth was a breath from hers, and her sigh was already filling him, when he heard his daughter's feet clattering on the stairs.

Boone jolted back as if she'd burned him. Speechless, they stared at each other, both of them stunned by what had nearly happened and by the force behind it.

What was he doing? Boone asked himself. Grabbing a woman in his kitchen when there was chicken on the stove, potatoes going cold on the counter and his little girl about to skip into the room?

"I should go." Ana set down her glass before it could slip out of her trembling hand. "I really only meant to stay a minute."

"Ana." He shifted, blocking the way in case she sprinted for the door. "I have a feeling what just happened here was out of character for both of us. That's interesting, don't you think?"

She lifted those solemn gray eyes to his. "I don't know your character."

"Well, I don't make a habit of seducing women in the kitchen when my daughter's upstairs. And I certainly don't make a habit out of wanting the hell out of a woman the minute I lay eyes on her."

She wished she hadn't set the wine down. Her throat was bone dry. "I suppose you want me to say I'll take your word for it. But I won't."

Both anger and challenge sparkled in his eyes. "Then I'll have to prove it to you, won't I?"

"No, you—"

"My hands are clean, clean, clean." Blissfully unaware of the tension shimmering in the air, Jessie danced into the kitchen, palms held out for inspection. "How come they have to be clean when I don't eat with my fingers anyway?"

Effortfully, he pulled himself back and tweaked his daughter's nose. "Because germs like to sneak off little girls' hands and into their mashed potatoes."

"Yuck." She made a face, then grinned. "Daddy makes the best mashed potatoes in the whole wide world. Don't you want some? She can stay for dinner, can't she, Daddy?"

"Really, I—"

"Of course she can." Mirroring his daughter's grin—but with something a great deal more dangerous in his eyes—Boone studied Ana. "We'd love to have you. We have plenty. And I think it would be a good idea for us to get to know each other. Before."

She didn't have to ask before what. That was crystal-clear. But, no matter how she tried, she couldn't make her temper overtake the quick panicked excitement. "It's very nice of you to ask," she said with admirable calm. "I wish I could, but—" She smiled down at Jessie's sound of disappointment. "I have to drive out to my cousin's and take care of his horses."

"Will you take me with you sometime, so I can see them?"

"If your father says it's all right." She bent down and kissed Jessie's sulky lips. "Thank you for my picture, sunshine. It's beautiful." Taking a cautious step away, she looked at Boone. "And the book. I know I'll enjoy it. Good night."

Ana didn't run out of the house, though she freely admitted she wasn't leaving so much as escaping. Back home, she went through the motions, giving Quigley his promised tuna, then changing into jeans and a denim shirt for the drive to Sebastian's house.

She was going to have to do some thinking, she decided as she pulled on her boots. Some serious thinking. Weigh the pros and cons, consider the consequences. She had to laugh, thinking how Morgana would roll her eyes and accuse her of being impossibly Libran.

Perhaps her birth sign was partially responsible for the fact that Ana could always see and sympathize with both sides of an argument. It complicated matters as often as it solved them. But in this case she was quite certain that a clear head and calm deliberation was the order of the day.

Maybe she was unusually attracted to Boone. And the physical aspect of it was completely unprecedented. Certainly she'd felt desire for a man before, but never this quick, sharp edge of it. And a sharp edge usually meant a deep wound to follow.

That was certainly something to consider. Frowning, she grabbed a jean jacket and started downstairs.

Of course, she was an adult, unattached, unencumbered, and perfectly free to entertain the thought of a relationship with an equally free adult man.

Then again, she knew just how devastating relationships could be when people were unable to accept others for what they were.

Still debating, she swung out of the house. She certainly didn't owe Boone any explanations. She was under no obligation to try to make him understand her heritage, as she had tried to do years before with Robert. Even if they became involved, she wouldn't have to tell him.

Ana got into her car and backed out of the drive, her thoughts shifting back and forth.

It wasn't deception to hold part of yourself back. It was self-preservation—as she'd learned through hard experience. And it was foolish even to be considering that angle when she hadn't decided if she wanted to be involved.

No, that wasn't quite true. She wanted. It was more a matter of deciding if she could afford to become involved.

He was, after all, her neighbor. A relationship gone sour would make it very uncomfortable when they lived in such close proximity.

And there was Jessie to consider. She was half in love with the girl already. She wouldn't want to risk that friendship and affection by indulging her own needs. Purely physical needs, Ana told herself as she followed the winding road along the coast.

True, Boone would be able to offer her some physical plea-sure. She didn't doubt that for a moment. But the emotional cost would just be too steep for everyone involved.

It would be better, much better, for everyone involved if she remained Jessie's friend while maintaining a wise distance from Jessie's father.

Dinner was over, and the dishes were done. There had been a not-too-successful session with Daisy—though she would sit down if you pushed on her rump. Afterward, there'd been a lot of splashing in the tub, then some horseplay to indulge in with his freshly scrubbed daughter. There was a story to be told, that last glass of water to be fetched.

Once Jessie was asleep and the house was quiet, Boone indulged himself with a brandy out on the deck. There were piles of forms on his desk—a parent's homework—that had to be filled out for Jessie's school files.

He'd do them before he turned in, he decided. But this hour, this dark, quiet hour when the nearly full moon was rising, was his.

He could enjoy the clouds that were drifting overhead, promising rain, the hypnotic sound of the water lapping against rock, the chatter of insects in the grass that he would have to mow very soon, and the scent of night-blooming flowers.

No wonder he had snapped this house up at the very first glimpse. No place he'd ever been had relaxed him more, or given him more of a sense of rightness and peace. And it appealed to his imagination. The mystically shaped cypress, the magical ice plants that covered the banks, those empty and often eerie stretches of night beach.

The ethereally beautiful woman next door.

He smiled to himself. For someone who hadn't felt much more than an occasional twinge for a woman in too long to remember, he was certainly feeling a barrage of them now.

It had taken him a long time to get over Alice. Though he still didn't consider himself part of the dating pool, he hadn't been a monk over the past couple of years. His life wasn't empty, and he'd been able, after a great deal of pain, to accept the fact that he had to live it.

He was sipping his brandy, enjoying it and the simple pleasure of the night, when he heard Ana's car. Not that he'd been waiting for it, Boone assured himself even as he checked his watch. He couldn't quite smother the satisfaction at her being home early, too early to have gone out on a date.

Not that her social life was any of his business.

He couldn't see her driveway, but because the night was calm he heard her shut her car door. Then, a few moments later, he heard her open and close the door to her house.

Propping his bare feet on the rail of the deck, he tried to imagine her progress through the house. Into the kitchen. Yes, the light snapped on, and he could see her move past the window. Brewing tea, perhaps, or pouring herself a glass of wine.

Shortly, the light switched off again, and he let his mind follow her through the house. Up the stairs. More lights, but it looked to Boone like the glow of a candle against the dark glass, rather than a lamp. Moments later, he heard the faint drift of music. Harp strings. Haunting, romantic, and somehow sad.

Briefly, very briefly, she was silhouetted against a window. He could see quite clearly that slim feminine shadow as she stripped out of her shirt.

Hastily he swallowed brandy and looked away. However tempting it might be, he wouldn't lower himself to the level of a Peeping Tom. He did, however, find himself craving a cigarette, and with apologies to his disapproving daughter he pulled one out of his pocket.

Smoke stung the air, soothed his nerves. Boone contented himself with the sound of harpsong.

It was a very long time before he went back into the house and slept, with the sound of a gentle rain falling on the roof and the memory of harpsong drifting across the night breeze.

Chapter 4

Cannery Row was alive with sounds, the chattering of people as they strolled or rushed, the bright ringing of a bell from one of the tourist bikes, the ubiquitous calling of gulls searching for a handout. Ana enjoyed the crowds and the noise as much as she enjoyed the peace and solitude of her own backyard.

Patiently she chugged along with the stream of weekend traffic. On her first pass by Morgana's shop, Ana resigned herself to the fact that the perfect day had brought tourists and locals out in droves. Parking was going to be at a premium. Rather than frustrate herself searching for a spot on the street, she pulled into a lot three blocks from Wicca.

As she climbed out to open her trunk, she heard the whine of a cranky toddler and the frustrated muttering of weary parents.

"If you don't stop that right this minute, you won't get anything at all. I mean it, Timothy. We've had just about enough. Now get moving."

The child's response to that command was to go limp, sliding in a boneless heap onto the parking lot as his mother tugged uselessly at his watery arms. Ana bit her lip as it curved, but it was obvious the young parents didn't see the humor of it. Their arms were full of packages, and their faces were thunderous.

Timothy, Ana thought, was about to get a tanning—though it was unlikely to make him more cooperative. Daddy shoved his bags at Mommy and, mouth grim, bent down.

It was a small thing, Ana thought. And they all looked so tired and unhappy. She made the link first with the father, felt the love, the anger, and the dark embarrassment. Then with the child—confusion, fatigue, and a deep unhappiness over a big stuffed elephant he'd seen in a shop window and been denied.

Ana closed her eyes. The father's hand swung back as he prepared to administer a sharp slap to the boy's diaper-padded rump. The boy sucked in his breath, ready to emit a piercing wail at the indignity of it.

Suddenly the father sighed, and his hand fell back to his side. Timothy peeked up, his face hot and pink and tear-streaked.

The father crouched down, holding out his arms. "We're tired, aren't we?"

On a hiccuping sob, Timothy bundled into them and rested his heavy head on his daddy's shoulder. "Thirsty."

"Okay, champ." The father's hand went to the child's bottom, but with a soothing pat. He gave his teary-eyed wife an encouraging smile. "Why don't we go have a nice, cold drink? He just needs a n-a-p."

They moved off, tired but relieved.

Smiling to herself, Ana unlocked her trunk. Family vacations, she thought, weren't all fun and frolic. The next time they were ready to snarl at each other, she wouldn't be around to help. She imagined they'd muddle through without her.

After swinging her purse behind her back, she began to unload the boxes she was delivering to Morgana. There were a half dozen of them, filled with sacks of potpourri, bottles of oils and creams, beribboned sachets, satiny sleep pillows and a month's supply of special orders that ran from tonics to personalized perfumes.

Ana considered making two trips, gauged the distance and decided that if she balanced the load carefully she could make it in one.

She stacked, juggled and adjusted, then just managed to shut her trunk with an elbow. She made it across the parking lot and down half a block before she began berating herself.

Why did she always do this? she asked herself. Two comfortable trips were better than one difficult one. It wasn't that the boxes were so heavy—though they were. It was simply that they were awkward and the sidewalk was jammed. And her hair was blowing in her eyes. With a quick, agile dance, she managed, barely, to avoid a collision with a couple of teenage tourists in a surrey.

"Want some help?"

Annoyed with herself and irresponsible drivers, she turned around. There was Boone, looking particularly wonderful in baggy cotton slacks and shirt. Riding atop his shoulders, Jessie was laughing and clapping her hands.

"We had a ride on the carousel and had ice cream and we saw you."

"Looks like you're still overloading," Boone commented.

"They're not heavy."

He patted Jessie's leg and, following the signal, she began to slide down his back. "We'll give you a hand."

"That's all right." She knew it was foolish to reject help when she needed it, but she had managed quite successfully to avoid Boone for the better part of a week. And had managed— almost as successfully—to avoid thinking about him. Wondering about him. "I don't want to take you out of your way."

"We're not going any way in particular, are we, Jessie?"

"Uh-uh. We're just wandering today. It's our day off."

Ana couldn't prevent the smile, any more than she could prevent the wariness from creeping into her eyes when she looked back at Boone. He was certainly looking at her, she realized, in that disconcertingly thorough way of his. The smile creeping around his mouth had less to do with humor than it did with challenge.

"I don't have to go far," she began, grabbing at a package that was beginning to slide. "I can just—"

"Fine." Overriding her objections, Boone shifted boxes from her arms to his. His eyes stayed on hers. "What are neighbors for?"

"I can carry one." Eager to help, Jessie bounced in her sneakers. "I can."

"Thank you." Ana handed Jessie the lightest box. "I'm going a couple of blocks down to my cousin's shop."

"Has she had her babies?" Jessie asked as they started to walk.

"No, not yet."

"I asked Daddy how come she got to have two in there, and he said sometimes there's twice the love."

How could anyone possibly have a defense against a man like this? Ana wondered. Her eyes were warm when they met his. "Yes, sometimes there is. You always seem to have the right answer," she murmured to Boone.

"Not always." He wasn't certain if he was relieved or annoyed that his hands were full of boxes. If they'd been free, he would have been compelled to touch her. "You just try for the best one at the time. Where have you been hiding, Anastasia?"

"Hiding?" The warmth fled from her eyes.

"I haven't seen you out in your yard in days. You didn't strike me as the type to scare that easily."

Because Jessie was skipping just ahead of them, she bit off a more acid response. "I don't know what you mean. I had work. Quite a bit of it, as a matter of fact." She nodded toward the boxes. "You're carrying some of it now."

"Is that so? Then I'm glad I didn't resort to knocking on your door and pretending I needed to borrow a cup of sugar. I nearly did, but it seemed so obvious."

She slanted him a look. "I appreciate your restraint."

"And so you should."

She merely tossed her hair out of her eyes and called to Jessie. "We'll go down this way, so we can go in the back. Saturdays are usually busy," she explained to Boone. "I don't like going through the shop and distracting the customers."

"What does she sell, anyway?"

"Oh." Ana smiled again. "This and that. I think you'd find her wares particularly interesting. Here we go." She gestured to a little flagstone stoop flanked by pots of bloodred geraniums. "Can you get the door, Jessie?"

"Okay." Anxious as ever to see what was on the other side, Jessie shoved it open, then let out a squeal. "Oh, look. Daddy, look!" Jessie set her package aside on the first available space and made a dive for the big white cat grooming herself on the table.

"Jessica!" Boone's voice was short and firm, stopping his

daughter in midstride. "What have I told you about going up to strange animals?"

"But, Daddy, he's so pretty."

"She," Ana corrected as she laid her boxes on the counter. "And your father's quite right. Not all animals like little girls."

Jessie's fingers itched to stroke the thick white fur. "Does she?"

"Sometimes Luna doesn't like anyone." With a laugh, Ana scratched the cat between the ears. "But if you're very polite, and pet her when she gives the royal consent, you'll get along well enough." Ana gave Boone a reassuring smile. "Luna won't scratch her. When she's had enough, she'll just stalk off."

But apparently Luna was in the mood for attention. Walking to the end of the table, she rubbed her head against the hand Jessie had held out. "She likes me!" The smile nearly split her face in two. "See, Daddy, she likes me."

"Yes, I see."

"Morgana usually keeps cold drinks back here." Ana opened the small refrigerator. "Would you like something?"

"Sure." He really wasn't thirsty, but the offer made it easy to linger. He leaned back against the counter of the kitchenette while Ana got out glasses. "The shop through there?"

When he gestured at a door, Ana nodded. "Yes. And through there's the storeroom. A great deal of what Morgana sells is one-of-a-kind, so she doesn't keep a large supply of inventory."

He reached over Ana's shoulder to finger the thin leaves of a rosemary plant on the windowsill. "She into this kind of thing, too?"

Ana tried to ignore the fact that his body was brushing hers. She could smell the sea on him, and imagined he and Jessie had gone down to feed the gulls. "What kind of thing?"

"Herbs and stuff."

"In a manner of speaking." She turned, knowing she'd be entirely too close, and pushed the glass into his chest. "Root beer."

"Terrific." He knew it wasn't particularly fair—and it was probably unwise, as well—but he took the glass and stood precisely where he was. She had to tilt her head back to meet his eyes. "It might be a good hobby for Jessie and me. Maybe you could show us how to grow some."

"It's no different from growing any living thing." It took a great deal of effort to keep her voice even when breathing was so difficult. "Care and attention, and affection. You're very much in my way, Boone."

"I hope so." With his eyes very intense, very focused, he lifted a hand to her cheek. "Anastasia, I really think we need to—"

"A deal's a deal, babe." The smug voice carried through the door as it opened. "Fifteen minutes of sit-down time every two hours."

"You're being ridiculous. For heaven's sake, you act as though I'm the only pregnant woman in the world." Heaving a sigh, Morgana walked into the back room. Her brows lifted when she saw the trio—and particularly when she saw the way Boone Sawyer was caging her cousin at the rear counter.

"You're the only pregnant woman in my world." Nash stopped short. "Hey, Ana, you're just the woman I need to convince Morgana to take it easy. Now that you're here, I can..." He glanced once at the man beside her, then back again to focus. "Boone? Well, I'll be damned. Boone Sawyer, you son of a—" He caught himself, mostly because Morgana shot an elbow into his ribs. There was a little girl, all eyes, standing at the table. "Gun," he finished, and strode across the room to shake Boone's hand and slap his back in a typical male greeting. "What are you doing here?"

"Delivering stock, I think." He grinned, gripping Nash's hand hard in his. "How about you?"

"Trying to keep my wife in line. Lord, what's it been? Four years?"

"Just about."

Morgana folded her hands on her belly. "I take it you two know each other?"

"Sure we do. Boone and I met at a writers' conference. It has to be ten years ago, doesn't it? I haven't seen you since—" Since Alice's funeral, Nash remembered abruptly. And he remembered, too, the devastation, the despair and the disbelief in

Boone's eyes as he'd stood beside his wife's grave. "How are you?"

"Okay." Understanding, Boone smiled. "We're okay."

"Good." Nash put a hand on Boone's shoulder and squeezed before he turned to Jessie. "And you're Jessica."

"Uh-huh." She beamed up at him, always interested in meeting someone new. "Who are you?"

"I'm Nash." He crossed to her, crouched down. Except for the eyes, eyes that were all Boone, she was the image of Alice. Bright, pretty, pixielike. He offered her a formal handshake. "It's nice to meet you."

She giggled and shook his hand. "Did you put the babies into Morgana?"

To his credit, he was speechless only for a moment. "Guilty." With a laugh, he picked her up. "But I'm leaving it up to Ana to get them out. So, what are the two of you doing in Monterey?"

"We live here now," Jessie told him. "Right next door to Ana's house."

"No kidding?" Nash grinned over at Boone. "When?"

"A little more than a week. I'd heard you'd moved here, and I figured I'd look you up once we got things together. I didn't realize you were married to my neighbor's cousin."

"A small and fascinating world, isn't it?" Morgana commented. She tilted her head at Ana, well aware that her cousin hadn't said a word since they'd come into the room. "Since no one's going to introduce me, I'm Morgana."

"Sorry," Nash said, jiggling Jessie on his hip. "Sit down."

"I'm perfectly—"

"Sit." This from Ana as she pulled out a chair.

"Outnumbered." Sighing, Morgana sat. "Are you enjoying Monterey?"

"Very much," Boone told her, and his gaze shifted to Ana. "More than I anticipated."

"I always enjoy having more than I anticipated." With a light laugh, she patted her belly. "We'll all have to get together very soon, so you can tell me things Nash doesn't want me to know."

"I'd be glad to."

"Babe, you know I'm an open book." He kissed the top of

Morgana's head and winked at Ana. "That the stuff Morgana's been waiting for?"

"Yes, all of it." Anxious to keep her hands busy, Ana turned to the pile of boxes. "I'll unpack it for you. Morgana, I want you to try out this new violet body lotion before you put it out, and I brought extra of the soapwort shampoo."

"Good, I'm completely out." She took the bottle of lotion from Ana and unstopped the bottle. "Nice scent." She dabbed a bit on the back of her hand and rubbed it in. "Good texture."

"Sweet violets, and the Irish moss Da sent me." She glanced up from her unpacking. "Nash, why don't you show Jessie and Boone the shop?"

"Good idea. I think you're going to find a lot of this right up your alley," Nash told Boone as he led the way to the door.

Boone shot a look over his shoulder before he passed through. "Anastasia." He waited until she glanced up from the boxes. "Don't run away."

"My, my, my." Morgana settled back and smiled like a cat with a direct line to Bossy. "Want to fill me in?"

With a little more force than necessary, Ana ripped through packing tape. "On what?"

"On you and your gorgeous neighbor, of course."

"There's nothing to fill in."

"Darling, I know you. When I walked into this room, you were so wrapped up in him I could have called out a tornado and you wouldn't have blinked."

Ana busied herself unpacking bottles. "Don't be ridiculous. You haven't called out a tornado since the first time we saw *The Wizard of Oz.*"

"Ana." Morgana's voice was low and firm. "I love you."

"I know. I love you, too."

"You're never nervous. Perhaps that's why it's so fascinating—and concerning—to me that you're so nervous just now."

"I'm not." She rapped two bottles together and winced. "All right, all right, all right. I have to think about it." She whipped around. "He makes me nervous, and it would be ridiculous to deny it's the fact that I'm very attracted to him that's making me so nervous. I just have to think about it."

"Think about what?"

"How to handle it. Him, I mean. I have no intention of making another mistake, particularly since anything I do that involves Boone also involves Jessie."

"Oh, honey, are you falling in love with him?"

"That's absurd." Ana realized too late that the denial was too forceful to be taken at face value. "I'm just jumpy, that's all. I haven't had a man affect me like this, physically, in..." Ever. Never before, and, she was very much afraid, never again. "In a long time. I just need to think," she repeated.

"Ana." Morgana held out both hands. "Sebastian and Mel will be back in a couple of days from their honeymoon. Why don't you ask him to look? It would relieve your mind if you knew."

Resolute, Ana shook her head. "No...not that I haven't considered it. Whatever happens, however it happens, I want it to be on equal terms. Knowing would give me an unfair advantage over Boone. I have a feeling those equal terms would be important, to both of us."

"You know best. Let me tell you something, as a woman." Her lips curved. "As a witch. Knowing, not knowing, makes no difference with a man, once he touches your heart. No difference at all."

Ana nodded. "Then I'll have to make sure he doesn't touch mine until I'm ready."

"This is incredible," Boone was saying as he surveyed Wicca. "Just incredible."

"I thought so, too, the first time I walked in." Nash picked up a crystal wand tipped at the end with a spear of amethyst. "I guess people in our line of work are suckers for this stuff."

"Fairy tales," Boone agreed, accepting the wand before running a finger over a bronze cast of a snarling wolf. "Or the occult. A fine line between the two. Your last movie chilled my blood even when it made me laugh."

Nash grinned. "The humor in horror."

"Nobody does it better." He glanced over at his daughter. She was staring at a miniature silver castle surrounded by a moat of rainbow glass, her eyes huge, her hands behind her back. "I'll never get out of here empty-handed."

"She's beautiful," Nash said, wondering, as he often did, about the children that would be his before much longer.

"Looks like her mother." He saw the question and the concern in his friend's eyes. "Grief passes, Nash, whether you want it to or not. Alice was a wonderful part of my life, and she gave me the best thing in it. I'm grateful for every moment I had with her." He set the wand down. "Now I'd like to know how you— the world's most determined bachelor—came to be married and expecting twins."

"Research." Nash grinned and rocked back on his heels. "I wanted to get out of L.A., and keep within commuting distance. I'd only been here a short time when I needed to do some research on a script. I walked in here, and there she was."

There was more, of course. A great deal more. But it wasn't Nash's place to tell Boone about the Donovan legacy. Not even if Boone would have believed him.

"When you decide to take the plunge, you take it big."

"You, too. Indiana's a long way from here."

"I didn't want to be able to commute," Boone said with a grimace. "My parents, Alice's parents. Jessie and I were becoming their life's work. And I wanted a change, for both of us."

"Next door to Ana, huh?" Nash narrowed his eyes. "The redwood place, with all the glass and decks?"

"That's the one."

"Good choice." He glanced toward Jessie again. She'd wandered around the shop and had worked her way back to the little castle. She hadn't once asked for it, and that made the naked desire in her eyes all the more effective. "If you don't buy her that, I will."

When Ana came out to restock a few shelves for Morgana, she saw not only the silver castle being rung up on the counter, but the wand, a three-foot sculpture of a winged faerie she'd had her eye on herself, a crystal sun-catcher in the shape of a unicorn, a pewter wizard holding a many-faceted ball, and a baseball-sized geode.

"We're weak," Boone said with a quick, sheepish grin as Ana lifted a brow. "No willpower."

"But excellent taste." She ran a fingertip over the faerie wings. "Lovely, isn't she?"

"One of the best I've seen. I figured I'd put her in my office for inspiration."

"Good idea." She bent over a compartment containing tumbling stones. "Malachite, for clear thinking." Her fingers walked through the smooth stones, testing, rejecting, selecting. "Sodalite to relieve mental confusion, moonstone for sensitivity. Amethyst, of course, for intuition."

"Of course."

She ignored him. "A crystal for all-around good things." Tilting her head, she studied him. "Jessie says you're trying to quit smoking."

He shrugged. "I'm cutting down."

She handed him the crystal. "Keep it in your pocket. Tumbling stones are on the house." When she turned away with her colorful bottles, he picked up the crystal and rubbed it with his fingers.

It couldn't hurt.

He didn't believe in magic crystals or stone power—though he did think they had plot possibilities. Boone also had to admit they looked kind of nice in the little bowl on his desk. Atmosphere, he thought, like the geode he'd bought to use as a paperweight.

All in all, the afternoon had had several benefits. He and Jessie had enjoyed themselves thoroughly, riding the carousel at the Emporium, playing video games, just walking down Cannery Row and Fisherman's Wharf. Running into Anastasia had been a plus, he mused as he toyed with the creamy moonstone. And seeing Nash again, discovering that they lived in the same area, was gold.

He'd been missing male companionship. Funny, he hadn't realized it, as busy as his life had been over the past few months, with planning the move, executing the move, adjusting to the move. And Nash, though their friendship had primarily been through correspondence over the years, was exactly the kind of companion Boone preferred. Easygoing, loyal, imaginative.

It would be a kick to be able to pass on a few fatherly hints to Nash once his twins were born.

Oh, yeah, he reflected as he held up the moonstone, watching it gleam in the bright wash of moonlight through his office window, it certainly was a small and fascinating world.

One of his oldest friends, married to the cousin of the woman next door. It would certainly be hard for Anastasia to avoid him now.

And, no matter what she said, that was exactly what she'd been doing. He had a very strong feeling—and he couldn't help being a bit smug about it—that he was making the fair maiden nervous.

He'd nearly forgotten what it was like to approach a woman who reacted with faint blushes, confused eyes and rapid pulses. Most of the women he'd escorted over the past couple of years had been sleek and sophisticated—and safe, he added with a little shrug. He'd enjoyed their companionship, and he'd never lost his basic enjoyment of female company. But there'd been no tug, no mystery, no illusion.

He supposed he was still the kind of man attracted to the old-fashioned type. The roses-and-moonlight type, he thought with a half laugh. Then he saw her, and the laugh caught in his throat.

Down in her garden, walking, almost gliding through the silvery light, with the gray cat slipping in and out of the shadows. Her hair loose, sprinkling gold dust down her back and over the sheer shoulders of a pale blue robe. She carried a basket, and he thought he could hear her singing as she cut flowers and slipped them into it.

She was singing an old chant that had been passed down generation to generation. It was well past midnight, and Ana thought herself alone and unobserved. The first night of the full moon in autumn was the time to harvest, just as the first night of the full moon in spring was the time to sow. She had already cast the circle, purifying the area.

She laid the flowers and herbs in the basket as gently as children.

There was magic in her eyes. In her blood.

"Under the moon, through shadow and light, these blooms I

chose by touch, by sight. Spells to weave to ease and free. As I will, so mote it be.''

She plucked betony and heliotrope, dug mandrake root and selected tansy and balsam. Blood roses for strength, and sage for wisdom. The basket grew heavy and fragrant.

"Tonight to reap, tomorrow to sow. To take only that which I've caused to grow. Remembering always what is begun. To serve, to aid, an it harm none.''

As the charm was cast, she lowered her face to the blooms, drawing in the ripe melody of the fragrance.

"I wondered if you were real.''

Her head came up quickly, and she saw him, hardly more than a shadow by the hedge. Then he stepped through, into her garden, and became a man.

The heart that had leapt to her throat gradually settled again. "You startled me.''

"I'm sorry.'' It must be the moonlight, he thought, that made her look so...enchanting. "I was working late, and I looked out and saw you. It seemed late to be picking flowers.''

"There's a lot of moonlight.'' She smiled. He had seen nothing it wasn't safe for him to see. "I would think you'd know that anything picked under the full moon is charmed.''

He returned the smile. "Got any rampion?''

The reference to Rapunzel made her laugh. "As a matter of fact, I do. No magic garden is complete without it. I'll pot some for you, if you like.''

"I rarely say no to magic.'' The breeze fluttered her hair. Giving in to the moment, he reached out, took a handful. He watched the smile in her eyes fade. What replaced it had his blood singing.

"You should go in. Jessie's alone.''

"She's asleep.'' He moved closer, as if the hair he'd twined around his finger were a rope and she were drawing him to her. He was within the circle now, within the magic she'd cast. "The windows are open, so I'd hear her if she called for me.''

"It's late.'' Ana gripped the basket so tightly that the wicker dug into her skin. "I need to...''

Gently he took the basket and set it on the ground. "So do

I." His other hand moved into her hair, combing it back from her face. "Very much."

As he lowered his mouth toward hers, she shivered and tried one last time to take control. "Boone, starting something like this could complicate things for all of us."

"Maybe I'm tired of things being simple." But he turned his head, just a fraction, so that his lips cruised up her cheek, over her temple. "I'm surprised you don't know that when a man finds a woman picking flowers in the moonlight he has no choice but to kiss her."

She felt her bones melting. Her body was pliant when she slipped into his arms. "And she has no choice but to want him to."

Her head fell back, and she offered. He thought he would take gently. The night seemed to call for it, with its perfumed breezes and the dreamy music of sea against rock. The woman in his arms was wand-slender, and the thin silk of her robe was cool over the warmth of satin skin.

But as he felt himself sink into that soft, lush mouth, as her fragrance whispered seductively around him, he dragged her hard against him and plundered.

Instantly desperate, instantly greedy. No rational thought could fight its way through the maze of sensations she brought to him. A sharp arrow of hunger pierced him, bringing on a groan that was only part pleasure.

Pain. He felt the aches of a thousand pricks of pain. Yet he couldn't pull himself away from her, couldn't stop his mouth from seeking more of hers. He was afraid, afraid that if he released her she would disappear like smoke—and he would never, never feel this way again.

She couldn't soothe him. Part of her wanted to stroke him and ease him and promise him that it would be all right, for both of them. But she couldn't. He devastated her. Whether it was her own grinding needs, the echo of his need seeping into her, or a mix of both, the result was a complete loss of will.

She had known, yes, she had known that this first meeting would be wild and strong. She'd craved it even as she'd feared it. Now she was beyond fear. Like him, she found the mixture of pain and pleasure irresistible.

Her trembling hands skimmed over his face, into his hair and locked there. Her body, shuddering from the onslaught, pressed urgently to his. When she murmured his name, she was breathless.

But he heard her, heard her through the blood pounding in his head, heard that soft, shaky sound. She was trembling—or he was. The uncertainty about who was more dazed had him slowly, carefully drawing away.

He held her still, his hands on her shoulders, his gaze on her face. In the moonlight, she could see herself there, trapped in that sea of blue. Trapped in him.

"Boone..."

"Not yet." He needed a moment to steady himself. By God, he'd nearly swallowed her whole. "Not just yet." Holding himself back, he touched his lips to hers, lightly, in a long, quiet kiss that wrecked whatever was left of her defenses. "I didn't mean to hurt you."

"You didn't." She pressed her lips together and tried to bring her voice over a whisper. "You didn't hurt me. You staggered me."

"I thought I was ready for this." He ran his hands down her arms before he released her. "I don't know if anyone could be." Because he wasn't sure what would happen if he touched her again, he slipped his hands into his pockets. "Maybe it's the moonlight, maybe it's just you. I have to be straight with you, Anastasia, I don't know quite how to handle this."

"Well." She wrapped her arms tight and cupped her elbows. "That makes two of us."

"If it wasn't for Jessie, you wouldn't go into that house alone tonight. And I don't take intimacy lightly."

Steadier now, she nodded. "If it wasn't for Jessie, I might ask you to stay with me tonight." She took a long breath. She knew it was important to be honest, at least in this. "You would be my first."

"Your—" His hands went limp. Now he felt both a lick of fear and an incredible excitement at the thought of her innocence. "Oh, God."

Her chin came up. "I'm not ashamed of it."

"No, I didn't mean..." Speechless, he dragged a hand

through his hair. Innocent. A golden-haired virgin in a thin blue robe with flowers at her feet. And a man was supposed to resist, and walk away alone. "I don't suppose you have any idea what that does to a man."

"Not precisely, since I'm not a man." She bent down for her basket. "But I do know what realizing that you may soon be giving yourself for the first time does to a woman. So it seems to me we should both give this some clear thinking." She smiled, or tried to. "And it's very difficult to think clearly after midnight, when the moon's full and the flowers are ripe. I'll say good night, Boone."

"Ana." He touched her arm, but didn't hold on. "Nothing will happen until you're ready."

She shook her head. "Yes, it will. But nothing will happen unless it's meant."

With her robe billowing around her, she raced toward the house.

Chapter 5

Sleep had been a long time coming. Boone hadn't tossed and turned so much as lain, staring up at the ceiling. He'd watched the moonlight fade into that final deep darkness before dawn.

Now, with the sun streaming in bright ribbons over the bed, he was facedown, spread out, and fast asleep. In the dream floating through his brain, he scooped Ana into his arms and carried her up a long curved staircase of white marble. At the top, suspended above puffy, cotton clouds, was an enormous bed pooled in waterfalls of white satin. Hundreds of long, slender candles burned in a drifting light. He could smell them—the soft tang of vanilla, the mystique of jasmine. And her—that quietly sexy scent that went everywhere with her.

She smiled. Hair like sunlight. Eyes like smoke. When he laid her on the bed, they sank deep, as if into the clouds themselves. There was harpsong, romantic as tears, and a whisper that was nothing more than the clouds themselves breathing.

As her arms lifted, wound around him, they were floating, like ghosts in some fantasy, bound together by needs and knowledge and the unbearable sweetness of that first long, lingering kiss. Her mouth moved under his, yielding as she murmured...

"Daddy!"

Boone came awake with a crash as his daughter landed with a thump on his back. His unintelligible grunt had her giggling and scooting down to smack a kiss on his stubbled cheek.

"Daddy, wake up! I fixed you breakfast!"

"Breakfast." He grumbled into the pillow, struggling to clear the sleep from his throat and the dream from his system. "What time is it?"

"The little hand's on the ten, and the big hand's on the three. I made cinnamon toast and poured orange juice in the little glasses."

He grunted again, rolling over to peer through gritty eyes at Jessie. She looked bright as a sunbeam in her pink cotton blouse and shorts. She'd done the buttons up wrong, but she'd brushed the tangles from her hair. "How long have you been up?"

"Hours and hours and hours. I let Daisy outside and gave her breakfast. And I got dressed all by myself and brushed my teeth and watched cartoons. Then I got hungry, so I fixed breakfast."

"You've been busy."

"Uh-huh. And I was real quiet, too, so you didn't have to wake up early on your sleep-in day."

"You were real quiet," Boone agreed, and reached up to fix her buttons. "I guess you deserve a prize."

Her eyes lit. "What? What do I get?"

"How about a pink belly?" He rolled with her on the bed, wrestling while she squealed and wriggled. He let her win, pretending exhaustion and defeat when she bounced on his back. "Too tough for me."

"That's 'cause I eat my vegetables. You don't."

"I eat some."

"Uh-uh, hardly any."

"When you get to be thirty-three, you won't have to eat your brussels sprouts, either."

"But I like them."

He grinned into the pillow. "That's only because I'm such a good cook. My mother was lousy."

"She doesn't ever cook now." Jessie printed her name with a fingertip on her father's bare back. "Her and Grandpa Sawyer always go out to eat."

"That's because Grandpa Sawyer's no fool." She was having trouble with the letter *S*, Boone noted. They'd have to work on it.

"You said we could call Grandma and Grandpa Sawyer and Nana and Pop today. Can we?"

"Sure, in a couple of hours." He turned over again, studying her. "Do you miss them, baby?"

"Yeah." With her tongue between her teeth, she began to print *Sawyer* on his chest. "It seems funny that they're not here. Will they come to visit us?"

"Sure they will." The guilt that was part and parcel of parenthood worked at him. "Do you wish we'd stayed in Indiana?"

"No way!" Her eyes went huge. "We didn't have the beach there, and the seals and stuff, or the big carousel in town, or Ana living next door. This is the best place in the world."

"I like it here, too." He sat up and kissed her brow. "Now beat it, so I can get dressed."

"You'll come right downstairs for breakfast?" she asked as she slid from the bed.

"Absolutely. I'm so hungry I could eat a whole loaf of cinnamon toast."

Delighted, she rushed for the door. "I'm going to make more, right now."

Knowing she would take him at his word and go through an entire loaf of bread, Boone hurried through his shower, opted not to shave, and pulled on cutoffs and a T-shirt that would probably have done better in the rag pile.

He tried not to dwell on the dream. After all, it was simple enough to interpret. He wanted Ana—no big revelation there. And all that white—white on white—was obviously a symbol of her innocence.

It scared the hell out of him.

He found Jessie in the kitchen, busily slathering butter on another piece of toast. There was a plate heaped with them, more than a few of them burnt. The smell of cinnamon was everywhere.

Boone put on the coffee before he snagged a piece. It was cold, hard, and lumped with sugary cinnamon. Obviously, Jessie had inherited her grandmother's culinary talents.

"It's great," he told her, and swallowed gamely. "My favorite Sunday breakfast."

"Do you think Daisy can have some?"

Boone looked at the pile of toast again, glanced down at the pup, whose tongue was lolling out. With any luck he might be able to pawn off half his Sunday breakfast on the dog. "I think she could." Crouching, Boone held out a second piece of toast close enough for Daisy to sniff. "Sit," he ordered, in the firm, no-nonsense voice the training books had suggested.

Daisy continued to loll her tongue and wag her tail.

"Daisy, sit." He gave her rump a nudge. Daisy went down, then bounded back on all fours to jump at him. "Forget it." He held the toast out of reach and repeated the command. After five frustrating minutes—during which he tried not to remember how simple it had been for Ana—he managed to hold the dog's hind-quarters down. Daisy gobbled up the bread, pleased with herself.

"She did it, Daddy."

"Sort of." He rose to pour himself some coffee. "We'll take her outside in a little while and have a real lesson."

"Okay." Jessie munched happily on her toast. "Maybe Ana's company will be gone, and she can help."

"Company?" Boone asked as he reached for a mug.

"I saw her outside with a man. She gave him a big hug and a kiss and everything."

"She—" The mug clattered onto the counter.

"Butterfingers," Jessie said, smiling.

"Yeah." Boone kept his back turned as he righted the mug and poured the coffee. "What, ah, sort of a man?" He thought his voice was casual enough—to fool a six-year-old, anyway.

"A really tall man with black hair. They were laughing and holding hands. Maybe it's her boyfriend."

"Boyfriend," Boone repeated between his teeth.

"What's the matter, Daddy?"

"Nothing. Coffee's hot." He sipped it black. Holding hands, he thought. Kissing. He'd get a look at this guy himself. "Why don't we go out on the deck, Jess? See if we can get Daisy to sit again."

"Okay." Singing the new song she'd learned in school, Jessie gathered up toast. "I like to eat outside. It's nice."

"Yeah, it's nice." Boone didn't sit when they were on the deck, but stood at the rail, the mug in his hand. He didn't see anyone in the next yard, and that was worse. Now he could imagine what Ana and her tall, dark-haired boyfriend might be doing inside.

Alone.

He ate three more pieces of toast, washing them down with black coffee while he fantasized about just what he'd say to Miss Anastasia Donovan the next time he saw her.

If she thought she could kiss him to the point of explosion one night, then dally with some strange guy the next morning, she was very much mistaken.

He'd straighten her out, all right. The minute he got ahold of her he'd—

His thoughts broke off when she came out the kitchen door, calling over her shoulder to someone.

"Ana!" Jessie leapt up on the bench, waving and shouting. "Ana, hi!"

While Boone watched through narrowed eyes, Ana looked in their direction. It seemed to him that her hand hesitated on its way up to return the wave, and her smile was strained.

Sure, he thought as he gulped down more coffee. I'd be nervous, too, if I had some strange man in the house.

"Can I go tell her what Daisy did? Can I, Daddy?"

"Yeah." His smile was grim as he set his empty mug on the rail. "Why don't you do that?"

Snatching up some more toast, she darted down the steps, calling for Daisy to follow and for Ana to wait.

Boone waited himself until he saw the man stroll outside to join Ana. He was tall, all right, Boone noted with some resentment. Several inches over six feet. He drew his own shoulders back. His hair was true black, and long enough to curl over his collar and blow—romantically, Boone imagined a woman would think—in the breeze.

He looked tanned, fit and elegant. And the breath hissed out between Boone's teeth when the stranger slipped an arm around Ana's shoulders as if it belonged there.

We'll see about this, Boone decided, and started down the deck stairs with his hands jammed in his pockets. We'll just see about this.

By the time he reached the hedge of roses, Jessie was already chattering a mile a minute about Daisy, and Ana was laughing, her arms tucked intimately around the stranger's waist.

"I'd sit, too, if someone was going to feed me cinnamon toast," the man said, and winked at Ana.

"You'd sit if anyone was going to feed you anything." Ana gave him a little squeeze before she noticed Boone at the hedge. "Oh." It was useless to curse the faint blush she felt heating her cheeks. "Good morning."

"How's it going?" Boone gave her a slow nod. Then his gaze moved suspiciously to the man beside her. "We didn't mean to interrupt while you have...company."

"No, that's all right, I—" She broke off, both confused and disconcerted by the tension humming in the air. "Sebastian, this is Jessie's father, Boone Sawyer. Boone, my cousin, Sebastian Donovan."

"Cousin?" Boone repeated, and Sebastian didn't bother to control the grin that spread over his face.

"Fortunately you made the introductions quickly, Ana," he said. "I like my nose precisely the way it is." He held out a hand. "Nice to meet you. Ana was telling us she had new neighbors."

"He's the one with horses, Daddy."

"I remember." Boone found Sebastian's grip firm and strong. He might have appreciated it if he hadn't seen the gleam of amusement in the man's eyes. "You're recently married?"

"Indeed I am. My..." He turned when the screen door slammed. "Ah, here she is now. Light of my life."

A tall, slim woman with short, tousled hair strode over in dusty boots. "Cut it out, Donovan."

"My blushing bride." It was obvious they were laughing at each other. He took his wife's hand and kissed it. "Ana's neighbors, Boone and Jessie Sawyer. My own true love, Mary Ellen."

"Mel," she corrected quickly. "Donovan's the only one with the nerve to call me Mary Ellen. Great-looking house," she added, with a nod toward the neighboring building.

"I believe Mr. Sawyer writes fairy tales, children's books, much in the manner of Aunt Bryna."

"Oh, yeah? That's cool." Mel smiled down at Jessie. "I bet you like that."

"He writes the best stories in the world. And this is Daisy. We taught her to sit. Can I come see your horses?"

"Sure." Mel crouched down to ruffle the pup's fur. While Mel engaged Jessie in conversation about horses and dogs, Sebastian looked back at Boone.

"It is a lovely house you have," he said. Actually, he'd toyed with buying it himself. Amusement lit his eyes again. "Excellent location."

"We like it." Boone decided it was foolish to pretend not to understand the meaning behind the words. "We like it very much." Very deliberately, he reached out to trail a fingertip down Ana's cheek. "You're looking a little pale this morning, Anastasia."

"I'm fine." It was easy enough to keep her voice even, but she knew very well how simple it would be for Sebastian to see what she was thinking. Already she could feel his gentle probing, and she was quite certain he was poking his nosy mental fingers into Boone's brain. "If you'll excuse me, I promised Sebastian some hawthorn."

"Didn't you pick any last night?"

Her gaze met his, held it. "I have other uses for that."

"We'll get out of your way. Come on, Jess." He reached for his daughter's hand. "Nice meeting both of you. I'll see you soon, Ana."

Sebastian had the tact to wait until Boone was out of earshot. "Well, well...I go away for a couple of weeks, and look at the trouble you get into."

"Don't be ridiculous." Ana turned her back and started toward an herb bed. "I'm not in any sort of trouble."

"Darling, darling Ana, your friend and neighbor was prepared to rip my throat out until you introduced me as your cousin."

"I'd have protected you," Mel said solemnly.

"My hero."

"Besides," Mel went on, "it looked to me as though he was more in the mood to drag Ana off by the hair than tackle you."

"You're both being absurd." Ana snipped hawthorn without looking up. "He's a very nice man."

"I'm sure," Sebastian murmured. "But, you see, men understand this territorial thing—which is, of course, an obscure concept to the female.''

"Oh, please." Mel shoved an elbow in his ribs.

"Facts are facts, my dear Mary Ellen. I had intruded on his territory. Or so he thought. Naturally, I would only think less of him if he had made no effort to defend it.''

"Naturally," Mel said dryly.

"Tell me, Ana, just how involved are you?''

"That's none of your business." She straightened, deftly wrapping the stems of the hawthorn. "And I'll thank you to keep out of it, cousin. I know very well you were poking in.''

"Which is why you blocked me. Your neighbor wasn't so successful.''

"It's rude," she muttered, "unconscionably rude, the way you peek into people's heads at the drop of a hat.''

"He likes to show off," Mel said sympathetically.

"Unfair." Disgusted, Sebastian shook his head. "I do not poke or peek at the drop of a hat. I always have an excellent reason. In this case, being your only male relative on the continent, I feel it's my duty to survey the situation, and the players.''

Mel could only roll her eyes as Ana's spine stiffened. "Really?" Eyes bright, Ana jammed a finger into Sebastian's chest. "Then let me set you straight. Just because I'm a woman doesn't mean I need protection or guidance or anything else from a male—relative or otherwise. I've been handling my own life for twenty-six years.''

"Twenty-seven next month," Sebastian added helpfully.

"And I can continue to handle it. What's between Boone and me—''

"Ah." He held up a triumphant finger. "So there is something between you.''

"Stuff it, Sebastian.''

"She only talks like that when she paints herself into a corner," Sebastian told Mel. "Usually she's extremely mild and well-mannered.''

"Careful, or I'll give Mel a potion to put in your soup that'll freeze your vocal cords for a week.''

"Oh yeah?" Intrigued by the idea, Mel tilted her head. "Can I have it anyway?"

"A lot of good it would do you, since I do all the cooking," Sebastian pointed out. Then he scooped Ana up in a hug. "Come on, darling, don't be angry. I have to worry about you. It's my job."

"There's nothing to worry about." But she was softening.

"Are you in love with him?"

Instantly she stiffened. "Really, Sebastian, I've only known him for a week."

"What difference does that make?" He gave Mel a long look over Ana's head. "It took me less than that to realize the reason Mel irritated me so much was that I was crazy about her. Of course, it took her longer to understand she was madly in love with me. But she has such a hard head."

"I'm getting that potion," Mel decided.

Ignoring the threat, he drew back to consider Ana at arm's length. "I ask because he definitely has more than a neighborly interest in you. As a matter of fact, he—"

"That's enough. Whatever you dug out of his head, you keep to yourself. I mean it, Sebastian," she said before he could interrupt. "I prefer doing things my own way."

"If you insist," he said with a sigh.

"I do. Now take your hawthorn and go home and be newlyweds."

"Now that's the best idea I've heard all day." Taking a firm grip on her husband's arm, Mel tugged him back. "Leave her alone, Donovan. Ana's perfectly capable of handling her own affairs."

"And if she's going to have one, she should know—"

"Out." On a strangled laugh, Ana gave him a shove. "Out of my yard. I have work to do. If I need a psychic, I'll call you."

He relented and gave her a kiss. "See that you do." A new smile began to bloom as he walked away with his wife. "I believe we'll stop by and see Morgana and Nash."

"That's fine." She shot a last glance over her shoulder. "I'd like to hear what they have to say about this guy myself."

Sebastian laughed and hugged her close. "You are a woman after my own heart."

"No, I'm not." She kissed him soundly. "I've already got it."

For the next several days, Ana busied herself indoors. It wasn't that she was avoiding Boone—at least not to any great extent. She simply had a lot to do. Her medicinal supplies had become sadly depleted. Just that day, she'd had a call from a client in Carmel who was out of the elixir for her rheumatism. Ana had had just enough to ship, but that meant she had to make more as soon as possible. Even now she had dried primrose simmering with motherwort on the stove.

In the little room adjoining the kitchen through a wide archway, she had her distilling flasks, condensers, burners and bottles, along with vials and silver bowls and candles, set up for the day. To the casual eye, the room resembled a small chemistry lab. But there was a marked difference between chemistry and alchemy. In alchemy there was ritual, and the meticulous use of astrological timing.

All of the flowers and roots and herbs she had harvested by moonlight had been carefully washed in morning dew. Others, plucked under different phases of the moon, had already been prepared for their specific uses.

There was syrup of poppy to be distilled, and there was hyssop to be dried for cough syrup. She needed some oil of clary for a specialty perfume, and she could combine that with some chamomile for a digestive aid. There were infusions and decoctions to be completed, as well as both oils and incense.

Plenty to do, Ana thought, particularly since she had the touch of magic from the flowers picked in moonlight. And she enjoyed her work, the scents that filled her kitchen and workroom, the pretty pink leaves of the flowering marjoram, the deep purple of foxglove, the sunny touch of the practical marigold.

They were lovely, and she could never resist setting some in vases or bowls around the house. She was testing a dilution of gentian, grimacing at the bitter taste, when Boone knocked on her screen door.

"I really do need sugar this time," he told her with a quick, charming grin that had her heart pumping fast. "I'm homeroom mother this week, and I have to make three dozen cookies for tomorrow."

Tilting her head, she studied him. "You could buy them."

"What homeroom mother worth her salt serves the first grade class store-bought? A cup would do it."

The image of him baking made her smile. "I probably have one. Come on in. Just let me finish this up."

"It smells fabulous in here." He leaned over to peek into the pots simmering on the stove. "What are you doing?"

"Don't!" She warned, just as he was about to dip a finger in a black glass pan cooling on the counter. "That's belladonna. Not for internal consumption in that form."

"Belladonna." His brows drew together. "You're making poison?"

"I'm making a lotion—an anodyne—for neuralgia, rheumatism. And it isn't a poison if it's brewed and dispensed properly. It's a sedative."

Frowning, he looked into the room behind, with its chemical equipment and its bubbling brews. "Don't you have to have a license or something?"

"I'm a qualified herbal practitioner, with a degree in pharmacognosy, if that relieves you." She batted his hand away from a pot. "And this is not something for the novice."

"Got anything for insomnia—besides belladonna? No offense."

She was instantly concerned. "Are you having trouble sleeping? Are you feverish?" She lifted a hand to his brow, then went still when he took her wrist.

"Yes, to both questions. You could say you're the cause and the cure." He brought her hand from his brow to his lips. "I may be homeroom mother, but I'm still a man, Ana. I can't stop thinking about you." He turned her hand over, pressing those lips to the inside of her wrist, where the pulse was beginning to jerk. "And I can't stop wanting you."

"I'm sorry if I'm giving you restless nights."

His brow quirked. "Are you?"

She couldn't quite suppress the smile. "I'm trying to be. It's hard not to be flattered that thinking about me is keeping you awake. And it's hard to know what to do.'' She turned away to switch off the heat on the stove. ''I've been feeling a little restless myself.'' Her eyes closed when his hands came down on her shoulders.

''Make love with me.'' He brushed a kiss on the back of her neck. ''I won't hurt you, Ana.''

Not purposely, she thought. Never that. There was so much kindness in him. But would they hurt each other if she gave in to what she wanted, needed from him, and held back that part of herself that made her what she was?

''It's a big step for me, Boone.''

''For me, too.'' Gently he turned her to face him. ''There's been no one for me since Alice died. In the past couple of years there was a woman or two, but nothing that meant any more than filling a physical emptiness. No one I've wanted to spend time with, to be with, to talk to. I care about you.'' He lowered his mouth to hers, very carefully, very softly. ''I don't know how I came to care this much, this quickly, but I do. I hope you believe that.''

Even without a true link, she couldn't help but feel it. It made things more complicated somehow. ''I do believe you.''

''I've been thinking. Seeing as I haven't been sleeping, I've had plenty of time for it.'' Absently he tapped a loosened pin back into her hair. ''The other night, I was rushing you, probably scared you.''

''No.'' Then she shrugged and turned back to filter one of her mixtures into a bottle, already labeled. ''Yes, actually, I guess you did.''

''If I'd known you were... If I'd realized you'd never...''

With a sigh, she capped the bottle. ''My virginity is by choice, Boone, and nothing I'm uncomfortable with.''

''I didn't mean—'' He let out a hissing breath. ''I'm doing a great job with this.''

She chose another funnel, another bottle, and poured. ''You're nervous.''

With some chagrin, he noted that her hands were rock-steady when she capped the next bottle. ''I think terrified comes closer. I was rough with you, and I shouldn't have been. For a lot of reasons. The fact that you're inexperienced is only one of them.''

"You weren't rough." She continued to work to hide her nerves, which were jumping every bit as much as his. As long as she had to concentrate on what she was doing, she could at least pretend to be calm and confident. "You're a passionate man. That's not something to apologize for."

"I'm apologizing for pressuring you. And for coming over here today fully intending to keep things light and easy, and then pressuring you again."

Her lips curved as she walked to the sink to soak her pans. "Is that what you're doing?"

"I told myself I wasn't going to ask you to go to bed with me—even though I want you to. I was going to ask if you'd spend some time with me. Come to dinner, or go out, or whatever people do when they're trying to get to know each other."

"I'd like to come to dinner, or go out, or whatever."

"Good." That hadn't been so hard, he decided. "Maybe this weekend. Friday night. I should be able to find a sitter." His eyes clouded. "Somebody I can trust."

"I thought you were going to cook for me and Jessie."

A weight lifted. "You wouldn't mind?"

"I think I'd enjoy it."

"Okay, then." He framed her face in his hands. "Okay." The kiss was very sweet, and if it felt as if something inside were going to rip in two, he told himself, he could deal with it. "Friday."

It wasn't difficult to smile, even if her system felt as if it had been rocked by a small earthquake. "I'll bring the wine."

"Good." He wanted to kiss her again, but he was afraid he'd scare her off. "I'll see you then."

"Boone." She stopped him before he'd reached the door. "Don't you want your sugar?"

He grinned. "I lied."

Her eyes narrowed. "You're not homeroom mother, and you're not baking cookies?"

"No, that was true. But I have five pounds in the pantry. Hey, it worked." He was whistling as he walked out the door.

Chapter 6

"Why isn't Ana here yet? When is she coming?"

"Soon," Boone answered for the tenth time. Too soon, he was afraid. He was behind in everything. The kitchen was a disaster. He'd used too many pans. Then again, he always did. He could never figure out how anyone cooked without using every pot, pan and bowl available.

The chicken cacciatore smelled pretty good, but he was uncertain of the results. Stupid, he supposed, absolutely stupid to try out a new recipe at such a time, but he'd figured Ana was worth more than their usual Friday-night meatloaf.

Jessie was driving him crazy, which was a rarity. She was overexcited at the thought of having Ana over, and she'd been pestering him without pause ever since he'd brought her home from school.

The dog had chosen that afternoon to chew up Boone's bed pillows, so he'd spent a great deal of valuable time chasing dog and feathers. The washing machine had overflowed, flooding the laundry room. He was much too male to consider calling a repairman, so he'd torn the machine apart and put it back together again.

He was pretty sure he'd fixed it.

His agent had called to tell him that *A Third Wish for Miranda* had been optioned for an animated feature by one of the major studios. That would have been good news at any other time, but now he was expected to fit a trip to L.A. into his schedule.

Jessie had decided she wanted to be a Brownie and had generously volunteered him as a Brownie leader.

The thought of having a group of six-and seven-year-old girls looking to him to teach them how to make jewelry boxes out of egg cartons chilled his blood.

With a lot of ingenuity and plenty of cowardice, he thought, he might be able to ease his way out of it.

"Are you sure she's coming, Daddy? Are you sure?"

"Jessica." The warning note in his voice was enough to make her lower lip poke out. "Do you know what happens to little girls who keep asking the same question?"

"Nuh-uh."

"Keep it up and you'll find out. Go make sure Daisy's not eating the furniture."

"Are you awfully mad at Daisy?"

"Yes. Now go on or you're next." He softened the order with a gentle pat on her bottom. "Beat it, brat, or I'll put you in the pot and have you for dinner."

Two minutes later, he heard the mayhem that meant Jessie had located Daisy, and girl and dog were now wrestling. The high-pitched yelps and happy squeals played hell with the headache pulsing behind his eyes.

Just need an aspirin, he thought, an hour or two of quiet, and a vacation on Maui.

He was on the point of giving a roar that would probably pop his head off his shoulders when Ana knocked.

"Hi. Smells good."

He hoped it did. She looked much better than good. He hadn't seen her in a dress before, and the swirl of watercolor silk did wonderful things for her slim body. Things like showing off those soft white shoulders under thin straps. With it she wore an amulet on a long chain that had the square of engraved gold hanging just below her breasts. Crystals glinted in it, drawing the eye, and were echoed by the tear-shaped drops at her ears.

She smiled. "You did say Friday."

"Yeah. Friday."

"Then are you going to ask me in?"

"Sorry." Lord, he felt like a bumbling teenager. No, he decided as he slid the screen open for her, no teenager had ever been this bumbling. "I'm a little distracted."

Ana's brows lifted as she surveyed the chaos of pots and bowls. "So I see. Would you like some help?"

"I think I've got it under control." He took the bottle she offered, noting that the pale green bottle was etched with symbols and that it carried no label. "Homemade?"

"Yes, my father makes it. He has…" Her eyes lit with secrets and humor. "…A magic touch."

"Brewed in the dungeons of Castle Donovan."

"As a matter of fact, yes." She left it at that, and wandered to the stove as he took out some glasses. "No Bugs Bunny this time?"

"I'm afraid Bugs met a fatal accident in the dishwasher." He poured the clear golden wine into the crystal glasses. "It wasn't pretty."

She laughed and lifted her glass in a toast. "To neighbors."

"To neighbors," he agreed, clinking crystal against crystal. "If they all looked like you, I'd be a dead man." He sipped, then lifted a brow. "Next time we'll have to drink to your father. This is incredible."

"One of his many hobbies, you might say."

"What's in it?"

"Apples, honeysuckle, starlight. You can give him your compliments, if you like. He and the rest of my family should be here for All Hallows' Eve. Halloween."

"I know what it is. Jessie's torn between being a fairy princess or a rock star. Your parents travel all the way to the States for Halloween?"

"Usually. It's a kind of family tradition." Unable to resist, she took the lid off the pan and sniffed. "Well, well, I'm impressed."

"That was the idea." Equally unable to resist, he lifted a handful of her hair. "You know that story I told you the day Daisy knocked you down? I find myself compelled to write it. So much so that I've put what I was working on aside."

"It was a lovely story."

"Normally I could have made it wait. But I need to know

why the woman was bound inside the castle all those years. Was it a spell, one of her own making? What was the enchantment that made the man climb the wall to find her?''

"That's for you to decide."

"No, that's for me to find out."

"Boone..." She lifted a hand to his, then looked down quickly. "What have you done to yourself?"

"Just rapped my knuckles." He flexed his fingers and shrugged. "Fixing the washing machine."

"You should have come over and let me tend to this." She ran her fingers over the scraped skin, wishing she was in a position to heal it. "It's painful."

He started to deny it, then realized his mistake. "I always kiss Jessie's hurts to make them better."

"A kiss works wonders," she agreed, and obliged him by touching her lips to the wound. Briefly, very briefly, she risked a link to be certain there was no real pain and no chance of infection. She found that, while the knuckles were merely sore, he did have real pain from a tension headache working behind his eyes. That, at least, she could help him with.

With a smile, she brushed the hair from his brow. "You've been working too hard, getting the house in order, writing your story, worrying if you made the right decision to move Jessie."

"I didn't realize I was that transparent."

"It isn't so difficult to see." She laid her fingers on either side of his temples, massaging in small circles. "Now you've gone to all this trouble to cook me dinner."

"I wanted—"

"I know." She held steady as she felt the pain flash behind her own eyes. To distract him, she touched her lips to his as she absorbed the ache and let it slowly fade. "Thank you."

"You're very welcome," he murmured, and deepened the kiss.

Her hands slid away from his temples, lay weakly on his shoulders. It was much more difficult to absorb this ache—this ache that spread so insidiously through her. Pulsing, throbbing. Tempting.

Much too tempting.

"Boone." Wary, she slipped out of his arms. "We're rushing this."

"I told you I wouldn't. That's not going to stop me from kissing you whenever I get the chance." He picked up his wine, then hers, offering her glass to her again. "Nothing goes beyond that until you say so."

"I don't know whether to thank you for that or not. I know I should."

"No. There's no more need to thank me for that than there is to thank me for wanting you. It's just the way it is. Sometimes I think about Jessie growing up. It gives me some bad moments. And I know that if there was any man who pushed or pressured her into doing what she wasn't ready to do I'd just have to kill him." He sipped, and grinned. "And, of course, if she thinks she's going to be ready to do anything of the kind before she's, say, forty, I'll just lock her in her room until the feeling passes."

It made her laugh, and she realized as he stood there, with his back to the cluttered, splattered stove, a dishcloth hanging from the waist of his slacks, that she was very, very close to falling in love with him.

Once she had, she would be ready. And nothing would make the feeling pass.

"Spoken like a true paranoid father."

"Paranoia and fatherhood are synonymous. Take my word for it. Wait until Nash has those twins. He'll start thinking about health insurance and dental hygiene. A sneeze in the middle of the night will send him into a panic."

"Morgana will keep him level. A paranoid father only needs a sensible mother to..." Her words trailed off as she cursed herself. "I'm sorry."

"It's all right. It's easier when people don't feel they have to tiptoe around it. Alice has been gone for four years. Wounds heal, especially if you have good memories." There was a thud from the next room, and the sound of racing feet. "And a six-year-old who keeps you on your toes."

At that moment, Jessie ran in and threw herself at Ana.

"You came! I thought you'd never get here."

"Of course I came. I never turn down a dinner invitation from my favorite neighbors."

As Boone watched them, he realized his headache had vanished. Odd, he thought as he switched off the stove and prepared to serve dinner. He'd never gotten around to taking an aspirin.

It wasn't what he would call a quiet, romantic dinner. He had lit candles and clipped flowers in the garden he'd inherited when he'd bought the house. They had the meal in the dining alcove, with its wide, curved window, with music from the sea and birdsong. A perfect setting for romance.

But there were no murmured secrets or whispered promises. Instead, there was laughter and a child's bubbling voice. The talk was not about what the candlelight did to her skin, or how it deepened the pure gray of her eyes. It centered on first grade, on what Daisy had done that day and on the fairy tale still brewing in Boone's mind.

When dinner was over, and Ana had listened to Jessie's exploits at school, along with those of Jessie's new and very best friend, Lydia, she announced that she and the child were assuming kitchen duty.

"No, I'll take care of it later." He was very comfortable in the sunset-washed dining alcove, and he remembered too vividly the mess he'd left behind in the kitchen. "Dirty dishes don't go anywhere."

"You cooked." Ana was already rising to stack the dishes. "When my father cooks, my mother washes up. And vice versa. Donovan rules. Besides, the kitchen's a good place for girl talk, isn't it, Jessie?"

Jessie didn't have any idea, but she was instantly intrigued by the notion. "I can help. I hardly ever break any dishes."

"And men aren't allowed in the kitchen during girl talk." She leaned conspiratorially toward Jessie. "Because they just get in the way." She sent Boone an arch look. "I think you and Daisy could use a walk on the beach."

"I don't..." A walk on the beach. Alone. With no KP. "Really?"

"Really. Take your time. Jessie, when I was in town the other day, I saw the cutest dress. It was blue, just the color of your eyes, and had a big satin bow." Ana stopped, a pile of dishes in her hands, and stared at Boone. "Still here?"

"Just leaving."

As he walked out in the deepening twilight with Daisy romping around him, he could hear the light music of female laughter coming through his windows.

"Daddy said you were born in a castle," Jessie said as she helped Ana load the dishwasher.

"That's right. In Ireland."

"A for-real castle?"

"A real castle, near the sea. It has towers and turrets, secret passageways, and a drawbridge."

"Just like in Daddy's books."

"Very much like. It's a magic palace." Ana listened to the sound of water as she rinsed dishes and thought of the squabbles and laughing voices in that huge kitchen, with a fire going in the hearth and the good, yeasty smell of fresh bread perfuming the air. "My father and his brothers were born there, and his father, and his, and further back than I can say."

"If I were born in a castle, I would always live there." Jessie stood close to Ana while they worked, enjoying without knowing why, the scent of woman, and the lighter timbre of a female voice. "Why did you move away?"

"Oh, it's still home, but sometimes you have to move away, to make your own place. Your own magic."

"Like Daddy and me did."

"Yes." She closed the dishwasher and began to fill the sink with hot, soapy water for the pots and pans. "You like living here in Monterey?"

"I like it a lot. Nana said I might get homesick when the novelty wears off. What's novelty?"

"The newness." Not a very wise thing to suggest to an impressionable child, Ana mused. But she imagined Nana's nose was out of joint. "If you do get homesick, you should try to remember that the very best place to be is usually where you are."

"I like where Daddy is, even if he took me to Timbuktu."

"Excuse me?"

"Grandma Sawyer said he might as well have moved us to Timbuktu." Jessie accepted the clean pot Ana handed her and began to dry, an expression of deep concentration on her face. "Is that a real place?"

"Um-hmm. But it's also a kind of expression that means far away. Your grandparents are missing you, sunshine. That's all."

"I miss them, too, but I get to talk to them on the phone, and Daddy helped me type a letter on his computer. Do you think you could marry Daddy so Grandma Sawyer would get off his back?"

The pan Ana had been washing plopped into the suds and sent a small tidal wave over the lip of the sink. "I don't think so."

"I heard him telling Grandma Sawyer that she was on his back all the time to find a wife so he wouldn't be lonely and I wouldn't have to grow up without a mother. His voice had that mad sound in it he gets when I do something really wrong, or like when Daisy chewed up his pillow. And he said he'd be damned if he'd tie himself down just to keep the peace."

"I see." Ana pressed her lips hard together to keep the proper seriousness on her face. "I don't think he'd like you to repeat it, Jessie, especially in those words."

"Do you think Daddy's lonely?"

"No. No, I don't. I think he's very happy with you, and with Daisy. If he decided to get married one day, it would be because he found somebody all of you loved very much."

"I love you."

"Oh, sunshine." Soapy hands and all, Ana scooted down to give Jessie a hug and a kiss. "I love you, too."

"Do you love Daddy?"

I wish I knew. "It's different," she said. She knew she was navigating on boggy ground. "When you grow up, love means different things. But I'm very happy that you moved here and we can all be friends."

"Daddy never had a lady over to dinner before."

"Well, you've only been here a couple of weeks."

"I mean ever, at all. Not in Indiana, either. So I thought maybe it meant that you were going to get married and live with us here so Grandma Sawyer would get off his back and I wouldn't be a poor motherless child."

"No." Ana did her best to disguise a chuckle. "It meant that we like each other and wanted to have dinner." She checked the window to make certain Boone wasn't on his way back. "Does he always cook like this?"

"He always makes a really big mess, and sometimes he says those words—you know?"

"I know."

"He says them when he has to clean it up. And today he was in a really bad mood 'cause Daisy ate his pillow and there were feathers all over and the washing machine exploded and he maybe has to go on a business trip."

"That's a lot for one day." She bit her lip. Really, she didn't want to pump the child, but she was curious. "He's going to take a trip?"

"Maybe to the place where they make movies, 'cause they want to make one out of his book."

"That's wonderful."

"He has to think about it. That's what he says when he doesn't want to say yes but probably he's going to."

This time Ana didn't bother to smother the chuckle. "You certainly have his number."

By the time they'd finished the kitchen, Jessie was yawning. "Will you come up and see my room? I put everything away like Daddy said to when we have company."

"I'd love to see your room."

The packing boxes were gone, Ana noted as they moved from the kitchen into the high-ceilinged living room, with its open balcony and curving stairs. The furniture there looked comfortably lived-in, bold, bright colors in fabrics that appeared tough enough to stand up under the hands and feet of an active child.

It could have used some flowers at the window, she mused. Some scented candles in brass holders on the mantel. Perhaps a few big, plump pillows scattered here and there. Still, there were homey family touches in the framed photographs, the ticking grandfather clock. And clever, whimsical ones, like the brass dragon's-head andirons standing guard on the stone hearth, and the unicorn rocking horse in the corner.

And if there was a little dust on the banister, that only added to the charm.

"I got to pick out my own bed," Jessie was telling her. "And once everything settles down I can pick out wallpaper if I want to. That's where Daddy sleeps." She pointed to the right, and Ana had a glimpse of a big bed under a jade-colored quilt—sans pillows—a handsome old chest of drawers with a missing pull, and a few stray feathers.

"He has his own bathroom in there, too, with a big tub that has jets and a shower that's all glass and has water coming out of both sides. I get to use the one out here, and it has two sinks and this little thing that isn't a toilet but looks like one."

"A bidet?"

"I guess so. Daddy says it's fancy and mostly for ladies. This is my room."

It was a little girl's fantasy, one provided by a man who obviously understood that childhood was all too short and very precious. All pink and white, the canopy bed sat in the center, a focal point surrounded by shelves of dolls and books and bright toys, a snowy dresser with a curvy mirror, and a child-sized desk littered with colored paper and crayons.

On the walls were lovely framed illustrations from fairy tales. Cinderella rushing down the steps of a silvery castle, a single glass slipper left behind. Rapunzel, her golden hair spilling out of a high tower window while she looked longingly down at her prince. The sly, endearing elf from one of Boone's books, and—a complete surprise to Ana—one of her aunt's prized illustrations.

"This is from *The Golden Ball.*"

"The lady who wrote it sent it to Daddy for me when I was just little. Next to Daddy's I like her stories best."

"I had no idea," Ana murmured. As far as she'd known, her aunt had never parted with one of her drawings except to family.

"Daddy did the elf," Jessie pointed out. "All the rest my mother did."

"They're beautiful." Not just skillful, Ana thought, and perhaps not as clever as Boone's elf or as elegant as her aunt's drawing, but lovely, and as true to the spirit of a fairy tale as magic itself.

"She drew them just for me, when I was a baby. Nana said Daddy should put them away so they wouldn't make me sad. But they don't. I like to look at them."

"You're very lucky to have something so beautiful to remember her by."

Jessie rubbed her sleepy eyes and struggled to hold back a yawn. "I have dolls, too, but I don't play with them much. My grandmothers like to give them to me, but I like the stuffed walrus my daddy got me better. Do you like my room?"

"It's lovely, Jessie."

"I can see the water, and your yard, from the windows." She tucked back the billowing sheer curtains to show off her view. "And that's Daisy's bed, but she likes to sleep with me." Jessie pointed out the wicker dog bed, with its pink cushion.

"Maybe you'd like to lie down until Daisy comes back."

"Maybe." Jessie sent Ana a doubtful look. "But I'm not really tired. Do you know any stories?"

"I could probably think of one." She picked Jessie up to sit her on the bed. "What kind would you like?"

"A magic one."

"The very best kind." She thought for a moment, then smiled. "Ireland is an old country," she began, slipping an arm around the girl. "And it's filled with secret places, dark hills and green fields, water so blue it hurts the eyes to stare at it for long. There's been magic there for so many centuries, and it's still a safe place for faeries and elves and witches."

"Good witches or bad ones?"

"Both, but there's always been more good than bad, not only in witches, but in everything."

"Good witches are pretty," Jessie said, stroking a hand down Ana's arm. "That's how you know. Is this a story about a good witch?"

"It is indeed. A very good and very beautiful witch. And a very good and very handsome one, too."

"Men aren't witches," Jessie informed her, giggling. "They're wizards."

"Who's telling the story?" Ana kissed the top of Jessie's head. "Now, one day, not so many years ago, a beautiful young witch traveled with her two sisters to visit their old grandfather. He was a very powerful witch—wizard—but had grown cranky and bored in his old age. Not far from the manor where he lived was a castle. And there lived three brothers. They were triplets, and very powerful wizards, as well. For as long as anyone could remember, the old wizard and the family of the three brothers had carried on a feud. No one remembered the why of it any longer, but the feud ran on, as they tend to do. So the families spoke not a word to each other for an entire generation.''

Ana shifted Jessie to her lap, stroking the child's hair as she told the story. She was smiling to herself, unaware that she'd lapsed into her native brogue.

"But the young witch was headstrong, as well as beautiful. And her curiosity was great. And on a fine day in high summer, she slipped out of the manor house and walked through the fields and the meadows toward the castle of her grandfather's enemy. Along the way was a pond, and she paused there to dangle her bare feet in the water and study the castle in the distance. And while she sat, with her feet wet and her hair down around her shoulders, a frog plopped up on the bank and spoke to her.

"'Fair lady,' he said, 'why do you wander on my land?'

"Well, the young witch was not at all surprised to hear a frog speak. After all, she knew too much of magic, and she sensed a trick. 'Your land?' she said. 'Frogs have only the water, and the marsh. I walk where I choose.'

"'But your feet are in my water. So you must pay a forfeit.'

"So she laughed and told him that she owed a common frog nothing at all.

"Well, needless to say, the frog was puzzled by her attitude. After all, it wasn't every day he plopped down and spoke to a beautiful woman, and he had expected at least a shriek or some fearful respect. He was quite fond of playing tricks, and was sorely disappointed that this one wasn't working as he'd hoped. He explained that he was no ordinary frog, and if she didn't agree to pay the forfeit he would have to punish her. And what forfeit did he expect? His answer was a kiss, which was no more and no less than she had expected, for as I said, she was young, but not foolish.

"She said that she doubted very much if he would turn into a handsome prince if she did so, and that she would save her kisses.

"Now the frog was very frustrated, and he plied more magic, whistling up the wind, shaking the leaves in the trees, but she merely yawned at this. At the end of his tether, the frog jumped right into her lap and began to berate her. To teach him a lesson for his forwardness, she plucked him up and tossed him into the water. When he surfaced, he wasn't a frog at all, but a young man, quite wet and furious to have had his joke turned on him. After he swam to shore, they stood on the bank and shouted at each other, threatening spells and curses, sending lightning walking the sky, and shooting the air with thunder. Though she threatened him with the hounds of hell and worse, he said he would have his forfeit regardless, for it was his land, his water, and his right. So he kissed her soundly.

"And it took only that to turn the heat in her heart to warmth, and the fury in his breast to love. For even witches can fall under that most powerful of spells. There and then they pledged to each other, marrying within the month right there on the banks on the pond. And they were happy, then and after, with lives full of love. Still, every year, on a day in high summer, though she is no longer young, she goes to the pond, dangles her feet and waits for an indignant frog to join her."

Ana lifted the sleeping girl. She had told the end of the story only for herself—or so she thought. But as she drew back the cover, Boone's hand closed over hers.

"That was a pretty good story for an amateur. Must be the Irish."

"It's an old family one," she said, thinking how often she had heard how her mother and father had met.

He expertly unlaced his daughter's shoes. "Be careful. I might steal it from you."

As he tucked the covers around Jessie, Daisy took a running leap and landed on the foot of the bed. "Did you enjoy your walk?"

"After I stopped feeling guilty for leaving you with the dishes—which took about ninety seconds." He brushed Jessie's hair from her brow and bent to kiss her good-night. "One of the most enviable things about childhood is being able to drop off to sleep like that."

"Are you still having trouble?"

"I've got a lot on my mind." Taking Ana's hand, he drew

her out of the room, leaving the door open, as he always did. "A lot of it's you, but there are a few other things."

"Honest, but not flattering." She paused at the top of the stairs. "Seriously, Boone, I could give you something—" She flushed and chuckled when she saw the light come into his eyes. "A very mild, very safe herbal remedy."

"I'd rather have sex."

Shaking her head, she continued downstairs. "You don't take me seriously."

"On the contrary."

"I mean as an herbalist."

"I don't know anything about that sort of thing, but I don't discount it." He wasn't about to let her dose him, either. "Why'd you get into it?"

"It's always been an interest. There have been healers in my family for generations."

"Doctors?"

"Not exactly."

Boone picked up the wine and two glasses as they walked through the kitchen and out onto the deck. "You didn't want to be a doctor."

"I didn't feel qualified to go into medicine."

"Now that's a very odd thing for a modern, independent woman to say."

"One has nothing to do with the other." She accepted the glass he offered. "It's not possible to heal everyone. And I...have difficulty being around suffering. What I do is my way of satisfying my needs and protecting myself." It was the most she felt she could give him. "And I like working alone."

"I know the feeling. Both my parents thought I was crazy. The writing was okay, but they figured I'd write the great American novel, at the very least. Fairy tales were hard for them to swallow at first."

"They must be proud of you."

"In their way. They're nice people," he said slowly, realizing he'd never discussed them with anyone but Alice. "They've always loved me. God knows they dote on Jessie. But they have a hard time understanding that I might not want what they want.

A house in the suburbs, a decent golf game, and a spouse who's devoted to me.''

"None of those things are bad."

"No, and I had it once—except for the golf game. I'd rather not spend the rest of my life convincing them that I'm content with the way things are now." He twined a lock of her hair around his fingers. "Don't you get the same sort of business from yours? Anastasia, when are you going to settle down with some nice young man and raise a family?"

"No." She laughed into her wine. "Absolutely not." The very idea of her mother or father saying, even thinking, such a thing made her laugh again. "I suppose you could say my parents are...eccentric." Comfortable, she laid her head back and looked at the stars. "I think they'd both be appalled if I settled for nice. You didn't tell me you had one of Aunt Bryna's illustrations."

"When you made the family connection, you were ready to chew me up and spit me out. It didn't seem appropriate. Then, I guess, it slipped my mind."

"Obviously she thinks highly of you. She only gave one to Nash after the wedding, and he'd been coveting one for years."

"That so? I'll be sure to rub his nose in it the next time I see him." Tipping up her chin with a finger, he turned her face toward his. "It's been a long time since I sat on a porch and necked. I'm wondering if I still have the hang of it."

He brushed his lips over hers, once, twice, a third time, until hers trembled open in invitation. He took the glass from her fingers, set it aside with his as his mouth moved to accept what was offered.

Sweet, so sweet, the taste of her, warming him, soothing him, exciting him. Soft, so soft, the feel of her, tempting him, luring him, charming him. And quiet, so quiet, that quick, catching sigh that sent a streak of lightning zipping up his spine.

But he was no sweaty, fumbling boy groping in the dark. The volcano of needs simmering inside him could be controlled. If he couldn't give her the fullness of his passion, then he could give her the benefit of his experience.

While he filled himself with her, slowly, degree by painful

degree, he gave back a care and a tenderness that had her teetering helplessly on that final brink before love.

To be held like this, she thought dimly, with such compassion
mixed with the hunger. In all of her imaginings, she had never
reached for this. His tongue danced over hers, bringing her all
those dark and dusky male flavors. His hands stroked persua-
sively while the muscles in his arms went taut. When his mouth
left hers to cruise down her jaw and over her throat, she arched
back, willing, desperately willing, for him to show her more.

It was surrender he felt from her, as clearly as he felt the night
breeze against his skin. Knowing it would drive him nearer to
the brink, he gave in to the fevered need to touch.

She was small, gloriously soft. Her heart beat frantically under
his hand. He could almost taste it, taste that hot satin skin on
his lips, on his tongue, deep within his mouth. It was torture not
to sample it now, not to drag her dress down to her waist and
feast.

The feel of her hardened nipples pressed against the silk had
him groaning as he brought his mouth back to hers.

Her mouth was as avid, as desperate. Her hands moved over
him as urgently as his over her. She knew, as she gave herself
fully to this one moment, that there would be no turning back.
They would not love now. It couldn't be now, on the starlit deck,
beneath windows where a child might wake and look for her
father in the night.

But there was no turning back from being in love. Not for
her. She could not change that tidal wave of feeling any more
than she could change the blood that coursed through her veins.

And because of it there would come a time, very soon, when
she would give to him what she had given to no other.

Overwhelmed, she turned her head, burying her face in his
shoulder. "You have no idea what you do to me."

"Then tell me." He caught the lobe of her ear between his
teeth, making her shudder. "I want to hear you tell me."

"You make me ache. And yearn." And hope, she thought,
squeezing her eyes shut. "No one else has." With a long, shuddering sigh, she drew away. "That's what we're both afraid of."

"I can't deny that." His eyes were like cobalt in the dim light.
"And I can't deny that the idea of carrying you upstairs now,

taking you into my bed, is something I want as much as I want to go on breathing.''

The image had her heart thundering. "Do you believe in the inevitable, Boone?''

"I've had to."

She nodded. "So do I. I believe in destiny, the whims of fate, the tricks of what men used to call the gods. When I look at you, I see the inevitable.'' She rose, pressed a hand to his shoulder to prevent him from standing with her. "Can you accept that I have secrets I can't tell you, parts of myself I won't share?'' She saw both puzzlement and denial in his eyes, and shook her head before he could speak. "Don't answer now.... You need to think it through and be sure. Just as I do.''

She leaned down to kiss him, and linked quickly, firmly. She felt his jerk of surprise before she backed away. "Sleep well tonight,'' she said, knowing that he would now. And that she would not.

Chapter 7

The one gift Ana always gave herself on her birthday was a completely free day. She could be as lazy as she chose, or as industrious. She could get up at dawn and gorge on ice cream for breakfast, or she could laze in bed until noon watching old movies on television.

The single best plan for the one day of the year that belonged only to her was no plan at all.

She did rise early, indulging herself in a long bath scented with her favorite oils and a muslin bag filled with dried herbs chosen for their relaxing properties. To pamper herself, she mixed up a toning face pack of elder flowers, yogurt and kaolin powder, lounging in the tub with harp music and iced juice while it worked its magic.

With her face tingling and her hair silky from its chamomile shampoo, she slicked on her personalized body oil and slipped into a silk robe the color of moonbeams.

As she walked back into the bedroom, she considered crawling back into bed and dozing to complete the morning's indulgence. But in the center of the room, where there had been nothing but an antique prayer rug when she'd gone in to bathe, stood a large wooden chest.

On a quick cry of pleasure, she dashed over to run her hands over the old carved wood which had been polished to a mirror gleam. It smelled of beeswax and rosemary and felt like silk under her fingers.

It was old, ages old, for it was something she had admired even as a child living in Donovan Castle. A wizard's chest, it was reputed to have resided once in Camelot, commissioned for Merlin by the young Arthur.

With a laughing sigh, she sat back on her heels. They always managed to surprise her, Ana thought. Her parents, her aunts and uncles...so far away, but never out of her heart.

The combined power of six witches had sent the chest from Ireland, winking through the air, through time, through space, by means that were less, and more, than conventional.

Slowly she lifted the lid, and the scent of old visions, ancient spells, endless charms, rose out to her. The fragrance was dry, aromatic as crusted petals ground to dust, tangy with the smoke of the cold fire a sorcerer calls in the night.

She knelt, lifting her arms out, the silk sliding down to her elbows as she cupped her hands, palms facing.

Here was power, to be respected, accepted. The words she spoke were in the old tongue, the language of the Wise Ones. The wind she called whipped the curtains, sent her hair flying around her face. The air sang, a thousand harp strings crying in the breeze, then was silent.

Lowering her arms, Ana reached into the chest. A bloodstone amulet, the inner red of the stone bleeding through the deep green, had her sitting back on her heels once more. She knew it had belonged to her mother's family for generations, a healing stone of enormous worth and mighty power. Tears stung the backs of her eyes when she realized that it was being passed to her, as it was only every half century, to denote her as a healer of the highest order.

Her gift, she thought, running her fingers over a stone smoothed by other fingers in other times. Her legacy.

She gently set it back in the chest and reached for the next gift. She lifted out a globe of chalcedony, its almost transparent surface offering her a glimpse of the universe if she should choose to look. This from Sebastian's parents, she knew, for she felt them as she cupped the globe in her hands. Next was a sheepskin, inscribed with the writing of the old tongue. A faery story, she noted as she read and smiled. As old as time, as sweet as tomorrow. Aunt Bryna and Uncle Matthew, she thought as she laid it back inside.

Though the amulet had been from her mother, Ana knew there would always be something special from her father, as well. She found it, and she laughed as she took it out. A frog, as small as her thumbnail, intricately carved in jade.

"Looks just like you, Da," she said, and laughed again. Replacing it, she closed the chest, then rose. It would be afternoon in Ireland, she mused, and there were six people who would be expecting a call to see if she'd enjoyed her gifts.

As she started toward the phone, she heard the knock at her back door. Her heart gave one quick, unsteady leap, then settled calmly. Ireland would have to wait.

Boone held the gift behind his back. There was another package at home, one that he and Jessie had chosen together. But he'd wanted to give Ana this one himself. Alone.

He heard her coming and grinned, the greeting on the tip of his tongue. He was lucky he didn't swallow his tongue, as well as the words, when he saw her.

She was glowing, her hair a rain of pale gold down the back of a robe of silver. Her eyes seemed darker, deeper. How could they be as clear as lake water, he wondered, yet seem to hold a thousand secrets? The gloriously female scent that swirled around her nearly brought him to his knees.

When Quigley rushed against his legs in greeting, Boone jolted as if he'd been shot.

"Boone." With a quiet laugh bubbling in her throat, Ana put her hand on the screen. "Are you all right?"

"Yeah, yeah. I... Did I get you up?"

"No." As calm as he was rattled, she opened the door in invitation. "I've been up quite a while. I'm just being lazy." When he continued to stand on the porch, she tilted her head. "Don't you want to come in?"

"Sure." He stepped inside, but kept a careful distance.

He'd been as restrained as could be over the past couple of weeks, resisting the temptation to be alone with her too often, keeping the mood light when they were alone. He realized now that his control had been as much for his sake as for hers.

She was painful to resist, even when they were standing outside in the sunlight, discussing Jessie or gardening, his work or hers.

But this, standing with her, the house empty and silent around them, the mysterious perfume of a woman's art tormenting his senses, was almost too much to bear.

"Is something wrong?" she asked, but she was smiling, as if she knew.

"No, nothing... Ah, how are you?"

"I'm fine." Her smile widened, softened. "And you?"

"Great." He thought that if he were any more tense he'd turn to stone. "Fine."

"I was going to make some tea. I'm sorry I don't have any coffee, but perhaps you'd like to join me."

"Tea." He let out a quiet breath. "Terrific." He watched her walk to the stove, the cat winding around her legs like gray rope. She put the kettle on, then poured Quigley's breakfast into his bowl. Crouching down, she stroked the cat as he ate. The robe slipped back like water, exposing one creamy leg.

"How's the woodruff coming, and the hyssop?"

"Ah..."

She tossed her hair back as she looked up and smiled. "The herbs I gave you to transplant into your yard."

"Oh, those. They look great."

"I have some basil and some thyme potted in the greenhouse. You might want to take them along, leave them on a windowsill for a while. For cooking." She rose when the kettle began to sputter. "I think you'll find them better than store-bought."

"That'd be great." He was almost relaxed again, he thought. Hoped. It was soothing to watch her brew tea, heating the little china pot, spooning aromatic leaves out of a pale blue jar. He hadn't known a woman could be restful and seductive all at once. "Jessie's been watching those marigold seeds you gave her to plant like a hen watches an egg."

"Just don't let her overwater." Setting the tea to steep, she turned. "Well?"

He blinked. "Well?"

"Boone, are you going to show me what's behind your back or not?"

"Can't fool you, can I?" He held out a box wrapped in bright blue paper. "Happy birthday."

"How did you know it was my birthday?"

"Nash told me. Aren't you going to open it?"

"I certainly am." She tore the paper, revealing a box with the logo of Morgana's shop imprinted on the lid. "Excellent choice," she said. "You couldn't possibly go wrong buying me something from Wicca." She lifted the lid and, with a quiet sigh, drew out a delicate statue of a sorceress carved in amber.

Her head was thrown back and exquisite tendrils of the dark gold hair tumbled down her cloak. Slender arms were raised, bent at the elbows, palms cupped and facing—mirroring the age-old position Ana had assumed over the chest that morning. In one elegant hand she held a small gleaming pearl, in the other a slender silver wand.

"She's beautiful," Ana murmured. "Absolutely beautiful."

"I stopped by the shop last week, and Morgana had just gotten it in. It reminded me of you."

"Thank you." Still holding the statue, she lifted her free hand to his cheek. "You couldn't have found anything more perfect."

She leaned in, rising on her toes to touch her lips to his. She knew exactly what she was doing, just as she knew even as he returned the kiss that he was holding himself on a choke chain of control. Power, as fresh and cool as rainwater, washed into her.

This was what she had been waiting for, this was why she had spent the morning in that ancient female ritual of oils and creams and perfumes.

For him. For her. For their first time together.

There were knots of thorny vines ripping through his stomach, an anvil of need ringing frantically in his head. Though their lips were barely touching, her taste was drugging him, making ideas like restraint and control vague, unimportant concepts. He tried to draw back, but her arms wound silkily around him.

"Ana..."

"Shh." She soothed and excited as her mouth played softly over his. "Just kiss me."

How could he not, when her lips were parting so softly beneath his? He brought his hands to her face, framing it with tensed fingers while he fought a vicious internal war to keep the embrace from going too far.

When the phone rang, he let out a groan that was both frustration and relief. "I'd better go."

"No." She wanted to laugh, but only smiled as she drew out of his arms. Never had she sampled a power more delicious than this. "Please stay. Why don't you pour the tea while I answer that?"

Pour tea, he thought. He'd be lucky if he could lift the pot. System jumbled, he turned blindly to the stove as she took the receiver from the wall phone.

"Mama!" Now she did laugh, and Boone heard the pure joy of it. "Thank you. Thank all of you. Yes, I got it this morning. A wonderful surprise." She laughed again, listening. "Of course. Yes, I'm fine. I'm wonderful. I— Da." She chuckled when her father broke in on the line. "Yes, I know what the frog means. I love it. I love you, too. No, I much prefer it to a real one, thank you." She smiled at Boone when he offered her a cup of tea. "Aunt Bryna? It was a lovely story. Yes, I am. Morgana's very well, so are the twins. Not very much longer now. Yes, you'll be here in time."

Restless, Boone wandered the room, sipping the tea, which was surprisingly good. He wondered what the devil she'd put into it. What the devil she'd put into him. Just listening to her voice was making him ache.

He could handle it, he reminded himself. They'd have a very civilized cup of tea—while he kept his hands off her. Then he'd escape, bury himself in his work for the rest of the day to keep his mind off her, as well.

His story line was all but finished, and he was nearly ready to start on the illustrations. He already knew just what he wanted.

Ana.

With a brisk shake of his head, he gulped more tea. It sounded as if she were going to carry on a conversation with every relative she had. That was fine, that was dandy. It would give him time to calm himself down.

"Yes, I miss you, too. All of you. I'll see you in a couple of weeks. Blessed be."

She was a little teary-eyed when she hung up, but she smiled at Boone. "My family," she explained.

"I gathered."

"They sent me a chest of gifts this morning, and I hadn't gotten a chance to call and thank them."

"That's nice. Look, I really— This morning?" he said with a slight frown. "I didn't see any delivery truck."

"It came early." She looked away to set her cup down. "Special delivery, you could say. They're all looking forward to visiting at the end of the month."

"You'll be glad to see them."

"Always. They were here briefly over the summer, but with all the excitement about Sebastian and Mel getting engaged and married so quickly, there wasn't much time to just be together." She moved to the door to let Quigley out. "Would you like more tea?"

"No, thanks, really. I should go. Get to work." He was edging toward the door himself. "Happy birthday, Ana."

"Boone." She laid a hand on his arm, felt his muscles quiver. "Every year on my birthday I give myself a gift. It's very simple, really. One day to do whatever I choose. Whatever feels right to me." Hardly seeming to move at all, she pulled the door closed and stood between it and him. "I choose you. If you still want me."

Her words seemed to ring in his ears as he stared down at her. She appeared so calm, so utterly serene, she might have been discussing the weather. "You know I want you."

"Yes." She smiled. At that moment she was calm, the eye of the hurricane. "Yes, I do." When she took a step forward, he took one in retreat. Was this seduction? she wondered, keeping her eyes on his. "I see that when I look at you, feel it whenever you touch me. You've been very patient, very kind. You kept your word that nothing would happen between us until I decided it should."

"I'm trying." Unsteady, he took another step back. "It isn't easy."

"Nor for me." She stood where she was, the silver robe shimmering around her in the sunlight. "You've only to accept me, to accept that I'm willing to give you everything I can. Take that, and let it be enough."

"What are you asking me?"

"To be my first," she said simply. "To show me what love can be."

He dared to reach out and touch her hair. "Are you sure?"

"I'm very sure." Offering and asking, she held out both hands. "Will you take me to bed and be my lover?"

How could he answer? There were no words to translate what was churning inside him at that moment. So he wasted no words, only lifted her into his arms.

He carried her as if she were as delicate as the amber enchantress he'd given her. Indeed, he thought of her that way, and he felt a thud of panic at the thought that he wouldn't be careful enough, restrained enough. It was so easy to damage delicacy.

When he reached the base of the stairs and started to climb, his pulse was throbbing in anticipation and fear.

For her sake, he wished it could have been night, a candlelit night filled with soft music and silvery moonglow. Yet somehow it seemed right that he love her, this first time, in the morning, when the sun was growing stronger in a deep blue sky, and music came from the birds that flitted through her garden and the tinkling bells of the wind chimes she had at her windows.

"Where?" he asked her, and she gestured toward her bedroom door.

It smelled of her, a mix of female fragrances and perfumed powders—and something else, something he couldn't quite identify. Like smoke and flowers. The sun streamed gaily through billowing curtains and splashed the huge old bed with the towering carved headboard.

He skirted the trunk, charmed by the rainbow of colors refracted by colored crystals suspended from thin wire in front of each window. Rainbows instead of moonbeams, he thought as he laid her on the bed.

Foolish to be nervous now, she told herself, but her hands trembled lightly when she reached out to hold him against her. She wanted this. Wanted him. Still, the calm certainty she had felt only moments ago had vanished under a wave of nerves and needs.

He could see the need, the nervousness, in her eyes. Could she possible understand that they were a mirror of his? She was so fragile and lovely. Fresh and untouched. His for the taking. And he knew it was vital for them both that he take with tenderness.

"Anastasia." Smothering his own fears, he lifted her hand, pressed his lips to the palm. "I won't hurt you. I swear it."

"I know that." She linked her fingers with his, wishing she could be sure if it was fear of the moment a woman experiences only once in her life, or fear of the overwhelming depth of her love for him, that left her shaky and unsure. "Show me."

With rainbows dancing around them, he lowered his mouth to hers. A deep, drugging kiss that both soothed and enticed. Time spun out, drifted. Stopped. Still there was only his mouth against hers.

He touched her hair, his fingers combing through, tangling in the luxurious length of it. To please himself, he spread it over the pillow, where it lay like a pool of gold dust against soft Irish linen.

When his lips left hers, it was to take a slow, lazy journey of her face until he felt her nervous trembling fall away into pliancy. Even as she surrendered her fears to the light, sweet sensations he brought her, he kept the pace slow, so slow that it seemed they had forever just to kiss.

She heard him murmur to her, reassurances, lovely, lovely promises. The low hum of his voice had her mind floating, her lips curving in a quiet smile as they met his again.

She should have known it would be like this with him. Beautiful, achingly beautiful. He made her feel loved, cherished, safe. When he slipped the robe from her shoulders, she wasn't afraid, but welcomed the feel of his mouth on her flesh. Eager now, she tugged on his shirt, and he hesitated only a moment before helping her remove it.

A groan ripped out of him as his body shuddered. God, the feel of her hands on his bare back. He fought back a wave of greed and kept his own hands easy as he parted her robe.

Her skin was like cream. Unbearably soft and fragrant with

oils. It drew him like nectar, inviting him to taste. As he closed his mouth over her breast, the quiet, strangled sound she made deep in her throat echoed like thunder in his head.

Gently he used tongue and lips to take her to that next degree of pleasure, while his own passions licked at him, taunting him, demanding that he hurry, hurry, hurry.

Her eyes were so heavy, impossible to open. How could he know just where to touch, just where to taste, to make her heart shudder in her breast? Yet he did, and her breath sighed out between her lips as he showed her more.

Quiet whispers, a gentle caress. The scent of lavender and fairy roses thickening the air. Smooth sheets growing warm, skin dampening with passion. A rainbow of lights playing against her closed lids.

She floated there, lifted by the magic they made together, her breath quickening a little as he eased her higher, just higher.

Then there was heat, searing, torrid. It erupted inside her so quickly, so violently, that she cried out and struggled against him. "No. No, Boone, I—" Then a flash, a lightning spear of pleasure, that left her limp and dazed and trembling.

"Ana." He had to dig his fisted hands into the mattress to keep from plunging into her, driving them both where he knew the rewards were dark and desperately keen. "Sweet." He kissed her, swallowing her gasping breaths. "So sweet. Don't be afraid."

"No." Rocked to the core, she held him close. His heart was thundering against hers, his body taut as wire. "No. Show me. Show me more."

So he slipped the robe away, driving himself mad with the sight of her naked in a pool of sunlight. Her eyes were open now, dark and steady on his. Beneath the passion just awakened, he saw a trust that humbled him.

He showed her more.

Fears melted away. There was no room for them when her body was vibrating from dozens of more vivid sensations. When he took her to the peak again, she rode out the storm, glorying in the flash of heat, desperate for the next.

He held back, gaining his pleasure from hers, stunned by the way she responded to each touch, to each kiss. Her innocence was his, he knew. With the breath laboring in his lungs, the blood pounding in his head, he entered her, braced for her to stiffen and cry out. Knowing he would have to stop, no matter how his body craved completion, if she asked it of him.

But she didn't stiffen, only gasped out his name as her arms came around him. The brief flash of pain was instantly smothered by a pleasure greater, fuller, than she had ever dreamed possible.

His, she thought. She was his. And she moved against him with an instinct as old as time.

Deeper, he slipped deeper, filling her, rocking her toward that final crest. When she did cry out, her body shuddering, shuddering from the glory of it, he buried his face in her hair and let himself follow.

He watched the dance of light against the wall, listening to her heart calm and slow. She lay beneath him still, her arms around him, her hands stroking his hair.

He hadn't known it could be like this. That was foolish, he thought. He'd had women before. More, he'd loved before, as deeply as anyone could. Yet this union had been more than he'd ever expected or experienced.

He had no way to explain it to her, when he was far from understanding it himself.

After pressing a kiss to her shoulder, he lifted his head to look at her. Her eyes were closed, and her face was flushed and utterly relaxed. He wondered if she had any idea how much had changed, for both of them, that morning.

"Are you all right?"

She shook her head, alarming him. Instantly concerned, he braced on his arms to remove his weight from her. Her lashes fluttered up so that he could see the smoky eyes beneath them.

"I'm not all right." Her voice was low and throaty. "I'm wonderful. You're wonderful." The smile curved beautifully on her lips. "This is wonderful."

"You had me worried." He brushed the hair away from her cheek. "I don't think I've ever been quite so nervous." Her lips were waiting for his when he bent his head to kiss her. "You're not sorry?"

Her brow arched. "Do I look sorry?"

"No." Taking his time, he studied her face, tracing it with a fingertip. "You look kind of smug." And the fact that she did brought him a rush of deep satisfaction.

"I'm feeling very smug. And lazy." She stretched a little, so he shifted to let her head rest on his shoulder.

"Happy birthday."

She chuckled against his throat. "It was the most...unique present I've ever been given."

"The thing about it is, you can use it over and over again."

"Even better." She tipped her head back, and now her eyes were solemn. "You were very good to me, Boone. Very good for me."

"It wasn't what I'd call an act of altruism. I've wanted this since the first time I saw you."

"I know. It frightened me—and excited me, too." She smoothed her palm over his chest, wishing for a moment they could stay like this forever, cocooned together in the sunlight.

"This changes things."

Her hand stilled, tensed. "Only if you want it to."

"Then I want it to." He sat up, bringing her with him so that they were face-to-face. "I want you to be a part of my life. I want to be with you, as often as possible—and not just like this."

She felt the old, niggling fear trying to surface. Rejection. Rejection now would be devastating. "I am part of your life. I always will be now."

He saw something in her eyes, sensed it in the tension suddenly blooming in the room with them. "But?"

"No buts," she said quickly, and threw her arms around him. "No ands. No anything now. Just this." She kissed him, pouring everything she could into it, knowing she was cheating them both by holding back. Not knowing how to offer it and keep him with her. "I'm here when you want me, as long as you want me. I promise you."

Rushing her again, he berated himself as she clung to him. How could he expect her to be in love just because they had made love? He wasn't even sure what he was feeling himself. It had all happened too fast, and he was riding on the emotion of the moment. He reminded himself, as he held Ana, that he didn't have only his own needs to consider.

There was Jessie.

What happened with Ana would affect his daughter. So there could be no mistaking, no acting on impulse, and no real commitment until he was sure.

"We'll take it slow," he said, but felt a twinge of resentment when Ana immediately relaxed against him. "But if anyone else comes to your door bearing gifts or needing a cup of sugar—"

"I'll boot him out." She squeezed him hard. "There's no one but you." Turning her head, she pressed her lips to his throat. "You make me happy."

"I can make you happier."

She laughed, tilting her head back. "Really?"

"Not like that." Amused, and flattered, he nipped her lower lip. "Not quite yet, anyway. I was thinking more along the lines of going down and fixing you lunch while you lazed around in bed and waited for me. And then making love with you again. And again."

"Well..." It was tempting, but she recalled too well what one of his meals did to a kitchen. And she had too many jars and bottles around that he might use incorrectly. "Why don't we do it this way—you wait for me while I fix lunch?"

"It's your birthday."

"Exactly." She kissed him before she slid out of bed. "Which is why I get to do everything my own way. I won't be long."

It was a pretty stupid man who wouldn't take a deal like that, Boone decided as he leaned back with his arms crossed under his head. He listened to her running water in the adjoining bath, then settled down to imagine what it would be like to spend the afternoon in bed.

Ana belted her robe as she walked downstairs. Love, she thought, did marvelous things for the spirit. Better, far better, than any potion she could brew or conjure. Perhaps in time, perhaps with enough of that love, she could give him the rest.

Boone wasn't Robert, and she was ashamed to have compared them, even for a moment. But the risk was so great, and the day so marvelous.

Humming to herself, she busied herself in the kitchen. Sandwiches would be best, she decided. Not terribly elegant, but practical for eating in bed. Sandwiches, and some of her father's special wine. She all but floated to the refrigerator, which was crowded now with Jessie's artwork.

"Not even dressed yet," Morgana said through the back screen. "I suspected as much."

With a boneless turkey breast in her hand, Ana turned. Not only was Morgana at her kitchen door, but crowded around her was Nash, Sebastian and Mel, too.

"Oh." She felt the flush blooming even as she set the lunch meat aside. "I didn't hear you drive up."

"Obviously too self-involved, with your birthday and all," Sebastian commented.

They piled in, bringing hugs and kisses and pushing ribboned boxes into her hands. Nash was already opening a bottle of champagne. "Find some glasses, Mel. Let's get this party started." He winked at his wife as she collapsed in a chair. "Apple juice for you, babe."

"I'm too fat to argue." She adjusted her weight—or tried to. "So, did you hear from Ireland?"

"Yes, a chest this morning. It's gorgeous. Glasses in the next cupboard," she told Mel. "Gifts inside. I talked to them..." Right before she'd gone upstairs to make love with Boone. Another flush heated her cheeks. "I, ah, I really need to..." Mel shoved a glass into her hand with champagne brimming up to the lip.

"Have the first glass," Sebastian finished for her. He cocked his head to the side. "Anastasia, my love, you look quite radiant. Turning twenty-seven certainly appears to agree with you."

"Keep out of my head," she muttered, and took a sip to give herself a moment to figure out how to explain. "I can't thank you all enough for coming by this way. If you'd just excuse me a minute."

"No need to get dressed for us." Nash poured the rest of the glasses. "Sebastian's right. You look fabulous."

"Yes, but I really need to—"

"Ana, I have a better idea." The sound of Boone's voice from just down the hall had everyone lapsing into silence. "Why don't we—'' Shirtless, barefoot and rumpled, he walked into the room, then stopped dead.

"Whoops," Mel said, and grinned into her glass.

"Succinctly put." Her husband studied Boone through narrowed eyes. "Dropping by for a neighborly visit, are we?"

"Shut up, Sebastian." This from Morgana, who rested both hands on her tummy and smiled. "We seem to have interrupted."

"I think we would have if we'd been any earlier," Nash murmured into Mel's ear, and made her choke back a chuckle.

Ana aimed one withering glance at him before she turned to Boone. "My family's brought along a little party, and they're all quite amused at the idea that I might have a private life—" she looked over her shoulder meaningfully "—that doesn't concern them."

"She always was cranky when you got her out of bed," Sebastian said, resigned to accepting Boone. For now. "Mel, it appears we'll need another glass of champagne."

"Already got it covered." Smiling, she stepped forward and offered it to Boone. "If you can't beat 'em," she said under her breath, and he nodded.

"Well." He took a long sip and sighed. It was obvious that his plans for the rest of the day would have to be adjusted. "Anybody bring cake?"

With a delighted laugh, Morgana gestured toward a large bakery box. "Get Ana a knife, Nash, so she can cut the first piece. I think we'll dispense with candles. She appears to have gotten her wish already."

Chapter 8

Ana was much too accustomed to her family to be annoyed with or embarrassed by them for long. And she was simply too happy with Boone to hold a grudge. As the days passed, they moved slowly, cautiously, toward cementing their relationship.

If she had come to trust him with her heart, with her body, she had not yet come to trust him with her secrets.

Though his feelings for her had ripened, deepened into a love he had never expected to experience again, he was as wary as she of taking that final step that would join their lives.

At the center was a child neither would have harmed by putting their own needs first.

If they stole a few hours on bright afternoons or rainy mornings, it was theirs to steal. At night Ana would lie alone and wonder how long this magic interlude would last.

As Halloween approached, she and Boone were caught up in their own preparations. Now and again her nerves would jump out at the idea of her lover meeting the whole of her family on the holiday. Then she would laugh at herself for acting like a girl on the point of introducing a first date.

By noon on the thirty-first, she was already at Morgana's, helping her now greatly pregnant cousin with preparations for the Halloween feast.

"I could have made Nash do this." Morgana pressed a hand

against the ache in the small of her back before she sat down to
knead bread dough from a more comfortable position at the
kitchen table.

"You could make Nash do anything simply by asking." Ana
cubed lamb for the traditional Irish stew. "But he's having such
fun setting up his special effects."

"Just like a layman to think he can outdo the professionals."
She winced and moaned and had Ana's immediate attention.

"Honey?"

"No, no, it's not labor, though I damn well wish it was. I'm
just so bloody uncomfortable all the time now." Hearing the
petulance in her own voice, she winced again. "And I hate whin-
ers."

"You whine all you like. It's just you and me. Here." Always
prepared, Ana poured some liquid into a cup. "Drink it down."

"I already feel like I'm going to float away—like Cleopatra's
barge. By the goddess, I'm big enough." But she drank, fingering the crystal around her neck.

"And you already have a crew of two."

That did the trick of making her laugh. "Talk to me about
something else," she begged, and went back to her kneading.
"Anything to take my mind off the fact that I'm fat and
grumpy."

"You're not fat, and you're only a little grumpy." But Ana
cast her mind around for a distraction. "Did you know that Sebastian and Mel are working on another case together?"

"No, I didn't." And it served to pique her interest. "I'm
surprised. Mel's very territorial about her private investigation
business."

"Well, she's lowered the gate on this one. A runaway, only
twelve years old. The parents are frantic. When I talked to her
last night, she said they had a lead, and she was sorry she
couldn't take this afternoon off to give you a hand."

"When Mel's in the kitchen, it's more like giving me a foot."
There was affection for her new in-law in every syllable. "She's
wonderful with Sebastian, isn't she?"

"Yes." Smiling to herself, Ana layered the lamb with potatoes and onions in Morgana's big Dutch oven. "Tough-minded, hardheaded, softhearted. She's exactly what he needs."

"And have you found what you need?"

Saying nothing at first, Ana added herbs. She'd known Morgana would work her way around to it before the day was over. "I'm very happy."

"I like him. I had a good feeling about him from the first."

"I'm glad."

"So does Sebastian—though he has some reservations." Her brows knit, but she kept her voice light. "Particularly after he cornered Boone and picked through his brain."

Ana's lips thinned as she adjusted the heat on the stove. "I haven't forgiven him for that yet."

"Well." Morgana shrugged and set the dough in a bowl to rise. "Boone didn't know, and it soothed Sebastian's feathers. He wasn't exactly pleased to have walked in on your birthday and found you fresh out of bed."

"It's certainly none of his business."

"He loves you." She gave Ana's arm a quick squeeze as she passed the stove. "He'll always worry about you more because you're the youngest—and simply because your gift makes you so vulnerable."

"I'm not without my defenses, Morgana, or common sense."

"I know. Darling, I…" She felt her eyes fill and brushed hastily at the tears. "It was your first time. I didn't want to probe before, but… Lord, I never used to be so sentimental."

"You were just able to hide it better." Abandoning her cooking for the moment, Ana crossed over to take Morgana into her arms. "It was beautiful, and he's so gentle. I knew there was a reason I had to wait, and he was it." She drew back, smiling. "Boone's given me more than I ever imagined I could have."

With a sigh, Morgana lifted her hands to Ana's face. "You're in love with him."

"Yes. Very much in love with him."

"And he with you?"

Her gaze faltered. "I don't know."

"Oh, Ana."

"I won't link with him that way." Her eyes leveled again, her voice firmed. "It would be dishonest when I haven't told him what I am, and haven't the courage to tell him how I feel myself. I know he cares for me. I need no gift to know he cares for me. And that's enough. When there's more, if there's more, he'll tell me."

"It never fails to surprise me how damn stubborn you are."

"I'm a Donovan," Ana countered. "And this is important."

"I agree. You should tell him." She gripped Ana's arms before her cousin could turn away. "Oh, I know. I despise it when someone gives me advice I don't want to hear. But you have to let go of the past and face the future."

"I am facing the future. I'd like Boone to be in it. I need more time." Her voice broke, and she pressed her lips together until she felt she could steady it. "Morgana, I know him. He's a good man. He has compassion and imagination and a capacity for generosity he isn't even aware of. He also has a child."

When Ana turned away this time, Morgana was forced to brace herself on the table. "Is that what you're afraid of? Taking on someone else's child?"

"Oh, no. I love her. Who wouldn't? Even before I loved Boone, I loved Jessie. And she's the center of his world, as it should be. There's nothing, absolutely nothing, I wouldn't do for either of them."

"Then explain."

Stalling, Ana rinsed the hard-cooked eggs she was going to devil. "Do you have any fresh dill? You know how Uncle Douglas loves his deviled eggs with dill."

On a hiss of breath, Morgana slapped a jar on the counter. "Anastasia, explain."

Emotions humming, Ana jerked off the tap. "Oh, you don't know how fortunate you are with Nash. To have someone love you that way no matter what."

"Of course I know," Morgana said softly. "What does Nash have to do with this?"

"How many other men would accept one of us so completely?

How many would want marriage, or take a witch as a mother for his child?''

"In the name of Finn, Anastasia." The impatience in her voice was spoiled a bit by the fact that she was forced to sit again. "You talk as if we're broomstick-riding crones, cackling while we curdle the milk in a mother's breast."

She didn't smile. "Don't most think of us just that way? Robert—"

"A pox on Robert."

"All right, forget him," Ana agreed with a wave of her hand. "How many times through the centuries have we been hunted and persecuted, feared and ostracized, simply for being what we were born to be? I'm not ashamed of my blood. I don't regret my gift or my heritage. But I couldn't bear it if I told him, and he looked at me as if—" she gave a half laugh "—as if I had a smoking cauldron in the basement filled with toads and wolfsbane."

"If he loves you—"

"If," Ana repeated. "We'll see. Now I think you should lie down for an hour."

"You're just changing the subject," Morgana began, then looked up as Nash burst in. There were cobwebs in his hair—simulated, fortunately—and an unholy gleam in his eyes.

"You guys have got to see this. It's incredible. I'm so good, I scare myself." He snatched a celery stalk from the counter and chomped. "Come on, don't just stand there."

"Amateurs," Morgana sighed, and hauled herself to her feet.

The two women were admiring Nash's hologram ghosts in the foyer when Ana heard a car drive up.

"They're here." Filled with delight at the prospect of seeing her family, she took one bounding leap toward the door. Then stopped dead. She was already whirling around when Morgana sagged against Nash.

Instantly he went as pale as his ghosts. "Babe? Are you—? Oh, boy."

"It's all right." She let out a long breath as Ana took her other arm. "Just a twinge, really." Leaning back against Nash, she smiled at Ana. "I guess having twins on Halloween is pretty appropriate."

"Absolutely nothing to worry about." Douglas Donovan was reassuring Nash. Like his son, he was a tall man, and his mane of raven hair was only lightly silvered. He'd chosen black tie and tails for the occasion, and had set them off with orange neon sneakers that pleased him enormously by glowing in the dark. "Childbirth. Most natural thing in the world. Perfect night for it, too."

"Right." Nash swallowed the lump in his throat. His house was full of people—witches, if you wanted to get technical— and his wife was sitting on the sofa, looking as if she weren't the least bit concerned that she'd been in labor for over three hours. "Maybe it was a false alarm."

Camilla wafted by in a sequined ball gown and tapped Nash on the shoulder with her feather fan. "Leave it to Ana, dear child. She'll take care of everything. Why, when I had Sebastian, I was in labor for thirteen hours. We joked about that, didn't we, Douglas?"

"After you'd stopped shouting curses at me, dear heart."

"Well, naturally." She wandered toward the kitchen, thinking she'd check on the stew. Ana never used quite enough sage.

"Would have turned me into a hedgehog if she hadn't been otherwise occupied," Douglas confided.

"That makes me feel better," Nash muttered. "Heaps."

Delighted to have helped, Douglas slapped him heartily on the back. "That's what we're here for, Dash."

"Nash."

Douglas smiled benignly. "Yes, indeed."

"Mama." Morgana gave her mother's hand a squeeze. "Go rescue poor Nash from Uncle Douglas. He's looking a little queasy."

Bryna obligingly set aside her sketchpad. "Shall I have your father take him out for a walk?"

"Wonderful." She gave a sigh of gratitude as Ana continued

to rub her shoulders. "There isn't anything for him to do quite yet."

Ana's father, Padrick, plopped down the moment Bryna vacated the seat. "How's the girl?"

"I'm really fine. It's all very mild as yet, but I'm sure it'll get rolling before too much longer." She leaned over to kiss his plump cheek. "I'm glad you're all here."

"Wouldn't be anywhere else." He put a pudgy hand on her belly to soothe and gave his daughter one of his elvish grins. "And my own little darling. You're pretty as a picture. Take right after your da, don't you?"

"Naturally." Ana felt the next contraction start and kept her hands steady on Morgana's shoulders. "Long, relaxed breaths, love."

"Will you want to give her some blue cohosh?" he asked his daughter.

Ana considered, then shook her head. "Not yet. She's doing well enough. But you could get me my pouch. I'll want some crystals."

"Done." He rose, then flipped his hand over. In the palm was a sprig of bell heather in full flower. "Now where did this come from?" he said, in the way he had since the laboring woman had been a babe herself. "Take care of this for me. I've business to tend to."

Morgana brushed the heather against her cheek. "He's the dearest man in the world."

"He'll spoil these two if you let him. Da's a pushover for children." With the empathic link, she knew Morgana was in more discomfort than she was letting on. "I'll have to take you upstairs soon, Morgana."

"Not yet, though." She reached over her shoulder for Ana's hand. "It's so nice being here with everyone. Where's Aunt Maureen?"

"Mama's in the kitchen, probably arguing with Aunt Camilla over the stew by now."

On a little groan, Morgana shut her eyes. "Lord, I could eat a gallon of it."

"After," Ana promised, and looked up as the rattle of chains and the moans of the suffering filled the room. "Somebody at the door."

"Poor Nash. He can't relax long enough to appreciate his own handiwork. Is it Sebastian?"

Ana craned her neck. "Uh-huh. He and Mel are critiquing the holograms. Whoops, there goes the smoke machine and the bats."

Sebastian strode in. "Amateurs."

"And Lydia was so scared she screamed and screamed," Jessie said, relating the chills and thrills of the elementary school's haunted house. "Then Frankie ate so much candy he threw up."

"Sounds like a red-letter day." To forestall exactly the same eventuality, he'd already hidden away half of the treats Jessie'd collected in her goodie bag.

"I like my costume best of all." As they got out of the car in front of Morgana's, Jessie twirled so that the starry pink material floated around her. Rather pleased with himself, Boone crouched to adjust her wings of aluminum foil. It had taken him the better part of two days to figure out how to tack and baste and tie the fairy costume together. But it was worth it.

She tapped her father's shoulder with her cardboard wand. "Now you're the handsome prince."

"What was I before?"

"The ugly toad." She squealed with laughter as he tweaked her nose. "Do you think Ana's going to be surprised? Will she recognize me?"

"Not a chance. I'm not sure I recognize you myself." They'd opted to dispense with a mask, and Boone had painted her cheeks with rouge, reddened her lips, and smudged her eyelids up to her eyebrows with glittery gold shadow.

"We're going to meet her whole family," she reminded her father—as if he needed reminding. He'd been worrying about the event all week. "And I get to see Morgana's cat and dog again."

"Right." He tried not to be overly concerned about the dog.

Pan might look like a wolf—disconcertingly so—but he'd been gentle and friendly with Jessie the last time they'd visited.

"This is going to be the best Halloween party in the whole world." Rising to her tiptoes, she pushed the doorbell. Her mouth fell open in a soundless gasp when the moans and clanking chains filled the air.

A husky man with thinning hair and jolly eyes opened the door. He took one look at Jessie and spoke in his best ghoul's voice. "Welcome to the haunted castle. Enter at your own risk."

Her eyes were big blue saucers. "Is it really haunted?"

"Come in...if you dare." He squatted down until he was at eye level with her, then pulled a fluffy stuffed bunny from up his sleeve.

"Ooh..." Charmed, Jessie pressed it against her cheek. "Are you a magician?"

"Certainly. Isn't everyone?"

"Uh-uh. I'm a fairy princess."

"That's good enough. And is this your escort for the evening?" he asked, glancing up at Boone.

"No." Jessie laughed gaily. "He's my daddy. I'm really Jessie."

"I'm really Padrick."

He straightened, and though his eyes remained merry, Boone was sure he was being measured. "And you'd be?"

"Sawyer." He offered a hand. "Boone Sawyer. We're Anastasia's neighbors."

"Neighbors, you say? Well, I doubt that's all. But come in, come in." He exchanged Boone's hand for Jessie's. "See what we have in store for you."

"Ghosts!" She nearly bounced out of her Mary Janes. "Daddy, ghosts!"

"Not a bad attempt for a layman," Padrick said kindly enough. "Oh, by the way, Ana's just taken Nash and Morgana upstairs. We've having twins tonight. Maureen, my passion flower, come meet Ana's neighbors." He turned to Boone as a striking amazon in a scarlet turban came striding down the hall.

"I imagine you'd like a drink, boyo," Padrick said to Boone.

"Yes, sir." Boone blew out a long breath. "I believe I would."

Hesitant and uneasy, Mel knocked on the door of Morgana's bedroom, then poked her head in. She wasn't sure whether she'd expected the clinical—and, to her mind, frightening—aura of a delivery room or the mystical glow of a magic circle. Either one she could have done without.

Instead, there was Morgana propped up in a big, cozy-looking bed, flowers and candles all around. Harp and flute music was drifting through the room. Morgana looked a bit flushed, Nash more than a bit pale, but the basic normality of it all reassured Mel enough to have her crossing the threshold when Ana gestured to her.

"Come on in, Mel. You should be an expert at this now. After all, you helped Sebastian and me deliver the foal just a few months ago."

"I feel like a horse," Morgana muttered, "but that doesn't mean I appreciate the comparison."

"I don't want to interrupt, or get in the way or— Oh, boy," she whispered when Morgana threw her head back and began to puff like a steam engine.

"Okay, okay." Nash gripped her hand and fumbled with a stopwatch. "Here comes another one. We're doing fine, just fine."

"We, hell," Morgana said between her teeth. "I'd like to see you—"

"Breathe." Ana's voice was gentle as she placed crystals over Morgana's belly. They hovered in the air, gleaming with an unearthly light that Mel tried to take in stride.

After all, she reminded herself, she'd been married to a witch for two months.

"It's all right, babe." Nash pressed his lips to her hand, wishing desperately for the pain to pass. "It's almost over."

"Don't go." She gripped his hand hard as the contraction began to ease. "Don't go."

"I'm right here. You're wonderful." As Ana had instructed

him, he cooled Morgana's face with a damp cloth. "I love you, gorgeous."

"You'd better." She managed a smile and let out a long, cleansing breath. Knowing she had a ways to go, she closed her eyes. "How am I doing, Ana?"

"Great. A couple more hours."

"A couple—" Nash bit off the words and fixed on a smile that was sick around the edges. "Terrific."

Mel cleared her throat, and Ana glanced over. "I'm sorry. We got a little distracted."

"No problem. I just thought you'd want to know Boone's here—with Jessie."

"Oh." Ana mopped her own brow with her shirtsleeve. "I'd forgotten. I'll be right down. Would you send Aunt Bryna up?"

"Sure. Hey, Morgana, we're all with you."

Morgana's smile was just a tad wicked. "Great. Want to change places?"

"I'll pass this time, thanks." She was edging toward the door. "I'll just get out of your way."

"You're not going to be gone long." Struggling against panic, Nash rubbed the small of Morgana's back and looked pleadingly at Ana.

"Only a minute or two. And Aunt Bryna's very skilled. Besides, we need some brandy."

"Brandy? She's not supposed to drink."

"For you," Ana said gently as she slipped out of the room.

The first thing Ana noted when she reached the parlor was that Jessie was being very well entertained. Ana's mother was laughing her lusty, full-bodied laugh as Jessie recounted her class's escapades at the school Halloween party. Since Jessie was already cuddling two stuffed animals, Ana deduced that her father had already been up to his tricks.

She certainly hoped he'd been discreet.

"Things are well upstairs?" Bryna said quietly as they passed in the doorway.

"Perfect. You'll be a grandmother before midnight."

"Bless you, Anastasia." Bryna kissed her cheek. "And I do like your young man."

"He's not—" But her aunt was already hurrying upstairs.

And there was Boone standing by the fireplace, where the flames crackled cheerily, drinking what was surely one of her father's concoctions and listening, with an expression of fascinated bemusement, to one of her Uncle Douglas's stories.

"So, naturally, we took the poor soul in for the night. Storm being what it was. And what did he do but go screeching out in the morning, shouting about banshees and ghosts and the like. Touched," Douglas said sadly, tapping a finger to his head, where an orange silk hat now resided. "A sad and sorry tale."

"Perhaps it had something to do with you clanging about in that suit of armor," Matthew Donovan commented, warming a brandy in his long-fingered hands.

"No, no, a suit of armor doesn't resemble a banshee in the least. I imagine it was Maureen's cat screeching that did it."

"My cats do not screech," she said, insulted. "They're quite well behaved."

"I have a dog," Jessie piped up. "But I like cats, too."

"Is that so?" Always willing to oblige, Padrick plucked a yellow-striped stuffed kitten from between her fairy wings. "How about this one?"

"Oh!" Jessie buried her face in its fur, then delighted Padrick by climbing onto his lap and kissing his rosy cheek.

"Da." Ana leaned over the sofa to press her lips to his balding head. "You never change."

"Ana!" Jessie bounced on Padrick's lap and tried to hold up her entire menagerie at once. "Your daddy's the funniest person in the world!"

"I like him myself." She tilted her head curiously. "But who are you?"

"I'm Jessie." Giggling, she climbed down to turn in a circle. "No, really?"

"Honest. Daddy made me a fairy princess for Halloween."

"You certainly sound like Jessie." Ana crouched down. "Give me a kiss and let's see."

Jessie pressed her painted lips to Ana's, flushing with pleasure at her costume's success. "Didn't you know me? Really?"

"You fooled me completely. I was certain you were a real fairy princess."

"Your daddy said you were his fairy princess 'cause your mama was a queen."

Maureen let out another peal of laughter, and winked at her husband. "My little frog."

"I'm sorry I can't stay and talk," Ana told Jessie.

"I know. You're helping get Morgana's babies out. Do they come out together or one at a time?"

"One at a time, I hope." She laughed, tousling Jessie's hair, and looked over at Boone. "You know you're welcome to stay as long as you like. There's plenty of food."

"Don't worry about us. How's Morgana?"

"Very well. Actually, I came down to get some brandy for Nash. His nerves are about shot."

With an understanding nod, Matthew picked up a decanter and a snifter. "He has my sympathy." When he passed them to her, she felt a jolt of his power and knew that, however calm his exterior, his mind and his heart were upstairs with his daughter.

"Don't worry. I'll take care of her, Uncle Matthew."

"No one better. You are the best I've known, Anastasia." His eyes held hers as he flicked a finger over the bloodstone she wore around her neck. "And I've known many." Then a smile touched his lips. "Boone, perhaps you'd walk Anastasia back up."

"Be glad to." Boone took the decanter from Ana before they started out.

"Your family," Boone began, shaking his head at the foot of the stairs, unaware that she'd stiffened.

"Yes?"

"Incredible. Absolutely incredible. It isn't every day I find myself plopped into the center of a group of strangers, with a woman about to give birth to twins upstairs, a wolf—because I swear that dog is no dog—gnawing what looks like a mastodon bone under the kitchen table, and mechanical bats flying overhead. Oh, I forgot the ghosts in the foyer.''

"Well, it is Halloween."

"I don't think that has much to do with it." He stopped at the top of the stairs. "I can't remember ever being more entertained. They're fabulous, Ana. Your father does these magic tricks—terrific magic tricks. For the life of me I couldn't figure out how he pulled it off."

"No, you wouldn't. He's, ah...very accomplished."

"He could make a living at it. I've got to tell you, I wouldn't have missed this party for the world." He cupped his free hand around her neck. "The only thing missing is you."

"I was worried you'd feel awkward."

"No. Though it does kind of scotch my plans to lure you into some shadowy corner and make you shiver with some bloodcurdling story so you'd climb all over me for protection."

"I don't spook easily." Smiling, she twined her arms around him. "I grew up on bloodcurdling."

"And uncles clanging around in suits of armor," he murmured as he brushed his lips over hers.

"Oh, that's the least of it." She leaned against him, changing the angle of the kiss. "We used to play in the dungeons. And I spent an entire night in the haunted tower on one of Sebastian's dares."

"Courageous."

"No, stubborn. And stupid. I've never been more uncomfortable in my life." She was drifting into the kiss, losing herself. "At least until Morgana conjured up a blanket and pillow."

"Conjured?" he repeated, amused by the term.

"Sent up," she corrected, and poured herself into the embrace so that he would think of nothing but her.

When the door opened beside them, they looked around like guilty children. Bryna lifted her brows, summed up the situation and smiled.

"I'm sorry to interrupt, but I think Boone is just what we need right now."

He took a firmer grip on the brandy bottle. "In there?"

She laughed. "No. If you'd just stay there, and let me send Nash out for a moment or two. He could use a little man talk."

"Only for a minute," Ana cautioned. "Morgana needs him inside."

Before Boone could agree or refuse, she slipped away. Resigned, he poured a snifter, took a good swallow himself, then refilled it when Nash stepped out.

He pressed the snifter on Nash. "Have a shot."

"I didn't think it would take so long." After a long breath, he sipped the brandy. "Or that it would hurt her so much. If we get through this, I swear, I'm never going to touch her again."

"Yeah, right."

"I mean it." Despite the fact he knew it was an expectant-father cliché, he began to pace.

"Nash, I don't mean to interfere, but wouldn't you feel better—safer—if Morgana was in a hospital, with a doctor and all that handy medical business?"

"A hospital? No." Nash rubbed a hand over his face. "Morgana was born in that same bed. She wouldn't have it any other way with the twins. I guess I wouldn't, either."

"Well, a doctor, then."

"Ana's the best." Remembering that relaxed him slightly. "Believe me, Morgana couldn't be in better hands than hers."

"I know midwives are supposed to be excellent, and more natural, I imagine." He moved his shoulders. If Nash was content with the situation, it wasn't up to him to worry about it. "I guess she's done it before."

"No, this is Morgana's first time."

"I meant Ana," Boone said on a chuckle. "Delivering babies."

"Oh, yeah. Sure. She knows what she's doing. It's not that. In fact, I think I'd go crazy if she wasn't here. But—" He took another swallow, paced a little more. "I mean, this has been going on for hours. I don't know how she can stand it. I don't know why any woman stands it. Just seems to me she could do something about it. Damn it, she's a witch."

Manfully masking another chuckle, he gave Nash an encouraging pat on the back. "Nash, it's not a good time to call her names. Women get a little nasty when they're in labor. They're entitled."

"No, I mean—" He broke off, realizing he was going over the edge. "I've got to pull myself together."

"Yep."

"I know it's going to be all right. Ana wouldn't let anything happen. But it's so hard to watch her hurting."

"When you love someone, it's the hardest thing in the world. But you get through it. And, in this case, you're getting something fantastic out of it."

"I never thought I could feel this way, about anybody. She's everything."

"I know what you mean."

Feeling better, Nash passed the snifter back to Boone. "Is that how it is with Ana?"

"I think it might be. I know she's special."

"Yeah, she is." Nash hesitated, and when he spoke again he chose his words with care. Loyalty, split two ways, was the heaviest of burdens. "You'd be able to understand her, Boone, with your imagination, your way of looking beyond what's considered reality. She is a very special lady, with qualities that make her different from anyone you've ever known. If you love her, and you want her to be a part of your life and Jessie's, don't let those qualities block you."

Boone's brows drew together. "I don't think I'm following you."

"Just remember I said it. Thanks for the drink." He took a steadying breath, then went back in to his wife.

Chapter 9

"Breathe. Come on, baby, breathe!"

"I am breathing." Morgana grunted out the words between pants and couldn't quite manage to glare at Nash. "What the hell do you call this if it's not breathing?"

Nash figured he was past his own crisis point. She'd already called him every name in the book, and had invented several more. Ana said they were nearly there, and he was clinging to that as desperately as Morgana was clinging to his hand. So he merely smiled at his sweaty wife and mopped her brow with a cool cloth.

"Growling, spitting, snarling." He touched his lips to hers, relieved when she didn't bite him. "You're not going to turn me into a slug or a two-headed newt, are you?"

She laughed, groaned, and let out the last puff of air. "I can come up with something much more inventive. I need to sit up more. Ana?"

"Nash, get in the bed behind her. Support her back. It's going to go quickly now." Arching her own back, which echoed the aches in Morgana's, she checked one last time to see if all was ready. There were blankets warmed by the fire, heated water, the clamps and scissors already sterilized, the glow of crystals pulsing with power.

Bryna stood by her daughter's side, her eyes bright with understanding and concern. Images of her own hours in that same bed fighting to bring life into the world raced through her head. That same bed, she thought blinking at the mists in her eyes, where her child now labored through the last moments, the last pangs.

"No pushing until I tell you. Pant. Pant," Ana repeated as she felt the contraction build within herself—a sweet and terrible pang that brought fresh sweat to her skin. Morgana stiffened, fought off the need to tense, and struggled to do as she was told. "Good, good. Nearly there, darling, I promise. Have you picked out names?"

"I like Curly and Moe," Nash said, panting right along with Morgana until she managed to jab him weakly with an elbow. "Okay, okay, Ozzie and Harriet, but only if we have one of each."

"Don't make me laugh now, you idiot." But she did laugh, and the pain eased back. "I want to push. I have to push."

"If it's two girls," he continued, with an edge of desperation, "we're going with Lucy and Ethel." He pressed his cheek against hers.

"Two boys and it's Boris and Bela." Morgana's laughter took on a slightly hysterical note as she reached back to link her arms around Nash's neck. "God, Ana, I have to—"

"Bear down," Ana snapped out. "Go ahead, push."

Caught between laughter and tears, Morgana threw her head back and fought to bring life into the room. "Oh, God!" Outside, lightning shot across a cloudless sky and thunder cracked its celestial whip.

"Nice going, champ," Nash began, but then his mind seemed to go blank as glass. "Look! Oh, Lord, would you look at that!"

At the foot of the bed, Ana gently, competently turned the tiny, dark head. "Hold back now, honey. I know it's hard, but hold back just for a minute. Pant. That's it, that's the way. Next time's the charm."

"It's got hair," Nash said weakly. His face was as wet with sweat and tears as Morgana's. "Just look at that. What is it?"

"I haven't got that end out yet." Ana sent a glittering smile to her cousin. "Okay, this is for the grand prize. Bear down, honey, and let's see if we've got Ozzie or Harriet."

With laughter, Morgana delivered her child into Ana's waiting hands. As the first wild, indignant cry of life echoed in the room, Nash buried his face in his wife's tangled hair.

"Morgana. Sweet Lord, Morgana. Ours."

"Ours." The pain was already forgotten. Eyes glowing, Morgana held out her arms so that Ana could place the tiny, wriggling bundle into them. In the language of her blood, she murmured to the babe, as her hands moved gently to welcome.

"What is it?" With a trembling hand, Nash reached down to touch the tiny head. "I forgot to look."

"You have a son," Ana told him.

At the first lusty wail, conversation in the parlor downstairs cut off like a switch. All eyes shifted to the stairs. There was silence, stillness. Touched, Boone looked at his own child, who slept peacefully on the sofa, her head nestled in Padrick's comfortable lap.

He felt a tremor beneath his feet, saw the wine slosh back and forth in his glass. Before he could speak, Douglas was removing his top hat and slapping Matthew on the back.

"A new Donovan," he said, and snatched up a glass to lift in toast. "A new legacy."

A little teary-eyed, Camilla walked over to kiss her brother-in-law's cheek. "Blessed be."

Boone was about to add his congratulations when Sebastian crossed the room. He lighted a white candle, then a gold one. Taking up a bottle of unopened wine, he broke the seal, then poured pale gold liquid into an ornate silver chalice.

"A star dawns in the night. Life from life, blood through blood to shine its light. Through love he was given the gift of birth, and from breath to death will walk the earth. The other gift comes through blood and bone, and is for him to take and own. Charm of the moon, power of the sun. Never forgetting an it harm none."

Sebastian passed the cup to Matthew, who sipped first. Fascinated, Boone watched the Donovans pass the chalice of wine from one to the other. An Irish tradition? he wondered. It was certainly more moving, more charming, than passing out cigars.

When he was handed the cup, he was both honored and baffled. Even as he began to sip, another wail sounded, announcing another life.

"Two stars," Matthew said in a voice thickened with pride. "Two gifts."

Then the solemn mood was broken as Padrick conjured up a party streamer and a rain of confetti. As he blew a celebratory toot, his wife laughed bawdily.

"Happy New Year," she said gesturing toward the clock that had just begun to strike twelve. "It's the best All Hallows' Eve since Padrick made the pigs fly." She grinned at Boone. "He's such a prankster."

"Pigs," Boone began, but the group turned as one as Bryna entered the room. She moved directly to her husband, who folded her tightly within his arms.

"They're all well." She brushed at happy tears. "All well and beautiful. We have a grandson and a granddaughter, my love. And our daughter invites us all upstairs to welcome them."

Not wanting to intrude, Boone hung back as the group piled out of the room. Sebastian stopped in the doorway, arched a brow. "Aren't you coming?"

"I think the family..."

"You were accepted," Sebastian said shortly, not certain he agreed with the rest of the Donovans. He hadn't forgotten how deeply Ana had once been hurt.

"An odd way to phrase it." Boone kept his voice mild to counteract a sudden flare of temper. "Particularly since you feel differently."

"Regardless." Sebastian inclined his head in what Boone interpreted as both challenge and warning. But when Sebastian glanced toward the sofa, he softened. "I imagine Jessie would be disappointed if you didn't wake her and bring her up for a look."

"But you'd rather I didn't."

"Ana would rather you did," Sebastian countered. "And that's more to the point." He moved to the doorway again, then stopped. "You'll hurt her. Anastasia sheds no tears, but she'll shed them for you. Because I love her, I'll have to forgive you for that."

"I don't see—"

"No." Sebastian nodded curtly. "But I do. Bring the child, Sawyer, and join us. It's a night for kindness, and small miracles."

Uncertain why Sebastian's words angered him so much, Boone stared at the empty doorway. He damn well didn't have to prove himself to some overprotective, interfering cousin. When Jessie shifted and blinked owlishly, he pushed Sebastian out of his mind.

"Daddy?"

"Right here, frog face." He bent and lifted his child into his arms. "Guess what?"

She rubbed her eyes. "I'm sleepy."

"We'll go home soon, but I think there's something you'd like to see first." While she yawned and dropped her heavy head on his shoulder, he carried her upstairs.

They were all gathered around, making a great deal more noise than Boone imagined was the norm even for a home delivery room. Nash was sitting on the edge of the bed beside Morgana, holding a tiny bundle and grinning like a fool.

"He looks like me, don't you think?" he was asking of no one in particular. "The nose. He's got my nose."

"That's Allysia," Morgana informed him, rubbing a cheek over her son's downy head. "I've got Donovan."

"Right. Well, *she's* got my nose." He peeked over at his son. "He's got my chin."

"The Donovan chin," Douglas corrected. "Plain as a pikestaff."

"Hah." Maureen was jockeying for position. "They're both Corrigans through and through. Our side of the family has always had strong genes."

While they argued over that, Jessie shook off sleep and

stretched forward. "Is it the babies? Did they get born? Can I see?"

"Let the child in." Padrick elbowed his brother out of the way. "Let her have a look."

Jessie kept one arm hooked around her father's neck as she leaned forward. "Oh!" Her tired eyes went bright as Ana took a babe in each arm to hold them up for Jessie to see. "They look just like little faeries." Very delicately, she touched a fingertip to one cheek, then the other.

"That's just what they are." Padrick kissed Jessie's nose. "A brand new faerie prince and princess."

"But they don't have wings," Jessie said, giggling.

"Some faeries don't need wings." Padrick winked at his daughter. "Because they have wings on their hearts."

"These faeries need some rest and some quiet." Ana turned to tuck the babies into Morgana's waiting arms. "And so does their mama."

"I feel wonderful."

"Nevertheless..." Ana shot a warning look over her shoulder that had the Donovans reluctantly filing out.

"Boone," Morgana called out. "Would you wait for Ana, drive her home? She's exhausted."

"I'm perfectly fine. He should—"

"Of course I will." He settled the yawning Jessie on his shoulder. "We'll be downstairs whenever you're ready."

It took another fifteen minutes before Ana was assured that Nash had all her instructions. Morgana was already drifting off to sleep when Ana closed the door and left the new family alone.

She was exhausted, and the powers of the crystals in her pouch were nearly depleted. For almost twelve hours, she had gone through the labor of childbirth with her cousin, as closely linked as it was possible to be. Her body was heavy with fatigue, her mind drugged with it. It was a common result of a strong empathic link.

She staggered once at the top of the stairs, righted herself, then gripped her bloodstone amulet to draw on the last of its strength.

By the time she reached the parlor, she was feeling a little steadier. There was Boone, half dozing in a chair by the fire, with Jessie cuddled against his chest. His eyes opened. His lips curved.

"Hey, champ. I have to admit I thought this whole setup was a little loony, but you did a hell of a job up there."

"It's always stunning to bring life into the world. You didn't have to stay all this time."

"I wanted to." He kissed Jessie's head. "So did she. She'll be the hit of school on Monday with this story."

"It's been a long night for her, and one she won't forget." Ana rubbed her eyes, almost as Jessie had before falling asleep again. "Where is everyone?"

"In the kitchen, raiding the refrigerator and getting drunk. I decided to pass, since I already had more than my share of wine." He offered a sheepish grin. "A little while ago I could have sworn the house was shaking, so I switched to coffee." He gestured toward the cup on the table beside him.

"And now you'll be up half the night. I'll just run and tell them I'm going, if you'd like to go put Jessie in the car."

Outside, Boone took a deep gulp of the cool night air. Ana was right, he was wide awake. He'd have to work a couple of hours until the coffee wore off, and he'd more than likely pay for it tomorrow. But it had been worth it. He glanced over his shoulder to where the light glowed in Morgana's bedroom. It had been well worth it.

He slipped Jessie's wings over her shoulders, then laid her on the back seat.

"Beautiful night," Ana murmured from behind him. "I think every star must be out."

"Two new stars." Bemused, Boone opened the door for her. "That's what Matthew said. It was really lovely. Sebastian made a toast about life and gifts and stars, and they all passed around a cup of wine. Is that an Irish thing?"

"In a way." She leaned her head back against the seat as he started the car. Within seconds, she was asleep.

When Boone pulled up in his driveway, he wondered how he

was going to manage to carry both of them to bed. He shifted, easing his door open, but Ana was already blinking awake.

"Just let me carry her inside, and I'll give you a hand."

"No, I'm fine." Bleary-eyed, Ana stepped out of the car. "I'll help you with her." She laughed as she gathered up the store of stuffed animals. "Da always goes overboard. I hope you don't mind."

"Are you kidding? He was great with her. Come on, baby." He lifted her and, in the way of children, she remained utterly lax. "She was taken with your mother, too, and the rest, but your father was definitely the hero. I expect she'll be bugging me to go to Ireland now, so she can visit him in his castle."

"He'd love it." She took the silver wings and followed him into the house.

"Just set those anywhere. Do you want a brandy?"

"No, really." She dropped the animals on the couch, put the wings beside them, then rolled her aching shoulders. "I wouldn't mind some tea. I can brew some while you settle her in."

"Fine. I won't be long."

A low growling emerged from under Jessie's bed when Boone carried her in. "Great watchdog. It's just us, you blockhead."

Desperately relieved, Daisy bounded out, tail wagging. She waited until Boone had removed Jessie's shoes and costume, then leapt onto the bed to settle at Jessie's feet.

"You wake me up at six and I'll staple those doggie lips closed."

Daisy thumped her tail and shut her eyes.

"I don't know why we couldn't have gotten a smart dog while we were at it," Boone was saying as he walked into the kitchen. "It wouldn't have been..." and then his words trailed off.

The kettle was on and beginning to steam. Cups were set out, and the pot was waiting. Ana had her head pillowed on her arms at the kitchen table, and was deep in sleep.

Under the bright light, her lashes cast shadows on her cheeks. Boone hoped it was the harshness of the light that made her look so delicately pale. Her hair spilled over her shoulder. Her lips were soft, just parted.

Looking at her, he thought of the young princess who had been put under a spell by a jealous faerie and made to sleep a hundred years, until wakened by true love's gentle kiss.

"Anastasia. You're so beautiful." He touched her hair, indulging himself. He'd never watched her sleep, and he had a sudden, tearing urge to have her in his bed, to be able to open his eyes in the morning and see her there beside him. "What am I going to do?"

Sighing, he let his hand fall away from her hair and moved to the stove to shut off the kettle. As gently as he had with Jessie, he lifted her into his arms, and, like Jessie, she remained lax. Gritting his teeth against the knots in his stomach, he carried her upstairs and laid her on his bed.

"You don't know how much I've wanted you here," he said under his breath as he slipped off her shoes. "In my bed, in the night. All night." He spread the covers over her, and she sighed, shifting in sleep and curling into his pillow.

The knots in his stomach loosened as he bent to touch his lips to hers. "Good night, princess."

In her panties and T-shirt, Jessie padded into the bedroom before dawn. She'd had a dream, a bad one about the haunted house at school, and wanted the comfort and warmth of her father.

He always made monsters go away.

She scurried to the bed, and climbed in to burrow against him. It was then that she noted it wasn't her father at all, but Ana.

Fascinated, Jessie curled up. Curious fingers played with Ana's hair. In sleep Ana murmured and tucked Jessie under her arm to snuggle her close. Odd sensations tugged through Jessie's stomach. Different smells, different textures, and yet she felt as loved and safe as she did when her father cuddled her. She rested her head trustingly against Ana's breast and slept.

When Ana woke, she felt arms around her, small, limp arms. Disoriented, she stared down at Jessie, then looked around the room.

Not her room, she realized. And not Jessie's. Boone's.

She kept the child warm against her as she tried to piece together what had happened.

The last thing she remembered was sitting down after she'd put on water for tea. Tired, she'd been so tired. She'd rested her head for a moment and...and obviously had fallen fast asleep.

So where was Boone?

Cautiously she turned her head, unsure whether she was relieved or disappointed to find the bed beside her empty. Impractical, of course, given the circumstances, but it would have been so lovely to be able to cuddle back against him even as the child cuddled to her.

When she looked back, Jessie's eyes were open and on hers.

"I had a bad dream," the girl told her in hushed morning whispers. "About the Headless Horseman. He was laughing and laughing and chasing me."

Ana snuggled down to kiss Jessie's brow. "I bet he didn't catch you."

"Uh-uh. I woke up and came to get Daddy. He always makes the monsters go away. The ones in the closet and under the bed and at the window and everywhere."

"Daddies are good at that." She smiled, remembering how her own had pretended to chase them away with a magic broom every night during her sixth year.

"But you were here, and I wasn't scared with you, either. Are you going to sleep in Daddy's bed at night now?"

"No." She brushed a hand through Jessie's hair. "I think you and I both fell asleep, and your father had to put both of us to bed."

"But it's a big bed," Jessie pointed out. "There'd be room. I have Daisy to sleep with me now, but Daddy has to sleep all alone. Does Quigley sleep with you?"

"Sometimes," Ana said, relieved at the rapid change of topic. "He's probably wondering where I am."

"I think he knows," Boone announced from the doorway. He was wearing only jeans, unsnapped at the waist, and he looked bleary-eyed and harassed, with the gray cat winding between his legs. "He howled and scratched at the back door until I let him in."

"Oh." Ana shoved her tumbled hair back as she sat up. "Sorry. I guess he woke you."

"Right the first time." He tucked his thumbs in his pockets while the cat leapt onto the bed and began to mutter and complain to his mistress. The knots in his stomach were back, doubled. How could he explain what he felt on seeing Ana cuddled with his little girl in the big, soft bed? "Jessie, what are you doing?"

"I had a bad dream." She leaned her head against Ana's arm and stroked the cat's fur. "So I came in to get you, but Ana was here. She made the monsters go away just like you do." Quigley meowed plaintively and made Jessie giggle. "He's hungry. Poor kitty. I can feed him. Can I take him down and feed him?"

"Sure, if you'd like."

Before Ana had finished the sentence, Jessie was bounding off the bed, calling to the cat to follow.

"Sorry she woke you." Boone hesitated, then moved over to sit on the edge of the bed.

"She didn't. Apparently she just climbed right on in and went back to sleep. And I should apologize for putting you to so much trouble. You could have given me a shake and sent me home."

"You were exhausted." He reached out, much as Jessie had, to touch her hair. "Incredibly beautiful, and totally exhausted."

"Having babies is tiring work." She smiled. "Where did you sleep?"

"In the guest room." He winced at the crick in his back. "Which makes getting a decent bed in there a top priority."

Automatically she pressed her hands on his lower back to massage and ease. "You could have dumped me in there. I don't think I would have known the difference between a bed and a sheet of plywood."

"I wanted you in my bed." His gaze met hers and locked. "I very much wanted you in my bed." He tugged on her hair to bring her closer. Much closer. "I still do."

His mouth was on hers, not so patient now, not so gentle. Ana felt a quick thrill of excitement and alarm as he pressed her back against the pillows. "Boone—"

"Just for a minute." His voice took on an edge of desperation. "I need a minute with you."

He took her breast, searing her flesh through the thin silk of her rumpled blouse. While his hands skimmed over her, his mouth took and took, swallowing her muffled moans. His body ached to cover hers, to press hard against soft, to take quickly, even savagely, what he knew she could bring to him.

"Ana." His teeth scraped down her throat before he gathered her close, just to hold her. He knew he was being unfair, to both of them, and he struggled to back off. "How long does it take to feed that cat?"

"Not long enough." With a shaky laugh, she dropped her head on his shoulder. "Not nearly long enough."

"I was afraid of that." He drew back, running his hands down her arms to take hers. "Jessie's been after me to let her spend the night at Lydia's. If I can work it out, will you stay with me? Here?"

"Yes." She brought his hand to her lips, then pressed it to her cheek. "Whenever you like."

"Tonight." He forced himself to release her, to move away. "Tonight," he repeated. "I'll go call Lydia's mother. Beg if I have to." He steadied himself and slowed down. "I promised Jess we'd go get some ice cream, maybe have lunch on the wharf. Will you come with us? If it all works out, we could drop her off at Lydia's, then go out to dinner."

She pushed off the bed herself, brushing uselessly at the wrinkles in her blouse and slacks. "That sounds nice."

"Great. Sorry about the clothes. I wasn't quite brave enough to undress you."

She felt a quick thrill at the image of him unbuttoning her blouse. Slowly, very slowly, his fingers patient, his eyes hot. She cleared her throat. "They'll press out. I need to change, go check on Morgana and the twins."

"I could drive you."

"That's all right. My father's going to pick me up so I can get my car. What time did you want to leave?"

"About noon, in a couple hours."

"Perfect. I'll meet you back here."

He caught her to him before she reached the doorway, then stopped her heart with another greedy kiss. "Maybe we could pick up some takeout, bring it back and eat here."

"That sounds nice, too," she murmured as she shifted the angle of the kiss. "Or maybe we could just send out for pizza when we get hungry."

"Better. Much better."

By four o'clock, Jessie was standing in Lydia's doorway waving a cheery goodbye. Her pink backpack was bulging with the amazing assortment of necessities a six-year-old girl required for a sleepover. What made the entire matter perfect in her eyes was that Daisy had been invited along for the party.

"Tell me not to feel guilty," Boone asked as he cast one last glance in the rearview mirror.

"About?"

"About wanting my own daughter out of the house tonight."

"Boone." Adoring him, Ana leaned over to kiss his cheek. "You know perfectly well Jessie could hardly wait for us to drive away so she could begin her little adventure at Lydia's."

"Yeah, but... It's not packing her off so much, it's packing her off with ulterior motives."

Knowing what those motives were brought a little knot of heat to Ana's stomach. "She isn't going to have less of a good time because of them—particularly when you promised her she could have a slumber party in a couple of weeks. If you're still feeling guilty think about how you're going to feel riding herd on five or six little girls all night."

He slanted her a look. "I kind of figured you'd help—since you have ulterior motives, too."

"Did you?" The fact that he'd asked pleased her enormously. "Maybe I will." She laid a hand over his. "For a paranoid father riddled with guilt, you're doing a wonderful job."

"Keep it up. I'm feeling better."

"Too much flattery isn't good for you."

"Just for that I won't tell you how many guys gave themselves whiplash craning their necks to get a second look at you when we were walking on the wharf today."

"Oh?" She skimmed back her blowing hair. "Were there many?"

"Depends on how you define many. Besides, too much flattery isn't good for you. I guess I could say I don't know how you could look so good today after the night you put in."

"It could be because I slept like a rock." She stretched luxuriously. A bracelet of agates winked at her wrist. "Morgana's the amazing one. When I got there this morning, she was nursing both of the twins and looking as if she'd just spent a reviving week at an expensive spa."

"The babies okay?"

"The babies are terrific. Healthy and bright-eyed. Nash is already a pro at changing diapers. He claims both of them have smiled at him."

He knew that feeling, too, and had just realized he missed it. "He's a good guy."

"Nash is very special."

"I have to admit, I was stunned when I heard he was married. Nash was always the go-it-on-your-own type."

"Love changes things," Ana murmured, and carefully screened all wistfulness from her voice. "Aunt Bryna calls it the purest form of magic."

"A good description. Once it touches you, you begin to think nothing's impossible anymore. Were you ever in love?"

"Once." She looked away, studying the shimmering ice plants along the banks. "A long time ago. But it turned out the magic wasn't strong enough. Then I learned that my life wasn't over after all, and I could be perfectly happy alone. So I bought my house near the water," she said with a smile. "Planted my garden, and started fresh."

"I suppose it was similar for me." He grew thoughtful as

they made the final turn toward home. "Does being happy alone mean you don't think you could be happy with someone?"

Unease and hope ran parallel inside her. "I guess it means I can be happy as things stand, until I find someone who not only brings me the magic, but understands it."

He turned into the drive, shut off the engine. "We have something together, Ana."

"I know."

"I never thought to feel anything this powerful again. It's different from what I had before, and I'm not sure what that means. I don't know if I want to know."

"It doesn't matter." She took his hand again. "Sometimes you just have to accept that today is enough."

"No, it's not." He turned to her then, his eyes dark, intense. "Not with you."

She took a careful breath. "I'm not what you think I am, or what you want me to be. Boone—"

"You're exactly what I want." His hands were rough as he dragged her against him. Her startled gasp was muffled against his hard, seeking mouth.

Chapter 10

A whip of panicked excitement cracked through her as he tore her free of the seat belt and yanked her across his lap. His hands bruised, his mouth branded. This was not the Boone who had loved her so gently, taking her to that sweet, sweet fulfillment with patient hands and murmured promises. Her lover of quiet mornings and lazy afternoons had become something darker, something dangerous, something she was helpless to resist.

She could feel the blood sizzling under her skin as he took those rough, impatient hands over her. This was the wildness she had tasted that first time, in a moonlit garden with the scent of flowers ripe and heady. This bursting of urgent needs was what he had only hinted at under all that patience and steady control.

In mindless acquiescence she strained against him, willing, eager and ready to race along any path he chose.

Her body shuddered once, violently, as he dragged her over a ragged edge. He heard her muffled cry against his greedy mouth, tasted the ripeness of it as her fingers dug desperately into his shoulders. The thought ran crazily through his mind that he could have her here, right here in the car, before reason caught up with either of them.

He tore at her blouse, craving the taste of flesh. The sound of ripping seams was smothered by her quick gasp as he feasted on her throat. Beneath his hungry mouth, her pulse hammered erratically, erotically. The flavor of her was already hot, already honeyed with passion.

On a vicious oath, he shoved the door open, yanking her out. Leaving it swinging, he half carried, half dragged her across the lawn.

"Boone." Staggered, she tried to gain her feet and lost her shoes. "Boone, the car. You left your keys—"

He caught her hair, pulling her head back. His eyes. Oh, Lord, his eyes, she thought, trembling with something much deeper than fear. The heat in them seared through to her soul.

"The hell with the car." His mouth swooped down, plundered hers until she was dazed and dizzy and fighting to breathe. "Do you know what you do to me?" he said between strangled gasps for air. "Every time I see you." He pulled her up the steps, touching her, always touching her. "Soft, serene, with something smoldering just behind your eyes."

He pushed her back against the door, crushing, conquering, those full, luscious lips with his. There was something more in her eyes now. He could see that she was afraid. And that she was aroused. It was as if they both were fully aware that the animal he'd kept ruthlessly on a choke chain for weeks had broken free.

With the breath coming harsh through his lips, he caught her face in his hands. "Tell me. Ana, tell me you want me. Now. My way."

She was afraid she wouldn't be able to speak, her throat was so dry and this new need so huge. "I want you." The husky sound of her voice had the flames in his gut leaping higher. "Now. Any way."

He hooked his hands in her blouse, watched her eyes go to smoke just before he rent it in two. When he kicked the door open, she staggered back, then was caught up in a torrid embrace. Like her blouse, his control was in shreds. His hands tight at her waist, he lifted her off her feet to take her silk-covered breast in his mouth. As crazed now as he, she arched back, her hands fisted in his hair.

"Boone. Please." The plea sobbed out, though she had no idea what she was asking for. Unless it was more.

He lowered her, only so that he could capture her mouth again. His teeth scraped erotically over her swollen lips, his tongue dived deep. Then his heart seemed to explode in his chest as she began to tug frantically at his clothes.

He stumbled toward the stairs, shedding his shirt as he went. Buttons popped and scattered. But his greedy hands reached for her again, yanking the thin chemise down to her waist as they reached the landing. "Here." He dragged her down with him. "Right here."

At last, he feasted, racing his mouth over her quivering flesh, ruthlessly exploiting her secrets, relentlessly driving her with him where he so desperately needed her to go. No patience here, no rigid control for the sake of her fragility. Indeed, the woman writhing beneath him on the stairs was anything but fragile. There was strength in the hands that gripped him, searing passion in the mouth that tasted him so eagerly, whiplike agility in the body that strained under his.

She felt invincible, immortal, impossibly free. Her body was alive, never more alive, with heat pumping crazily through her blood. The world was spinning around her, a blur of color and blinding lights, whirling faster, faster, until she was forced to grip the pickets of the banister to keep from falling off the edge of the earth.

Her knuckles whitened against the wood as he tore her slacks away, then the thin swatch of lace beneath. His mouth, oh, his mouth, greedy, frantic, fevered. Ana bit back a scream as he sent her flying into hot, airless space.

Her mindless murmurs were in no language he could understand, but he knew he had taken her beyond the boundaries of the sane, of the rational. He wanted her there, right there with him as they catapulted into the madness of vivid, lawless passion.

He'd waited. He'd waited. Now her slim white body bucked. A thoroughbred ready to ride. Quivering like a stallion, he mounted her, driving himself into that wet, waiting heat. She arched to meet him and, hips moving like lightning, raced with him into the roaring dark.

Her hands slid weakly off his damp back. She was too numb to feel the slap of wood against them as they fell against the stairs. She wanted to hold him, but her strength was gone. It wasn't possible to focus her mind on what had happened. All that came were flashes of sensations, bursts of emotions.

If this was the darker side of love, nothing could have prepared her for it. If this terrible need was what had lived inside him, she couldn't comprehend how he could have strapped it back for so long.

For her sake. She turned her damp face into his throat. All for her sake.

Beneath his still-shuddering body, she was as limp as water. Boone struggled to get a grip on reality. He needed to move. After everything else he'd done to her, he was probably crushing her. But when he started to shift, she made a little sound of distress that scraped at his conscience.

"Here, baby, let me help you."

He eased away, picking up a tattered sleeve of her blouse with some idea to cover her. Biting off an oath, he tossed it down again. She'd turned slightly on her side, obviously seeking some kind of comfort. For God's sake, he thought in disgust, he'd taken her like some kind of fiend, and on the stairs. *On the stairs*.

"Ana." He found what was left of his own shirt and tried to wrap it around her shoulders. "Anastasia, I don't know how to explain."

"Explain?" The word was barely audible. Her throat was wild with thirst.

"There's no possible... Let me help you up." Her body slid like wax through his arms. "I'll get you some clothes, or... Oh, hell."

"I don't think I can get up." She moistened her lips, and tasted him. "Not for a day or two. This is fine, though. I'll just stay right here."

Frowning at her, he tried to interpret what he heard in her

voice. It wasn't anger. It didn't sound like distress. It sounded like—very much like—satisfaction. "You're not upset?"

"Hmmm? Am I supposed to be?"

"Well, for… I practically attacked you. Hell, I *did* attack you, almost taking you in the front seat of the car, tearing off your clothes, dragging you in here and devouring what was left of you on the stairs."

With her eyes still closed, she drew in a deep breath, then let it out again on a sigh through curved lips. "You certainly did. And it's the first time I've been devoured. I don't think I'll ever go up and down a staircase the same way again."

Gently he tipped a finger under her chin until her eyes opened. "I had intended to at least make it to the bedroom."

"I guess we'll get there eventually." Recognizing concern, she put a hand on his wrist. "Boone, do you think I could be upset because you wanted me that much?"

"I thought you might be upset because this wasn't what you're used to."

Making the effort, she sat up, wincing a little at the aches that would surely be bruises before much longer. "I'm not made of glass. There's no way we could love each other that wouldn't be right. But…" She linked her arms around his neck and her smile was wicked around the edges. "Under the circumstances, I'm glad we made it into the house."

He skimmed his hands down to her hips for the pleasure of bringing her body against his. "My neighbor's very open-minded."

"I've heard that." Experimentally she caught his lower lip between her teeth. Remembering how much pleasure it gave her to feel his lips cruise over her face and throat, she began a lazy journey over his. "Fortunately, my neighbor's very understanding of passions. I doubt anything would shock him. Even if I told him I often fantasize about him at night, when I'm alone, in bed."

It was impossible, but he felt himself stir against her. The deep, dark wanting began to smolder again. "Really? What kind of fantasies?"

"Of having him come to me." Her breath began to quicken as his mouth roamed over her shoulder. "Come to my bed like an incubus in the night, when a storm cracks the air. I can see his eyes, cobalt blue in a flash of lightning, and I know that he wants me the way no one else ever has, or ever will."

Knowing very well that if he didn't take some kind of action now they'd remain sprawled on the stairs, he gathered her up. "I can't give you the lightning."

She smiled as he carried her up. "You already have."

Later, hours later, they knelt on the tumbled bed, feasting on pizza by candlelight. Ana had lost track of time and had no need to know if it was midnight or approaching dawn. They had loved and talked and laughed and loved again. No night in her life had been more perfect. What did time matter here?

"Guinevere was no heroine." Ana licked sauce from her fingers. They had discussed epic poetry, modern animation, ancient legends and folklore and classic horror. She wasn't sure how they had wound their way back to Arthur and Camelot, but on the subject of Arthur's queen, Ana stood firm. "And she certainly wasn't a tragic figure."

"I'd think a woman, especially one with your compassion, would have more sympathy with her situation." Boone debated having a last piece from the cardboard box they'd plopped in the center of the bed.

"Why?" Ana picked it up herself and began to feed it to him. "She betrayed her husband, helped bring down a kingdom, all because she was weak-willed and self-indulgent."

"She was in love."

"Love doesn't excuse all actions." Amused, she tilted her head and studied him in the flickering light. He looked gloriously masculine in nothing but a pair of gym shorts, his hair tousled, his face shadowed with stubble. "Isn't that just like a man? Finding excuses for a woman's infidelity just because it's written about in romantic terms."

He didn't think it was precisely an insult, but it made him

squirm a little. "I just don't think she had control of the situation."

"Of course she did. She had a choice, and she chose poorly, just as Lancelot did. All that flowery business about gallantry and chivalry and heroism and loyalty, and the two of them justified betraying a man who loved them both because they couldn't control themselves?" She tossed her hair back. "That's bull."

He laughed before he sipped his wine. "You amaze me. Here I've been thinking you were a romantic. A woman who picks flowers by moonlight, who collects statues of faeries and wizards, and she condemns poor Guinevere because she loved unwisely."

She fired up. "Poor Guinevere—"

"Hold on." He was chuckling, enjoying himself immensely. It didn't occur to either of them that they were debating about people most considered fictional. "Let's not forget some of the other players. Merlin was supposed to be watching over the whole business. Why didn't he do anything about it?"

Fastidiously she brushed crumbs from her bare legs. "It's not a sorcerer's place to interfere with destiny."

"Come on, we're talking about the champ here. One little spell and he could've fixed it up."

"And altered countless lives," she pointed out, gesturing with her glass. "Skewed history. No, he couldn't do it, not even for Arthur. People—witches, kings, mortals—are responsible for their own fates."

"He didn't have any problem abetting adultery by disguising Uther as the Duke of Cornwall and taking Tintagel so that Igraine conceived Arthur in the first place."

"Because that was destiny," she said patiently, as she might have to Jessie. "That was the purpose. For all Merlin's power, all his greatness, his single most vital act was bringing Arthur into being."

"Sounds like splitting hairs to me." He swallowed the last bite of pizza. "One spell's okay, but another isn't."

"When you're given a gift, it's your responsibility to know

how and when to use it, how and when not to. Can you imagine how he suffered, watching someone he loved destroyed? Knowing, even as Arthur was being conceived, how it would end? Magic doesn't divorce you from emotion or pain. It rarely protects the one who owns it.''

"I guess not.'' He'd certainly had witches and wizards suffering in the stories he wrote. It gave them a human element he found appealing. "When I was a kid, I used to daydream about living back then.''

"Rescuing fair maidens from fiery dragons?''

"Sure. Going on quests, challenging the Black Knight and beating the hell out of him.''

"Naturally.''

"Then I grew up and discovered I could have the best of both worlds, living there up here—'' he tapped his head with a fingertip "—when I was writing. And having the creature comforts of the twentieth century.''

"Like pizza.''

"Like pizza,'' he agreed. "A computer instead of a quill, cotton underwear. Hot running water. Speaking of which...'' he said, fingering the hem of the T-shirt he'd given her to wear. He moved on impulse, and had her shrieking out a laugh as he tossed her over his shoulder and climbed out of bed.

"What are you doing?''

"Hot running water,'' he repeated. "I think it's time I showed you what I can do in the shower.''

"You're going to sing?''

"Maybe later.'' In the bathroom, he opened the glass shower doors and turned on the taps. "Hope you like it hot.''

"Well, I—'' She was still over his shoulder when he stepped inside. With the crisscrossing sprays raining, she was immediately drenched, front and back. "Boone.'' She sputtered. "You're drowning me.''

"Sorry.'' He shifted, reaching for the soap. "You know, this shower really sold me on the house. It's roomy.'' He slicked the wet bar of soap up her calf. "Pretty great having the twin shower heads.''

Despite the heat of the water, Ana shivered when he soaped lazy circles at the back of her knee. "It's a little difficult for me to appreciate it from this position." Then she shoved her dripping hair out of her face and noticed that the floor was mirrored tiles. "Oh, my."

He grinned, and moved slowly up to her thigh. "Check out the ceiling."

She did, tilting her head and staring at their reflections. "Ah, doesn't it just steam up?"

"Treated glass. Does get a little foggy if you're in here long enough." And he intended to be in there just long enough. He began sliding her down his body, inch by dangerous inch. "But that only adds to the atmosphere." Gently he pressed her against the back wall, cupping her breasts through the clinging shirt. "Want to hear one of my fantasies?"

"It— Oh." He was rubbing a thumb over an aching nipple. "Seems only fair."

"Better idea." He brushed his lips over hers, teasing, retreating, until her breath began to hitch. "Why don't I show you? First we get rid of this." He dragged the wet shirt over her head, tossing it aside. It landed with a plop that had another tremor jerking through her system. "And I start here." Toying with her mouth, he rubbed the slick soap over her shoulders. "And I don't stop until I get to your toes."

She had a feeling showers were going to join staircases in the more erotic depths of her imagination. Gripping his hips for balance, she arched back as he circled wet, soapy hands over her breasts.

Steam. It was all around her, it was inside of her. The thick, moist air made it all but impossible to breathe. A tropical storm, water pounding, heat rising. The creamy soap had flesh sliding gloriously against flesh when their bodies moved together. Her hands foamed with it as she ran them over his back, over his chest. Even as his mouth raced to possess, his muscles quivered at her touch, and her laugh was low and softly triumphant.

If she burned, so did he. That was power clashing against power. There was no longer any doubt that she could give back

the wild, wanton, wicked pleasure he brought to her. A pleasure
so much sweeter, so much richer, because it grew from love, as
well as passion.

She wanted to show him. She would show him.

Her hands slid down him, over strong shoulders, the hard
chest. She murmured in approval as she traced fingertips over
his rib cage and down to the flat plane of his stomach.

He shook his head to try to clear it. He had expected to seduce
her here, yet he was being seduced. The delicate hands flowing
over his slick skin were shooting arrows of painful need through
his system.

"Wait." His hands groped for hers, held them firm. He knew
that if she touched him now he would never be able to hold
back. "Let me…"

"No." With the new knowledge brimming inside, her mouth
seared over his and conquered. "Let me."

Her fingers closed around him, sliding, stroking, squeezing
lightly, while his breath sounded harshly in her ear. A fresh flash
of triumph exploded inside her as she felt his quick, helpless
shudder. Then greed, to have him, all of him, deeply inside her.

"Ana." He felt the last wisps of reality fading. "Ana, I
can't—"

"You want me." Delirious with power, she threw her head
back. Her eyes were hot with challenge. "Then take me. Now."

She looked like a goddess newly risen from the sea. Wet ca-
bles of hair slicked like dark gold over her shoulder. Her skin
glowed, shimmered with water. In her eyes were secrets, dark
mysteries no man would ever unlock.

She was glorious. She was magnificent. And she was his.

"Hold on to me." Bracing her against the wall, he lifted her
hips with his hands. "Hold on to me."

She locked her arms around him, keeping her eyes open. He
took her where they stood, plunging into her as the water showered over them. Gasping out his name, she let her head fall back.
Through the rising mists, she saw their reflections—a wonderful
tangle of limbs that made it impossible to see where he left off
and she began.

On a moan of inexpressible pleasure, she dropped her head to his shoulder. She was lost. Lost. Thank God for it. "I love you." She had no idea if the words were in her head or had come through her lips. But she said them again and again until her body convulsed.

He emptied himself into her, then could only stand weakly against the wall as the strength ran out of him. His heart was still roaring in his ears as he closed his hands over her shoulders.

"Tell me now."

Her lips were curved, but she swayed a little and stared up at him through clouded eyes. "Tell you what?"

His fingers tightened, making her eyes clear. "That you love me. Tell me now."

"I... Don't you think we should dry off? We've been in the water quite a while."

With an impatient jerk, he switched off the taps. "I want to look at you when you say it, and have at least some of my wits about me. We're going to stay right here until I hear you say it again."

She hesitated. He could have no idea that he was forcing her to take the next step toward having him—or losing him. Destiny, she thought, and choices. It was time she made hers. "I love you. I wouldn't be here with you, couldn't be here, if I didn't."

His eyes were very dark, very intense. Slowly his grip lightened, his face relaxed. "I feel as though I've waited years to hear you say that."

She brushed the wet hair away from his brow. "You only had to ask."

He caught her hands in his. "You don't." Because she was beginning to shiver, he drew her out of the stall to wrap her in a towel. He caught it close around her, then wrapped his arms tight for more warmth. "Anastasia." Tenderness swelled inside him as he touched his lips to her hair, her cheek, her mouth. "You don't have to ask. I love you. You brought something I thought I'd never have again, never want again, back into my life."

On a broken sigh, she pressed her face to his chest. This was real, she thought. This was hers. She would find a way to keep it. "You're everything I've ever wanted. Don't stop loving me, Boone. Don't stop."

"I couldn't." He drew her away. "Don't cry."

"I don't." The tears shimmered, but didn't spill over. "I don't cry."

Anastasia sheds no tears, but she'll shed them for you.

Sebastian's words rang uncomfortably in Boone's head. Resolutely he blocked them out. It was ridiculous. He'd do nothing to hurt her. He opened his mouth, then closed it again. A steamy bathroom was no place for the proposal he wanted to make. And there were things he needed to tell her first.

"Let's get you another shirt. We need to talk."

She was much too happy to pay any heed to the curl of uneasiness. She laughed when he took her back to the bedroom and tugged another of his shirts over her head. Dreamily she poured two more glasses of wine while he pulled on a pair of jeans.

"Will you come with me?" He held out a hand, and she took it willingly.

"Where are we going?"

"I want to show you something." He took her down the shadowy hall, into his office. Delighted, Ana turned a circle.

"This is where you work."

There were wide, uncurtained windows framed with curving cherrywood. A couple of worn, faded scatter rugs had been tossed on the hardwood floor. Starshine sprinkled through the twin skylights. An industrious-looking computer, reams of paper and shelves of books announced that this was a workplace. But he'd added charm with framed illustrations, a collection of dragons and knights that intrigued her. The winged faery he'd bought from Morgana had a prominent place on a high, carved stool.

"You need some plants," she decided instantly, thinking of the narcissus and daffodils she was forcing in her greenhouse. "I imagine you spend hours in this room every day." She glanced down at the empty ashtray beside his machine.

Following her gaze, he frowned. Odd, he thought, he hadn't

had a cigarette in days—had forgotten about them completely. He'd have to congratulate himself later.

"Sometimes I watch out the window when you're in your garden. It makes it difficult to concentrate."

She laughed and sat on the corner of his desk. "We'll get you some shades."

"Not a chance." He smiled, but his hands went nervously to his pockets. "Ana, I need to tell you about Alice."

"Boone." Compassion had her rising again to reach out. "I understand. I know it's painful. There's no need to explain anything to me"

"There is for me." With her hand in his, he turned to gesture at a sketch on the wall. A lovely young girl was kneeling by a stream, dipping a golden pail into the silver water. "She drew that, before Jessie was born. Gave it to me for our first anniversary."

"It's beautiful. She was very talented."

"Yeah. Very talented, very special." He sipped his wine in an unconscious toast to a lost love. "I knew her most of my life. Pretty Alice Reeder."

He needed to talk, Ana thought. She would listen. "You were high school sweethearts?"

"No." He laughed at that. "Not even close. Alice was a cheerleader, student body president, all-around nice girl who always made the honor roll. We ran in different crowds, and she was a couple of years behind me. I was going through my obligatory rebellious period and kind of hulked around school, looking tough."

She smiled, touched his cheek where the stubble was rough. "I'd like to have seen that."

"I snuck cigarettes in the bathroom, and Alice painted scenery for school plays. We knew each other, but that was about it. I went off to college, ended up in New York. It seemed necessary, since I was going to write, that I get myself a loft and starve a little."

She slipped an arm around him, instinctively offering comfort, waiting while he gathered his thoughts.

"One morning I was in the bakery around the corner from where I was living, and I looked up from the crullers and there she was, buying coffee and a croissant. We started talking. You know...what are you doing here, the old neighborhood, what had happened to whom. That kind of thing. It was comforting, and exciting. Here we were, two small-town kids taking on big bad New York."

And fate had tossed them together, Ana thought, in a city of millions.

"She was in art school," Boone continued, "sharing an apartment only a couple of blocks away with some other girls. I walked her to the subway. We just sort of drifted together, sitting in the park, comparing sketches, talking for hours. Alice was so full of life, energy, ideas. We didn't fall in love so much as we slid into it." His eyes softened as he studied the sketch. "Very slowly, very sweetly. We got married just before I sold my first book. She was still in college."

He had to stop again as the memories swam back in force. Instinctively his hand closed over Ana's. She opened herself, giving what strength and support she could.

"Anyway, everything seemed so perfect. We were young, happy, in love. She'd already been commissioned to do a painting. We found out she was pregnant. So we decided to move back home, raise the child in a nice suburban atmosphere close to family. Then Jessie came, and it seemed as though nothing could ever go wrong. Except that Alice never seemed to really get her energy back after the birth. Everyone said it was natural, she was bound to be tired with a new baby and her work. She lost weight. I used to joke that she was going to fade away." He closed his eyes for a minute. "That's just what she did. She faded away. When it had gone on long enough for us to worry, she had tests, but there was a mess-up in the lab and they didn't detect it soon enough. By the time we found out she had cancer, it was too late to stop it."

"Oh, Boone. I'm sorry. I'm so sorry."

"She suffered. That was the worst. She suffered and there was nothing I could do. I watched her die, degree by degree.

And I thought I would die, too. But there was Jessie. Alice was only twenty-five when I buried her. Jessie had just turned two.'' He took a long breath before he turned to Ana. ''I loved Alice. I always will.''

''I know. When someone touches your life that way, you never lose it.''

''When I lost her, I stopped believing in happy-ever-after, except in books. I didn't want to fall in love again, risk that kind of pain—for myself or for Jessie. But I have fallen in love again. What I feel for you is so strong, it makes me believe again. It's not the same as I felt before. It's not less. It's just...us.''

She touched his cheek. She thought she understood. ''Boone, did you think I would ask you to forget her? That I could resent or be jealous of what you had with her? It only makes me love you more. She made you happy. She gave you Jessie. I only wish I had known her.''

Impossibly moved, he lowered his brow to hers. ''Marry me, Ana.''

Chapter 11

She froze. The hands that had reached up to bring him close stopped in midair. Her breath seemed to stall in her lungs. Even as her heart leapt with hope, her mind warned her to wait.

Very slowly, she eased out of his arms. "Boone, I think—"

"Don't tell me I'm rushing things." He was amazingly calm now that he'd taken the step—the step he realized he'd already taken in his head weeks before. "I don't care if I'm moving too fast. I need you in my life, Ana."

"I'm already in your life." She smiled, trying to keep it light. "I told you that."

"It was hard enough when I only wanted you, harder still when I started to care. But it's impossible now that I'm in love with you. I don't want to live next door to you." He took a firm grip on her shoulders to keep her still. "I don't want to have to send my child away so I can spend the night with you. You said you loved me."

"I do." She gave in to desperate need and pressed herself against him. "You know I do, more than I thought I could. More than I wanted to. But marriage is—"

"Right." He stroked a hand down her damp hair. "Right for us. Ana, I told you once I don't take intimacy lightly, and I wasn't just talking about sex." He drew her back, wanting to see her face, wanting her to see his. "I'm talking about what's inside me every time I look at you. Before I met you, I was content to keep my life the way it was. But that's no good anymore. I'm not going to keep running through the hedges to be with you. I want you with me, with us.''

"Boone, if it could be so simple." She turned away, struggling to find the right answer.

"It can be." He fought against a quick flutter of panic. "When I walked in this morning and saw you in bed, with your arms around Jessie—I can't tell you what went through me at that moment. I realized that was what I wanted. For you to be there. Just to be there. To know I could share her with you, because you'd love her. That there could be other children. A future.''

She shut her eyes, because the image was so sweet, so perfect. And she was denying them both a chance to make the image reality, because she was afraid. "If I said yes now, before you understand me, before you know me, it wouldn't be fair.''

"I do know you." He swept her around again. "I know you have passion, and compassion, that you're loyal and generous and openhearted. That you have strong feelings for family, that you like romantic music and apple wine. I know the way your laugh sounds, the way you smell. And I know that I could make you happy, if you'd let me.''

"You do make me happy. It's because I don't want to do any less for you that I don't know what to do." She broke away to walk off the tension. "I didn't know this was going to happen so quickly, before I was sure. I swear, if I'd known you were thinking of marriage…''

To be his wife, she thought. Bound to him by handfast. She could think of nothing more precious than that kind of belonging.

She had to tell him, so that he would have the choice of accepting or backing away. "You've been much more honest with me than I with you.''

"About?''

"About what you are." Her eyes closed on a sigh. "I'm a coward. So easily devastated by bad feelings, afraid, pathetically afraid, of pain—physical and emotional. So hatefully vulnerable to what others can be indifferent to."

"I don't know what you're talking about, Ana."

"No, you don't." She pressed her lips together. "Can you understand that there are some who are more sensitive than others to strong feelings? Some who have to develop a defense against absorbing too much of the swirl of emotion that goes on around them? Who have to, Boone, because they couldn't survive otherwise?"

He pushed back his impatience and tried to smile. "Are you getting mystical on me?"

She laughed, pressing a hand to her eyes. "You don't know the half of it. I need to explain, and don't know how. If I could—" She started to turn back, determined to tell him everything, and the sketchpad on his desk slid off at the movement. Automatically she bent to pick it up.

Perhaps it was fate that it had fallen faceup, showing a recently completed sketch. An excellent one, Ana thought on a long breath as she studied it. The fierce and wicked lines of the black-caped witch glared up at her. Evil, she thought. He had captured evil perfectly.

"Don't worry about that." He started to take it from her, but she shook her head.

"Is this for your story?"

"*The Silver Castle,* yes. Let's not change the subject."

"Not as much as you think," she murmured. "Indulge me a minute," she said with a careful smile. "Tell me about the sketch."

"Damn it, Ana."

"Please."

Frustrated, he dragged a hand through his hair. "It's just what it looks like. The evil witch who put the spell on the princess and the castle. I had to figure there was a spell that kept anyone from getting in or out."

"So you chose a witch."

"I know it's obvious. But the story seemed to call for it. The vindictive, jealous witch, furious with the princess's goodness and beauty, casts the spell, so the princess stays trapped inside, cut off from love and life and happiness. Then, when true love conquers, the spell's broken and the witch is vanquished. And they live happily ever after.''

"I suppose witches are, to you, evil and calculating." Calculating, she remembered. It was one of the words Robert had tossed at her. That, and much, much worse.

"Goes with the territory. Power corrupts, right?"

She set the sketch aside. "There are those who think it." It was only a drawing, she told herself. Only part of a story he'd created. Yet it served to remind her how large a span they needed to cross. "Boone, I'll ask you for something tonight."

"I guess you could ask me for anything tonight."

"Time," she said. "And faith. I love you, Boone, and there's no one else I'd want to spend my life with. But I need time, and so do you. A week," she said before he could protest. "Only a week. Until the full moon. Then there are things I'll tell you. After I do, I hope you'll ask me again to be your wife. If you do, if you can, then I'll say yes."

"Say yes now." He caught her close, capturing her mouth, hoping he could persuade her by his will alone. "What difference will a week make?"

"All," she whispered, clinging tight. "Or none."

He didn't care to wait. It made him nervous and impatient that the days seemed to crawl by. One, then two, finally three. To comfort himself, he thought about the turn his life would take once the interminable week was over.

No more nights alone. Soon, when he returned restlessly in the dark, she would be there. The house would be full of her, her scent, the fragrances of her herbs and oils. On those long, quiet evenings, they could sit together on the deck and talk about the day, about tomorrows.

Or perhaps she would want them to move into her house. It wouldn't matter. They could walk through her gardens, under her arbors, and she could try to teach him the names of all of her flowers.

They could take a trip to Ireland, and she could show him all the important places of her childhood. There would be stories she could tell him, like the one about the witch and the frog, and he could write about them.

One day there would be more children, and he would see her holding their baby the way she had held Morgana and Nash's.

More children. That thought brought him up short and had him staring at the framed picture of Jessie smiling out at him from his desktop.

His baby. Only his, and his only, for so long now. He did want more children. He'd never realized until now how much he wanted more. How much he enjoyed being a father. It was simply something he was, something he did.

Now as his mind began to play with the idea, he could see himself soothing an infant in the night as he had once soothed Jessie. Holding out his arms as a toddler took those first shaky steps. Tossing a ball in the yard, holding on to the back of an unsteady bike.

A son. Wouldn't it be incredible to have a son? Or another daughter. Brothers and sisters for Jessie. She'd love that, he thought, and found himself grinning like an idiot. He'd love it.

Of course, he hadn't even asked Ana how she felt about adding to the family. That was certainly something they'd have to discuss. Maybe it would be rushing her again to bring it up now.

Then he remembered how she'd looked with her arm cuddling Jessie in his bed. The way her face had glowed when she'd held two tiny infants up so that his daughter could see and touch.

No, he decided. He knew her. She would be as anxious as he to turn their love into life.

By the end of the week, he thought, they would start making plans for their future together.

For Ana, the days passed much too quickly. She spent hours going over the right way to tell Boone everything. Then she would change her mind and struggle to think of another way.

There was the brash way.

She imagined herself sitting him down in her kitchen with a

pot of tea between them. "Boone," she would say, "I'm a witch. If that doesn't bother you, we can start planning the wedding."

There was the subtle way.

They would sit out on her patio, near the arbor of morning glories. While they sipped wine and watched the sunset, they would talk about their childhoods.

"Growing up in Ireland is a little different than growing up in Indiana, I suppose," she would tell him. "But the Irish usually take having witches in the neighborhood pretty much for granted." Then she'd smile. "More wine, love?"

Or the intellectual way.

"I'm sure you'd agree most legends have some basis in fact." This conversation would take place on the beach, with the sound of the surf and the cry of gulls. "Your books show a great depth of understanding and respect for what most consider myth or folklore. Being a witch myself, I appreciate your positive slant on faeries and magic. Particularly the way you handled the enchantress in *A Third Wish for Miranda*."

Ana only wished she had enough humor left to laugh at each pitiful scenario. She was certainly going to have to think of something, now that she had less than twenty-four hours to go.

Boone had already been more patient than she had a right to ask. There was no excuse for keeping him waiting any longer.

At least she would have some moral support this evening. Morgana and Sebastian and their spouses were on their way over for the monthly Friday-night cookout. If that didn't buck her up for her confrontation with Boone the following day, nothing would. As she stepped onto the patio, she fingered the diamond-clear zircon she wore around her neck.

Obviously Jessie had been keeping an eagle eye out, for she zipped through the hedge, with Daisy yipping behind her. To show his indifference to the pup, Quigley sat down and began to wash his hindquarters.

"We're coming to your house for a cookout," Jessie announced. "The babies are coming, too, and maybe I can hold one. If I'm really, really careful."

"I think that could be arranged." Automatically Ana scanned the neighboring yard for signs of Boone. "How was school today, sunshine?"

"It was pretty neat. I can write my name, and Daddy's and yours. Yours is easiest. I can write Daisy's, but I don't know how to spell Quigley's, so I just wrote *cat.* Then I had my whole family, just like the teacher told us." She stopped, scuffed her shoes, and for the first time since Ana had known her, looked shy. "Was it okay if I said you were my family?"

"It's more than okay." Crouching down, Ana gave Jessie a huge hug. Oh, yes, she thought, squeezing her eyes tight. This is what I want, what I need. I could be a wife to him, a mother to the child. Please, please, let me find the way to have it all. "I love you, Jessie."

"You won't go away, will you?"

Because they were close, because she couldn't prevent it, Ana touched the child's heart and understood that Jessie was thinking of her mother. "No, baby." She drew back, choosing her words with care. "I would never want to go away. But if I had to, if I couldn't help it, I'd still be close."

"How can you go away and still be close?"

"Because I'd keep you in my heart. Here." Ana took the thin braided gold chain with the square of zircon and slipped it over Jessie's neck.

"Ooh! It shines!"

"It's very special. When you feel lonely or sad, you hold on to this and think of me. I'll know, and I'll send you happiness."

Dazzled, Jessie turned the crystal, and it exploded with light and color. "Is it magic?"

"Yes."

Jessie accepted the answer with a child's faith. "I want to show Daddy." She started to dash off, then remembered her manners. "Thank you."

"You're welcome. Is— Ah, is Boone inside?"

"Uh-uh, he's on the roof."

"The roof?"

"'Cause next month is Christmas, and he's starting to put up the lights so we know how many we have to buy. The whole house is going to be lit up. Daddy says this is going to be the most special Christmas ever.''

''I hope so.'' Ana shielded her eyes with the flat of her hand and looked up. There he was, sitting on top of the house, looking back at her. Her heart gave that quick, improbable leap it always did when she saw him. Despite nerves, she smiled, lifting one hand in a wave while the other rested on Jessie's shoulder.

It would be all right, she told herself. It had to be.

Boone ignored the tangle of Christmas lights beside him and pleased himself by watching them until Jessie raced back across the yard and Ana went inside.

It would be all right, he told himself. It had to be.

Sebastian plucked a fat black olive from a tray and popped it into his mouth. ''When do we eat?''

''You already are,'' Mel pointed out.

''I mean real food.'' He winked down at Jessie. ''Hot dogs.''

''Herbed chicken,'' Ana corrected, turning a sizzling thigh on the grill.

They were spread over the patio, with Jessie sitting in a wrought-iron chair carefully cradling a cooing Allysia in her lap. Boone and Nash were deep in a discussion on infant care. Morgana had Donovan at her breast, comfortably nursing, while she listened to Mel relate the happy ending of the runaway she and Sebastian had tracked down.

''Kid was miserable,'' she was saying. ''Sorry as hell he'd taken off, scared to go back. When we found him—cold, broke and hungry—and he realized his parents were scared instead of angry, he couldn't wait to get home. I think he's grounded till he's thirty, but he doesn't seem to care.'' She waited until Morgana had burped her son. Her hands had been itching to touch. ''Want me to put him back down for you?''

''Thanks.'' Morgana watched Mel's face as she lifted the baby. ''Thinking about having one of your own. Or two?''

''Actually.'' Mel caught the special scent of baby and felt her knees go weak. ''I think I might...'' She cast a quick look over her shoulder and saw her husband was busy teasing Jessie. "I'm not sure yet, but I think I may have already started."

"Oh, Mel, that's—"

"Shh." She leaned down, using the baby for cover. "I don't want him to know, or even suspect, or I'd never be able to stop him from looking for himself. I want to be able to tell him about this." She grinned. "It'll knock his socks off."

Gently Mel laid the child in his side of the double carriage.

"Allysia's sleeping too," Jessie pointed out, tracing a finger over the baby's cheek.

"Want to put her down with her brother?" Sebastian leaned over to help Jessie stand with the baby. "That's the way." He kept his hands under hers as she laid Allysia down. "You'll be an excellent mother one day."

"Maybe I can have twins, too." She turned when Daisy began to bark. "Hush," she whispered. "You'll wake the babies."

But Daisy was lost in the thrill of the chase. Heading for open ground, Quigley shot through the hedges into the next yard, yowling. Delighted with the game, Daisy dashed after him.

"I'll get him, Daddy." Making as much racket as the animals, Jessie raced after them.

"I don't think obedience school's the answer," Boone commented, tipping back a beer. "I'm thinking along the lines of a mental institution."

Panting a bit, Jessie followed the sounds of barks and hisses, across the yard, over the deck, around the side of the house. When she caught up with Daisy, she put her hands on her hips and scolded.

"You have to be friends. Ana won't like it if you keep teasing Quigley."

Daisy simply thumped her tail on the ground and barked again. Halfway up the ladder Boone had used to climb to the roof, Quigley hissed and spat.

"He doesn't like it, Daisy." On a sigh, she squatted down to pet the dog. "He doesn't know you're just playing and wouldn't really hurt him ever. You made him scared." She looked up the ladder. "Come on, kitty. It's okay. You can come down now."

On a feline growl, Quigley narrowed his eyes, then bounded up the ladder when Daisy responded with another flurry of barks.

"Oh, Daisy, look what you've done." Jessie hesitated at the foot of the ladder. Her father had been very specific about her not going near it. But he hadn't known that Quigley would get so scared. And maybe he'd fall off the roof and get killed. She stepped back, thinking she would go tell her father to come. Then she heard Quigley meow.

Daisy was her responsibility, she remembered. She was supposed to feed him and watch him so he didn't get in trouble. If Quigley got hurt, it would be all her fault.

"I'm coming, kitty. Don't be scared." With her lower lip caught between her teeth, she started up the rungs. She'd seen her father go right on up, and it hadn't looked hard at all. Just like climbing the jungle gyms at school, or up to the top of the big sliding board. "Kitty, kitty," she chanted, climbing higher and giggling when Quigley stuck his head over the roof. "You silly cat, Daisy was only playing. I'll take you down, don't worry."

She was nearly to the top when her sneakered foot missed the next rung.

"Smells wonderful," Boone murmured, but he was sniffing at Ana's neck, not the chicken she'd piled on a platter. "Good enough to eat."

Nash gave him a nudge as he reached for a plate. "If you're going to kiss her, move aside. The rest of us want dinner."

"Fine." Slipping his arms around a flustered Ana, he closed his mouth over hers in a long, lingering kiss. "Time's almost up," he said against her mouth. "You could put me out of my misery now, and—"

The words shut off when he heard Jessie's scream. With his heart in his throat, he raced across the yard, shouting for her. He tore through the hedges, pounded across the grass.

"Oh, God! Oh, my God!"

Every ounce of blood seemed to drain out of him when he

saw her crumpled on the ground, her arm bent at an impossible angle, her face as white as linen.

"Baby!" Panicked, he fell beside her. She was too still—even his fevered mind registered that one terrifying fact. And when he reached down to pick her up, there was blood, her blood, on his hands.

"Don't move her!" Ana snapped out the order as she dropped beside them. She was breathing hard, fighting back terror, but her hands clasped firmly over his wrists. "You don't know how or where she's hurt. You can do more harm by moving her."

"She's bleeding." He cupped his hands on his daughter's face. "Jessie. Come on, Jessie." With a trembling finger, he searched for a pulse at her throat. "Don't do this. Dear God, don't do this. We need an ambulance."

"I'll call," Mel said from behind them.

Ana only shook her head. "Boone." The calm settled over her as she understood what she had to do. "Boone, listen to me." She took his shoulders, holding tight when he tried to shake her off. "You have to move back. Let me look at her. Let me help her."

"She's not breathing." He could only stare down at his little girl. "I don't think she's breathing. Her arm. She's broken her arm."

It was more than that. Even without a closer link, Ana knew it was much more than that. And there was no time for an ambulance. "I can help her, but you have to move back."

"She needs a doctor. For God's sake, someone call an ambulance."

"Sebastian," Ana said quietly. Her cousin stepped forward and took Boone's arms.

"Let go of me!" Boone started to swing and found himself pinned by both Sebastian and Nash. "What the hell's wrong with you? We have to get her to a hospital!"

"Let Ana do what she can," Nash said, fighting to hold his friend and his own panic back. "You have to trust her, for Jessie's sake."

"Ana." Pale and shaken, Morgana passed one of her babies

into Mel's waiting arms. "It may be too late. You know what could happen to you if—"

"I have to try."

Very gently, oh, so gently, she placed her hands on either side of Jessie's head. She braced, waiting until her own breathing was slow and deep. It was hard, very hard, to block out Boone's violent and terrified emotions, but she focused on the child, only the child. And opened herself.

Pain. Hot, burning spears of it, radiating through her head. Too much pain for such a small child. Ana drew it out, drew it in, let her own system absorb it. When agony threatened to smother the serenity needed for such deep and delicate work, she waited for it to roll past. Then moved on.

So much damage, she thought as her hands trailed lightly down. Such a long way to fall. A perfect image clicked in her mind. The ground rushing up, the helpless fear, the sudden, numbing jolt of impact.

Her fingers passed over a deep gash in Jessie's shoulder. The mirror image sliced through her own, throbbed, seeped blood. Then both slowly faded.

"My God." Boone stopped struggling. His body was too numb. "What is she doing? How?"

"She needs quiet," Sebastian muttered. Stepping back from Boone, he took Morgana's hand. There was nothing they could do but wait.

The injuries inside were severe. Sweat began to bloom on Ana's skin as she examined, absorbed, mended. She was chanting as she worked, knowing she needed to deepen the trance to save the child, and herself.

Oh, but the pain! It ripped through her like fire, making her shudder. Her breath hitched as she fought the need to pull back. Blindly she clutched a hand over the zircon Jessie still wore and placed the other over the child's quiet heart.

When she threw her head back, her eyes were the color of storm clouds, and as blank as glass.

The light was bright, blindingly bright. She could barely see the child up ahead. She called, shouted, wanting to hurry, knowing that one misstep now would end it for both of them.

She stared into the light and felt Jessie slipping further away.

"This gift is mine to use or scorn." Both pain and power shimmered in her voice. "This choice was mine from the day I was born. What harms the child bring into me. As I will, so mote it be."

She cried out then, from the tearing price to be paid for cheating death. She felt her own life ebb, teetering, teetering toward the searing light as Jessie's heart began to beat tremulously under her hand.

She fought back, for both of them, calling on every ounce of her strength, every vestige of her power.

Boone saw his daughter stir, watched her lashes flutter as Ana swayed back.

"Jess—Jessie?" He leaped forward to scoop her into his arms. "Baby, are you all right?"

"Daddy?" Her blank, unfocused eyes began to clear. "Did I fall down?"

"Yeah." Weak with relief and gratitude, he buried his face against her throat and rocked her. "Yeah."

"Don't cry, Daddy." She patted his back. "I'm okay."

"Let's see." He took a shaky breath before he ran his hands over her. There was no blood, he discovered. No blood, no bruise, not even the smallest scratch. He held her close again, staring at Ana as Sebastian helped her to her feet. "Do you hurt anywhere, Jessie?"

"Uh-uh." She yawned and nestled her head on his shoulder. "I was going to Mommy. She looked so pretty in all the light. But she looked sad, like she was going to cry, when she saw me coming. Then Ana was there, and she took my hand. Mommy looked happy when she waved goodbye to us. I'm sleepy, Daddy."

His own heart was throbbing in his throat, thickening his voice. "Okay, baby."

"Why don't you let me take her up?" When Boone hesitated, Nash lowered his voice. "She's fine. Ana's not." He took the already dozing child. "Don't let common sense get in the way, pal," he added as he took Jessie inside.

"I want to know what happened here." Afraid he'd babble, Boone forced himself to speak slowly. "I want to know exactly what happened."

"All right." Ana glanced around at her family. "If you'd leave us alone for just a minute, I'd like to..." She trailed off as the world went gray. Swearing, Boone caught her as she fell, then hoisted her into his arms.

"What the hell is going on?" he demanded. "What did she do to Jessie?" He looked down, alarmed by the translucent pallor of Ana's cheeks. "What did she do to herself?"

"She saved your daughter's life," Sebastian said. "And risked her own."

"Be quiet, Sebastian," Morgana murmured. "He's been through enough."

"He?"

"Yes." She laid a restraining hand on her cousin's arm. "Boone, Ana needs rest, a great deal of rest and quiet. If you'd prefer, you can bring her home. One of us will stay and take care of her."

"She'll stay here." He turned and carried her inside.

She was drifting in and out, in and out of worlds without color. There was no pain now, no feeling at all. She was as insubstantial as a mist. Once or twice she heard Sebastian or Morgana slip inside her deeply sleeping mind to offer reassurance. Others joined them, her parents, her aunts and uncles, and more.

After a long, long journey, she felt herself coming back. Tints and hues seeped back into the colorless world. Sensations began to prickle along her skin. She sighed once—it was the first sound she had made in more than twenty-four hours—then opened her eyes.

Boone watched her come back. He rose automatically from the chair to bring her the medication Morgana had left with him.

"Here." He supported her, holding the cup to her lips. "You're supposed to drink this."

She obeyed, recognizing the scent and the taste. "Jessie?"

"She's fine. Nash and Morgana picked her up this afternoon. She's staying with them tonight."

With a nod, she drank again. "How long have I been asleep?"

"Asleep?" He gave a half laugh at her prosaic term for the comalike state she'd been in. "You've been out for twenty-six hours." He glanced at his watch. "And thirty minutes."

The longest journey she'd ever taken, Ana realized. "I need to call my family and tell them I'm well."

"I'll do it. Are you hungry?"

"No." She tried not to be hurt by his polite, distant tone of voice. "This is all I need for now."

"Then I'll be back in a minute."

When he left her alone, she covered her face with her hands. Her own fault, she berated herself. She hadn't prepared him, had dragged her feet, and fate had taken a hand. On a tired sigh, she got out of bed and began to dress.

"What the hell are you doing?" Boone demanded when he walked in again. "You're supposed to rest."

"I've rested enough." Ana stared down at her hands as she meticulously buttoned her blouse. "And I'd just as soon be on my feet when we talk about this."

His nerves jittered, but he only nodded. "Have it your way."

"Can we go outside? I could use some air."

"Fine." He took her arm and led her downstairs and out on the deck. Once she was seated, he took out a cigarette, struck a match. He'd hardly closed his eyes since he'd carried Ana upstairs, and he'd been subsisting on tobacco and coffee. "If you're feeling up to it, I'd appreciate an explanation."

"I'm going to try to give you one. I'm sorry I didn't tell you before." Ana linked her hands tight in her lap. "I wanted to, but I could never find the right way."

"Straight out," he said as he dragged deeply on smoke.

"I come from a very old bloodline—on both sides. A different culture, if you like. Do you know what wicca is?"

Something cold brushed his skin, but it was only the night air. "Witchcraft."

"Actually, its true meaning is wise. But witch will do." She looked up, and her clear gray eyes met his tired, shadowed ones. "I'm a hereditary witch, born with empathic powers that enable me to link emotionally, and physically, with others. My gift is one of healing."

Boone took another long drag on his cigarette. "You're going to sit there, look me in the face and tell me you're a witch."

"Yes."

Furious, he flung the cigarette away. "What kind of a game is this, Ana? Don't you think after what happened here last night I deserve a reasonable explanation?"

"I think you deserve the truth. You may not think it reasonable." She held up a hand before he could speak. "Tell me how you would explain what happened."

He opened his mouth, closed it again. He'd been working on that single problem for more than twenty-four hours without finding a comfortable solution. "I can't. But that doesn't mean I'm going to buy into this."

"All right." She rose, laid a hand on his chest. "You're tired. You haven't had much sleep. Your head's pounding and your stomach's in knots."

He lifted a brow derisively. "I don't think you have to be a witch to figure that out."

"No." Before he could back away, she touched a hand to his brow, pressed the other to his stomach. "Better?" she asked after a moment.

He needed to sit down, but he was afraid he wouldn't get up again. She'd touched him, barely touched him. And even the shadow of pain was gone. "What is it? Hypnotism?"

"No. Boone, look at me."

He did, and saw a stranger with tangled blond hair billowing out in the wind. The amber enchantress, he thought numbly. Was it any wonder it had reminded him so much of her?

Ana saw both shock and the beginning of belief on his face. "When you asked me to marry you, I asked you to give me time so that I could find the right way to tell you. I was afraid.'' Her hands dropped away. "Afraid you'd look at me exactly the way you're looking at me now. As if you don't even know me.''

"This is bull. Look, I write this stuff for a living, and I know fiction from fact.''

"My skill for magic is very limited.'' Still, she reached into her pocket, where she always carried a few crystals. With her eyes on Boone's, she held them out in her palm. Slowly they began to glow, the purple of the amethyst deepening, the pink of the rose quartz brightening, the green of the malachite shimmering. Then they rose, an inch, two inches, up, circling, spinning in the air and flashing with light. "Morgana is more talented with such things.''

He stared at the tumbling crystals, trying to find a logical reason. "Morgana is a witch, too?''

"She's my cousin,'' Ana said simply.

"Which makes Sebastian—''

"Sebastian's gift is sight.''

He didn't want to believe, but it was impossible to discount what he saw with his own eyes. "Your family,'' he began. "Those magic tricks of your father's.''

"Magic in its purest form.'' She plucked the crystals out of the air and slipped them back in her pocket. "As I told you, he's very accomplished. As are the rest of them, in their own ways. We're witches. All of us.'' She reached out to him, but he backed away. "I'm sorry.''

"You're sorry?'' Rocked to the core, he dragged both hands through his hair. It had to be a dream, a nightmare. But he was standing on his own deck, feeling the wind, hearing the sea. "That's good. That's great. You're sorry. For what, Ana? For being what you are, or for not finding it important enough to mention?''

"I'm not sorry for being what I am.'' Pride stiffened her spine. "I am sorry for making excuses to myself not to tell you. And I'm sorry, most sorry of all, that you can't look at me now the way you did only a day ago.''

"What do you expect? Am I supposed to just shrug this off,

pick up where we were before? To accept the fact that the woman I love is something out of one of my own stories, and think nothing of it?''

''I'm exactly what I was yesterday, and what I'll be tomorrow.''

''A witch.''

''Yes.'' She folded her hands at her waist. ''A witch, born to the craft. I don't make poisoned apples or lure children into houses of gingerbread.''

''That's supposed to relieve my mind?''

''Even I don't have the power to do that. As I told you, all of us are responsible for our own destinies.'' But she knew he held hers in his hands. ''You have your choice to make.''

He struggled to get a grip on it, and simply couldn't. ''You needed time to tell me. Well, by God, I need time to figure out what to do about it.'' He started to pace, then stopped dead. ''Jessie. Jessie's over at Morgana's.''

Ana felt the crack in her heart widen. ''Oh, yes, with my cousin the witch.'' A single tear spilled over and ran down her cheek. ''What do you think Morgana's going to do? Cast a spell on her? Lock her in a tower?''

''I don't know what to think. For Lord's sake, I've found myself in the middle of a fairy tale! What am I supposed to think?''

''What you will,'' Ana said wearily. ''I can't change what I am, and I wouldn't. Not even for you. And I won't stand here and have you look at me as if I were a freak.''

''I'm not—''

''Shall I tell you what you're feeling?'' she asked him as another tear fell. ''Betrayed, angry, hurt. And suspicious of what I am, what I can do, or will do.''

''My feelings are my own business,'' he shot back, shaken. ''I don't want you to get inside me that way.''

''I know. And if I were to step forward right now, reach out to you as a woman, you'd only back away. So I'll save us both. Good night, Boone.''

When she walked off the deck, into the shadows, he couldn't bring himself to call her back.

Chapter 12

"I guess you're still a little dazed." Nash lounged against the rail of Boone's deck, enjoying a beer and the cool evening breeze.

"I was never a *little* dazed," Boone told him. "Look, maybe I'm just a narrow-minded sort of guy, Nash, but finding out the lady next door is a witch kind of threw me off stride."

"Especially when you're in love with the lady next door."

"Especially. I wouldn't have believed it. Who would? But I saw what she did with Jessie. Then I started piecing other things together." He laughed shortly. "Sometimes I still wake up in the middle of the night and think I dreamed the whole thing." He walked over to the rail, leaning out toward the sound of water. "It shouldn't be real. She shouldn't be real."

"Why not? Come on, Boone, it's our business to stretch the envelope a little."

"This blows the envelope wide open," Boone pointed out. "And what we do, we do for books, for movies. It's entertainment, Nash, it's not life."

"It's mine now."

Boone blew out a breath. "I guess it is. But didn't you...don't you even question it, or worry about it?"

"Sure, I did. I thought she was pulling my leg until she tossed me up in the air and left me hanging there." The memory made him grin, even as Boone shut his eyes. "Morgana's not the subtle type. Once I realized the whole thing was on the level, it was wild, you know?"

"Wild," Boone repeated.

"Yeah. I mean, I've spent most of my life making up stories about this kind of thing, and here I end up marrying an honest-to-goodness witch. Elfin blood and everything."

"Elfin blood." The term had Boone's head reeling. "It doesn't bother you?"

"Why should it bother me? It makes her who she is, and I love her. I have to admit I'm a little dubious about the kids. I mean, once they get going, I'll be outnumbered."

"The twins." Boone had to force his mouth to close. "Are you telling me those babies are...will be..."

"A pretty sure bet. Come on, Boone, they aren't going to grow warts and start to cackle. They just get a little something extra. Mel's expecting, too. She just found out for sure. She's the most down-to-earth lady I know. And she's handling Sebastian as if she's been around a psychic all her life."

"So you're saying, 'Loosen up, Boone. What's your problem?'"

Nash dropped down on the bench. "I know it's not that easy."

"Let me ask you this.... How far into the relationship were you when Morgana told you about her—what do I call it?—her heritage."

"Pretty much right off the bat. I was researching a script, and I'd heard about her. You know how people are always telling me about weird stuff."

"Yeah."

"Not that I believed it, but I thought she'd make a good interview. And—"

"What about Mel and Sebastian?"

"I can't say for sure, but she met him when a client of hers wanted to hire a psychic." Nash frowned into his beer. "I know what you're getting at, and you've got a point. Maybe she should have been straight with you earlier."

He gave a choked laugh. "Maybe?"

"Okay, she should have been. But you don't know the whole story. Morgana told me that Ana was in love with this guy a few years back. She was only about twenty, I think, and really nuts about him. He was an intern at some hospital, and she got the idea that they could work together, that she could help him. So she told him everything and he dumped her. Hard. Apparently he was pretty vicious about it, and with her empathic thing she's really vulnerable to, well…bad vibes, let's say. It left her pretty shaky. She made up her mind she'd go it alone." When Boone said nothing, Nash blundered on. "Look, I can't tell you what to do, or how to feel. I just want to say that she wouldn't have done anything to hurt you or Jessie on purpose. She's just not capable of it."

Boone looked toward the house next door. The windows were blank and dark, as they had been for more than a week. "Where is she?"

"She wanted to get away for a little while. Give everybody some room, I guess."

"I haven't seen her since the night she told me. For the first few days, I figured it was better if I stayed away from her." He felt a quick pang of guilt. "I kept Jessie away from her, too. Then, about a week ago, she took off."

"She went to Ireland. She promised to be back before Christmas."

Because his emotions were still raw, Boone only nodded. "I thought I might take Jessie back to Indiana before the holidays. Just for a day or two. Maybe I'll be able to work all this out in my head by the time we all get back."

"Christmas Eve." Padrick sampled the wassail, smacked his lips and sighed. "No better night in the year." Filling a cup, he handed it to his daughter. "Put color in your cheeks, my darling."

"And fire in my blood, the way you make it." But she smiled and sampled. "Isn't it incredible how the twins have grown?"

"Aye." He wasn't fooled by the bright note in her voice. "I can't stand to see my princess so sad."

"I'm not." She squeezed his hand. "I'm fine, Papa. Really."

"I can turn him into a purple jackass for you, darling. I'd be pleasured to."

"No." Because she knew he was only half joking, she kissed his nose. "And you promised we wouldn't have to talk about it once everyone got here."

"Aye, but—"

"A promise," she reminded him, and moved away to help her mother at the stove.

She was glad her house was filled with the people she loved, with the noise of family. There were the scents she had always associated with this holiday. Cinnamon, nutmeg, pine, bayberry. When she'd arrived home a few days before, she'd thrown herself into a flurry of preparations. Tree trimming, present wrapping, cookie baking. Anything and everything to take her mind off the fact that Boone was gone.

That he hadn't spoken to her in more than a month.

But she would survive it. She had already decided what to do, and she refused to let her own unhappiness ruin the family celebration.

"We'll be pleased to have you home with us back in Ireland, Ana." Maureen bent to kiss her daughter's head. "If it's truly what you want."

"I've missed Ireland," Ana said simply. "I think the goose is nearly ready." After opening the oven and taking a heady sniff, she nodded. "Ten minutes more," she predicted. "I'll just go see if everything's on the table."

"Won't even discuss it," Maureen said to her husband when Ana slipped out.

"Tell you what I'd like, my dove. I'd like to take that young man and send him off to some nice frozen island. Just for a day or two, mind."

"If Ana wasn't so sensitive about such matters, I could brew up a nice potion to bring him around."

Padrick patted his wife's bottom. "You have such a delicate touch, Reenie. The lad would be bound by handfast before he could blink—which would be the best thing to happen to him and that darling child of his.'' He sighed, nibbling his way up his wife's arm. ''But Ana would never forgive us for it. We'll have to let her work this out her own way.''

Frustrated by a day of canceled flights and delays, Boone slammed the car door. What he wanted was a long hot bath, and what he had to look forward to was an endless night of dealing with those terrifying words *Some Assembly Required.*

If Santa was going to put in an appearance before morning, Boone Sawyer was going to have to put in some overtime.

''Come on, Jess.'' He rubbed his tired eyes. He'd been traveling for more than twelve hours, if you counted the six he'd spent twiddling his thumbs in the airport. ''Let's get this stuff inside.''

''Ana's home.'' Jessie tugged on his arm and pointed toward the lights. ''Look, Daddy. There's Morgana's car, and Sebastian's, and the big black car, too. Everybody's at Ana's house.''

''I see that.'' He felt his heart begin to trip a little faster. Then it all but stopped when he saw the For Sale sign in her front yard.

''Can we go over and say merry Christmas? Please, Daddy. I miss Ana.'' She closed her hand around the zircon she wore. ''Can we go say merry Christmas?''

''Yeah.'' Glaring at the sign, he gripped his daughter's hand. ''Yeah, let's go do that. Right now.''

Move away, would she? he thought as he strode across the lawn. In a pig's eye. Sell her house when he wasn't looking and just take off? They'd just see about that.

''Daddy, you're walking too fast.'' Jessie had to trot to keep up. ''And you're squeezing my hand.''

''Sorry.'' He drew in a long breath, then let it out again. He scooped her up and took the stairs two at a time. The knock on her door wasn't so much a request as a demand.

It was Padrick who answered, his round face wreathed in a fake white beard, and red stocking cap on his balding head. The minute he saw Boone, the twinkle in his eyes died.

''Well, well, look what the cat dragged in. Brave enough to

take us all on at once, are you, boyo? We're not all as polite as my Ana."

"I'd like to see her."

"Oh, would you now? Hold it right there." He gave Jessie his charming smile and lifted her out of Boone's arms. "Looks like I got me a real elf this time. Tell you what, lass, you run right on in and look under that tree. See if there's not something with your name on it."

"Oh, can I?" She hugged Padrick fiercely, then turned back to her father. "Please, can I?"

"Sure." Like Padrick's, his smile faded as soon as Jessie raced inside. "I came to see Ana, Mr. Donovan."

"Well, you're seeing me. What do you think you'd do if someone took your Jessie's heart and squeezed it dry?" Though he was more than a head shorter than Boone, he advanced, fists raised. "I won't use nothing but these on you. You've my word as a witch. Now put 'em up."

Boone didn't know whether to laugh or retreat. "Mr. Donovan..."

"Take the first punch." He stuck his whiskered chin out, looking very much like an indignant Santa. "I'll give you that much, and it's more than you'd be deserving. I've listened to her crying in the night over the likes of you, and it's boiled my blood. Told myself, Padrick, if you get face-to-face with that weasel of a man, you'll have to demolish him. It's a matter of pride." He took a swing that spun him completely around and missed Boone by a foot. "She wouldn't let me go after that other slimy bastard when he broke her poor heart, but I've got you."

"Mr. Donovan." Boone tried again, dodging the peppery blows. "I don't want to hurt you."

"Hurt me! Hurt me!" Padrick was dancing now, fueled by the insult. His Santa cap slipped over his eyes. "Why, I could turn your insides out. I could give you the head of a badger. I could—"

"Papa!" With one sharp word, Ana stopped her father's babbling threats.

"You go on inside, princess. This is man's work."

"I won't have you fighting on my doorstep on Christmas Eve. Now you stop it."

"Just let me send him to the North Pole. Just for an hour or two. It's only fitting."

"You'll do no such thing." She stepped out and put a warning hand on his shoulder. "Now go inside and behave, or I'll have Morgana deal with you."

"Bah! I can handle a witch half my age."

"She's sneaky." Ana pressed a kiss to his cheek. "Please, Papa. Do this for me."

"Could never refuse you anything," he muttered. Then he turned glittering eyes on Boone. "But you watch your step, mister." He jabbed out a plump finger. "You mess with one Donovan, you mess with them all." With a sniff, he went inside.

"I'm sorry," Ana began, fixing a bright smile on her face. "He's very protective."

"So I gathered." Since he wasn't going to have to defend himself after all, he could think of nothing to do with his hands but shove them in his pockets. "I wanted to—we wanted to say merry Christmas."

"Yes, Jessie just did." They were silent for another awkward moment. "You're welcome to come in, have some wassail."

"I don't want to intrude. Your family..." He offered what almost passed for a grin. "I don't want to risk my life, either."

Even the faint smile faded from her eyes. "He wouldn't really have harmed you. It's not our way."

"I didn't mean..." What the hell was he supposed to say to her? "I don't blame him for being upset, and I don't want to make you or your family uncomfortable. If you'd rather, I could just..." He turned slightly, and the sign on her lawn caught his eye. His temper rose accordingly. "What the hell is that?"

"Isn't it clear enough? I'm selling the house. I've decided to go back to Ireland."

"Ireland? You think you can just pack up and move six thousand miles away?"

"Yes, I do. Boone, I'm sorry, but dinner's nearly ready, and I really have to go in. Of course, you're welcome to join us."

"If you don't stop being so bloody polite, I'm going to—" He cut himself off again. "I don't want dinner," he said between his teeth. "I want to talk to you."

"This isn't the time."

"We'll make it the time."

He backed her through the doorway just as Sebastian came down the hall behind her. Placing a light hand on Ana's shoulder, he sent Boone a warning glance. "Is there a problem here, Anastasia?"

"No. I invited Boone and Jessie for dinner, but he isn't able to join us."

"Pity." Sebastian's smile glittered with malice. "Well, then, if you'll excuse us, Sawyer."

Boone slammed the door behind him, causing all the ruckus inside to switch off like a light. Several pairs of eyes turned their way. He was too furious to note that Sebastian's were now bright with amusement.

"Stay out of my way," Boone said quietly. "Each and every one of you. I don't care who you are, or what you are." More than ready to fight a fleet of dragons, he grabbed Ana's hand. "You come with me."

"My family—"

"Can damn well wait." He yanked her back outside.

From her perch under the Christmas tree, Jessie stared wide-eyed after them. "Is Daddy mad at Ana?"

"No." Happy enough about what she'd seen to burst at the seams, Maureen gave the little girl a squeeze. "I think they've just gone off to take care of another Christmas present for you. One I think you'll like best of all."

Outside, Ana labored to keep up. "Stop dragging me, Boone."

"I'm not dragging you," he said as he dragged her through the side yard.

"I don't want to go with you." She felt the tears she'd thought she was finished with stinging her eyes. "I'm not going through this again."

"You think you can put up a stupid sign in your yard and solve everything?" Guided by moonlight, he tugged her down the rock steps that led to the beach. "Drop a bombshell on my head, then take off for Ireland?"

"I can do exactly as I please."

"Witch or no witch, you'd better think that one over again."

"You wouldn't even talk to me."

"I'm talking to you now."

"Well, now I don't want to talk." She broke away and started to climb back up.

"Then you'll listen." He caught her around the waist and tossed her over his shoulder. "And we're going to do this far enough from the house so that I know your family isn't breathing down my neck." When he reached the bottom, he flipped her over and dropped her to her feet. "One step," he warned. "You take one step away and I'll haul you back."

"I wouldn't give you the satisfaction." She struggled with the tears, preferring temper. "You want to have your say. Fine. Then I'll have mine, as well. I accept your position on our relationship. I deeply regret you feel it necessary to keep Jessie away from me."

"I never—"

"Don't deny it. For days before I left for Ireland you kept her at home." She picked up a handful of pebbles and threw them out to sea. "Wouldn't want your little girl too near the witch, after all." She whirled back to him. "For God's sake, Boone, what did you expect from me? Did you see me rubbing my hands together and croaking out, 'I'll get you, my pretty—and your little dog, too'?"

His lips quirked at that, and he reached out, but she spun away. "Give me some credit, Ana."

"I did. A little later than I should have, but I did. And you turned away. Just as I'd known you would."

"Known?" Though he was getting tired of the choreography, he pulled her around again. "How did you know how I'd react?

Did you look in your crystal ball, or just have your psychic cousin take a stroll through my head?''

"Neither," she said, with what control she had left. "I wouldn't let Sebastian look, and I didn't look myself, because it seemed unfair. I knew you'd turn away because..."

"Because someone else had."

"It doesn't matter, the fact is you did turn away."

"I just needed to take it in."

"I saw the way you looked at me that night." She shut her eyes. "I've seen that look before. Oh, you weren't cruel like Robert. There were no names, no accusations, but the result was the same. Stay away from me and mine. I don't accept what you are." She wrapped her arms tight and cupped her elbows for warmth.

"I'm not going to apologize for having what I think was a very normal reaction. And damn it, Ana, I was tired, and half-crazy. Watching you lie there in bed all those hours, and you were so pale, so still. I was afraid you wouldn't come back. When you did, I didn't know how to treat you. Then you were telling me all of this."

She searched for calm, knowing it was the best way. "The timing was bad all around. I wasn't quite strong enough to deal with your feelings."

"If you had told me before—"

"You would have reacted differently?" She glanced toward him. "No, I don't think so. But you're right. I should have. It was unfair, and it was weak of me to let things go as far as they did."

"Don't put words in my mouth, Ana. Unless you're, what do you call it—linked? If you're not linked with me, you don't know what I'm feeling. It hurt that you didn't trust me."

She nodded, brushing a tear from her cheek. "I know. I'm sorry."

"You were afraid?"

"I told you I was a coward."

He frowned, watching the hair blow around her face as she

stared out at the moon-kissed sea. "Yes, you did. The night you came across my sketch. The one of the witch. That upset you."

She shrugged. "I'm oversensitive sometimes. It was just the mood. I was..."

"About to tell me, and then I scared you off with my evil witch."

"It seemed a difficult time to tell you."

"Because you're a coward," he said mildly, watching her. "Let me ask you something, Ana. What did you do, exactly, to Jessie that day?"

"I linked. I told you I'm an empath."

"It hurt you. I saw." He took her arm, turning her to face him. "Once you cried out, as if it were unbearable. Afterward, you fainted, then slept like the dead for more than a day."

"That's part of it." She tried to push his hand away. It hurt too much to be touched when her defenses were shattered. "When the injuries are so serious, there's a price."

"Yes, I understand. I asked Morgana. She said you could have died. She said the risk was very great because Jessie..." He could hardly say it. "She was gone, or nearly. And you weren't just fixing some broken bones, but bringing her back from the edge. That the line is very fine, and it's very easy for the healer to become the victim."

"What would you have had me do? Let her die?"

"A coward would have. I think your definition and mine are different. Being afraid doesn't make you a coward. You could have saved yourself and let her go."

"I love her."

"So do I. And you gave her back to me. I didn't even thank you."

"Do you think I want your gratitude?" It was too much, she thought. Next he would offer her pity. "I don't. I don't want it. What I did I did freely, because I couldn't bear to lose her, either. And I couldn't bear for you—"

"For me?" he said gently.

"For you to lose someone else you loved. I don't want to be thanked for it. It's what I am."

"You've done it before? What you did with Jessie?"

"I'm a healer. I heal. She was..." It still hurt to think of it. "She was slipping away. I used what I have to bring her back."

"It's not that simple." His hands were gentle on her arms now, stroking. "Not even for you. You feel more than others. Morgana told me that, too. When you let your defenses down, you're more vulnerable to emotion, to pain, to everything. That's why you don't cry." With his fingertip, he lifted a teardrop from her cheek. "But you're crying now."

"You know everything there is to know. What's the point of this?"

"The point is to take a step back to the night you explained it all to me. The point is for you to take another chance and open yourself up. For me."

"You ask too much." She sobbed the words out, then covered her face. "Oh, leave me alone. Give me some peace. Can't you see how you hurt me?"

"Yes, I can see." He wrapped his arms around her, fighting to soothe while she struggled for release. "You've lost weight, you're pale. When I look into your eyes, I see every ounce of pain I caused you. I don't know how to take it back. I don't know how your father kept himself from cursing me with whatever was in his arsenal."

"We can't use power to harm. It's against everything we are. Please let me go."

"I can't. I almost thought I could. She lied to me, I told myself. She betrayed my trust. She isn't real." He kept a firm grip on her arms as he pulled her away. "It doesn't matter. None of it matters. If it's magic, I don't want to lose it. I can't lose you. I love you, Ana. All that you are. Please." He touched his lips to hers, tasting tears. "Please come back to me."

The shaft of hope was almost painful. She clung to it, to him. "I want to believe."

"So do I." He cupped her face, kissing her again. "And I do. I believe in you. In us. If this is my fairy tale, I want to play it out."

She stared up at him. "You can accept all of this? All of us?"

"I figure I'm pretty well suited to do just that. Of course, it might take a while for me to convince your father not to do something drastic to my anatomy." He traced his fingers over her lips as they curved. "I didn't know if you'd ever smile for me again. Tell me you still love me. Give me that, too."

"Yes, I love you." Her lips trembled under his. "Always."

"I won't hurt you again." He brushed away tears with his thumbs. "I'll make up for everything."

"It's done." She caught his hands. "That's done. We have tomorrow."

"Don't cry anymore."

She smiled, rubbing her fists across her cheeks. "No, I won't. I never cry."

He took those damp fists and kissed them. "You said to ask you again. It's been longer than a week, but I'm hoping you haven't forgotten what you said your answer would be."

"I haven't forgotten."

"Put your hand here." He pressed her palm to his heart. "I want you to feel what I feel." He linked his free hand with hers. "The moon's almost full. The first time I kissed you was in the moonlight. I was charmed, enchanted, spellbound. I always will be. I need you, Ana."

She could feel the strength of that love pouring into her. "You have me."

"I want you to marry me. Share the child you gave back to me. She's yours as much as mine now. Let me make more children with you. I'll take you as you are, Anastasia. I swear I'll cherish you as long as I live."

She lifted her arms to him. Hair like sunlight. Eyes like smoke. Shafts of moonglow shimmered around her like torchlight.

"I've been waiting for you."

Epilogue

Alone on a wild crag facing a stormy sea stood Donovan Castle. This dark night, lightning flashed and shuddered in the black sky, and the wind set the leaded glass to shaking in the diamond panes.

Inside, fires leaped and glowed in the hearths. Those who were witches, and those who were not, gathered close, waiting for the indignant wail that would signal a new life.

"Are you cheating, Grandda?" Jessie asked Padrick as he perused his cards.

"Cheating!" He gave a merry laugh and wiggled his brows. "Certainly I am. Go fish."

She giggled and drew from the pile. "Granny Maureen says you always cheat." She tilted her head. "Were you really a frog?"

"That I was, darling. A fine green one."

She accepted this, just as she accepted the other wonders of her life with the Donovans. She petted the snoring Daisy, who rested her big golden head in Jessie's lap. "Will you be a frog again sometime, so I can see?"

"I might surprise you." He winked and changed her hand of cards into a rainbow of lollipops.

"Oh, Grandda," she said indulgently.

"Sebastian?" Mel hustled down the main stairs and shouted

into the parlor, where her husband was sipping brandy and watching the card game. "Shawn and Keely are awake and fussing. I have my hands full helping with Ana."

"Be right there." The proud papa of three months set down his snifter and headed up to change diapers.

Nash bounced one-year-old Allysia on his knee while Donovan sat in Matthew's lap playing with his pocket watch. "Be careful he doesn't eat it," Nash commented. "Or make it disappear. We're having a little trouble keeping him in line."

"The lad needs to spread his wings a bit."

"If you say so. But when I went to get him out of his crib the other day, it was full of rabbits. Real ones."

"Takes after his mother," Matthew said proudly. "She ran us ragged."

Allysia leaned back against her father and smiled. Instantly Daisy woke and trotted over. Within seconds, every dog and cat in the house was swarming through the room.

"Ally," Nash said with a sigh. "Remember how we said one at a time?"

"Doggies." Squealing, Ally tugged gently on the ears of Matthew's big silver wolf. "Kittycats."

"Next time just one, okay?" Nash plucked a cat off his shoulder, nudged another off the arm of the chair. "A couple of weeks ago she had every hound within ten miles howling in the yard. Come on, monsters." He rose, tucking Allysia, then Donovan, under his arms like footballs. They kicked and giggled. "I think it's time for bed."

"Story," Donovan demanded. "Uncle Boone."

"He's busy. You'll have to settle for one from your old man."

He was indeed busy, watching a miracle. The room was scented with candles and herbs, warmed by the fire glowing in the hearth. He held tight to Ana as she brought their son into the world.

Then their daughter.

Then their second son.

"Three." He kept saying it over and over, even as Bryna

settled an infant in his arms. "Three." They'd told him there would be triplets, but he hadn't really believed it.

"Runs in the family." Exhausted, elated, Ana took another bundle from Morgana. She pressed her lips gently to the silky cheek. "Now we have two of each."

He grinned down at his wife as Mel settled the third baby in the crook of Ana's arm. "I think we need a bigger house."

"We'll add on."

"Would you like the others to come up?" Bryna asked gently. "Or would you rather rest awhile?"

"No, please." Ana tilted her head so that it rested against Boone's arm. "Ask them to come up."

They crowded in, making too much noise. Ana made room in the big bed for Jessie to sit beside her, then placed a baby in her arms.

"This is your brother, Trevor. Your sister, Mauve. And your other brother, Kyle."

"I'm going to take good care of them. Always. Look, Grandda, we have a big family now."

"You do indeed, my little lamb." He blew heartily into his checked kerchief. He wiped his runny eyes and looked mistily at Boone. "Just as well I didn't flatten you when I had the chance."

"Here." Boone held out a squealing infant. "Hold your grandson."

"Ah, Maureen, my cheesecake, look at this. He has my eyes."

"No, my frog prince, he has mine."

They argued, with the rest of the Donovans throwing their weight to one side or the other. Boone slipped his arm around his wife, held his family close as his son suckled greedily at his first taste of mother's milk. Lightning flashed against the windows, the wind howled, and the fire leapt high in the grate.

Somewhere deep in the forest, high in the hills, the faeries danced.

And they lived happily ever after.

* * * * *

#1 *New York Times* bestselling author

NORA
ROBERTS

continues *The Donovan Legacy* with a
brand-new story in this intriguing series:

ENCHANTED

Dark and mysterious Liam Donovan is destined
to love sweet Rowan Murray—if he dares
to taste a beauty so innocent, so forbidden....

AVAILABLE IN NOVEMBER AT YOUR
FAVORITE RETAIL STORE

Only from Silhouette Intimate Moments.

Here's a sneak preview of ENCHANTED

"Just a storm, it's just a storm. No big deal." Rowan all but chanted the words as she lighted more candles.

She wasn't afraid of the dark, not really. But it was so *damn* dark, and the lightning had struck so close to the cabin. The thunder rattled the windows until she was certain they would just explode.

And if she hadn't been sitting outside, daydreaming while the storm blew in, she'd have a fire built. She'd have the warmth and light from that *and* the candlelight, and it would be sort of...cozy. If she really worked on believing it.

And now the power was out, the phones were out and the storm appeared to be at its peak directly over her pretty little cabin.

There were candles, she reminded herself. Dozens and dozens of candles. White ones, blue ones, red ones, green ones. She could only think that Belinda had bought out a candle store. Some were so lovely, with odd and beautiful symbols carved into them, that she held back from lighting them. And after all, she must have had fifty flaring away by now, with adequate light and marvelous scents to settle her nerves.

"Okay. All right." She set yet one more candle on the table in front of the sofa and rubbed her chilled hands. "I ought to be able to see enough to get a fire going. Then I'll just curl up right here on the couch and wait it out. It'll be fine."

But even as she crouched in front of the hearth and began to arrange the kindling, the wind howled. Her door banged open like a bullet out of a gun and half the cheery candles behind her blew out.

She leaped up, whirled around. And screamed.

Liam stood a few paces away, the wind swirling through his hair, the candlelight gleaming in his eyes. She dropped the kindling on her stockinged feet, yelped and fell backward into a chair.

"I seem to have startled you again," he said in that mild and beautiful voice. "Sorry."

"I—you. God! The door…"

"It's open." He turned, crossed to it and closed out the wind and rain.

She'd been certain she'd locked it when she'd rushed in out of the storm. Obviously not, she thought now and did her best to swallow her heart and put it back in its proper place.

"I thought you might have been having some trouble with the storm." He stepped toward her, each movement graceful as a dancer's. Or a stalking wolf. "It seems I was right."

"Power's out," she managed.

"So I see. You're cold." He picked up the scattered kindling and crouched to build a fire with wood and match. He thought she'd had enough surprises for one night, even if it did take quite a bit longer that way.

"I wanted to get some light before I built a fire. Belinda has lots of candles."

"Naturally." The kindling caught with a quick crackle, and flames licked obligingly at the logs he arranged. "This'll warm the room soon. There's a small generator out back. I can start it for you if you like, but this will pass before long."

He stayed where he was, the firelight dancing over his face. And looking at him, she forgot about the storm and fears of the dark. She wondered if all that gorgeous hair that nearly fell to his shoulders was as soft as it looked, wondered why it seemed she knew exactly how it would feel under her fingers.

Why she had an image of him leaning over her, leaning close, with his mouth a breath away from hers, she couldn't comprehend. Only a breath away.

"You're daydreaming again, Rowan."

"Oh." She blinked, flushed, shook herself clear. "Sorry. The storm's made me jumpy. Would you like some wine?" She pushed herself up, began backing quickly away toward the kitchen. "I have a very nice Italian white I tried last night. I'll just...pour some. Won't be a minute."

For Lord's sake, for Lord's sake, she berated herself as she dashed into the kitchen where a half-dozen candles glowed on the counter. Why did being around him make her so skittish and stupid! She'd been alone with attractive men before. She was a grown woman, wasn't she?

She got the bottle out of the refrigerator by the light of the candles, found glasses and filled them. When she turned, a glass in each hand, he was there just behind her, and she jolted.

Wine sloshed over the rim and onto the back of her hand.

"*Must* you do that!" She snapped it out before she could stop herself, then watched that fast, fabulous grin flash over his face, bright and blinding as lightning in a storm.

"I suppose not." Ah, the hell with it, he decided. He was entitled to some small pleasures. With his eyes on hers, he lifted her damp hand, bent his head and slowly licked.

The best she could manage was a small, quiet moan.

"You're right. It's very nice wine." He took the glass and when her freed hand fell limply to her side, he smiled. Sipped. "You've a lovely face, Rowan Murray. I've thought of it since I last saw you."

"You have?"

"Did you think I wouldn't?"

She was so obviously befuddled it was tempting to press his advantage, to go with the urge grinding in him to take before she knew all he wanted, and what he refused to want. One step closer, he mused, the slow slide of his fingers around the base of her neck where the flesh was warm and smooth. Fragile. His mouth to hers while the taste of her was still mixed with wine on his tongue.

And he wouldn't be in the mood to leave it at something quite so simple, or quite so innocent....

Don't miss Silhouette's newest cross-line promotion,

Four royal sisters find their own Prince Charmings as they embark on separate journeys to find their missing brother, the Crown Prince!

Royally Wed

The search begins
in October 1999 and
continues through February 2000:

On sale October 1999: **A ROYAL BABY ON THE WAY**
by award-winning author **Susan Mallery** (Special Edition)

On sale November 1999: **UNDERCOVER PRINCESS**
by bestselling author **Suzanne Brockmann** (Intimate Moments)

On sale December 1999: **THE PRINCESS'S WHITE KNIGHT**
by popular author **Carla Cassidy** (Romance)

On sale January 2000: **THE PREGNANT PRINCESS**
by rising star **Anne Marie Winston** (Desire)

On sale February 2000: **MAN...MERCENARY...MONARCH**
by top-notch talent **Joan Elliott Pickart** (Special Edition)

ROYALLY WED
Only in—
SILHOUETTE BOOKS

Available at your favorite retail outlet.

Visit us at www.romance.net

SSERW_T5

THE FORTUNES OF TEXAS

*Membership in this family has
its privileges…and its price.
But what a fortune can't buy,
a true-bred Texas love is sure to bring!*

Coming in December 1999…

A Willing Wife by

JACKIE MERRITT

Dallas Fortune lived alone and liked it that way. So he
was shocked by the deep emotions single mother
Maggie Perez and her young son awakened within him.
But would the eligible rancher's wounded heart allow
him to join this ready-made family?

In January 2000
THE FORTUNES OF TEXAS continues with
CORPORATE DADDY by Arlene James.

Available at your favorite retail outlet.

Return to Whitehorn

Look for these bold new stories set in beloved Whitehorn, Montana!

CINDERELLA'S BIG SKY GROOM by Christine Rimmer
On sale October 1999 (Special Edition #1280)
A prim schoolteacher pretends an engagement
to the town's most confirmed bachelor!

A MONTANA MAVERICKS CHRISTMAS
On sale November 1999 (Special Edition #1286)
A two-in-one volume containing
two brand-new stories:

"Married in Whitehorn" by Susan Mallery
and
"Born in Whitehorn" by Karen Hughes

A FAMILY HOMECOMING by Laurie Paige
On sale December 1999 (Special Edition #1292)
A father returns home to guard his wife and child—
and finds his heart once more.

***Don't miss these books, only from
Silhouette Special Edition.***

Look for the next **MONTANA MAVERICKS** tale, by
Jackie Merritt, on sale in Special Edition May 2000.
And get ready for
MONTANA MAVERICKS: Wed in Whitehorn,
a new twelve-book series coming from Silhouette Books
on sale June 2000!

Available at your favorite retail outlet.

Temperatures rise and hearts sizzle in

TEXAS HEAT by MARY LYNN BAXTER

Bestselling author **Mary Lynn Baxter** brings you three tempting stories about the power of mutual attraction.

Passions ignite when three fiery women meet the Western heroes they've always dreamed of. But will true love be found?

Find out in **TEXAS HEAT,** on sale November 1999 at your favorite retail outlet.

Silhouette ®

Visit us at www.romance.net

PSBR31299_T5

In December 1999
three spectacular authors invite you to share the
romance of the season as three special gifts are

Delivered by Christmas

A heartwarming holiday anthology featuring

BLUEBIRD WINTER
by *New York Times* bestselling author

Linda Howard

A baby is about to be born on the side of the road. The single
mother's only hope rests in the strong arms of a dashing doctor....

And two brand-new stories:

THE GIFT OF JOY
by national bestselling author **Joan Hohl**

A bride was not what a Texas-Ranger-turned-rancher was
expecting for the holidays. Will his quest for a home lead to love?

A CHRISTMAS TO TREASURE
by award-winning author **Sandra Steffen**

A daddy is all two children want for Christmas. And the
handsome man upstairs may be just the hero their mommy needs!

*Give yourself the gift of romance in
this special holiday collection!*

Available at your favorite retail outlet.

Visit us at www.romance.net

PSDBC_T5

**Start celebrating Silhouette's 20th anniversary
with these 4 special titles by
New York Times bestselling authors**

Fire and Rain
by Elizabeth Lowell

King of the Castle
by Heather Graham Pozzessere

State Secrets
by Linda Lael Miller

Paint Me Rainbows
by Fern Michaels

On sale in December 1999

Available at your favorite retail outlet

™ *Silhouette*®

Visit us at www.romance.net

PSNYT_T5